ALCHEMISED

SenLinYu

Forever

FSC
www.fsc.org
MIX
Papier | Fördert
gute Waldnutzung
FSC® C014496

PRODUZIERT MIT VERANTWORTUNG

www.ullstein.de

English Edition by Forever
Forever ist ein Verlag der Ullstein Buchverlage GmbH, Berlin

ISBN 978-3-98978-027-9

Bei Fragen zur Produktsicherheit wenden Sie sich bitte an
produktsicherheit@ullstein.de.
Illustration auf Seite 1024: © Avendell
Symbole im Satz: © Alex Hovey (Sonne); © Francesca Baerald
(Drache, Rosen); © antondzyna/Adobe Stock (Rosen); © A-R-T-U-R/iStock
(Vignetten); © Lazarev/iStock (Mondphasen)
Vorsatz und Nachsatz: © Regina Flath; © seamartini/iStock, © Freepik/
luckycreative, © Yevheniia Lytvynovych/shutterstock, © Golden Shrimp/
shutterstock, © Evgenia Pichkur/shutterstock
Gesetzt aus der Adobe Caslon und Felina Gothic
Satz: © Del Rey, Penguin Random House LLC, New York. Wir danken
Penguin Random House LLC für die freundliche Zusammenarbeit.
Druck und Bindearbeiten: GGP Media GmbH, Pößneck

SenLinYu

ALCHEMISED

To Jame, for finding me

Author's Note

This is a work of fiction which explores many of the darker aspects of war and survival. Reader discretion is advised. For more details, please see the back of the book for content notes.

PART ONE

PROLOGUE

HELENA WONDERED SOMETIMES IF SHE STILL HAD eyes. The darkness surrounding her never ended. She thought at first if she waited long enough, some glimmer of light would appear, or someone would come. Yet no matter how long she waited, there was nothing.

Just endless dark.

She had a body; she could feel it wrapped around her like a cage, but no amount of effort or determination could make it move. It floated inert and unresponsive except when jerking violently as the surges hit—jolts of electricity tearing through her, beginning at the base of her neck and making every muscle in her body seize violently. As suddenly as they came, they'd be gone. They were her only sense of time.

They were done to ensure her muscles couldn't deteriorate altogether while she was in stasis. Helena remembered that detail. Remembered that she'd been placed there as a prisoner, kept preserved, but someday, someone would come for her.

At first, she'd counted the time in between surges to calculate their frequency. Second by second. Ten thousand, eight hundred. Every three hours without fail. Always the same. Then she'd counted the surges, but as the number grew and grew, she stopped, afraid to know.

She forced herself to focus on other things, not the wait. Not the endlessness. Not the dark. She had to wait, so she gave herself a routine to keep her mind fresh. Imagined walks. Cliffs and sky. Visited all the places she'd ever wandered. All the books she'd read.

She had to endure. To stay alert. That way she would be ready. She *had* to stay ready.

She would not let herself fade away.

CHAPTER 1

When light came, it nearly split Helena's brain open.

There was screaming.

"Fuck! How's this one awake?" A voice broke through the sensory agony.

Light was stabbing her. A spike driven through her eyes, burrowing into her skull. Gods, her eyes.

She writhed. The brightness blurred, careening. The burn of fluid rushed down her throat. A roar in her ears.

Slick fingers dug into her arms, against bone, dragging her up. Air hit her lungs, sending them seizing as the fluid came back up.

"Fuck this stasis gel. Can't get a decent grip. Make her shut up! She's about to drown herself."

Her head slammed into something as she was dropped. Rough stone tore her hands. She scrabbled blindly, trying to push herself up. Her eyes squeezed shut, but the light was still a knife in her skull. A hard object was ripped off the back of her neck, and something warm and wet ran across her skin.

"How the fuck is she awake? Someone must've fucked the dosage on this one. Don't let her crawl off."

Her arms were gripped again, and she was heaved up from the ground.

She tore herself free, forcing her eyes open. All she could make out was blinding white. She lunged towards it.

"You fucking bitch, you cut me!"

Pain exploded across the back of her head.

THERE WAS STILL LIGHT WHEN she regained consciousness.

It came slowly, as though she were underwater, swimming towards a surface that rippled just beyond reach, consciousness seeping back in. Her eyes were closed; the light was just beyond them. She could feel the pain of it already.

She was lying on something hard. A cold table, its metal inert beneath her fingers.

She could dimly make out voices, muffled but close.

"Well?" A woman's voice. "Any others?"

"No." A man's voice. That first voice from earlier. "We've pulled the rest out. It was just this one stored wrong."

"And she was conscious when you opened the tank?"

"Sure was. Started screaming when we lifted the top and pulled her up. Gave me a heart attack, I can tell you. Willems was so startled, he nearly drowned her, and when we did get her out, she was fucking feral. Scratched the shit out of me until we got her knocked out. Had the intravenous and all, but the sedation was turned off. Someone must've bumped it."

"That doesn't explain the lack of records for this one," said the woman. "Seems odd."

"Probably done in a hurry. Couldn't have been kept for long. Even the ones properly done are mostly dead. Lot of the tanks are just soup and bones." The man laughed nervously.

"We'll know more once I have her in Central," the woman said. She sounded disinterested. "You were right to call this in. It's anomalous. Let me know how many of the rest wake. Any corpses intact enough for reanimation go to the mines. The living stock goes to the Outpost."

"Of course. And you'll put in a good word for me, right? It would mean a lot if it comes from you." The man sounded hopeful, and his chuckle was forced. "Not getting any younger, you know."

"The High Necromancer has many petitions to consider. Your work will not be forgotten. Have a lorry made ready for transport."

There were retreating footsteps followed by an irritated sigh.

"There's no need to feign unconsciousness; I know you're awake. Open your eyes," the woman said. "I've altered your senses, so the light shouldn't be too much."

Helena peered cautiously through her lashes.

The world around her was greenish dusk, every form shadow-like. The vague shape of a person moved on her right side.

Her eyes followed sluggishly.

"Good. You're following instructions *and* tracking motion."

Helena tried to speak, but a low gasping emerged.

There was a click of a pen and papers shuffling.

"So, Prisoner 1273, or are you Prisoner 19819? You have two inmate numbers, and there's no record of either in this facility. Do you happen to have a name?"

Helena said nothing. Now that the mere concept of light was not a terror, she could think a little. She was still a captive.

The woman gave an impatient huff. "Do you understand me?"

Helena gave no response.

"Well, I suppose I can't expect much. We'll know soon anyway. You, bring her."

The shape blurred away, and new figures appeared. Cold skin pressed against her wrists. The stench of chemical preservatives and old meat burned in her nose. Necrothralls. She tried to make out the faces, but her eyes kept sliding off, refusing to focus.

The table began vibrating as it was rolled across a stone floor, radiating through her skull into her teeth.

Then it was so bright, it was like needles being driven into her retinas. She gave a muffled scream, squeezing her eyes shut again.

There was a nauseating lurch upwards, and everything grew darker again, a motor rumbling to life somewhere beneath her.

She needed to escape. She tried to shift and felt the clank of metal.

"Lie still." The woman's voice was suddenly back. Very close.

Helena jerked away, breath coming in rapid pants and her hands and feet twisting against the restraints. She had to run. She had to—

"Don't make my day harder," the woman said, her voice icy.

Fingers gripped the base of Helena's skull, and a pulse of energy flooded through her brain.

Darkness again.

JOLTING AGONY AND SUDDEN TERROR ripped Helena back into consciousness.

She lurched upwards, eyes wide, just in time to see a syringe pulled away. There was a snap of chains, and she fell back, heart racing, every beat a throb of pain as though it'd been stabbed through.

"There now." There was the clatter of the syringe being dropped onto a metal tray somewhere to her right. "That should get you lucid and talking."

It was the woman from earlier.

Helena was no longer on the table or in a lorry. There was a hard mattress under her, and the strong sterile scent of antiseptic everywhere. A dim grey ceiling loomed overhead.

Through the pain, energy was suddenly roaring through her veins, growing into a searing heat that burned in her hands as they flexed. She could feel her consciousness sharpening and everything growing brighter, clearer. She twisted, and metal bit into her wrist.

"None of that. You'll break your bones before you break out of those shackles. Answer my questions and I might let you get up before that drug wears off. I understand it can be quite painful otherwise."

Unable to move, Helena felt her mind begin to race instead. An injection, some kind of harsh stimulant. Trapped inside her, the energy poured into her brain, and her scattered, panicked thoughts were narrowing into crystalline focus.

"Helena Marino. You"—there was a sound of shuffled pages—

"should be dead according to your 1273 file. You were marked for culling, due to unspecified 'extensive injuries.' But the 19819 designation means you were selected for stasis." More pages were shuffled. "However, there's no record that you ever arrived there or underwent processing." The woman sucked her teeth. "You have not existed anywhere in our file system since Augustus of last year. Fourteen months. And now we find you in the very stasis warehouse you never arrived at. How is that?"

Helena blinked slowly, trying to process the information. Fourteen months?

"Obviously no one can survive in stasis that long. Even at six months with perfect conditions it's nearly impossible, and you weren't even stored properly. So where did you come from? And who put you there?"

Helena turned her head away, refusing to answer.

The woman hummed, stepping closer. "You're not in any trouble. Tell me the truth and this will all be over. Where were you before you were placed in stasis?"

The question was enunciated slowly.

Helena said nothing, although her jaw was burning to move. Her body started to tremble as her heartbeat drove the drug deeper into her veins.

There wasn't anyone left to protect, but she refused to cooperate with her captors. To make anything easy for them, even their filing system.

Besides, she hadn't been anywhere else.

"Where. Were. You. Before stasis?" The woman was speaking loudly.

Helena's throat tightened, trying not to even think about the answer, because it tore her apart to remember.

Before the warehouse, she'd been captured along with everyone else, crammed into cages outside the Alchemy Tower, where all the prisoners had been brought so they could witness the "celebrations" of the war's end.

She could still smell the smoke and blood in the summer heat, hear the raucous cheers as Resistance leaders died, their screams fading. Watching them die, and knowing it was still not over, even then.

Some necromancer in the crowd would hurry forward, eager to show off, and in a matter of seconds that dead body would get up again. Someone Helena had trusted or served under, brought back with reanimation. A necrothrall, an empty automaton corpse. They'd be slit open, their skin in ribbons, organs excised, eyes blank, face slack, and they would be used to kill the next "traitor" in an even more brutal way.

The executions had not stopped until the air was red with a mist of blood.

General Titus Bayard's dead body was used to kill his wife. Slowly. Making him eat the strips of her as he cut them off.

Each death had carved out a piece of Helena until there was a cavern of grief inside her chest. When there wasn't anyone left worth publicly killing, they'd put her in that stasis tank.

The other prisoners had been unconscious as they were paralysed, needles inserted in their veins, tubes shoved down their noses, breathing masks adhered to their faces. Not Helena.

She had been kept awake, aware of the claustrophobic horror of all that was happening to her, as she was locked inside her body and left in the dark. Waiting for someone to come for her.

No one ever did.

Fingers snapped in front of Helena's face, jolting her from her memories. The woman was glaring at her.

"I'm not having a filing error damaging my reputation. If you won't answer, I'll stop doing this the *easy* way."

Helena flinched.

"See? You do understand me."

Her stomach shrivelled, but she locked her jaw.

The woman stepped closer. Helena's eyes strained to make her out. A squarish face with impatiently pursed lips. A medical uniform.

"Perhaps an example is in order." The woman's hand pressed against Helena's neck. Helena gave a sharp gasp as burning-cold energy surged through her, towards her spine.

It wasn't an electric jolt like in the tank; it burrowed from the woman's hand and into Helena like a needle. The channel of energy sang through her like a tuning fork, until both resonated along the same wavelength.

The woman clenched her fingers. Pain burst through every nerve in Helena's body. She gave a gasping, garbled scream, body seizing, hands wrenching at the cuffs.

"Be still."

A flick and Helena went limp. She couldn't feel anything below her chest. As if her spine were severed. Her blood roared in panic.

A wave of the woman's hand, and the void of numbness vanished.

Soap-roughened fingers trailed dangerously along Helena's arm.

"Understand now?"

The woman's resonance was still running through her like a current, a visceral warning. Helena managed to nod shakily. She should have realised: The woman was a vivimancer. Necromancy's inverse twin, wielded on the living rather than the dead.

"I knew you'd catch on. Let's try again."

Helena's throat grew thick, her eyes burning. Every nerve twinged, her blood roaring in her ears. What was the harm in answering?

"Where did you come from?"

"Wsss—th—w-housss—" Helena fought to make her tongue cooperate.

"None of that foreign nonsense. Speak Paladian," the woman said sharply.

There was no such thing as a Paladian language; the woman was speaking in Northern dialect. Helena wanted to tell her that but didn't think it would help. She swallowed and tried again, but her tongue slurred everything together.

The woman sighed. "Why do you Resistance fighters always waste my time? Perhaps if we jolt your brain, you'll remember how to speak a proper language."

She gripped Helena's head this time. A wave of resonance surged through from both sides like cymbals slammed together.

Everything went red. The scream wrenched from Helena's throat was animal.

The hands were snatched back. "What on earth?"

Helena wasn't sure if the woman was running in circles overhead or if the room was spinning.

"What is this? Who did this to you?"

Helena stared dazedly up as the red faded from her vision. Her hands were twitching and spasming, convulsively jerking against the chains. She didn't know what the questions meant.

"Something has been done to your mind," the woman said, sounding bewildered but also strangely excited. "Some kind of transmutation. I have never encountered anything like it. I'm going to have to report this. I'll need a specialist. You have—" The woman paused. "There's no name for this! *I'll* have to come up with a name . . ."

She seemed to be talking mostly to herself. "Transmutational barriers inside a brain. How is that possible? I have never—there are—patterns in it."

She touched Helena again. Helena flinched, but the resonance was not for torture this time, just a frisson of energy through her brain that turned everything luridly red again.

"This is elaborate, beautiful, professional work. A vivimancer manually rewiring the human consciousness."

Helena lay there, not understanding.

The woman's face came close enough that Helena could make out blue eyes with deep creases between them and around the mouth. She stared at Helena with avid fascination.

"If Bennet were still here, he would marvel at the precision of this work." Resonance ran through Helena's mind as tangibly as if fingers were gliding inside her skull. The woman's pale eyes lost focus as she worked. "The smallest mistake anywhere, and you'd be vegetative, but whoever did this kept you *almost* completely intact. This is genius."

"Whaa—tt?" Helena finally managed a clear word.

"I wonder . . . What does it look like?" The woman walked away, then returned a minute later, carrying a sheet of glass.

Helena squinted and recognised the object. A resonance screen. They were frequently used for academic presentations and alchemical medical procedures. The gas used reactive particles to mirror the shape and pattern of a resonance channel.

The woman held the glass overhead, her other hand resting on Helena's forehead, and ran resonance through Helena's skull. Her vision turned red again, but Helena squinted through and watched as the dim cloud between the panes morphed into the vague shape of the human brain and then into an incomprehensible spiderweb of lines that wound all over.

"I doubt you understand any of this, but imagine your mind is a—a city. Your thoughts run along various streets to reach their destinations. Those lines you see are your streets that have been rerouted. There are barriers, transmutationally crafted, and so instead of following a natural pattern through the brain, someone has created alternative routes. Some areas are cut off entirely. I can't even imagine how . . . The skill this would take . . ."

Her words trailed off. She set the screen aside and peered probingly at Helena.

"Who worked on you?" The question was loud, slow, and over-enunciated.

Helena just shook her head.

The woman's expression hardened dangerously, but then she seemed to reconsider. "I suppose you wouldn't know, given the state of your brain. You're probably lucky to remember your own name. You were an alchemy student, I presume." She idly tapped a metal cuff around Helena's wrist.

Helena gave a wary nod.

"And foreign. Obviously." She gave Helena a pointed once-over.

Helena swallowed. "Etras."

"Ah, quite far from home then. Do you remember your resonance repertoire?"

"Div . . . erse."

"Hmm." The woman's eyebrows furrowed, and she studied Helena more carefully. "Wait. I remember hearing about you. You're that little savant the Holdfasts sponsored. That must have been more than a decade ago, so you must be what, twenty-something now?"

Helena's eyes burned, and she gave a stilted nod.

The woman raised an eyebrow. "Do you remember what happened to your sponsor, Principate Apollo?"

"Killed."

"Mhmm. And the war. I'm sure you remember that. Did you help the Holdfast boy burn down the city? Your darling Luc, as you all liked to call him?"

Helena's throat tightened. "I didn't—fight."

The woman gave a small sound of surprise, and her eyes narrowed. "But the final battle? I assume you remember that?"

Helena's mouth parted several times, her tongue struggling to untangle. "We—the—the Resistance lost. There were—executions. M-Morrough came—at the end. He—he had Luc. K-Killed him—there. Then—then they—they took me to the warehouse."

"Who's they?"

Helena swallowed bitterly. "L-Liches."

The woman chuckled. "I haven't heard anyone dare use that word in a long time. All of the Undying, regardless of their forms, are the High Necromancer's most ascendant followers. Their immortality is the reward for their excellence. In this new world, death claims only the unworthy. No matter what insults you attempt, it is your friends who are nothing but ashes to be forgotten."

She tapped Helena's forehead. "You do seem mostly intact, though. So why go to all the effort? And who could have even—?" The woman picked up the resonance screen, glancing at it once more, and then disappeared through the curtains.

Helena was relieved to see her gone.

Her memory or mind had been altered?

She would have thought it a trick, but she'd seen the resonance screen. She knew what a brain should look like. It would have required a highly specialised and extensive degree of vivimancy to transmute a mind into that state.

It wasn't something a person would forget having happened to them.

Yet she didn't *feel* like she'd forgotten anything, except the mention of an extensive injury.

She couldn't remember any injury, just shock, and grief, and horror.

She swallowed and blinked hard, trying not to think about it.

Looking around, she tried to make out her surroundings. Whatever she'd been injected with was a brutally effective drug. There was a sharp bruise forming on her chest where the needle had punctured its way to her heart. It hurt with every beat.

She looked down. There were bars along each side of the bed, and the metal cuffs around her wrists were shackled to them. The skin was raw and bruised, and beneath the cuffs chaining her to the bed, a greenish band of metal was also locked around each wrist.

Those at least were familiar. They'd been snapped around her wrists during the celebration.

In the darkness, thick with blood, with little torchlight and too many bodies in a cramped cage, she'd barely been able to make them out. But she remembered them.

Inside the stasis tank, she'd been constantly aware of them clamped around her wrists. Their existence had persisted along the edge of her consciousness, an inescapable presence that stifled her resonance, preventing any transmutational manipulation that might have let her escape.

Even in the tank, she could feel the lumithium inside them.

By its nature, lumithium bound the four elements of air, water, earth, and fire together, and in that binding, resonance was created.

The Sacred Faith held that resonance was a gift, intended by Sol, godhead of the elemental Quintessence, to elevate humanity. Resonance was a rare ability in many parts of the world, but not in Sol's chosen nation of Paladia. The pre-war census had estimated nearly a fifth of the population possessed measurable resonance levels. The number had been expected to rise further with the next generation.

Usually, resonance was channelled into the alchemy of metals and inorganic compounds, allowing for transmutation or alchemisation. However, in a defective soul which rebelled against Sol's natural laws, the resonance could be corrupted, enabling vivimancy—like what the woman had used on Helena—and the necromancy used to create necrothralls.

As the element of resonance, lumithium could increase or even create resonance in inert objects through exposure, making them alchemically malleable. However, pure lumithium was too divine for mortals; overexposure caused wasting sickness, and for individuals with resonance, direct exposure could result in a raw, metallic pain within their nerves.

The lumithium in the manacles didn't seem to make Helena sick. Which meant that something had altered it. The sharp energy inside was keyed into her resonance, but rather than turn it raw, it blurred her senses. She could feel her resonance, but when she tried to control it, the cuffs were like static in her nerves. No matter how she tried, she could not push beyond it.

All she knew was that as long as those manacles remained locked in place, she wasn't an alchemist at all.

CHAPTER 2

There was a necrothrall somewhere nearby. Alone and able to focus, Helena could smell the rotting meat and chemical preservatives. The Undying used the dead like puppets to perform any undesirable or menial tasks. Chained and waiting, she wondered what this one was being used for. She peered around, looking for any shadows beyond the curtains.

"Marino?"

Her name was whispered so softly, it could have been a breeze.

Turning, Helena made out a face peeking through the dividing curtain. She squinted hard, and her eyes managed to focus enough to make out a pale face and hair.

"Marino, is that you?"

Helena nodded, still trying to see who it was.

"It's Grace. I was an orderly in the hospital." She crept through the curtains as she spoke. She had a heavy Northern accent, the kind that pulled hard on the consonants.

"Sorry, I'm—disoriented," Helena said.

"I didn't expect to see you here." Grace came closer, youthful yet sunken features emerging from the dimness, her expression both frightened and curious.

Helena's eyes widened.

Grace's face was disfigured with scars, long cuts that bisected her cheeks and chin and nose. Not the accidental marring of injury. They were intentional.

Helena tried to lift a hand, but the shackles on her wrists were too short. "What happened?"

Grace looked confused, and then—following Helena's stare—reached up to touch her face. "Oh, the cuts? We all have them."

"What? Why would the liches—"

Grace shook her head sharply. "*Keep your voice down.*" She glanced around quickly, sniffing at the air before looking back at Helena again, her eyes angry. "They use the greys for listening sometimes. There's one in here, can't you smell it? You can't call the Undying *liches.*" The word came out barely a whisper. "If they hear—there'll be—consequences."

Helena nodded quickly, afraid Grace might flee if she wasn't careful.

Grace crept closer.

"The Undying didn't do this." She gestured at her face. "We did it ourselves. The Undying can do anything they want to us—to anyone labelled Resistance. It's the thing nowadays to keep greys instead of staff. Other times—they just want something to play with. At a party or—after a night out." Her face twisted. "No one interferes. Even the ones who aren't Undying or in the guilds will go along with it because they all hope it'll give them a better chance of earning immortality, too."

Grace gave a jerky, stilted shrug. "But if you're messed-up looking, they won't keep you for long." She drew a shaky breath and then peered hard at Helena. "Where have you been?"

Helena shook her head, trying to absorb everything Grace had said. "They took me to a warehouse—after—"

Grace's eyes narrowed.

Helena stared at her searchingly. "Is the Eternal Flame still—"

"No." Grace shook her head violently, and her expression turned angry. "They're all dead. Every one of them. After Luc was dead, they sent the rest of us out to the factory Outpost below the dam. Most of us can't leave. Takes months of good behaviour to get permission, and we have to wear these." She held up a wrist cuffed with a copper band, brighter and more fitted than Helena's. "We have to check in morning and night. There's a curfew. If anyone's missed for more than twenty-four hours—" She swallowed. "If they don't turn up, the High Reeve's sent to hunt them down, and they're always dead by the time he brings them back. The Warden likes to string them up, leaves them hanging for days sometimes, and then when they're starting to rot, she'll reanimate them and have them 'work' with us for a while before they go to the mines. Says it's so we don't forget the rules."

"Who—" Helena forced herself to ask, even though she was afraid to know.

Grace hesitated, eyes softening slightly. "Lila Bayard was the first one he brought back."

Grace was saying something else, but Helena couldn't hear her. All she heard was "*Lila Bayard was the first,*" over and over.

Not Lila . . .

Grace's voice came slowly back. "The Warden had her put into paladin armour and stationed at the gate. She'd been dead awhile already. Must've gotten pretty far. More than half of her face was missing, and she didn't have the prosthetic leg anymore, so they welded a steel bar on to keep her upright. She— It can't really move. Just stands there. We go past every day." Grace seemed to finally notice Helena's expression; she looked down. "She's mostly bones now. The Warden thinks it's—funny."

Helena shook her head, struggling to accept it, but of course Lila was dead. For Luc to be captured and killed, his paladins had to be killed. That was the oath they took, to die for the Principate.

Helena swallowed hard. "But surely somewhere—the Resistance—"

"There's no Resistance!" Grace said in a harsh whisper. "You think the rest of us were going to keep fighting, with everyone in the Eternal Flame dead? There's no point. The High Reeve kills everyone. Any hint, even whispers get people killed. He has this—this monster he uses for hunting. There's no point in running away or resisting or organising unless you want to be the next corpse."

Helena fell silent. Grace watched her warily, fidgeting and seeming ready to bolt at any moment.

"Who's the High Reeve?" Helena hoped it was a safe question to ask. She didn't remember the title.

Grace shook her head. "I don't know. He still wears a helmet the way the Undying did during the war. The High Necromancer's too important for public appearances, so he sends the High Reeve instead. He's some kind of vivimancer, but not like the rest. He kills people without even touching them."

"Resonance doesn't work like that," Helena said, correcting her reflexively. "Without an array, a stable channel has to be formed through contact, and then—"

"I know how resonance works," Grace said sharply. "But I've seen him do it. Last week—" Grace's voice failed; her throat bobbed several times. "There was a smuggling ring. There's been a grain shortage. Most of what we get on the Outpost is rotten. A few people were bringing in extra food. It wasn't even a lot, but the Warden heard rumours about the prisoners organising. Ten people in all. Public execution. The High Reeve did all of them at the same time. Did it 'clean' so they'll last longer in the lumithium mines."

Grace seemed to shrivel as she spoke, as if the memory were enough to paralyse her. "All there is now is surviving. *That's all that matters.*" She whispered the last words as if they weren't for Helena, but for herself.

"Why are you here, Grace?" Helena asked, glancing half-blindly around. "This isn't—we're not at the Outpost, are we?"

Grace shook her head. "No. They call this Central now. Houses all the Undying's experimentation. I—" She choked. "I have three brothers. They're littler than me. None of them were old enough to enlist, so they weren't in the Resistance rosters. My brother Gid, he'll be old enough to work soon, and he can come off the Outpost. He'll get real wages when he does. We—we just have to make it till then."

"Grace . . ."

"They're offering really good money for eyes. Just one, and it'd cover us for months."

Helena looked at her, bewildered. "What do they want eyes for?"

Grace shook her head. "I don't know. I just want the money."

If she weren't chained to the bed, Helena would have reached towards her.

"Grace, if you do this—that's not ever going to be healable—"

Grace gave an abrupt, almost wild laugh. "I *know* eyes don't grow back. That's why the pay's good."

"Yes, but—"

"Why should I keep them?" Grace sounded nearly hysterical. "So I have two eyes to watch my brothers starve? There's no food!" She wasn't whispering anymore. The scars on her face reddened, growing stark. "You don't know—you don't have any idea what it's like now. Where have you been? Why didn't you save Luc? You were supposed to, but you didn't. He died! We all watched it. And the Bayards are dead. And everyone in the Eternal Flame is dead—except you. And you think I should care about my eyes?"

Before Helena could answer, or Grace could say more, the sound of footsteps drew close.

Terror washed across Grace's face, and she fled.

The curtains on Helena's other side were shoved aside, and several figures filled the space. As one came towards the bed, Helena recognised her interrogator. The lines on the woman's face were stark with tension.

Helena couldn't make out the others behind her, but they were an unnatural grey that instantly made her skin crawl, the space within the curtains filling with the smell of preservatives.

"It's this one," the woman said. "Quite secure, as I assured you." She glanced nervously towards the figures, which seemed to move as a collective.

Necrothralls. They were all necrothralls.

She looked at Helena. "The High Necromancer has sent for you. He wishes to watch your examination personally."

Helena's chest clenched, and she pulled against the restraints. "No."

She couldn't. She couldn't see him again. The only time she'd ever seen the High Necromancer, Morrough, he'd killed Luc.

Luc, who'd been the whole world to her.

Helena had enlisted in the Resistance and sworn fealty to the Order of the Eternal Flame—not out of faith, but because of Luc Holdfast. Because she might not believe in the gods, but she had believed in him, that he was good and kind and cared about everyone.

She'd promised she'd do anything for him.

But he'd died before her eyes.

Her throat was closing. "No," she said again as the bed jolted and began to roll, her captors paying her no mind.

It was at the lifts that Helena recognised her surroundings, realised what Central was. The murals and art had been scraped from the walls, the portraits and gilding all gone, leaving the interior brutal and raw, but she knew the intricate metalwork of the lift gate.

She'd seen it every day since she was ten.

She was *in* the Alchemy Tower. In the very heart of the Alchemy Institute that the Holdfasts had founded.

This was Central.

"What did you do?" Her voice shook with horror and grief. "What did you do?"

"Calm down," the woman said through gritted teeth, glaring at Helena. She kept glancing at the necrothralls around them.

Helena couldn't be calm. It was like coming home and finding all the comfort it had once offered torn apart, the beauty flensed, everything once familiar peeled off into ruin.

Helena had come halfway across the world to study in this Tower. Luc had been so proud of the Institute his family had built. It had been the heart of Paladia. She'd known it through his eyes, all the history and meaning of it. Now it was ravaged and mutilated.

The breadth of Luc's loss was more than she could hold, but somehow she had the capacity to grieve this fragment of it. A sobbing, screaming moan tore from her.

Fingers gripped the base of Helena's skull until nails bit into her skin.

She was spiralling down. Down.

A long tunnel. Twisting darkness.

Cold dead hands and the smell of death.

When her mind cleared, she was strapped down on a table. A bright light hung overhead, the beam directed at Helena so that the room beyond disappeared.

There was a small man beside her with a pinched nose, and he kept touching Helena's face with sweaty, damp fingertips, prodding between her eyes, at her temples, poking through her hair to her skull.

"This is—quite a marvel of human transmutation, I must say," the man was saying in a high, rapid voice. He had an accent—not the Northern dialect, but something more western sounding. "Vivimancy of this skill is—miraculous. Very right to call me."

There was a long, oppressive silence.

He coughed. "The—the thing is. This is—impossible. This—can't be done."

"It's obviously possible. The evidence is right here," the woman said sharply from Helena's other side, barely visible in the severe shadows.

"Yes, quite right, Doctor Stroud. Of course, it is as you say. But—the use of vivimancy on a brain has always been a most delicate procedure. Transmutation of this scale and complexity is beyond all known scientific possibility. Memory is a mysterious thing, very changeable as it's moved around. Not a place, it is—the mind's journey. A path. The more important, more journeyed, the stronger the path. The less journeyed"—fingers fluttered—"it fades."

"Get to the point," said the woman—Doctor Stroud.

"Yes, yes. There are areas of the brain that can be altered. In the laboratories, we have vivisected countless human brains and reassembled them in various ways, to some success and also . . . failure. This transmutation, however, is upon—thought. M-M-Memory. What has been done here—" Something wet fell onto Helena's face, and she realised the man was perspiring on her. "This is alteration of the unalterable. Someone—has disassembled the pathways of her mind and created alternative routes for them. How could it be done without knowing all her thoughts and memories? No. No. This is scientifically impossible."

"I thought the mind was your specialty." A voice emerged from the darkness, low and rasping.

The man whimpered and looked ready to weep. "The—the brain is,

Your Eminence." He bowed towards the shadows. "But this work is beyond me. Bennet and I, you remember our labours for your cause? I hope . . . Memories cannot simply be regenerated; the mind and spirit must forge them. The spirit cannot be altered by external force—the—the fevers—"

"Is there any way to uncover what is hidden?"

The man opened and closed his mouth as if he were a fish, staring into the darkness as though he expected to be swallowed by it.

"The Holdfasts are dead," the rasping voice said, "the Eternal Flame erased from this earth. What would they have hidden within her mind?"

The question was met with silence.

"Who placed her in that warehouse?"

Stroud stepped forward. "There's nothing confirming it, but based on the records, Mandl was overseer at the time. It was shortly before her ascendance and transfer to the Outpost."

"Send for her."

Stroud nodded and disappeared. As she did, the shadows moved.

Helena could only see from the corner of her eyes, but she could not fail to notice when Morrough emerged from the darkness.

The High Necromancer was not what she remembered. When he'd killed Luc, he'd been human. Now he was mutated. His limbs stuck out in ways that were impossibly jointed, and he was nearly the size of two men.

She thought, at first, that he was wearing a mask. The High Necromancer had been masked during the celebration, wearing a huge golden crescent that concealed half his face like an eclipsed sun.

As he drew nearer however, she realised it wasn't a mask she was staring at. Morrough's face was skull-like, his features so sunken, the skin so translucently pale, that she could see through to the bone.

Where his eyes should have been were two blackened, empty hollows, as if they'd been burned out with live coals.

Somehow, he still seemed to see Helena.

He walked forward, one hand outstretched, but there was something wrong about it, over-jointed, the skin bizarrely stretched. Too many bones inside it. Before his fingers grazed her skin, the pain of his resonance lanced through her skull.

Her vision turned red.

Screaming surrounded her, blistering her eardrums and going on and on as her memories detonated inside her brain. A cascade of images tore through her consciousness.

Everywhere she looked, people were dying. Her hands were covered in blood. There were bodies everywhere.

She was kneeling on the floor, holding together torsos and faces and limbs, trying to put them back together, knitting them into wholeness. Again and again and again. Bodies raw with burns, so consumed by fire that she couldn't find their features.

Always another body, and another.

The resonance burrowed deeper and deeper, and the screaming grew louder.

She saw Luc. Vivid as if he were there with her. His beautiful face, and eyes as blue as a summer's sky, golden sunlight reflecting in them.

Then Luc was gone. Blood was everywhere. All she could see was a reddened light, fractured and disjointed, swimming overhead. And the screaming.

Her screams. Her vocal cords were shredded, raw pain tearing through her lungs and throat. A lancing pain through her heart each time she gasped for air.

The small man was muttering, "I wouldn't recommend—" over and over with his arms cradled defensively around his own head.

There was a knock on a door, and Stroud reappeared, barely glancing at Helena.

"Mandl is on her way. And—" She hesitated. "I brought Shiseo. I thought he might have some insight into our prisoner. He did consult with the Eternal Flame. She needs a new nullification set anyway; I thought he might apply them before his departure."

There was a quiet shuffling in the dark. Helena craned her neck as much as she could, eyes straining for a glimpse of the traitor.

A round-faced man with dark hair emerged, carrying a small case. He paused to bow reverently before the High Necromancer.

Morrough waved him towards Helena. "What kinds of vivimancy did the Eternal Flame utilise?"

Shiseo drew closer, and Helena realised he was Eastern. Far Eastern. He only met Helena's accusing stare for a moment before he averted his gaze.

"I am sorry." He bowed slightly once again. "I was only consulted on occasion due to my metallurgical knowledge."

Helena released a small breath of relief.

"Surely you know something—you did work in their laboratories," Stroud said, impatiently. "Do you recognise her, at least?"

Shiseo barely glanced at Helena.

"I believe she was a healer," he said quietly as he returned his attention to his case.

Helena fought back a wince.

Stroud looked sharply at Helena, her eyes narrowed.

"Really? A healer, you say?" The way Stroud spoke was venomous. She cleared her throat, glancing around. "Of course I knew there were vivimancers who supported the Eternal Flame. As if martyring themselves could earn acceptance, even though the Faith spurned their gifts as an abomination." Her eyes were scathing. "I just didn't realise *this* was one of them."

No one said anything. Stroud's face reddened. "I'm sure I would have realised if I'd had more time to retrieve the Resistance's records. But why would someone transmute a healer's mind?"

Shiseo bowed to Stroud now. "I could not say."

A growing sense of agitation permeated the room.

Morrough sighed like a gusting bellows. "He knows nothing. Apply the nullification and get him out."

Shiseo bowed and lifted Helena's hand as far as it would go, inspecting her wrist and the cuff around it. He had soft hands for a metallurgist.

"These are—a very old model. They do not fully suppress the resonance," he said. He slid the manacle up Helena's forearm as far as it would go, and it was as if the static of the suppression was pushed up towards her brain along with it.

His fingers pressed deftly along her arm, finding the dip just below her wrist between the two bones of her forearm.

Her pulse beat against his fingers. He felt it for a moment and moved his fingers away from it, squeezing briefly before he turned to Stroud. "Just here."

Stroud's dry, hard fingers wrapped around her wrist. Helena felt a brief tingle of Stroud's resonance before all sensation from hand to elbow vanished and her body went limp with paralysis. Without explanation or warning, Stroud plucked something out of the case. It gleamed in the light, revealing the bulbous handle and long pointed spike of an awl.

With practised ease, Stroud drove the tip straight through Helena's wrist. Helena felt nothing, but her throat closed, stomach inverting as she watched Stroud work the awl in slow circles as it sank between the bones, the tip emerging on the other side.

When Stroud pulled it out, there was a drop of blood on the tip and a hole running straight through Helena's wrist. The wound was bloodless, all the torn skin, muscle, and broken vessels instantly closing in the process.

Setting the awl aside, Stroud manipulated Helena's hand, bending and arching it back, checking for range of motion. Sensation returned, but the paralysis lingered.

"Nerves and veins are all intact," Stroud said, letting go.

Helena could do nothing but watch as Shiseo stepped over and pushed a tiny, notched tube through the hole now running through her wrist until the ends protruded on each side. The moment the tube slipped into place, the blurred sense of resonance in Helena's left hand vanished completely.

It was as if one of her senses had been ripped out.

She could feel the tube inside her, a deadening sense of inertia emanating from it.

Shiseo pulled out a ribbon of metal. It was smooth and shining on one side, grooved on the other. He slid the groove over one notched end of the tube before wrapping the ribbon around her wrist and sliding it over the other, locking the tube in place before he wrapped the rest of the metal ribbon around and around.

He inspected the tension and fit, lined up all the layers, and with little more than a flick of his fingers, the layers morphed into a solid ring of metal, perfectly fitted.

No lock, no way to open it without resonance.

Shiseo slid a strangely shaped wire into a tiny opening on the old cuff. A mechanism inside clicked, and it fell off.

He picked it up as if it were a curious antique and put it in his case before moving around to Helena's right side.

Helena grasped desperately at her dim sense of remaining resonance, trying to focus, to remember the sensation of who and what she was, knowing it would be gone in minutes.

Shiseo was just removing the second old manacle when the door opened and a guard entered.

"Warden Mandl."

A woman in uniform strode into the room with a quick, confident step that faltered when her eyes landed on Helena.

She had a wide mouth, and it dropped open in shock.

"What did you do to this prisoner, Mandl?" Morrough asked. He had disappeared back into the shadows, but his voice emerged, even more dangerous now.

Mandl flung herself prostrate, disappearing from Helena's range of vision.

"Your Eminence . . ." Her pleading voice rose from the floor.

"I saved you from the Holdfasts and the Faith. Saved all the necromancers and vivimancers like you who lived like rats fearing the Eternal Flame's punishment for your 'unnatural gifts.' I let you ascend above those who had sought to subdue you. Now I learn you betrayed me?"

"No! It was not a betrayal! I am loyal. Loyal to our cause, and loyal to you! It was my foolish desire for vengeance—I confess it. I wanted her to suffer. But I would never betray you."

"Explain yourself."

Mandl pushed herself up, still kneeling, her head bowed but her voice shaking with emotion. "She is a traitor to vivimancers! She tormented me! Thought herself better than me for having been a part of the Holdfasts' Institute, her vivimancy blessed by the Eternal Flame. She had to be punished!"

Helena stared at the woman in dazed bewilderment.

"You tampered with a prisoner and her records out of—jealousy?" Stroud looked astonished. "Why didn't you report her abilities?"

Mandl shrank back. "I feared that she would be favoured if it was known. That you might find her useful and not punish her as she deserved to be punished."

Stroud leaned over her. "And what kind of punishment did you think she deserved?"

Mandl swallowed nervously. "I—left her conscious—in the stasis tank. I intended to return. I wanted her to be trapped, knowing and dreading what I would do to her, but then I was assigned to the Outpost and selected for ascendance. I was afraid my temporary lapse in judgement would disappoint, so I did not disclose it. But I would never betray our great cause!"

"She has been in that warehouse for the fourteen months since you were reassigned. Why are there no records?" Stroud sounded highly sceptical.

"I'd intended to complete her records once I was—done with her. When I left, I assumed she would die and then no one would ever know. Forgive me! I did nothing else, I swear it." Mandl flung herself back down onto the floor.

"I see now I have been too generous," Morrough said. His nightmarish face and looming eye sockets emerged from the shadows. He tilted his head as though staring down at Mandl. "You were not worthy of my gift."

"Please! Your Eminence, I beg of you—give me—"

Mandl stopped speaking as she was jerked up onto her feet by an unseen force. The front of her grey uniform tore open as her ribs unfurled in a gush of blood, her chest rent apart.

Helena's skin crawled, terror slithering like a worm through her gut as the warm wet smell of fresh blood and exposed organs permeated the room. There was a sensation like a hum in the air that she could feel all the way into her own lungs.

But Mandl, split open as she was, was not dead.

Her hands rose up, and she tried to claw her ribs closed with one hand and ward off Morrough with the other, her exposed lungs pulsing. "Another chance—please! I will not fail you! I swear. You will not regret it."

"No, you will not fail me again," Morrough said, his rasping voice almost gentle as he reached into Mandl's open chest, fingers sliding beneath her lungs and extracting a gleaming piece of metal from somewhere near her heart. Little tendrils of viscera were wrapped around it, clinging to both the metal and Morrough's fingers as it was torn free.

When it came loose, Mandl's body dropped to the ground. Silent. Dead.

Morrough gave a low sigh and seemed to shrink momentarily as he stood, cradling the metal in his hand. Through the blood, the piece had a sharp, bright, lumithium gleam.

He gestured with his other hand. A necrothrall crawled from the shadows like an animal. It was a young woman in the early stages of necrosis, still wearing the tattered remains of the Eternal Flame's hospital uniform. Her expression was blank. A rip in the uniform exposed a chest latticed with blackening veins.

When the corpse reached Morrough, she stood, and he shoved the metal piece into her. There was a soft crunch of breaking bone that left a hole purpled with old blood in the centre of her chest.

The corpse-woman shuddered, and then her expression morphed, the blankness vanishing.

She stumbled and gave a wild screeching moan as she looked down at her blackened fingers and deteriorating body.

"No! Please, no—it wasn't my—"

"Do not fail me again, Mandl," Morrough said, "and in time perhaps I will permit you a better reliquary. Perhaps your original."

He gestured at Mandl's corpse on the floor. The air hummed again as his fingers curled, and the ribs closed. Mandl's body stood. The front of the uniform was ripped open, exposing her, and she was covered in blood. The skin knit back together, but her face showed nothing. The corpse-woman fell to the floor moaning and pleading, clawing at the oozing wound in the middle of her chest as if trying to rip the metal back out while Morrough walked back towards Helena.

Stroud kicked Mandl. "Thank the High Necromancer for his mercy in allowing you a vivimancer's corpse, and a return to the Outpost, Warden."

The corpse-woman gave one last guttural moan and struggled to her feet.

"Thank you, Your Eminence," she rasped, and stumbled from the room.

Stroud joined Morrough, appearing unfazed by what had transpired.

"Is it possible for someone to survive fourteen months in stasis?" Stroud asked.

Morrough said nothing, but the nervous, perspiring man spoke up from where he'd been cowering against the wall. "Ac-Actually that idea does have some potential," he said, stepping forward and then shrinking back as Morrough's eyeless attention turned to him.

He adjusted the collar on his shirt several times. "Our good friend from the Far East"—he gestured towards Shiseo, who was absorbed in cleaning his awl—"mentioned that the suppression she was wearing was an old model, without a complete resonance block. Perhaps that explains both her mind—*and* her survival."

Stroud's eyes narrowed. "How?"

"The transmutation done to her isn't something another person could do. Those memories are too deeply enmeshed with her mind. However, if you had someone capable of such complexity—a healer, as our friend says she was—perhaps she . . ."

"You're saying *she* did this to herself?" Stroud gestured towards Helena with scathing disbelief.

He choked on his saliva. "Well—it seems the most likely explanation. In my opinion." His face was gleaming with perspiration.

Stroud sucked on her teeth. "And the survival?"

"She—did not let herself die. Per-Perhaps a low level of internalised resonance in a competent healer would provide a sufficient means of self-sustenance when ordinarily a body would perish under such conditions."

"That's absurd!" Stroud snapped.

“That is immaterial. Can we recover the memories?” Morrough said. “The Eternal Flame would not go to such lengths unless the information was of vital importance.”

“Your Eminence.” Stroud sounded pleading. “The Order of the Eternal Flame is gone. Their ashes are all that remain.”

“I did not ask you,” Morrough said, his focus on the man, who'd turned a sickly green.

“I don't—believe—”

“*Get out.*” The air hummed.

The man blanched and bowed repeatedly, thanking Morrough for his mercy and patience as he walked backwards out of the room with visible relief on his face.

“What are you hiding?” Morrough loomed above her.

Her heart beat faster and faster. She had no answer.

Stroud leaned over as well, eyes narrowed in appraisal. “Your Eminence, perhaps if we removed the frontmost section of her brain, we might be able to penetrate some of the memories before the fevers become detrimental,” she said, trailing her finger thoughtfully across Helena's forehead. “Or it might alter the pathways enough to revert things. I would be honoured to maintain her vitals while you perform the vivisection.”

Terror sliced through Helena as Morrough nodded. Stroud stepped to the side, adjusting the light overhead, as though intending to begin immediately.

“Pardon,” a soft voice interrupted, and Helena felt a rush of relief until she realised it was the traitor, Shiseo, standing with his case gripped in his hands. “I have just remembered one small thing. There was a General Bayard. His head was injured in the war.”

“Yes.” Stroud seemed irritated by the interruption.

“The brain was healed, but”—he paused as if struggling to find the right words—“it blocked him from who he was—his mind, his true self.”

“Yes. We are aware of what happened to Bayard. Nonverbal. Dependent. His wife had to care for him like a child,” Stroud said, her voice waspish.

"Of course, I apologise. It was probably nothing." Shiseo bowed and appeared to be on the verge of leaving.

"Wait." Stroud sounded conciliatory. "You've begun now. Tell us what your point is."

Shiseo stopped. "I don't know all the details, but I believe they pursued a cure for him late in the war. A complicated procedure of the mind."

"By a healer or by a surgeon?" Stroud leaned forward.

Shiseo tilted his head as if trying to recall. "A healer."

Stroud pursed her lips. "Elain Boyle, I imagine."

Shiseo tilted his head again, no recognition in his face.

"She was Luc Holdfast's personal healer. The Eternal Flame was rather lax in their record keeping, but Elain Boyle's name appeared frequently in the last year of the war. She seemed to have become unusually distinguished." Stroud tapped her fingers on her lips, sucking at her teeth again.

"Where is Boyle now?" Morrough asked.

"Killed when we seized the Institute. I believe her body was sent to the mines. We could see if there are any remains." Stroud's attention returned to Shiseo. "What did the Eternal Flame do with Bayard that you think is somehow relevant?"

Shiseo bowed again.

"I was only aware of this because they hoped there were similar techniques used in the Eastern Empire. The healer, I was told, had a special ability to—to alter not just the brain but the mind. They proposed to enter the mind of Bayard and heal him from within."

The mood in the room suddenly shifted, growing electrified.

"That would be animancy, not healing," Stroud said with slow incredulity.

"I do not know, the words were—different," Shiseo said. "The mind, I was told, resisted another's presence, but this healer believed that with many small treatments, it was possible. Like learning to tolerate a poison."

"Mithridatism," Morrough said slowly. He straightened into his full, tremendous height. "Soul mithridatism . . ."

He advanced on Shiseo as if intending to rip the answers out of him. "The Eternal Flame found a way to make living subjects survive soul transference? And you never thought to mention this?"

Helena thought she was about to watch another rib cage be torn open.

Shiseo remained eerily calm and bowed again. "I apologise. They asked me many questions. It is hard to remember."

Morrough seemed appeased by this excuse and turned back, considering Helena once more as if still inclined to vivisect her in search of answers.

"If the Eternal Flame did have an animancer who developed a temporary transference method . . . could that explain this form of memory loss? If another person could enter someone's mind like that, they might be able to alter thoughts and memories, just as we see here. It would explain everything," Stroud asked, gesturing at Helena. "And . . . I must say it seems more likely than far-fetched notions of self-transmutation."

"If the Eternal Flame discovered a viable method of transference, that has more significance than mere memory loss," Morrough said. Helena could feel his resonance in her marrow, as if it were burrowing into her flesh, attempting to peel her apart, layer by layer.

He looked towards Stroud. "Record every detail Shiseo remembers of this procedure before his departure east. We will begin testing this gradual transference method. I want it perfected. If it is possible, we'll use it to remove the transmutation on her and see what the Eternal Flame was so desperate to hide from me."

Morrough drew a breath that rattled as he turned away.

"Your Eminence," Stroud said, her voice nervous. "This transference procedure you wish to begin testing, it would require an animancer, I believe?" She gave a weak cough. "I'm sure Bennet would have been thrilled by the opportunity, but unfortunately souls are not within my resonance repertoire, and there's only one other. Would this be something that you and I—" Her voice lifted hopefully.

"Let the High Reeve manage it."

Stroud's face fell. "But I found h—"

"I have other work for you."

Stroud straightened but still looked disappointed.

"The High Reeve was Bennet's favourite after all." Morrough waved a dismissive hand as he vanished into the shadows. "It's time he's given more to do than hunting."

CHAPTER 3

When Helena was rolled back into the lift at Central, she counted the floors of the Tower as they passed.

The Alchemy Tower had been an architectural wonder for centuries. It was only five storeys when initially constructed as a memorial to the first Necromancy War. Back then, alchemical resonance was an arcane ability, regarded as magic. Its practitioners, figures cloaked in myth and mystery, like Cetus, the first Northern alchemist.

The Holdfasts and the Institute had changed that, establishing alchemy as the Noble Science, something to be studied and mastered. When the Alchemy Institute threatened to outgrow the Tower, it was raised with alchemically wrought pulley systems to add additional storeys to the base. It had stood as the tallest building on the Northern continent for almost two centuries, growing ever taller as the city around it expanded and alchemists flocked through its gates.

The study of Northern Alchemy itself was entwined with the Tower structure. The lowest five levels with the largest lecture halls were the "foundations," filled with initiates still discovering their resonance and mastering basic transmutation principles. Annual exams were required to ascend. After five years, most students would depart with their certification to join the guilds, with only qualifying undergraduates ascending to the next tier in the narrowing Tower to study more technical fields and subjects. Even fewer would rise past the graduate and research floors to achieve the rank of grandmaster.

The lift stopped somewhere amid the former research floors.

Helena strained her eyes, forced to peer through an aura of pain steadily fogging her vision. The walls blurred, her eyes failing to focus until she was rolled to a stop in the centre of a sterile room.

It had probably been a private laboratory once.

The straps pinning her in place were unfastened, and Stroud paused, checking Helena's wrists.

The tubes running between her ulna and radius were nauseating, evoking a deep sense of wrongness. She couldn't even twitch her fingers without feeling the way her muscles, tendons, veins, and nerves in that narrow space were all forced to accommodate the nullification driven through her.

"Very good," Stroud said to herself before she turned to leave. Just before the door shut, Helena heard her say, "No one enters this room without my approval."

There was a heavy click and the grind of a lock, and Helena was left alone.

She lurched up, but the drug had burned itself out of her blood and her muscles were cramping, contracting as though pulled taut. She tried to straighten, but the instant her feet touched the ground, her legs collapsed under her.

She slumped to the floor.

Run, a voice kept telling her. But she couldn't; her arms and legs couldn't hold her. In the absence of any physical ability, her thoughts turned inwards.

Had she really forgotten something?

Perhaps the Eternal Flame was not gone but remained as a hidden ember, waiting until the time was right. The possibility sparked a glimmer of hope. But how had she been made to forget?

Transference. Animancy.

Both words were unfamiliar.

She turned them over in her mind. Trying to contextualise the comments that had been made. Souls and minds and occupying the mental landscape of another person to transmute them from within. And the Eternal Flame had discovered this?

Surely not. Souls were considered inviolable among those of faith. The Eternal Flame considered even the physical alterations of vivimancy and necromancy a risk to an immortal soul.

Alteration of a mind, the transference of a soul: Surely that would be seen as infinitely worse.

Yet Shiseo claimed that the Eternal Flame had developed a way to perform this animancy-transference process. Something that Morrough, who'd unlocked the secrets of immortality, had not discovered.

Who was Elain Boyle? Helena didn't know the name, and she was sure there had never been any other healers, much less a personal one, designated for Luc alone.

Luc would never have consented to receiving anything that wasn't equally distributed to all the rest of the Resistance, and that included medical care and healing. He'd struggled with having paladins sworn to protect him, despite it being a tradition older than Paladia.

Stroud had to be mistaken.

Yet there *was* something hidden, changed about her. A secret so painstakingly concealed, Helena could not even guess at what it was.

Her muscles cramped harder. She lay on the floor, her body curled and contorted inwards like a dead spider, but her mind raced on.

What would Luc do if he were the one still alive? Captive. He'd already have a plan. He would have charmed Grace into passing a message for him, begun coordinating a way to escape, and plotted to rescue everyone on the Outpost.

That's what he would do. Now it was up to Helena.

She couldn't fail him. Not again.

HELENA HAD EXPECTED THE TRANSFERENCE to begin immediately, but instead she spent what felt like days barely able to move as her muscles gradually un-cramped.

"Withdrawal," Stroud said with a look of condescension as she forced a feeding tube down Helena's nose and inserted a saline drip into her arm to keep her sedated. "No matter. I imagine they taught you to enjoy suffering. After all, sacrifice is a healer's calling, isn't it?"

Stroud was unveiled in her disdain for Helena with the revelation that they were both vivimancers, but on opposite sides in the war.

Stroud considered her a traitor.

"I don't like those spasms," Stroud later said during an examination, her mouth pursed when Helena's fingers seized, making her drop a cup. "It's not caused by the nullification set; do you remember when they began?"

Helena shook her head, flinching as the cold burning sensation of Stroud's resonance sank into her left wrist, winding through the bones as she twisted and manipulated it for several minutes.

"From the condition of it, it appears you've broken this wrist several times. There's old nerve damage. Do you remember when it happened?"

Helena had no recollection of ever seriously injuring her hands. Dexterous hands were vital for channelling and controlling resonance in both an alchemist's practice and a healer's work. She'd always been very careful with them.

"There wasn't any mention of it in your student files, so it must have been during the war, but there's no records there, either."

Helena's academic records had been unearthed, and Stroud liked to use them to interrogate her about the smaller details of her life. She suspected it was because Stroud was allowed to punish her for refusing to answer.

Where was her alchemy resonance first tested? At the Paladian embassy in her homeland, the southern islands of Etras. How old was she when she immigrated to Paladia to study at the Alchemy Institute? Ten.

How many years of education did she complete at the Institute? Six.

Did she remember Principate Apollo Holdfast's death? Yes, she had been in class with Luc.

When did she join the Resistance? When the guilds overthrew legitimate government and there was a Resistance to join.

Stroud had not liked that answer.

When did she become a member of the Order of the Eternal Flame? Helena tried to avoid answering, but Stroud had the book of members, with Helena's vows and name all written in her blood.

"Did the Eternal Flame's Council know you were a vivimancer when you joined?"

Helena shook her head.

Stroud sat glaring at her, waiting for a verbal response.

"I didn't know I was a vivimancer," Helena finally said. "And after—once everyone knew—Luc didn't care. He didn't think a person's abilities changed who they were, only what they did with them."

"How magnanimous." Stroud's voice was chilly. Her fingers were creasing the file in her hand. "A pity he didn't also step down. A great many people might still be alive then."

"His family was Called," Helena said, despite knowing there was no point in arguing.

"Yes, by the sun," Stroud said, scoffing, her voice growing sharp. "I know they didn't teach modern astronomy at the Institute, but did you ever study the newer astrological theories? You're from the trade islands after all; you must have been exposed to all kinds of ideas. Did you really believe that the sun looked at the earth and chose a favourite? That a drop of sunlight endowed Orion Holdfast with such godlike abilities that all his descendants deserved to rule Paladia like gods themselves?"

Helena set her jaw, but Stroud would not stop.

"According to your academic records, you were considered bright. Surely you didn't swallow every story you were told about the Holdfasts. Look me in the eyes and tell me: Do you *really* think the Holdfasts had a right to rule?"

Stroud's fingers dug beneath Helena's chin, forcing her to look up.

She stared squarely into Stroud's face, feeling the threat of her resonance. "Better them than people like you."

Stroud's hand dropped, her resonance vanishing before she slapped Helena across the face so hard her head cracked against the wall.

"If you'd joined our cause, you could have been great." Stroud was breathing heavily as she stood over Helena. "You would have been somebody. You're nothing now. You spent yourself on the wrong side. No one will ever remember you. You're ash, like all the rest. And a traitor to your kind."

Once she was alone, Helena cradled the swollen side of her face, head throbbing.

The Resistance had considered the war a holy war—a divine battle between good and evil, a testing of the Faith. But Helena's motives had been more personal than that.

Luc didn't need to be divine for her to want to save him. He could have been entirely ordinary, and she would have made all the same choices.

Was there something she could have done that could have changed things?

When she'd first immigrated to Paladia, she'd thought it was paradise. Etras did not have much metal as a natural resource. Resonance was rare. There were a few alchemy guilds, but they offered no formal training. Reaching Paladia had felt like coming home; like finding the place where she'd always been meant to be.

She'd been vaguely aware that there was a hierarchy among alchemists that divided even the student body, splitting the devout families in close alliance with the Holdfasts apart from the guilds, but she wasn't familiar enough with the city-state's politics to understand the intricacies of it.

All she knew was that some students wouldn't speak to her, laughed when she asked questions, and mocked her accent and way of gesturing with her hands when she talked. Later she learned that those were the guild students and to be wary of them.

It was Luc who'd had to explain that the guild students thought Helena's enrolment had taken a spot that should have gone to the guilds—though Luc assured her that they were wrong. His family's Institute hadn't been founded for guilds but for people like her, the ones who didn't have opportunities to study alchemy on their own. The guild students didn't even need to attend; their places and futures were all assured. For them, enrolment at the Institute was a status symbol. Once they had their certification, they'd all leave.

Helena was special, though. She'd be the one who'd stay beyond Year Five, who'd study more than just the principal foundations of alchemy. She'd ascend to the highest floors, make discoveries, and do the kind of work that would change the world. Her name remembered forever.

Why would his family want another guild student at their Institute when they could have someone like her?

Luc had always had a talent for making Helena feel like she was special rather than painfully out of place. She'd wanted to prove him right—that she was something, that she'd be worth believing in. His family wouldn't be wrong about her.

She'd focused on her education and ignored the political hostilities around her.

Luc would mention things from time to time, how the guilds were convinced that his family was stifling alchemy's scientific progress and preventing industrialisation, and then he'd wave towards the factories below the dam filling the sky with black clouds of smoke. That his father was being accused of allowing the country to fall behind because of his derelict governance. Or that the guilds had proposed that the Principate's power be limited to religious affairs, and that *they* be the ones to run the country.

It had seemed that nothing Principate Apollo did was ever enough for the guilds; their complaints and demands were endless.

When Principate Apollo was murdered, the guilds didn't see a tragedy at all, but an opportunity. They used Luc's age, only sixteen, as a pretext for declaring a reformation: No longer would religious elites and a warrior class rule Paladia. The city-state would be governed by the newly formed Guild Assembly.

The guilds' sedition would have been easy for the Order of the Eternal Flame to stop if it hadn't been for Morrough. He appeared amid the upheaval seemingly from nowhere, offering immortality. Not an endless life of decay, but one impervious to age and injury, discovered not through any divine power but through science.

The guilds seized the opportunity, and the Undying began to appear.

A select few at first, revealing themselves to be not only immortal but also capable of advanced forms of alchemy. Power and eternal life were suddenly within the grasp of anyone prepared to prove themselves loyal to Morrough. Aspirants flocked to join them, aligning with the guilds.

The ideas of "New Paladia" being promised by the Guild Assembly spread through the population like a disease.

When the Eternal Flame moved to restore order, the Undying revealed another ability: necromancy. On a scale never seen before. Rather than recruiting heavily from among the Aspirants, when attacked they'd kill the Eternal Flame's soldiers, and then use reanimation to turn them back on their own compatriots, building an army with the Eternal Flame's dead.

Luc, newly crowned as Principate, had been certain that the citizens of Paladia would be shocked into reason once they realised they were aligning themselves with necromancers. Necromancy had been a mortal crime throughout most of the continent for centuries. Not even the guilds would go so far.

He had been wrong.

"If you were a healer, why aren't you mentioned more in the hospital records?"

Stroud had returned in a state of high dudgeon, a stack of files with her.

Helena's name was almost nowhere to be found. Stroud had only managed to find her signature on inventories of medical supplies, an application for a base-level alchemy knife, and a few request forms for the chymistry and metallurgy departments for certain compounds. The only interesting thing in the entire stack was a preliminary casualty list that had Helena listed among the presumed dead.

All told, in years of military files, Helena had scarcely existed at all. Stroud seemed personally affronted by it.

"Well?"

"Healing is a miracle; it's not something you're supposed to put your name on," she said, reciting what she'd been told long ago. "There's a symbol placed on medical records to indicate acts of—intercession."

"Do you mean—" Stroud flipped through a file and turned it towards Helena. In the corner was a crescent shape with a slash across it. "This?"

Helena gave a short nod.

Stroud stared at it. "Then how on earth do you keep track of procedures?"

Tightness spread from her chest to her throat. "Healing's not a procedure."

Falcon Matias, the spiritual counsellor of the Eternal Flame's Council and Helena's direct superior, had been strict in his demands that the use of vivimancy not be documented in any ways which might glorify it. The act of vivimancy, he said, could only be purified through intentions of selflessness.

Although healers were relatively common in the remote parts of Paladia, vivimancy was rare enough that there were all kinds of claims about what vivimancers were capable of—that they could enthral the living just as necromancers enthralled the dead, for instance, and perform unspeakable transmutations upon living flesh.

Helena used to think these views of vivimancers unreasonably harsh, but now as Stroud's subject, she began to understand.

Stroud was not enthralling, but she was expert in paralysing and transmutationally manipulating Helena at the slightest provocation. If Helena twitched too much, Stroud would fuse her bones together to keep her still. She seemed to take delight in the technicality of it not being torture. Sometimes she left Helena like that for hours.

It was a relief when Stroud finally seemed to lose interest, announcing that she had no more time to deal with Helena. Several times each day, two necrothralls would come to retrieve her and make her walk along the corridor that ran around the lift.

Her vision recovered, the necrothralls were horrifying to see. The adipocere gave a taut waxy sheen to the greyish-purple mottling of their skin, and the sclera around their clouding pupils were red or vivid yellow. Their fingertips were blackened and rotting off. The smell of chemical preservatives and rot made Helena sick, but they wouldn't let her stop walking until her legs gave out and they had to drag her back into the cell.

The walks blurred together along with the days. Helena didn't know how long she'd been in Central; the lights never went out, and all the windows were covered and sealed.

"Is this her?" A man with a ghastly pale face and a sharp, needle-thin nose suddenly stepped out from a room and into Helena's path as she was being shoved along the perpetual route.

Helena gave a gasp of shock. Standing before her, in elaborate embroidered clothes and jewellery, was Jan Crowther, one of the five members of the Eternal Flame's Council.

"Crowth—"

A heavily ringed hand shot out, gripping her by the shoulder and dragging her close, peering at her.

"You knew him?" he asked, his fingers and rings digging into her skin.

She tried to pull free, but the necrothrall escorts held her in place as Crowther leaned in, closer and closer, drawing a deep breath, and a thick purple tongue flicked out as if he meant to lick her.

She recoiled, but he was close enough now that she could make out details. There was a slight yellowing in his sclera and faint patterns of dark veins beneath his vaguely clouded eyes. His skin was powdery, smelling strongly of lavender.

This wasn't Crowther.

One of the Undying was wearing his corpse.

On the rare occasions when they couldn't regenerate anymore, so grievously wounded in battle that their immortal bodies could no longer heal, the Undying could move themselves into their necrothralls instead. It was why the Resistance had called them liches.

It was an imperfect solution; even when maintained, the bodies rotted slowly around them and lacked the regenerative qualities of the near-impervious originals. Helena suspected this was why Morrough was so interested in transference—the method had the potential to allow the Undying to move into living bodies instead.

The lich using Crowther's body drew back. He looked at her again, a strange expression sweeping across his face.

"I know you," he said softly.

He gripped her face, twisting her head so that light fell on it from different angles. His eyes were crawling over her skin as if looking for something. He grabbed one of her hands, the dark heavy rings digging against her bones, shifting the manacle and sending a shock of pain down her arm. He looked at her fingers and then back to her face.

The necrothralls did nothing.

Was this the High Reeve?

"Yes. That's her." Stroud had appeared, her voice much softer than Helena was accustomed to. She looked irritated at the way Helena was being manhandled but seemed reluctant to protest. "She'll be ready soon."

The lich gripped Helena by her hair, his expression twisting as he leaned in again, a hungry, desperate look in his eyes unlike anything she'd ever seen on Crowther's impassive face.

"I've seen her somewhere." He gripped her tighter, shaking her so hard that her head snapped back. "Where did I see you?"

"This was the Holdfasts' pet, Guildmaster. You probably saw her at the Institute."

The lich's face contorted with contempt at the mention of the Holdfasts, and he let go, abruptly losing interest. Now he looked angry, a deep purple rising along his neck, mottling his face. "I expected more than this. I was told this assignment was something special."

Stroud sucked at her teeth. "Appearances are not everything. You can tell the High Reeve she'll be ready for him soon. Now, you wanted to see the preparations for the chambers." Stroud gestured towards the lifts. "I intend to begin with a test batch very soon to see how quickly we can get things started. The interest has been almost overwhelming. I have dozens of applications, and the announcement is still weeks away." Stroud gave a nervous laugh but caught herself, clearing her throat as she pressed her hand against a panel on the lift. "It's been difficult to determine the most promising combinations. I've taken what I can from the hospitals' records. The guilds' archives are quite useful, too, truly ahead of their time. But you're the only one who produced exactly what we're hoping to replicate here, so I'm very eager for your insight."

The lich's expression grew stony despite the praise. The lift arrived, and he and Stroud were gone before he gave an answer.

The necrothralls nudged Helena forward. She released a slow breath. Not the High Reeve, then. It was a relief that the first reanimated body she'd recognised had been Crowther, one of the more detached members of the Council, and not someone she'd known well.

She looked up and flinched at the sight of the only portrait that hung in the corridor.

The Tower used to be full of art and decorations, lined with portraits of significant alchemists who'd studied or taught at the Institute. Now there was only one, and it depicted a sallow, sullen-looking man with a large forehead and heavy chin.

The name ARTEMON BENNET was hammered into the plaque beneath it, with two dates below, spanning more than eighty years.

Helena remembered with visceral clarity the reports associated with that name. Once the Undying had established a strong position in the city, they put out a call for all the vivimancers and necromancers in hiding to join their cause, setting up laboratories where such supporters could explore their powers, freed from the oppression of the Faith.

When Resistance fighters weren't simply killed and reanimated into necrothralls, they were sent to those laboratories as research subjects. Artemon Bennet had been the head of New Paladia's science and research departments. It was reported that he had a particular interest in experimentation on alchemists.

The only good thing about the portrait was knowing that Bennet was somehow dead.

Another walk was finally coming to its end. Helena still struggled with breathing deeply, a habit ingrained by the stasis tank's limited oxygen and worsened by the necrothralls' stench. Her head was growing light, vision threatening to blur. Her footsteps began to falter.

The necrothralls gripped her, not letting her slow. Her feet began to drag across the floor.

A strangled gasp jolted her to alertness.

"Marino?" A dark-haired girl in a wheeled chair was passing her. She was gaunt, almost collapsed in on herself, but she straightened, leaning forward as her eyes fastened on Helena's face. She had scars like Grace's, and there was a blanket over her lap. She wore the same manacles around her wrists that Helena did. She was being pushed down the hall in the direction of an operation theatre that Helena had vaguely noticed was open.

Helena staggered, trying to find her feet. "Penny."

Penny was a year older than Helena. One of the few other girls at the Institute to pursue undergraduate studies in alchemy. She'd been among the first to enlist with the Resistance, determined to go to the front lines and fight.

The orderly pushing Penny walked faster, turning the chair to block the exchange.

Helena and Penny both craned their necks, trying to keep sight of each other as they were pushed apart.

"Penny, what are they—" Helena didn't get the whole question out as she was shoved towards her room.

Penny leaned over the arm of the chair, looking back, her face stricken. "You were right. I'm so sorry. We should have listened to you."

There was no time to ask what she meant. The orderly sped up, and Penny disappeared.

"I'm delivering you today," Stroud said, walking in with a stack of files she was immersed in. She'd been increasingly distracted every time Helena saw her. "Get ready."

"I'm leaving?"

Stroud looked up and gave an irritated, nervous smile. "Yes. Central has other purposes. The High Reeve has been waiting for you. Come. Now."

There was no readying for Helena to do. She was bundled into the lift with nothing but the clothes on her back and a pair of wool slippers too large for her feet.

The lift descended to the fifth floor, where the Alchemy Tower was connected by skybridges to the surrounding Institute buildings. In a city as vertical as Paladia, skybridges were frequently used to interconnect buildings, some like slender passages, others large enough to hold plazas and gardens dozens of storeys above the rest of the city. As the city had grown, the lower parts saw their sky almost blotted out, creating a damp, darkened underbelly that festered with diseases.

She could see the commons below, grassy patches bisected by geometric footpaths that ran between the dorms and the Tower and the Science Main.

White marble steps led up to the vast Tower doors. Helena's memory instantly superimposed the wave of blood and gore and bodies that had covered it when she'd seen it last.

She looked away.

She had to focus on the present.

HELENA WAS PUSHED INTO THE back seat of a motorcar, a necrothrall cramming her towards the middle as it seated itself beside her. The smell of rot immediately began to fill the enclosed space.

Her throat convulsed, and she clamped a hand over her nose and mouth.

Stroud climbed in on the other side, seemingly immune to the stench, flipping through her perpetual stack of files.

The motorcar drove down a long tunnel, amber light from the electric lanterns flickering across Helena's lap, giving way to drab grey when the motorcar emerged from underground. She peered out, taking in the sky. It was dark and overcast, a grey that seemed to leach the world of colour. Looking out at the city, she was shocked by the scars still starkly visible from the war: huge gaps in the skyline, burned-out buildings, and collapsed ruins. It hardly looked as if any rebuilding had begun. The road was the only thing that appeared new.

When the motorcar crossed from the East Island to the West Island, nearly all traces of the war disappeared behind them.

Paladia had been founded on a river delta in the basin of the Novis Mountains. The original island had a high northern plateau which sloped down to the southern tip. The Alchemy Tower had been built on the highest point of the island, and the town—eventually a city—had grown around it until every inch of land had been built on. The island of Paladia, later called the East Island, was home to industry, trade, government, the perihelion cathedrals, and the Alchemy Institute.

The West Island was built centuries later, engineered to accommodate the exploding population. All of it was newer, bigger.

During the war, the Undying held diluted control over the West Island, while the Resistance had headquartered in the Alchemy Institute, giving them an established point of defence on the East Island and splitting the city-state in two. Because the East Island held most of the crucial infrastructure and the main ports, it had borne the brunt of the war as the Undying tried to seize control.

Contrasted with the ruins of the East Island, the West Island looked almost unscathed, its vast interconnected buildings vaulting up towards the sky, gleaming and unmarred.

When Helena had first sailed up the river and seen Paladia, it had looked as if some great deity had laid their crown in the dip of the mountains, the spires and gleam of the city reflecting across the water. She hadn't thought anywhere on earth could be so beautiful.

The motorcar felt tiny as it sped through the West Island, crossing another bridge towards Paladia's mainland, which spanned the miles from the river shore to the mountain tree line.

The mainland was mostly mines and agriculture, and the little that wasn't commercial was owned by the oldest families who'd joined the Institute centuries ago, at the time of its founding.

If she was being taken to the mainland, then the High Reeve must have an estate of some kind. Either one was seized and bestowed post-war, or perhaps he was from one of the wealthy guild families. There had been a number who'd seen their fortunes explode from the industrialisation of the last century.

She leaned forward, looking towards the front window, searching for any signs of their destination.

Removed from Central, she was finally beginning to develop a vague shape of a plan.

Realistically, her chances of escape were negligible. Even without the manacles impeding her dexterity and suppressing her resonance, she had minimal combat training. Her resonance had always been her greatest asset. Assuming she could somehow escape, she had nowhere to go, no idea who was alive or who could be trusted, or who would trust her.

If she was cooperative, there was a chance she'd survive transference, but if she did survive, she'd be betraying the Eternal Flame, giving up information she'd sacrificed her own memory to protect.

Her hands clenched, pain sparking like fire in her wrists.

In the stasis tank, she'd told herself over and over that she'd survive, that she had to hold on. She couldn't explain why.

After all, the whole point of her healing had been to ensure the survival of the others, to be a fail-safe so that Luc would not die. There was no use in a healer when everyone was dead.

She wouldn't be a traitor. Whatever she'd allowed to be hidden in her mind, she wouldn't let the Undying discover it. Surviving didn't matter. She'd kill herself before they learned anything from her.

Perhaps her violent captor could be her means to that end.

If what Grace had said was true, the High Reeve preferred murder to strategic choices like interrogation. Men prone to violence were generally thoughtless, acting with emotion first and applying reason after.

If she could provoke him, he might kill her on impulse. One mistake was all she'd need, and her secrets would be lost. No amount of necromancy could bring a mind back from death.

What would Morrough do to the High Reeve then? Undoubtedly something even worse than what was done to Mandl.

Helena hoped it would be.

She might not be able to avenge Luc, but she could get justice for Lila.

The thought of Lila Bayard, dead, her face ripped off, her corpse used to imprison the people she'd once protected, made Helena's chest grow so tight, it ached.

Lila had been one of the few who wasn't bothered by Helena being a vivimancer. During the war, they'd even shared a room. They hadn't been close—as a paladin, Lila was often gone, fighting at the front—

but she'd never treated Helena like she was lesser for not being in combat.

Lila had been considered a once-in-a-lifetime talent as a combat alchemist. She'd joined the crusades of the Eternal Flame at fifteen, travelling the continent, investigating rumours of necromancy. Her life had revolved around becoming a paladin and serving the Principate.

People used to call Lila the embodiment of Lumithia, the warrior goddess of alchemy.

Helena couldn't imagine how anyone could have killed Lila, especially not *after* Luc had been killed. Lila would have died a thousand times over before she'd live to see Luc captured. She had lived and breathed her vows of protection.

Helena blinked as they stopped at a checkpoint.

The trees along the road were all skeletal, bare-limbed. The motorcar drove a few miles farther and turned off the main road.

A building loomed through the trees as they drove down a long lane and a heavy, ornate gate swung open. The motorcar drove through, towards a towering house.

It was an old thing, its façade covered in bare vines which crawled up the front like blackened veins. The architecture was far from the modern elegance in the city. There was a dark, heavy quality to the ornate details, which appeared to have weathered at least a century. It bore five dark spires that jutted across the sky, three on the main portion of the house, and one on each wing that sprawled forward to form a half circle.

The gate and wall and other buildings all curved in to create an enclosed courtyard with an overgrown garden in the centre. The motorcar crunched over white gravel as it pulled around and stopped.

At the top of a wide flight of stone steps stood a young woman.

Helena was shoved out of the car behind Stroud. She drew a deep breath of clean air and shivered. It was bitterly cold, the damp country air immediately seeping into her bones. She'd forgotten the brutality of Northern winters.

The woman on the steps was barely more than a girl, and she stood out starkly in the drab surroundings. She had light-brown hair that fell in perfect ringlets around her pale face. Her dress was poison green, embellished with a black external corset resembling a rib cage, and a gleaming plated bird skull was fastened so that the long beak ran down between her breasts. Several of her fingers bore alchemy rings, and she swung a short staff idly in her hand as she watched the party ascend the stairs towards her.

She stared past Stroud to Helena, pale-blue eyes narrowing. "Well," she said as they reached her. "I suppose fanatics must come in all sizes."

Her attention turned to Stroud, and she donned a brittle smile. "Welcome to Spirefell. My husband is waiting for you."

Stroud fell in step with the lady of the house, while the necrothrall guard nudged Helena to follow.

The door of the house was held for them by a dead butler, and the sight made Helena's blood run cold.

Unlike the necrothralls in Central, the butler was freshly deceased and immaculately dressed. She thought for a moment he was alive, or that he was a lich. His skin lacked the waxy adipocere sheen, and he moved with none of the sluggishness she'd come to associate with necrothralls. But his expression and eyes were completely blank.

He must have been recently killed. Grace had said the Undying kept necrothralls as staff, and a wealthy family wouldn't want to deal with the smell, which meant they'd be replaced frequently.

Her stomach knotted as she stepped inside and took in the trappings of the house.

The foyer was large and cold, and the first thing she saw was a bright smear of blood.

Helena gasped, eyes and head instinctively averting.

"What's the matter?" Stroud asked sharply.

"The blood," she forced herself to say, unable to look again. All the executions flooded through her mind, the smells and sickening taste in the air, washing like a flood across the white marble.

Stroud glanced around the room. "Where?"

Helena tried to indicate, and Stroud only looked confused. She looked again and discovered her mistake. There was no blood.

A bouquet of roses sat arranged on a table in the centre point of the room. She flinched just looking at them.

"Never mind," she muttered.

The girl in green was watching. She looked between Helena and the roses, and then a slight smile tugged at the corner of her mouth as she turned away, heading towards a set of doors across the foyer.

"Wait here," Stroud said. The door shut, leaving Helena with the dead. She glanced around, trying to look anywhere but at the roses.

The gloom felt heavier inside than under the oppressive grey sky. Spirefell was a cavernous thing, shadowed with filigree metalwork. There was a large, ornate stairway to the right, leading to multiple landings that looked out over the foyer.

Darkened hallways led farther into the house, illuminated by weak electric sconces that hummed and hardly penetrated the gloom. The windows high overhead seemed designed to direct the light only to the table at the centre. There was a distorted black shape inlaid as a mosaic into the marble floor, encircling the table. From her angle, Helena couldn't work out what it was.

The house felt dirty. There was no visible dust, but Helena couldn't shake the sense that the place was untended. The air was stale, as if the building also were a mouldering corpse.

The door across the way opened. "Come, Marino," Stroud said as if summoning an animal.

The room she entered had two immense latticed windows looking out into gardens with a large hedge maze. The winter curtains were drawn back to let in cold light. The girl in green had set the short staff aside and was seated on the edge of a spindly-looking chair, her skirts spread to show off the fabric. Across the room, by the windows, stood a dark figure.

The hair on her arms rose.

Stroud pulled her past the spindly chairs and chaises towards the figure.

Winter light silhouetted him, and it wasn't until she drew near that Helena could begin to make out any details.

Pale skin. Silver-white hair.

He was old, then. He must be one of the guild patriarchs.

She'd met a few of them at the Institute. They were always the same.

Prideful, obsessed with their power and perceived status, always demanding more respect.

This was exactly the kind of person who would be easy to manipulate. Helena would only need to be insufficiently cowed, and he'd snap her neck.

With luck, she might be dead within a fortnight.

He turned. Helena's throat closed as the world around her vanished, footsteps faltering.

He was not old at all.

It was the iron guild heir. Kaine Ferron.

She stared at him in stunned recognition.

He'd been one of the few guild students who'd stayed at the Institute for undergraduate study. They'd been the same year, shared classes, even worked as assistants on the same research floors.

Her mind refused to accept what it was seeing, because it could not be Kaine Ferron.

His hair had been dark, now it was colourless. While the pallor of his skin didn't come from age, he looked as if he'd been bleached in moonlight.

For an instant she thought he must be a corpse, like Crowther's body at Central, but the silver-grey eyes that met hers were sharp, the sclera white, pupils black, no darkened veins anywhere beneath his skin. There were no veins visible at all, as if his blood were quicksilver.

"The last member of the Order of the Eternal Flame for you, High Reeve," Stroud said, as if presenting him with a medal. "I believe you knew each other at the Alchemy Institute."

His eerie silver eyes flicked away. "Hardly."

"I know you've made preparations," Stroud said, seating herself, "but I wouldn't worry much; she has no training or combat experience to speak of. She'll be quite manageable for you."

He looked at Helena again, no emotion on his face, but there was a predatory calculation in his eyes, like a wolf. "I'm sure."

Stroud cleared her throat, seeming uncomfortable with Ferron's terseness. "Now then. The High Necromancer wishes to have results before the winter solstice. Per his commands, you're to perform the temporary transference method upon her as frequently as possible to achieve singularity without extinguishing her soul. Once that is accomplished and you've accustomed yourself to her mind, I believe that reversing the transmutations of her memory should be a small matter for you. You may examine what's concealed, and when it's done, I'll come to retrieve her. The High Necromancer intends to extract the memories as well."

Ferron gave an idle nod.

"I'm sure you know, but this is an absolute priority. All other obligations should be considered secondary until completion."

The girl in green made an abrupt sound, and all her perfect ringlets trembled.

"You mean, we really have to keep her?" she burst out. "I just don't see how it's fair. She's not even Paladian. Why can't she stay at the Outpost with the rest of them? Why are we keeping her here? I had all these parties planned this season. I've already had to cancel three dinners and make up excuses about why. No one asked me if I wanted a prisoner." Her voice was fluting with a note of tearful petulance. "And what is she wearing? If anyone sees her, it'll be all anyone talks about."

"Shut up, Aurelia," Ferron said, his voice like ice, not even bothering to look over.

"I—wasn't sure what clothes would be appropriate," Stroud said, her voice tight with embarrassment. "Of course, you don't have to keep her in that. It was simply what was on hand."

The windows rattled, and a low meandering howl of wind floated through the house. Stroud jumped. Ferron and Aurelia didn't seem to notice it.

"It's hardly a concern," Ferron said. "I'm sure we'll find something for her to wear. Aurelia has so much."

Aurelia's eyes went wide. "You want me to give her *my* clothes?"

"We don't want anyone mistaking her for staff. Unless you prefer I have something made?"

Aurelia gave a horrified gasp, as if the idea were more scandalous than keeping a prisoner or running a house with dead servants.

"Excellent," Stroud said in a bright voice as everyone pretended not to notice that Aurelia was on the verge of spontaneous combustion. "Now then, you're free to examine her, High Reeve. She's all yours." She gestured towards Helena.

Ferron looked at Helena without moving. "Here?"

"Just a preliminary exam, to see if you have questions before I go. Do you—prefer privacy?"

"No. You're welcome to watch." He stepped towards Helena. He was all in black, dressed in city clothes. His coat and waistcoat were intricately detailed with black embroidery that only showed when it caught the light. At his throat, he wore a pristine white cravat.

Helena had never seen a guild alchemist wearing so little metal. Alchemists tended to keep metal everywhere: as jewellery, and woven into their clothes, walking sticks, weapons. Unusual alchemists like pyromancers always wore their ignition rings unless they were forced to remove them.

Aurelia was covered in metal, but not Ferron.

He pulled off a black glove, revealing a pale, long-fingered hand.

A vivimancer, Grace had said. Of course he didn't need metal.

Helena tried to flinch back, all too familiar with the danger of Stroud's grasping fingers, but when she tried to move, she couldn't.

Without Ferron touching her, a frisson of resonance fine as spider silk had insinuated itself through her body, so subtle she hadn't felt it. Now it held her fast. It wasn't like Morrough's; it didn't fill the air until everything hummed. If she hadn't tried to move, she wouldn't have realised it was there.

Ferron's eyes gleamed, as if he could feel her struggling. His index finger barely touched her temple, and then she truly felt his resonance, vivid as a live wire.

Sharp and finely honed, it sank through her skull. The room and Ferron all vanished as her memories sprang up before her eyes like a zoetrope.

The drive to Spirefell. Penny. Stroud's interrogations. The lich in the Tower wearing Crowther's body. The discussions of how best to extract the memories from Helena's mind. Shiseo emerging from the darkness with his little case and awl. As Ferron went further back, the memories dimmed, flashing by as though her mind were a book he was flipping through to see if there was anything of interest inside.

He went all the way back to the stasis and the nothing that went on and on and on, then even further to the Tower and blood and the years in the hospital.

She hadn't realised how small and repetitive her life was until she experienced it being skimmed through like that.

When it stopped, Helena's mind was reeling. Ferron's touch remained a moment longer, and she could feel his resonance through her brain, turning her vision red.

Finally, his hand dropped away and he stood there, staring at her.

"Well," he said at last.

"Extraordinary, isn't it?" Stroud said from somewhere behind him.

"Quite," he said, his gaze splinter-sharp. He raised an eyebrow, still looking at Helena. "The war is over. What is it you think you're protecting in that brain of yours?"

She met his stare without flinching.

Luc. She was protecting Luc.

"Holdfast is dead," he said sharply, as if he'd seen the answer in her eyes. "The Eternal Flame extinguished. There's no one left for you to save."

He turned away, his expression venomous.

"Anything else?" he asked Stroud.

She shook her head.

The paralysis on Helena vanished. She'd been fighting it, and it happened so suddenly her knees gave out. She dropped, trying to catch herself, and the weight of her body slammed into her hands. Tearing pain exploded through her wrists, white-hot fire searing all the way to her shoulders.

She hit the floor.

Aurelia stifled a laugh.

"You met with Shiseo and went over everything several times before he left, I believe," she heard Stroud saying. "After the first session, I'll send someone for appraisal, so we can establish a timeline for results."

"Yes, this plan has all been laid out for me in excruciating detail," Ferron said tonelessly. "I'll get it done. Now if you'll excuse me."

He stepped over Helena's body and walked out of the room without a backwards glance.

Helena tried to sit up. Without use of her hands, she had to roll carefully onto her side and use her elbows, cradling her wrists protectively near her chest.

When she finally looked up, Stroud had gone, and Aurelia was standing impatiently a few feet away. The short staff was clasped in her hands.

"Get off the floor," she said. "I'm to show you your room."

Helena stood and followed Aurelia warily back into the foyer. Her wrists were throbbing. The necrothrall from Central was still there and shadowed them as Aurelia led the way down a hallway, up a flight of stairs, through a series of rooms, and into another hallway.

It was darker there. A different wing based on the angle of the light. Most of the windows were heavily draped, the furniture shrouded with dustcloths.

"To be clear, just because we have to keep you doesn't mean I want to see you," Aurelia said, walking quickly.

Helena already felt short of breath from the stairs and could barely keep up.

"I understand those bracelets keep you from using alchemy. Although that hardly matters here. The Ferrons built this house with pure iron, and there's a reason I was chosen as Kaine Ferron's wife."

Aurelia paused and looked back at Helena, lifting one hand. Her wrist swished dramatically, and the alchemy rings decorating her fingers transformed, lengthening into knives that made her fingers look spider-like.

Helena watched the transmutation with trained interest. Natural iron resonance was considered somewhat rare among alchemists—though not as unusual as gold resonance or pyromancy. Raw iron was naturally intractable, to the point of being considered generally inert. Most alchemists couldn't transmute iron without having it repeatedly exposed to lumithium emanations in an Athanor Furnace, and even then they fared better with steel than iron alone.

Aurelia's transmutational work was quick and flashy. In class, she would have been docked for excess movement and imperfect iron distribution, but the ease with which she'd transformed her rings meant she had an extremely high degree of iron resonance, and if the house was iron, that meant Aurelia could wield it like a weapon, too.

Helena looked down, noticing then the wrought iron running through the floor and decorating the walls.

"We don't use this wing," Aurelia said, continuing down the hall. Her rings were pretty bands around her fingers once more. "I don't want you seen, particularly when I have guests. Stay out of the way unless you're sent for. The thralls all have instructions to keep an eye on you, so we'll know if you cause problems."

Aurelia stopped, setting the short staff on one of the iron bars in the floor and giving it a little twist. The iron shifted with a groan, and a door, heavily decorated with more iron, swung open.

It was a large room with two long windows and a canopied bed between them. There was a single wing-backed chair next to one window and an ornate table beside it. A large wardrobe sat against the far wall, a heavy rug covering most of the floor.

There was nothing on the walls except a clock too high to reach, but it was all clean and smelled freshly aired out.

Helena stepped into the room, taking it in carefully.

"Meals will be sent," Aurelia said, and the door closed behind her.

It was only when she was alone that it struck Helena as odd that Aurelia had escorted her.

Perhaps the Ferrons weren't as wealthy as their home would make them seem.

The house did appear understaffed. Their butler was a corpse—perhaps all the servants were. If they were desperate for money, that would explain why they had no choice but to keep Helena, and why Ferron spent his time hunting down Resistance fighters rather than managing his family's guild and factories.

She remembered the Ferrons being among the wealthiest families in Paladia. They'd invented industrial steel manufacturing, allowing them to monopolise more than just Paladia's steel industry. Most neighbouring countries had sourced from the Ferrons, too.

Clearly their fortunes must have turned if their house was in a condition like this.

She went to the nearest window. There was a radiator bolted beneath it, and the window was latticed with wrought iron and locked tight. No jumping, then.

She touched the iron with a fingertip and felt nothing. No connection to the cold metal, just that dead, empty feeling emanating through her wrist.

She pressed the length of her hand against it, bitterly missing her resonance. The world she'd known was always full of energy, humming with power that she'd been attuned to since birth.

Now everything was still. The constant sense of inertia was disorienting.

Peering through the paned glass, she saw wilderness and mountains.

She reconsidered her plans. If the necrothralls were there to watch her, they'd likely been commanded to keep her from killing herself.

She drummed her fingers on the windowsill, ignoring the little shocks of pain it sent up her arm.

Ferron, unfortunately, was not the stupid, deluded patriarch she'd hoped for.

His resonance was like Morrough's, beyond anything she'd known was possible, but what worried her most was the way he'd gone through her memory. Morrough had done something similar, but that mental violation had been brutal and haphazard; Ferron had been surgical.

She'd assumed his quick kills were a sign of impulsiveness, but there'd be no need to keep prisoners if he could look inside their minds and take the answers.

How could she outwit someone like that? Could he see memories alone or her thoughts, too?

She turned from the window, surveying the room, wondering if his strange appearance was an effect of his abilities.

The Undying didn't change after their ascendance. It was a part of the "gift." Unless their bodies were so destroyed that they became liches, they were immutable. They could lose entire limbs and grow them back.

What would make Ferron look like that?

He seemed—distilled. As though he'd been taken and sublimated until all that was left was an essence—something deathly cold and gleaming. The High Reeve.

Not a person, but a weapon.

Well, Helena would be sure to treat him as one.

CHAPTER 4

It took Helena mere minutes to explore every corner of her room and the adjoining bathroom. She was provided with only the most essential objects: soap, towels, a toothbrush, and a metal cup for water. She squeezed the cup, trying to bend it and work it. If she could break it, she'd have a nice sharp edge to slit her arteries open.

After several minutes of trying, all she had were dents in her thumbs and throbbing pain in both wrists.

Next she tried pulling down the mirror, but it was welded to the wall so firmly she couldn't even get her fingers under it. It didn't break when she tried hammering it with the cup, either.

She stepped back, glaring at the glass, and winced at her reflection.

She scarcely recognised the person scowling back. Sallow skin that had seen no light in more than a year, long black hair tangled almost to mats around her face. Her features were all sunken. She'd look like a necrothrall herself if not for her furious dark eyes.

She went back to the bedroom and was disappointed to find that there weren't any drape cords for her to try to hang herself with. She checked behind all the curtains, in case one had been missed.

Just live, Helena, a voice in her mind begged.

She paused, fingers tracing the pattern on the curtain, trying to stifle it.

Luc . . . oh, Luc. Of course he would haunt her, refusing to accept a pragmatic choice. If he were there, he'd be telling her that her plan was terrible. He'd hated that kind of thing. People sacrificing themselves because of him or his family. He always felt responsible, convinced that if he was better, he could save everyone.

She could hear him now, telling her stubbornly that she wasn't going to die. She could come up with a better plan if she'd just stop fixating on this one.

She shook her head. "I'm sorry, Luc. This is the best I can do."

She went to the door leading to the hallway.

The instructions to stay out of sight implied she could leave her room. Her body trembled in anticipation, heartbeat quickening.

She gripped the knob, and it turned easily. The heavy door swung open, revealing a long corridor spilling into darkness, but rather than exhilaration at this freedom, Helena's heart stopped.

The sconces along the wall were no longer illuminated. She hadn't noticed how ominous the corridor was, thin and winding, full of creeping shadows like teeth that gave way to a mouthlike darkness.

She was used to constant light in Central.

She stood frozen. It was irrational. It was a house. She'd seen too many real, awful things to be afraid of shadows and hallways, but her legs wouldn't move. The doorknob rattled in her hand.

The darkness was like a pulsing oesophagus, the long shadows swaying with the wind, threatening to swallow her. If she stepped out, she'd fall into the cold, awful, unending dark again.

She would never be found.

Terror coursed through her as the shadows stirred again, crawling towards her.

Her chest spasmed, sending a shock of pain through her lungs. She shrank back into the room and shut the door, her body pressed close against the reassuring surface of it, lungs and heart pulsing. She couldn't breathe.

She knew the terror of the stasis tank would haunt her, but she had not realised the way it had rooted itself inside her, grown through her nerves and organs to paralyse her.

She stayed crouched, without sense of time, until there was a rap at the door, the soft clatter of dishes, and retreating footsteps.

She cracked the door open and found a cloth bundle and a tray of food. Pulling them inside quickly, she tried not to see the vanishing darkness again.

The door safely closed, she stared in revulsion. The meal was pig slop, as if someone had taken kitchen scraps and the day's leftovers, put them in a pot, and boiled them. She'd sooner starve.

She shoved the tray aside.

Untying the bundle, she found sets of underclothes, wool stockings, and one dress, red as blood.

There were stitch marks along the hems and the neck and bodice from where the details and lace had been carelessly ripped off to make it as plain as possible.

Helena wished bitterly she hadn't flinched at the sight of those roses.

She looked over at the food again. She'd have to be careful around Aurelia.

At the bottom of the bundle were three sets of slippers. Dancing slippers by the look of them, impractically thin-soled and delicate shoes with ribbon laces, cast off because the fabric on the toes was wearing thin and they'd lost their satiny sheen.

Aside from the stockings, Helena put it all into the wardrobe, preferring to remain in the thin scratchy dress from Central.

Another tray arrived the next morning, somehow worse. Helena was hungry enough by then to pick out the few bites that hadn't been so boiled that the colour had leached out.

She wanted to try leaving her room again, but the thought made her stomach twist into a vicious knot.

Instead, she preoccupied herself with exercise, performing callisthenics. She needed to at least be able to climb a flight of stairs without having her legs threaten to give out. Her arms were weak, too, but anything that required her to put weight on her wrists was out of the question.

She stared bitterly at the manacles. She'd always been so proud of her hands—all the things she could do with them.

The longer she spent preoccupying herself with excuses not to leave the room, the guiltier she grew.

Anyone else in the Resistance would have already mapped the house, identified potential weapons, and murdered both the Ferrons.

Lila would never allow herself to be so weak. It wouldn't matter what she was scared of. But Helena had never been much like Lila. She had to do things her way. Better to wait, let Ferron come to her.

He was sure to turn up soon.

She could only guess at what transference would entail.

She thought of Crowther's corpse in Central with the lich inside it. Perhaps that would be her soon, except still alive, aware of what was happening to her as Ferron took over, possessing her mind and body.

At least if she had to see Ferron frequently, she'd have opportunities to figure out what made him tick. To find a weakness.

She racked her memory for what she knew of the family. The Ferrons were entwined with the alchemical industrialisation of the last century.

They had formed the very first iron guild shortly after Paladia's founding. Iron was one of the eight traditional metals associated with the eight planets: lead for Saturn, tin for Jupiter, iron for Mars, copper for Venus, quicksilver for Mercury, silver for Luna, lumithium for Lumithia, and gold for Sol.

Being intractable and highly prone to corrosion, iron was regarded as lowly and ignoble, especially when compared with incorruptible substances like silver, lumithium, and gold. The Ferrons themselves had also been common. Blacksmiths and ironworkers making ploughs and farm tools more often than holding illustrious jobs like forging steel weapons for the Eternal Flame the way other iron alchemists had.

As time passed and new metals were discovered, iron remained a stubborn and base fixture until the Ferrons developed a method of efficient alchemical steel manufacturing. With the precision of their iron resonance, they could assure quality at an industrial scale that no one else could match. It had changed the world, and it had changed the Ferrons. They'd transformed from trade workers to a new and incredibly wealthy working class, the world transforming with them.

It didn't matter whether theologically iron was classified as celestially inferior; the modern world was built with Ferron steel. Factories, railway lines, motorcars, even Paladia itself as its architecture shot skywards, climbing with the industrial boom.

Spirefell, deteriorated as it now was, had clearly been built as a monument to that growing influence and wealth, and the family's immense pride in it.

Helena's first memory of Kaine Ferron was during Year Two, not as a person but merely a name on a list. Helena had ranked first on the National Alchemy Exam for their year, beating out Ferron, who'd taken the spot the year before.

Luc had been so proud of her, loudly proclaiming that Year One barely counted, because it had been Helena's first year ever studying alchemy, and she was doing it in her second language.

Helena had almost fainted with relief. Her scholarship at the Institute depended on her academic performance, and the exam was a significant part of her evaluation. Her father had given up everything in Etras to bring her to Paladia; they would have been ruined if she'd lost her scholarship.

During the six occasions Helena took the national exam, top rank had swung like a pendulum. Helena Marino. Kaine Ferron.

A rivalry, albeit an indirect one, never openly acknowledged.

He was guild. Guild students didn't speak to "the Holdfast pet."

She couldn't imagine how he'd become High Reeve.

He'd been academic track like her. Not a specialised combat alchemist like Lila, or double track, the way Luc had been. Why would a guild heir be hunting down and killing all the surviving Resistance members?

The more time she had to think about it, the more a seething sense of hatred filled her at knowing, even distantly, someone so evil.

In a way, it was strangely poetic that it was Helena who'd been brought as a captive to Spirefell.

She'd beaten Ferron before. If she was careful, and clever, she would do it again.

WHEN FERRON DIDN'T APPEAR ON the second day, Helena forced herself into the hallway, ignoring the way her organs shrivelled and her throat closed. She hugged the wall, letting her fingers trace the wainscotting, not caring that the dust crept into the grooves of her fingerprints, blackening them like an infection.

You can do this, she told herself as she edged slowly towards the darkness, trying to evade the sharpest shadows. She tried the nearest door along the hallway and found it locked. She kept going, just a little farther.

The wind moaned through the halls, twisting into a scream, windows rattling. The house creaked like shifting bones.

Helena tried to breathe but she couldn't, not in the hallway with the shadows crawling up her like fingers.

After the third door, she couldn't go any farther. She turned back, the hallway swaying, the dark moving closer.

Before she reached the open door, her legs gave out. Everything blurred, blackening around her.

Lila Bayard emerged from the darkness.

It was not the Lila that Helena remembered. Not the beautiful, statuesque girl in armour who wore her pale-blond hair plaited in a crown around her head like the statues of Lumithia.

Lila's hair was cropped short as a boy's. She looked shrunken, despite her unusual height.

She stared at Helena. The right side of her face and neck was mottled with scarring, a long cruel gouge across her cheek that ran down her throat. Her eyes were red.

"Lila. Lila, what's wrong. What happened?"

Helena felt herself growing cold, fingers numb as she reached out.

Lila opened her mouth to answer but then faded away.

"Lila . . ."

When Helena opened her eyes, she was lying on the floor in her room, head throbbing.

Something niggled in the corner of her mind, dangling just past the edge of recollection.

She tried to focus, but sharp red pain splintered her mind. Whatever it was vanished like water through sand.

The windows rattled, and the house groaned, sending a vibration through the floor as though it were coming alive. She pushed herself up, favouring her hands, and went to the window.

The mountains were white, but snow hadn't reached the river basin yet. The winter solstice to mark the new year must be at least a few weeks away.

Fourteen months. She tried to remember the last date she could recall during the war. It would have been late summer when the final battle occurred, but she couldn't remember the month or lunar phases at the time. The hospital ward did not change with the seasons.

As she was peering out, the door behind her opened. Her spine prickled as she turned, anticipating Ferron.

Instead it was Aurelia, who entered in a swirl of blue fabric, gilded in metal once more as if she were a filigreed exoskeleton. If the Ferrons were short on money, it was likely because Aurelia's skirts required a dozen yards of imported silk.

Aurelia might have an unusual resonance for iron, but she seemed new to money. Not that Helena had ever had any herself, but it was unavoidable knowledge when among the noble families that served the Holdfasts and the Eternal Flame.

Country dress was supposed to be less formal. Luc used to always tell her about his family's country home in the mountains, how much more comfortable the clothes were. Every year after the summer solstice parades that celebrated the Principate's birthday, he'd invited her to come, to escape the city's heat and the river sicknesses that came with the warm season.

She'd always chosen to stay with her father.

Years later, she did see the country home, but she'd gone there alone. Luc had been right. It had been beautiful, the clothes comfortable, but she'd hated every minute of it.

Aurelia stood staring at Helena in disgust. "Why are you still wearing that? Haven't you washed since you got here?"

Helena hadn't. It felt safer to be dirty.

"I knew you were foreign, but I assumed there was basic hygiene in whatever hovel the Holdfasts found you in."

Helena's jaw clenched.

"Stroud called. That procedure is to happen tonight. Be washed and do something with that awful hair of yours before I come back, or I'll have the thralls strip you and do it instead. We have some nice stinking ones now, and I'll call them in if I ever see you looking like this again."

She turned, skirts swishing as she walked out.

Helena went to the bathroom, tearing off the slip dress and quickly twisting the taps for the shower. The pipes spat several times before water finally emerged with a hissing whine. She scrubbed herself from head to toe with a cloth as quickly as possible and tried to work her fingers through her hair. There was no comb anywhere.

Did Ferron think she could somehow slit her throat with it?

Not a bad idea, actually.

When she was suitably clean, she dressed in the clean, scratchy undergarments and then forced herself to pull on the dress, trying not to look at the red.

Then she sat, wrestling the remaining knots out of her hair. Her hands and wrists were aching, but she didn't want to find out if Aurelia meant her threat.

Paladians had always found Helena's hair disorderly. Northern hair was generally fine and extremely straight; curls were only acceptable when forged with a heated iron bar that singed the hair into the shape of a corkscrew.

When Helena had been a healer, she'd learned to keep it in two tight braids coiled at the base of her neck. She tried to plait her hair now, but her wrists couldn't manage the twisting motion.

The door swung open with an abrupt bang, and Aurelia stood in the doorway, her sharp blue eyes flicking up and down with overt disdain. Helena sat tense, bracing for the verdict.

Aurelia gave a sniff, lips tightening. "Come."

Helena followed Aurelia, silently, trying to focus on the intricate metal filigree of her clothing and not on the shadows around her.

Her escort did not appear to enjoy the silence. "Kaine says all that's valuable about you is your brain." She looked over at Helena as if expecting the pronouncement to be hurtful in some way. "I figure that means I can do whatever I want with all the rest of you."

She transmuted her iron-ringed fingers as she said this.

For all the power of her iron resonance, Aurelia's movements were all for show. The weapons she'd transmuted would break half her fingers if she tried to use them.

Helena doubted she had any formal training. In general, the guilds only sent sons to the Institute; daughters were for marriage. They might be taught alchemical parlour tricks, but they were rarely certified.

Still, Helena pretended to flinch back, her eyes carefully averted so they wouldn't betray her critical appraisal.

Aurelia's corseted chest swelled as the rings transformed again. "I bet you wish you hadn't joined the Holdfasts now. The guilds were always going to win. You all tried to hold us back, and look at what that got you."

She tossed her head and continued on.

The foyer was empty. Aurelia ascended the steps quickly, hurrying down the second-floor corridor before stopping short outside the first door to the left, touching a panel on the door above the knob. There was a click of the lock unfastening.

"Here. Go in and wait," Aurelia said, her eyes darting around, and it dawned on Helena far too late that she was walking into a trap.

"Kaine will be along shortly. *Don't* come out until he arrives," Aurelia added.

With that, Aurelia hurried on towards the far end of the hallway, leaving Helena in the corridor with the overwhelming sense that she was *not* supposed to go into this room.

She glanced around. Should she try to go back? Or was there a chance that this would get her in enough trouble that Ferron would kill her?

Before she could weigh her options, the corridor began to stretch, ballooning until every surface started to slide out of reach. The doorknob was shrinking away from her, leaving her in the open amid the gaping shadows.

She lunged forward and caught the knob, managing to twist it and drag herself into the room.

Inside, it was smaller than the corridor.

She leaned against the door, palms and fingers tracing the grain of the wood as the enclosed space settled around her.

Helena was surprised to find the room like hers. Two windows. A bed and wardrobe, but a desk and chair rather than an armchair. It could have belonged to an ascetic.

She went to the desk by the window. There was a neat stack of paper.

She lifted the top sheet of paper, holding it up in the dim light to see if Ferron's correspondence might have pressed through to the lower page, but the paper was thick and pristine. She ran her fingers across the surface of the desk; there was delicate silverwork across it, intricate leaves and vines set in the wood with perfect alignment. Undoubtedly the work of a talented silver alchemist.

The desk was perfectly maintained. A stark contrast with the cobwebs coating the iron filigree throughout the rest of the house.

She turned away, tense and trapped inside a room she was nearly certain she was not supposed to be in. She doubted she could make it back to her own room, and if Aurelia caught her disobeying, she was sure to do something nasty.

But what might Ferron do when he found her? Would intruding into a locked room merit lethal punishment? She doubted he was that impulsive, and if Stroud knew so many vivimancy punishments that weren't technically torture, Ferron undoubtedly did, too.

Her mouth went dry.

She still didn't know what transference would entail. Despite the frequent references made to it, no one had explained to her what Ferron would be doing. Helena could only guess based on the comments Shiseo had made, even though they made no sense because Helena had been the one who'd healed General Bayard when he was first injured. She'd tested the limits of her knowledge and abilities trying to save him, painstakingly regenerating the damaged brain tissue. When he'd survived, people had called it a miracle, declaring Helena's hands to be blessed by Sol.

That praise had ended when General Bayard woke. He was like a child. A huge, powerful general with the emotions of a toddler. A once brilliant tactician who couldn't find his way through a door without help.

Helena had saved his body and learned the bitter lesson that a mind was a thing apart and she had not saved it. She'd tried and failed for years to fix what she'd done. Somewhere in the hidden spaces of her memory, Elain Boyle had materialised, a cure in hand, a procedure then used on Helena as well. Now the Undying had learned of it.

The door clicked, breaking Helena from her thoughts. She turned as Ferron strode in. His hand was at his throat, pulling the collar loose.

He stopped short at the sight of her.

"Well," he said, "this is a surprise."

CHAPTER 5

Helena said nothing. She had no idea what to expect or what to do, so she watched Ferron like a cornered animal.

His eyes flicked from her to the door.

"Aurelia brought you here, I presume." He sighed. "I suppose it is time that we begin."

He came forward. Helena stiffened, but he strode past her to the wardrobe and jerked it open.

Apparently, he was not quite an ascetic. The door of the wardrobe held an entire row of decanters. He snatched one up and poured several fingers of amber liquid into a tumbler before turning back, taking a long sip as he stared at her over the glass, his gaze starting at the floor and working slowly up.

His attention turned away when he reached her shoulders. He looked down at the tumbler with another sigh as if the situation were deeply inconvenient for him.

"Let's get this over with."

Helena didn't move.

His gaze lifted. "Come here."

When she didn't obey, a slow smile curved along his lips. "I can make you, if you don't."

He raised his hand and gestured lazily, long fingers curling with perfect precision, knuckle by knuckle.

Helena's limbs began moving against her will, like a puppet manipulated across a stage. Her legs bent, lifted, weight shifting, step, another step. She fought against it, tensing, but it only made her bones feel like they'd snap.

It stopped once she was within arms' reach. He tilted her chin up with a fingertip, their eyes meeting.

"See?" he said. "It'll be easier if you obey."

She would have spat at him, but when she tried, her jaw clenched, teeth locking together. His eyes gleamed.

"Don't test me; it won't get you what you want," he said, his eerie eyes hooded. "You know, this is new for me. I don't generally keep prisoners."

He drained his glass and set it down.

"Sit." He gestured towards the chair.

Her limbs came free. She considered trying to bolt, if for no other reason than to be annoying, but she could feel his resonance through her nerves like a trip wire.

She sat, and the instant she was in place, she couldn't move again.

Ferron stepped behind her. She could hear him but not see him, which made her heart beat faster, ears straining for any sound.

One of his hands caught her jaw, tilting her head back until she was staring at the ceiling. She couldn't see his face, only his other hand, which bore a dark ring that glittered in the low light. Two fingers pressed against her temple, and his thumb settled between her eyes.

He leaned forward just enough that she could glimpse his face.

"Now then, let's see what it's like to be you."

She tensed as a weight enveloped the front of her skull, pushing down with slowly increasing pressure. It grew and grew until something gave way, as though Ferron's fingers had gone through her forehead and into her brain.

Her mind and body were abruptly sheared apart. She could sense that her skull was still intact, his hands still on the surface, but it *felt* as though her head had been broken open, cracked like an egg, her brain exposed as Ferron's resonance poured inside.

It wasn't a channel of energy like normal resonance, but something immense and fluid that pushed into the space until she was suffocating under it, the grooves and crevices of her mind filled with the oppressive, growing sense of an Other trying to occupy the plane of her cerebral existence. When there were no more crevices, her consciousness was crushed as though collapsing in on itself.

Everything went red.

She was screaming.

She could hear it. Feel it. The physical part of herself still immobilised in the chair was screaming, but Helena's mind was elsewhere, fissuring beneath the growing pressure of Ferron's consciousness.

Ferron didn't stop. He pushed deeper. She was drowning inside her brain, trapped as the water rose and the pressure grew and there was nowhere to go. He swallowed her whole.

There was a seismic hum, then light like a mist evaporating.

She was still staring up, eyes locked on the ceiling. A pale face hung straight above her, staring down.

Her eyes moved jerkily, startled at Ferron's cruel features, at how alien and unnatural he was. She realised sluggishly that he was *in* her mind, looking at himself through her eyes.

Then he was gone. His resonance and mind ripped out like an invasive taproot.

Everything inside her mind collapsed around the empty space, the integrity of her own consciousness crumbling.

She fell sideways out of the chair, the room tumbling with her.

Her thoughts rolled like dice in her skull.

Where was she?

"Get out."

She knew the words, but they came from far away. Sounds. Not Etrasian. Etrasian was prettier. Melodic.

This was—

Dialect.

Her thoughts were very slow.

She tried to lift her head, but the room kept moving.

She must be on a ship. Crossing the sea. Leaving the cliffs and islands behind.

Where was she going?

To school. Yes, she was going to study alchemy.

There was something wet on her face. She tried limply to lift her hand and managed to smear it away.

Her fingers came away red. Why red?

"Get out!"

The room shook. Helena was picked up by an unseen force and shoved towards the door. She collapsed dazedly, but the jolt knocked her back into herself, remembering.

Ferron. The transference.

Her stomach turned over. If it hadn't been empty, she would have vomited.

She looked back. He was right there, his face white and terrifying, twisted with fury. The room hummed.

"*I said get out!*" He looked like an animal, ready to lunge and rip her throat open with his bare teeth.

Absolute terror flung Helena into action. She pushed herself up, wrenched the door open, and fled.

The ground rolled beneath her feet. Her vision was stained red no matter how much she blinked, as if the walls were dripping with blood, shadows turned to gore. She kept smearing her hands across her eyes as she tried to find her way.

All she could hear was her panicked breathing and her feet on bare wood, the iron in the floor like ice.

She reached the top of the stairs. She could feel herself going into shock, her limbs turning leaden, dragging her down. Her body growing colder and colder as a feverish chill consumed her.

She swayed and nearly toppled down the steps, clinging to the banister to keep upright, staring down into the foyer.

The roses rippled as if underwater, floor shifting, and around it circled a black dragon.

It was curled inwards around the table, wings spread out, head curved down so that its tail was caught within its teeth, consuming itself.

An ouroboros.

In her red-stained vision, it looked as if it were swimming in blood.

What if she just threw herself over the balcony?

There was no one to stop her. The secrets Luc had entrusted to her would be safe, and Ferron would have failed.

She leaned forward, hands trembling.

Headfirst.

Dead on impact or Ferron could use vivimancy to keep her alive.

Just a little—

A vise-like grip closed around her arm and wrenched her back an instant before she toppled over the railing.

She whirled and found Ferron glaring at her.

"Don't. You. Dare."

She tried to jerk loose, lunging towards escape, but he dragged her back from the railing and down the stairs as she beat and clawed at him, trying to rip herself free. He didn't stop. He pulled her through the house, practically kicking in the door of her room before shoving her onto the bed.

Helena collapsed, breathing unsteadily, hands and wrists throbbing.

"Did you think I didn't know you'd try to kill yourself?" Ferron asked venomously. "As if there's *anything* the Eternal Flame loved more than dying for their causes."

"I thought you liked us dead." Her head hurt so much, she wanted to vomit.

He gave a barking laugh. "Consider yourself the sole exception to that rule. The High Necromancer wants your secrets, and until he has them, you will not die."

He glanced around her room, and his eyes seemed to glow.

He closed them, shaking his head. "I thought transference would be enough for one night, but it seems you're determined to make this as difficult for yourself as possible."

He leaned over her.

Helena stared at him in dread.

"Let's see what other ideas you've had." His cold fingers pressed against her temple.

It wasn't transference, and she was so relieved that she almost relaxed when she realised he was only violating her memories.

His resonance swept through her mind like a breeze, sending her thoughts fluttering.

He moved slowly. Instead of a long pass across time, he took interest only in recent events, winding through her memories like a current.

He seemed to pore over every detail. Exploring her room. The way the hallway frightened her, and her musings over him and his family. Her attempts at exercise.

When he finally stopped, the blood on her face had dried in tracks down her cheeks.

"Industrious as always," he said mockingly, pulling his hand away.

Her jaw clenched.

He was still leaning over her, hand pressed into the mattress by her head. "Do you really think you can trick me into killing you?"

She stared stonily at the canopy.

"You're welcome to try." He turned to leave, then paused as if just remembering something. "Don't enter my room again. If I want to deal with you, I'll come here."

Once he was gone, Helena didn't move.

She hadn't placed much faith in her plans. She'd known the odds of success were impossibly small, and yet she'd tried to convince herself otherwise. Luc wouldn't give up. If it were him, he'd fight to the very last. How could she betray him by doing less?

But Luc was dead.

No matter what she did, it wouldn't bring him back.

Her shivering grew uncontrollable. She curled onto her side, burrowing into the bedding. The wounded feeling in her head grew until it was a sinkhole drawing her inwards, her skin growing taut like a membranous exoskeleton.

The sheets became damp with her sweat as her fever rose. Her body was freezing, but her brain was on fire.

Time morphed, twisting, and she lost track of everything beyond her misery.

There were voices. So many voices. Vile things were poured down her throat, making her gag, burning concoctions that blistered her organs. Hot and cold and slimy things on her skin. She was picked up and plunged into ice-cold water, dragged out to breathe, and then shoved under again.

Her mind burned on like an ember, charring everything around it.

There were needles. Little pricks she hardly felt, then large agonising lances of pain that punctured her arms.

The pain in her head grew until it blotted out all thought.

Finally, she slipped away, her mind untethering itself in a free fall.

There was blood everywhere.

She was in the hospital in Headquarters. The bells were ringing. There were bodies being rushed in by nurses and medics whose faces blurred as they passed.

There was a boy in her arms, dying. She tried to calm him, trying to focus, not to feel the building panic of the room catching like claws through her lungs, but he wouldn't let her heal him. No matter how she tried, he'd shove her back. Blood kept pouring out in dark spurts. The sticky warmth seeping into her skin. People kept calling her amid the clamour, but she had to save this boy.

She was right here.

Finally, he stopped fighting. She felt him through her resonance. A rush of hope in her heart at the vibrant sense of living. Then he was gone, like a fist through her chest. Too late.

She looked up at the bodies piled around her, one on top of the next, a wall rising endlessly, rivulets of blood running down it as it swayed, threatening to crush her.

She tried to breathe. The smell of bile, charred flesh and blood, sweat, filth, and antiseptic burned in her nose and lungs, suffocating her.

Everywhere she turned, there were more bodies, even under her feet. She crushed them when she moved.

Choose.

Who lives and dies. She had to decide.

It would be her choice.

She reached out, fingers trembling, but a hand caught hers, stilling it.

It was Luc.

She gave a panicked gasp of relief, clutching at him.

He was standing in his golden armour, helmet off so she could see his face. He smiled at her. For a moment the nightmare vanished.

Then blood began to trickle down his face.

Lila was just behind him, glaive in hand, pale hair a crown around her head, but half her face was rotted away, peeling back to reveal her skull. Someone else stood just beside her, but Helena couldn't remember his face.

Beside them were Titus and Rhea, and after them the Council and the Eternal Flame, all standing in a ring around her.

Their faces were blank except Luc's.

Luc was still alive. He was bleeding, but she could heal him. Her hand shook as she reached out, but he spoke.

"I'm dead because of you."

She shook her head, voice failing her.

"Look, Hel," Luc said. He touched his breastplate, and the golden armour melted away, revealing his bare chest. A gleaming black knife was shoved between his ribs, a bloodless wound. The incision grew, running down his torso until the knife fell, shattering on the ground, and his organs came sliding out, blackened with gangrene, the smell of decay filling the air as if he'd been rotting for months.

"See?"

"No. No . . ." She tried to reach for him anyway, but he melted away, leaving her fingers stained with his blood.

Her mother was there now. Helena couldn't make out her face, but she knew it was her mother. The scent of dried herbs clung to her as she stood in front of Helena.

Helena reached for her, but her mother vanished into mist.

Then her father.

He stood out among the Northerners. His eyes were dark, and his black hair curled just like hers.

He wore his white medical coat, and when she met his eyes, he smiled at her. Just below his jaw was a gash mimicking the curve of his smile, running from ear to ear.

"Helena," he said, "I'm dead because of you."

He stepped towards her, a scalpel gleaming in his hand.

She didn't move, didn't resist this time when he took her in his arms and slit her throat.

WHEN THE WORLD SWAM BACK into focus, Helena wished she'd died.

Her head throbbed, and her hair was plastered to her cheeks and forehead. The room was stiflingly hot. Her mouth was so dry, her tongue threatened to crack.

She managed to roll onto her side. The bedside table bore a pitcher, a cup of water, and several vials. She fumbled for the cup, gulping it down.

She slumped back, kicking off the blankets. The smell of a mustard poultice burned in her nose. She craned her head, looking at the vials on the table again. There were iron and arsenic tablets, smelling salts, and ipecac.

She reached for the arsenic, but she'd no sooner lifted her hand than the door opened, and that nervous stuttering man from Central entered, accompanied by Ferron.

"It's unlikely the fevers will improve as the procedure continues," the man was saying, looking as terrified of Ferron as he'd been of Morrough.

Ferron didn't appear to be listening; his gaze had gone instantly to the table and the vial that Helena had been about to steal. He strode across the room, sweeping up all three vials and pocketing them with the barest glance down at her.

Bastard.

"I'm expected to put up with this every week?" Ferron asked, scowling down at Helena as if she were a stray he wanted to drown.

The man's head bobbed. "As I understand, the assimilation process of transference that the Eternal Flame developed was intended to cultivate a progressive degree of tolerance. As with traditional mithridatism, there will be side effects. The next time should result in further progress on your part, but as a result the brain fevers will likely be of a similar magnitude. You must understand, it's hardly a natural state of being. A living body surviving even a brief presence of another soul has never been achieved before. That she's alive at all should be considered a miracle. As the purpose of this is only to keep her alive long enough to reverse the transmutations, the long-term deterioration will be immaterial."

"I don't have time to play nurse," Ferron said, sneering at him. "Your cure was nearly as bad as the disease. At this rate, I can't see how she'll survive long enough for me to find anything. Getting her to tolerate transference and manage a full reversal of what's been done to her memory will only be the first steps. I'll still have to find the information. That could take months. I will not be set up for failure because you've decided something is 'immaterial.'"

The man shrivelled, his neck seeming to sink into his chest cavity, shoulders rising past his ears. "I assure you, High Reeve, the arsenic is unlikely to kill her. She may begin to show symptoms of poisoning, but based on our theories, this procedure will be complete before she develops any serious necrosis or—significant liver damage."

"How do you know how long this procedure will take? We don't even know if it worked on Bayard." Ferron's voice had grown deadly. "If you're certain that she will not die before the High Necromancer has his answers, and I am to follow your advice, then you will go attest to this, now, before our preeminent leader, and make clear to him that I am acting on your advice and assurances."

The man lost all remaining colour. "W-Well, when considered in that light, it's possible that if the sessions were spaced out more generously, we might reduce the side effects and brain fevers. But I would not dare make recommendations on my own. I'm no expert in this new science. This would be for Stroud or the High Necromancer himself to decide."

"I was sent you. I'd expect you to at least have enough expertise to have an opinion," Ferron said.

The man mopped his forehead. "I will strongly advise Stroud to visit so that she can make a recommendation," he said, avoiding Ferron's stare.

"Get out!"

Helena flinched.

Ferron watched him disappear through the door before glancing scathingly down at her, as if it were all her fault.

He reached towards her and she shrank back, but his hand passed harmlessly and slid under the pillow instead, searching the bed to ensure she hadn't managed to squirrel away any of the arsenic. She glared at him until he was satisfied that she had no poison hidden anywhere and left again with a slam of the door.

Her legs were wobbly when she got up. She had to sit on the floor under the shower spray because it was too tiring to stand, but she felt vaguely human again when all the sweat and smell of poultices had washed away.

The awful red dress had been washed, pressed, and put away in her wardrobe, along with several more dresses, also all red. Some were almost burgundy, while others were luridly bright. Freshly dyed. There were hints of the original sage green and pale pink barely visible along the hems.

Clearly Aurelia did not move on once she had an idea in her head.

STROUD ARRIVED THE NEXT DAY, followed into the room by a dead servant and Mandl, or rather the corpse that Mandl now occupied.

The servant was an older woman, dressed as household staff of some kind. She had light-brown hair that was neatly combed back and age lines around her mouth and eyes. Her eyes had an eerie lack of focus which contrasted sharply with the glowering resentment in Mandl's new face.

"Sit up," Stroud said to Helena, setting a medical bag on the table.

Helena obeyed without a word, remaining impassive while Stroud prodded her, noting the way Helena's wrists had shrunk inside the manacles, and checking her vital signs, tsking with irritation.

"Well, this is disappointing," she said at last. "I'd really hoped you'd handle it better."

Helena said nothing, a gleam of triumph rising in her chest.

"I suppose it was too much to hope you had the physical resilience of a man like Bayard," Stroud added with a disgruntled huff after another minute of running her resonance intrusively through Helena's organs.

She pressed her fingers against Helena's head, pushing a little frisson of energy into her mind, making Helena wince. Her mind still felt raw. "This degree of inflammation after seven days is worrying."

She sucked her teeth and glared at Mandl. "A pity you didn't report her at the time. This would all be so much easier."

Mandl bobbed her head stiffly, which was not enough penitence for Stroud.

"You should be grateful that I haven't pointed out to His Eminence that if we'd learned about her sooner, we might have retained Boyle's corpse and had an animancer for one of the Undying to use."

"I said I was sorry," Mandl said. "I don't know what else you want me to do, or why you dragged me here."

"You were gifted ascendance on my recommendation. If I am going to be inconvenienced by this, then so will you," Stroud said. "And if this costs me anything, I will see that it costs you more."

Stroud turned back to Helena, examining her again with an increasingly sour expression. "We'll need to delay the next procedure until she's stronger. If she dies prematurely, we'll lose the information."

She turned to the other necrothrall in the room. "High Reeve!"

The servant turned her head, cloudy eyes focusing on Stroud.

"I will speak with you. Privately."

The necrothrall servant nodded and gestured towards the door.

Of all the uses of necromancy that Helena had witnessed, the creation of the Ferrons' servants seemed a particularly vile choice. In a war, she could see the horrific rationale leading to the act, but the servants in Spirefell were all civilians, murdered for the sake of cheap convenience.

With every minute she spent in the house, her hatred of Ferron deepened, because she knew his history—the luxury and privilege of his family. His easy life. The Ferrons would have been nothing without the

Holdfasts and the Alchemy Institute; their wealth would never have existed.

They should have been grateful, loyal to Luc for what his family had enabled them to become, but they'd turned traitor and chosen Mor-rough.

Perhaps that ouroboros dragon was not merely a pretentious decoration but something the Ferrons prided themselves on. An omen of a destructive, insatiable hunger which left nothing but ruin in its wake.

FERRON STRODE INTO HER ROOM the next day. Helena's body went rigid, dread sweeping through her like a tide. The physical pain of trans-ference twinged inside her psyche like an aftershock.

He stopped at the door, and his pale eyes slid over her, flickering as they paused on her fingers, which spasmed uncontrollably when she was startled. She hid them behind her skirts.

"Stroud wants you going outside," he said. "She believes fresh air will improve your constitution." He tossed a bundle towards her. "Put it on."

Helena unfolded it and found it was a thick cloak, dyed crimson. She grimaced.

"Something wrong?"

She looked over. "Is red the only dye you have in this house?"

"It'll make you easy for the thralls to spot. Come!" Ferron stalked into the hallway.

She followed tentatively. The sconces in the hallways were lit, driving back the shadows as he headed to the far end of the wing, descending a new flight of stairs to a set of doors that opened onto a veranda in the courtyard.

It was raining, and a gust of wind swirled along the house, whipping across her face. She gave a startled gasp.

Ferron turned sharply. "What?"

"I—" Her voice cracked, and she swallowed. "I'd forgotten what wind feels like."

He turned away. "The courtyard's enclosed. You may wander as you wish."

She looked around, taking in the details of the house and the other buildings. The veranda they stood on continued past the end of the wing and became a cloister walkway, connecting the main house to the other buildings, walling them in. A person could travel all the way to the gate without stepping into the rain, the house and buildings forming an iron ring.

"Go." Ferron waved her off and then seated himself at a nearby table with two small chairs, pulling a newspaper out of his overcoat.

Helena's eyes instantly locked onto the headlines.

ETERNAL FLAME TERRORIST SEIZED! screamed the words at the top of the fold in all-capitals.

She stepped closer without thinking.

Who had they found?

Grace said they were all dead. But here was proof of survivors. Ferron hadn't killed them all.

He looked up. She froze in her tracks, unable to tear her eyes away from the paper, looking desperately for a name.

"Care to see?" he asked in a slow drawl that made her skin prickle.

He snapped the paper open, and Helena stared dumbfounded at a photograph of herself, drugged and sedated in Central. Her face was gaunt, her expression contorted, strained from the withdrawal of the interrogation drug, her hair tangled around her face.

It was clearly intended to make her look like a dirty, feral extremist.

The last fugitive of the Eternal Flame terrorists has been apprehended and taken for interrogation, proclaimed the lede just above the fold.

"You're finally famous, and look—I'm included, too." Ferron's eyes glittered with malice as he indicated a photo of himself farther down the column, in that very courtyard, the spires of the house silhouetted behind him. "Just in case anyone wants to know where you are. Or who's keeping you."

Helena looked at him in confusion. Why would they want to publicise her capture and location? And why now? She'd been in Central for weeks. Her apprehension was old news.

"I thought it was a rather obvious trap," Ferron said with a sigh, flipping past the front page. "Then again, your Resistance was never known for its intelligence. Anything more subtle would elude them. The High Necromancer hopes that if there's anyone left, they'll feel morally obligated to rush in and save the Flame's last ember." He glanced sidelong at her. "I have my doubts, but no harm in trying, I suppose."

He leaned back, idly returning his attention to the next column.

Helena staggered back.

Was that why they'd sent her to Spirefell rather than keeping her in Central? To be used as bait?

A strangled sound tore from her throat. She turned and stumbled down the steps out into the rain. There was nowhere to go, but she had to go somewhere.

The cloak, clasped at her throat, choked her, dragging her back. Her fingers tore at it until it came loose, setting her free. She ran across the courtyard.

The icy rain soaked through the thin, fashionable fabric of her dress, but she scarcely felt it. She could see the towers from the city, rising beyond Spirefell. She looked for the beacon, the light that had always shone from the top of the Alchemy Tower, the Eternal Flame which had been kept burning since the day of Paladia's founding, but it was not there. It was gone.

Still she went towards them, but as she neared the far side of the courtyard, all the towers vanished behind the wall. She moved back and forth, looking for some way out, finally going to the gate, knowing it would be futile but unable to help herself.

It was locked tight, made of wrought iron too ornate to squeeze through. She rattled it so hard, it made her wrists spasm.

She tried to climb it but her slippers shredded, the iron cold enough to burn her skin, and when she tried to pull herself up, the pain inside her wrists left her hands numb.

Across the courtyard, Ferron was reading the paper, unconcerned by Helena's attempts at escape.

She wanted to scream. She gripped the gate, rattling it again.

What if someone came, not knowing they were being lured into a trap?

Someone who'd managed to survive all this time, captured because of her.

She drew in a gasping breath. Her chest felt as though it might split open. She slumped, shaking the gate again and again, as if the iron might bend for her if she were only persistent enough.

Finally, she turned back to the house in despair.

Everywhere she looked was grey: the dead grass and leafless, skeletal trees, the dark house with its black vines and spires, even the washed-out slope of the mountains, white peaks shrouded by the mist of an overcast sky.

It was as if all colour had been leached from the world. Except her. She stood there in blood red, stark against the monochrome.

The wind drove the rain into her, striking like droplets of ice, making her shudder. She was drenched through. Her hands were turning white, the tips of her fingers aching with every gust of wind. The metal from the manacles sent a chill radiating into her bones.

She pressed her fingers over her eyes, trying to think. What could she do? Surely there was something.

No. Her plan remained the same. Die, by Ferron's hand or her own.

The rain was streaming through her hair and down her face as she forced herself to walk back towards the house. There were two necrothralls stationed outside, at the top of the stairs leading to the main wing. She recognised them from Central. Weathering outside, they were so decrepit that they almost blended in with the stones, but both watched as she neared Ferron.

Ferron glanced up, his eyes hard. "You haven't been out long enough. Keep walking."

She slunk back into the courtyard. There were a few trees in the centre that hid her from view as she huddled in the cloistered walkway across the courtyard, trying to warm herself. She could see her cloak lying in the gravel, soaked with rain. She wrapped her arms around her chest, trying to conserve body heat.

Gradually the shivering stopped. Another gust of wind tore through her. She felt thin as paper, so tired she could fall asleep out there.

Which might indicate hypothermia . . .

If she fell asleep, her organs would begin to shut down, and she'd die. She'd read it was a gentle way to go. She let herself sink into the oblivion until everything grew comfortingly vague.

"Creative." Ferron's voice was colder than the wind. Fingers gripped her arm, and heat surged through her, her heart suddenly racing, hot blood pulsing through her body.

She gave a startled gasp, wrenching herself away from him, but it was too late.

He glared at her. "Get up."

She pushed herself awkwardly to her feet, wrists twinging. She was still blue with cold, limbs stiff with chill, but now too warm to die.

"Don't make me drag you," he said through clenched teeth as he turned and walked away.

She followed him sullenly. There was a servant waiting at the door. The third she'd seen. Dead like all the rest. This one was younger, uniformed as a housemaid. She was holding a brush and cloth. Helena tried to slink past but found herself trapped in place.

"Aurelia will throw a fit if you track mud into her house. Sit."

"I can clean myself," Helena said stiffly.

"I didn't ask," Ferron said. His resonance twanged through her nerves, and Helena's knees gave out, dropping her onto a chair. The maid knelt and began cleaning Helena's wet slippers while Helena sat rigidly, torn between horrified fascination and shame.

The Faith said that a soul and body remained joined together as one until cremation. It was only when fire consumed the flesh that the ethereal soul was untethered from the crude earthly form. A person who had lived devoutly and without vice would release a pure soul that could ascend to the highest of the heavenly realms.

If a body was not burned, the soul was left trapped, unable to ascend and in danger of becoming tainted by the body's putrefaction. Left too long, the impurity of the body could metamorphise the soul into maggots and insects, plagues, and other grotesque forms of evil, doomed to sink beneath the surface of the earth to be consumed forever in the dark wet fire of the Abyss.

Reanimation risked that metamorphosis. Tethering both body and soul to a necromancer meant that even the purest souls could become too corrupted to ever ascend unless they were freed with sacred fire.

Helena couldn't help but peer into the maid's face, looking for any sign that there might be a soul still inside, slowly decaying, trapped in a state of neither life nor death. The maid's gaze was empty. If there was any trace of her soul, it was smothered beneath Ferron's will.

She looked up at him. "You're a monster."

He raised an eyebrow. "Noticed that, have you?"

CHAPTER 6

FERRON LEFT AS THE MAID FINISHED WITH Helena's slippers, and Helena immediately stood, refusing to let the corpse touch her further.

The maid headed inside. The instant her back was turned, Helena snatched up Ferron's discarded newspaper, hiding it behind her back as she drew a deep breath and stepped inside.

She focused on the paper in her hand as she hurried towards the stairs.

The shadows loomed but Helena refused to let herself look at them, counting each step, hand pressed against the banister and then along the wall, focusing on the amber pools of light cast by the sconces, until she reached her room.

In her absence, it had been aired out. The bed stripped, linens changed. The air was almost as cold as it had been outside, but the windows were closed and locked again.

Helena was drenched and freezing but Ferron might realise he'd left the newspaper and come for it. She had no time to waste.

She huddled near the window where the light was strongest, her eyes drinking in every word, starting at the very top. NOVEMBRIS 1788.

She stared at the date in shock. That couldn't be right. Her last memory with a clear date was the hearing about Lila Bayard resuming paladin duties and returning to combat early in 1786.

If the war had ended fourteen months ago, that would have been in late summer of 1787. Which meant that she had no memory of nearly nineteen months of the war. It blurred out of focus when she tried to think back, to remember anything more than the hospital shifts. She had no recollection of anything, not of conversation or the seasons, or Lumithia's Ascendance and Abeyance, of anything but the endless loop of shift after shift in the hospital, like an eternal scream.

She squeezed her eyes shut, racking her brain. There must be something. She couldn't have lost that much, but it was like trying to catch the wind with her fingers. A sharp pain splintered through her skull.

She blinked, vision flickering red as her eyes opened.

There was a newspaper in her hands.

She clutched it tightly. She had to read quickly before Ferron noticed she'd taken it. Her eyes raced to the first article.

> The last fugitive of the extremist group calling themselves the Order of the Eternal Flame has been apprehended and faces interrogation. New Paladia's Central office has confirmed the identity of Helena Marino, a foreign alchemy student from the southern islands of Etras. The Etrasian government denies any involvement in or support of the Eternal Flame's terrorist activities. To protect the citizens of New Paladia from further violence, Marino has been imprisoned outside the city at Spirefell while her fate is decided.
>
> Spirefell, the renowned Ferron estate, was built of iron by Urius Ferron. With a unique structure, built as a celebration of the family's exceptional resonance, the house makes a secure location for dangerous prisoners.
>
> The Ferrons, one of New Paladia's oldest families, have a history in the region that predates the Holdfasts. They were frequent victims of the Eternal Flame's persecution. Iron

> Guildmaster Atreus Ferron was arrested and executed for speaking against the Holdfasts' oppressive regime, and his son, Kaine Ferron, was baselessly accused of assassinating Principate Apollo Holdfast. All charges against father and son were later dropped . . .

Ferron had been accused of killing the Principate? The assassination responsible for causing the war?

She stared at the words until they blurred.

She remembered Principate Apollo's death. He was found brutally murdered in the Alchemy Institute's commons, and an investigation had immediately been opened. She didn't remember there being any conclusion. There'd been so much happening at the time: the funeral, the preparations for Luc to be crowned Principate. What should have been a joyous occasion was shrouded by grief and shock, Luc in denial even as his friends were swearing oaths to die protecting him. The ceremony was barely over before the sedition and the Undying, and the war that never seemed to end.

Had Ferron killed Principate Apollo? Surely not, he would have been only sixteen. Perhaps the claim had been fabricated to further portray the Ferron family as victims of the Holdfasts? That seemed more likely.

She read the rest of the article, hoping for more information but finding simply a reiteration of the Undying's usual narrative about the war: that they had not started it; that in fact there had never been a "war" but instead civil unrest caused by a small group of religious extremists who refused to acknowledge the democratically elected Paladian Guild Assembly.

It made Luc out to be a power-hungry monster who'd tried to burn down the entire city rather than let anyone else have it.

Luc, who'd gone up onto the roof of the Alchemy Tower the night before becoming Principate, standing alone on the very edge.

Helena had followed him and stood as close as she dared, promising him that she would do anything for him if he would just step back and take her hand.

He hadn't listened, not until she swore that if he jumped, then she would, too. He'd stepped back to save her.

They'd sat together there on the roof until sunrise. She'd gripped his hand and talked the whole night, telling him about Etras, the cliffs, and the little villages with the donkeys pulling painted carts, the olives, all the farms, and the sea on summer days. They'd go there someday, she told him. Once everything was better, she'd take him and he'd see how beautiful it was.

Luc had never wanted to be Principate. If there had been anyone else, he would have given it up in a heartbeat.

Helena turned the page of the newspaper, blinking hard.

A column within listed executions performed by the High Reeve the previous week. There was a picture of wretched-looking men and women on their knees on a platform. Dressed all in black, with an intricate helmet obscuring his face and hair, stood Ferron, one pale hand outstretched.

She could tell it was Ferron just by his posture and the familiar tilt of his long fingers, but the article only referred to him as *the High Reeve.*

There was no reference anywhere to Kaine Ferron being the High Reeve.

Was that a secret?

Who would benefit from that? If the deteriorating condition of the estate was anything to go by, it was not the Ferrons.

No. Morrough must be responsible. After all, keeping the High Reeve's identity hidden provided the High Necromancer with an exceptionally powerful tool. If the High Reeve could be anyone, people were kept paranoid, always wondering. It would also prevent Ferron from gathering his own followers or accumulating enough power to overthrow Morrough.

Perhaps Ferron had ambitions that Morrough feared. That was a tantalising possibility. Something Helena might take advantage of.

It also made Spirefell the perfect trap. If anyone tried to save Helena, they would assume they were attacking a guild heir; they'd have no idea who her captor truly was.

She read the rest of the paper quickly. There were some vague allusions to grain shortages. It was strange. The countries on both sides of Paladia were significant agricultural exporters. The Novis monarchy had historical ties with the Holdfasts, so an embargo by Novis was predictable, but Hevgoss, their western neighbour and a heavily militaristic country, had been angling for better trade agreements with the guilds for decades.

The Holdfasts had always blocked the negotiations, refusing to have alchemy used for industrialised warfare. Guilds found to be violating the trade restrictions with Hevgoss had their access to lumithium cut off, preventing them from alchemical processing on an industrial scale.

Why wouldn't Hevgoss be pouring grain into Paladia now?

The political section of the paper was almost funny in a horrible way. The Guild Assembly, whose formation was ostensibly the reason for the war, was three weeks into negotiations over the lift fare, as if New Paladia had nothing more urgent to do before the hibernal solstice ushered in the new year.

More interesting was a paragraph mentioning that a Paladian envoy had arrived at the Eastern Empire and been permitted to cross the border. It was the first time any Paladians had been allowed into the Eastern Empire in several hundred years. Was that where that traitor Shiseo had been headed?

Helena mostly skipped the society pages, but she couldn't help noticing how often Aurelia Ferron's name was mentioned. Quite the socialite, it seemed.

Then an editorial caught her eye. It was almost innocuous, describing the current labour shortage and lamenting the recent loss of so many talented alchemists in the "conflict" caused by the Eternal Flame. There were statistics presented about how Paladia's economy was expected to continue to shrink due to a multigenerational loss of alchemists. The solution, the author declared, was sponsored births. The article suddenly stopped being editorial and read more like an advertisement. The head of the new science and alchemy department at Central, Irmgard Stroud, was heading up a program to bolster the next generation of alchemists using new scientific selection methods to give them the best start.

Volunteers were wanted. Participants would be provided food and lodgings, and upon completion of the program, those with criminal convictions would be eligible for retrial.

Helena read the editorial several times, hardly able to believe what she was seeing. It was a breeding program being passed off as an economic solution. As if alchemists were dogs to mate in pursuit of economically desirable transmutation abilities.

It wasn't an entirely new concept. *Marrying into the resonance* was a well-known term for the guild families' tendency to marry those with either the same or a complementary alchemical resonance. Aurelia and Ferron were just such an example.

While an alchemist's resonance repertoire was as heritable as hair or eye colour, resonance could also appear or vanish at random.

Neither of Helena's parents had been alchemists. Her father had possessed a minor resonance for steel and copper, but not enough to merit training or qualify for a guild. Her mother had no resonance at all that Helena could remember. Luc's great-aunt, Ilva Holdfast, was famously a Lapse, a child of alchemists who never manifested resonance.

Now it seemed Stroud had every intention of testing exactly how heritable resonance was or wasn't, and she intended to use the prisoners on the Outpost to do it. After all, who else would volunteer for a breeding program because of incentives like food, lodgings, and a retrial?

She thought of Grace, starving and desperate, with brothers too young to work, willing to sell an eye. Helena could only guess how many others were like her.

All those files Stroud had been constantly going through. This must have been what she was working on, winnowing out eligible candidates from the Resistance records.

Helena hid the newspaper in her wardrobe, resolving to drop it somewhere when she next left her room. Her joints were stiff with cold, and she went to the shower, peeling off her wet clothes.

She stood under the hot water until feeling seeped back into her body and the bone-deep cold faded away. She began washing slowly, in no hurry to go back into her freezing room.

As she looked down, she discovered scars that she had no memory of.

The largest was right in the middle of her chest, running between her breasts. The roping scar was raised, slightly puckered, as if her sternum had been split open and stapled back together.

She traced her fingers across it, finding a divot in the bone, the odd sensation of severed nerves.

It didn't seem like healing had been used. The bone could have been regrown. She could have easily knit the nerve endings back together to avoid the loss of sensation, and then arranged the matrices so that the scarring was less visible.

None of that had happened. The wound had been left to heal without any vivimancy.

Perhaps this was the extensive injury Stroud had mentioned.

No, she couldn't have been placed in stasis with an injury like that. She began to search her body carefully and found more scars.

Her mind seemed trained to overlook them, but she focused, taking note of each one.

There were traces of a large circular wound that went straight through her calf. Hairline scars, one on her stomach and another between two ribs. Vivimancy had undeniably been used to heal them.

In her right palm there were more scars. Slits in the palm and fingers, as if she'd gripped a knife blade in her hands, and more oddly, seven tiny punctures. They were perfectly spaced into a circle in her palm. Not large but distinct in the way they marred the skin. She stared at them. The shape felt familiar.

She put her hand down, unsettled, and finally reached up to find the one scar that she did remember.

It was hardly visible, hidden below the shadow of her jaw. It ran long and thin across the left side of her neck, stopping just short of her throat.

Ferron brought Helena's dried and cleaned cloak with him when he arrived the next day and threw it at her head.

Helena followed him, surreptitiously dropping the newspaper along the way. On the veranda, he pulled out another paper. The cover story was about a monument the governor, Fabian Greenfinch, was having built in honour of Morrough as New Paladia's liberator. It would be unveiled the following year.

It was raining again. Helena glanced around, not sure what to do, finding no appeal in strolling about in circles under Ferron's supervision.

Perhaps she could find a very sharp stick somewhere and stab him with it.

She wandered along the veranda until she was bored, and then sat observing the stillness of the house, trying to guess at how many rooms there must be in a place so large.

She'd thought the Bayards' house, Solis Splendour, enormous. It had been one of the few freestanding houses in the city, a remnant from long ago. Spirefell was much larger.

When Ferron stood and left, she assumed it was a sign to go back inside. She cast her eyes around and was disappointed to find he hadn't forgotten his newspaper.

She went to the door. The winter light spilled like quicksilver across the dark floor, but the hallway beyond disappeared into darkness like the opening of a mouth. With the winter drapes, the light was blotted out, creating the dusty suffocating feeling of a tomb. The lights were off.

She groped along the wall, trying to find a dial or switch.

Wind rushed out of the dark, and the smell of dust and rot struck her face like a cold breath, followed by a low, shifting groan that made the house vibrate.

Helena stumbled back outside, heart racing.

If the clouds would lift, it would get brighter. She huddled on the veranda, waiting. Through the obscuring rain, the house around her looked almost like an immense slumbering creature, curved inwards, the spires like spines.

The rain did not cease. Instead the sky dimmed as dusk fell. At this point in the lunar cycles, even Lumithia, the brighter moon, had waned too much for her light to penetrate the cloud cover.

The light in the doorway had shrunk and weakened.

Helena drew a deep breath; she'd taken the route before. There were steps not far into the shadows. If she found them, she could feel her way back.

It was only shadows. It wasn't the tank. It wasn't the nothing. Just shadows.

She wavered in the doorway, and everything grew darker, the remaining light outside beginning to vanish.

Helena felt herself disappearing into it. Terror sharp as talons clawed through her as she forced herself forward. She stumbled, colliding with a table, barely feeling the pain that shot up her shin.

Find the stairs.

It's only a house.

But she *felt* the darkness swallowing her, dragging her in, the endlessness so close. She gripped the table, hands shaking so violently that the wood rattled. Something fell, crashing onto the floor.

Breathe. Just breathe.

She fought to breathe but pain splintered her chest. Her heart was racing, beating like a caged bird inside her, breaking itself against her ribs.

She made it a few steps before her legs gave out. She curled up on the floor, the wood like bones beneath her hands. She was disappearing into the nothing again. Into the nothing where she couldn't move . . . couldn't scream . . . and no one ever came . . .

She was gripped by the arms and wrenched off the floor.

"What are you doing?"

She blinked in the sudden light, staring into Ferron's incensed face.

An electric sconce on the wall glowed, a halo in the dark illuminating only them.

She focused on his face, trying not to see the ocean of black surrounding her.

"It was—dark," she forced out.

"What?"

Her breathing was so rapid, her head swam.

"*You're* scared of the dark?" His silver eyes were burning, his voice thick with disbelief.

She tried to pull away—she'd rather suffocate in the hallways than be near Ferron—but he didn't let go, pulling her over to the stairs, mere steps away, and dragging her to her room, refusing to let her collapse back onto the floor.

"Calm down," he snarled at her as soon as she was inside the familiar space.

The door slammed.

Helena dropped into the chair, doubling over and gripping the fabric. Her fingers kept twitching, sending shocks of pain to her arms, but she didn't care. She needed to feel that things were real and tangible, not an abyss of nowhere with her body and nothing else.

The air sliced through the inside of her lungs.

She was in her room. The house had not eaten her, because houses did not eat people. Her mind cleared slowly, that suffocating terror gradually ebbing away, allowing reason to seep back in.

It was almost worse to be rational again, to sit knowing her fear made no sense. It didn't matter. The part of her that was afraid did not care about being rational.

"What's wrong with you?"

She started, looking up.

Ferron was still in the room, apparently having lingered to interrogate her now that her fit of panophobia was over.

She averted her eyes.

"If you won't tell me, I'll pull the answer out of your head."

Helena flinched. The thought of his resonance set her teeth on edge. There were parts of her brain that still felt bruised, caved in from the transference.

Her mouth twisted, throat going taut. "I don't like places I can't see."

"Since when? I haven't noticed you keeping the light on in here constantly. Or are these shadows different?"

Heat rose across the back of her neck. She stared at the iron bars in the floor. "I know this room. It's the places I don't know, that I can't see the end of. I-In the stasis tank, it was always dark no matter how hard I tried to see, and I couldn't feel anything around me, just my body floating and not moving. It felt—endless. Like I was nowhere. I was—I was there so long. I kept thinking that eventually someone would come but—" She shook her head. "When I see dark places and I don't know where they end, I feel like I'll disappear inside them, but this time, I'll never be found."

She sounded irrational. She *was* irrational, but there was no help for it; there was a schism between her reason and her mind, a fault line shearing them forever apart. Her mind did not care whether the fear made sense; it just wanted to never go back.

Ferron was silent for so long that she finally looked up at him, morbidly curious, but he was unreadable. Still as a statue as he stared at her.

It was the first time she'd bothered to just look at him, to see him for what he was, rather than *who* he was.

His clothing hid it well, but he was strangely slight. Not at all built like an iron alchemist. He didn't even have the look or presence of a combat alchemist. She couldn't imagine him with a heavy weapon in hand.

Aside from the predatory intensity to his eyes, his features were almost too fine, like a statue carved a stroke too far.

Everything about him was slim and sharp-edged.

"You know," Ferron said, jolting her from her thoughts, "when I heard it was you I'd be getting, I was looking forward to breaking you."

He shook his head. "But I don't think it's possible to exceed what you've done to yourself."

CHAPTER 7

Ferron took her to and from the courtyard each day. His mood was always dark after that, and he'd mockingly point out the location of the various light switches that she was "too dense" to observe on her own.

He was so condescending, she wanted to throw a rock at him and was disappointed when she found nothing outside but little pieces of finely milled white gravel.

The courtyard bored her. It was tedious and bitterly cold, the winter snow bearing down in the clouds, although there was never more than a dusting on the ground—enough to leave her feet numb with cold.

When alone, she ventured out of her room, determined to find a passable weapon; even a furniture nail would do. If Ferron wouldn't slip up and do it, she'd kill herself before another transference session arrived.

In the hours when light trickled through the east windows, if she stayed near the walls and thought very carefully about breathing, she could manage the excursions.

But whenever she left her room for long, the necrothralls began materialising. They didn't try to stop her or herd her back into her room; they just watched her, hovering like ghostly apparitions.

She tried to ignore them along with the creaks and groans of the house, the shifting shadows, but they made it impossible for her to find any means of suicide. She persisted doggedly, but most of the rooms were locked tight, and those that weren't held nothing but old furniture and useless knickknacks.

In one old room, she found a painting crammed behind a disassembled bed frame. It was covered by a dustcloth. She pulled it out, curious.

Drawing the fabric back, it was a portrait of the Ferron family. Not Ferron and Aurelia, but Ferron as a boy with his parents.

Atreus Ferron, the former patriarch, was a large man Helena vaguely remembered seeing at the Institute. He had hawkish features, a harshly lined face, and heavy brows that shadowed pale-blue eyes. He was elegantly dressed, but the family's lineage as blacksmiths and ironmongers was plain to see in his build, his broad shoulders and huge hands with heavy iron rings decorating the fingers.

Kaine Ferron stood beside his father. He looked exactly as she remembered him from the Institute, so unlike the distilled iteration he would become. His face was fuller, and while he was almost the same height as his father, he had none of the build that made the patriarch so intimidating. Ferron was gangly, with the air of a colt. His manners were a clear imitation of the man looming beside him. His brown hair was lighter than his father's but styled identically, his expression and posture also mirroring Atreus, dark brows drawn down over hazel eyes.

The central figure of the portrait was a woman in a pale-grey dress. She wore an iron ring on her wedding finger, but her hands were so delicate that it looked out of place on her. She was slight as a willow, with a heart-shaped face, grey eyes, and a small chin framed by ash-brown hair. If Helena had seen a portrait of her alone, she would never have guessed that this was Ferron's mother, but side by side, she could see her influence in his build, the way her features softened Ferron's, erasing the harsh hawkish angles and build he would have inherited from his father; but there was the greatest likeness in their mouths and something in the light and tilt of their eyes.

Helena studied the faces for a long time before noticing that the portrait was incomplete. The details of their clothing and the motifs usually included in such portraiture were all absent. As if something had interrupted it, and that was why it was abandoned.

She let the dustcloth slip from her fingers and tucked the painting back into its hiding place. Her mind flipped like a coin between the dark-haired Ferron in the painting and the silvery-pale iteration that now existed.

"THE INFLAMMATION IS NEARLY GONE," Stroud announced two weeks later, bringing Mandl with her once again, and pressing her resonance intrusively into Helena's brain until her vision turned red. "I think monthly sessions will do. Although"—she picked up Helena's wrist, inspecting her muscle tone with disapproval—"you're not recovering the way I'd hoped. Are you going outside daily?"

"Yes. The High Reeve has been ensuring it."

"And exercising? The stronger your constitution is, the more likely you'll handle transference without any more febrile seizures."

Helena stared at Stroud in speechless disbelief at this revelation that no one had seen fit to reveal previously. She'd had seizures?

Stroud stared back expectantly, and it took her a moment to remember that the woman thought walks might prevent them.

"Yes," Helena bit out.

"Good. It's been noted that you have a nervous disorder."

Helena's jaw tensed. Of course Ferron would have told Stroud.

"Yes. I don't like—dark places I don't know."

There was a snort of laughter from Mandl.

"Well, not much to be done about that," Stroud said, and resumed her examination of Helena. "You know, it's a pity I can't use you as one of my program's trial subjects. I was rereading your admission paperwork. You had a remarkable repertoire."

Helena's throat closed.

"The Holdfasts did love collecting rare alchemists," said Mandl.

Helena bit her tongue until she tasted blood.

Stroud nodded. "Once the High Reeve is done with you, I think I might request to have you next."

Helena's chin snapped up. "Well, you won't have much luck with me. I'm sterilised."

She winced as Stroud's resonance suddenly jabbed into her lower abdomen. A moment later, disappointment and anger lit Stroud's face.

"When did this happen?"

Helena looked away, staring across the room so hard, her vision blurred. "It was one of the conditions the Falcon had for allowing me in the city. Since vivimancy is a corruption of the soul that begins in the womb, it could—it could be passed on. I'd already taken vows as a healer that I wouldn't ever marry or have children, but he—" She swallowed. "He wanted to be sure."

"And of course you agreed," Stroud said, withdrawing her hand. "Because you thought they'd accept what you are if you only reduced yourself enough."

Heat spread along Helena's jaw. "There wasn't any point in refusing. Like I said, I'd already made the vows."

Stroud chuckled. "Usually, it was children who fell for that lie."

Helena looked at her, eyes narrowing.

Stroud had an arch expression and glanced at Mandl again. "Didn't you know? Your Eternal Flame was quite adept at identifying potential vivimancers not even born. It was, what, thirty years ago that Principate Helios mandated that all pregnancies be managed by the Faith's hospitals. Devout doctors trained to know what to look for and what solutions to offer. What kind of parents would want to keep a monster once they're warned of the danger?"

Helena's stomach clenched.

"Mandl here was abandoned at birth, raised as an orphan in one of the aeries. Children like her were told their soul's corruption must be purified, and that if they did what was asked, they might be wanted someday." Stroud shrugged. "Of course, neither the Faith nor Paladia ever did want them for anything but forced labour. And look, they handled you the same way."

"No," Helena said, shaking her head. "Luc wasn't like that. He didn't even know about the conditions for me becoming a healer. Or how healing worked. He wouldn't have let me, if he'd known. People like Falcon Matias had harsh views, but Luc was always reining people like the Falcon in. Once it was over, he wanted to—"

"If he didn't know, all that means is that he was a puppet and a fool. And you're still one," Mandl said, her dead face seething with hatred, before she turned to Stroud. "You should tell her what His Eminence did with Holdfast after he killed him."

Helena's stomach dropped like a stone. She looked quickly between them, but Stroud shook her head. "Remember your place, Mandl."

When they were gone, Helena sat, frozen and wondering what had happened to Luc.

Of course it was no surprise they hadn't cremated him properly, but—what had been done that Mandl wanted Helena tortured with knowledge of?

Luc had never deserved the cruelty and hatred he'd been subjected to.

She'd admit he hadn't known everything, but that wasn't because he was a puppet. The position of Principate was complex. Being a religious head and ruler was a difficult task, especially during war when he was expected to be fighting and governing. He couldn't be weighed down by everyone else's personal decisions.

Some choices had to be made without him, certain sacrifices that would have paralysed him to make or even know of. That didn't make him a puppet. It made him human.

Helena had loved him for how human he was. He didn't need to be Principate or favoured by the gods. He'd been good enough just as he was.

Ferron made his routine appearance after Helena's inedible lunch. She went resignedly to fetch her cloak.

"No need today," he said. She paused, looking at him warily.

The door closed behind him with a soft click.

His fingers spun, and his resonance seized hold of her. She was pulled forward. Once she was near the bed, his hand flicked, toppling her back onto the mattress.

Ferron sauntered over, expression bored, the only emotion a glint in his eyes.

Helena bit her lip to keep quiet, willing her breathing to steady as she fought against his resonance.

He stared down at her through hooded eyes.

She hadn't even considered this. She should have. She knew he was a monster, but he'd never shown interest.

As if interest had anything to do with it. Her mind raced. Why now? Why today? Had Stroud mentioned that Helena was sterile, and he'd seen that as an opportunity? Something he could exploit without consequence?

A whimper crept up her throat. She wished she could sink through the surface of the mattress and suffocate there. Wished she could scream. Her fingers managed to flex, but in the place where her resonance should be, there was nothing but a gaping wound.

His right hand pressed into the mattress by her head, and he turned her chin until she was looking straight up at him.

Her heart shuddered.

His pupils were contracted, the grey of his irises like a storm.

His cool fingers followed the curve of her jaw to her temple. She lay, viscerally aware of the almost-weight of his body as his resonance pierced her mind.

Her mind was like an upturned snow globe, all her thoughts whirling like snow flurries through her consciousness.

It wasn't transference, but she could still vaguely sense his mind through the connection. Endured his amusement at all her ideas for killing him—it had grown into a veritable constellation of fantasies. He skimmed through them all without concern, and then sank deeper into her mind, watching her tentative explorations of the house, the courtyard, the necrothralls, the newspaper she'd stolen, Stroud. The only moment in which she felt any glimmer of a reaction from him was at her constant thoughts of Luc, the scale of her grief.

Then she was in her room reaching for her cloak, and he was closing the door, and she knew what was about to happen.

The memory evaporated like fog beneath bright sun, and she found herself lying on the bed, Ferron staring down at her with a scathing expression on his face. He snatched his hand away.

"I have no desire to touch you," he said, sneering. "Your presence here is offensive enough."

"Small mercies," Helena said in a dry voice. It wasn't a very clever retort, but her head was throbbing again, as if the scab on a wound had been peeled off while the skin was fresh.

He straightened, and she thought he'd walk out in offence, so she quickly asked the question haunting her.

"Did you kill Principate Apollo?"

He paused and leaned against the bedpost, crossing his arms and cocking his head to the side. "Not . . . officially."

"But it was you. Wasn't it?" The more she'd thought about it, the more convinced she'd become.

"You don't remember?" He shook his head. "Did you even do anything during the war? The way the Holdfasts used to parade you around, you'd think you would have at least tried to be useful, but you have the most unexceptional personnel file I've ever seen." He scoffed. "How many years of your life did you spend in that hospital? And for what? Saving people who would have been better off if you'd let them die. But no, you put them back together and sent them right back out to suffer a bit more." He gave a slow smile. "Perhaps Stroud's wrong, and you were sympathetic to our cause."

He couldn't have hurt her more if he'd struck her.

All those years. All the people she'd healed, her resonance knitting them back together so they could live to fight another day, and for what? So they could be tortured to death, or enslaved, or—worse?

Until that moment, healing had been the only thing she hadn't felt guilt over. Luc might be dead, but she had done some good. Now Ferron had ripped that shred of comfort away from her, turning the act into its own form of atrocity.

She clamped her hands over her mouth until she could feel the outline of her teeth, curling onto her side.

He laughed. "You Resistance fighters are always easy to break."

He turned to leave.

The grief swelled inside her lungs, but she fought it back. "You didn't answer my question," she said through gritted teeth.

He paused.

"Right . . . Well, I suppose there's no harm in telling you. The High Necromancer personally requested that I kill the Principate. He'd been in Paladia for some time already, quietly gathering followers, but with Apollo in power, the Guild Assembly would never have garnered enough public support. The country needed to be destabilised, the future made to feel uncertain. The Principate was impossible to target in public with his paladin, guards, and everyone else flocking around, worshipping his radiance. But the Holdfasts were always careless at the Institute, convinced that anyone who walked through those gates would be too dazzled by their magnificence to lay a finger on them."

She watched from the corner of her eye as Ferron held up his left hand, studying it. "I'm sure you know what a fascinating resonance vivimancy is. Sinking my hand into his chest cavity was like breaking the surface of water. Slipped right in"—his fingers curled—"then I pulled out his beating heart. You should have seen the shock on his face. I hadn't realised he'd still be alive for a moment, but he lived just long enough to know exactly who killed him."

Principate Apollo had been a warm, generous man with an easy smile, jokes ready for any nervous student who approached. Luc had been so much like him. The same crooked smile. Being near them felt like standing in the summer sun.

"I suppose your master was quite pleased with you," she said dully, not wanting to give him the satisfaction of witnessing her horror.

"He was indeed. They were all waiting for me when I returned. We had a celebratory dinner with him, my mother and I. I was declared a prodigy . . ."

Helena glanced up. His eyes were locked on the window, as though his mind had gone elsewhere.

He roused himself, glancing down.

"Any other questions?" He arched an eyebrow as if daring her.

"No," she said quickly, looking away. "You've done enough."

CHAPTER 8

Luc Holdfast sat on the rooftop of the Alchemy Tower, hunched back against the tilt of the tiles as he absently spun an opium pipe in his fingers. The spire of the Tower, lit with the Eternal Flame, burned above him, a beacon of white light.

The sun was setting, the world hued with bronze shadows as Helena clambered across to join him.

He was so gaunt, he already looked older than his father. The war had chewed him down to the bone. The tendons along his neck stood out like cords when he swallowed, looked over, and then away again.

"What happened to us, Hel?" he asked as she crouched down beside him.

She stared at the horizon, past all the towers, towards the south.

"A war," she said.

"You used to believe in me. What did I do to make you stop?" His voice was faraway.

"I still believe in you, Luc," she said. "But we have to win this war; we can't make choices because we want a certain story to tell later. There's too much at stake."

"No," he said. "This is how we win. This is how we've always won. My

father, my grandfather, all the Principates going all the way back to Orion. They won by trusting that good would triumph over evil, and I have to do the same."

His thumb flicked against his index finger, ignition rings sparking. Pale flames flared to life, filling his palm, a light like a small sun. His fingers closed around them, leaving only a tongue of fire along a fingertip as he tucked the opium pipe between his lips and brought the flame close to the bowl.

Helena looked away, listening to him inhale.

"What if it's not that simple, though?" she said. "Everyone who wins says they were good, but they're the ones who tell the story. They get to choose how we'll remember it. What if it's never that simple?"

He shook his head. "Orion became sun-blessed because he refused to break his faith."

Helena exhaled, burying her face in her hands.

She heard his rings spark, and the pipe hissed as the opium vaporised.

"Luc—please, let me help you." She tried to reach towards him.

He flinched away. "Don't—touch me."

He was teetering dangerously close to that immense fall, as if the Abyss still called to him. She didn't know how to draw him back anymore, what to say that he'd still hear.

"Do you remember what I promised you, Luc, that night you came out here?" she asked, her voice pleading.

He gave no response. His gaze had settled back into a dim stupor, the sunset limning his gaunt features as though gilding him.

"I promised I'd do anything for you." She curled her fingers into a fist. "Maybe you didn't realise how far I was willing to go."

THE MEMORY OF LUC LINGERED in Helena's mind when she woke in the morning.

She lay in bed, replaying it. It was a forgotten memory, which should have frightened her, but there seemed to be no information in it that Ferron could find useful, and she missed Luc desperately, even if it was a memory bitter as seawater.

He'd been smoking opium. How had that happened? He must have been horrifically injured to be allowed drugs like that. His great-aunt Ilva, who'd acted as steward for the Principate when Luc was at the front, had always been reluctant to allow him drugs, preferring to utilise Helena's abilities than to risk addiction.

But he wouldn't even let Helena touch him.

She lay in bed, turning the memory over and over, taking note of every detail. The evening light, the way it bronzed his features and illuminated his eyes. The nervous, intense way his fingers moved as he'd sparked his rings, bringing the flames to life.

She'd loved his pyromancy. It always felt more like magic than alchemy, the way he could make fire an extension of himself with those sun-bright flames.

The Holdfasts were always depicted wreathed in fire. The creation of sacred fire and the alchemisation of gold were the two unique gifts which Sol bestowed upon the Holdfasts.

Alchemisation, the transformation of one metal into another, was the most difficult form of alchemy. Prior to Orion Holdfast's founding of the Institute, early alchemical writing was more entwined with mythological ideas than science.

The mythical Cetus, often called the first Northern alchemist, was credited with hundreds, even thousands of the earliest alchemical writings, which spanned centuries. Scholars had speculated that Cetus was the name of a school or an alchemical sect. The mystery was later revealed to be a consequence of superstition. Early alchemists were forced to write pseudonymously, initially to avoid persecution, while later novice alchemists used the names of more famous alchemists in their attempts to legitimise their theories and discoveries. As a result, "Cetus" had written almost all the surviving alchemy texts.

While the works of Cetus were considered historically seminal, they were highly inaccurate, and it was doubted that any alchemist by the name had even existed, but with no one else to credit, almost all early alchemical theories and discoveries prior to Paladia's founding remained attributed to him.

It was Cetus's early writings that established the alchemical principle that a metal could only be alchemised into a less noble form, often in keeping with the planetary hierarchy.

Later, Orion Holdfast discovered the modern principles of alchemisation, overturning Cetus's claims and laying forth the methods and array principles needed to transform the ignoble metals into those less corruptible.

In Orion's work, alchemisation was predicated upon spiritual purity; only an alchemist with a soul as pure as the metal they sought to create could alchemise it.

It was Sol's own light and purity bestowed in blessing upon the Holdfasts that endowed them with the divine ability to turn lead into pure gold.

However, Luc had always preferred pyromancy. There were strict rules the family had to abide by when alchemising gold. The heavenly metal could not be abused or used for selfish purposes; after all, the neighbouring countries' and Paladia's own currency had to be respected. There were rules about fire, too, but not nearly so elaborate as those involving gold production.

She remembered the first time Luc showed her his fire. She'd been sure the flames would burn him, but they simply danced across the surface of his fingers, shining like a star in his hand.

Even without the flames, she'd always felt warm near Luc; even the cold Paladian winters were thawed by his presence. All alone now, she missed him so intensely, her bones and skin ached for the familiarity and comfort of a hug.

HELENA HAD FINISHED WITH HER exploration of the second-floor wing and resolved to explore the downstairs next.

She stood staring down the shadowy twist of the stairs as the windowpanes rattled like chattering teeth, the wind moaning through the corridor.

Her fingers curled tight around the banister, smooth as bone against her palm. She squeezed until she could feel the wood grain, wrist twinging against the manacle.

She refused to let her eyes sink into the shadows as she stepped forward.

She thought about the cliffs on Etras, the endless roar of the sea. In her memory, she was a child again, scrambling among tide pools during the summer Abeyance when Lumithia waned and the sea retreated, leaving its bed laid bare and full of treasures. The brilliant summer sun radiating across her skin.

Helena would go south. Run away and follow the river from the mountains all the way to the sea and sail home.

She reached the bottom of the stairs and found a necrothrall waiting, all the amber lights already aglow. Ferron's wordless reminder that she could do nothing and go nowhere without his knowledge.

She swallowed hard, letting go of the fantasy. She would die in Spirefell.

The rooms on the main floor flowed from one to the next. Spirefell seemed to have more rooms than the Ferrons had ever known what to do with.

"Come back here, I'm not done with you." A harsh voice made Helena freeze before she realised it was not directed at her.

"There's nothing more to say," came Ferron's voice. "I'm not interested."

"Don't walk away from me! Disobey me and I'll have you disowned, your name stricken from the guild!"

Helena peeked out into the corridor to see Ferron turning to face the lich that she'd seen with Stroud at Central, the one using Crowther's body.

"You're dead, Father. Perhaps you forgot. That corpse has no claim to my estate or my inheritance. And"—Ferron's voice grew pointed—"you have no iron resonance inside that body. Regardless of the titles the guild indulges you with, you have no real power. It took nearly a year before anyone even remembered you, and longer before they wanted you back. The only reason I let you continue as guildmaster is because I have better things to do with my time than dealing with the minutiae of factory management."

The lich's face darkened until it was almost purple with rage. Helena would never have guessed this was Atreus Ferron. Crowther was a different build entirely, so slight he was needle-like and more than half a head shorter than Ferron.

"I should have refused your mother's pleas and had you killed in the womb," Atreus said, his face contorted with rage. "You deserve none of the suffering we endured for you."

Ferron seemed unfazed, even slightly bored.

"A pity you didn't, if it would have spared me this tedious conversation." He turned away, his grey eyes still alight with scorn. "Get out of this house, Father, before I have it throw you out."

Helena ducked back out of sight, dreading discovery. The necrothrall tailing her blinked placidly.

"You'll regret this. The High Necromancer will remember that you did not volunteer yourself."

"The High Necromancer knows exactly where I am and what I'm doing. If he wants something, he won't have it relayed by the likes of you. After all, how many times did you manage to fail him to be banned from receiving a corpse with iron resonance? Was it the second time or the third?"

There was a snarl, followed by the sudden scream of metal and a thud. She peeked out again. Atreus was on the ground; one of the bars of iron in the floor had caught around his leg, pulling him back towards the main wing of the house.

He was clawing at the ground, scrabbling, trying to escape but only succeeding in nearly ripping his fingers off. Atreus screamed with rage, mouth frothing, the noises practically animal.

Ferron idly followed. "I'd be careful with that corpse. Pyromancy is a rare ability, you know. Give yourself a few more months, and I'm sure you'll manage a spark."

HELENA SCUTTLED BACK TO HER room once they were gone; just a glimpse of the house in action had made her far more wary. She'd understood in theory that it was malleable, but seeing the reality of it turned every bit of wrought-iron filigree ominous.

It was not her imagination: The house was almost alive.

And so was Atreus—or reanimated. She would have sworn he'd been executed before the Undying had appeared.

She kept trying to piece together the bits and pieces of her missing memories, but it was difficult to know if she'd forgotten something or never been informed in the first place. After all, a healer didn't merit much in the way of security clearance. Her only knowledge of the battles and military strategy was trying to staunch the sea of blood that followed.

Despite knowing how dangerous it was, she couldn't help but try to unravel the mystery of what she'd forgotten. Her mind itched for context. Yet she was playing a cat-and-mouse game with Ferron, and her ignorance was her only defence. But it didn't feel protective. It felt like walking blind, with her skin sheared off.

Her mind circled relentlessly, treating every new piece of information as a potential clue, turning it one way and then the other, trying to see if it fit into any of the gaps. What could she have possibly known that would need to be hidden like this?

Stop thinking. She slotted her feet under the wardrobe and began doing sit-ups until her abdominal muscles burned. Lila used to do it in their room when she was anxious and off duty.

Helena needed to focus on Ferron, on finding some way to provoke him into killing her.

He had to have some kind of weakness she could exploit.

Kaine Ferron, where is the chink in your perfect armour?

As if on cue, the door opened, and he walked in.

He stared down at where her feet were tucked under the wardrobe and the way she was laid out, panting from exertion.

"You've found something to do with yourself, I see."

She forced herself to roll over and stand, biting back a wince when she pushed herself up.

He was early for their walk, and this aberration in the daily routine made her suspicious.

"Come here," he said, withdrawing a vial containing several small white tablets, watching her reaction to it.

"What are those?" she asked when he unscrewed the top and tapped one out.

He raised an eyebrow. "I'll tell you if you swallow it like a good girl."

Helena pressed her lips tightly together.

Despite healers generally lacking formal medical training, Helena was intimately acquainted with medicine. She knew very well the power and danger in something as innocuous as a small white tablet.

"You know I'm not going to kill you," Ferron said, his eyes glittering with amusement. "After all, if I were, you'd feel obliged to come running."

Helena glowered at him. Poison was only one of the innumerable possibilities.

Ferron didn't give her an opportunity to choose between compliance and resistance. His resonance settled in her bones and pried her mouth open. He lifted her chin with a finger and dropped the tablet onto the back of her tongue, forcing her to swallow.

It slid like a pebble down her oesophagus.

She expected him to release her immediately, but instead he pulled off his gloves and took her face in his hands, fingertips pressing along her jaw.

The hairs on the back of her neck stood on end, and she kicked him violently in the shin.

His jaw twitched, but he didn't let go. Her legs simply stopped moving.

"I hate you," she forced out between her clenched teeth.

He paid her no mind as his eyes went out of focus.

She could tell that he was doing some kind of complex transmutation to her. Something was happening. She should have been panicking, trying to resist as Ferron's resonance sank into her biochymistry. Instead, she became completely calm.

She could feel him altering her as if she were an instrument he was tuning; tampering, adjusting, manipulating her until she felt empty.

He let go.

She jerked away, expecting the feelings to come rushing back. Vivimancy of that type was practically useless because it required a constant resonance connection to maintain.

Yet her emotions didn't come back.

They were somewhere else. Present but distant. Removed.

Ferron watched as she stood there, left intellectualising her confusion.

It was as though a piece of glass had been slotted between them. She was aware she hated him. This was a piece of information that seemed of utmost importance, and yet she couldn't feel it. Hatred was a construct rather than an emotion.

"How do you feel?" His sharp eyes were cataloguing her every detail.

Her skin prickled with awareness of his scrutiny, a shiver running down her spine, but she didn't feel the corresponding wash of fear. Just awareness. Her hands had stopped spasming.

"I feel cold," she said. "Numb. What are those tablets?"

"They were developed during the war. It's a sort of holding effect on physiological transmutations that would otherwise be temporary."

Helena blinked, wondering at how that could work. It must have been developed using chymiatria in tandem with vivimancy; developed in stages, addressing each of the various hormones and—

Ferron snapped his fingers in front of her face. "The purpose of this is to acclimate you to the house so I don't have to waste my time escorting you everywhere, not so you can have something to reverse-engineer. Out."

Helena was unfazed. It was bizarre how empty she felt. Scarcely human. As if nothing meant anything or had any consequences. The tablets took away the good feelings as much as the bad. She was carved out and empty. An abyss instead of a human.

"Is this what it's like to be you?"

He gave a dry laugh. "Like it?"

She considered. It was certainly easier to be near Ferron now that she didn't feel overwhelmed by how much she hated him, and afraid of his capacity to hurt her. She was still excruciatingly aware of how dangerous he was, but without the sickening physical reaction of that knowledge.

"It feels like I'm dead," she said.

He made an odd sound. "Well, the effect is temporary. It'll only last a few hours."

He gestured towards the door, but Helena remained where she was, eyes narrowing.

"You're being different to me now. You're less mean." She furrowed her eyebrows in confusion—a feeling she was still, apparently, capable of experiencing.

He stepped towards her and leaned so close, his breath ran along the length of her neck.

"Why would I torture you when you won't react?" he asked softly in her ear.

He straightened, raising an eyebrow. "See? Nothing. No elevated pulse, no pounding heart. I could bring in one of your little friends, and peel their skin off right here in front of you, and you wouldn't react." He shook his head. "There's no fun in that."

Helena nodded, her own ideas developing. This would be the perfect state to be in to finally kill herself without any sense of self-preservation holding her back.

"Outside," he said again, a look of irritation flashing across his face as if somehow reading her intentions. Helena retrieved her cloak with a sigh. The lights in the hall were all off, only the dim illumination of daylight trickling through the windows, but she was unafraid. She knew they were only shadows.

She descended the stairs and went to the veranda, standing in the doorway for a moment, but the courtyard was of no interest to her.

She turned to explore the house. She couldn't help but wonder at Ferron's choice to drug her. Wasn't it more convenient for her to be afraid?

He had to have some kind of fail-safe, some trick of keeping an eye on her that she hadn't realised yet.

She stopped in her tracks, a sudden thought occurring to her, one which had never entered her mind when she'd been consumed by thoughts of shadows.

She turned around and walked back towards the west wing. Ferron was on the veranda, reading a book. He glanced through the open door, but she ignored him, ascending the stairs, scanning every corner as she went towards her room.

She'd rarely looked up. The ceilings were shadowy, the darkness always pressing down on her when she looked too long. She'd focused on her most immediate surroundings, the walls within reach, the next place she'd step, the space between the shadows. She didn't look up.

There were two dead maids in her room, turning down the bed, the windows thrown open. They dropped the duvet and instantly snapped the windows shut, locking them as Helena entered.

She ignored them, seizing hold of the armchair and dragging it over to the far corner of the room as the manacles bumped against the bones inside her wrist. She stood on the chair and finally resorted to tilting it against the wall, clambering up the back so she could get a good look at the high-up corner nearest the door.

Tucked into the shadow was an eye encased in glass. It swivelled, the pupil contracting, as if it were still alive, and stared straight at her.

The iris was a beautiful, deep blue.

They're offering a lot of money for eyes, Grace had said.

The upholstery of the chair was slick. Helena slid back, and it thunked onto four legs as Ferron walked in.

"Took you long enough," he said.

"Are you always watching me?" she finally asked, still staring at the corner. The eye was so cleverly concealed that she could scarcely make it out. How many did he have in the house? It couldn't be the only one if the speed at which the necrothralls found her was anything to go by.

He scoffed. "Hardly. You're terribly boring."

She should be horrified. She would be—but it would have to happen later. In the moment, all she felt was curiosity. She looked at him. He had a book on poisonous plants in hand, index finger marking his page.

"How does that work? I didn't know you could—reanimate parts."

"It's actually easier than thralls," he said, coming to stand beside her. "Reanimation is like electricity. Just channelling the right kind of energy to where it needs to go and keeping it there. It takes barely anything to maintain something so small once it's encased in the proper preservatives."

That was less interesting than she'd hoped. She turned to watch the maids, who were finishing with the room.

They were remarkably reanimated. A person might not notice they were dead. They were agile and precise in their tasks and without any signs of decomposition. It was undeniable that Ferron had a horrific talent for necromancy.

It had to take a tremendous amount of mental resources to maintain and independently monitor them to behave like that. There was a reason necrothralls were mostly used for repetitive labour and battle hordes: Complex tasks were beyond their limited mental capacity.

How was that possible?

She looked at Ferron, scrutinising him.

"You're not a homunculus, are you?" She felt ridiculous asking the question. Artificial humans were considered as mythical as chimaeras or philosopher stones. One of the many ideas attributed to Cetus in the prescientific era.

Of the three, homunculi were a particularly enduring concept. The idea was that by placing a man's seed in a cucurbit with the proper environment of stable warmth, it could come to life on its own. After being fed distilled blood, it could grow into a human of limitless alchemical potential and utterly without flaws because it was unspoiled by the inferior environment and contributions of a female womb—the source of all humanity's flaws.

Ferron stared. "Pardon?"

"Never mind," she said quickly. Obviously, he wasn't; she'd known him as an ordinary boy, and a "flawless" human would not be a mass murderer. "I'm just trying to figure you out."

He laughed. "I suppose I should be flattered that that's what you came up with, but no, I'm not a homunculus." There was a pause. "Although Bennet did spend years trying to grow one. All he ended up with was a lot of cucurbits of putrefied sperm."

She grimaced but eyed him again.

There was undeniably something done to Ferron. With Morrough in his monstrous and distorted form, it made sense that he'd have unnatural abilities as a result of whatever transmutations he'd performed on himself, but Ferron looked mostly human.

Where did the power come from? She studied him.

Supposedly there were crystals and precious stones with properties useful for resonance. In early myths of Orion Holdfast, Sol's blessing was described as a huge celestial stone. Amulets featuring crystals had been long popular as a result. Necklaces and brooches had been sold in Paladian shops and stands to visiting pilgrims who considered the city-state as particularly sacred to the Faith, often with promises that they would strengthen or expand an alchemist's resonance or repertoire, ensuring admission to the Institute.

Many students wore heirloom jewellery, and the official figures of the Faith often wore items set with sunstones.

She studied Ferron for any jewellery or signs of an amulet. Guild families usually wore signet rings and a variety of pins and brooches to indicate their orders and exclusive clubs, but in stark contrast with his wife and father, Ferron usually wore nothing, not even a wedding band. The only piece visible was a slender, dark metal ring on his right hand.

Her eyes narrowed as she studied it.

"What kind of ring is that?" she asked.

He looked down. "This?" he asked, as if there were any other rings she could have been referring to. He turned his hand. "Just an old piece."

He slipped it off and tossed it to her. She caught it reflexively, disappointed to discover that it wasn't an unusual black metal at all, but a severely tarnished silver ring, as if he never took it off to care for it. It was hand-forged rather than transmutationally crafted; she could see the hammer marks that had beaten a scaled, almost geometric pattern onto it.

A bizarre thing for an iron alchemist to wear.

She could feel him watching and wondered what he'd do if she swallowed it.

"Don't swallow it."

She looked up.

He gave her a sidelong look. "You're lucky the national exam never tested for an ability to lie. You have a transparent face."

He held out his hand for the ring. Helena debated popping it into her mouth solely to provoke him.

Irritation flickered in his eyes. "Try it, and I'll bring it back up again. All you'll get is a sore throat."

She dropped the ring into his palm, and he slid it back onto his finger.

"Why all this sudden interest in me?" he asked.

She shrugged. "You don't make sense."

He raised an eyebrow. "Oh, is that all? And here I was hoping you were plotting to seduce me."

She stared at him blankly.

He gave a mocking smile. "Steal my heart with your wit and charms."

Helena scoffed.

"Who knows, perhaps I have a proclivity for—" He paused, studying her, trying to find something.

Helena walked away. "Maybe tomorrow."

ON HER OWN, IT WAS nice, feeling like a functioning person again. Helena had forgotten how easy it was to exist when her mind and body couldn't betray her.

She was determined not to waste the effects of the tablet and moved through the house quickly, puzzling over the drug's composition as she went.

Her parents had practised medicine. Her mother as an apothecary, and her father as a traditional surgeon trained in Khem. Helena had grown up surrounded by herbs and tinctures and medical procedures. It wasn't formal training, but it was enough that she'd been a quick study as a healer, much to the distaste of her religious superior, Falcon Matias.

She'd once tried to tell him that the principles of healing followed the same rules as any form of medicine, citing her parents' work. It was like manual versus alchemical metallurgy: The use of resonance did not alter the fundamental principles.

He'd been so incensed, he'd made Helena spend two days in a chantry offering penance for daring to compare her corrupted resonance to that of the Noble Art.

According to Matias's stringent understanding of the Faith, necromancy, in addition to its violation of the dead, was also a violation of the natural cycle and natural law, and vivimancy stemmed from the same corrupt form of resonance.

Healing was permitted within limits because it was categorised as a spiritual intercession, something selfless and divinely led.

Helena had never understood why, but the Institute, which generally treated science and the Faith as complementary to each other, strictly banned the study of vivimancy even for healing. Most healers tended to appear in remote places in the Novis Mountains and were only taught to work by intuition, their success or failure left to the will of Sol. No "science" about it.

Helena learned to hold her tongue and pretend that her unusual talent for healing was divine and not because she understood the systems and functions of the human body.

The tablet Ferron had forced down her throat was a clear demonstration of the potential if healing were allowed to be scientific. It seemed to have some kind of vasoconstriction component. A glycoside, perhaps synthesised from foxglove. She tried to remember if she'd noticed anything that might have indicated mineral acids, and maybe . . .

"Awful, aren't they?" Aurelia's voice floated down the hallways from the foyer. "They were inside at first, but it doesn't matter how much they're doused, they just reek. I told Kaine I'd set them on fire if they stayed inside another day."

"He won't just get you new ones?" It was a man's voice.

"No." Aurelia's tone was petulant. "I've asked and asked, but they're Central's, so we must keep them. Everyone else has new thralls all the time, but Kaine never wants to change them. Then he finally brings some new ones, and they're those awful things."

"For the prisoner, I suppose."

"Of course." Aurelia's voice turned sour. "The whole house has been turned upside down because of her. Just look at the banisters. They make the foyer look like some giant birdcage, but Kaine insists we keep them like this now. He bites my head off if I even leave a door open, and the thralls are never around when I need them. It's so embarrassing. I saw Lotte Durant the other day. Her husband gets her new thralls as soon as the old ones start getting ugly. Lets her pick them out and everything. They do whatever she tells them. Even awful things sometimes—it's so funny. One of the girl ones scorched Lotte's new silk, and you should have seen what Lotte had all the rest of them do to it. Chills just thinking about it. I wanted to punish one of mine once, and Kaine showed up saying they're his and if I want to torture any, I'd have to make my own . . . Well, I would if I could."

Helena followed Aurelia's voice and discovered that the foyer had been transformed since she'd last seen it. The rails had been reshaped into iron bars stretching all the way up to the ceiling, making it impossible to jump from the landings or from the stairs. Ferron was clearly taking no risks.

Down below, Aurelia and her companion walked into the next room, still discussing how unfair and unsympathetic Ferron was as a husband.

The details of the ouroboros on the foyer floor showed up better from the third floor, even with the bars. Helena stared down, studying the wings, the spines, the fangs, and the sleek body curving into a circle as it consumed itself.

THE NEXT MORNING, HELENA LAY pinned to her mattress as if a boulder had been dropped onto her chest. A lash of despair, and grief, and anger—all the feelings she'd been unable to experience the day before—had come back, redoubled, so heavy she could barely breathe.

The period of respite made it all hurt even more; the momentary relief making the magnitude of its weight even more tangible. She could feel herself crumbling.

Her spine and neck were overheated while the rest of her body was clammy and ice-cold, the sheets and nightclothes damp with a strong mineral scent. There'd definitely been mineral salts in the tablet.

She rolled onto her side and was violently sick on the floor.

She slumped down, shivering, limbs leaden. She wanted to strangle Ferron and then crawl into a hole and die. She was hot and cold and thirsty and pathetically desperate for comfort.

If even one of the necrothralls had walked in and stroked her hair, she probably would have wept.

A wave of loneliness struck so sharply, she gave a heaving sob and almost burst into tears anyway.

The door opened, and one of the necrothralls did enter, but only to clean the mess.

She lay in bed sick until evening, shivering and sweating until she passed out from exhaustion.

When Ferron arrived the next day, Helena glared daggers at him. He could have warned her about the withdrawal.

He waited for her to retrieve her cloak, but rather than lead the way, he stood and let her walk past.

The hallway was unlit. She could feel the shadows, the dark looming, but she kept her fingers tracing along the wainscotting and her focus on her next step. She knew her way. Even in the dark, she could find it now.

When she reached the courtyard, Ferron appeared on the veranda, observing her like a scientist with a test subject.

She sighed and began a tedious walk around the courtyard. When she finished the first loop, he was already gone.

CHAPTER 9

A NOTE ARRIVED ON HELENA'S LUNCH TRAY A few days later.

Transference tonight was written on the card in a brusque script.

Ferron entered the room at eight. He said nothing, he just went and stood next to her chair, waiting.

She could have tried to struggle, but she knew it was futile. She went over, nauseous with dread, the memory of the fevers and the nightmares already gripping her.

As she seated herself, he slid his gloves off and stepped into place behind her.

She kept her eyes straight ahead until he tilted her head back.

He was more careful than he'd been the first time. Apparently febrile seizures were enough to merit a degree of caution.

The pressure from his resonance developed more gradually. It felt like diving too deep underwater, and when the weight finally began to crush her, it was too late to escape. His resonance smothered her consciousness until her thoughts fragmented, flattened. Her vision turned red, and something warm ran from the corners of her eyes and over her temples.

There was a horrible humming pressure, and then Ferron was melded into her consciousness as if they'd coalesced.

For better or worse, she was brutally conscious and coherent this time.

"I hate you," she rasped out, and let him feel every ounce of her loathing. If there was a time to provoke him, it was surely now. During a procedure this dangerous, he couldn't afford to make any mistakes, but she couldn't move.

I hate you. Traitor. Coward. I hate *you.*

Ferron paid no notice. He was eerily still, as if distracted by the alien plane of existence he had forced himself into. He didn't do anything this time, didn't even look around.

After an eternal moment, he untangled himself. He didn't rip himself free but withdrew slowly. It was worse because it took so long. Like being flayed from the inside out.

The room tunnelled, all red and scraped raw, her mind like flensed skin.

She toppled forward.

A FACE SWAM BEFORE HER eyes. Red then white. She blinked and the red smeared. Her eyes refused to focus. Her hands and feet had gone numb. The right side of her face and body was rigid.

The face in front of her was strangely pale, emotive for an instant and then blank as she managed to focus her eyes on it.

It was a man.

"You're all right. You had a seizure. It's over now."

He touched her jaw, and she felt warmth under her skin where the muscles were so rigid that they might crack, coaxing them to relax.

"Can you speak? You were screaming for several minutes."

She fought to swallow, head throbbing, a wet membranous pulsing in her skull. Her mouth tasted like copper.

She tried to talk but the muscles on the right side of her jaw were still so tight, she could scarcely part her teeth. She pressed her face into the warmth of the hand, wanting to cry.

She felt so cold, as if something poisonous was spreading through her, freezing her solid. A low, gasping sound emerged from the back of her throat.

She didn't understand. She didn't remember—

"Who are you?" she slurred through her teeth.

Myriad emotions flashed across his face. He opened his mouth, then shut it firmly.

"I'm in charge of your care," he finally said very slowly, saying each word precisely. His hand slid across the side of her neck, making her tremble. His fingertips touched the dip at the base of her skull. "Go to sleep. You'll remember when you wake."

Helena wanted answers, not sleep, but the warmth seeped under her skin like water. The room blurred, the edges disappearing. The face softening as it faded away.

"Do I know you?" she asked as her eyes slid closed.

"I suppose you do."

WHEN SHE WOKE AGAIN, SHE did remember, and she was screaming. Her mind was aflame with fever. She veered in and out of lucidity. Sometimes remembering transference, other times lost and confused.

Run away.

She was supposed to run away, to go somewhere. But she needed—something.

She wouldn't go without it.

In the middle of the night, she wandered outside into the courtyard, icy rain pouring from the sky, searching. She lay on the ground, trying to make her head cool from the fire raging inside it. If her mind were cool, she'd remember what she was looking for.

"What are you doing? You're freezing yourself to death, you idiot." Ferron carried her inside.

Her skin was so cold that even the servants' dead hands burned as they stripped off her wet clothes.

When they finally left her, she tried to get back out, but the door and windows were locked fast. Eventually they bound her to the bed so she would stop clawing her fingers raw on the door, trying to escape.

She was left, trapped, forced to endure the lurid, blood-drenched nightmares as she burned away.

Every time she closed her eyes she was at the Institute, bright and golden and gleaming as it had once been, hurrying up the Tower steps for a class, her textbooks pressed tight against her chest, Luc ambling beside her. There was someone else with them, but even her dreams flinched away from the face.

Then Helena would blink or look down to take notes, and when she looked again, the world would be in ruins. All the students slumped over in their seats, cut open, their blood spattered across the room. Helena the lone survivor amid the carnage.

In one dream, Penny was laid out on a medical table, strapped down and screaming as faceless figures vivisected her before the assembly of dead students.

In another, it was Ferron at the front of the room as if called up for a demonstration. He stood there, morphing steadily from a dark-haired boy into a pale silvery nightmare, his colour turning into blood that dripped from his hands.

When the fever broke, Helena's limbs had atrophied again. She had no idea how much time had passed. She stumbled and trembled like a kitten when she walked. It was as if the synapses in her brain were misaligned.

She was grateful that Ferron did not come and harass her about going outside. She didn't want to see him again because she had a very clear memory of pressing her face against his hand without any idea of who he was.

In charge of her care? A very generous way of describing himself.

She paused, replaying the interaction. His slow enunciation as he'd answered her question. She'd been speaking in Etrasian.

As she recovered, she kept having dreams about Luc, memories. Not forgotten ones but moments from the past that made her chest ache at their recollection.

"Come on," Luc whispered after finding her studying in the library,

"you've been in here for two days. You're going to start growing mushrooms out of your ears." He tugged one of them teasingly. "You need sunshine. I need sunshine."

"I need to finish analysing this array structure," she hissed, trying to elbow him away as he began stealing her pens. "Go away."

Luc never went away no matter how she threatened him. He'd mope and sulk, making progressively more and more noise until the librarians ordered Helena to take him outside, as though the next Principate were a recalcitrant pet.

When they were older and she'd started doing lab work, he couldn't just make noise to disrupt her, so instead he'd threaten to go off and get into trouble, and hadn't she promised his father to keep him out of trouble?

They would go into the city, and he'd show her all the best places. The prettiest fire chapels and immense perihelion cathedrals, hidden water gardens, little bookstores and cafés.

All the towers and gardens and views of Paladia that she had ever loved, she had known because Luc had shown them to her. She had loved the city through his eyes. She wished she'd given in more often.

When Helena finally managed to leave her room again, her mind played tricks on her. The house seemed wrong somehow, different from what she remembered. The light was from the wrong angles, the windows in the wrong places, doors where they shouldn't be.

"The brain inflammation is much better this time," Stroud said when she came to examine Helena. Her resonance was moving beneath the surface of Helena's skull like a worm. "I don't like that you had a seizure again, but only one is an improvement. I think a monthly schedule will be about right."

Stroud was barely gone when Ferron arrived and stood at the foot of her bed, hands clasped behind his back, studying her through languid eyes.

"Did you know it's nearly solstice?" he said at last.

No. She had no idea of the date. She knew there was a month between transference sessions, but she hadn't been sure of when she'd arrived.

The winter solstice marked the end of the year in the North. It was one of the most significant events of their calendar. Southern coastal countries, where the days did not ebb and grow so dramatically, tracked the year by Lumithia's lunar tides.

"You were supposed to be gone by now." His eyes flicked towards the window. "Seems I'll be keeping you through the winter."

There was no emotion in Ferron's voice or face as he said it. It was one of the things that Helena realised was most strange about him: how little his body and tone communicated at times.

Etras had an animated culture and language, using expressions and hand gestures. It had been one of the many things that had made Helena a clear outsider. She'd learned to lace her fingers tightly together under the desk when speaking in class or else risk the room rippling with laughter as her hands started gesticulating.

Paladians valued stillness. Expert alchemists would only move their fingers for precise and controlled use of their resonance. It was culturally ingrained. Expressions were also valued most when they were subtle; insults often came in the form of sarcastic flattery that didn't translate easily for a newcomer.

Helena had learned to be still and watch for subtle tells. To understand that when the pupils got small, and the eyes skipped over her face, and the feet pointed away, that the smiling and nice-sounding words didn't mean that she was liked or her presence wanted.

Ferron was more difficult to read than most Paladians, not because his mouth said one thing and his body another, but because his body sometimes didn't say anything at all.

He stood there, body still, expression flat, hands concealed. Helena couldn't work out his mood.

"There are a few things scheduled to arrive tomorrow, to spare myself any additional inconvenience from all this. *Please*"—he placed overt emphasis on the word—"do not mistake it for a sign of affection."

A PAPER PACKAGE WAS LEFT at her door along with the breakfast tray the next morning. Inside was a pair of boots.

She pulled them out, running her fingers over the details.

They were beautiful, gleaming leather, with sturdy soles and a row of buttons to fasten them up. She could see the craftsmanship in all the details.

When Ferron had referred to something sparing himself "additional inconvenience," she had not expected shoes, although the slippers were in tatters from the wet gravel.

She slipped her feet into them, already looking forward to walking the halls without the ice-cold iron in the floors seeping through her feet.

It was then she realised there was more in the package. A pair of shearling gloves made with an odd design, very long in the wrist. Not formal length, but strangely proportioned, rather like a hawking glove.

She pulled one on curiously and realised the shape and length was to cover the manacles, preventing the metal from growing frigid and burning her skin.

When she went out for her walk, it was the first time her hands and feet didn't begin immediately aching from the cold.

Still she refused to feel any gratitude towards Ferron. It would only get colder after the solstice passed. If she was there all winter, she'd probably develop nerve damage or frostbite from going outside. It was in his best interest to keep her healthy.

She was not so foolish as to mistake calculation for kindness.

CHAPTER 10

HELENA SAT BY THE WINDOW IN HER room, trying and failing to make out any sense of resonance in her fingers. If she focused very intensely, sometimes she thought there was still a glimmer of it.

She stood and went to the window. The days were short and terribly dark, sunsets at midday.

She closed her hand into a fist, eyes shut, concentrating, and then flexed her fingers, pressing them against the window's icy iron lattice, straining until her eyes blurred.

Nothing.

She fidgeted with the manacle around her wrist until the spike between her wrist bones twinged in warning.

Despite centuries of alchemical study, there was still much unknown about resonance.

Prior to the Faith, there had been a cult of alchemy devoted to a masculine version of Lumithia.

The cult claimed that mankind itself was the first product of the alchemy, created by Sol at the beginning of time and scattered across the earth. However, the human beings created were lowly and corruptible, much like the most ignoble of metals, and Sol for all his power could not make them better. Then came Lumen, whose alchemical processes were much harsher. Lumen joined together the other four elements of fire, earth, water, and air, using the entire earth as an alembic, with the creatures of earth as the prima materia. The Great Disaster, two millennia past, which nearly shattered both earth and humanity, had been the processes of alchemisation itself.

First the fires that rained upon the earth: the calcination. The rising tides that swallowed the great cities were the dissolution. The earthquakes that shattered even the mountains were the separation. The aftermath as the survivors emerged from the destruction: the conjunction. The plagues and sickness and starvation that followed: the fermentation. The death toll, so immense that humanity nearly blinked from existence: the distillation. And finally in culmination, the result of Lumen's great experiment, mankind itself manifesting alchemical resonance was the coagulation.

This process was the method of alchemisation that Cetus's early writings referred to.

The Faith and the Institute both rejected the cult almost entirely, although they did accept Lumen as Lumithia, and acknowledge her as one of the elemental deities in the Quintessence. However, the Faith held a strict view that resonance was not a reflection of spiritual purity but merely an expression of it. All humans were flawed, alchemist or not, and therefore all humans must strive towards purification. A step which Cetus conveniently left out of his alchemical process.

Additionally, it wasn't difficult to predict where large numbers of alchemists would appear. It was correlated with regions that had large lumithium deposits. The Northern continent's largest mine was in the mountains, upriver from Paladia, and the number of children with measurable resonance born in the city was more than double the rates of neighbouring countries.

Paladia's lumithium mines had made for complicated politics. Lumithium could only be safely excavated by those without resonance; otherwise the symptoms and wasting sickness came quickly. But the work was limited to a single generation. Miners' children were almost always born with measurable resonance. Paladia was constantly bringing in new labourers to work the mines, resulting in a perpetual population explosion. That was the reason for the city-state's incredible density.

The guilds depended on lumithium for processing, but they disliked the competition that mining created. The Alchemy Institute had been at maximum capacity for decades, which functioned as a limit on the number of alchemy certificates in any given year. Without certification, people could not professionally call themselves alchemists or use their resonance without a credentialled supervisor.

The guilds wanted the certification and admissions of the Alchemy Institute to remain limited, both because it increased the value of their credentials, and because those without formal certification were cheap to hire for alchemical factory work. However, the guilds also wanted assurance that their heirs would be the ones entering the Institute, no matter whose resonance or aptitude was greater.

It had created a perpetual cycle of grievances in which everyone found the current circumstances unfair, but no one would agree to a solution. Principate Helios had tried for decades, and it had resulted in mass riots and labour strikes.

The Undying had seemingly solved the mining issue by using necrothralls, avoiding both lumithium shortages and exponential competition, which made for bitter irony: The war had so decimated the alchemist population that now they needed a breeding program to revive it.

She squinted, trying to see the tube running through her wrist more clearly, to work out what it was. It appeared to be encased in ceramic. Which might mean it was breakable, although more likely it meant the metal was corrosive.

Lumithium wasn't corrosive, though. It was categorically noble, an incorruptible metal, less perfect than gold but superior to silver, which tarnished. Perhaps a lumithium alloy?

She couldn't think of many lumithium alloys, though, as it was predominantly used in the emanations needed to increase or stabilise the resonance of other metals.

She suspected that the resonance suppression was some kind of

Eastern alchemy. The Eastern Empire was very secretive of their alchemy, and Shiseo had been the one who'd put the manacles on her.

While she was still scrutinising, the door opened. She glanced over, expecting Ferron, but found a stranger staring at her, his face alight.

He slipped in, shutting the door softly, looking around, as if he expected to be immediately stopped. When nothing happened, a slow smile spread across his face.

He came towards Helena on quick, quiet steps.

He was solidly built, with wheat-coloured hair and a square face. He was dressed in a deep-blue frock coat and cape that had geometric embroidery decorating it, and a deep-burgundy cravat at his throat.

Helena's instinctive response to the sight of him was absolute terror.

It had never occurred to her that a stranger might one day walk into the room. Her hands spasmed, sending a shock of pain up her arms.

He paused.

"You don't remember me," he said in disbelief. There was a hint of offence in the way he said it, as if she should know him instantly.

Helena studied him wildly, trying to guess at who he could be. His voice was vaguely familiar, but she couldn't place where she'd heard it.

His expression grew eager, triumphant as he got closer. His hand extended, fingers curved and grasping.

The door slammed open so abruptly the room seemed to jolt.

"Lose your way, Lancaster?" Ferron said as he entered, his eyes burning an irate silver.

A flood of relief rushed through Helena.

Lancaster straightened instantly, the hurried shiftiness falling away as he pivoted to face Ferron, giving a careless shrug. Ferron passed him without a glance.

"Just exploring this mansion of yours," he said. "Got curious when I saw her."

He nodded towards Helena just as Ferron stepped between them. Helena shrank towards Ferron without thinking, so close she could smell the scent of juniper on his clothes.

"She's not available for entertainment," Ferron said, his voice chilly.

"You'll have to find someone else to amuse yourself with. I'm sure you'll manage."

Lancaster laughed. "But you got her in the papers and everything." He pouted. "Surely you allow her visitors?"

"No, I don't," Ferron said after giving Helena a perfunctory glance. "And in the future, if you're curious about something of mine, you may ask. We should return to the party. I imagine Aurelia misses us."

He rested a gloved hand on Lancaster's shoulder and steered him firmly towards the door. Lancaster glanced back at Helena, the intensity returning to his eyes, as if there was something he was trying desperately to communicate to her.

Helena watched him vanish through the doorway, trying to place the name.

Lancaster.

A guild name. Nickel. Yes, the nickel guild. There'd been a Lancaster in her year, or perhaps the year above? Erik Lancaster.

Why would he expect Helena to recognise him?

As she stood wondering over this, the faint sound of music drifted through the closed door.

It dawned on her then why there was someone in the house. The Ferrons were hosting a solstice eve party.

She had no idea they hosted anything. The parts of the house she'd seen were so dirty, she'd be embarrassed to admit guests. However, the hibernal solstice was one of Paladia's most significant holidays, and given how closely the summer solstice was tied to the Holdfasts, it was probably the only major holiday the Undying were still allowed to celebrate.

She went to the door. Despite the danger, she was burning with curiosity. She knew there'd be Undying and liches present. Anyone invited would be an Aspirant or at least supportive of the regime.

It might be her best chance to get herself killed. She gripped the knob, then paused; it was more likely that they'd just torture her. She wavered. In that case, unless Ferron intervened, there'd be little she could do to protect herself.

Her instinctive relief at his appearance unsettled her in more ways than she wanted to think about, and she would think about it if she spent the entire evening in her room.

She opened the door.

Even though her exploration of the house while drugged by that tablet had made it possible for her to pass the hallway shadows without panicking, she still had to take several steadying breaths before she could make herself cross the threshold.

She went towards the main wing.

The music grew louder. She paused, checking to ensure all was clear.

She scarcely recognised the house. The sconces and chandeliers were all lit and gleaming, everything sparkling in a way Helena hadn't known Spirefell could.

She crept down the hall, but before she could turn the corner, she heard the rustle of fabric and a woman's hushed giggle. She shrank back, holding her breath as she melted into the shadows, trying not to feel them closing around her. Aurelia darted around the corner, pulling someone along by their wrist, drawing him into the darkness at the far end of the corridor.

It was not Ferron.

Helena couldn't see much from her vantage point, but the build and hair were unmistakably wrong.

Aurelia leaned against the wall with an eager laugh, and the man closed in on her until Helena couldn't see her anymore. There was more rustling fabric, and then the giggling gave way to breathy gasps and hushed moans and audible groaning.

Helena stared in horrified disbelief, not sure what to do until the thought occurred to her: Ferron would watch his wife having an affair when he checked Helena's memories.

She scrambled away from the shadows and fled silently up the nearest stair.

With her preferred route cut off, she resigned herself to approaching from a higher floor. She could hear the hum of voices like a hive of bees. It was a large party.

She'd peeked into an abandoned ballroom during her drugged exploration of the house. On the third floor there was a cramped, twisty little stairway that led to the balcony alcove over the ballroom where the chandelier could be pulled up for cleaning.

She crept up the stairs and then knelt, peeking over the railing, her loose hair falling around her face. She noticed with irritation that there was a mesh safety net over the opening, as if Ferron had somehow foreseen that she'd go there and might attempt suicide during his party.

She hadn't even been thinking about it, but she was annoyed at finding herself preemptively thwarted.

She peered past the net. The ballroom was filled with people and corpses. Everyone was gleaming, decked with fabric, jewels, and finery. Even at a distance, she could tell their clothing was covered in intricate decorations. Silver fine as moonlight, and platinum and gold that seemed to glow amid the gemstones and yards of richly dyed fabrics. The wealth of the guests dripped off them.

The high society of New Paladia. There were dozens of liches in attendance, the death of their bodies apparent in the waxy pallor of their skin and yellowing sclera. As Helena watched, she began to suspect that some were living people who'd powdered and oiled their skin in imitation. As if it were something to aspire to.

There were two girls, clearly sisters. The younger one had sharp features and a canny look about her, while the older sister looked as if she'd been cast from the same mould but softened somehow, her edges worn down, like a statue left to weather.

The older girl wore a pale-bluish paint on her skin and seemed disinterested in the party around her. When people tried to talk to her, she'd ignore them. Sometimes she'd drift away as if caught by an invisible current, and the younger sister would immediately break off her conversation and go after her, coddling her and snatching things off passing trays and feeding her canapés as if she were a baby bird, holding her hand to keep her close.

An odd pair.

Helena caught sight of Stroud and Mandl. Mandl had clearly used vivimancy to improve her appearance. The corpse no longer bore any visible signs of rot. The blackening veins still showed through the bloodless skin, but she'd seemingly accentuated it, as if to make her appearance seem intentional.

There were several photographers with large cameras. Flashes like small explosions kept going off as they tried to capture the room.

Helena recognised the governor, Fabian Greenfinch, who'd been named head of the Guild Assembly during the "reformation."

She searched for Ferron and found him standing towards the far side of the room. It was like spotting a panther amid a flock of exotic birds.

He was in black, as always, and it made the silvery whiteness of his hair and skin starker. Not the grey of death like the liches and their imitators; he gleamed somehow.

There was something so distinctly strange about him.

"The new year is almost here!" said a woman with a grey-painted face, spinning around. She let out a wild giggle as she held a crystal goblet overhead, the contents splashing onto her dress and the floor.

Aurelia swept back into the room. Her dress was also black, and she was ornamented all over with silver rather than her usual iron, as if trying to look more like her husband. Her bodice was detailed with scaled armour. The geometry of the pattern was embroidered in silver up her sleeves. She wore silver alchemy rings crafted to make her fingers look longer.

Yet there was a faint sense of dishevelment about her. The stain on her lips was smudged so that it softened her mouth, and her skirts had odd creases. She sauntered over to Ferron with a smug expression, reaching out to straighten his collar and draw him towards her.

Ferron stared at his wife, his expression not changing.

"Ten! Nine! Eight! Seven!" The room began chanting a countdown for the solstice and the new year it heralded.

As the numbers wound down, Ferron reached out and ran his thumb across his wife's mouth.

At zero, he leaned forward and pressed his lips against Aurelia's. A camera flashed. The room exploded with cheers, and kissing, and clinking glassware.

Ferron's lips remained pressed against Aurelia's, but as he kissed her, he raised his eyes, and his gaze locked onto Helena's face.

She stared back, forgetting to breathe, frozen in place.

Her stomach flipped, and her heart began pounding until her blood roared in her ears. She wanted to draw back, to disappear, but she was trapped by that cold silver.

He didn't look away until Aurelia broke off the kiss, turning from him. His eyes immediately dropped, and a false, indulgent smile curved across his lips as he scanned the room, clapping without enthusiasm until one of the dead servants approached with a tray of drinks. He snatched up a flute and knocked back the contents as if it were a mouthwash.

Helena sat back, pressing her hands against her chest, willing her heart to stop pounding.

"And now," a loud voice said, interrupting the hum of conversation, "some entertainment to inaugurate this new year."

The music broke off as the musicians looked around, uncertain if they were supposed to keep playing.

Helena followed the voice and spotted a man with long sideburns curving down his jaw, as ornately dressed as the rest of the guests, entering from the far side of the room and gleefully dragging a line of people behind him. A man, woman, and three children, ranging in age, all chained together.

They were clearly not guests; their clothes were too plain, and their faces stricken with terror.

The speaker turned, facing the watching crowd as he gestured at his prisoners. "These are the last surviving relatives of one of the Eternal Flame's noble families."

Shock rippled through the room. Helena scrutinised the faces of the people chained together but didn't recognise them.

"Distant relatives, I'll admit, but very careful to try to hide this illustrious connection, weren't you?" He turned to the captives, wagging a finger.

"Please—" It was the father who spoke. "My wife's grandmother was a Lapse, we had no—"

The father was backhanded across the face with a jewellery-covered hand, knocking him off his feet, and he dragged the family to the ground as he fell. He lay, the side of his face pocked with wounds.

"I told you not to talk. You're ruining my fun." The speaker's voice was almost singsong. "Now then, I know you'll all want a turn, but I say we choose an order and do them one by one. Youngest first, I think. Or . . . last?" He looked around expectantly, as if to see what the popular vote would be.

"Durant." Ferron's voice was icy. "I told you no."

Durant pivoted, buying himself a moment by running a finger along his cheeks to smooth his sideburns as he drew up and faced Ferron. The room held its breath.

"Oh, come on, it'll be fun, and they deserve it. By law, it's required that all citizens disclose any relation to the Eternal Flame. They didn't. They need to be made an example of."

"Then they'll be formally executed," Ferron said. "I don't need your ideas of entertainment staining the marble."

"Come on, it's the perfect start to the new year, putting the last of them in the ground. Everyone wants to watch them die. Are you going to be a shit host and disappoint all your guests?"

Ferron rolled his eyes. "Fine."

Faster than Durant could move, Ferron stepped forward and snapped the neck of the youngest prisoner. A boy of ten or twelve. The crack was audible all the way up to where Helena watched in horror.

The mother screamed, lunging forward and catching her son as Ferron let go of him. Then Ferron had his hands around her neck and snapped it, too.

The whole family was dead within a minute, bodies left sprawled across the floor, still linked by their chains.

It happened so fast, everyone in the ballroom was left standing in shock, unable to process that it was already over. Helena could scarcely believe it. It didn't seem real that something like that could happen without warning. Five people.

Ferron hadn't even used resonance or a weapon, just his bare hands.

He straightened, adjusting his cuffs with the flick of his wrist. "Executions are required to be clean now, Durant. His Eminence has been quite clear on that point. I hope you weren't expecting to break the law here on my property and in front of our illustrious governor and a dozen journalists."

Ferron patted Durant on the shoulder, his expression impassive, as if it were nothing that he'd done. He raised two fingers, signalling, and several servants hurried through the dazed crowd to drag the bodies away. Durant stood looking like a child whose toy had been stolen.

The silence was broken by hushed voices as the crowd woke from their stupor. The music began falteringly, and after some slight hesitation, the party resumed.

In a few minutes, it was as if the deaths had been forgotten.

Helena almost left, not wanting to witness what might happen next, but equally afraid to miss something important. She'd been cut off from everything for so long.

The party did not end until dawn, although the numbers dwindled as those who had work the next day were forced to excuse themselves. Eventually only the most affluent remained. Helena tried to notice everything she could, to identify as many faces as possible. She looked for signs of tension or familiarity. Trying to construct a sense of the social hierarchy that existed.

From overhead, unable to hear words, it was easy to notice the ways people lied to one another. She just watched their bodies move, observing the contradictions between their expressions and their subconscious gestures, slowly picking out who among the guests were the Undying. There was a kind of fearfulness they tended to evoke after even short conversations.

Ferron also watched the room, only conversing when approached. He did not mingle, and he never sought anyone out. The entire room seemingly oriented itself around him instead.

It grew readily apparent which people in attendance knew him to be the High Reeve and who were unaware. There was a reverence and delicacy in how certain people approached, while some of the liches who spoke to him seemed overtly resentful. Atreus did not appear to be there at all, assuming he was still in Crowther's body.

Ferron smiled smiles that never reached his eyes, engaging in endless small talk as if he were a benevolent ruler. To Helena, unable to make out his words and simply watching him from a distance, he looked completely bored.

Morning light was streaming through the windows when the last guests finally began to leave.

Helena turned to make her way back to her room and nearly jumped out of her skin. One of the servants was standing silently beside the steps, watching her. She was an older servant, one of Helena's most regular minders. Not a housekeeper but something senior. Helena had been so absorbed by the party, she hadn't even noticed when the necrothrall had come.

Halfway to her room, they paused at the sound of an angry voice.

"Still?" It was a man speaking.

"It's not like it's something I can just do on my own," Aurelia's sharp voice retorted.

"The only reason you exist is to give the Ferrons an heir. If they cast you aside, do you think anyone else would ever take you?"

"There's nothing else I can do! I've tried everything."

"Get him drunk. Drug him if you must, or find someone else to put a child in your womb. I will not let you bring our family to ruin."

"He can't get drunk!" Aurelia snapped. "Do you think I haven't tried? I've gone to every shop, used every drug and perfume, and nothing ever works. If I get pregnant, he'll know it's not his."

"Useless girl. I should have kept your sisters instead of you."

There was no response to that.

Helena heard rapid footsteps and barely managed to shrink into an alcove before a viper-faced man with thick sideburns came around the corner. He was markedly less lavish in his clothing than the other guests.

Helena heard the clatter of Aurelia's heels on the wood floor, and a door in the distance slammed.

She released a slow breath. She'd known the Ferrons were an arranged marriage, but she hadn't realised how dysfunctional they were.

When she reached the hallway leading to her room, she peeked warily around the corner and found Ferron standing outside the door, waiting for her. Her blood ran cold, the crack of the boy's neck still ringing in her ears. She'd known what he was, but seeing it was different.

It had happened so fast, and in front of everyone.

He hadn't even hesitated.

He glanced over. "Enjoy your spying?"

She swallowed hard and made herself walk towards him. "It was—something new."

He inclined his head, studying her beneath lidded eyes. "Are you bored?"

Of course she was bored. There was little for her to do but frantically search his decrepit house and worry over her inability to find anything. "Imprisonment is not particularly diverting."

"You do realise you're allowed to ask for things. Within reason."

She most certainly did not. "I am?"

He nodded as if it were obvious. "Ask the servants if you want something. They know what you're allowed." His eyes narrowed. "Why is Lancaster interested in you?"

Of course that was why he was there.

"I don't know." She shook her head, a curl falling across her face, suddenly tired. "I don't think I knew him. Guild students never spoke to me."

Curiosity bloomed in his eyes, real interest rather than the feigned attention he'd employed during the party. "You're full of surprises."

"Do you say that to every girl?" The words popped out thoughtlessly.

Ferron gave a short laugh, his gaze sharpening, eyes darting across her face.

"I think you should go to bed," he said.

She looked at him in confusion, feeling as if the encounter had suddenly veered off course, but she wasn't sure how.

She was tired, though. She hadn't expected to be up the whole night. She looked at him for another moment, then went into her room without looking back. When she climbed into her bed, she could still see Ferron's shadow outside her door.

Somehow, knowing it was his, the sight of it didn't frighten her even though it should have.

THE NEXT DAY WHEN HELENA spotted one of the maids, she stopped her. "Can I have a knife?"

The maid shook her head.

Helena cocked her head, eyes widening innocently. "What about scissors?"

Another no. Well, she'd expected as much.

"Books? Or the day's newspaper?"

The maid hesitated then nodded slowly.

Helena stared at her, torn between triumph and abject frustration. Had she really been allowed reading materials the whole time? And Ferron had assumed she'd know she was allowed to order the servants around?

"Then I would like them," she said, her jaw tense. "Please."

The paper arrived with her next meal.

It featured a photograph of Ferron and Aurelia's kiss on the cover. For all the world, they looked like a happy young couple, especially since the black-and-white photo made Ferron appear more human than he was in person. His hand was resting on his wife's waist, and her embellished fingers were curved up around his shoulder as if she were clinging to him.

It looked romantic and delightfully celebratory.

The article made no references to Ferron murdering a family for his guests' entertainment, as if it wasn't even notable.

The next page had a picture of the High Reeve executing several more "insurgents." Apparently in anticipation of the new year, public executions had been held on all eight days of the week leading up to the solstice.

There was also an article about the repopulation program "showing promise."

Ferron arrived that afternoon to check Helena's memories. It hadn't happened since before the latest transference, as if he'd been waiting for her brain to recover enough to handle the intrusion.

He was disinterested in what he found aside from the moment that Lancaster had entered her room. He watched the encounter over and over, forcing Helena to repeatedly relive the abject mortification of her thoughtless relief when he'd stormed in. He took no interest in Aurelia's affair, and when he encountered the conversation between Aurelia and her father, he chuckled as he broke the connection with Helena's mind.

If he had eyes and necrothralls all throughout the house, there was likely little he didn't know.

He pulled out a vial of the small white tablets. Helena cringed at the thought of the withdrawal but opened her mouth obediently.

In a matter of minutes, every feeling within her was gone; she felt placid as a frozen lake.

"That will be the last one," he said before he left.

Helena resolved to explore the remainder of the house. She'd yet to venture into the east wing, and after such a large party there was a chance that something useful to her might have been left out.

She slipped through the house, listening carefully for the sound of Aurelia's heels on the wood floor, starting on the top storey and making her way down. The east wing was not a mirror of the west wing but similar enough that Helena almost felt as though she'd already explored it.

The servant from the previous night was following her once again.

As Helena explored the main floor, the servant paused to close the door, and Helena noticed that a large door across the way had been left ajar.

That was unusual. Locked or unlocked, the doors were almost always closed.

On impulse, Helena made a lunge, darting through the door and slamming it behind her. There was a lock on the inside, and she twisted it an instant before the knob rattled.

If she weren't drugged, her heart would be racing.

She knew she had minutes at best before the key would be retrieved, so she turned away, eager to experience the freedom of exploring on her own and hopefully finding something she wasn't intended to.

There was a switch on the wall. A dusty chandelier overhead came to life, the bulbs humming, barely illuminating the room. The lights flickered unsteadily, casting shadows that scrabbled across the floor like rats.

She was standing in a large drawing room. The windows were covered, not merely curtained but boarded up, and the smell of dust and metal and something uncomfortably organic lingered in the air. There was a pungent metallic ozone scent that she could taste on her tongue, a thick sensation caused by heavy alchemy use. When resonance was channelled deeply, the air itself was left with traces of the transmutation.

It had been a long time since she'd encountered a smell like that.

She couldn't help but feel that the heaviness about the house was stronger in that room.

There was a large cage welded into the floor, gleaming when the light flickered; the bulb filaments gave soft buzzing clicks each time.

She approached cautiously. The cage was too narrow for an animal but slightly shorter than Helena. A prisoner would be forced to huddle inside it.

It was iron, but roughly wrought, made with manual smithing not alchemy, which meant the iron was probably inert, not transmutable at all. She touched it, feeling the rough telltale traits that no alchemist would leave behind.

A pattern on the floor beyond caught her attention.

There was an alchemical array carved into the wood. The largest Helena had ever seen.

Transmutational arrays were often simply illustrative, to record processes, but they were also used for transmutation when the process was too complex for simple resonance manipulation. Alchemisation always required the stabilisation of an array. Proprietary arrays were what allowed the guilds to produce alchemical products inside industrial-sized forges.

Helena had never seen anything as elaborate as what was carved into the floor of Spirefell. Within the containment circle were nine smaller arrays which met to form the nine points, rather than a celestial eight or an elemental five.

Each inner array was marked with numerous symbols, and they all channelled towards a series of concentric circles in the centre.

It was not an iron forge array. The symbols and lines were all wrong for any kind of ironwork.

The light in the room kept cutting out. She knelt, trying to see more clearly.

Alchemists often used unique symbols to protect their discoveries from anyone without proper training and devotion to the subtle arts, but alchemical energy favoured certain patterns. A scholar with a wide repertoire and sufficient experience could usually parse them. It was like reading shorthand: If the fundamentals were there, an educated alchemist could divine the meaning through reason.

She traced her fingers along the lines, trying to envision the resonance flow.

There was a click and grind behind her.

She glanced back to see Ferron's silhouette filling the doorway.

CHAPTER 11

Helena knew she was about to be dragged out of the room, but rather than stand, she turned back to the array, wanting to unravel at least a fragment of it.

Her life was an incomprehensible mystery enough.

Rather than pull her from the room, Ferron came and stood watching as she tried to make sense of the symbols on the floor. After failing at one, she tried the next, and then another. It took a minute before she realised that they'd all been meticulously defaced to obscure any trace of what they'd originally been.

Unsolvable puzzles seemed fated to be her primary occupation.

She looked up at Ferron in resignation.

He was glaring at her. "It's impressive how determined you are to be difficult."

"Were you expecting something else?" she asked with a loose shrug.

He didn't answer, but there was a hardening fury visible around his eyes.

She stared at him, calm enough to glimpse at what was beneath: a sea of seething rage. There was something about this room that he seemed particularly averse to. If she was lucky, maybe he'd snap her neck.

She looked over towards the cage. "Keep a lot of people in cages, Ferron?"

His jaw clenched, throat dipping as he swallowed.

"Only you," he said, glancing around at the intricate, iron interior of his ancestral home. "Haven't you noticed?"

Helena's lip curled and she stood. She'd hoped to needle him, but he'd already seen through it. Better to behave so he'd leave her alone.

She walked out into the main hall, expecting to find the necrothrall waiting, placid as always. Instead, the woman was all the way across the room, clouded eyes wide as if in fear. The necrothrall's lips moved, mouthing something silently as she looked at Ferron.

Kaine, Helena realised. The woman was saying Ferron's name over and over.

Ferron gave a sharp flick of his hand, and the woman fled.

Helena watched her disappear, feeling a vague sense of guilt. "Don't hurt her."

"She's dead," Ferron said coolly as he closed the door. She heard it lock from within, and then the iron in the wall screeched, warping. The door would not reopen for anyone without iron resonance. "She can't be hurt."

He said it almost glibly, but Helena suspected he was not as indifferent as he tried to appear.

Helena rounded on him. "Why keep them?"

He shrugged. "It's hard to find good staff nowadays."

Her eyes narrowed. "How long have you had them?"

His mouth split into a grin. "Interested in keeping a few of your own? I doubt necromancy would agree with you."

She lifted her chin, watching him archly. "You're avoiding the question."

His eyes flickered, but he shook his head. "I've reanimated so many, I don't keep track anymore. Now, are you done in this wing, or are you still holding out hope that there are weapons lying around for you to find?"

She refused to rise to his baiting; a trick like that didn't work when she was drugged. He was usually so direct, it was interesting to catch him being evasive.

"I assumed I was allowed in any rooms I found unlocked. Aurelia never said I shouldn't go anywhere, just to keep out of sight."

"Well," he said, fingers spanning her lower back as he pushed her firmly away from the now warped door. "I doubt Aurelia would feel much disappointment if you met an unfortunate end. It might spell my demise as well, and then she'd be a wealthy widow, free to conduct her tawdry affairs even more publicly than she already does."

Helena eyed him appraisingly as they walked. "You don't care?"

He didn't look at her. "I was commanded to marry her, so I married her. I was never commanded to care."

Helena stopped in her tracks. "You sound as enslaved as I am."

He paused and turned slowly to face her. "Are you trying to provoke me? Or sway my allegiance?" He gave a dark chuckle. "How terribly audacious of you."

"You've already thought it," she said, relishing how clearly she was able to think when she wasn't overcome with the need to scan and watch for every shadow, when she wasn't perpetually suffocating. "If you hadn't, you'd be offended right now."

He seemed momentarily impressed by her drug-induced bravado, but then glanced dismissively away. "It's a pity the way you wasted yourself."

She wasn't sure she followed the line of thought but responded anyway. "Luc was worth it."

"Why?"

The question caught her off guard. She shook her head. "Some people just are. You look at them, and you know it."

"Blind adoration, then," he said, turning to walk away.

"It wasn't blind. I chose him," she said.

He stepped back, and something about his expression sharpened. "Did you? Remind me, how many other choices were there?"

Her hand curled into a fist, the scars in her palm pressing against her fingertips. "Not many, I admit, but I knew whose fault that was."

He began circling her idly. "You think the guilds invented the divide between us and the Eternal Flame? The Holdfasts claimed all their preferences were divinely moral and treated any concessions as a violation of their consciences; where exactly did that leave the wants and needs of the rest of us? When anything we wanted became a sin or form of vice simply because it inconvenienced them for us to have it? All we did was become what they'd already convinced themselves we were. Ignoble and corrupt." He stopped, hands clasped behind his back. "You think it was an accident that we hated sponsored students like you? If we hadn't, how would they have kept you so lonely and desperately grateful to them?"

She shook her head. It wasn't true. The guilds *were* the ones who'd started it. Luc had always tried to see the best in everyone. To him, his family's responsibilities were a weight he'd had no choice but to accept for the sake of everyone else. He'd tried to solve the problems that plagued the city, but none of the solutions were ever good enough for the guilds.

Ferron was a snake, trying to present himself as though he were on Helena's side. As if her morality were dictated based on who was nicest to her.

She looked at him in disbelief, but after a moment the vague emotion faded, her attention drawn away by new questions. Staring up at him, she couldn't help but wonder again at what he was.

He would have been sixteen when he murdered Principate Apollo. Something like that should have been enough to become one of the Undying, but Ferron did not look sixteen.

Overlooking his colouring, his general appearance was that of someone in their twenties. Yet if his ascendance was so recent, he should look more aged by the years of war. He was almost pristine, as though all the death and destruction he'd caused had never touched him. The only sign that he'd even seen battle was his eyes: There was a hollow rage lurking behind them that she'd only ever seen in those who'd spent a long time at the front lines.

As if Ferron had any reason for that kind of anger.

Even locked out from her emotions, the hatred Helena felt for him was an inescapable structure in her mind.

Why do any of it? He didn't seem to find any enjoyment in what he did. There'd been many sadistic Undying who fought in the war; Helena had cared for their victims. Ferron seemed devoted to brutal efficiency and yet seemed to derive neither pleasure nor benefit from it.

As High Reeve, he was merely a weapon, not permitted the prestige of his abilities. He was the *only* anonymous figure; no one else was kept hidden behind a title.

That must chafe, particularly when the rest of the Undying were filling their days with debauchery while Ferron still lived at the beck and call of the High Necromancer. Obedient as a dog.

What did he gain from it? Surely he was too intelligent to be so void of ambition. He had to be playing a long game. And if Helena could only deduce it, that would give her leverage, a means of manipulating him.

Or perhaps that was merely Helena's vanity distorting her assessments—needing her captor to be cunning, because how pathetic was she, as his prisoner, if he was not?

She opened her mouth, wanting to prod, but reconsidered.

He smirked. "Analysing me again?"

Before she could reply, the sharp click of hurrying heels echoed down the hall. Helena moved to disappear, but Aurelia had already swept around the corner, her expression eager until she caught sight of Ferron.

Her eyes instantly narrowed, her lips pursing as she drew up, looking accusingly at them. The ringlets framing her face trembled.

"Are we all socialising together now?" she asked, her voice like sweetened arsenic.

"Just touring the house," Ferron said, gesturing idly around the large hall, which was full of dusty portraits and busts of men who'd presumably been important members of the family.

Aurelia's lips pressed together, turning white.

"I thought you had business today. You said your afternoon was quite full when I asked you to stop by the fundraiser." She tossed her head, the perfect curls bouncing like springs. "And yet"—she was speaking through clenched teeth—"here you are, 'touring the house.' I thought we weren't beholden to the Eternal Flame anymore."

Helena stood very still.

Ferron's eyes flicked upwards for a moment. "The High Necromancer was quite clear that this assignment takes precedence over everything else. Those are my orders."

Aurelia gave a sharp, shattering laugh. "But you've already killed the rest of the Eternal Flame, so why does she matter?"

"Whatever the High Necromancer wishes to be done, I fulfil," Ferron said with the impatience of someone who'd had this argument many times already. "If he wanted handmade paper clips, I'd do that with equal devotion."

He wasn't even looking at his wife anymore. His gaze passed over Aurelia's head, staring at a mirror that reflected himself and Helena.

"Ah, and that's supposed to explain why you spend so much time with her. And when you're not, it's the thralls following her." Aurelia scoffed. "As if she'll disappear otherwise." She cast a hateful glare at Helena. "There's no need to act as if she's anything precious. I asked Stroud, and she told me: She was a nobody. No one's coming for her, but you're still hovering about like you're hoarding her."

Ferron gave a dark laugh, and a glint entered his eyes as they dropped from the mirror to Aurelia. Uncertainty flashed across her face, as if she was caught off guard by the weight of his attention.

"I thought you didn't want to lay eyes on her, Aurelia." The way he said his wife's name was unnervingly intimate.

Aurelia flushed, the colour rising from her neck and staining her cheeks.

Ferron stepped towards her. "If you feel that I'm hoarding her, keeping her all to myself, perhaps I should include you more. She could have dinner with us. I could move her into our wing of the house, bring her when we visit the city. Perhaps we should have included her in that solstice photo that you bought."

Aurelia was turning paler and paler.

"The world already knows she's mine," Ferron said, his words pointed, "but if you'd like, I can remind them. I wouldn't want you to think I'm hiding anything, my dear."

Aurelia trembled as if on the verge of imploding.

"I don't care *what* you do with her, just keep her out of my sight!" She turned on her heel, storming away.

Ferron stared after her with a look of annoyance, then turned and directed his scowl at Helena.

"You irritate my wife," he said.

"Seems I do," she said blandly. "If you want to do something about it, you could kill me."

He snorted, amusement lighting his face for an instant.

"Those tablets really do a number on you."

"I feel like I can breathe again," she said, wishing she could feel this calm without being frozen. "Like I'd been drowning so long, I'd forgotten what oxygen feels like." Then she grimaced. "The withdrawal leaves something to be desired, though."

"Well, I'm not the one to blame for that." He turned to walk on. "Besides, if I didn't leave you on the floor retching, you might make the mistake of thinking I care."

Helena inclined her head. "Yes. You seem strangely concerned about me thinking such a thing."

Ferron froze for an instant, then turned back, a cruel smile thawing his face. "Your friends must have thought very little of you, if this seems like care."

Helena was so stunned by his words, she *felt* her heart try to beat faster.

"Yes, they did," she said quickly. "Of course they cared."

He tilted his head. "Who?"

She swallowed. "Luc, and Lila, and—" There was a name on the tip of her tongue, but her mind seemed to swerve around it until she focused. "And S-Soren. Lila's twin brother. He was—he was my friend, too."

How had she forgotten Soren? She barely had time to wonder. Ferron seemed to be waiting for more names.

"Ilva Holdfast, Luc's great-aunt. She advocated for me when my vivimancy was discovered. And—and Matron Pace. She managed the hospital."

Ferron still seemed to be waiting, and it upset her so much that her anger broke through for an instant.

"Having a vivimancer as part of the Eternal Flame wasn't something everyone was going to be comfortable with. Especially since I was—

foreign. It was too much for some people. I didn't have the same kinds of connections that others did. If there'd been problems, it could have—it could have undermined Luc."

He raised an eyebrow. "Well, you seem to have it all very thoroughly rationalised for yourself. Congratulations. It was clearly all worth it in the end."

He flashed an insincere smile and walked away.

Helena was tempted to fling a marble bust after him and ask exactly who cared about him. His own father wanted to disown him, his wife couldn't stand him, and he couldn't even keep living staff on to run his house.

If she hadn't been drugged, she would have, but she was rational enough to know it was pointless, and her time was limited.

The necrothralls appeared and vanished like ghosts as she resumed her exploration. When she finished with the east wing, she fetched her cloak and gloves, determined to spend her remaining time on the outbuildings.

The sky was unusually clear, a stark winter blue. The reborn sun was a pale golden disc, too feeble for much warmth but a comfort to see.

The garden shed was locked. The next building was a small iron forge. Locked too. Hardly surprising. So were the connecting storehouses. She tried the stable, feeling the eyes of the necrothralls on her as she tested the large sliding doors and found them locked. She tugged at them a few more times, wishing they'd give.

She'd always liked horses. They reminded her of the donkeys in Etras that were always nuzzling into people's pockets with their velvety noses, looking for treats.

Animals were rare on Paladia's islands. The city was so dense and multi-levelled, there was no place for them except as pets, and there'd been no pets allowed at the Institute. The highroads became exclusively for motorcars and lorries, and so horses were only brought into the city for ceremonial events and parades.

Luc had the handsomest white destrier named Cobalt, who'd loved carrots but hated the city, and he was always taken back out to the countryside as soon as the summer solstice parade passed. Luc had told her that if she ever visited their country estate, they'd go riding.

Helena tried a smaller stable door around the corner and was surprised when it opened.

She slipped inside. The sweet smell of hay filled the air, and another scent she couldn't place. She squinted into the dark. All the stalls seemed empty; no stomping or snorting greeted her.

She clicked her tongue and heard shuffling at the far end of the stable. The sound of something very large getting up.

She clicked again and heard a deep, huffed breath, but she couldn't see anything.

"Hello," she said tentatively, stepping a little farther in.

The door behind her swung wide open. Bright light spilling in.

She expected Ferron, but it was the two necrothralls from Central shoving their way in.

A snarl—almost a roar—rolled through the darkness. Every hair on Helena's body rose on end.

There was the sound of a heavy chain being dragged, another snarl, more furious than the first, and Helena saw what was in the shadows. An enormous creature, black as night, lunged towards them.

It was a wolf.

No. Bigger than a wolf. It was larger than a destrier. So immense it seemed to fill the stable.

Grace had said the High Reeve had a monster, but Helena had not taken that literally.

The creature was monstrous. Fangs longer than her fingers flashed in the light. Wind rushed across the room. The smell of blood struck her face as a foaming mouth burst from the shadows, jaws snapping.

There was the sharp sound of a chain reaching its end. Taloned claws scrabbled across the wood floor as the monster lunged again.

The necrothralls grabbed Helena by the hair and dragged her back out into the courtyard, dumping her on the gravel.

Helena scrambled to her feet, heart trying to beat with fear but unable to. She was stunned by what had happened. Her captivity was so rigidly controlled, it was startling to brush with danger.

She couldn't help but wonder if the stable door being unlocked was also Aurelia's doing.

The creature was still snarling, and then a low gusting howl emerged, a sound like moaning wind.

She caught her breath and looked back at the necrothralls, who'd both stationed themselves in front of the stable, watching her as the creature inside quieted.

She moved away. The next building was a small, geometric one. Helena tried the door, and it clicked, swinging inwards. As soon as she saw the interior's five walls, she knew what it was. A chantry.

She stepped inside, letting the door close behind her. Helena had always struggled with the rigidity of Northern religion, but now, at the end of everything, there was a bittersweetness to a place like this.

Paladia had been a culture shock for Helena in many regards. In Etras, gods didn't require being believed in any more than the mountains did. They existed. A person accommodated them respectfully, and sometimes made little offerings and prayers requesting favour, but the gods represented facets of life on Etras, not purpose itself.

Things were different in Paladia. While the ancient gods were said to have required blood for their sacrifices, Sol required life itself, lived out in service to him. Northerners were expected to devote their every moment in ritual sacrifice so that in death their souls might ascend to the heavens. Everything revolved around what Sol did or did not allow.

Luc had tried everything to earn the favour Sol had extended to his forefathers. He'd possessed the alchemical gifts, sun-blessed like all the rest, but he never received the miracles his ancestors had enjoyed, which had ensured their triumphs in battle and the riches of their rule.

Luc would have given up all his gifts for one miracle, anything to bring the war to an end, but his prayers were never answered, his devotion never acknowledged.

He'd always blamed himself for that.

If he were still alive, he'd pray even now, but the ritual words stuck in Helena's throat.

Each wall was for one of the five gods of the Quintessence. The radiant, unconquerable Sol, giver of life, was at the centre, flanked by the rest. The altar brazier that should have been burning ceaselessly with a flame from the eternal fire was cold, its amiantos wick dusty and dry.

The Ferrons had probably had a chantry built for their private worship and interments because that was something the upper classes did—although given the number of spires decorating the house, it did seem that the family had been religious at some point. Paladians loved decorating in sets of five even though their venerations and celebrations were primarily for Sol and Lumithia.

Along the walls there were dozens of stones with plaques bearing names and dates. With limited land, Paladians kept the ashes of their dead for generations rather than burying them in cemeteries as some countries did.

Despite the visible neglect, the chantry was not entirely abandoned. One plaque was brighter than the rest, carefully polished. It sat beneath the altar of Luna, the lesser moon goddess.

ENID FERRON. ALWAYS BELOVED. A WIFE AND MOTHER.

Based on the celestial dates, she'd died during the war, 1785, three years into Luc's reign. She must have been Ferron's mother.

Helena studied the inscription, finding it ironic. However "beloved" Enid Ferron had been by her husband and son, it had not been enough to be granted the immortality they enjoyed.

Then again, the guilds had always been intensely patriarchal.

Ironically, the one thing the guilds thought the Holdfasts weren't traditional enough about was women. Girls had been welcomed to study at the Institute for decades. There were female lecturers, instructors, and board members in the school. It had been with Principate Apollo's blessing that Lila Bayard had trained from childhood to become paladin primary.

The guilds, for all their talk of progress and equality, and freedom from rigid traditionalism, had very specific ideas about precisely who deserved that equality and freedom.

A low view of women was common in the North, especially among those of faith. Prior to the pressure exerted by the Principate, the Faith regarded women as categorically lesser, and even after the official distancing occurred, the belief remained pervasive.

It had been viewed as a fact of nature. Men were of Sol, active, hot and dry, full of vitality, and the source of life's seed. Women, it followed, were an inferior human form. Wet and cold, passively bound to the monthly cycle of Luna, the lesser moon. While their bodies were the necessary vessels for birth, it was their blood that was the source of all defects. Both vivimancy and necromancy were regarded as a corruption of resonance caused by a "poisonous womb."

Hence the long-standing obsession with creating homunculi even among the Faith, to erase women's defective hold on humanity.

However, not all women were doomed to cold passivity. To avoid such categorisation, a girl could devote herself to the cult of Lumithia, goddess of warfare and alchemy, who'd been born from the heart of Sol. Women associated with Lumithia were not expected to be traditional; they could be alchemists, surgeons, paladins, anything.

But there was a price. Were they to marry or bear children, they had to give it all up. Lumithia was a virgin goddess. Mothers and married women were not welcome at her altar.

When Helena was done exploring, she stayed outside despite the cold, watching the winter sun sink behind the mountains. The stars appeared in the night sky, shining briefly before the moons rose. Luna first, a deformed quarter moon in the far horizon with her soft light, ushering in a gentle twilight.

Then Lumithia rose. She was a waning crescent, but still more than double Luna's size and so bright it hurt to stare directly at her. She ascended into the sky like a white sun, the constellations vanishing behind her light until only the planets and a few stars remained visible in the black abyss of sky. Glimmers fine as diamond dust.

CHAPTER 12

HELENA OPENED THE DOOR, A PIECE OF crystal clutched in one hand, and found Lila sitting on the floor, curled up like a child trying not to be found. She was out of her armour. Her eyes were red-rimmed, her long pale hair cropped short, and when she turned to look at Helena, it brought the right side of her face into view.

A roping scar tore through the side of her face and throat.

"Lila. Lila; what's wrong? What happened?"

Lila stared at Helena without responding for a long time.

"I made a mistake," Lila finally said, her voice barely a whisper, "I've made such a mistake."

"It's—all right. I'm sure it'll be all right. Whatever you've done—I'm sure it can't be that bad."

"No." Lila shook her head. "I've been lying to everyone—"

Helena woke abruptly, lurching up as the dream was cut short.

The withdrawal from the tablet hit like a brick wall, and she collapsed again, emotions crushing her. Even breathing hurt.

She tried to ignore it, to focus on the memory.

What had Lila been about to say? And what had happened to her?

The injury had looked recent, the scarring reminiscent of what was on Helena's own chest, no vivimancy used.

Helena couldn't imagine why. Lila wasn't someone who'd ever refused healing. As Luc's paladin primary, there was a tremendous pressure on her to keep him safe, to prove that she deserved her rank.

She would often grow short-tempered when she wasn't allowed to recover as quickly as she wanted to, brushing off Helena's warnings about the balance of things, that healing took a much greater toll on the body than natural recovery did; too much and it could kill her. That there was a price that had to be paid, somehow, by someone.

Lila never cared about any of that. Protecting Luc was all that mattered to her.

MOUNTAIN SNOW BLANKETED THE ESTATE a few days later, cutting Spirefell off from the rest of the world, and life fell into a monotonous routine until the third session of transference arrived.

Once again, Helena's consciousness was crushed down to the brink of oblivion, all the way to that moment of singularity as Ferron enmeshed his mind with hers.

This time, she felt him blink, and her own eyes closed. She was being puppeteered not physically but across her now shared mental landscape. She could feel his mind orienting itself within the patterns of hers, his consciousness attempting to sway her.

With his presence, she could finally feel the strange shape of her thoughts, the unnatural ways they swerved.

Much of it was seamless, smooth channels of evasion that refused to veer from their course, but there was a fault line, as if one part had been constructed separately.

She *felt* Ferron notice it, and before he could push towards it, she reacted.

A self-destructive wave of desperation exploded from inside her, like a bomb going off in her head.

Ferron vanished. Everything vanished.

When she regained consciousness, she could barely form thoughts. The vibrations of her own breathing hurt like the tongue of a whip lashing through her mind.

She wasn't particularly feverish, but she also didn't get better after several days.

In her dreams, there were people crowded around her. Dozens of them. Each time she slept, they'd drag her underwater and drown her. Bloodless hands grasping at her. Icy water filled her lungs. Her arms and legs were twisted and wrenched at. Splintered nails clawing at her skin. Fingers hooking inside her mouth, pulling down on her jaw until it came loose. Fingernails sinking into her eyeballs, and she never died.

She just kept drowning.

She'd wake, choking and gagging as her body tried to expel the phantom water from her lungs. She couldn't make her mouth work. Her vision was upside down.

She recognised the voice of the stuttering mind specialist, saying things about the mind being complex and not fully understood, that Helena's condition was unprecedented, and there was little to be done but wait and see what would happen.

When she finally began to recover, she felt as though a part of her had died.

Ferron's encroachment was inevitable, progressing a little further with each month, the cracks in her mind widening to accommodate him. She had neither the strength nor the will to keep resisting.

The war was lost. Her suffering would not bring anyone back, not any more than Luc's had saved them.

When she was no longer bedridden, she braved the cold and went out to the stables. The side door was unlocked, and she entered quickly before the thralls could stop her.

It was empty. Death slipping from her fingers again.

The winter deepened, sinking into an oppressive cold that crawled into the recesses of the house, the iron acting like veins, carrying the midwinter frost into every hallway and inner room, leaving the house frigid no matter how much the radiators hissed.

The Ferrons fled to the city, leaving Helena behind. In their absence, the meals were improved by the lack of table scraps, and the bread was less stale, although the inclusion of protein was scarcer.

For several weeks, newspapers became her only glimpse into the world beyond. The repopulation program, which had initially been treated as an economic necessity, was gradually reframed as the new scientific frontier. New Paladia would forge its own future; no longer would alchemical repertoires be left to chance. Parentage in the program was to be selected based on the strength and variety of resonance. Tests were being done to discover the ideal combinations.

The guild families, editorials effused, had the right ideas about marrying into resonance. Without the interference and backwards notions of the superstitious, there would be a new world order. Resonance-based abilities would achieve heights never before seen.

Scientific terminology and the overuse of words like *genius* and *groundbreaking* tried to frame the program as if it were an obvious next step. There were never any explanations about where these assets would go, or who'd raise them, or that they were people, just that they would exist and be industrially and economically valuable resources.

New Paladia sounded more like a factory than a city, intended to produce exactly the variety of alchemists the guilds wanted.

The society pages, which Helena had taken only a passing interest in, gradually became the sections that she read most avidly as she noticed a pattern. Over the course of several weeks, several familiar names vanished. Paladian guild society only had so many visible members, which made their abrupt disappearances noticeable, especially when pages usually brimming with gossip were reticent to speculate about their whereabouts.

Helena couldn't help but wonder if it was a sign of a growing insurrection. Perhaps New Paladia's cracks were finally beginning to show.

She began having dreams of herself sitting across from Ilva Holdfast, with Crowther beside her. Her eyes darting back and forth between Ilva's strained expression and Crowther's appraising stare.

She could feel that they were waiting for her to say something, but she always woke before she'd answered.

As Helena was left to her own devices, Spirefell became her domain. With Aurelia gone, she spent little time in her room, accustomed to ignoring the necrothralls' constant orbit around her. She avoided the largest rooms and spaces with deep shadows, and it became an ingrained habit to open the doors and pick things up gingerly so that it didn't agitate the manacles.

Her familiarity was fortunate, because when Aurelia returned from the city, Helena knew every hidden alcove and servants' passage to hide in.

Aurelia had not come alone. She'd brought a companion, the same broad-shouldered man Helena had glimpsed during the solstice party. The first time Helena encountered them together, Aurelia was entirely naked, splayed out across a bearskin rug, giggling beneath the body of her paramour. Ferron was still in the city, and they seemed to be taking liberal advantage of his absence.

It was more than a week before Helena finally saw the pair of them fully clothed. At the rear of the house sprawled an enormous hedge maze. Helena would sometimes pass the time trying to navigate through it with her eyes. She was nearly to the centre when Aurelia exited the maze, her companion close behind.

Aurelia was speaking animatedly, the first time Helena had ever seen her happy, while her companion seemed absorbed by the house, peering up and giving Helena a clear look at his face.

Lancaster.

Helena shrank from sight instantly.

Lancaster was Aurelia's lover? The same person who'd just happened to find her room during the party.

That couldn't possibly be a coincidence.

Could he—

Helena was afraid to even allow the possibility to exist in her mind where Ferron might return and discover it, but she couldn't stop herself from wondering.

Could Lancaster be a spy? What if he was from the Resistance and that was why he'd looked for Helena? Was that what he'd been trying to communicate to her?

Was he a piece of her hidden memory? He must be. It would explain his surprise when she didn't recognise him.

She went back to the window, but he and Aurelia had moved on.

Helena began watching for Lancaster, growing increasingly convinced that he had ulterior motives in visiting. He'd often try to slip away from Aurelia, eyes and attention constantly wandering.

Helena weighed the risk of approaching him. If her suspicions were correct, it would be vital that she escape before Ferron returned. If she acted prematurely, she might doom them both.

Better unconfirmed suspicions than anything concrete for Ferron to discover.

She was grateful for the choice when Ferron returned without warning.

He seemed tired. A sense of exhaustion hung about him, but he grew sharp and focused once Helena was in his sights.

"Stroud will be here tomorrow," he said at last. "She's concerned about your physical condition."

Helena stiffened. "I've been walking. There's been nothing different."

"She'll arrive after lunch," was all he said before leaving. "Make sure you're in your room."

Stroud arrived without Mandl and made Helena strip to her underclothes and stand shivering in front of her. Stroud walked around her, fingers trailing over Helena's shoulders, resonance sinking into her skin.

"Don't they feed you?" Stroud finally asked, sucking her teeth as she paused, squeezing Helena's arm and then pushing two fingers against her stomach. "You're showing signs of malnutrition. What are you eating?"

Helena's skin hurt from the cold, the air piercing straight to her bones. "K-Kitchen scraps," she said, shivering.

"What?" Stroud drew back, looking Helena up and down. "Describe exactly what you've been eating."

Helena swallowed, trying to concentrate. "Um. It's all boiled together, some grains, vegetable peels, cores, and sometimes meat trimmings. When they're here, I think what's left on the plates is put in, too. But they haven't been, so there's not been much meat lately."

"That's what we feed the thralls. Why are you eating that?"

Helena blinked at this revelation. It made sense, but she was too cold to muster emotion at the news. "Because I'm a prisoner. I don't think they thought it necessary to feed me well."

"You are a"—she paused as though debating what to call Helena—"an asset. The Ferrons are supposed to be feeding you properly. That is not nearly enough nutrition, it's no wonder you've been so sickly." Stroud's expression grew irate. She turned and went to the door. One of the necrothrall maids was waiting outside.

"I want the High Reeve. Here. In person. Now."

Ferron entered a few minutes later wearing a scowl, barely glancing at Helena, who was still shivering in her underclothes. "You *summoned* me?"

"Is there a reason you're starving her?" Stroud said, her hard fingers digging into Helena's arm, lifting it and turning her. "Look at her. You complain about her fevers while feeding her little more than kitchen scraps."

Ferron finally looked at Helena properly. "Pardon?"

"She isn't a necrothrall," Stroud said sharply. "She needs real food. You can't expect her to handle transference if you're starving her."

Ferron said nothing, but Helena could have sworn he'd somehow paled. "I assumed she'd been eating as Aurelia and I do." His fingers flexed. "Aurelia has always managed the menu. I will make enquiries."

"I want her eating full meals. As much as she wants, with proper cuts of meat and vegetables. And porridge or broths in between until she's healthy."

Ferron gave a tight nod. "She'll be fed properly. I will ensure it."

"Thank you, High Reeve. See that she does." Stroud turned back to Helena.

Ferron didn't move, still looking at Helena until Stroud glanced over her shoulder at him. "Perhaps go see if there'll be a proper meal tonight."

He blinked, gave a short nod, and left.

"Lie down," Stroud said as soon as the door closed. "I want to examine things more closely."

Helena was so cold, she was grateful to climb onto her bed. Even Stroud's cold fingers felt warm as she appraised Helena's limbs and then worked up to her abdomen, pressing down with the heel of her hand, feeling at Helena's organs.

Helena hadn't really considered malnutrition as something happening to her. Food had often been in short supply during the war, and those who fought were prioritised; they needed consistent and high-quality food. Noncombatants made do with what was left.

After the Resistance lost the ports, there'd been shortages of almost everything.

Stroud's resonance made Helena's stomach lurch. She gagged and tried to sit up.

"None of that. Lie still."

Before she could protest, Stroud's fingers were digging in against the base of her skull, and Helena's eyes rolled back, unconsciousness swallowing her.

When Helena woke, Stroud was gone. She felt terrible with a heavy sense of disorientation throughout her body, her vision blurring, and there was a sharply painful bruise near her left hip as if she'd been stabbed with a needle. Helena rubbed at it, trying to think what kind of injections might be necessary to treat malnutrition, but her mind was too foggy for much coherence.

That night, there was a knock, and the maid brought in a tray with a full meal. Meat in a red wine sauce, two different vegetable dishes, one with cheese, and thick slices of soft fluffy bread with butter spread in a generous layer across each one, and even a stewed pear for dessert.

Helena gorged herself, despite knowing she might end up sick from it. She was starving.

She was still eating when Ferron walked in, standing over her to inspect her meal.

"It would seem that I'm obliged to personally see to everything," he said with a scowl as he stepped back. "You could have mentioned it."

"If I were to start complaining, the food would not be the first thing I'd bring up," she said, dragging her spoon down the side of the pear and eating it in tiny savouring bites, refusing to be hurried by him.

He inclined his head, expression still irritated, and went over to the nearer window. Helena deliberately took slower bites, chewing luxuriantly.

When she was finally finished eating, she thought she might pop. She wanted to curl up and sleep, but Ferron nodded pointedly at her head. She sighed and seated herself on the edge of her bed, hating how routine it had all become. Even her dreams felt routine.

She kept dreaming of Ilva and Crowther. And Lila crying. Over and over, the memories seemed to haunt her.

Ferron also seemed to find them interesting. He watched them several times before he moved on to the time she'd spent spying on Lancaster, wondering if he might be there to save her.

He drew his hand away.

As her vision returned, she found herself lying flat on her back in the bed, his face just above hers.

"Lancaster will be one of the Undying soon," he said. "In belated recognition for his *exceptional* services during the war."

There was something sneering in the way he said it, but if he meant to plunge Helena into despair, he failed. If Lancaster wasn't one of the Undying yet, that made it even more likely that he might be a spy for the Resistance. He'd have to seem trustworthy to get this close to Helena without raising suspicion.

"Are you one?" she asked. She'd assumed for so long, but she'd begun to wonder if he might be something else entirely.

He gave a slow smirk. "What do you think?"

She shook her head, uncertain.

The smirk faded, but he kept looking at her, and his eyes grew darker than she'd ever seen them.

She realised then that she was lying on a bed beneath him. Heat flooded under her skin, and her spine prickled as she sat up quickly, folding her arms.

He stepped back, straightening. "If you have any hopes involving Lancaster, you should let them die."

LILA WAS SEATED ON THE *edge of Helena's bed, eyebrows knit together, studying her. No scar on her face.*

"Are you—" Lila looked away and seemed to be choosing her words carefully. "Are you not all right, anymore? Is that why you spoke and why there's all the trainees now?"

Helena looked sharply at Lila, but Lila was unfastening a buckle and didn't meet her stare.

"No. I'm fine. The trainees are because Matias hopes to get rid of me."

"Oh, good. I mean, not good, but that makes sense," Lila said, and cleared her throat. "I can see why you're not thrilled about them, then."

Helena forced a laugh.

"You know, you can talk about—anything with me, if you want." Lila looked over at her.

"No." Helena shook her head. "I don't need to talk. There's—no point in talking, and as I have now been reminded publicly, I'm not a fighter. I don't know anything about what war really is. So—what would I even have to say?"

Lila's prosthetic leg clicked as she shifted and then said, "I think the hospital's worse than the battlefield."

Helena went very still.

"I realised it when I was in there for my leg." Lila's gaze was faraway, eyebrows furrowing. "At the front—everything's so focused, you know. The rules are simple. We win some. We lose some. You get hit sometimes. You hit back. You get days to recover if it's bad. But—" She looked down, her fingers tapping absently along the place where her prosthetic was joined to her thigh. "—in the hospital, every battle looks like losing. I can't imagine what that's like." She looked at Helena. "All you see in there is the worst of it."

Helena said nothing.

Lila sighed and unclasped more pieces of her armour, leaving them all over Helena's bed. "When Soren told me what you said—I don't agree, but I get it."

Lila nudged her with her elbow and stood. "Even if the trainees are just because of Matias meddling, I'm glad you're getting more time off. I think you've needed that—some space from it all."

HELENA SPENT DAYS REPLAYING THE conversation. She bitterly missed having people to talk to, who cared about what she said.

She'd had trainees?

She remembered Stroud mentioning there being other healers like Elain Boyle, but Helena had assumed they'd come from somewhere else.

She couldn't imagine Falcon Matias approving the addition of more healers.

Ilva Holdfast had worked very hard to make Helena's vivimancy palatable to the Resistance. She'd declared that it was the gods' will that the Eternal Flame had a vivimancer in their ranks, and that Helena had been born, found, and brought to Paladia destined to become a healer, so that if Luc was struck down in battle, vivimancy might save him; a resonance of corruption purified by Sol's will.

Helena had needed to leave the city and go into the mountains to train with an ascetic monk. Matias had been a Shrike at the time, living in a hut near the Holdfast estate, acting as a spiritual advisor for the family.

He'd disliked healers on principle and hated Helena the moment he laid eyes on her.

Nothing about her fell in line with what he regarded as appropriate for a healer. He'd been more an obstacle than a teacher, but Helena was stubborn, and familiar enough with medicine to manage her own training. She was determined to become a healer, whether he wanted it or not.

When Ilva began demanding that Helena be sent back to the city because Luc had gone to the front lines, Matias tried to resist, denying Helena's suitability until Ilva practically bribed him with the offer that Luc would make him Falcon, a religious rank high enough to join the Council, and even then he agreed only on the condition that if Helena was to be the Eternal Flame's healer, then she would heal all who served Sol's sacred cause.

The Principate, after all, was not above others, but first among equals.

What would make Matias approve trainees?

Helena couldn't help but think wistfully about Lila.

When Helena came back as a healer, it had been inadvisable for her to seem too close to Luc. A childhood friendship was all very well, but someone like Helena couldn't appear to have undue influence over a figure like the Principate.

Paladia's survival depended on the Resistance's unwavering faith in Luc. If his judgement was questioned, all Paladia would suffer the consequences. Certain sacrifices had to be made.

Lila as Luc's paladin primary had been the closest to Luc that Helena was allowed to be after that. Lila had been primary . . .

Helena blinked.

There'd been a paladin secondary. Soren. Lila's twin brother. Where was Soren?

Helena's head throbbed.

Why would she forget Soren? He—

A face briefly flickered in her memory. Helena's mind swerved violently, as if recoiling. No. She tried to focus.

Soren. Remember Soren. What happened to him?

Her skin crawled, a painful ghastly ache rose through her body, her lungs seized as if there were water inside them, and her vision turned a violent red.

When her head cleared, her temples were throbbing.

What had she been thinking about?

Something about—Lila?

CHAPTER 13

It was the misplaced gleam of silver that caught Helena's attention as she was passing along the outer edge of the main foyer. On the far side of the room, she spotted a door left ajar—a door which she knew was always kept locked.

She pretended not to notice, making her way there slowly. All too aware of the eyes everywhere.

The dining room was well lit and in the process of being arranged for a dinner party. Dishes and chests of cutlery had all been laid out for selection.

Helena only gave herself a moment to draw a steadying breath before slipping through the door.

She knew better than to lock it, knowing that would draw in every necrothrall like a lure.

Instead, she walked calmly, exploring as she always did, heading towards the large display cabinet filled with intricate silver candlesticks and epergnes, not letting herself look too closely at the silverware chests on display.

When she was hidden behind a large floral arrangement, her right hand shot out, snatching up a beautifully sharp-edged table knife with one smooth motion. Her hand dropped again, hiding the knife amid her skirts as she kept walking.

Her heart began pounding violently in her chest.

All these months, and she'd finally managed to get her hands on a weapon.

One of the maids was close behind her. Helena knew better than to attack a necrothrall unless she was sure she could sever the head completely. Better to smuggle the knife back to her room.

Then what? Her temples pulsed.

Should she kill herself? A month before, the answer would have been obvious, but the possibility of rescue tugged at her. Luc's insistent voice haunting her, begging her to live.

Perhaps she only needed to wait a little longer.

No. No more waiting.

She squeezed the knife, feeling the weight of it tucked in her palm until her wrist nearly spasmed.

If she went into her bathroom and lodged herself between the door and sink, she would have enough time to slash her wrists and throat before anyone reached her.

She'd just need a minute, enough time to lose as much blood as possible before there was any intervention, which wouldn't be too hard because Paladia, for all its scientific medical advancement, was superstitiously terrified of blood transfusion or anything else involving the bodies or fluids of others. They thought it would contaminate their resonance.

A vivimancer could force blood regeneration, but with enough blood loss, the energy and materials for new blood would take their own lethal toll. Stroud might be knowledgeable enough to avoid it, but someone like Ferron wouldn't be.

If she severed her carotid arteries, even if he did manage to keep her alive, her brain wouldn't be usable.

The room threatened to sway, but she steeled herself. She kept moving idly, pausing to pretend she was studying the silver dishes displayed. They were beautiful, intricate pieces made with elegant, organic lines, a stark contrast with the heavy ironwork.

The butler entered the room, gesturing towards the door.

Helena turned and headed out, careful to keep the knife from sight, moving only a little quicker than usual as the front door opened and Ferron walked in, followed by Atreus, whose mood had turned Crowther's thin face sour.

Ferron paused, his eerie eyes instantly alighting on Helena, his gaze flicking to the open dining room doors.

"I didn't realise you let your prisoner have free rein in the house," Atreus said, looking at her with distaste.

Ferron raised a silencing hand, his focus on Helena, a predatory intensity illuminating his eyes.

Her instincts screamed for her to flee, but she didn't want to find out how fast he could set the house on her; the cage of iron bars in that foyer could easily chase her down.

Best to avoid suspicion.

She forced herself to stop and face them, burying her hand in her skirts.

Ferron drifted towards her. His gaze seemed to be cataloguing her, as if there was a checklist he was reviewing. He idly pulled his gloves off, pocketing them.

She took an involuntary step back, the pattern of the knife hilt biting into her palm.

"I don't often see you in this part of the house." His voice was casual. "Was that your first time in the dining room?"

Her mouth went dry. "I was—looking at the flowers."

He glanced towards the dining room again, eyes narrowing. "Were you, now?"

She used his distraction to adjust her grip on the knife. "Yes. I like—flowers."

Heat rushed along her neck, a cold pit forming in her stomach.

"Let's see it, then." His eyes were on her hand where it was hidden amid her skirts.

Helena's heart dropped like a stone as she tried not to react, to appear innocent.

"What did you take?" He held out his hand.

She could try lying. He wouldn't believe her. She could try running. He'd catch her.

She could try killing him.

Yes. She'd do that.

She let her eyes widen, jaw slackening with surprise. His mouth curved into a faint smirk.

She lunged.

She had minimal training in combat alchemy, but her body moved on instinct. The blade sliced through the air as she flung herself at him.

Ferron dodged, as she'd known he would. A perfect basic defence dodge.

She let go of the knife, sending it spinning through the air.

Resonance would have made it easier, but she could do without.

She caught the hilt in her left hand, ignoring the pain that shot up her arm. With resonance she would have transmuted the length, but it took a split second longer to slam the blade into his chest, straight for his heart.

Pain exploded through her wrist. She'd thrown all her weight into the blow, but she could have been stabbing granite; the blade barely pierced him.

Ferron gave a low gasp as if she'd knocked his breath out, catching her by the shoulders as he doubled over. She used both hands and pushed harder as something inside her left wrist tore, trying to force the blade through his heart.

Ferron laughed, his lips close enough to her neck that his breath ran down her spine.

"And here I thought you'd use poison," he said, his voice mocking.

Rage ignited inside her. She flung herself backwards, taking the knife with her.

Atreus was crossing the room, hands outstretched, face contorted with fury.

She had no chance against two.

Her left wrist was on fire. She could barely manage to grip the handle, but she wouldn't let go.

She angled the blade back and drove it towards her own throat, meeting Ferron's eyes with savage triumph.

Ferron moved so fast he blurred.

The world morphed, going silver as resonance exploded outwards and the knife was ripped away from her throat, pain tearing up her arm all the way into her shoulder.

Her mind struggled to catch up.

Ferron had caught the blade in his fist, wrenching it up overhead. His other hand was wrapped around her throat, holding her back.

She couldn't move. His resonance had her frozen, every bone, muscle, and tendon under his control. She couldn't even breathe. Her heart was constricted. Atreus, a few feet away, was trapped in place as well.

This was how Ferron killed.

His hand around the knife blade was seeping blood, running over her fingers and down her arm. His eyes were a reflective silver so bright, they appeared to glow.

"Why don't you ever stop?" He let go of her, shoving her back.

Her hand, numb with pain, lost its grip.

"Why don't you die?" There was no point in being coy. She wanted to kill him; they both knew it.

Blood was still flowing down the hilt of the knife, dripping scarlet across the white marble floor, spattering across the ouroboros mosaic.

His lips curved into an insincere smile. "Prior commitments, I'm afraid."

He glanced back at his father, coming towards them again. Ferron's expression turned vicious. "Did I ask for your help?"

He turned back to Helena, examining the knife in his hand. It had sliced into his palm so deep, it was lodged in the bones. He didn't even wince as he pulled it free, holding it up so the blade caught the light, scarlet blood gleaming along the edge.

"How good of Aurelia to have these freshly sharpened and left within your reach."

With a careless flick of his wrist, he tossed it back towards the dining room. With the lazy way he threw it, it shouldn't have made it across the room, but his resonance still sang in the air.

The knife gained velocity as it flew straight through the barely open doorway and into the large vase in the centre of the table. It shattered on impact, glass flying in all directions as the water flooded across the table.

He glanced down at his hand. The wound was already gone.

Helena knew the Undying could regenerate but it was still startling to witness. It would have taken her at least half an hour to heal a wound like that; hands were delicate, intricate, full of nerves.

Her left wrist hurt so much she could hardly think straight. A stream of blood ran down from beneath the manacle into her palm, joining Ferron's on the floor.

She watched dully as Ferron curled his fingers. Then his eyes alighted on her hand. His jaw tensed. "You would injure the one place that is difficult to repair. I'll have to call in Stroud."

He turned towards one of the necrothralls.

"Take our prisoner to her room," he said in a cool voice. "Be sure she stays there until tomorrow."

Helena didn't wait to be nudged along. She turned and left.

"I've seen that girl somewhere," she heard Atreus say as she reached the hallway.

"She was the only southerner at the Institute, rather hard to miss, I'd say," Ferron said, not seeming to care.

The rush of adrenaline was ebbing from Helena. When she reached the stairs, her legs trembled, almost giving out. She listed towards the nearest wall, fingertips seeking the surface and wincing as they made contact. Her blood smeared along the wallpaper.

She should have cut her throat open the instant she'd gotten her fingers on that knife.

IT WAS MIDWINTER WHEN GOVERNOR Fabian Greenfinch was nearly assassinated.

It happened during the unveiling ceremony for Morrough's new statue. The governor was giving a speech about New Paladia's liberation, and Mandl, Warden of the re-education centre on the Outpost, whose "members" had built the statue, had been standing beside him on the dais. As the ribbon cutting commenced, a crossbow bolt emerged from one of the nearby buildings. It narrowly missed the governor, instead striking Mandl.

Mandl died.

In front of a crowd of reporters and international visitors, citizens, and foreign dignitaries, one of the Undying, whose appearance marked her as undeniably and visibly among the immortal, *died.*

The death sent shock waves across Paladia and beyond. The newspaper headlines were almost audibly hysterical. The Resistance terrorists believed to have been wiped out had reappeared in a spectacular manner, before an audience that could not be as easily cowed into silence as the national press was.

Lancaster's visits to Spirefell abruptly ceased. Aurelia floated around the house, wan and paranoid, starting at every sound as if expecting Resistance fighters to emerge from the walls and murder her next. Several times Helena heard her interrogating Ferron about what protections the estate had, and couldn't they have more necrothralls?

Ferron, when Helena caught glimpses of him, was no longer in coats and cloaks and pristine white shirts or even armour, but what appeared to be a combination of light combat gear and hunting clothes. He regularly returned to the house covered in mud, soaked from rain, and pale with rage.

Helena was thrilled.

She read the coverage obsessively, her heart soaring. The Resistance was still out there.

The papers emphasised over and over that it was a *failed* assassination attempt, trying desperately to gloss over the fact that someone ostensibly immortal had been killed by accident instead.

Helena knew the continent had to be alight with speculation of how it had been done, and how it might be replicated.

There was a way to kill the Undying.

Her steps were light for days.

Stroud visited again. Unlike Ferron and Aurelia, she seemed unfazed by the upheaval and new danger.

The butler accompanied her, carrying in a folding medical table, setting it up in the middle of the room before leaving.

"Strip and seat yourself," Stroud said, patting the table and then turning to review a file.

Helena set her jaw as she obeyed.

"I would have thought you'd have more urgent concerns than coming here," Helena said, hoping to lure out some new information.

Stroud glanced over. Her "no" was casual, like she couldn't think of anything.

"You're not worried you might be targeted?"

"I'm not one of the Undying," Stroud said with a careless shrug.

"You're not?" Helena was startled. She'd assumed anyone so close to Morrough must be.

"No. Someday, perhaps, but I have no interest at present. The High Necromancer empowers me to carry on his work so that I will not weaken or fade so long as I am faithful."

"I didn't know that was possible." Helena's fingers ached; her left hand was still in a splint, recovering from her attempt on Ferron's life.

"There are many things you don't know. The Toll of extensive vivimancy is reversible for those who know the means." Stroud glanced derisively at Helena.

Helena watched her curiously. "But why not become Undying?"

Stroud shook her head. "The Undying have their own—limitations. Bennet was one of the earliest to ascend. He used the High Necromancer's great knowledge to experiment beyond what was believed possible. He spent decades seeking to unlock the secrets of transference. Anyone who knew him could not help but appreciate his genius. I was among the few who worked most closely beside him . . ."

Visible emotion swept across Stroud's face, and she cleared her throat. "But even I could not deny that near the end, he began slipping. He poured tremendous resources, including his own vitality, into experiments, and the more he did it, the more obsessed he became. The Undying frequently develop a tendency towards sadism over time. Some more quickly than others. I don't want my work marred by such preferences. Perhaps once transference is perfected, I will request ascendance. But until then, the High Necromancer provides what I need. He knows it makes me even more loyal than the others."

The Undying had always seemed psychotic, but Helena hadn't realised it was a side effect of their immortality.

Stroud touched Helena with her hard, soap-rough hands, mur-

muring to herself that Helena was already showing signs of eating properly.

"Take these." Stroud held out several tablets.

"What are they for?"

Impatience flashed across Stroud's face. "The High Necromancer wishes to see you."

Helena recoiled. "Why?"

Stroud ignored the question. "If you don't take them yourself, I have a tube here." She pulled it out of her medical satchel. "I can paralyse you and shove it down your throat all the way to your stomach and then pour the tablets down. I've done it many times before. It will bruise the oesophagus, and you'll struggle to swallow or speak for a few days. It's your choice."

Helena shoved the tablets into her mouth, dry-swallowing them and ignoring the way they tried to stick in her throat. As they dissolved, they burned against the tissue.

Stroud turned away, rummaging through her bag again. She'd brought considerably more items with her than on previous visits. Helena squinted, trying to make out what they were, but her vision was suddenly fogging.

"Wait—"

Stroud pulled out several vials and large syringes, laying them out in a row.

"What are you—" Her face was going numb.

She blinked. Stroud had filled a syringe and stood before her, flicking it to remove air bubbles.

Helena tried to read the words on the vial. The letters blurred.

"Don't . . ." she managed to say.

"It's all to get you ready, like I said," Stroud said as she jabbed the needle into Helena's arm, injecting it.

Helena scarcely felt it.

Stroud picked up the next vial and a larger syringe.

Helena's head lolled back, and she swayed, nearly falling off the table as she tried to get away.

"Lie down." Stroud's words ballooned around her.

It only took slight pressure, and Helena collapsed sideways. The table was cold against her temple as another needle sank into her arm. The room had gone dark.

She heard the flick of Stroud's fingers against another syringe.

Then she didn't remember anything.

WHEN HER EYES OPENED, IT was dark. She was in her bed, her arms and legs aching with injection bruises. The splint on her hand was gone.

It was like someone had kicked her repeatedly in the lower abdomen and then stabbed her all over for good measure. Her whole body had a taut, swollen feeling, as though her skin was stretched too tight. She wanted to curl into a ball, but it hurt too much to lie on her arms.

In the bathroom mirror, she found her eyes wildly dilated, the sclera bloodshot. Her mouth was parched, but water hurt inside her stomach. She nearly collapsed on the floor of the bathroom.

Ferron arrived the next day, or perhaps two days later. Helena had lost track of time.

"The High Necromancer wishes to see you," he said. "What's wrong with you?"

Helena had no idea what was wrong, she just knew she'd been dosed with something horrible.

"Stroud," she muttered.

He swore and left, then came back looking incensed.

He had her carried to a motorcar idling in the courtyard. She was bundled in blankets and tucked into the back seat. The fresh air made her feel marginally better, enough that she could sit up and look out the windows, arms still throbbing from the bruises.

Rather than head to Central, the bridge they took turned towards the lower parts of the city and into a tunnel. The car drove on and on and didn't emerge. Instead, it stopped somewhere in the gloom. Dim amber lights shone weakly through a sort of vaporous mist that hung over the ground, darkness pressing in on all sides.

The air was stale and damp. She could smell the river threatening to seep in.

Ferron got out and opened the far passenger door, his expression tense. "Can you walk?"

The few figures Helena could make out were old, rotted necrothralls. She swallowed hard and nodded.

Don't look at the shadows.

"Come, then." He took her by the arm. He didn't grip hard, but it still made the bruises throb.

Helena had no choice but to follow, her breath growing short. His silver-white hair became the only thing visible in the dark. She reached out, trying to ground herself by finding a wall to touch.

A damp, slimy surface met her fingertips. She snatched her hand back.

The tunnel finally opened into a large room with green glass sconces illuminating it; dozens of other tunnels all opened into it, as if they were in the centre of a warren. The walls were covered with intricate but faded murals. It looked almost like an abandoned temple.

She'd never seen this place. She knew Paladia had been built on the ruins of a city long ago destroyed by plague. Rivertide. The site of the first Necromancy War. She'd thought all traces of it gone.

The air was thick with the smell of decay, a vile miasma that came from the far end of the room.

Her every instinct screamed to run, but Ferron pulled her forward. Her feet slipped across the floor until they reached the far end of the room.

"Your Eminence." Ferron knelt, pulling Helena to the ground with him. "I've brought the prisoner. My deepest apologies for the delay."

There was a long silence, so long Helena began to doubt there was anyone there.

"Bring her closer." The words floated, blurred and mumbled, from the darkness.

Ferron pulled Helena to her feet and dragged her up a series of steps she could barely make out before shoving her to her knees again.

Helena stared in horror at the sight before her. She barely recognised the grotesque shape.

Morrough lay reclined upon a throne of bodies. Necrothralls, contorted and twisted together, their limbs transmuted and fused into a chair, moving in synchrony, rising and falling as they breathed in tandem, squeezing and releasing around him. Morrough seemed shrunken somehow from the immense distorted being he'd been.

Now he looked as though the skin was rotting off him.

One of the faces in the throne was briefly illuminated in the dim light, and Helena thought it might be Mandl's old face, but she couldn't be sure because the throne shifted, lifting Morrough towards her.

Morrough tilted his head, his empty sockets like blackened holes. "Have I thought too well of you, High Reeve? I wanted those memories by now, and you've brought me only scraps."

There was something wrong with Morrough's tongue, the words slurred as if he were speaking around some large object in his mouth.

"I apologise. I will strive to do better."

"Yes, you are always striving, aren't you?" The words did not seem kindly meant. "I shall inspect these memories myself. Hold her fast."

There was a pause, and the only sound was the heaving of the decayed bodies. Another face appeared, half rotted, but she recognised the wide scar that ran along the side of Titus Bayard's skull.

Before she could shrink back, Ferron's knee lodged between her shoulder blades and his hands wrapped around her jaw, holding her in place.

Morrough extended his decrepit right hand, over-large with fingers jointed like spider legs. The bones were emerging through the tips of his fingers, except for two which hung limp, dangling strips of flesh.

The resonance that struck Helena was blistering in its power. It jolted through her like a live wire, charring her from the inside. Her body spasmed, jerking violently.

She screamed through her teeth as it ravaged its way through her skull.

Morrough's examination of her memories wasn't some disorienting state of reliving; it was like having her consciousness flayed. Morrough peeled her mind apart, ripping her memories from wherever he found them.

While he'd said he wanted to see the lost memories, he seemed in no hurry to find them, instead focusing his attention on her imprisonment at Spirefell. The claustrophobic monotony, the endless isolation, punctuated only by Ferron's occasional appearance to check her memories or perform transference.

Morrough seemed particularly interested in the transference sessions and the nightmares and fevers that followed. He found her fears amusing and the agony of transference a novelty, replaying it over and over, Ferron crushing and consuming her until there was no end or beginning of either of them.

It was only when she'd stopped screaming and gone limp, no longer struggling at all, that he finally turned to the glimmers of memory, but even those he distorted.

Luc on the roof, but stripped of all the details that had made the memory beautiful: the white fire, the light in his eyes, the gilding of the city at sunset, each disappeared until all that remained was the distance between them, the way Luc recoiled from her, the reproach in his voice, and the drug washing him away.

Morrough watched the memory of Lila asking about the trainees several times with a sort of idle curiosity, but it was her memory of Lila scarred and crying that he took the greatest interest in.

When he tired of it, she hoped he was done, but he was not. He went back to the last transference session.

Whatever power she'd briefly possessed to push Ferron from her mind failed her now. Morrough stretched the memory, drawing out every excruciating moment of Ferron's mental violation, the backlash from her attempted resistance, until she didn't even realise when he finally stopped.

Her mind was awash in so much pain that it blotted out everything else until she grew aware of her lungs seizing. Her eyes unable to focus. She had no sense of where she was until she felt her pulse fluttering against the pressure of Ferron's fingers, his knee pressed against her spine.

"So . . ." Morrough's voice came from somewhere in the dark. "The Eternal Flame's animancer is not dead after all."

"You believe Boyle is still alive?" Ferron sounded startled.

"Who?"

Ferron loosened his grip on Helena, and she slumped against him in the suffocating darkness. "Stroud mentioned her. Based on the Resistance records of Elain Boyle, it was presumed that she—"

"Boyle was no one. Haven't you noticed that the transference was different with the others?"

Helena's eyebrows furrowed. Others?

"I was told that the transmutations in her mind would cause difficulty," Ferron said.

"Those difficulties are because she is resisting, because she *can* resist. This—she is the animancer."

There was a pause punctuated only by the heaving rhythm of necrothralls. Ferron seemed frozen with surprise.

"You did not notice, or even suspect?" Morrough sounded so enraged, he had to pause to catch his breath. "I had wondered at your progress, the reported intensity of the brain fevers in her, unlike our test subjects. How could so much be concealed if the mere penetration of her mind is so difficult?"

Morrough spoke so slowly that dread seemed to build with his every word. Ferron remained silent.

"There is only one answer: She is the animancer. Even now, with her resonance all but gone, she is still resisting. She erased her memory of what she is in an attempt to escape me."

The pressure growing in Helena's head was so intense, her vision disappeared.

"Surely not." Ferron's voice broke through. "Stroud said it was impossible for any person to erase their own—"

"What does Stroud know of anything? She cannot imagine talent beyond her own abilities. This is the animancer. I could *feel* her attempts to resist me." The corpses oozed Morrough towards Helena again, his eye sockets looming, his resonance a sharp hum in her bones.

"I beg your forgiveness for my failure," Ferron said, his voice sounding hoarse with shock. "I never considered it."

Morrough was silent for a long time, his skeletal face bloated and rippling in her vision.

"Your father was recently here, begging for an audience as you now beg for forgiveness. He claims he tried to tell you what he remembered, but you did not listen."

Ferron's grip on Helena tightened again. "His memory is hardly reliable, Your Eminence. It seemed imprudent to indulge his fits of paranoia. I did not realise he would disturb you with his claims. However . . . I did quietly begin a reinvestigation due to his comments."

"And . . ."

"It would seem that she was apprehended near the West Port shortly after the bombing."

"To rescue the Bayard paladin?"

"A bombing seems a careless method of rescue. The paladin's escape may have been coincidental. As you recall, Bayard was already dying when I captured her."

"It *was* because of Bayard. I am sure."

Helena's mind throbbed as she tried to understand what they were saying.

A rasping, wheezing sigh rose from all the bodies at once. "All this time we thought Hevgoss . . . but it was the Eternal Flame after all. They must have caught on to him."

"Surely if they'd realised, they wouldn't have allowed their Headquarters to be so easily taken."

"Perhaps . . ." Morrough did not sound convinced. "But that is not for you to decide. I determine what was pointless. This proves that the Eternal Flame was more cunning than we thought. I suspect our captive animancer knows far more than she realises."

"Then I will continue to break her," Ferron said. He started to pull Helena up from the floor to drag her away.

"Did I give you leave to go?" Morrough's body was suddenly raised high, his massive, distorted form now looming over them both. He was barely clothed, and his skin sagged, rotting off him so that Helena could see his organs pulsing where it tore away. Bright beneath the decaying flesh. She stared dazedly.

There were too many bones, some greyish and crumbling, others white.

Morrough's wasted hand fell on Ferron's shoulder. "You are growing presumptuous, High Reeve."

Ferron instantly released Helena. She dropped to the ground at his feet. It was warm, and something wet clung to her skin, seeping through her clothes. She could smell viscera and old blood. In the darkness, cold fingers tugged at her dress as the throne morphed with another rasping, rotting heave.

"How can I trust someone who presumes and overlooks as much as you have of late?"

Ferron drew a sharp breath.

"Your failures seem to be multiplying. Overlooking your prisoner's signs of animancy. Ignoring your father's counsel. And where are the assassins that I ordered you to find?"

The copper-tanged rot in the air choked Helena as the darkness closed around her, cold dead fingers scrabbling, trying to drag her deeper. All her fears coming to life.

"I am your most loyal servant. I will not fail you. If it was the Eternal Flame, I will find them."

"It *was* the Eternal Flame. Who else could it be? Who would dare to kill the Undying? The weapon was obsidian. Crowther is ours now, but he must have shared the secrets with someone overlooked during the purge. Perhaps their identity is one of the secrets our captive animancer is trying so hard to keep from us."

As Morrough spoke, the resonance in the air became a solid, weighted mass bearing down. Helena's ribs bowed under the pressure, threatening to snap inwards and shred her lungs.

"Mandl's death was a humiliation. For one so illustrious, you should have *foreseen* it."

The pressure eased enough for Helena to manage one desperate breath, but the miasma coated her throat, choking her.

"I am investigating all potential avenues," Ferron said, breathing heavily. "The records indicate that Crowther collaborated with a metallurgist killed during the final battle. I have assigned cryptologists to re-evaluate his research for any hints of other collaborators."

"That is old information," Morrough snarled. "How many weeks have you been investigating the deaths with nothing to show for it? Have you forgotten what happens when I am disappointed?"

"I—"

The thrumming of Morrough's resonance concentrated and vanished. There was a crack, sharp and sudden like branches snapping. Ferron gave a broken gasp and dropped like a stone, falling not prone but over Helena, one arm braced just above her head.

She could just barely make out his face. His silver eyes above her seemed to glow as blood spurted from his mouth, dripping from his lips and onto the floor. His expression twisted, his body contorting and his pupils dilating until his irises were narrow bands of silver.

Then he screamed and went limp, collapsing on top of her.

The weight of his body, the jut of broken bones, pressed down on her, but she couldn't feel a heartbeat.

No hint of breathing. He was completely still.

He jerked, a garbled gasp rattling in his lungs as his chest began pulsing. He convulsed as though drowning, coughing up blood, as he pushed himself off her.

"I-I will not f-fail you, I swear." His voice shook, barely more than a whisper, and he rose unsteadily back to his feet.

"Be sure that you don't," was all Morrough said.

Ferron reached down, fingers spasming as he pulled Helena up from the ground again. Her head lolled back.

"Watch her carefully. The Eternal Flame will come for her soon, I am certain of it."

"I will die before I lose her," Ferron said, his grip tightening.

"I want them alive this time, High Reeve. These last embers who dare mock me. You will bring them to me, to kill at leisure."

"You will have them. As I have given you all the rest." Ferron's voice had grown steadier. He bowed low.

Helena craned her neck, peering through her swimming vision at the green, rotted faces visible on the throne, terrified of how many she'd recognise if she could see them clearly.

She tried to rip herself free, but she couldn't escape. Ferron squeezed harder as he dragged Helena out of the hall, pulling her through winding tunnels, not stopping even when her legs failed, feet tripping. He wouldn't let go.

Finally he stopped and, without releasing her, allowed Helena to slide to the floor. She crumpled, gasping, still struggling to breathe. The air was cleaner, damp and swampy, but there was no more scent of blood. The stones in the tunnel were dry.

Her head hurt so much that trying to think was like touching a raw wound, but she had so many questions.

"I—" Her throat closed, convulsing. "I—attacked a prison?"

"It was after the final battle," Ferron said, sounding far away. "Seems you were captured after levelling more than half the West Port Laboratory. You'd disguised yourself as a Hevgotian during the attack, and then disappeared into that tank afterwards, resulting in contradictory reports. The investigation was considered inconclusive until my father realised where he recognised you from. He was present that night."

She shook her head. "I was a healer," she said. "I wasn't—they didn't let me fight."

Ferron said nothing.

She still didn't understand. "And Lila was there?"

"Yes."

"But she was dying when you—caught her."

"The West Port Laboratory was Bennet's experimental research site."

A low sound of horror tore from Helena. She doubled over, retching. Ferron had to prop her up.

"Drink this," he said, pressing a vial of something into her hand. "It'll help."

Helena's hand shook, but she swallowed without question. There was nothing he could give her that could make things worse. Instead pain relief so bitter it was mouth-numbing washed across her tongue. She sat breathing unsteadily as it took effect.

She tried to focus but felt concussed. With brain injuries it was important to remain conscious. Conversing was supposed to help, keeping patients talking. She kept herself talking.

"Did this happen to you?" Her tongue was sluggish. She felt Ferron look at her, his pale eyes gleaming briefly in the darkness.

"More than once . . ." he said after a long silence. "My training was rigorous."

"Why?"

He shifted, muffling a low groan. "To see if I'd be better than my father, or if I'd break under interrogation, too."

She furrowed her eyebrows. "Was that—before you killed Principate Apollo?"

He released a huffing breath, as if suppressing a laugh.

"Are you wanting a confession?" he finally asked. "Shall I tell you everything I've done?"

She could only make out the vaguest shape of him, crouched in front of her. His breathing was still strained as he held her upright.

She wondered then if they'd paused there so she could recover, or so he could. The dose of laudanum she'd taken had eased the pain splintering her head.

A question rose to her lips, and she felt as if it was vital that she ask. She leaned forward, trying to see his face. "Do you want to?"

He was silent for a long moment, and then stood without answering, pulling her to her feet. Her body was half numb, and he had to nearly carry her the rest of the way to the motorcar.

In the light, she found she was covered in putrefied remains, rotted blood and gore smeared around her clothes and hands. All the necrothralls were watching as Ferron pulled her over to the car, handing her off to one of his own servants, letting it strip off her dress and wrap her in a wool lap cloth. She collapsed across the back seat.

Ferron sat up front. When the motorcar emerged from the tunnel, she was almost blinded by the vivid white of the overcast sky, but she managed to make out his profile. He was slumped forward, eyes closed. Pale as death.

IT TOOK TWO DAYS BEFORE Helena could see reliably, and three before she could sit up without feeling dizzy. She tried to read but the words swam, leaving her with nothing but her thoughts to preoccupy her.

One the third day, one of the maids brought a tray of porridge to her bed. She looked at it, meeting the cloudy blue eyes.

"Ferron, will you come here?"

The maid stared at her, and then looked away, leaving without acknowledgement, but that evening as she was picking at her dinner, the door opened and Ferron entered.

"You called?" His tone was sardonic.

"I had a question I wanted to ask you," she said, sitting forward even though it made her head throb until her eyes threatened to pop.

She drew a slow breath, gathering up all the threads of information she'd collected over the months. As if without realising it, she'd been weaving a tapestry, and only now could she make out the image forming at her fingertips.

"Mandl wasn't the first of the Undying to be killed," she said at last. "They've been dying for weeks. I didn't realise what the disappearances had in common until now. I thought it was censorship, that maybe they were dissidents, but it's the Undying. They're disappearing because they're being killed, and you're the one who's been covering it up."

Ferron said nothing, his expression carefully blank.

She swallowed hard. "You know, the Undying have never made much sense to me. Scientifically or logically. Immortality seems like a dangerous thing to just—gift to people, and Morrough's hardly the altruistic type. I know how vivimancy works. There's a price for complex regeneration, and someone always has to pay it. There's no way around that. In order to regenerate the way the Undying can, someone is paying for it."

"I thought you had a question," Ferron said.

"I'm getting there," Helena said calmly, trying to ignore the throbbing in the back of her head. "When the Undying are in dead bodies, they don't retain their old resonance; they get whatever resonance the new body has. Like your father: He's an iron alchemist, he doesn't know anything about pyromancy. So if someone like you, an animancer, lost their body, you'd lose that ability, and if you thought being a lich was a punishment, something you do to teach someone a lesson, you'd cling to your body no matter what condition it was in and be desperate to figure out transference. But even if you did, you'd still need to find an animancer. But someone like that would fight the transference."

She winced, pressing her hand against her forehead as if she could push back the pressure. "So . . . that's where the repopulation program comes in," she said unsteadily. "Morrough doesn't care about the economy or what kind of alchemists there are in New Paladia. The real reason Stroud's using selective breeding is to find a way to control what resonance children are born with. That's why they brought back your father and I saw him at Central. She's trying to produce an animancer for Morrough. If transference is perfected by the time she does, he'd have the means and the perfect vessel to use, but he's—he's running out of time."

Ferron's eyes narrowed.

She drew a deep breath. "Something's wrong about him. He's too old, and that should affect resonance, but it hasn't with him. He's got some other source for his power, something he can draw from. But he's deteriorating anyway. I saw him only a few months ago, and he wasn't like that. That throne is now keeping him alive. I kept trying to guess what could possibly hurt someone like him. It's not like anyone could get close. Then I thought, maybe the source of his power is right in front of us, but it's been disguised, so that people wouldn't realise. Perhaps it's presented as a gift, something people are desperate to earn, but really he's the one who needs it."

Pain shot through Helena's head. Her vision turned red. She gave an agonised gasp, toppling sideways. Ferron was moving towards her.

She looked up, forcing her question out.

"The Undying. You're his source of power, and the Resistance—we figured that out, didn't we? How to kill him. How to kill all of you."

CHAPTER 14

Helena was seated on a stool in a laboratory. Lying on the table before her were rows and rows of transmuted metals and compounds, some shaped into hollow spheres, others still in small vials, waiting for testing.

Directly across from her sat Shiseo, studying a sphere grasped in his fingers, as he made notations on a slip of paper.

"You have an interesting repertoire," he said in a quiet voice as he reached towards a vial in the third row. "Very unusual. Good attention to detail. I am surprised you are not a metallurgist."

"I wasn't sure what to do," Helena said, handing another sphere over for grading. "It felt like whatever I chose, someone was disappointed. Everyone—" She started to move her fingers but stopped, folding her hands. "Everyone wanted a lot for me, and I'm not sure I ever knew what I wanted." She shrugged. "Probably good that I didn't, since it didn't matter in the end."

Shiseo didn't reply. He was studying his notes; then he looked at her folded hands before his impassive eyes reached her face. "I don't think a steel weapon would suit you."

"What?"

"You are exceptional with titanium. I met the titanium guildmaster once, and even his work was not so perfect." Then he picked up a piece of her nickel work, studying it as well. "Have you ever tried nickel-titanium alloy?"

She shook her head.

"It would make a better weapon for you. Very light. You'd waste your strength with steel."

"This isn't for a weapon," Helena said quickly. "It's just—curiosity."

Shiseo made a little click with his tongue. "Well . . . if you wanted a weapon, I would advise you to use nickel and titanium. Don't limit yourself to what Paladians do."

THE ENTIRE RIGHT SIDE OF Helena's body was vaguely sore, and her tongue had the sensation of oversensitive, newly regenerated tissue across its surface as she struggled to wake.

She stared dazedly at the canopy over her, trying to remember what had happened.

Ferron—she'd been talking to Ferron. She looked around for him, but he was gone.

She'd been telling him that Morrough was dying, that killing the Undying somehow hurt him; she'd finally pieced it all together and then—

There was nothing after that.

She sat up slowly. It must have been another seizure. She shifted her shoulders, opening her mouth cautiously, expecting the muscles to catch, residual tension holding her back, but it didn't.

She looked down at herself. She'd been treated.

Seizures were not something she'd encountered much in a military hospital, but Titus Bayard had suffered from them after his brain injury.

Muscle tension wasn't something that could be treated with a mere touch of vivimancy. Resonance could loosen the knotted muscles, but the tension had to be manually massaged away to help the limbs to stretch and extend again.

Which meant that someone had, at minimum, touched the entire right side of her body. She shuddered and hoped it hadn't been one of the necrothralls—but then reconsidered when she reviewed the alternatives.

She took a long shower until all the remaining aches in her body faded, tilting her back and letting the water stream through her hair, replaying the memory.

Shiseo. So, she had known him. She didn't want to believe it, but he was right there in her mind now.

They couldn't have known each other well. He probably performed resonance tests for lots of people. Maybe he'd done it as a way of spying on the Resistance.

But why hide that memory? She was bewildered by the span of her memory loss.

Why would the Undying trust Shiseo if he'd worked and lived among the Resistance for the entire war? Countless Paladians had been killed or imprisoned for less, but instead he was entrusted as envoy.

It made no sense.

After its founding, Paladia had courted foreigners from the world over. The Holdfasts had wanted the Institute to be the alchemy capital of the world, where alchemists of every kind might come and study and share their techniques and methods. Paladia had quickly outgrown that dream, though.

Especially once the Institute neared capacity, sentiments of welcome soured.

After Principate Apollo's death, when talk of war began, Helena's father had wanted to return south. He'd said it wasn't their fight, and his responsibility was keeping her safe, but Helena had already promised Luc she'd stay, and so her father had stayed because of her.

And died because of her.

She drew a sharp breath, tracing along the scar on her throat as she stepped out of the shower.

As she towelled off, she froze at the sight of her reflection.

Since the meals had improved, she'd begun avoiding her reflection, hating the changes she saw, as the version of herself that she knew vanished.

In her memories, she'd been gaunt from stress. Her skin sallow from the absence of sunlight. Her nearly black hair always carefully restrained by two tight braids coiled at the back of her head. Bony and thin-limbed. Her eyes, large and dark, but with fire in them.

When she'd come to Spirefell, there was still something of that girl in her reflection.

Now her face was no longer gaunt, or her cheeks hollowed, and her eyes weren't sunken from exhaustion. Her colour had improved. Without a comb or ties for her hair, it hung loose, cascading past her elbows. Her bones barely jutted out.

She looked healthy.

Pretty, even.

A Helena from a different life.

But her eyes—

Her eyes were dead. There was no fire in them.

The spark she'd once regarded as the most intrinsic part of who she was had gone out.

She was a vibrant corpse, hardly different from the necrothralls haunting Spirefell.

Ferron reappeared a day later while Helena was eating dinner.

He was wearing his "hunting" clothes, but they were clean, so she assumed he was heading out rather than returning. She watched him warily as he entered. Without his coat and normal layers, he was noticeably slender.

As he came closer, her eyes narrowed. His clothes were a dark grey, made to blend into the city shadows, but there was a metallic sheen in some places. It was most obvious over his forearms, chest, and legs.

A woven body armour. That was why she hadn't been able to stab him.

He stopped in front of her, his expression unreadable, hands somewhere behind his back. "What made you realise?"

The tines of her fork caught against the plate. "Realise what? That

Morrough's dying or that he's been creating the Undying as some sort of power source?"

His mouth curved. "Let's start with the latter."

She looked towards the window. "Everyone always acted like the war was inevitable, a part of the cycle in the eternal battle of good and evil, but I just—never understood. Why did Morrough want Paladia? The Council thought Hevgoss was involved, that they were creating a pretext for their military intervention so they could absorb Paladia into their borders. But what did Morrough get out of it, then? No one ever seemed to wonder. There's just always an evil necromancer somewhere that the Eternal Flame needs to kill. No one talks about why, what could drive someone to that." She shook her head. "I just don't think immortality seems like much of a gift, especially not one that someone would give away like Morrough does, unless there was more of an advantage for him than everyone who got it. Things that seem too good to be true usually have a price you don't know about until it's too late."

Ferron said nothing.

"Am I right?" she asked.

His expression and posture were unreadable. "Does it matter?"

She looked away.

"Actually, I'll tell you . . . *if* you tell me what it was that ended up being too good to be true for you."

She swallowed hard, staring at the mountains. "Paladia."

She drew a deep breath and looked at him. "Well?"

He met her stare, eyes glittering with a strange look of satisfaction. "Yes, he's dying."

CHAPTER 15

HELENA'S CAPTIVITY SANK BACK INTO MONOTONY.

She only saw Ferron when he came to check her memory, and then a few days later to perform transference again.

She didn't struggle. Her mind still felt tenuous as spider silk. She was afraid that if she unravelled, Ferron would have free rein.

He didn't try to push into the hidden spaces but simply settled himself into the landscape of her mind and stayed there. He blinked, and her eyes fluttered. Her left hand rose; she watched it open and close. Her consciousness was split between herself and him, but with every passing second, she felt more like him than she did herself. Slowly devoured.

She tasted blood.

It was streaming from her eyes and nose.

When it was over, she stayed limp where she was, head tilted back, gazing at the ceiling until the necrothralls came and picked her up, putting her to bed.

Because of her lack of resistance, she was only mildly feverish for a few days. It seemed she was the animancer after all.

The realisation lay like a stone on her chest. She'd been sure her memory loss had been part of the Resistance strategy, intended to protect some vital secret for Luc. That it was something grandly self-sacrificing that she had cooperated with, entrusting her mind and memories to the mysterious Elain Boyle.

Had it just been her, hiding herself all this time? Was that all it was in the end? Surely there was something, but nothing she remembered, none of her glimmers of returning memory, hinted at anything of importance.

Ferron was constantly busy, spending most of his time trying to hunt down the last members of the Eternal Flame. When she did happen to see him from the courtyard windows, he looked visibly ground down. Sometimes he came back covered in blood.

She couldn't help but notice the strain around his eyes and the stiff way he often moved.

She began to suspect that Morrough was torturing him regularly.

Since Ferron couldn't stay dead, Morrough got the pleasure of killing him over and over.

He wasn't returning to the house pale with fury; he was in shock from torture. The symptoms showed more distinctly every time she caught sight of him. It was as though he were mentally eroding as the physical ramifications vanished.

She tried not to notice. When she couldn't help it, she tried not to care.

He was trying to hunt down the Resistance. Every time he was tortured was a sign he had failed. Hadn't she wanted him punished?

He'd chosen this, after all. Morrough was dying, and Ferron knew it, and yet he still chose to serve him, carrying out everything that Morrough now lacked the strength to do himself.

He deserved to suffer.

WHEN SHE FOUND SPOTS OF blood between her legs, she sat staring in total incomprehension until it dawned on her that *she* was menstruating. Even before the war, the stress of her scholarship had kept her irregular. It had stopped completely after the assassination.

She'd forgotten that it was something her body was supposed to do.

When she'd been sterilised, Matias had wanted her womb removed, but Ilva had insisted that the procedure be as non-invasive as possible. A ligature. Which meant she could still bleed.

She shoved a cloth between her legs, and when her lunch was brought, she had to ask the maid if she could have something for her monthlies. If it had happened sooner, she might have enjoyed thinking about Ferron's discomfort at being forced to deal with the reality of a female prisoner, but now Ferron's discomfort was something she tried not to think about.

Ten days after transference, when he came to her room to check her memories again, he seemed less on edge. When he encountered Helena's reluctant but fixated concern over him, he broke the connection.

She blinked and found him staring down at her.

"Worrying about me?" His face twisted into a gloating smile. "I never thought I'd see the day."

Her face burned. "Don't take it as a compliment. I hate torture."

"What a saint," he said dryly, laying a hand across his chest. "I'm sure sweet Luc would be touched by your tender heart."

"Don't use his name," she said sharply. "You were never his friend."

She sat up even though her head was still swimming.

He leaned against the bedpost. "You know, I wonder sometimes who's responsible for more Resistance deaths, Holdfast and his morals or me. What do you think?"

"It's not the same."

His fingers twitched. He almost managed to hide it by crossing his arms. "Is there really a difference between having someone die for you and killing them?"

Anger flared in her chest. "Yes. I'm sure you'd love to imagine there isn't to soothe your conscience, but you are nothing like him."

He gave a thin smile. "I don't believe I have a conscience, but tell me, do you wish I'd kept them alive?" He asked the question softly. "Leaving the Eternal Flame members alive, letting people hope, would that be kinder?"

"They should hope, because there is someone out there. Someone from the Eternal Flame that you haven't caught."

"Not for long."

The blood drained from her face. "Did you—?" Her voice wavered.

He shook his head. "Not yet. But I can guarantee it." There was anger in his smile. "Whatever happens to Morrough, the killer will be dead and gone long before he is."

"You don't know that," she said fiercely.

"I do, though," he said, his expression so hard he could have been carved from granite. "This is a story with only one ending. If your Resistance wanted something else, they should have made different choices. Perhaps some hard, realistic ones, and given up their fanatical notions that the righteousness of their cause made their victory inevitable. They were fools, every one of them." He sneered. "If the gods were real, they would have made Apollo Holdfast harder to kill."

Helena stared at him, watching the way his face twisted, the tangible fury in his eyes.

"Who do you hate so much?" Until then, she hadn't realised the depths of his anger. It was like the ocean that went on and on, and all its promises were death.

He seemed briefly startled by the question, then his emotions vanished like a box snapped shut.

"Many people," he said with an insolent shrug. He smiled, mouth curving like a scythe. "Most of whom are dead now."

LANCASTER'S VISITS TO SPIREFELL RESUMED as winter faded. Helena paid little attention. If there was any chance that he was a member of the Resistance, Ferron would have gone after him by now.

When she heard frequent footsteps, she knew that the Ferrons must be hosting some new event. The main wing of the house was bustling with activity. New necrothralls were brought in, and the decaying corpses constantly stationed outside the main doors were banished to elsewhere.

There were boxes of flowers scattered all over the foyer to be arranged. They were shipped from somewhere farther south or grown indoors; Spirefell's garden beds were still bleak.

Helena calculated the date and realised that it was the vernal equinox.

Aurelia would have a party.

There were large braziers set alight in the courtyard as the motorcars began pulling in. Helena watched from a high window as the guests emerged. It was a smaller party than the winter solstice. The solstices were Paladia's most significant celebrations, while the equinoxes tended to be heralded more in agricultural countries. Novis was said to have grand parades each spring in celebration of Tellus, the earth goddess.

When all the guests were inside, Helena waited for half an hour before she slipped towards the main wing. The thralls were too busy with the guests to supervise her, leaving only the eyes in the walls to watch.

She could hear the voices before she reached the dining room. The party sounded drunk. She crept into the next room. The voices were muffled through the walls, but when she strained, she could still make out the conversation.

"It's a ghost, I'm telling you. Holdfast has come back for vengeance. No other explanation," came a loud slurred voice. "Straight through the damned walls."

"Do shut up," drawled someone. "There's no such thing as ghosts, you fuck."

"You wouldn't say that if you'd seen Vidkun. He'd bricked himself up in his house with nothing but his thralls with him. A rat couldn't get in there. How'd anyone kill him?"

"Just because you can't transmute anything that isn't half copper doesn't mean the rest of the world can't. Everyone knows the Holdfasts collected alchemists from all over. It's probably one of those freaks. Besides, Vidkun was an idiot. He stayed home and lived alone. If you don't want to die, just fuck someone in their bed instead of your own."

There was braying laughter.

"Speaking of fucking," came a new, sly voice, "how many of you have been to Central lately? Stroud show you the works?"

There was audible chuckling.

Helena went still, not even breathing.

"Always glad to perform my civic duty. Paladia can never have too many alchemists," replied a leering voice.

"Stroud lets you have anyone you want?"

"Well," the sly voice replied, "it probably depends on your repertoire. She'll give you a list of room numbers to choose from. There's this one girl, pretty thing, scars weren't too bad. Little bitch managed to bite me, but she was *very* cooperative after I broke her jaw. I told Stroud to let it heal the old-fashioned way." There was a dramatic sigh. "I'll go back again this week, make sure she's knocked up, and if not, I guess I'll try again. I rather hope it didn't take, I think I'll like her better with her mouth wired shut."

Helena felt as though someone had stabbed her. Pain twisted through her chest and stomach.

"Is that all? I thought from the papers that there'd be more of a process. I'll have to go see what I can get."

There was more laughter then.

"You been in, Ferron? With your repertoire, they must have you working through every room."

Helena's mouth went dry.

"No," came Ferron's cold voice. "I've better things to do."

"Right, no need to commute to the city when you've got one here."

"The prisoner's not for that," Aurelia broke in. "We'll be done with her soon, anyway. And really—she's nothing to look at. All she does is skulk around like a rat. I had to threaten her just to make her wash."

"I saw the picture in the paper. Bit feral but I don't think I'd mind," the sly voice replied.

There was raucous laughter then.

"Have you noticed the flowers?" Aurelia asked loudly.

A woman's voice, much softer than the men's, replied, and then Aurelia's voice dropped, too. Helena strained her ears but only made out a few words about import taxes.

The conversation returned to the most recent murder.

"Ghastly. Couldn't even sleep after I saw him. Cut him to bits, sliced so thin, light shines through the pieces. Stuffed it all down his throat."

"After, though? Right?" A new, nervous voice. "He was already dead when—"

"No, they did it before. He had the alloy in his blood. Blocked the regeneration. Whoever we missed, they're psychotic."

"You've noticed the pattern, haven't you?"

There was a pause and uneasy muttering.

"The Celebration Purge," Ferron said when no one spoke. "The killer's imitating the executions. Vidkun was a copy of Bayard and his wife."

"So it's all revenge, then?" It was the nervous voice again. "Durant, Vidkun, and all the rest, those are the Undying who were there that night. The rest of us are safe."

There were murmurs of relief.

"Fuck . . ." came the sly voice. "That means they won't go after that frigid little bitch. I was hoping she'd be next."

"Well, I'm not risking it," boomed another voice. "Just had a safe room built. Inert iron and solid lead for the walls, ceiling, and floor. I'm the only one with the combination. Nothing can get through that."

They spent a long time describing various precautions they were taking—trick steps and hidden defences within their homes, all keyed to their repertoires.

Helena tried to listen carefully, but the conversation splintered into several smaller ones overlapping into an unintelligible murmur. Finally, there came the sound of chairs moving, and Aurelia saying something about flowers in the hothouse, and the voices dispersed into another room.

Helena slid down against the wall, unable to do anything but sit frozen with horror at the thought of everyone in Central.

There had been so many women in the Resistance. Not many in combat, but everywhere else; they'd staffed the hospital, gone to the front lines as field medics and dragged the wounded bodies to safety, operated the radios and relayed messages, washed and repaired the clothes and uniforms, and cooked the meals. All the ordinary tasks that never ended, not even when a war began. It had been women doing them.

They would have been in Headquarters, and they wouldn't have been important enough to execute.

All this time, Helena had thought her imprisonment terrible. Now she was left guilt-stricken by how little she'd had to endure.

The house was quiet, the conversation a buzz several rooms away. She slowly headed back to the west wing, still in the stupor of horror.

She was almost around the corner when she heard footsteps pounding behind her.

She turned just in time to see a blur. Something struck her.

The breath left her lungs as she was slammed to the ground, head striking the wood floor. The world swung out of view, the arched ceiling a cavernous maw hanging above her.

She lay half dazed, trying to breathe as the thing on top of her righted itself, revealing the face of Lancaster.

"Got you," he said, panting, his weight pinning her in place. He laughed quietly. "Who knew slipping off to take a piss would make me so lucky? Ferron always has your wing crawling with his thralls. I didn't know if I'd ever reach you. Had to get a party big enough to keep 'em all busy."

His thumb dragged across her chin and cheek, his breath hot and thick with wine. "Fuck. Look at you. You've filled out since last time."

Helena's head was swimming. *Do something.*

"If I was Ferron, I'd keep you chained to my bed." A hand slithered down to her breasts, squeezing hard, and then harder. "You were supposed to be mine. I'm the one who caught you while you were busy gutting Atreus. When I saw you in the ruins of the lab, everything in flames, the sky blazing, and all those thralls around you. You looked like Lumithia born from fire."

Helena tried to shift and twist free but couldn't make her arms move properly. She wanted to scream, but knew he'd smother the sound too fast. She had to wait for the right moment.

He leaned close, whispering, "I should have been made Undying then; they wouldn't have caught you without me. But you disappeared. I won't lose you this time. We're finally going to have our fun."

Helena's heart was slamming against her ribs. She bit her tongue, biding her time.

One chance.

"You've heard me scream plenty now," he said huskily. "I wonder what it sounds like when you do." He laughed softly. "I guess we'll have to stay quiet for now. Don't want Ferron interrupting us again."

He reached into a pocket, fumbling as he searched for something.

Helena rammed her hips up, knocking him off balance, slamming her elbow into his jaw. She scrambled up, pain searing through her wrists as the core of the manacles bit against muscle and bone. Agony lanced up her arms.

She ran. The door at the end of the hallway was closed. Her hands were on fire, and she could barely feel the knob, fingers fumbling, scrabbling for purchase.

Her head was wrenched back as she was dragged away by her hair. Stars flashed in her vision, and an arm crammed hard over her mouth when she tried to scream, a thick coat muffling her terror.

"Clever little bitch." He dragged her backwards a little farther and jerked her head to one side. A needle sank into her neck.

CHAPTER 16

SOMETHING WASN'T RIGHT ABOUT THIS.

Helena's thoughts were dim, struggling to arrange themselves as she was dragged across the floor and shoved into a dark corner.

"Don't make a sound," someone said.

A shadow closed in. A mouth pressed against hers, thick and wet, the tongue pushing past her teeth until she choked on it. A sharp pain consumed her lip, hot, salty blood filling her mouth.

"I've got to get the gate open. Wait here," said the shadow, but then it lingered, closing in and around her throat.

Her fingers twitched, spasming. Sharp pain like a fresh wound radiated up her arms as teeth sank into the side of her neck. Her body jerked. A hand clamped over her mouth, muffling her scream.

The shadow finally let go. "Wait here. Don't make a sound."

She sat. Pain clustered along her neck and shoulders. When she tried to brush it away, her hands grew sticky and wet.

A thought dangled just out of reach as she sat waiting in the dark. The shadow came back. She tried to speak, but the shadow clamped a hand over her mouth and dragged her outside. Both moons were nearly full, hanging like two luminous discs in the black.

Her wrist was yanked, pulling her forward. Pain shot up her arm as she stumbled.

She was dragged through the gravel as a strangled scream escaped her. A gaping mouth loomed over her.

The gate. It was open.

"Almost there. Gods, I'm going to turn you inside out."

The shadow's face was close again. She could see it in the moonlight. Red lips and teeth. Lancaster. A grin like a jackal.

She tried to speak. There was something she *needed* to say, but the words wouldn't form. They were trapped, pulsing in her throat. There was a sudden jerk. Her legs gave out as Lancaster vanished.

Then a loud crash.

She turned, eyes dazed, and found Lancaster crumpled against the wall as Ferron stood over him, kicking so violently that bones cracked each time.

Ferron picked up Lancaster by the throat until they were eye-to-eye. The moonlight illuminated them both as if they were cast in silver.

"Going somewhere, Lancaster?"

Lancaster's lungs gave a wet rattle. "I assumed you wouldn't mind if I borrowed her, seeing how you let Aurelia out to play. I'm the one who caught her. She should be mine."

"She'll never be yours."

Without lowering Lancaster from where he was holding him, Ferron shoved his hand into Lancaster's abdominal cavity as easily as if his hand were breaking water. He pulled out Lancaster's organs, winding them slowly around his fist.

Lancaster screamed, his legs thrashing.

Ferron drew out the intestines so far that they twitched, glittering in the moonlight.

"If I ever see you again, I will strangle you with these," Ferron said in a voice of deadly calm. "Pity you're not immortal yet. I could do it so slowly then."

He dropped the intestines so that they hung down Lancaster's front like watch chains, then pulled out a handkerchief and wiped his hands as Lancaster stumbled through the mouth of the gate, whimpering and trying to stuff his organs back into his stomach.

When Lancaster had disappeared, Ferron turned towards Helena. His face was rigid with fury.

"You idiot—why did you come out tonight?"

Helena just looked at him.

She thought she should say something. What she'd tried to tell Lancaster.

"Ferron always comes for me," she whispered.

He stopped short. His jaw locked, fists clenching, saying nothing for a moment. Then his throat dipped, and he sighed.

"What did he do to you?" he asked in a low voice, kneeling next to her.

Helena looked down at herself. Her dress was ripped open, her stockings shredded. All her things were ripped. There was blood and white gravel all over.

Ferron reached out towards her, just barely touching her shoulder, and she felt a little flush of warmth. She huddled towards him, but he drew away.

"Drugged," he said. "Did he make you swallow something?"

She shook her head.

"An injection, then. Let's go to your room." His eyes went briefly out of focus, and then he helped her up to her feet. Helena gasped as pain shot up her arms.

Ferron said nothing, but he draped his coat over her shoulders, covering up her ruined dress.

The necrothrall woman was in Helena's room with a bowl of water and a cloth in hand.

"Clean her up," he said, going to the window, standing still as a statue while the necrothrall led Helena to sit on the edge of the bed and began dabbing at the gravel and blood.

The necrothrall's fingers were cold, and she smelled vaguely of raw meat left out too long. Helena flinched away, but every time she shrank back, the woman followed until Helena was trapped against the bedpost. She started shaking.

"Stop," Ferron finally said, his voice tense.

Helena froze and so did the necrothrall, stepping back as Ferron came over.

Helena stared at his shoes. They were so perfectly polished, they shone.

"What's wrong?" he asked.

Lots of things were wrong. More things than Helena's brain could presently remember.

"I don't like when people are dead," she said in a small voice.

He sighed and sat down beside her, taking the cloth away from the necrothrall.

"I'm not going to hurt you," he said in a tense voice. He took her by the shoulders, turning her towards him.

She knew he wouldn't. He only hurt her on certain days, and this wasn't one of them, so she sat very still.

Moving slowly, he started along her shoulder, removing the bits of white gravel and washing the wounds before his fingers brushed across her skin. She felt a tingle of warmth as the skin knit together, regenerating into delicate new tissue. He worked across her shoulders and up her neck, to her throbbing lip.

His lips were pressed into a flat line, his expression clinical and intent.

When he finished, his attention turned to her hands. Her wrists were aching, the skin hot and taut.

He turned one hand over. Her palm was scraped raw, pocked with bits of gravel.

It took longer to fix her hands and wrists, and even when the cuts were gone, they still hurt. He kept going over them, making her move all her fingers.

He finally sat back and looked away. "Did he do—anything else to you?"

She shook her head.

He exhaled slowly. He was staring across the room. "I'm required to spend the next several days in the city. I think it's best that you stay in your room until I return."

Helena said nothing. Eventually he stood and left. She heard the door bolt for the first time.

She sat staring blankly at the wall, not sure what she felt. Her mind only seemed to work in fragments.

She was dirty.

She went and stood under the water, letting it stream hot down her face and over her shoulders.

She still felt teeth sinking into her skin, the way the flesh tore under the pressure. The places were still oversensitive. She wanted to stick her fingers inside them and tear it all out.

She found a cloth. She scrubbed and scrubbed until all her skin was so raw the water hurt.

There was a white flannel nightgown draped over the chair, and a cup of tisane by the bed. She recognised the scent of chamomile, but when she sipped it, it was bitter enough to make her tongue curdle.

Laudanum.

She drank all of it before sinking into a deep, empty sleep.

THE MENTAL FOG WAS GONE the next morning.

Her lungs contracted, chest heaving, panicking over what had almost happened, and her lack of comprehension at the time.

If Lancaster had gotten her out of Spirefell, what would he have done to her? What would she have just lain there and let him do?

She huddled in a tight ball and didn't get up when she heard the door unlock and the maid come in, setting the tray beside Helena's bed.

Breakfast and a pot of tisane with the recognisable scent of chamomile. The maid poured a cup and then pulled out a small vial with a few drops of reddish liquid inside.

She shook her head but regretted the choice once the maid was gone and she was left with her thoughts.

She kept thinking about the girls in the repopulation program, lured in by the promise of food and pardon.

If Helena hadn't been sterilised and missing memories, she'd be there, too.

Compared with what the rest of the survivors suffered, Ferron was almost kind. It was such a horrible thought.

How was it that the High Reeve was somehow one of the least monstrous of the Undying? No. That wasn't true. She'd witnessed his killing, watched him calmly unspool Lancaster's organs with his bare hands.

There was plenty of monster in Ferron, lurking beneath the surface.

Her head throbbed, and she closed her eyes.

The door was rebolted each time the servants left, and so Helena made no effort to leave her bed. She lay curled beneath her blankets, smothered in her despair, until the quiet was split by the sudden scream of metal and the door burst open.

Helena shot up to see Aurelia stride in, a newspaper clutched in one hand, the iron short staff in the other. There were several necrothralls out in the hallway. They all moved to follow Aurelia.

Aurelia stopped short, turning back, then she gripped the staff, twisting it against one of the iron bars running through the floor. The door slammed shut, nearly severing one of the maids' arms. There was a grating sound of metal as the frame around the door warped, sealing the room.

Aurelia turned back to Helena.

"Come here." Her voice was bright with anger.

Helena slipped out of bed and walked over without a word, heart pounding.

Aurelia was pale. Brittle as a stalk of grass in midwinter. She was impeccably dressed and groomed as always, but there was a sense of unravelling about her. Her earrings, intricate little chandeliers of tiny pearls, trembled.

"Did you know I was the third daughter my mother had?"

Helena didn't know anything about Aurelia.

"My family's been pure iron for nearly a century, had a guild member in every generation, but we never got very high. It's hard, competing with a family like the Ferrons. My father always said that in Paladia, you have to be satisfied with scrap metal until you can make something of it. We were going to make something of it."

Aurelia drew a quick breath. "People thought there was something wrong with Kaine when he was born. Thought maybe he was a Lapse, or he didn't have iron resonance. No one was sure, just knew the family was secretive about him. My father saw an opportunity. My mother and father were cousins. He thought they could easily have a girl with pure iron resonance, and the Ferrons would be desperate to marry Kaine to her. To stay in control of the guild."

Aurelia gave a panting breath, her chest heaving.

"Mother said the first two were tiny. *Little bits of things.*" Her blue eyes shone. "My father paid a vivimancer to come in early to see if they were girls, but when they didn't show any signs of iron resonance in the womb, he didn't let her keep them. If they'd come to term, he said, another iron family might beat us to the marriage contract. I was the third girl. My mother always said the first two babies were hers, and I was—Kaine Ferron's. She burned them in the fireplace and buried the ashes in the garden. Spent all her time out there with them."

Helena studied Aurelia in stunned sympathy, but that only seemed to enrage her.

"I know you snoop. Have you seen *this* story?" Aurelia lifted the newspaper up so that Helena could see the front page.

It was a gruesome photo, even in black and white. Kneeling down, his face plain to see, Ferron was calmly disembowelling Lancaster in the lobby of the Central Hospital.

She could only stare a moment before Aurelia twitched her hand, folding the newspaper away, knuckles whitening as she gripped the short staff. The house groaned, trembling.

"I have to admit," Aurelia said in a voice of unnatural calm, "when I first heard that Kaine had killed Erik, I was so happy. I thought, *He's finally noticed.*"

The chandelier earrings were trembling more visibly.

"I tried to be a perfect wife. I knew it wasn't a love match, but I thought he'd realise I was *made* to be his wife. How many men can say that? I did everything, all the things, just the way I was supposed to."

She tossed her hand, still clutching the paper, her alchemy rings gleaming dully.

"People don't know, but he didn't live here. On our wedding day, he left me in the foyer. Disappeared for a whole month before I heard he was back in the city. I thought it was a test. I decorated and threw parties, but he never came to them. Then I thought I'd get his attention if I made him jealous, but he didn't care. I figured he preferred men or preferred nothing, and I couldn't do anything about that but accept it."

The bitterness in Aurelia's expression grew ugly.

"I accepted it." Her voice shook with resentment. "Until you came along, and suddenly he moved in, and he turned every inch of this estate upside down for you; took you out for walks and gave *you* a tour of the house."

Helena opened her mouth, trying to explain that Ferron was ordered to do all those things.

"Shut up! I don't want to hear from you!" The newspaper crumpled in her fist. "Then Erik Lancaster started paying attention to me." Aurelia looked on the verge of tears. "He was so sympathetic, kept me company at all the events that Kaine never showed for. He wanted to know all about me. He noticed all the things I did to impress Kaine. He wanted to see the house, how I'd decorated it. He was the one who said I should throw all the parties again so everyone could see how wonderful I was, even if Kaine didn't. The winter solstice was all his idea. That big guest list. And all the dinner parties. Even the equinox party."

Aurelia's voice trailed off and she stared towards the windows for several moments.

"When I heard Kaine had killed Erik, I thought, *He's finally noticed. He was just busy before. He does care.* But then—" A tremor ran through Aurelia. "—then it crossed my mind that Erik approached me the week after that vile article was written about you being here. He was always wanting to come here, even in the winter when it's ghastly. Then I thought about how he'd disappear. During the solstice party, and the dinner parties, and the equinox. And he'd always be so worked up when he'd come back and find me."

It was a terrible silence.

"It was all because of you," Aurelia said at last. "Erik came here because of you. Kaine killed him because of you. Erik was using me! He used *me* so he could get to *you*!"

She flung the paper onto the floor, the pages splayed out, revealing Ferron and his pale hair and skin. Hands stained black with blood, and Lancaster's blank stare, face still contorted.

KAINE FERRON PUBLICLY KILLS INITIATE

"Why do they care so much about you?" Aurelia demanded, stepping towards Helena. "What's so special about you that Kaine would move here, into this house he clearly hates? With all these servants he can't stand to be around but won't ever get rid of? Why would Erik spend months using me to reach you? Why does anyone care about you?"

"I—"

Aurelia slapped her across the face, the iron rings cracking against her cheekbone. "I don't want to hear from you!"

There was a loud bang outside the door, as if someone was trying to break it down. Aurelia jumped.

There was another boom.

Aurelia smiled. "I think he's noticed I'm in here," she said. "But they're never going to get through that door in time. Not when I have this."

Aurelia set the short staff directly onto one of the iron bars in the floor, and they twisted up like vines, wrapping around Helena's wrists and jerking down. Her knees hit the floor with a sickening lurch that shuddered up her spine.

Aurelia stood over her. "I told you not to cause problems for me."

The banging on the door had grown louder. Aurelia tilted her head to the side.

"You know, Kaine's terribly hard to shop for. I can never find anything he wants, but there is one thing that he started collecting . . . Do you know what it is?"

Helena's heart was racing. She shook her head.

Aurelia nodded towards the far corner of the room. "Eyes. There's one right over there. I bet he's watching us now. I don't think he's got any brown ones."

"Please don't." Helena tried to wrench her hands free, but the iron around her wrists did not yield.

"Don't worry," Aurelia said. "This way Kaine will still have pieces of you once you're sent back."

Helena tried to jerk free, but Aurelia made the iron pull her lower until her shoulders threatened to dislocate.

Ferron will come. Ferron will come.

The words ran through her mind in a relentless loop. He would; he had to know what was happening. He wouldn't let Aurelia—

He was in the city. She knew how long that journey was.

Aurelia grasped Helena by the chin. Her rings had lengthened into threatening points. "Open your eyes wide."

Helena trembled. "Please—"

"Shut up," Aurelia said, dropping the short staff and gripping Helena's jaw tighter, the tips of her rings sinking into Helena's cheek.

The banging outside the door grew louder.

Aurelia pressed the tip of one of her ring spikes against the outer corner of Helena's left eye, digging the tip back into the socket. She smiled, eyes alight with malice. "I hope I'm there when Kaine sees you next. Even if he kills me, the satisfaction of this will be worth it."

Helena jerked her head back as Aurelia's ring sliced along her cheek.

"Aurelia!"

The scream shattered the air. Not one voice but several all at once. All in unison.

"Aurelia!"

The thralls were screaming through the door. Inhuman, tearing rage in their voices.

Aurelia started and gave a panicked laugh as she glanced towards the door. "I didn't know they could do that. Guess you get all the special treatment."

She turned back to Helena, her fingers digging into Helena's hair to hold her in place as she dug the spike into the side of Helena's eye again.

Pain and pressure grew; Helena could feel that her eyeball was on the verge of being pulled from its socket. The thralls were still screaming, but Helena barely heard them above her own heartbeat. She was struck by the surreal thought that Aurelia Ferron's face would be the last thing she ever saw.

She was going to be left in the dark forever.

Her eye gave, and her vision became one-sided.

The whole house shook as the floor rippled, like a creature come to life.

Aurelia let go, turning in bewilderment. Before she could do anything, iron bars tore themselves out of the floor and walls, darting towards Aurelia like striking serpents, closing around her and dragging her away.

Aurelia screamed in terror as she was dragged off the floor, fighting to free herself with her own resonance, but the iron bars wrapped tighter and tighter until Helena heard bones breaking and Aurelia went limp, her iron-taloned fingers splayed and contorted where they'd been trying to push back against the bars.

Everything stopped.

As quickly as it had come alive, the house sank back into stillness.

CHAPTER 17

HELENA'S ARMS WERE STRAINING AGAINST THE IMPLACABLE iron, the edges scraping across her skin, shoulders screaming as she struggled, trying to wrench herself free. The room around her was only half visible, and all in ruins. Her terrified breathing was the only sound. The house was utterly quiet.

It seemed an eternity before Helena heard the distant sound of footsteps in the hall. The door warped, opening, and then Ferron was kneeling in front of her, blocking the ghastly sight of Aurelia from view as the iron around her wrists melted away. She collapsed towards him.

Her chest was spasming with suppressed panic.

He tilted her face up towards his, and his expression grew horrified. He touched her cheek and held her face as he drew several deep breaths.

"Your eye is out of the socket, and you have a deep puncture in the white," he said, his voice shaking. "How do I fix it?"

Helena stared dazedly at him, shuddering as tears tracked down her face, running along his fingers. Her breath came faster and faster.

She should know the answer to the question, but she couldn't remember. She could only feel the spot where Aurelia's iron talon had punctured her eye.

Ferron gripped her firmly by the shoulders. "Look at me. I need you to stay calm and tell me how to fix this. You know how to do it."

She choked back a sob.

Think, Helena. She was a healer. Someone had an injured eye. She needed to work efficiently if she was going to preserve their sight. *Focus.*

"F-F-For a punctured sclera," she said in a wobbling voice, casting her mind back, trying to recall the technique. She had no idea how to explain it to a novice vivimancer; she'd never taught anyone to heal.

It was pointless anyway. Ferron might be able to repair damaged tissue, but he wouldn't restore her vision. She'd still be blind in one eye. She crumpled.

Ferron gripped her tighter, holding her firmly upright. "Come on. You know how you'd do it. Tell me."

She swallowed hard. "The resonance has to be very close," she said, her voice barely more than a whisper. "You start at the deepest part and replicate the tissue exactly like the surrounding tissue; it won't matrice the way skin will on its own. You have to regenerate each structure fully. Layer by layer."

That answer alone would have been enough to deter any knowledgeable healer. Basic regeneration was one thing, but matricing tissue was technically taxing and mind-numbingly repetitive, like watching one's skin being rubbed off. It made the brain itch, but concentration had to be maintained the entire time.

Ferron was ignorant of this.

He placed his hand over hers, their fingers aligning, and she could dimly feel his resonance through her own fingertips before it cut off at her wrists.

"Show me."

Her wrists were ringed with bruises. Pain shot through the bones as she moved her fingers. She ignored it, focusing on the intuitive sensation that had been absent for so long, dimly feeling her eye where his resonance ran through her fingertips.

Transmutation always started with an initial touch to forge the connection. Once it was established, the alchemist could allow their fingers space to manipulate the channel.

Her fingers moved cautiously, prompting his, weaving invisible filaments of energy into a lattice of fragile tissue.

Ferron's silver eyes were almost luminous as he imitated the motions.

A tug came from the centre of her eye.

She whimpered, trying to hold still.

It was like a needle being poked into the puncture, a thread pulled through, on and on.

It took all her willpower not to jerk away, to focus on the feeble sense of resonance, to keep creating the complex regenerative structure.

Despite how small the wound was, it took ages. Ferron didn't stop even when Helena's fingers cramped and failed and fell away, the sensation leaving her ready to scream.

"And now?" Ferron asked the moment it was finally over, not giving her even a moment's respite.

She drew a deep breath.

"For—for a—a luxated eye," she said in a voice far calmer than she felt, "you have to morph and retract it carefully or you'll strain the optic nerve—more."

The motion was like turning a dial. Her eye slid back, squeezing and morphing before settling back into place with a nauseating pop.

She blinked slowly. Her eye hurt; it had grown dry and sticky after being so long exposed.

"H-How much can you see?" Ferron asked, tilting her face up towards his, his fingertips pressed against her jaw, his thumb running along the place where Aurelia had sliced her cheek open.

She stared at him and covered her right eye with her hand. His face was mere inches away, but there was only a dark blur.

"I can't—" Her voice cut off, chest constricting. Her hand slid from her eye to clamp over her mouth as she fought not to sob.

"What else do I need to do? How do I fix it?" He gripped her shoulders, still not letting her slump.

She shook her head, pressing her hands against her temples. "The optic nerve's probably damaged. I can't—help, though—it'll be too—"

His fingers pressed around her eye socket, and she could feel his resonance moving along the nerve towards her brain. Her body convulsed violently at the sensation, but he held her still. She felt heat and the same agitating regeneration process as he found the damage hidden between her eye and brain. An animal-like whimper escaped through her clenched teeth.

He pulled his hand away and stared at her. It was lighter now, like peering through a heavily fogged window.

"Anything?" His voice was hoarse.

"Your hair's pale. I think—I can make out your eyes and mouth a little—"

"Good, we're getting somewhere, then. Now what?"

He wanted to do more?

"Um . . . Atropine drops, from belladonna. It would dilate the pupil, keep it from straining while the tissue's recovering."

"Get the kit," Ferron said to the servants, all of whom had been frozen in place, inanimate while Ferron's full attention was on Helena. One of them sprang to life and hurried down the hallway.

"I need to deal with Aurelia now," Ferron said. "Wait here."

Helena nodded, slumping back.

She watched through her blurred vision as Ferron turned to face his wife.

He didn't even need to touch the twisted metal that wrapped around her. A flick of his hand and the tangle of iron slipped away, slithering back into the floor and walls.

Ferron knelt, pressing two fingers against Aurelia's neck.

The imbalance in Helena's vision made it hard to track how injured Aurelia was as Ferron began setting bones and popping dislocated joints back into place as easily as if he were assembling a puzzle.

He set a hand on Aurelia's chest, and Helena expected to watch Ferron create a new necrothrall. Instead, Aurelia screamed, lurching up from the floor, her eyes wild with terror.

"What? How did you—?" Aurelia was spluttering, her hands flying to her chest and sides, touching herself all over in confusion. "How? How are you *here*?"

"This is *my* house." The rage in Ferron's voice was palpable in every word.

"But you—you were in the city!" Aurelia seemed more hysterical about that than anything else.

Did she not remember what Ferron had done to her? Or was it simply too much for her to comprehend?

"Yes, I was. It was incredibly inconvenient of you, forcing me to leave in the middle of a ceremony."

"But—how did you—" Aurelia looked around the ruins of Helena's room.

"Did you think the thralls were the only things I can control from a distance? This is my house, and my family metal."

Helena stared at him in shock. What he was claiming wasn't possible.

There was no way that anyone could possibly transmute iron from a distance, especially not in that manner.

Ferron's resonance might be beyond anything Helena had ever seen, but even he couldn't reach all the way from the city and control the inner workings of Spirefell with such accuracy. He would have been acting blind, with no idea of what he was doing, unless—

She looked towards the eye in the corner.

No. It still wasn't possible, even with that. Every inch of distance from a transmutational target increased the effort. Even if he'd merely been in a different wing of the house, he'd be dead, dissolved into nothingness like a collapsing star, to use that much power.

It happened sometimes in the factories when the transmutational array sourcing was too powerful. The alchemists would disintegrate.

"That's impossible," Aurelia said, echoing Helena's thoughts.

"Underestimating your husband twice in one day? That's not very wifely of you."

"Oh, are you here for me? No, you aren't, you're here because of her." She pointed accusingly at Helena. "You nearly killed me, and you did kill Erik Lancaster, because of her!"

"Yes, I did. Do you know why? Because she is the last member of the Order of the Eternal Flame, which means that she is important. Infinitely more so than you will ever be. More important than Lancaster dreamed. My job is to keep her mind intact. When your father had you educated, did he ever mention that the eyes have a nerve connecting directly to the brain? What do you think happens if you just rip them out?"

Aurelia glanced towards Helena in horror.

Ferron kept talking in his cold, unsympathetic voice. "I've tried to be patient with you, Aurelia. I've been willing to overlook your indecent behaviour and petty interferences, but do remember, aside from being somewhat decorative, you are useless to me. If you ever go near her again, or speak to her, or so much as set foot in this wing again, I will kill you, and I will do it slowly, perhaps over the course of an evening or two. That isn't a threat. It's a promise. Now get out of my sight."

Aurelia scrambled up clumsily, her face contorted in fear and pain as she fled, limping, from the room.

Ferron stood, breathing deeply before he turned back to Helena. His eyes were still blazing silver.

He approached her slowly and knelt, turning her face up towards his again, studying her eyes. "The pupils are different sizes," he said. "I'll call a specialist. See if there's anything else to be done."

She stared back at him. He looked haggard, his skin pallid grey, his eyes too bright in contrast, but maybe it only seemed that way because of how her vision blurred.

"Were you in the house when you—" She gestured at the wreckage of the room.

He glanced over. "No. Or I might have managed it more neatly. I'd reached the edge of the property."

"How—?"

He gave a tired grimace. "The ability came compliments of Artemon Bennet, although he didn't have any idea at the time of what he was doing. It was intended to be a punishment."

Helena's eyebrows furrowed. She had no idea what could be done to make a person's resonance so powerful that they could control iron from a distance like that.

"How could anything—?"

"I don't want to discuss it right now," he said, cutting her off.

There was a pause. She still felt like she should say something.

"How did you know I'd be able to fix my eye?"

"You were a healer."

"Yes, but . . ." Her voice faded. She was unable to explain why she felt dissatisfied with the answer.

"Where did you learn to heal?" she asked, thinking back not only on how easily he'd imitated her directions but also how he'd dealt with Aurelia, and repaired the nerve damage on his own.

"Well, you see, there was a war, and I was a general. Picked up a few things."

A headache was developing in Helena's temples from her imbalanced vision.

"Well, you—you have a natural talent for it. In another life, you could be a healer."

"One of life's great ironies," he said, glancing towards the door, his jaw tight.

The maid had returned carrying a satchel, the kind that field medics wore, strapped over the shoulder and belted at the waist.

Ferron took it, rummaging through the pockets. She heard the rattle and clink of glass vials.

"Just atropine?" he asked, looking towards her with a vial in hand.

She shook her head. "Five drops of atropine diluted in a teaspoon of saline."

There was more tinkling, unscrewing, pouring, and then he pocketed something and snapped the satchel shut. The maid immediately took it back.

Helena started pushing herself unsteadily to her feet.

"I should—lie down so it doesn't run," she said. Her balance felt off and her hands and arms shook, refusing to bear her weight. She sank back to the floor. Perhaps she'd just lie there.

A hand closed around her elbow and drew her to her feet.

"I'm not leaning over you on the floor," Ferron said in an irritated voice. Rather than pull her to the bed, he led her out of the room and down the hallway to another room.

The air was stale, the bed stripped and bare. Ferron wrenched a dust-cloth off a sofa, and Helena lay down flat on it.

He leaned over her, vial in hand. His face went in and out of focus every time she blinked. Dark. Light. Dark. Light.

"How many drops?"

"Two, twice a day, for two days. Then euphrasia compresses for a week."

Ferron leaned closer, dripping two drops of the belladonna atropine into her eye. She closed her eyes to keep from blinking it away.

His fingers brushed against her cheek, and she felt the cut there vanish. "The servants will have this room made up."

She counted his receding footsteps, covering her left eye so she could see.

He stumbled as he left the room, catching himself against the door-frame and righting himself slowly, as if unsteady on his feet.

She closed her eyes again, listening to the heavy silence of the house.

Don't cry. Don't cry, she told herself.

She listened as the servants arrived and the bed's mattress was flipped and made up with fresh sheets and bedding. The radiators were turned on, hissing as the room warmed. Helena's few possessions were brought in and put into a new wardrobe. The curtains were left drawn, permitting only a splinter of light.

When they were gone, Helena made her way over to the bed and tried to sleep.

Ferron returned a few hours later, followed by an older man with a case filled with innumerable contraptions.

"I warn you, sclera punctures are quite a nasty business," he said with a wheezing voice as he glanced over Helena. "Not much that can be done. We'll be lucky if she can keep the eye. I brought some patches, or if you're willing to spend the money I have some glass ones which will do nicely."

He sat down heavily in a chair that the butler had brought over.

"She instructed you in the vivimancy to try to repair it?" he asked Ferron, who was leaning against the wall, watching from hooded eyes.

Ferron gave a wordless nod.

The optician leaned closer, prying Helena's eye open and holding various mechanical contraptions up, peeling the lid back as he studied the injury.

He was quiet for a long time.

"This is—quite exceptional work," he finally said in a voice full of surprise. "Vivimancy, you say? Well."

He sat back heavily and stared at Helena, rubbing his chin. "Where'd you learn this trick?"

"I was a healer," Helena said.

The doctor made an incredulous wheezing sound. "But you're—" He gestured towards her wordlessly. "How would you know about medical procedures like that?"

"My father was a surgeon, trained in Khem, before he moved to Etras."

"Khem? Really. They have doctors there?"

Helena gave a tight nod.

"Fancy that. I've never known anyone from Khem. And he crossed all the way from the lower continent? I can't imagine. The sea is—" He shuddered. "Tides like mountains? No thank you. Even during the summer Abeyance, they say it's a treacherous passage. I can't imagine living in the coastal regions. You must be grateful to be inland now, away from all that."

Helena stared at him.

He peered at her through a series of lenses, muttering to himself and twisting various screws and then holding a small light near her face before sitting back. "I believe you may make a full recovery."

He glanced towards Ferron. "Keep her out of the light, apply the belladonna twice a day, and there's a good chance she'll have little impairment."

Helena watched one-eyed as he stood, packing his instruments away before he turned to Ferron, straightening his coat pompously.

"I must say, that's an exceptional healer you have there. When you told me what happened, I didn't think there was much chance of keeping the eye. We have a few vivimancers at the hospital now, and they cause more trouble than they're worth. Always sure they know better than the doctors, but then only addressing the symptoms and never bothering to understand how anything works. Useless lot."

The doctor looked down at Helena again. His eyes resting on the manacles around her wrists.

"What a pity," he said to himself. "Such a waste of talent."

Ferron made a noncommittal grunt. The doctor turned to face him, flushing. "And you, sir. Remarkable that you could manage such delicate healing through imitation. Very impressive. You should work in the hospital."

"So I'm told," Ferron said with an insincere smile. "Do you think they'll still hire me after I murdered someone in the lobby?"

The man blanched. "Well—what I mean is—"

"If there's nothing else, I'll see you out," Ferron said, striding away.

HELENA WORE A PATCH OVER her left eye. Ferron came like clockwork to administer the atropine drops, apparently not trusting even his servants around Helena with belladonna. Once she no longer needed the eye drops, she was brought cool compresses made from eyebright.

She'd just stopped wearing the patch when Stroud returned.

"You've had a rather unfortunate month, I hear," she said as Helena automatically stripped for the examination.

Helena's vision was still imbalanced, making things swing out of focus as Stroud began examining her. Stroud noted something in her file, and then made Helena lie back and spent more than a minute kneading her stomach and lower abdomen.

"Perfect," Stroud finally said, stepping back and taking several more notes. "You're finally ready."

Helena stared dully at the ceiling, debating whether to give Stroud the satisfaction of asking what she meant. Stroud stood waiting, and finally she relented.

"Ready for what?"

"Enrolment in my repopulation program."

Helena looked at her blankly.

"Didn't I mention it?" Stroud inclined her head smugly. "It must have slipped my mind."

Helena blinked slowly. Her uneven vision left her off kilter, as if reality itself were out of alignment. "I was sterilised."

"Yes, I know." Stroud just nodded. "I believe I may be the first vivimancer to manage a full ligation reversal."

The room threatened to tilt. "No. They said it would be—"

"Well, they did try to make things difficult. I had to practise several times on a few of the extra girls we had in the program. It wasn't any loss, don't worry. Not every resonance is worth replicating, and it's good to have a few spares for consolation; some of the sires don't take it well when we don't have any availability for their repertoires."

Helena's throat convulsed. "What?"

"Anyway, I didn't want to say anything until I was sure. I thought you'd figure it out. I suppose you're not as bright as everyone says."

Helena tried to scramble up and escape, but Stroud paralysed her limbs with a careless touch.

"The High Necromancer is convinced that you're an animancer. If he's right, we can't let a girl like that go to waste. Do you have any idea how rare they are? And here you are at the critical moment, when we need one most."

Her body shook. "I thought—the transference—"

"Oh, so now you want to cooperate with transference?" Stroud laughed. "Don't worry, we'll still try to recover your memories afterwards. We're simply reprioritising for a little while."

Stroud went to the door where the maid was waiting. "High Reeve, a word."

Helena lay there, unable to move. Ferron wouldn't let this happen. He'd spent months practising transference; Stroud couldn't come and upend everything.

She tried to make herself breathe steadily. If she started hyperventilating, Stroud would probably sedate her or knock her out completely. What if she woke up back in Central, waiting for someone to come through the door to—

Her vision swam, terror crawling through her like insects.

What was she going to do? Try to argue that her memories were more valuable than a pregnancy?

If she had to choose one or the other, what was worse? Cooperating with Ferron's extraction of the Eternal Flame's secrets, or letting herself be raped to produce the child Morrough needed for his own transference?

Even if she did stop resisting transference, if she cooperated with Ferron, wouldn't they just forcibly impregnate her afterwards?

"You called," Ferron said as he entered, his tone clipped with irritation.

"High Reeve, yes, I wanted to inform you that I've been able to reverse Marino's sterilisation. The High Necromancer wants her transferred into the repopulation program," Stroud said.

Ferron's expression did not so much as ripple, but he went uncannily still.

"You did what?" he finally said.

Stroud laid a hand proudly on Helena's stomach. "You know how rare animancers are. If she really is one, it would be a waste not to use her. I've spent the last few months experimenting with a reversal process, and it's finally complete. They were careless, really; they should have taken out the womb, although I would have replaced it if they had. I have plenty of healthy subjects to choose from. It was a relatively minor process compared with what Bennet and I used to do to the chimaeras."

"You didn't mention this." Ferron's voice had grown dangerous.

"The program is not your purview, and you talk so frequently of how fragile she is, I thought it better to wait until I was sure. However, the High Necromancer wants her enrolled immediately. The matter of transference will resume once we have the child. I suspect she'll be much more cooperative about it then." She looked down at Helena. "Won't you?"

Ferron was silent.

"Now, I could take her back to Central. We have a long list of promising sires, and Marino here has such an unusual repertoire that we could pair her with practically anyone." Stroud looked squarely at Ferron. "However . . ." Her voice was idle, meandering like a summer brook. "When it comes to resonance, there is one candidate who stands out from the rest."

"Get to the point," Ferron's voice was flat, but Helena could hear murder ringing underneath.

Stroud straightened imperiously. "It's time you had children. I know your family's concern is with iron, but you have a wife for that. As our other animancer, the High Necromancer has chosen you to be the first to make an attempt with Marino here. If she becomes pregnant, we'll look for signs of animancy. Your father was a great help in detailing your mother's condition, so we know just what symptoms to look for. However, given how tight our timeline has become, the High Necromancer considers it best to keep alternatives under consideration. You'll have two months to produce results, or she'll be transferred to Central, and we'll see if we have better luck with other candidates."

CHAPTER 18

Everything around Helena blurred. Stroud removed the paralysis after Ferron icily excused himself, but Helena still didn't move.

The grating, scratching sound of Stroud's pen on paper was the only sound in the quiet room.

Helena's mouth had gone parched, but she struggled to swallow, trying to think of some way to reverse what had so suddenly happened.

Her fingers flexed, running across the linen sheets as she tried to focus on external sensations. A half-whimpering rasp escaped her throat.

She thought she might scream. Just scream and scream and never stop.

"What's wrong?" Stroud asked, glancing up from Helena's medical file.

Helena stared at her.

"I would have thought you'd be pleased to have a break from transference. With the way you've been resisting, you'd likely have liver failure before the year's out." Stroud tapped absently on Helena's file. "I'm very particular about the alchemists in my program. The war cost us so many priceless lineages. You should be grateful to still provide something with such lasting significance."

"You're having me raped, and you expect me to be grateful about it?" Helena's voice was dead, coming from far away.

Stroud's expression soured. "I'm giving you an opportunity for your life to mean something."

Helena's rage was the only thing keeping her from losing her mind. "If it's such a great thing, it's a wonder you don't volunteer yourself."

Stroud froze, anger flashing like lightning across her face, darkening every line. Helena braced herself to be struck, but Stroud's mouth pressed into a thin-lipped smile and she leaned over Helena almost tenderly.

"The High Reeve has been married for more than a year without any children to show for it. His Eminence insists Ferron be your first candidate, but I doubt anything will come of it. After everything Bennet did to him, he's scarcely what I'd call human. After he's made his attempts, you'll come back to Central, and I'll be the one to decide who goes next. For however long it takes."

Helena's blood ran cold.

Stroud touched Helena's chin with the tip of her finger. "With that in mind, I think you'd best learn to watch that tongue of yours. I don't have to let you keep it."

Helena did not make another sound until Stroud was gone. Dread welled up inside her like poison, corroding her organs, burning her lungs. She went through the house, every unlocked door, searching the rooms in a desperate frenzy to find something, anything. There had to be something.

Ferron did not reappear until the following evening. When he did, his expression was hard, but his eyes seemed to slide off her, as if he couldn't bring himself to look at her anymore.

Her hands started spasming over and over, nerves twinging.

"It's not tonight," he said abruptly. "I'm told"—he was still not looking at her—"you won't be fertile for three more days."

She wasn't surprised—

He was a murderer and a necromancer. What reason did she have to think he'd be above this?

Yet somehow, irrationally, she'd thought he was . . . safe.

Stupid.

"Come here," he finally said.

She walked mechanically, staring at the buttons on his coat and shirt. He reached out, leather gloves pressing against her jaw, tilting her face up until her eyes met his.

"How much can you see?" he asked, gaze flickering from one eye to the other in comparison.

Helena laughed.

She had no idea when she'd last laughed. A lifetime ago. But the question was funny. Hilarious even.

Every good thing she had ever had in her life was destroyed, every scrap of solace ripped away as though there was nothing left of her now except hurting. She had been imprisoned and violated in almost every way imaginable, and now he would inflict this final atrocity upon her, but he was worried about her *eyesight.*

She laughed and laughed and then she wasn't laughing anymore, she was crying. She was crying until she was rocking, back and forth, half screaming, and Ferron just stood there.

She didn't stop until she was hollow, as though she'd sobbed out everything inside her and now the only thing left was a shell. She was so tired of existing.

"Feel better?"

She swallowed, her throat aching. "No."

His fingers spasmed, and she watched him curl them into a fist, tucking it behind his back. She knew that trick.

She looked up at him, noticing then the odd pallor and haggard set of his jaw.

Well, at least they were both suffering.

"What were you tortured for this time?" she asked dully, relieved to wonder about something, anything else.

He gave a slight hum. "It was for a few things. As I am frequently reminded, I am a constant disappointment, and now the public, through their vast collective intelligence, has deduced that I'm the High Reeve."

The news piqued her curiosity. "Was it because you killed Lancaster?"

"I imagine that played a part, and Aurelia's little fit didn't help. I had to leave suddenly, and the High Reeve was supposed to be in attendance. International papers are less reluctant to print such theories, so word's gotten out. I'll soon be acknowledged as the High Necromancer's successor." He gave a grimacing smile. "This previous anonymity was all for my protection, you see."

"Of course," Helena said. "So you were only tortured a little bit."

"It was nothing," he said, but his hands were both behind his back.

He shifted, as if he was about to leave. Even though she didn't want to be anywhere near him, the alternative was being alone with her thoughts.

"Why'd you kill Lancaster?" she asked.

"He endangered my assignment. I would have done a formal execution, but I was busy, and I wanted him taken care of."

"So you killed him in the middle of the hospital?" she said, eyeing him doubtfully.

"I was going to kill him in his hospital room, but he tried to run." He shrugged. "I improvised."

The image of Lancaster lying split open while Ferron gutted his remains was seared into Helena's mind.

Ferron rolled his neck. "If you have no more questions, we should get this over with. Sofa, or bed?"

The words were like a steel rod rammed down the length of her spine, and it took her a moment to realise he intended to check her memories.

She'd assumed that was over now. "I thought—"

Thought what? That she wasn't still a prisoner and that in exchange for her body, she'd now be permitted her mind? She swallowed her words and went to the sofa.

He followed her, expression unreadable as he extended his hand, fingers barely grazing her forehead before his resonance slid through her skull.

By the time he stopped, Helena felt as though she'd collapsed inwards upon herself. Reliving all the recent days made her jaw clench until her teeth threatened to crack.

She lay slumped back on the sofa, Stroud's threat echoing in her head.

She pressed her face into the fabric of the sofa, smelling the age and dust, and tried to shut out the surrounding world. Ferron left without a word.

HELENA'S EYE HAD RECOVERED ENOUGH to finally handle light again, so she pushed the curtains back, her new room revealing a view of the courtyard rather than the mountains. Outside, the world had metamorphosed, showing early signs of spring. The deadened grey she was accustomed to now showed pricks of colour amid the toppled grass and the tree branches.

A few weeks before, she would have been comforted by it, but there was a pit inside her now, even beauty turned to horror.

Two days. Her thoughts circled relentlessly, like a trapped animal ready to gnaw off her own limbs to escape.

In war, rape had always loomed as a possibility. There were stories about the prisoners in the laboratories, warnings of what could happen to women captured from Resistance territory. But rape for the purpose of pregnancy was a layer of intention that she still had not fully wrapped her mind around.

Her experiences in the matter of pregnancy had never been favourable.

Precautionary measures were in short supply during the war. Girls would show up at the hospital from time to time, nervously asking to talk to Matron Pace. Oftentimes, that was the end of it, but other times, they'd keep coming back.

Helena had been an only child. As an apothecary, her mother mostly prevented pregnancies. It was the village midwives who handled the rest. Mothers only came to a surgeon like Helena's father when things had gone wrong. Most of the babies Helena saw growing up were deformed, or deathly sick, or stillborn.

That pattern continued during the war. As a healer, Helena was only summoned when a baby was born too early or had gotten stuck in the wrong position, or the milk wouldn't come in because there wasn't enough food. She would be asked if she could do something. Most often she couldn't. The babies were tiny and fragile, and even vivimancy couldn't fix everything.

She'd watch the mothers break, something seismic inside them rupturing. They'd scream sometimes. Others would be silent, and that was often worse in the end.

Helena had been grateful that it would never be her. She would never marry or have children, so would never have to endure losing them.

It was the one thing she'd thought herself safe from.

She lay in bed unable to sleep. Lumithia was nearing her biannual Ascendance, waxing so full that the night glowed silver, the light stark against the black shadows. The air had a nearly constant feeling of resonance.

Helena flexed her fingers, wishing she could shove her hand inside her body as easily as Ferron had into Lancaster's belly. She'd rip out her organs right there in the bed.

The thought of her body's forced complicity made her sick, and yet the idea of not becoming pregnant left her frozen with fear. Stroud's threat kept ringing in her head.

Faced with the choice of struggling or cooperating with her own rape so that it would not be as bad as it could be made her feel so guilty, her mind threatened to shear apart. If the destination was inevitable, her only choice was in how horrifying the journey would be.

The night dragged like sandpaper across her skin until she was nearly raw from it.

When Ferron walked into her room, she gave a ragged gasp and nearly burst into tears.

When he saw her, he seemed to almost turn, as if to walk out.

She started to reach a hand forward, then snatched it instantly back, clenching her fingers into a fist. The movement was enough to still him.

His eyes flicked between her and the door as if still debating with himself.

What if he refused and just let Stroud take her?

The room swam. Her hands had already gone numb.

If he left, she would let him. She would go to Central. She would not be so complicit as to ask.

She couldn't read the expression on his face. It was impassive, as if he wasn't fully there.

Finally he turned away. Helena didn't know if she should laugh or cry that this was the line he wouldn't cross. The sole command he'd refuse. After all, he was known to be the High Reeve now; Morrough couldn't kill him.

He pulled a small tin case out of his pocket, putting something from it under his tongue.

"Bed," he finally said without looking at her.

Helena didn't move.

He turned to face her, his eyes flat.

"Wait—" She held her hands out, as if she could ward him off. "What if you just kill me?" she asked, her voice shaking. "You could now. You said that everyone knows now that you're the High Reeve. Morrough wouldn't be able to justify killing you because of me. I'm no one."

Ferron's attention sharpened. For a moment, he stood considering it, calculation visible in his eyes.

Her pulse sped up.

"I can do it myself, if you want, so he won't realise," she offered. "If you just—give me something. It doesn't need to be easy, or quick; it could be something small. You can say you left briefly and—"

She knew the instant she misspoke. Ferron's expression abruptly hardened, his eyes going flat and his gaze sliding through her again.

"Bed," he said again, this time through clenched teeth.

Her hands fell to her sides. She turned slowly, eerily disconnected from her body as she walked over. She bit down on her inner lip, harder and harder, trying to feel something. Blood gushed across her tongue as she lay down, but her body remained numb.

Ferron approached a few moments later. He'd only removed his coat.

She tensed as soon as he got close, trying not to grind her teeth.

His expression was set like granite; he stood at the foot of the bed, staring at the headboard.

"Close your eyes," he said.

She forced herself to obey and tried to focus on breathing. *Don't think.* She could smell him in the room, the scent of juniper, metal, and the decay of the house.

The mattress dipped to her right. Her breathing stuttered and sped up.

"Don't—open your eyes."

She squeezed them tighter. There was a pause as her skirts pushed up towards her hips, underclothes stripped down. Her heart seemed to stop.

She heard Ferron inhale. She could feel his body through the air.

"Breathe," he said near her left ear.

There was a touch between her legs, something warm and slippery. She flinched away, then realised it was oil.

She drew a rasping breath, squeezing her eyes so tight, they throbbed as his weight pressed against her hips.

She choked back a garbled whimper.

She closed her eyes tighter. Her mind scrabbled, trying to find an escape. In stasis, in the tank, she'd learned to take herself away when her mind teetered on the edge.

That was how she'd survived. She'd learned she could endure.

Now that escape didn't work.

She was trapped inside her body, as if someone had nailed her consciousness in place with a spike.

This is better than Central, she reminded herself, struggling to keep from hyperventilating, from clawing and screaming and trying to shove him off.

Her chest spasmed. There were tears sliding from the corners of her eyes.

Better than Central.

What if this failed? What if Stroud was right about him, that it wasn't even possible, but Helena had cooperated anyway? What if it was all for nothing?

She gave a frantic, panicking gasp, unable to keep from recoiling just as he jerked and stilled.

He was gone so suddenly, it was as if he'd evaporated.

Helena opened her eyes and couldn't see him anywhere. The violent sound of retching emerged from the bathroom.

Eventually she heard the toilet flush and the sound of water running from the tap for several minutes.

She managed to shove her skirts down but couldn't make herself move beyond that. Her body was numb.

It's over, she kept telling herself, trying to make herself calm down, but she couldn't stop trembling. Her nails had carved crescents into her palms.

Ferron emerged from the bathroom, his tense expression faded, as if he couldn't maintain it. His face was drawn, his eyes stark and reddish.

He looked strangely mortal. She wished he didn't.

She looked away.

He crossed the room silently, picked up his coat, and left.

Helena sat up slowly, trying not to feel her body.

Going into the bathroom, she turned on the shower's spray and curled up beneath it without taking her clothes off. When the water ran cold, she still didn't move.

CHAPTER 19

HELENA TRIED TO MAKE HERSELF GO OUTSIDE the next day. She was desperate for fresh air, to escape the oppressive weight of the house, but when she reached the doorway, a warm spring breeze rushed across her face, filling her lungs with the scent of loam and spring blossoms. She could see little clusters of crocuses and snowdrops peeking through the dead grass. The blackened vines covering the house were tipped with specks of green, and flocks of birds chirped as they soared overhead.

It was beautiful, and it felt like a betrayal.

The world was not supposed to be beautiful any longer. It was supposed to be dead and cold, forever mirroring the misery of Helena's life. Instead it had moved on, tilting into a new season, and she could not. She was trapped forever in winter, in the season of death.

She retreated into the house.

When the door to her room opened in the afternoon, she was relieved to see Stroud instead of Ferron.

Stroud looked amused. "I thought I'd stop by and make sure there wasn't any damage from this first time. We wouldn't want an infection interfering. Was there blood?"

Helena hadn't looked, but she shook her head slowly.

Stroud's eyes flicked curiously up and down. "Well, you are over twenty. There isn't always."

Helena tried not to react to Stroud's resonance when she laid her hand on Helena's pelvis, but when she felt the resonance wave glide through the most intimate parts of her body, she shuddered uncontrollably.

"We likely won't know if you're pregnant for a few weeks after, but we will know soon enough. I've grown quite adept at detecting them early." There was the most unnerving sensation of something inside her lower abdomen being adjusted, and Helena gave a sharp gasp. "Yes, this is definitely the right window. You're as ready as I can make you."

Helena's skin crawled until Stroud stopped.

"So, how was it?"

"Horrible," Helena said, looking away.

Stroud made a sound of false sympathy. "Not surprising. You're high-strung."

Helena stared towards the window, her jaw trembling.

Stroud's lips stretched like rubber, and she set the file down, running her fingers idly across Helena's name and the two prisoner numbers stamped across the front.

"Did you know, I studied in the Alchemy Tower. It was years before your time, obviously. My repertoire and resonance levels weren't *good* enough to keep ascending, but I was allowed to transfer to the science department and study as a medical assistant. That's where I first heard of vivimancy. It wasn't until years later that I realised what power I had and began the struggle of mastering it. I would never have imagined I'd become one of the few vivimancers to survive the war."

Helena didn't understand why Stroud was telling her this.

Stroud rummaged in her bag and pulled out a vial of tablets, breaking one in half. "Open."

"Why?" Helena asked, locking her jaw.

Stroud did not answer, she just stepped forward and, using her fingers and resonance to pry Helena's mouth open, pushed a crumbling piece into her mouth and forced her to swallow as it began dissolving. Helena recognised the taste as it moved down her throat.

"Artemon Bennet saved people like me. Gave us a chance to test our abilities openly and be proud of them." Stroud was still gripping Helena's jaw; her fingers were digging into the skin.

Helena could feel Stroud tinkering with her physiology, tuning her. It was wholly different from what Ferron had done when acclimating her to the house. Rather than feel physiologically detached from her mind, she realised that her skin had begun to warm, starting at the surface and slowly sinking deeper.

Stroud kept talking. "I'm not saying he was perfect; Bennet considered other vivimancers too feeble-minded to appreciate his genius." Her pale eyebrows rose. "But I served him without question, gave up my personal ambitions to stay by his side. That's why I'm still here, even though everyone *always* underestimated me."

Helena tried to pull away, but Stroud's resonance had strangled her motor nerves. A pulsing tension bloomed from her lower abdomen, and her skin was growing so sensitive, it ached.

"There." Stroud let go, letting Helena topple sideways on the bed. "You'll enjoy it much more now."

Helena lay paralysed, unable to resist or scream as Stroud arranged her on the bed, flat on her back, legs parted.

No. No. No.

"I'll tell the High Reeve you're ready for him on my way out," Stroud said as she left.

Helena waited for what felt like hours, want carving itself into her bones. Her body screamed for movement, for touch, for friction, need crawling beneath her skin.

When Ferron finally arrived, if she could have moved, she would have shuddered just at the vibration of the door shutting, but she could only lie there, eyes fastened on him, begging him to notice that something was wrong.

He wasn't looking at her, though. He was staring past her, through her, his gaze in an unseeing mid-distance as he slid off his coat and draped it over the sofa.

She watched him move, her eyes suddenly ravenous, intent on cataloguing all the details about him. The wait had left her hollow inside, a pit of harrowing want that kept growing.

His hands, she knew, were warm.

A tremor swelled inside her.

Stop thinking.

She squeezed her eyes shut, but the need she felt corroded her willpower.

The bed shifted. A shiver ran down her spine. Her skirts were shifted, pushed up, and the brush of fabric against her thighs made her inhale raggedly. The only reaction she could muster.

"Breathe," Ferron said, as he had the night before.

She was keenly aware of him, more so than the day before, except now her wants were inverted. She could barely feel his weight. She wanted to arch up, press into him even as an endless scream throbbed inside her skull. Her eyes snapped open, and she stared up at him.

She felt as though she'd never truly looked at him before.

There'd always been a sharp and wary distance between them. When she observed him, it was in search of tells, for weakness. She'd never looked at him as something human or hot-blooded.

Now he felt very human to her. She *wanted* him to touch her. She remembered what his hands felt like, the press of his fingertips along her jaw. She craved it so much, her skin ached. The weight she'd been desperate to escape from the night before—she wanted it.

Tears burned a hot trail down her temples.

For the briefest moment, Ferron's eyes flicked to her face before averting again. He went still and looked at her again.

"What's wrong?" he asked.

She stared at him, willing for him to understand.

He drew away, wrenching a glove off. He was still wearing them, even now.

He barely touched her, but that was all it took. The paralysis melted away.

Helena's body shuddered back into motion, and she instantly curled onto her side with a sob, pressing her legs tight together as her body throbbed, gasping raggedly. Even her breath burned in her lungs.

"What did she do to you?"

She couldn't look at him.

"She said it was to make it b-better." Her voice shook uncontrollably.

"Because I—complained. H-How long do those tablets you gave me last?"

"Eight hours."

"She gave me half." She drew a ragged breath. "Can you—change it to something else?"

"Not once it's taken effect," he said. "It has to wear off on its own."

She nodded. She'd assumed as much but hoped to be wrong.

She tried to draw another breath.

"Can we—can we wait till—after?" Her voice was strangled.

There was a silence.

"I have to leave after this. I won't be back until late tomorrow."

She lay there, trying to think clearly, not sure that she was rational anymore.

This, or maybe not pregnant. For all the accidental pregnancies she'd treated, she knew that children didn't always come easy. For her parents, it had taken years; she'd arrived after they'd given up. A miracle, they'd said.

Two months, and then she'd go to Central, to Stroud, and—

She was going insane. She couldn't do this. A choice like this—it wasn't fair to make her choose between things like this. No good choices, just worse and worse, which way to hate herself forever.

This was the cruellest thing Stroud could have done.

"Just—do it now," she said, rolling back onto her back, refusing to look at him.

She stared up at the canopy, willing her mind away. There was a long pause before the bed shifted.

She hadn't thought it could be worse the second time, but it was a thousand times worse. Now her body *wanted* him.

She tried closing her eyes, but she was restless. She couldn't keep them shut. They fluttered open and she looked at Ferron again, taking in all the details she'd never cared to notice before. His sharp cheekbones and eyes, his thin lips, the precise lines of his jaw, and the way his pale throat disappeared in the collar of his shirt. She wanted to press close and breathe against his skin, to *feel* the warmth of another body.

"Hurry up," she said through clenched teeth, trying to hold herself rigid.

There was no need for oil, but he used it anyway. She arched back until she could see the headboard, spine trembling, burying her face in her hands, biting down viciously on her palm, and felt ruined.

Whimpers formed in her throat when he moved. Her fingers twisted, clawing the duvet, threatening to tear it.

She was nauseous with horror. She hated every fibre of her being—the physicalness of herself that she could not overcome, that was perpetually scared, and weak, and now wanting—and she could not escape from any of it. Perhaps Matias had been right all along, and it was her nature to be feeble.

She wished she could tear herself out of her body. Slice it to pieces and watch it burn away so that she was not human anymore.

Her body contracted against her will. Ferron gave a ragged gasp, and the sound burned through her. His weight pressed down, and she broke with a despairing sob.

He thrust a few more times and shook with a tortured groan.

In an instant, he was gone, recoiling as if he couldn't get away fast enough.

She barely opened her eyes in time to see him as he vanished through the door.

She caught only a glimpse of his face just before the door slammed. He looked grey, as though he was going to faint.

He was gone. The room was empty, and she was alone.

She curled onto her side and sobbed into her hands. The desperation burning beneath her skin was temporarily dulled by the magnitude of the horror she felt. She crawled into the bathroom, retching until nothing else would come up.

She'd always known of sex. In Etras, it was part of life—like birth and death—but in the North, sentiments were different, the subject kept rigidly behind closed doors.

Boys could get into trouble for going to the entertainment districts, but it was considered an irrepressible part of their nature to hunger, and a sign of their vitality, and so punishments were usually light, more a consequence of being caught than for the act itself. The expectations were different for girls, even those allowed beyond the traditional confines of Paladian society. Lumithia was a virgin goddess, pure and gleaming. Women associating with her cult and the opportunities it permitted were required to be likewise.

Helena's life at the Institute revolved around her scholarship, which, in addition to being dependent on her academic performance, had included a morality clause. She'd adhered to it more devoutly than she would have any faith, in greater terror of earthly consequences than of divine threats. Her fear stifling even the smallest potential spark of desire towards anyone.

She'd thought sometimes that someday, when she'd repaid her debts, accomplished all that was expected, and reached her own goals, she would like to be loved. To know what it was to feel wanted.

Now this sick shame was all she knew.

WHEN THE DRUG FINALLY WORE off, Helena lay trying to make herself think of something, anything else, but there was little to turn her mind to. The only question left to wonder over was why she was somehow a piece in a labyrinthian conspiracy.

She could mostly make out Morrough and Stroud's motives, what use they found in her, but no matter what angle Helena considered things from, she could not place Ferron's motives in all this, even though he was the last person she wanted to think about at all. At least wondering at his political motives kept her from thinking about him as a human.

She was certain he'd somehow engineered the revelation that he was High Reeve. There may have been extenuating circumstances, but if he hadn't wanted the rumour to spread, he would have contained it. He wanted Paladia and the surrounding countries to know that it was Kaine Ferron.

Why? Could it be an attempt to escape Morrough's punishments? To make himself harder to replace? There had to be more to it than that.

New Paladia was presently surrounded by enemies.

The Novis monarchy across the river to the east had age-old ties to the Holdfasts: Luc's mother had been the queen's distant cousin. Novis was unlikely to ever acknowledge the Guild Assembly. Hevgoss, looming over Paladia from the west, had a long history of surreptitiously interfering with nearby countries to provoke a crisis as context in which to "intervene." Interventions which usually resulted in a government beholden to them.

The Eternal Flame had suspected from the beginning that Morrough was being used by Hevgoss, but it seemed something, possibly Helena, had soured that relationship.

Paladia's economy and legitimacy depended on alchemy, and the war had decimated both the population and the industry. The natural resources and centuries of alchemical science remained, but the country was weak, and the wolves were closing in. It was only the fear of the Undying that held their enterprising neighbours at bay, but now that myth was shattered. Morrough had all but vanished from the public eye; the High Reeve was the only true power that remained.

Perhaps Ferron was secretly negotiating with Hevgoss to overthrow Morrough.

Terrifying as the High Reeve was, the Ferrons were an old family, considered a part of Paladia's history even before they'd made their fortune. The Undying maintained their regime entirely through fear, and those in Paladia still benefitting from it could fit in Spirefell's ballroom. The disillusionment was reaching its climax. Once it finally crumbled, people would want someone familiar, someone with power they could take pride in.

The whole world knew the revolutionary power of Ferron steel. It had forged the industrial era.

At this point, Paladians might consider Ferron a saviour if he usurped Morrough. He could blame the bulk of his atrocities on Morrough, and take responsibility only for what benefitted him.

From everything Helena knew, Ferron had no competition. Greenfinch was little more than a puppet, and the Guild Assembly was a joke. Ferron was Morrough's only visible crutch.

It would explain why Morrough was torturing him so much: out of resentment for his own failing immortality. He was critically dependent on Ferron and without alternatives.

Yet Helena couldn't shake the sense that she was missing something.

How did *she* fit into Ferron's plans?

Whatever machinations were in place, she somehow played a role. He was too invested in her safekeeping for it to be otherwise. Ferron devoted an excessive degree of effort to ensuring her well-being while trying not to appear so.

She kept thinking about his hesitation when she asked him to kill her. He *had* considered it. Why? If she was a necessary part of his plan, how could killing her possibly be an option? But if she wasn't, why all the effort?

IT WAS AFTER NIGHTFALL WHEN Ferron returned. When he entered the room, they stared at each other, neither speaking.

There was nothing to say.

He turned, slipped a tablet under his tongue, and when he turned back, his gaze went through her.

Helena lay, eyes fastened on the canopy.

She didn't flinch when she felt the bed shift. She didn't make a sound when her skirts were pushed up to her waist. He moved between her legs, and she stared straight up so intently, her vision blurred.

When he entered her, she gave a small choking gasp and turned her face towards the wall, writhing with internal anguish.

Her body had anticipated it. Just as the drug had acclimated her to the house, it had attuned her body to this.

It was such a profound betrayal.

She thought of shoving him off. If he'd physically force her, pin her down, or paralyse her, then she might hate herself less.

But she was so tired of being hurt, and so she didn't move.

When it was over, he left without a word. She didn't look at his face.

After five days, the door stayed shut, and the house was silent. It was finally over, but she scarcely felt any relief.

She was going mad. She could feel herself fragmenting with anxiety, coming apart, consumed by the cage holding her.

What if it worked? What if it failed?

She didn't know what she was more afraid of.

AS THE DAY LENGTHENED INTO evening, Helena grew increasingly agitated, but it wasn't until it grew briefly dark and then searingly bright again that she realised why.

Lumithia had reached full Ascendance. The world outside lay cast in silver almost bright as day, radiating light from amid a black sky. Every star and planet erased. Luna, halfway across the sky, looked like a broken piece of pottery in contrast.

Lumithia's slow orbit meant she waxed full only twice each year, in the spring and autumn, while entering her Abeyance in summer and winter.

When she was in Ascendance, it had an intense effect on alchemists.

For those with low resonance, Ascendance was the only time of year when they could transmute, while alchemists with strong abilities found themselves disoriented by her radiance. Moon-drunk, people called it.

Ascendance had a particularly heightened influence on Paladians. A sign of Paladia's deep connection to the gods, according to the Faith. Luc and Lila used to get so intoxicated from it, they'd have trouble walking straight, while Helena—in the true fashion of a foreign unbeliever—had only ever felt anxious, a heavy sense of dread pressing down on her.

That night, dinner failed to appear.

It was the first time in all the months of her imprisonment that there was no meal.

Something was wrong. Even with Ascendance, the necrothralls should still be present and somewhat active. She looked out into the courtyard and saw the two necrothralls stationed by the front doors, still as statues. But there were no sounds of footsteps outside the door, and when she left her room, no one appeared.

Helena went towards the foyer, staying within the path of Lumithia's silver gleam, constantly expecting one of the necrothralls to emerge. The shadows were black as ink, their edges crisp against the bright white light.

The foyer was empty, the white marble practically glowing under the moonlight. The dragon ouroboros on the floor gleamed as though it had scales, its dark body shimmering amid the white marble.

The weight of Lumithia was oppressive. Helena's resonance sang in her blood, as though attempting to overpower the nullification, creating a sensation like being in a cage too small to turn in.

She scanned the space, looking for any signs of movement. Necrothralls didn't need to be consciously maintained. According to research, they could be given orders and then they'd fulfil them repetitively ad infinitum. Even if Ferron was drunk off the Ascendance, they should operate as usual.

Unless Ferron was dead . . .

She froze in her tracks. What if the Eternal Flame had come during the Ascendance, taking advantage of his disorientation to kill him? The Undying at the party had said the murderer was like a ghost, in and out without a trace except for the body left behind.

She looked around the foyer more slowly. The stark silver-white and black surrounding her made her vision swim as she went towards the front door.

Her fingers trembled as she tried the knob. It wouldn't turn. She twisted at the lock beneath the handle, but it spun. She jerked, ignoring the pain that shot up her arms, trying to rattle the door, but it wouldn't budge. It was sealed shut.

Her chest clenched, but she forced herself to head towards the next exterior door.

Locked tight.

She moved through the house, breath coming faster and faster with each door she found sealed.

Was Ferron dead somewhere in Spirefell? Was she going to stumble across his corpse? She braced herself each time she entered a room, certain she'd find blood seeping from the shadows.

Surely the Eternal Flame wouldn't have left her, though. If they'd come here, they would leave a door or window unlocked. Give her that much at least.

She just had to find it.

She tried another door. Jerking at it over and over until a bright shock of pain left her hand numb.

The longer she searched, the more convinced she grew. Ferron was dead. She was trapped alone in this house.

Soon Stroud would come to retrieve her. Helena would be taken to Central, and if she wasn't pregnant, Stroud would find someone else to rape her.

Her arms were going numb, her head growing light. She went to the second floor and down the first corridor. She'd avoided this part of the house because both Ferron's and Aurelia's rooms were down that hallway.

If Ferron was dead, she had to see it with her own eyes. She had to know, or he'd haunt her.

She reached the first door on the left and stood trying to breathe, to make her hand steady enough to grasp the knob.

It opened silently.

The room was swallowed by shadows. The moonlight poured like a molten silver river through the windows. Her eyes went to the bed. It was empty.

As she stood in the doorway, the air in the room shifted.

She turned sharply towards the desk. It was mostly in shadows, the edge covered in bottles. Then a shadow moved, and the moonlight fell across Ferron's face, catching his pale hair and skin so that he seemed to glow.

"Helena," he said softly.

She stood frozen, not sure if she felt relief or terror at the sight of him.

He had never called her anything before. "The prisoner" was the only way he'd ever referred to her in all the months she had been at Spirefell.

Stroud called her Marino, but Ferron never called her anything. It had been so long since she'd heard anyone use her name.

"I—" She felt foolish. "I thought you were dead."

She should turn and leave, but he looked so unearthly that she couldn't tear her eyes away. His expression was one of utter despair, but as he stared at her, a look of starvation filled his eyes.

He stood slowly.

There was an uncharacteristic looseness to the way he moved. She looked past him, towards the desk, finally understanding.

He was drunk. Excessively intoxicated, under the influence of both Lumithia and actual inebriation. With his regenerative abilities, he probably needed the combination.

As he came towards her, she tried to back away, but then the wall met her shoulders, and there was nowhere to go, and then no space left between them.

He raised a pale hand, and his fingers wrapped around her throat.

His eyes were dark, ringed in glowing silver. Her pulse fluttered against his grip as he stared down at her.

It was no wonder the servants had disappeared. Maybe everyone else knew to hide from him on these nights. Except her.

"Oh, Marino." His thumb trailed along her neck, following the scar below her jaw. "If I'd known what pain you'd cause me, I never would have taken you."

He sighed, and she could smell the liquor on his breath as his head dipped closer. She had no idea what he meant, if she was supposed to apologise.

"But at this point I suppose I deserve to burn. I wonder if you'll burn, too."

His face was so close the words brushed against her lips, and his mouth crashed against hers.

CHAPTER 20

IT WAS A PUNISHING KISS.

The moment their lips touched, he crushed her body against his. The hand on her throat slid into her hair, tangling in the curls, gripping them tight as the kiss deepened, angling her head back so that he could consume her. He kept kissing her, hard enough to hurt but not bleed, like a storm poured down her throat.

When she was gasping for breath, he pulled away from her lips, kissing along her jaw and the side of her neck. His other hand curled around her waist.

Helena stood frozen in shock. Pliant and stunned in his possessive hands.

He pulled at her dress until the buttons snapped, giving way. Her back was against the wall, his knee pressed between her legs, pinning her by her skirts while his hands worked quickly, fabric ripping open, and she was stripped to the waist.

Cool air bit across her skin for an instant before the warmth of his hands and mouth erased it. An ache shuddered through her. His face was buried against her throat, lips pressed below her ear, kissing down the length of her neck to the juncture of her shoulder, nipping, and he reached a spot, and she—moaned.

The sound shattered the quiet.

They both froze. Ferron wrenched himself away.

Helena stared at him, too dazed to move. Moonlight poured through the window, a stark and damning silver path to where she was slumped against the wall, half stripped and—aroused.

Ferron's eyes were wide with shock, his pale hair falling across his face. As he stood staring at her, his eyes developed that eerie light to them that seemed to illuminate him from within. He ran a hand across his face, combing his hair back, and his jaw tightened, rolling, a look of derision spreading across his face even before he opened his mouth to speak.

Before he could say anything, a sob of horror tore from Helena. Her fingers scrabbled, trying desperately to pull her dress back on. It was rent open, buttons gone, so she clutched at the fabric, using her arms to cover herself, backing away until she reached the door.

She bolted, fleeing through the house as the reality of what she'd done nearly ripped her legs from beneath her.

She'd been receptive to Ferron.

He'd come towards her and kissed her and she had let him. In the moment, it hadn't even occurred to her to push him away. Instead, she'd melted at the warmth of being held.

Trapped in Spirefell, she was latching on to any glimpse of kindness, any sense of tenderness her mind could fabricate.

But it wasn't kindness.

He wasn't kind; he simply wasn't cruel. He wasn't as monstrous as he could be.

And for Helena's fracturing mind, an absence of cruelty was sufficient solace. For her starved heart, it was enough.

She fled to her room, tearing off the ruined dress in the damningly bright silver light, pulling on new clothes as if they could hide what she'd done.

She was better than this. She clutched at her chest, nails biting into her skin as if she could claw the resolve into herself.

"I'm so—sorry, Luc." Her voice was strangled with guilt.

She couldn't do this. She couldn't.

She wasn't going to let her mind trick her into wanting the attention of the person responsible for starting the war. His harm was incalculable. Everything. All of it. It was all his fault, but she could feel herself eroding, desperate to have something in her life that was not pain. That was not dead and gone.

But she couldn't.

She could bear the horror of being betrayed by her body, but she wouldn't let herself be betrayed by her mind.

She'd sooner break it.

She stared out the window at the enclosed courtyard, her inescapable prison, pressing her trembling hand against the cool glass and iron lattice, reaching for the power that was no longer there. There was nothing.

It was gone, like everything else.

She gave a broken, despairing sob and then drew her head back and smashed it against the glass and iron as hard as she could.

She did it again.

And again.

There was blood streaming into her eyes, but she kept going.

An arm closed around her waist, and a hand clamped over both wrists as she was dragged away from the window. A wash of red ran down the glass.

She fought, trying to twist her hands free, ignoring the pain that shot through them, digging her toes into the iron bars in the floor, trying to lunge free.

"Don't—don't." Ferron's voice was in her ear.

Her vision had gone red as blood flooded down her face, and she was screaming. All the guilt and anguish that she had pressed down swallowed her whole. She screamed as if she could shatter the world with it.

She wanted to be done.

She couldn't betray everyone. Luc. Lila. Soren. Matron Pace. Her father . . .

"I can't—" She strained again to get free, clawing empty air as she grasped towards the window.

His hand around her wrists let go, and then his palm was pressed against her forehead.

"No—!"

It was too late. His resonance poured through her. It was as if she were a tapestry. He found the threads of emotion and ripped them out.

He didn't sedate or paralyse her. It was worse, more violating than that. He took away all the things she felt, leaving her mind scrambling, trying to reconcile the dissonance.

It was like the tablets, except he only used his resonance to keep her there for as long as it took, until her body finally lost all the drive of those now vanished emotions.

The fight drained out of her. She hung limp against him. There was blood streaming down her face, dripping from her chin. His hand was stained with it when it fell away. He used just the tips of his fingers to heal the splits and gouges across her forehead. She could feel his resonance in her skull.

"Slight fracture," he said, and the remaining pain had mostly seeped away before he finally let her go.

She stood, empty and lost. He'd gutted her emotions so deeply, it was like trying to reach into the bottom of a well.

She looked towards the bloodstained window and considered a second attempt, but there was no point. He'd just do it again until she was hollowed out and compliant. A statue worn featureless.

Ferron turned her to face him, his eyes still silver-bright. "Why?"

She stared dully back at him; her head was still throbbing. At least something hurt.

"Why what?" she asked.

"Why this sudden need to go so far?" There was movement behind him. One of the necrothralls entered the room, both hands full, the door left open behind her. It was the older woman, but for a moment there was something strangely lifelike about her.

She was not as stilted and blank as Helena was accustomed to; she moved more like a lich.

Under Helena's scrutiny, she slowed and grew more mechanical as she brought a bowl and cloth over and began wiping Helena's face clean.

"Why not?" Helena said in a dead voice. "I've always been trying to kill myself. You know that."

His eyes narrowed. "You know as well as I do that that wouldn't have killed you."

She made no response.

"If you won't tell me, I'll look for myself," he said when she refused to reply.

Helena recoiled, jerking her face away from attempts to get the remaining blood from the corners of her eyes.

She opened her mouth several times before she could speak. "I think there's something wrong with me," she said at last.

He gave her a sidelong glance which communicated that this was obvious.

"It's a survival instinct or"—her body was so taut with humiliation that the words choked her—"a coping mechanism, maybe."

She looked away. "I read this research proposal once at the Institute. The author had an idea of trying to make test subjects emotionally attached to their—superior."

Her voice was straining, threatening to fail.

"He believed that with his methods, he could make subjects proactively compliant. That if they were conditioned with a sufficiently strong sense of dependence, they would begin to rationalise and justify any—any harm they suffered, and even try to form an emotional connection or even feelings towards the person controlling them, as a sort of survival instinct."

She felt as though she might pass out. She could feel the weight of Ferron's eyes on her.

"It was just a proposal, I don't know that there was any truth to it, but lately, I can't stop thinking about it," she said, her voice straining.

She stared across the room to the bloodstained window. "I would rather spend the rest of my life being raped in Central than spend a minute of it having feelings for you."

The air in the room seemed to freeze.

"Well," Ferron said after a long silence, "with luck you're pregnant, and there will be no need for either choice. You'll be left to yourself."

He turned away, and Helena's resolve shattered. Her hand darted out, catching hold of his coat to stop him.

Her body was shaking but she couldn't let go. She gripped harder. She didn't want to be alone; she couldn't bear it.

His hand rose, resting on her shoulder, and that was all it took. She crumpled, huddling closer. She could barely feel his fingers on her arm, but breathing no longer felt like a rope burn dragged through her lungs. She dropped her head against his chest.

She was so tired of the space around her always being cold and empty and endless.

Ferron's head suddenly whipped around as he shoved her away. Helena stumbled back, falling against the bed. His eyes had gone wide and there was something strained in his expression, his gaze flicking around the room and then towards the open door.

Then he gave a soft, bitter laugh.

"Oh, you're pathetic, aren't you?" he said. "Survival? Really?"

She didn't know what he meant.

He laughed again. "You expect me to believe that *you* suddenly care about surviving? When everyone in the Resistance has always been so rabid to die for their cause? But you're different? Even though you've been fantasising a grand murder-suicide for the two of us for months?"

He crouched in front of her, and she had never seen his face this vicious. There was a raw malice in his eyes. "No, the thing eating you alive isn't surviving or some subconscious instinct to appease me. What you can't bear is the isolation. The Eternal Flame's lonely little healer, with no one left to save. No one needs you, and no one wants you."

He smiled at her, his grin almost fanged. "That's all this is. You can't bear being alone. You'll do anything for the people who'll let you love them." He raised an eyebrow. "Wasn't that what the war was? You wanted to fight, but when they realised what you were, Ilva Holdfast decided you were better suited as Holdfast's sacrificial lamb. They put you on death row before Holdfast even saw combat."

"That's—not—how—it—was." Helena's hands were clenched into fists, the punctures in her palm beneath her fingers.

"That is exactly how it was. You know, Falcon Matias left his quarters almost entirely intact. He had a whole stack of correspondence from Ilva dated from when you were in training. She knew all she had to do was dangle Holdfast's life over your head, and you'd do whatever she asked." He tilted his head back. "You would have done anything for your friends: made all the hard choices, paid the price without complaint, whored yourself for the war effort. But tell me . . . because I am sincerely curious, what did Holdfast ever do for you to deserve it?"

She glared at him through burning eyes. "Luc was my friend. He was my best friend."

"So?"

Helena drew a shuddering breath, looking away. "My father gave up everything so I could study at the Institute, but—it was—it was hard. I—I didn't want him to know how hard it was." There was a feeling like a stone lodged in her throat. "But I was—so afraid I'd fail and I—I didn't know anyone. Luc could have been friends with anyone, but he picked me. I wouldn't have had anyone without him."

"So, what now?" Ferron said, straightening his coat, erasing the divots in the fabric where Helena's fingers had crumpled it. "I'm your replacement Holdfast, is that it? If anyone makes the mistake of speaking to you, you can't help but latch on to them?"

Helena shrank away, but Ferron wasn't done. "Let me be very clear, then. I don't want you. I *never* wanted you. I am not your *friend.* There is nothing I want more than the moment I'm finally done with you."

He turned and left.

WHEN STROUD RETURNED TWO WEEKS later, Helena sat wordlessly for examination. The time had passed in such a dull haze, she'd scarcely even been aware of the days. Like a ghost, she'd let the world slip by around her while she remained frozen in time.

"You're looking rather grey," Stroud said, her mouth quirking. "How did the High Reeve's efforts progress?"

Helena's throat closed and she said nothing, staring down at her lap, rolling the thin linen fabric of her slip between her fingers.

"Lie back," Stroud said, setting her satchel on the bedside table.

Stroud pulled Helena's slip up and aside, setting a cold hand on the lowest part of her abdomen. "It might be too early to tell, but sometimes I'm able to. In your case, the sooner we know, the better."

Helena's head pulsed with her heartbeat.

Stroud's eyebrows furrowed her face into rows of wrinkles as her resonance prodded deeper. A look of surprise swept across her face. "You're pregnant."

Helena felt nothing at first. The words were abstract. Conceptual.

Then they ran her through like a longsword.

There were no emotions built up inside her, though; Ferron had ripped them out, and she was still empty.

So she fell inwards.

It was like being forced deep under freezing water: no air, simply unending pressure that crushed her on all sides. Her heart surged until the roar of her blood was all she could hear.

Stroud was still speaking. Helena couldn't make out the words.

No.

Please, no.

No. No. No.

This was her fault. She'd complied, she hadn't struggled.

Stroud was still talking to her, speaking more loudly. The words muffled away, the sounds rounded and indecipherable.

The room blurred, threatening to dim. Helena's throat compressed, strangling her. A sharp stabbing pain ripped through her chest, something tearing open inside of her.

No. Please. No.

Stroud reached out, fingers pressing against the side of Helena's neck, and Helena started screaming.

Not with anguish as she had with Ferron, but shattering screams like a dying rabbit. Sharp, quick, repetitive. They kept bursting out of her.

Stroud seemed bewildered. She slapped Helena hard across the face.

Helena couldn't stop screaming.

Everything was bleeding together, the edges of her vision fading.

Ferron was in front of her, his hands on her shoulders.

"Calm down." His voice was hard, but his hands weren't. He pulled her close until the world narrowed into the space between them. "Breathe."

He squeezed her shoulders hard enough to reach through the numbness.

"Come on. You have to breathe."

Helena managed one ragged breath and burst into tears.

"No . . ." Her voice rose staccato. "No, no, no. Please. *No!*"

"Keep breathing, that's all you have to do. You breathe," Ferron said, his expression drawn. The muscles in his jaw were taut.

He turned to glare at Stroud without letting go.

"You know she is prone to fits. You cannot spring something like that on her," he said in a low voice.

Stroud straightened. "You said she was afraid of shadows. If she's going to keep adding things perpetually, you should make a list and put them up on the wall somewhere." She rolled her eyes, arms crossed at her chest. "Shouldn't she be glad to know the conception efforts are over?"

"No. And you should have known that. I'm beginning to think you're purposely torturing her. Why is that?"

"I'm not," Stroud said, too quickly.

Ferron's eyes narrowed. "Do be honest. You won't enjoy the way I take answers."

Stroud paled, eyes darting towards the door, as if measuring the distance. "The High Necromancer says that she's the one who bombed the West Port Lab. We'd won. It was our victory day, and she—she killed Bennet! His years of work. My work. All our experiments. She destroyed all of it."

There was a long pause, and Ferron's eyes turned to slits.

"I appreciate you have a fanatical devotion to his memory, but psychologically torturing a prisoner does very little when she has no memory that it even happened. Neither your program nor your rank grant you personal revenge on *my* prisoner."

He let go of Helena, turning on Stroud, pulling off his gloves. "You appear to have forgotten that I do not suffer fools tampering with her. I have gone to considerable expense and effort to maintain her environment, regardless of how inflated your sense of importance is over being outside of the lab when it exploded. The only reason you hold any rank whatsoever is because those more suited to the task are all dead. If anything, you should be grateful to her. You'd be no one now if anyone else had survived."

Stroud went white, nostrils flaring. "I worked at Bennet's side. My repopulation program is—"

"A farce. A convenient cover for the High Necromancer to achieve his ends and sate the endless appetites of his loyalists," Ferron sneered at her. "The only reason you survived was because you were a glorified lab assistant, sent off to retrieve new subjects. Without Shiseo, you'd have nothing to show for your time running Central. You think it isn't noticeable how little you've produced since his departure? It's no wonder you were so eager to launch your repopulation program."

Ferron had that same scathing, unrelenting intensity that he'd levelled upon Aurelia. "After you threatened to commandeer my assignation, I investigated your little project. You boast so freely to the papers, I was curious to see what remarkable data you must have to show for it. I was something of an academic myself once. Do you mind telling me about your controls? Or the statistics and historical data? No matter where I look, I can only find anecdotes in unsubstantiated newspaper articles."

"Things—are st-still in the early stages—" Stroud stammered, her face now a stark combination of white with red-stained cheeks. "I am a legitimate—"

"Your 'program' is a spectacle." Ferron's voice grew low and taunting. "Your lab assistants are better qualified than you are. Vivimancy is the only unique skill you possess, and I am far more competent in that field than you."

Ferron gestured towards the butler, standing near the door. "Show Stroud out, and don't ever let her inside this house again unless I'm present to personally escort her."

Stroud huffed, muttering about speaking to the High Necromancer, but her hands trembled violently as she gathered her files. When the door shut, Ferron turned back to Helena.

She could feel his stare without looking up.

He reached towards her, and she went stiff. He didn't touch her face; instead, his fingers slid along the nape of her neck, finding the dip of her skull.

She looked up then, but there was no emotion on his face. He could have been marble.

"I don't trust you to be conscious right now," he said.

She felt his resonance, delicate as the prick of a needle.

Heaviness swept through her like a black tidal wave, dragging her down.

"No . . ." she choked out, not sure what she was protesting. Everything.

But the world slipped from her grasp. She was dimly aware of her legs being lifted onto the bed, the duvet pulled over her.

"I'm so sorry."

CHAPTER 21

IT WAS A STRUGGLE TO WAKE AGAIN. The room was dim and heavy, Helena's vision sluggish and disoriented. It felt as if she had been unconscious for a long time. Her mouth was parched.

Turning her head, she spotted Ferron standing with the lady's maid. He was speaking quickly to her in a low voice, as though explaining something complicated.

Her eyes drifted shut, head swimming.

When they opened again, Ferron was looking at her, and the necrothrall was across the room.

Now that she wasn't panicking anymore, Helena thought she was going to be sick from the sight of him. She squeezed her eyes shut, curling into a defensive ball as he walked over.

"You are not allowed to hurt yourself or do anything that might cause an abortion or miscarriage," he said. "You'll be monitored full-time now, just in case your newfound desperation drives you to previously unknown heights of creativity."

The words were caustic, but he sounded more tired than anything else.

Helena said nothing, waiting for him to leave.

She curled protectively around her stomach. She knew there was little more than nothing there, but eventually there would be, and she could do nothing to stop it.

When she wouldn't get up for several days, Ferron returned.

"You cannot lie in bed moping for nine months," he said when she refused to acknowledge him. "You need to eat and go outside."

She ignored him.

"I have something for you," Ferron finally said.

Something heavy pressed onto the duvet. She glanced over.

There was a thick book beside her. *The Maternal Condition: An In-Depth Study on the Science and Physiology of Gestation.*

She looked away. "Why?"

"Because you'll wear your brain smooth if you don't find answers to all the things you want to know." He sounded resigned.

There was a pause; clearly, he'd hoped for some reaction.

"I'll expect you out of bed tomorrow," he said, and left.

When his footsteps had finally faded, Helena reached towards the book and almost shoved it off the bed, then hesitated and pulled it against her chest, holding it tightly.

The next day, she got out of bed and sat by the window, where the light was strongest. The book was brand new, with a leather spine that creaked when she lifted the cover and pages that still smelled of machine oil and ink.

It was a medical textbook, not a housewife's guide that would have avoided technical and medical terminology in favour of the more accessible explanations of pregnancy.

She was several chapters in when he returned.

She clutched at her book reactively, but he simply studied her.

"When did you last go outside?" he asked.

She looked down. "I—went out—"

She didn't know how long the necrothralls retained information, whether they could observe the passage of time. If she lied, would he know?

"Last week," she said.

"No, you didn't. You haven't been outside in weeks."

She stared down at her book, not blinking until the words began to blur. She didn't want to go outside. She didn't want to see the spring or smell the scent of the world coming to life.

"Put your shoes on."

She stood, holding her book tightly against her chest. He sighed with irritation.

"You cannot bring that; it weighs nearly five pounds."

Helena only held it tighter. Other than her shoes and gloves, it was her only possession.

Ferron gripped his temples as though he had a migraine.

"No one is going to steal your book," he said as if he was trying very hard to be patient. He gestured around. "Who even would? If they do, I will buy you a new one. Leave it."

She placed it carefully on the table, fingers lingering on the cover a moment longer before she went to retrieve her boots.

The courtyard was reborn by spring. There was grass, and little red buds covered the trees. The vines on the house had bright-green leaves, transforming their previously gruesome appearance.

It was beautiful, Helena couldn't deny it, but every detail felt tainted and poisonous.

Ferron said nothing, but he walked with her around the courtyard a few times and then back to her room.

As he turned to leave, she forced herself to speak.

"Ferron." Her voice wavered.

He was already in the hall, but he paused and turned slowly back. His expression was closed, eyes guarded.

"Ferron," she said again, voice barely more than a whisper. Her jaw trembled uncontrollably, and she gripped the post of the bed, trying to steady herself. "I—I will never ask anything of you—"

His expression went flat and cold, and something inside her broke but she kept speaking.

"You can do anything you want to me. I'll never ask for any mercy from you, but please—don't do this . . ."

He stood, impassive.

"It—this baby—it'll be half yours. Don't let them—" she said in a broken voice. "I'll do anything you want—I'll—I'll—"

She didn't have anything to offer. Her heart was racing too fast, and her voice cut off when she couldn't breathe. She clawed at her chest, trying to force her lungs to inhale.

Ferron's eyes flickered, and he stepped into the room, shutting the door. He walked over and took her by the shoulders, practically holding her up as she fought to breathe.

"No one is going to hurt your baby," he said, meeting her eyes.

She gave a small gasp of relief. It was what she'd so desperately wanted him to say.

She dropped her head, her hair falling and concealing her face.

"Really?" She let her desperation fill her voice.

"Nothing will happen to it. You have my word. Calm down."

What an empty promise. There was no point in begging. He had every reason to lie to her, to say whatever was necessary to lull her into compliance, to keep her calm and docile with reassurances that meant nothing.

She jerked free, backing away.

"You'll say anything, won't you?" she said, her voice shaking. "I guess you have to, whatever it takes to 'maintain my environment.'"

She wrapped her arms around herself and sank to the floor.

"Stay away from me," she said. "I'll only exercise and eat if I don't have to see you."

SHE WENT OUTSIDE ALONE THE next day, intent on poisoning herself with everything and anything she could find. Spring was a good time for it. With a garden so overgrown, there was a chance of white hellebore being somewhere in the overgrowth. She crawled through the beds, ignoring the pain in her hands and arms, searching everywhere, but there was nothing abortive or poisonous.

Even the crocuses and snowbells that she was certain she'd seen were gone, the soil loose in their wake. She raked through it with her fingers, but there wasn't a single bulb left behind.

She went out searching every day, desperate to find some overlooked sprout as she began to develop headaches and nausea. What was briefly a grinding pain in the back of her skull seemed to expand by the hour. It worsened week by week until she couldn't read, her vision swimming in an aura of pain.

The heavy winter drapes were kept closed, blotting out all light. She ate less and less. When she couldn't eat or drink or get out of bed for two days, Ferron reappeared.

"You said you'd eat," he said.

She scoffed, and her head throbbed so painfully it was as though someone had driven a metal rod into her skull. Her vision turned blood red. She moaned, hardly able to breathe until it passed.

"If I could even think of anything that sounded edible, I doubt I could keep it down," she said in a strained voice. "Sickness isn't unusual in early pregnancy. It'll pass. Statistical probability indicates I'm unlikely to die from it."

She felt the air shift as Ferron stiffened, as if her words had startled him.

"My mother nearly did," he said.

She felt as if there was something she was meant to realise at the comment, but her head hurt too much to wonder.

Ferron didn't leave. He was still standing beside her bed when she fell into exhausted sleep.

He brought Stroud a few days later.

"I can't imagine that the Toll of the animancy is already manifesting," she was saying loudly as she entered the room. "It generally doesn't develop until the final months. However, she was a healer. Perhaps she has less vitality left than we'd realised."

She stopped beside Helena, not really looking at her at all. She flipped the duvet back and shoved Helena's nightgown up to her stomach without warning.

Helena flinched, and Ferron looked away.

"Now, it's still early, but I think—" Stroud rummaged in her bag and pulled out a resonance screen.

Stroud held the screen up in her left hand while her right rested on Helena's lower abdomen. Stroud's resonance sank through her skin, and the gas within the glass morphed into a series of nebulous shapes. In the negative space, there was something small, pulsing so rapidly it seemed to flutter.

Helena stared, stricken.

"There." Stroud sounded pleased. "Your heir—" She caught herself. "Well, progeny, I suppose we should say."

Ferron's face had gone ashen.

Stroud pulled her hand away. "It all appears normal, nothing irregular that I can detect. Have you checked her brain recently?"

Ferron shook his head.

Stroud clicked her tongue but nodded. "Given the seizures she's had, it's probably for the best not to disrupt things at such a fragile juncture." She rested her hand on Helena's head, sending out the barest wave of resonance. Helena shuddered from the pain. "If she really is an animancer, I suspect the headaches are self-inflicted, so there's not really anything to be done about it. In fact, it might prompt the recovery of her memories."

Ferron's eyes narrowed. "What do you mean?"

Stroud pulled the covers back over Helena. "If the High Necromancer is correct, she's keeping the memories hidden by internalising her resonance. Which means that she's probably been putting most of her energy into maintaining it. It might explain her lethargy, since it's unlikely that it's being done efficiently. Now she's pregnant. She doesn't have the strength to sustain both, especially if this embryo is an animancer. The High Necromancer says that his power was so great, he'd claimed every drop of his mother's life while still in the womb and was birthed from her corpse upon the funeral pyre. We'll have to be sure to maintain Marino. Perhaps if we're lucky, we'll end up with both a baby and the memories before she succumbs to the Toll."

"You didn't think to mention this until now?" Ferron's words were fine and sharp as a razor.

Stroud gave a tight shrug. "It's not as though I have much data to theorise on." She shot him a snide look. "You should ask your father. He's our resident expert, you know."

Something unreadable flashed across Ferron's face. "I wouldn't rely on his cooperation in this case."

"Well, I can have an intravenous drip put in, but that's as much as I can do."

Stroud left, but Ferron stayed behind.

Helena closed her eyes. Now she understood: She was expected to die, and they'd all known. She only hoped it would happen too early for the pregnancy to be viable.

That fluttering negative space in the resonance screen danced in her mind's eye.

Her chest tightened, heart pounding as if she were running.

The mattress shifted, and cool fingers touched her cheek, brushing back her hair and resting against her forehead.

A few days later, a doctor visited, and an intravenous drip was inserted into her left arm. Her days became ruled by the unending drip of saline and drugs inside the glass vial.

The morning sickness seemed to fade, but the headaches didn't; if anything, they grew worse. Helena could barely move. She was poked and prodded by countless doctors, but none offered useful advice.

When they'd gone, Ferron would sit on the edge of the bed and smooth her hair. Sometimes he would take her hand, his fingers moving absently against hers. The first time he did it, she thought he was playing with her fingers; then she realised he was massaging them.

He always started at her palms, careful not to bend her wrists or bump the manacles, working slowly to her fingertips, knuckle by knuckle. It made them spasm less, so she let him, but she told herself she didn't like it.

She grew thin, until the manacles were loose enough that she could see the tubes where they penetrated her wrists, and the necrothrall maid who most frequently watched her grew fretful to the point that Helena began to doubt that the woman was a necrothrall at all.

She'd hover over Helena, wordlessly offering mint and ginger tisanes, clear broths, and bits of toast, giving her sponge baths, and carefully combing and plaiting Helena's hair into a loose braid so it wouldn't mat. She seemed strangely experienced in nursing for a lady's maid.

Ferron began to hover, too. He had to leave to hunt and perform whatever duties Morrough still gave him, but he was often in her room. Sometimes he'd come in, completely filthy, verifying that she was still alive before even cleaning up.

He didn't speak or meet her eyes, but he was there constantly. Sitting sometimes for hours with her hand in his as if it could keep her from slipping away.

Stroud visited again when Helena was barely conscious. She heard comments about not expecting it to take such a toll already, blaming the transmutation in Helena's brain, and complaining that it was far too early for viability.

Atreus was mentioned again.

Helena dreamed that her room was filled with moonlight, except instead of coming through the windows, the light came from Ferron. His eyes had that eerie silver glow as he sat next to her, her hand in his once more, but this time her palm was pressed against his chest so that she could feel his heartbeat.

She couldn't help but think something was supposed to happen, but nothing did. The dead sensation in her wrists was like a pit.

She felt like an hourglass, the final grains of sand finally running down. It was almost over. She could feel herself slipping away.

The room flipped as she was dragged up and crushed tight.

"Stay . . . please . . . stay."

The light grew and the strangest sensation came over her, a glow inside her chest, familiar even though she was certain she'd never experienced anything like it before. The constant feeling of strain inside her chest, like a thread pulled to the verge of snapping, slowly faded away.

She closed her eyes, drawing a struggling breath, and the dream dissolved into nothingness.

HELENA WOKE WITH A START, panic gripping her. She pushed herself up in bed, swaying as the room swam around her. She braced herself, ripping the needle from her arm, and tumbled from the bed.

There was something important she needed to do—

Her legs nearly gave out when they hit the floor. She stumbled, catching herself. A shock of pain lanced through her arms, but she ignored it.

She was supposed to be doing something.

What was it, though?

She couldn't remember.

She was waiting. She needed to be ready for . . .

The knowledge danced just beyond reach, but she could feel it.

Don't break.

She'd promised . . .

What? What had she promised? *Think, Helena.*

She *had* to remember now. She pressed her hands against her temples.

There were red spots dancing in her vision. Pain ballooning until it was larger than she was.

Ferron appeared in front of her. "What's—"

She stared at him wildly. "I'm waiting—I promised I'd wait—"

Pain sheared through her brain, and the world split in two.

When her vision cleared, Ferron was still there, but his eyes had turned a flat grey, his hair darkened by shadows as he lunged towards her.

She fell back instinctively, fingers scrabbling, trying to find—

He vanished.

The room splintered.

Ilva Holdfast was sitting in front of her, her expression tense. "*We're losing the war.*"

Before Helena could answer, Ilva was gone. Helena was falling.

No . . . She wasn't falling.

Ferron had her by the throat, and he was slamming her onto the floor. His eyes narrowed into slits.

Cold water filled her mouth.

Everything was dark, ice-cold. She was surrounded by water. She could see Luc. He was clawing at his own throat, fingers leaving gouges in his skin.

Lila, with her hair cropped short, curled up against the wall, crying. "*I made a mistake.*"

"Surely I deserve something in return, to warm my cold heart."

A hard kiss where she was pinned against a wall.

"You seem pleased, to have successfully whored yourself."

Matron Pace standing, looking over her shoulder. "*Lila Bayard is not the only person that the Eternal Flame would suffer greatly for losing.*"

"*You're mine. You swore yourself to me.*" The words were growled in her ear.

Jan Crowther, alive, his eyes narrowed and furious. "*You're more likely to destroy the Eternal Flame than save it.*"

Helena herself crying. "*I'm sorry. I'm sorry. I'm sorry I did this to you.*"

Everything was falling in fragments around her as Ferron reappeared, his face white with rage, his eyes glowing that bright unearthly silver.

"I have warned you, if something happens to you, I will personally raze the Eternal Flame. That isn't a threat. It is a promise. Consider your survival as much a necessity to the Resistance as Holdfast's. If you die, I will kill every single one of them."

It was like falling. The past broke free, surging through her mind and swallowing her.

PART TWO

CHAPTER 22

Four Years Prior
Solstice Eve, 1785 PD

On the upper plateau of the East Island, not far from the Alchemy Institute, stood one of the few freestanding houses on the Paladian islands.

Solis Splendour, the Bayard family's grand old house, was one of the few to survive the city's stratospheric architectural climb. As most of the city gave way to vast, interconnected towers, climbing ever higher, the Bayards had kept their original home on its original land. The city and the more newly monied loomed high overhead, but Solis Splendour had never tried to rise, content to flourish in the shadow of the Alchemy Institute and Tower.

The Bayards were such fixtures at the Institute that Helena sometimes forgot how near their family seat was, and how wealthy they were.

Even in a war, barely maintained, Solis Splendour was beautiful and startling in size, even as a convalescent home. Its many spacious rooms were now filled with rows of beds for those too injured to return to combat, so that Headquarters would not overflow with the wounded. Rhea Bayard had been offering such care even before her husband became one of the permanent residents.

Helena stood at the bottom of the steps leading to the front door, trying to summon the will to knock. The air was so cold that her nose had gone numb, and her fingertips ached through her kid gloves. The first day of winter, but it had already been bitterly cold for months.

The hibernal solstice was supposed to be all about looking ahead to brighter days, but after five years of war, it was difficult to believe that things would ever get better no matter how much the days lengthened or warmed.

When Helena was too cold to keep loitering outside, she ascended the steps and rapped hesitantly.

The door immediately swung open, revealing Sebastian Bayard, Lila and Soren's uncle. He was a tall man, with an agile build, and pale skin and hair that almost blended into each other. The only colour to him was his soft blue eyes that always seemed to be searching for something that wasn't there.

He'd been Principate Apollo's paladin primary, among other things, and now, in reserve, he always had a sort of tragic alertness about him, like a dog waiting for its master to return.

"Helena," Sebastian said, inviting her in, "we're glad you made it. I know Rhea hoped you would."

Helena's stomach twisted into a hard knot as she stepped into the warm interior of the house, discarding her coat but leaving on her gloves.

Several children scampered by, quiet and wan-faced but with shining eyes. Some were so young, they'd never known a day outside the war. They were all accustomed to staying out from underfoot and minding themselves, but solstice was magical for them.

The front rooms were still functional, and they were full of people, some with wheeled chairs, crutches, or bandages, and others in good health, if not spirits. The mood of the party failed to match the cosy light and warmth, or the cheerful music emanating from the gramophone; the voices and conversation were all low and sombre.

"There she is." Lila's voice suddenly broke through the hum as she rose from the far side of the sitting room. Her pale hair was braided as always into a crown around her head, which made her seem even taller than she was. Groups parted as Lila crossed the room, hopping agilely on her gleaming prosthetic leg to avoid chairs and tables.

It was uncharacteristically showy, but Helena knew that Lila was desperate to prove that she was more than sufficiently recovered from her injury and ready to return to combat.

The decision would be made by the Council in three days. There would be a full hearing, and as healer and one of the alchemists involved in developing the titanium base of the prosthetic, Helena would be among those consulted about whether Lila was competent to resume her duties as paladin primary.

Lila's ice-blue eyes scanned Helena's face in an instant. "You look nearly frozen. Come over here. Luc's got a fire, he'll make it warm for you."

They reached the group that Lila had broken away from, all members of the same battalion. They were gathered around the fireplace, and in the centre sat Luc, their god-touched Principate, slouched like a schoolboy and teasing the flames with his fingertips. With the flick of his fingers, the flames took shapes and danced across the logs like acrobats, their light gilding him.

Luc was smaller in both build and height than almost all of them, barring a few of the girls. Even Lila's twin brother, Soren, who was regarded as small for a paladin, had a good several inches on Luc.

People said it was something about pyromancers, they just tended to be slight, but the sneering few pointed out that the Principate being expected to marry someone shorter than him might also have something to do with their generationally dwindling stature.

Helena knew almost nothing about Luc's mother, much less how tall or short she'd been. She'd died of a wasting sickness when he was too young to remember her.

"Make some space for Helena," Lila said, nudging her forward. "Hel, I'll get you some mulled wine, that'll get you warm."

Lila disappeared again.

"I don't think I've ever seen Lila so helpful," said one of the boys, a wry smirk on his face.

Helena wasn't sure of his name. He was newer. A defence specialist.

His predecessor had been killed during the same battle against Blackthorne that cost Lila her leg.

"Shut up, Alister," Luc and Soren, who was sitting just behind Luc, said simultaneously.

Fire flashed in Luc's eyes, while Soren seemed to lengthen like an ominous shadow. Everyone glared at Alister.

Alister shifted and forced a smile. "It was a joke. I think we'd all be acting just like her if we needed a hearing to resume combat. I just don't know why she's worried. She could have lost an arm, too, and she'd still fight better than most of us."

Soren relaxed, rolling his eyes, but Luc stared stonily at the fire.

Penny Fabien had shifted her legs to the side and, meeting Helena's eyes, patted a spot next to Luc, but Helena hesitated.

Sit there and in a matter of days, Ilva Holdfast would call Helena in "just for a chat," and during the conversation she'd make a series of remarks about how tenuous things presently were. About the need to make sacrifices, and how sometimes caring about someone meant staying away from them. She would talk about loyalty, how the members of the Eternal Flame had followed the Holdfasts for generations. The Principate was held to certain standards, and it would be devastating to the cause if their faith in Luc was shaken; if he seemed to prioritise others more than them.

Helena shook her head, mumbling something about finding Lila as she backed away.

The next room was quieter, filled with more severely wounded convalescents. They paid no attention to her.

Sitting among them was former general Titus Bayard.

Although he'd never been a paladin himself, he was taller and broader than his brother, with a wide forehead filled with furrows and creases. He'd served as military commander for the Eternal Flame for most of Luc's life, training and approving new members, including his own children, choosing their positions and combat designations.

Now, with that same intense care and concentration, he very slowly wound a ball of yarn in his huge hands.

"Hello, Titus," Helena said in a low, even voice, kneeling beside him. "It's Healer Marino, do you remember me?"

He gave no indication of hearing her. He only ever minded Rhea.

"Do you mind if I look at your brain? Won't hurt a bit, just a little touch."

He gave a noncommittal grunt. She slipped a glove off and reached out, fingers trailing along the wide scar that started at his temple and disappeared into his hair. Her resonance unspooled from her fingertips like tendrils of energy cast in a net, examining the tissue and bone and into the brain, looking desperately for any signs of change.

Everything was the same.

There was almost nothing wrong with Titus physically. Even his brain showed little sign of anything being wrong with it except inactivity. All the carefully, perfectly regenerated tissue Helena had spent shift after shift reconstructing had saved his life but trapped him inside his own mind. She didn't know how to get him out. If he was even still in there.

"You're very strong," she said conversationally as she smoothed his hair to conceal the scar again.

His concentration on the ball of yarn broke off briefly so he could give her a grimacing smile. Their eyes met, and she felt the same pang in her chest again, an overwhelming desire to tell him, *I'm sorry. I was trying to save you. I didn't mean to do this to you.*

"Helena."

Her stomach clenched in dread as she turned to face Rhea Bayard. Titus's wife was a tall woman with raven-like features, all long and sharp, and deep-set green eyes that Soren had inherited. According to the stories, she'd been an alchemist at the Institute, and a good one, but she'd retired to marry and have children.

"You came in so quietly, I didn't realise you were here. Have you already seen Titus?" Rhea was smiling, but it was strained.

Helena knew when she received the invitation that this was why she was invited. Rhea lived in the desperate hope that eventually Helena would find a way to heal Titus. She used to bring him to the hospital constantly, even after everyone else had given up, convinced that with time and new science, someone with Helena's abilities could restore him.

Helena had been afraid that Rhea would blame her for failing to heal Titus, but her enduring conviction that Helena would find a cure felt worse at times.

"Yes, just now," Helena said, even though she knew that wasn't what Rhea was really asking. "You take such good care of him."

Rhea's smile faded when Helena added nothing else. She looked down, twisting her fingers.

"Good. Good. Yes. That's good to hear." Rhea cleared her throat as she stepped over to a shelf and took a package down, holding it out. "I'm glad you came. You missed the earliest festivities, but this one's for you."

Helena stared at the outstretched gift, her face growing hot. "Oh, but I didn't—I didn't realise there'd be—presents. I didn't bring—"

"You keep my children alive. We'll call it even."

Helena sat down and pulled off the paper string, opening it. Inside the package lay a knitted green pullover, intricately made with raised patterns reminiscent of alchemy symbols. "Oh. This is beautiful. This is too much; I can't take something like this."

Rhea seemed pleased by how stunned Helena was. "I wasn't sure about your colours, or your resonance aside from titanium, but Lila mentioned you like the barrens, so I thought the green would suit."

"This must have taken so much time."

Rhea sighed. "Knitting keeps my hands busy. My parents are from the lowlands in Novis; lots of sheep there. My mother always sends me skeins along with her letters, trying to convince me to bring Titus to live with them." She pressed her lips together. "He would like the sheep. But the twins are here. Besides, there's not much chance of a cure for Titus if we go."

Helena ran her fingers along the patterns nervously. "I'll try to do some more research, see if I can find anything new."

"Thank you—" Rhea began but then broke off. "Titus, no! We don't do that."

Helena watched as Rhea hurried over and tried to pry someone's crutch from Titus's hands.

"Helena, can you find Sebastian?" Rhea said, her voice forcefully cheery as she half wrestled with her husband, who, while usually gentle, was twice her size and sometimes threw tantrums.

Helena hurried from room to room, looking for Sebastian. He was in the little entry at the front door, avoiding everyone under the pretence of acting as a welcoming committee.

Helena barely opened her mouth before he seemed to know. "Titus?"

He was gone in an instant. Helena stood, clutching the knitted pullover in her hands. Her opportunity to exit was clear before her. No one would notice if she slipped away.

"You're already going?"

She looked around guiltily and found Luc standing behind her, two mugs of mulled wine in his hands.

"I have another shift soon," she said, grateful that it was the truth. Luc had always teased her for being a terrible liar. Her face, he'd once said, was disastrously honest.

His eyebrows knit together. "They have you back-to-back like that today?"

"Not usually, but everyone wanted the solstice off," she said. "And they know it's not really a tradition in the south, so they just assume I don't have any plans, and—they're right. I don't really have people like they do."

His eyebrows rose. "Am I not people anymore?"

She managed a smile. "Of course you are, but you're busy. Everyone wants you."

He dropped down on the slender bench by the door and held out one of the mugs. "Stay. You haven't even been here ten minutes."

She glanced towards the other rooms to see if anyone had noticed, knowing they undoubtedly had because Luc would always be immediately missed. If Soren and Lila weren't shadowing him, that was only because they already knew where he was and were giving him the space he'd asked for.

She could hear Lila in the next room, her voice raised dramatically, telling the story of Orion and the great battle against the Necromancer during the first Necromancy War. The children were scampering in from all corners to listen.

Lila had a mysterious allure when it came to children; she could be in armour and covered in blood, and toddlers would still want her to pick them up. And she would, and a minute later she'd be playing peekaboo with her helmet visor.

Soren was standing near the doorway, wearing a look of grave interest in a story he'd heard a hundred thousand times. Helena caught the corner of his eye for an instant before he pretended not to notice her or Luc.

This interception was carefully coordinated.

"I miss you," Luc said as she took the mug, resigning herself to Ilva's impending lecture. Luc nudged her with his elbow as she sat beside him. "Every time I look for you, you're busy or slipping off somewhere."

She gripped the mug tighter. "Well, my job starts when yours ends. That's probably why," she said. "But I'm always here when you need me."

She sipped the wine. It was warm but also sour and barely spiced; the shortages were eating into all the supplies.

"Same goes for you. Just because you're a healer doesn't mean you don't get breaks. If you're getting called in for too many shifts, tell me. I'll get it fixed."

She shook her head. "Don't worry, Ilva always looks after me."

After all, Ilva considered Helena a vital asset. The Eternal Flame had only one healer, and while they couldn't afford to lose her, they also couldn't afford *not* to use her. They couldn't take any more losses.

"That's good. It's nice knowing there's one person I never have to worry about," he said, eyes fluttering closed for a moment, exhaustion visible in his face.

Lila's voice rose, deep and dramatic. "The dead surrounded them on all sides. Orion and his faithful paladins stood back-to-back. Darkness all around, the only light the fire in Orion's hands . . ."

Luc sighed. "You're going to clear Lila, aren't you?"

Helena peered into her mug. "She's ready. There's no reason not to, and she's the best at what she does, which is keeping you alive."

There came a series of gasps from the children in the next room as Lila described the paladins battling horde after horde of necrothralls while Orion fought the Necromancer alone.

"What if the reason is that I don't want her cleared?" Luc said, his voice barely audible.

Helena looked over. Now he was the one avoiding her eyes, his jaw jutting stubbornly forward.

"You know," he said, "when she took the vows, I thought, at least if she was always there to protect me, it meant I'd be there to protect her, too." He rubbed the ignition ring on his thumb against the rim of the mug. "But I'm not—not always. She acts like that's the job, getting chopped into bits in front of me. She's already saved my life more times than I can count, and that's supposed to be fine"—his eyebrows furrowed together—"because I'll win the war, so it'll all even out in the end. Just like Orion. Except I don't know *how* to do that. And she just keeps getting hit and I'm supposed to keep letting her."

He swallowed hard.

There were too many people, too many lives, balancing on his shoulders. Everyone was always watching, waiting for him to intuitively manifest a miracle like the one Lila was presently describing in vivid detail to gasps and cheers.

Luc's sense of failure ran through him like a fault line, waiting to rupture. Every death and every scar that Lila and Soren bore adding to it.

He spoke again. "Everyone keeps saying, *We're almost there,* and *It has to get worse before it gets better,* and *It's a crucible,* and I just have to prove true . . . but what if I can't? What if that's why things are like this?"

He looked at her, his face stricken, guilt written across it, all the doubt he was not supposed to feel. The Principate was supposed to be unwavering, faith manifest, Sol's divinity come to earth.

Everyone went out ready to die for him at any moment, so how could he betray their faith by doubting himself.

"Holy white flames rose everywhere, consuming every necrothrall," Lila's voice boomed grandly.

Sitting there beside Helena, Luc was an orphan with centuries of legacy resting on his shoulders, and no more idea of how to single-handedly win a war than anyone else.

Helena shook her head. "Luc, I don't believe in you because anyone ever said I should. I'm here because there's no one braver or kinder than you. You're all the good things that anyone ever hopes to be. We're not here because you tricked us." She touched his wrist with her gloved fingers for just a moment. "The reason we believe in you is because if you're not good enough, then no one is."

He shook his head. "Orion was. All my forefathers were. Nothing like this ever happened to any of them. A necromancer showed up, and they stopped them, simple as that, but I've tried everything, and I can't—"

"Their wars were easier than this one," Helena said forcefully. "None of them were anything like this, except maybe Orion's, but even then, it was simpler, because, like Lila just said, he could fill the valley with fire that reached the mountaintops and burn down everything. Even if you could do that, there's a city with thousands and thousands of people around you. Orion only fought one necromancer in his whole life. There's no reason to think any of them could fight this war better. You're doing your best, and if the gods don't see that, they're blind—"

"Don't say things like that," he said, cutting her off. "That's not helping."

Her mouth snapped shut, and she didn't know what else to say; nothing ever seemed to be right.

"Where the Necromancer had stood, there was nothing but ashes," Lila said in a climactic voice.

"What was the Necromancer's name?" came a small piping voice.

"No one knows," Lila said with an air of mystery. "Anyone who knew, he'd killed. Where was I? Oh yes, even now, Orion's whole body was arrayed in holy sunfire, and using his pyromancy, he took that fire and lit a brazier."

"I thought you said everything was burned up in the great waves of fire except the paladins and Orion," the little voice interrupted again.

There was a mixture of laughter and shushing.

"Well, as it happened, this iron brazier was not burned away in the great waves of fire," Lila said in a mock-solemn voice. "And so Orion placed the holy fire into it, and before his paladins and the dawning sun, he swore a solemn oath that so long as he and his descendants drew breath, the fire would not go out, and the flames would be carried to destroy the rot of necromancy wherever it festered, and—"

"I thought there was a stone," came the piping voice once more, apparently revolting against the shushing. "When my dad tells the story, *his* version has a stone in it."

"Well, this version doesn't have a stone," Lila said quickly, trying to finish the story. "Anyway—"

"I like it better when it has the stone," contributed another small voice.

Helena set the mug down, glancing at Luc, who was clearly distracted by Lila's squabbling over his family history with a pack of children.

"Luc, I have to go now," she said. "Don't lose hope, though. We're always here for you. The days will get brighter."

He gave a wan smile and a listless nod. "I know."

The nearly moonless sky loomed overhead as she stepped outside, bright with winter stars. She let out a harsh breath which rose like a fog, blotting them out.

She turned her eyes to the Alchemy Tower ahead, still and always illuminated by Orion Holdfast's Eternal Flame.

Luc was the only Holdfast left now to keep that promise and sustain the fire, but after five years, the war had become a battle of attrition. No amount of healing, or fire, or paladins was enough to win against the ever-growing army of necrothralls.

She stared at the beacon of light, heart clenching at the thought that it might go out, that Luc would be the last because no one could save him from his destiny.

She looked down at her hands, curling her fingers inside the gloves and slowly opening them, drawing a deep breath.

"You promised you'd do anything for him."

CHAPTER 23

Februa 1786

Helena's jaw was taut, her teeth grinding together as her fingers twisted through the air, pulling, tugging at the feeble connection threatening to melt away from her.

Her right hand was cramping, sharp pain shooting along the tendon to her elbow, but if she broke the connection, let her hand rest for an instant, her patient would die.

"Come on," she said under her breath as her fingers spun through the air, refusing to give up. "Where is it?"

As if she'd needed to just verbalise her desperation, she found it: internal bleeding where the pressure was pooling.

"Got you. Got you," Helena said with a little gasp of relief, her fingers moving faster now, manipulating the tissue, repairing the artery, drawing the blood away so that she could focus on the task before her: a rib cage which had been split apart.

She'd been transmuting regenerative lung tissue with one hand and maintaining the heartbeat with the other when she'd realised there was something else wrong, and now, finally, her resonance was not screaming at her that death was imminent.

She gave herself a moment to flex her right hand once before guiding the shattered bones back over the new lungs, knitting together the places where they'd broken, regenerating what was missing. She pushed the mangled skin back, repairing it as best she could. Finally, she rested both hands on the healed chest, drawing it up, making it rise for breath, letting out her own sigh.

There would still be weeks of recovery ahead, at least a month of convalescence at Solis Splendour. The lung tissue was new and delicate, the repaired bones fragile, but he would live to fight another day.

She let herself look at the face, now that she knew he wouldn't die, checking the intravenous drip before she gestured for the medics to take over again.

He was young. She knew so many of the faces, but she'd never seen his before. A new recruit, or maybe newly of age. No, he couldn't be of age. He looked barely fourteen.

She had no time to wonder. She had to wash her hands, douse them in antiseptic, and move to the next bed with a ribbon designating the need for intercession.

Don't look at the face, she reminded herself as the medics and nurses scattered to make space for her.

She didn't know anymore how long she'd been on shift. A day or two? It was hard to say.

It had been mostly battle injuries at first, cuts and gouges, stab wounds, broken bones. Then it became burns, charred-off limbs, scorched lungs, skin a charcoal crisp that cracked to ooze blood.

The hospital smelled like roast meat, blood, the stench of gut wounds, and the lavender oil they disinfected with.

Helena used to like the smell of lavender.

Her last patient, she lost. The organs failed more quickly than Helena could regenerate them. She was so tired that her hands trembled uncontrollably with every twist of her resonance. She wasn't fast enough.

Her resonance rebounded on her, a pulse of energy like a blow straight through her chest. Ghostly cold rushed through her and dissipated.

Gone.

Helena slumped, breathing unsteadily, wanting to scream. A minute more and she could have—

She pushed herself up, hands shaking as she stepped back, looking at the face before she could stop herself.

The body was so badly burned, she couldn't tell if it had been a boy or a girl. It was horrifyingly small. She looked around, searching for another ribbon, but finding none.

She walked stiffly towards the nearest wall, her knees giving out. Her mouth was parched, and her hands shook as an orderly paused and handed her a cup of water.

She was one of the young ones, with bright-blue eyes. New enough to still be eager at her job.

Helena clutched the cup in her hands, staring dully across the casualty ward, the rows of beds, and the piles of blood-soaked clothes and bandages and sheets on the floor. She could feel that same blood on her face and hair. Only her hands were mostly clean. The only thing she'd washed in at least a day.

She pressed her hand against her chest, finding the sunstone amulet under her filthy uniform. The fabric was so stiff with blood, it almost cracked as she squeezed the amulet, trying to ground herself.

"You should have been on break hours ago."

She looked up to find Matron Pace standing beside her, mopping her forehead with a mostly clean cloth, a chipped cup in her other hand.

The matron's apron was as blood-spattered as Helena's, and red-stained wisps of greying hair clung to her flushed, swollen face.

"I didn't see you on break, either." Even Helena's voice shook with exhaustion.

Pace had been in medicine longer than the Paladian Central Hospital had existed. Helena heard she'd been a midwife before the national medical licensing laws came into effect. Women needed alchemy certification to qualify, and Pace wasn't an alchemist, so she'd become a nurse.

Helena sat, the joints in her hands aching from the constant repetitive flexing. Inside her chest, there was a feeling like a rope pulled taut. She dreaded the thought of beginning to feel her feet again.

"Go rest," Matron Pace said.

Helena shook her head, her eyes fastened on the door where any new casualties would be brought in. "I should stay in case of an emergency. Is Maier still in the surgery?"

Maier was one of the most accomplished alchemical surgeons Paladia had ever produced. He'd left a hospital in Novis to join the Resistance and keep their hospital running after the Undying wiped out all the field hospitals and clinics.

Maier was a genius surgeon and a hard worker, but also short-tempered, and he did not like women. Unfortunate when the war hospital was predominantly staffed and run by women. He kept to himself and the few male assistants he'd brought with him, leaving the management of the hospital and any dealings with medics, nurses, or orderlies to Pace.

"Marino, there are plenty of accomplished medics here. You've worked longer than you should have, go rest."

Helena watched a sheeted gurney pass, already on its way to the crematorium. "I don't want to sleep right now. I'll just dream of being in here."

Pace sighed. "I don't know that I should tell you this, but there's a meeting in session. The Council asked for a report from the hospital. If you'd like to go."

Exhaustion had dulled Helena's mind to near incomprehension, but the thought of giving a report in the war room left her numb.

She hated going into that room where everything was reduced to figures and zones of interest. The dead were only numbers in that room.

"Do we *have* the numbers yet?" she asked.

"Just the preliminary ones." Pace picked up a file, holding it out.

THE MEETING WAS UNDER WAY when Helena entered the war room. The Resistance Headquarters were based in what had once been the Holdfast Institute of Alchemy and Science. The war room was previously the faculty boardroom; now it was an audience chamber. Spanning a wall was a tiered map of the full city-state, the two main islands, and the mainland abutting the mountains, the levels and water districts all marked out.

Most were coloured black or red, a tide of blood closing in on the blue area centred in the upper half of the East Island. There was a gleam of gold in the sea of blue marking the Institute itself.

The Council of Five sat at a dais behind a long marble table. Two chairs were empty. Falcon Matias sat on the far right, beside him was Steward Ilva Holdfast, a gaunt, grey-haired woman with a large sunstone pin affixed over her heart.

The seat of honour, in the centre, sat empty. It had been weeks since Helena had even glimpsed Luc. Was he still fighting?

The fourth seat was also empty, its occupant standing beside the map, a long staff in his hand. As General Althorne touched parts of the map with his staff, areas which had been black turned red, indicating the active combat zones.

To the far left of the dais sat Jan Crowther, his eyes scanning the room, watching the audience rather than Althorne.

Everyone else was seated in rows of chairs split in the centre to form an aisle. Helena hung back. Those in attendance were all clean, and Helena was covered in blood and other fluids.

"If we continue to push back in the upper trade district, we should be able to press our advantage . . ." Althorne was saying, indicating a series of buildings near the ports.

"Hold, Althorne," Ilva spoke up. "We finally have the hospital report."

All eyes turned to Helena, eyebrows rising at the sight of her. She should have cleaned up more before coming. It had felt so urgent when she was on her way.

"Marino, you have the floor."

Helena swallowed and looked down at the file in her hands, chest tight as she walked towards the centre of the room where there was a large mosaic of the sun, rays spanning out around it. Speakers were supposed to stand in the centre.

"These are only the initial estimates," she said, her voice hardly loud enough to carry, but it carried anyway; the spot where she stood had been designed to capture any sound and amplify it due to the oddly stepped ceiling overhead.

"An estimate is fine," Ilva said.

Helena opened the file. The numbers felt so incomprehensible, they threatened to stretch and distort as she read them out. Estimated casualties, estimates on how many would be permanently removed from combat, estimates on how many might recover enough to return to the front. Every number but the last too large.

The report was met with a long silence.

Althorne cleared his throat. "Would you say those estimates are likely to rise or drop in the final report?"

"Rise," she said in a dull voice. "The hospital resorted to triage care per protocol and prioritised the patients most likely to survive, but preliminary reports are usually conservative."

There were concerned murmurs.

"Thank you, Marino," Ilva said, a note of tension in her voice as she nodded towards the map. "Althorne, you may resume."

"Wait," Helena said. Her heart was pounding as she forced herself to look up from the numbers, staring at the empty seat where Luc was supposed to be. Anything. Anything. Anything. "I submitted a proposal to the Council a week ago, along with my report on the hospital inventory, and several weeks before, too. I never received an answer."

There was a tense silence. She plunged on.

"I know—it is hard to consider, but I believe we should offer Resistance members the choice of donating their bodies to the cause in the event that they're killed in combat," she said. "Rather than burning the bodies, we could—" She hesitated a moment, knowing she could never take back what she was about to say. "—reanimate them and use them as an infantry in order to protect our living combatants. This would be done only with their written permission—"

"Absolutely not," Ilva said, cutting her off.

"That is treason!" came another voice.

Helena looked up and met the eyes of Falcon Matias, who glared down at her, his face livid.

"You stand before us and propose a desecration of the natural cycle. This is the reason why vivimancers can never be trusted, not even for a moment. They are corrupt from conception! This is why this country faces war even now. One moment of leniency and their corrupted natures will seek to spread their contamination." He turned to the Council members seated beside him, inclining his head. "I am ashamed that such apostasy could be uttered by my oblate. I beg the Council's forgiveness. She will be taken in hand, placed in chains, and stripped of all—"

"We are fighting a war against the dead and the Undying," Helena said. She'd known they wouldn't listen, but surely by now they understood the Eternal Flame couldn't possibly win if things continued as they were. "It wouldn't be done to anyone who didn't consent while they were still alive. Our soldiers are willing to die for the cause; why not at least give them the choice to keep fighting and spare the living?"

"What do *you* know about fighting?"

The question came from behind her. She looked back, but there were so many people glaring at her, she couldn't even guess at who'd spoken.

"Your proposal is a violation of everything the Eternal Flame has stood for since the moment of its founding," Ilva said in a cold voice. "You want us to consider the damnation of our soldiers' souls? You took oaths, Marino. Did I misjudge you? Have your abilities made you forget your humanity?"

"No!" Helena said, ragged with frustration. The file in her hands was crumpling as she gripped it. "I am loyal to the cause. My vows are to protect life and fight against necromancy no matter the cost. This would be to that end. I would sacrifice my soul for the Eternal Flame. There might be others who would as well. Can't we ask?"

Falcon Matias stood up. He was a tiny, bony man, and he looked prepared to launch himself over the dais at Helena and strangle her. "The Order of the Eternal Flame, created by Orion Holdfast himself, was founded on Sol's principles of the natural cycle of life and death. It was for Orion's bravery and willingness to sacrifice his life that he was blessed by the heavens and made victorious. Any use of necromancy is a violation of the cycle. Your thoughts and words are a stain upon the Eternal Flame and history itself."

"Who are we saving right now?" Helena said, her voice rising. "How many more can we lose before—"

There was the firm smack of a flat hand on the marble table, and the ceiling overhead abruptly rearranged itself. Helena's words were swallowed, leaving a deadly silence.

Jan Crowther lifted his hand away from the dais, his eyes narrowed into slits as he studied her.

"Marino, your voice is no longer recognised by this body," Ilva said after a moment, her voice cool and deliberate. "However, it is plain to see that you are—hysterical. Given that you are clearly not sound of mind, we will not have you disavowed for this." As she spoke, Ilva looked sharply at Matias, who looked ready to protest. "In gratitude for your years of service, I will have this outburst stricken from the records." She closed her eyes briefly as if in prayer. "I'm only grateful that Principate Lucien was not here to witness this betrayal of faith. Tell Matron Pace she will handle all future reports from the hospital. You are dismissed."

Without another glance in Helena's direction, Ilva turned towards the map once more. One of her hands rested on Matias's arm to calm him. "Moving on now. Althorne, you may continue."

Althorne's voice was a distant rumble in Helena's ears as she turned and left the war room.

STANDING IN THE CORRIDOR OUTSIDE, Helena looked down at herself.

Except for the clean gloves she'd pulled on as she left the hospital, she was covered in blood.

The file slipped from her fingers onto the floor, and she clamped her hands over her mouth to keep from keening as her chest started to heave.

A heavy hand landed on her shoulder. "Not here. Sweet fire, you're a dunce."

She was guided, blindly, down the hallway into the adjoining corridor before being let go. She sagged against the wall, sliding to the floor, head pressed against her knees as she sobbed until her head felt hollow.

She looked up at Soren, who stood a foot away, leaning against the wall, watching her with his deep-set eyes.

If he was here, it meant Luc must be back, too. He must have crashed from exhaustion if they'd run the meeting without him.

Soren shook his head. "You should have cried before you went in for your report, unless you were betting on Ilva forgiving you for reasons of temporary insanity."

"Shut up," she said, shrinking smaller, her chest hitching.

"You could've at least washed up if you wanted to be taken seriously."

"Shut—up," she said again.

"You knew it wasn't going to work," he said, folding his arms. "You had to have known. They're never, ever, ever in a million years going to approve using necromancy on our soldiers. Or on anyone not our soldiers, before you get any other ideas."

She pulled her knees tight against her chest. "You have no idea what it's like in the hospital."

"No, I don't," Soren said in a flat voice, "and neither does anyone else in there, so I don't know why you thought screaming at them while looking like that would change their minds."

She was too tired to argue.

"You know what your problem is?"

Helena said nothing. He'd tell her whether she wanted him to or not. He'd always possessed all the sharp edges and wariness that Luc lacked.

"You don't have faith in the gods."

"Yes, I do," she said quickly.

"No. You don't. You think you do because you think they probably exist, but that's not faith. You don't trust them."

"Why would I? They haven't done anything to deserve being trusted," she said, her voice thick. "I've tried everything, Soren. I try to believe, but it's never enough. Even if I did really believe—if my soul's the price of saving you, of saving everyone"—she choked—"that's not a price. That's a bargain."

He dropped into a squat in front of her so that their faces were almost level. "That doesn't matter, though. They'll never agree. No one will. You're just hurting yourself."

She looked down. "Then we're going to lose," she said in a dull voice. "And I'm going to be the one who puts you back together, over and over, until I have to watch you die instead. And we *still* won't win."

Soren gave a heavy sigh. "I'm guessing no one told you, but this battle was actually quite the victory for us."

She should have felt something at this news, but she was empty. "Whether you win a battle or lose it, all I see is the cost."

"Just figured you'd want to know, because Luc thinks it's a sign that things are finally taking a turn."

Helena felt as if her chest had caved in.

"Don't take that from him. Please."

She nodded silently. Soren rested a hand on her shoulder. She could tell he wanted to say something else, but he just stood up instead.

"We're back for a few days. I'm sure we'll see you around. You should clean up and get some sleep. You need it."

He walked away.

Helena stayed curled against the wall, too crushed beneath her despair to move.

"Marino."

A cool voice jolted Helena awake.

Her eyes snapped open, and she found Ilva Holdfast standing before her, both hands resting idly on the head of her cane. Helena was still huddled against the wall where Soren had left her.

"Let's have a private chat," Ilva said, her tone even and emotionless.

Helena's stomach shrivelled as she stood stiffly.

They went up a floor to Ilva's office, and she produced a little key from her pocket to unlock it.

Helena had always admired that Ilva never tried to hide her lack of resonance, never acted ashamed or apologetic about it. Even though most people didn't possess measurable resonance, once swept into the world of alchemy, the absence sometimes felt startling to encounter. The guild families staked everything upon their alchemy; their future and fortunes depended on maintaining their traditional resonance. They were borderline superstitious about their children's abilities, and so a Lapse in the family was often taken as a sign that the bloodline was weak.

But Ilva had never been hidden away by the Holdfasts. The Faith had long held that resonance was no form of superiority; it was Sol's will to endow whom he would.

The Holdfasts had given Ilva as many opportunities as any other Holdfast. She'd been one of the first women to study in the science department before deciding her interests lay elsewhere, and the first female non-alchemist to join the Eternal Flame when her brother Helios, Luc's grandfather, had become Principate.

Now she was the only family Luc had left, and he had made her steward, entrusting her to act on his behalf when he was absent.

Helena entered the office and stopped short.

Jan Crowther was seated in one of the two chairs across from Ilva's desk.

He was a needle of a man, plainly dressed, with ash-brown hair combed back from his face. A red flame pyromancer, Crowther had fought in the Eternal Flame's crusades against necromancy in the surrounding countries until his right arm was paralysed.

He rarely spoke in the public meetings. He managed logistical matters, supplies, rations, and dispatching and assigning the Resistance's noncombatants. Helena didn't know why he was there; if she was going to be censured, it made more sense for Falcon Matias to be present.

"Sit down," Ilva said, seating herself behind the desk, which was covered in files.

Helena sat in the chair beside Crowther's. She was so tired it was difficult not to slump.

"Seems I'm doomed never to have an easy conversation with you," Ilva said.

Helena said nothing. There was a long silence, as if Ilva was debating where to begin.

"We're losing the war," Ilva finally said.

Helena blinked, the room coming into sharp focus. Her eyes darted between Ilva and Crowther, who remained silent, both watching for her reaction.

She didn't know what to say. Most people regarded it as a preordained fact that the Resistance would win. Eventually. The Eternal Flame was always victorious. In the battle of good and evil, good always won in the end.

"I know," Helena finally said.

Ilva inclined her head, her gaze seeming to go through Helena. "Luc is—exceptional. The best of all the Holdfasts, I've always said. When you've lived as long as I have, you learn how rare it is that anyone with such capacity for greatness is actually truly good, but Luc is one of those rare few. It's a tremendous burden, trying to protect someone like that." Ilva closed her eyes for a moment, her age showing in every line of her face. "I never expected to be steward to the Principate. I've spent so much time wondering what Apollo would do, or my brother, or father, but it's no use—none of them were anything like Luc. He's so earnest, it pains me." She pressed her hand over her heart and looked directly at Helena. "I am grateful you at least did not make that proposal with Luc present."

Helena just pressed her lips together, knowing Ilva's gratitude wasn't because Helena would have hurt Luc but because he might have agreed with her. Because he trusted her, valued her perspective even when they disagreed.

But if she'd spoken with Luc present, and he had listened, everyone else would have seen her as a serpent, dripping poison in his ears, corrupting their golden heir.

"I stand by what I said."

Crowther let out a breath like a hiss, and the fingers of his hand twitched. Her eyes caught on the ignition rings decorating his fingers.

"You know it's impossible," Ilva said.

Helena shrugged. "Even when we're losing?"

"Yes, even then," Crowther said, speaking at last through clenched teeth.

"I know you want to help," Ilva said, "but we're not only fighting for ourselves, but for the soul of Paladia. As Principate, Luc cannot allow the principles of his forefathers to be betrayed." Ilva looked down at her hands, folded before her on the desk. "However, the country has been exhausted by this war. The moral outrage towards necromancy has only dulled further with time. There are many people like you in the city who prefer the idea of necrothralls fighting instead of their sons. The Undying do not ask for food or soldiers, or for their citizens to do without, and that has allowed their Guild Assembly to legitimise themselves and claim that they are the ones for the people."

"So what do we do?" Helena asked.

Ilva pursed her lips, drawing a deep breath. "Do you remember Kaine Ferron?"

Helena stifled an incredulous laugh. Everyone remembered Kaine Ferron. He'd murdered Luc's father by ripping out his heart at the foot of the Alchemy Tower.

Ferron had been sixteen, just another student, and without warning he'd committed the worst crime in Paladia's history.

He was never arrested or charged, even though the investigation had yielded multiple witnesses positively identifying him as the murderer, because he'd disappeared.

There were a few reports later listing him as likely among the Undying, but little else was known since.

"Yes, I remember Ferron," she said, realising that Ilva was waiting for an answer.

"Kaine Ferron has offered to spy for the Resistance," said Crowther.

Helena's head swivelled sharply. "What?"

Crowther's upper lip curled. "He says it's to avenge his mother." He inclined his head. "A strange motive, given that Enid Ferron died peacefully in the family's city residence a year ago. When he was reminded of that, he admitted he has a few—conditions for the services he's offering."

Helena stared at him expectantly, but it was Ilva who spoke.

"He wants a full pardon for all of his wartime activities."

That seemed an obvious demand, although entirely out of the question. Luc would never pardon his father's murderer.

There was something about the way Ilva said it that made Helena feel that a pardon was not all Ferron had asked for.

"And . . . ?"

"He wants you, Marino," Crowther said. "Both now and after the war."

Crowther said it casually, but Ilva's lips went white.

Helena sat looking between them, certain she was misunderstanding, but there was only silence.

"His information would be invaluable to us," Ilva said without meeting Helena's eyes.

Helena shook her head slowly, not ready for the conversation to move on to estimates of value.

Crowther and Ilva were seated too far apart to look at simultaneously. She had to keep glancing between them; Ilva was not looking at her, while Crowther studied her with a look of impassive curiosity.

Helena's voice failed twice before she managed to speak. "But—why would he—I don't think Ferron knows who I am."

Crowther gave a slow reptilian blink. "The two of you were academically competitive, weren't you?"

"W-Well, yes, technically, but—it was just the national exam scores. We never—never spoke. He was guild, and you know how they were—and I was—I was . . ."

The thirty-six-hour hospital shift had dulled her brain to the point that it was only then that she realised Ilva had not brought her into the office to censure her at all.

She looked between them again. "Are you asking me to—"

"We *need* that information," Crowther said. "We have spies, but none at the level Ferron can offer. This would be direct access to intelligence we often spend months trying to piece together." He tilted his head, studying her sideways. "Given your impassioned advocacy today that the Resistance do whatever is necessary to win this war without thought to personal cost . . ." He smiled. "We thought you might be interested."

Helena's mouth was so dry, she could barely swallow. Her words stuck in her throat.

"We won't force you," Ilva said quickly. "It's only if you agree. You *can* say no."

"Yes," Crowther said with another thin, empty smile. "Ferron was quite specific that you have to be willing."

This had to be a test. They wouldn't do this, not after everything . . .

Ilva wouldn't *sell* her.

"You can have a day to think it over," Ilva said.

"But an answer now would be preferable, for all parties involved," Crowther said pointedly.

Ilva's fingers curled into a fist. "She should have time to think, Jan."

Those words finally made it real.

Ilva had never offered Helena time to think about any of the irreversible decisions she'd been asked to make. Helena almost felt the now nearly invisible incision scar just below her navel. Ilva, who was always calm, who always did whatever she considered best for Luc regardless of the cost, had finally found a choice that even her conscience struggled with.

Not a test, then.

"I don't need time to think," Helena said. "You say we're losing the war, and this is the only option, so—I'll do it." As she spoke, she could feel the blood draining from her face, head and body growing light.

Ilva stared at her and then at Crowther, and she gave a sharp nod. "All right."

Helena's fingers had gone numb at some point during the conversation. She swallowed hard, forcing herself to speak again. "How will you explain it—once I'm gone?"

Ilva cleared her throat. "Oh, you won't be leaving. Not immediately anyway. To start, you'll act as liaison between the Resistance and Ferron. You'll see him—what was it?"

"Twice weekly," Crowther said.

"Yes. You'll go every four days, acting as his point of contact, and pass the information he gives you to Crowther, who will ensure it reaches the right members of the Council and the commanders. The rest of the time, you'll remain here, and everything will operate as usual."

"Oh," was all Helena could say.

She should feel relieved by that, but she didn't feel anything. The room was tunnelling; Crowther and Ilva were down a long telescope. Even their voices were far away.

"Given the sensitive nature of this arrangement, there will be no official records or acknowledgement of any kind," Crowther said. "And under absolutely no circumstances are Luc or any other friends or acquaintances you may possess to have any idea of this. Do you understand, Marino?"

"Yes." Her ears were ringing.

Crowther said something else about healing herself as necessary to avoid raising questions. She couldn't make out all the words.

She just nodded and said yes again.

CHAPTER 24

Februa 1786

It was dawn when Helena reached the top floors of the Alchemy Tower. What had once been the Holdfast family's city residence was now rooms for Luc and the paladins and a few other alchemists.

As Helena came around the bend of the hallway, the door ahead swung open, and Luc walked out.

"Hel!" His face lit up for an instant, but then he stopped short. "What happened?"

She stared at him, stunned that he'd read everything in her expression so quickly. Then she realised he was staring at her clothes.

She looked down. She was still covered in dried blood.

Soren and Lila both emerged from the room behind Luc, fully armed. The paladins would never make the mistake of believing anywhere was safe for the Principate after what happened to Apollo.

"It's not my blood," Helena said. "Hospital shift. I just got off."

"Oh, that's a relief." Luc was clearly distracted; he took her by the shoulders. "Did you hear the news?"

His voice was buoyant, and his eyes alight.

Helena couldn't remember the last time he'd looked like this.

"We retook the trade district during the battle, means we're on track to get the ports by summer."

"Really?" She tried to force some excitement into her voice.

If Soren hadn't mentioned that the battle had been considered a success, she would have sounded completely disbelieving. She knew it was strategically significant. City warfare was fraught with danger and complicated logistics. All the levels and districts and zones of the city were porous. Attacks could come from any direction. To have captured such a large district was a remarkable success.

But how could that battle be a victory, when so many had died?

Because the ports meant food, resources, and medical supplies. Everything that had been rationed for months. The supplies smuggled from Novis only ever took the edge off their shortages. If they had the ports in time for summer, they'd be able to get the quantities they were desperate for.

"We've got a new trick," he said, and smiled again. "You know those lumithium pieces we find sometimes after burning the liches and Undying? If you can rip it out, it kills them. All their necrothralls, too."

Helena stared at him in surprise. "How'd you figure that out?"

The only reliable method for permanently removing the Undying from combat was by burning them so hot and fast that they couldn't regenerate, but when on fire, the Undying and the necrothralls would often plunge straight into the nearest cluster of combatants.

That was why there were always so many burn wounds.

"Heard a rumour about it, so we figured we'd give it a try. Lila got the first one." Luc grinned, nodding over his shoulder. "We're going out to celebrate. Just a few of us. You want to clean up and come?"

The *no* she knew she should give stuck in her throat. She didn't want to be left alone with her thoughts. It would be so nice to see Luc happy.

"I—" she started to say, but she caught sight of Soren's face, and he gave the faintest warning shake of his head.

The words died in her throat. Of course she couldn't go. How had she already forgotten what she'd just done in front of the Council?

Even if people had been ordered to forget it, they wouldn't if she was seen anywhere near Luc.

"I can't," she said.

His face fell. "Just for a little while," he said, and attempted a conspiratorial smile, the way he used to grin when he was coaxing her away from homework. "You don't have to stay long."

Soren spoke up. "Let her sleep, Luc. She was probably in the hospital longer than we were fighting."

Luc ignored him. "Breakfast," he said, setting his jaw stubbornly. "At least breakfast. You're never in the mess. Go wash up. We'll wait."

"No. I really can't," she said. "I need to sleep. Maybe next time, all right?"

Her voice wobbled.

His face fell. "All right, if you really don't want to." He stepped back and forced a smile. "I'm holding you to that, though. Next time."

HELENA'S NORMALLY TIDY ROOM LOOKED as though a tornado had blown through. Lila had returned in full force, which meant there was a pile of filthy clothes, fireproof amiantos under-armour, and padding piled in one corner, while armour, weaponry, and holsters and harnesses were spread across Lila's unmade bed as if she'd emptied her entire trunk getting dressed.

Despite the impression of coolheaded, sharp-eyed talent that Lila radiated as paladin, behind closed doors she could be chaos personified. Off duty, she was twitchy and incapable of keeping still or on any task that didn't interest her, and she left things everywhere. Weeks after Lila departed, Helena would find her things in odd places. Mostly padding or pieces of scale mail or little gears for her rappelling harness that Helena had to hope weren't important.

Helena stood, staring tiredly at the mess for a moment before wincing at the sight of her reflection in Lila's vanity.

She was covered in dried blood. She wasn't sure if her uniform could even be bleached clean. It was a pity that only amiantos fabric could be whitened by being thrown in fire.

She forced herself to sit down at Lila's vanity and remove the pins holding her braids in place before she stripped for a shower. Her sunstone amulet, tucked under her uniform, was warm from her skin as she lifted it off. She paused, cradling it in her palm, throat working as she studied the golden sunrays and the shimmering red surface of the stone in the centre.

The Holdfast Suncrest, with seven points rather than eight, representing each of the seven planets, except the sun, centre of all.

Ilva had given it to her when Helena returned to the city and formally made her vows as a healer.

It had been a private ceremony, an informal recitation beneath the Eternal Flame's light with only the steward and Falcon present as witnesses because Ilva did not want Luc to have any idea about the kinds of promises Helena made in his name. He already chafed against the traditional vows his paladins had made about protecting him. Luc didn't want anyone to die for him, and certainly not to promise to as his paladins did.

Helena had also promised to.

Most healers could practise for decades without consequence, but to heal injuries that cheated death came with a price. It was called the Toll.

To heal a mortal wound or reanimate the dead required vitality, a drop of life itself. The greater the scale of the work, the greater the cost. Healing came with the highest cost; that was why the Faith considered it a purifying act and allowed its practice while forbidding all other forms of vivimancy.

Becoming a healer would slowly carve away Helena's life span, like a candle being burned at both ends. Someday, she didn't know when, her resonance would begin to wither and fade, and Helena would go with it. She felt it sometimes while healing, a sensation like sand in an hourglass being diverted, flowing from her fingertips and into her patients.

She never knew how much was left, just that she was spending it.

After the avowal ceremony, when Matias had gone, Ilva had stopped her and draped an amulet around Helena's neck, tucking it under the neckline of her uniform.

"It's traditional for a healer to wear a holy amulet," Ilva had said. "This crest is only worn by the Holdfasts and their paladins, but I think it right that you wear it, too."

Now Helena stood, staring at the amulet, cold and hollow inside. The protruding sunrays bit against her palm, leaving a circle of indentations, threatening to break skin. She squeezed harder until they sank into her palm and her blood ran across the gold.

HELENA WOKE BECAUSE HER HANDS hurt, a bone-deep ache radiating from her palms to fingertips. Repetitive strain injuries were common in alchemists. She started to massage her right palm to try to loosen the muscles, wincing. The circle of cuts from the amulet reopened, blood trickling down her wrist. She should heal them—blood poisoning was a severe risk in the hospital—but instead she lay there staring at them until they stopped oozing.

Finally she dressed and braided her hair and headed for the hospital—only to be informed that she had no shifts for the next two days. The news should have been a relief, but being left to her thoughts was the last thing she wanted.

Helena departed reluctantly, compiling a list of tasks she'd been putting off. She'd check the hospital inventory first, and then—

As she came around the corner, she found Crowther standing in the hallway, studying a mural of Orion Holdfast.

Every corner of the Institute was beautifully decorated with various forms of the alchemical arts, but that mural was Helena's favourite. She often found herself in front of it after her worst shifts, or when Luc hadn't come back for a long time.

In most of the depictions of the Holdfast Principates, there was a sort of indifference in the expressions, likely intended to make them look regal and divine. In this mural, there was a tenderness to Orion's face, a hint of a smile.

It made him look like Luc.

The sun's rays were a halo behind Orion, and he wore the radiant crown on his head. His flaming sword was laid aside, still piercing the Necromancer's skull, while cradled in his palms was a large orb of brilliant light.

Whenever Helena stood in front of it, she told herself that someday there would be paintings of Luc like that.

"I can see why you like this one," Crowther said, glancing sidelong at her.

Helena knew little about Jan Crowther, even though he'd joined the faculty at the Institute when Helena was fifteen.

He'd been a sponsored student, like her, brought to Paladia as a child after being orphaned by a necromancer in the far north-eastern reaches of the continent. He'd attended the Institute, joined the Eternal Flame, and fought in the crusades, where he'd been injured. When he'd joined the Institute faculty, students expected he was there to train Luc, given the rarity of pyromancers, but Luc had nothing to do with Crowther. After less than a year, Crowther left again, only to immediately return after Principate Apollo's assassination.

He turned and stared at her. His right arm was strapped tightly against his torso with a harness. Although he still wore ignition rings on his left hand, she'd never seen him use them.

"My office, I think," he said, gesturing down the hall towards the Alchemy Tower. Helena said nothing. They rode the lift to one of the faculty floors, and he led the way to a door with his name on it.

His hand brushed across a metal panel, and the door clicked and opened.

The office within was clearly lived in. One wall was covered in maps, not only of Paladia but also of the neighbouring countries and other continents. A dilapidated sofa was crammed in a corner.

There was scarcely floor space to walk.

"Sit," he said, slipping around his desk and seating himself. The only window in the room was directly behind him, leaving him cast in shadow. "What do you know about the Ferron family's history?"

Helena sat staring at her lap rather than trying to make out Crowther's expressions.

"Just the general things," she said. "They were one of the early common guild families. Their resonance is mostly for steel alloys. They have iron mines, and a few generations back they developed the methods of industrial steel manufacturing. Most of the infrastructure in Paladia nowadays is made with Ferron steel."

Crowther's silhouette nodded. "The Ferron family is arguably older than Paladia. They were iron alchemists when the basin was still a floodplain; their early resonance and techniques were developed finding bog iron."

Helena wasn't sure how that information was relevant, but she supposed anything about the Ferrons was useful to know.

"I was Kaine Ferron's academic advisor here at the Institute."

She peered at him. "You knew him? Do you think his offer to spy is legitimate?"

Crowther sighed, pressing his fingertips down on the desk so the joints bowed inwards. "Ferron was a remarkable liar and an impersonal student. I believe he hated this institution. Our conversations were rarely more than minimally cordial."

"Why?"

"Why? I should think it obvious. The Ferrons are ambitious. They've made no effort to hide their inflated opinions of themselves. Did you ever see the crest they bought with their fortune?"

Helena tried to remember. "Is it a lizard?"

"No." Crowther shoved a slip of paper towards her.

Helena picked it up and stared. It was a dragon curled into a perfect circle, long fangs tearing apart its own tail. On the upper right, taloned wings arched above the curved body.

"It's an ouroboros," she said, doubtful about what character insights a family crest would reveal. Crowther remained silent, so she hazarded a guess. "In Khemish alchemy, a serpent ouroboros is supposed to represent infinity or rebirth. Perhaps that's how the Ferrons saw their new fortune. Although in Cetus's writing, it can also be used to represent greed and self-destruction. Maybe that's why they chose a dragon instead of the serpent. A mythical creature is an unusual choice either way."

She tried to hand it back.

"Look. Again."

She sighed, not sure what Crowther wanted her to see.

"Squint if you need to."

She narrowed her eyes, letting the image blur. "Oh." She felt like an idiot. "They chose a dragon because the wings make it look like the symbol for iron."

"Yes," Crowther said. Her jaw clenched at the condescension in his voice. "It says a great deal about how the family sees themselves. A circle is without hierarchy, and yet in this crest, it is iron that forms it." Crowther drummed his fingers on his desk. "Iron will never be a noble metal, but it is indisputable at this point that Ferron steel has built as much of Paladia as Holdfast gold. The Holdfasts ruled for nearly five hundred celestial years by divine right, but the rest of the world has been catching up with our technological revelations. The tension between past ideals and present realities is what enabled this war."

"What do you mean?"

Crowther's eyes gleamed in the shadows.

"I mean that time has allowed this country to begin questioning what is divine, and whether it matters. Our Principate can alchemise gold and wield holy fire. Two gifts of exceptional rarity. Once, that was miracle enough. But the world has changed, and the Principate has not. Morrough can raise the dead and grant immortality. The Ferrons have found a way to turn their lowly iron into seemingly infinite mountains of wealth. In a world like that, what purpose is there in fire or endless gold?"

Helena was dumbstruck to hear such criticism uttered by a Council member.

"If you think that, why are you here?"

"Because I wish to see every necromancer wiped from the face of this earth. That is the purpose of the Eternal Flame and the reason for the Principate's crown. I will see this city burned to ash sooner than allow necromancers to use it as their stronghold," Crowther said, baring his teeth. "As long as the Eternal Flame is faithful to ridding the world of necromancers, I will be faithful to it."

His words were chilling.

"Then taking Ferron's offer is a compromise—working with one necromancer to stop others."

"That and because we have no other options at this point," Crowther said, waving his hand.

Helena refrained from mentioning her alternative. "Still, I would like to know that there's some tangible purpose to this deal. I am the only healer the Resistance has, and if Ferron—" She couldn't bring herself to verbalise what Ferron could do. "Based on everything you've said, Ferron doesn't seem to have any reason to help the Eternal Flame. I don't understand how it could be worth it to trust him."

Crowther only scoffed. "I'm sure Ilva has filled your head with pretty stories about your importance, but you're easily replaced. We already have several candidates under consideration."

The room went briefly out of focus, and Helena felt as if she'd been kicked in the stomach.

Crowther's features were just visible enough that she could see his cheeks stretch as he smiled. "As to why I believe in the legitimacy of Kaine's offer, it is *because* I know he is not loyal or concerned with our cause that I believe him earnest in this. The Ferrons have spent the last century digging into their family lineage and convincing themselves of some imaginary right to rule that was usurped by the Holdfasts. They were not looking for someone else to serve when Morrough appeared; they thought he was a means to an end, an outsider with the resources to challenge and undermine the Principate for them. But now Morrough holds too much of an advantage. Ferron is making the gamble that he can sabotage the Undying by aiding us until the scales even."

"Because if the Undying and the Eternal Flame destroy each other, then—"

"Who better to rule the ashes than the family whose steel can rebuild this city?"

Helena straightened, starting to see the strategy. "So he'll betray us eventually, but not until we're more of a threat to the Undying."

"Yes."

She nodded slowly, ignoring the sick knot in her stomach.

"He won't ever be loyal, but I expect he'll be an excellent spy if for no other reason than his vanity. He's already done more for us in a day than the Resistance has accomplished in the last year."

"What do you mean?"

Crowther flicked two fingers; they were so long they reminded Helena of harvestman spiders. "When he made his offer and set his terms, as proof of his—sincerity, he told us how to kill the liches and Undying without fire."

"The lumithium," Helena said, remembering Luc's words, the "rumour" they'd heard about.

"Yes. The vulnerability of the 'talismans,' as he calls them, was Ferron's sample of the information he could offer. It's likely to be a very beneficial arrangement for us in the immediate future."

And when it wasn't? What would happen to her then?

"However . . . I have no interest in accepting Ferron's crumbs. We *will* take advantage of this."

Helena leaned forward. "How?"

Crowther raised his eyebrows, an odd smile playing at his lips. "Because he made a mistake when he asked for you."

Helena's heart stuttered.

"He wanted us to believe the reason for his spying was his mother. When I wouldn't let him get away with that lie, he was forced to improvise, and he did so by inventing an excuse of wanting you. Quite the misstep, I'd say."

Her hand clenched, and she could feel the punctures in her palm begin to bleed, sticking to the inside of her glove. "Why?"

Crowther leaned forward, his thin features emerging from the shadows.

"It's an odd request, don't you think? Why would Kaine Ferron, the iron guild heir, want Helena Marino?"

She shook her head.

"He could have asked for anything, cited a crisis of conscience, demanded a mountain of gold, but instead, he wants . . . *you*? It's an irrational choice." Crowther drummed his fingers thoughtfully. "A sign of some kind of subconscious obsession perhaps."

His eyes flicked over Helena appraisingly. "An obsession is a weakness, and a weakness is an opportunity for us. As we established, you'll go to Ferron twice a week and bring his missives safely back to me, and during those visits, you will do *anything* he wants."

"I *know*."

"You will also make a study of him. It is your job now to notice everything. Discover his weaknesses, his secret desires. Make use of that allegedly clever mind of yours. Let him think he has all the power and gradually make him begin craving things he can't demand from you. Whatever passing interest prompted this, I want you to turn it into an obsession that consumes him."

She stared at him, incredulous. "I don't have any idea of how to do that."

"Well, then it's fortunate that you have an advantage over him."

Helena stared at Crowther, at a loss.

"Ferron was already gone when your vivimancy was discovered. He doesn't know what you are. With your abilities, you can make him feel however you want him to feel about you. Enthral him."

Helena sat stunned. "I've *never* used my vivimancy to—"

"But you could, couldn't you?" His face hardened, dark eyes narrowing. This was the point of the conversation, the destination he'd been leading her to the whole time. "Your job, Marino, is to use any means necessary to bring Ferron to his knees. You will use those cursed abilities of yours to make him forget he ever wanted anything but you."

Her throat closed, her face burning. "I don't think that's even possible—"

"Then make it possible. Or are you just the compliant lamb that Ilva sees you as?"

Helena flinched.

"If you only want to be a victim, then by all means, go. Or you can do things my way, and Kaine Ferron will not be your owner, he'll be your target, and your job will be to get as much information out of him as possible until it is *we* who have no more need of him." He gave a thin smile. "The choice is yours."

When Crowther finally let her leave, Helena felt as drained as if she'd just pulled another three-day hospital shift. He told her he'd "send word" when he had a date and location for the first liaison, and until then she was to behave as usual.

She went to the library archives and found old copies of the newspapers that had been printed after Principate Apollo's assassination. There'd been a picture of Ferron included. His student portrait, taken only a week before.

She stared at the boy in the black-and-white photograph.

He was in his student uniform, the crisp white collar that kept the chin up, and the pins on his jacket with his guild sigils, iron and steel. Guild students only ever wore their guild metals, while Helena had been required to wear a sash with pins for all the metals she was ranked as competent in, as if she didn't already stick out enough.

He had dark hair but pale Northern skin and eyes, and his expression was tense with just a hint of prideful defiance in it, as if he'd known then what the photo would be used for.

She studied him, memorising the details, trying to imagine what he'd be like now, more than five years later.

When she ran out of newspapers to read, she checked out several medical textbooks, as well as studies and theories on human behaviour and the mind.

She couldn't find a reason why she wouldn't be able to emotionally and physically enthral him with vivimancy the way Crowther wanted, but that didn't necessarily mean it was doable. Only theoretically possible.

It couldn't be anything too overt, only enough to alter the heart rate and stimulate certain hormones and reactions to stimuli until there was an ingrained physiological response. Using vivimancy would simply be taking a shortcut in old behavioural experiments.

Helena knew from years of healing that most people couldn't tell when resonance was being used on them unless the manipulation was overt. That was part of what made people so afraid of vivimancers: the idea that something could be done without their knowledge.

But if Ferron ever suspected it, he'd kill her in a heartbeat.

Which meant it would be a gradual process, requiring her to know Ferron intimately, to be able to read his body and emotions. The feelings she evoked would have to seem natural. Subtle as poison until he was too far gone for a cure.

CHAPTER 25

Februa 1786

THE LIAISON POINT SELECTED WAS ON THE factory Outpost north of Headquarters. The Outpost was a huge satellite structure built in the river just below the hydroelectric dam, erected atop enormous pillars that held it above even the highest storm floods, but near enough to benefit directly from the electricity generated there.

The factories there had been shuttered by the war, and the Outpost decimated by both sides during early attempts to control it for potential weapons manufacturing. There'd been such massive and extensive destruction, it was eventually rendered virtually defunct. Once in ruins, it wasn't strategic enough for either side to prioritise holding it, and since disputing the territory further could have endangered the dam, it was mutually abandoned.

Neither side wanted Paladia without electricity, or waist-deep in water.

Even before the war, Helena had considered the Outpost one of the ugliest things she'd ever seen, a brutal black stain on a picturesque landscape. In addition to being an eyesore, the Outpost had filled the skies with black smoke, poisoned the water, and left vile bogs of foul sludge throughout the wetlands that flooded into the water slums and low districts during Ascendance.

She'd never gone anywhere near it.

In the late evening on the designated day, she changed out of her uniform, leaving all her possessions carefully packed in her trunk, including the sunstone amulet. She hadn't worn it since the meeting, the mere sight of it making her feel sick.

She dressed in civilian clothes that were as nondescript as possible. With her hood pulled up, hiding how dark her hair was, she was hardly memorable. Just a person trying to stay out of the war's path. The Undying didn't usually bother civilians; they preferred Resistance soldiers as their necrothralls because they came armed and trained to fight.

The route was relatively simple. She only had to walk north from Headquarters and cross the bridge to the mainland. Because the northern tip of the island was built on the plateau, she didn't have to navigate through the various levels of the city. The roadway gate was closed. The guards stationed at the pedestrian door checked the papers and identification Crowther had provided and let her through.

The river swirled below, not even flood season yet, just all the water from the mountain storms.

She reached the mainland and followed the road to the dam, then took a second bridge across the water to the Outpost. She was startled by the number of people there. Because the facility was abandoned, many of the poorer civilians who weren't alchemists and were afraid to ally with either side had fled there: The Outpost was the only place removed from the fighting that didn't require enduring the winter brutality of the mountains.

The Outpost was a combination of a labyrinth and a city. The huge metal and concrete walls made it claustrophobic. The factories were heavily sabotaged in ways only possible with alchemy. Bizarre transmutations and alchemisation used to destroy complex machinery. The tenements were more intact, and heavily occupied. The building she'd been directed to find had the alchemical symbol for iron set into its decorative mosaic doorway.

Helena entered, trying not to seem lost.

There'd been a skylight far overhead, but now its glass covered the floor. Only a few of the units had doors. Second floor, to the left, the fourth door. The number beside it was scratched off.

Helena removed her gloves and knocked firmly, trying not to be too loud.

Nothing happened. She waited and checked the map. Perhaps she was too early.

Well, she'd wait. She stood, externally calm while her heart beat her blood into a storm.

The door abruptly swung open, an electric lantern's light spilling out into the landing. Kaine Ferron stood framed in the doorway.

He looked identical to his portrait in the paper, as if he had not aged a day. Five years and time had not touched him.

He didn't even look seventeen. There was a coltishness to his build, the kind that boys had just after a growth spurt before filling out. Even his dark hair was combed in the same way he'd worn it at the Institute, as if he'd stepped straight through the years.

He was in a stone-grey uniform that almost matched the hazel-grey of his eyes. It was the uniform of upper-middle-ranked members of the Undying. The higher the rank, the darker the uniform. The generals wore all black.

He stared languidly down at her with his eerily youthful face.

The circumstances were already odious, but somehow what she felt least prepared for was that he'd look so young.

She stood gaping at him until he finally moved, holding the door slightly wider in invitation, creating just enough space for her to squeeze by if she brushed against him.

Her heart caught in her throat when she stepped inside.

As she crossed the threshold, she was torn between wanting to scan the unit and being afraid to take her eyes off Ferron for an instant.

In the split second it took her to pivot, her eyes raced across the room, taking in as much detail as possible. It was simple and empty. One room with dirty walls and a cracked tile floor, furnished with only a wooden table and two chairs. No bed, no sofa. She didn't know if she should be relieved or terrified.

Her body threatened to tremble uncontrollably. She barely heard the door closing over the blood roaring in her ears.

She faced him, trying to mirror his languid indifference, to keep from betraying how scared she was. His fingers barely brushed the surface of the door, but she heard a mechanism shift inside it before the click of the lock, trapping her.

As he turned to face her, she spoke.

"Ferron, I understand you want to help the Resistance." Her voice came from somewhere far away. Her mind was churning. Racing ahead.

How many people had he killed? He was clearly one of the Undying and had been for years now. How many necrothralls did he control? Why did he ask for her? Why would he want her? If he hurt her, would she be able to heal it all before curfew or would she be trapped there on the Outpost overnight?

The questions were clamouring in her head as dread crawled through her like a parasite. She felt it insinuating in her bones, finding every crack in her resolve to burrow into.

"You understand the terms?" he asked, tilting his head appraisingly. His face might be deceptively young, but his eyes weren't.

She met them. "A full pardon. And me. In exchange for your information."

"Now and after the war." His eyes glittered as he said it.

Helena didn't let herself react. After years in the hospital, she'd learned to ignore her feelings and do her job.

"Yes," she said, without emotion. "I'm yours."

Ferron might own her in body, but her mind and feelings were her own. If he wanted them, he'd have to work harder than that.

Get closer, Ferron. Become so obsessed with finding my vulnerabilities that you don't notice the ones I'm making in you.

He smirked, and as he did, his true age suddenly showed starkly, not a physical vanishing but a look of spite so unmistakably hardened with time that it temporarily erased the façade of youth.

"Promise?" he asked.

"If you want."

He flashed a quick grin, the expression slicing like a scythe across his face, more a wound than a real emotion. "Swear it, then. I want to hear you say it as a vow."

She didn't let herself pause or think, just pressed a hand over her heart. "I swear it, on the spirits of the five gods and my own soul, Kaine Ferron, I'm yours as long as I live."

It was only after she'd spoken that she thought about the other vows she'd made in her life. All the contradictory things she'd promised. She'd have to find a way to reconcile them somehow.

At those words, he stepped towards her.

There was a predatory curiosity in his eyes, like a wolf stalking prey.

Before he could touch her, she blurted out, "Until we win, you can't do anything to me that will interfere with—with my other responsibilities in the Resistance. I have to be able to go back without—without drawing attention."

He paused, an eyebrow rising. "Right . . . I'll have to keep you alive until this is over." He sighed. "Well, I suppose that gives us something to look forward to." He leaned towards her, bringing his face close to hers. "We'll save the real fun for later."

"I want you to swear it," she said, and her voice shook.

He laid a hand over the place a heart should be. She wasn't sure if the Undying had hearts.

"I swear," he said, exaggeratedly reverent, his breath ghosting across her neck, "on the gods and *my soul*"—he laughed as he said it—"I won't interfere."

She craned her head back, eyes narrowed, suspicious of his cooperation. She knew it was an empty vow, but why play along? He had all the leverage, and instead of exploiting it, he was pretending like this was some kind of mutual agreement.

Noticing her scrutiny, he straightened and walked around her, tsking when she tried to keep him in her line of sight. His eyes were aglow with amusement.

"My, but you're suspicious of me, aren't you? Let me guess: You think this is all a ploy on my part, and that I'll change my mind the moment I've gotten what I want."

Helena went violently still.

"Yes, that's exactly what you think." He stopped short. "How's this? As a token of my—sincerity, I won't touch you. Yet." His eyes trailed lazily down. "After all, I did specify willing, and you don't *look* very willing."

She should have felt relief but instead she was horrified by his proposal. This wasn't what she wanted. She was supposed to begin her mission at once; the longer it took to start, the more likely it was that Ferron would lose interest before she had a hold on him. But how was she supposed to say that without making *her* intentions obvious?

He seemed to notice her discomfort at the offer and gave a slow, wolfish smile. "In the meantime, I'll let you go running back to your precious Eternal Flame with my information and find other means of enjoying your company."

The thought of consenting to whatever awful thing he wanted was bad enough, but being forced to remain dreading it was worse.

She slid a hand behind her back, curling it into a tight fist until her nails bit into her palm, the almost healed cuts all throbbing, threatening to split open again.

"That's—generous of you," she said in what she hoped was a convincingly meek voice.

"Yes, I am generous. However." Ferron suddenly looked appraising. "I do think you should give me *something*, at least." The smile he flashed was viperine. "After all, I did have to give up some rather precious information to earn you. Surely I deserve something in return, to warm my cold heart."

Helena's stomach dropped, her equilibrium vanishing.

"What—what do you want?" she asked in a stiff voice.

She tried to calculate the likely options, but she was already drowning in possibilities. She didn't like to think about the kinds of things men considered a favour.

"You don't sound very enthusiastic." He pulled an expression of mock grief, pouting and looking so young that she almost physically recoiled.

"What do you want me to do?" she asked through gritted teeth. "Tell me, and I'll do it."

He gave a barking laugh. "My gods, Marino. You *are* desperate."

"I'm here. I assumed that was obvious," she said in a deadened voice, unable to look at him anymore.

"Well, since you're a void of creativity when it comes to gratitude: Kiss me like you mean it," he said, and then as if it were an afterthought, he added, "Based on your performance, I'll decide how much information I feel inspired to part with."

A kiss? Just a kiss? That was better than she'd expected, but she still didn't want to go anywhere near him.

He was goading her. That was obvious. From the moment she'd knocked on that door, everything he'd done was intended to keep her on edge.

This kiss was intended to compound that. To seal her sense of humiliation and cement her resentment towards him, the belief that she was only being spared further shame through his leniency. He expected her to hate him, to be so distracted by her emotions that she was easy to manipulate into fuelling her own misery.

It was a game. None of *this* was real. She was a toy, something he'd thrown into his list of demands as a diversion tactic. She wasn't a part of his real plan.

She had to remember that.

She stepped towards him.

Ferron was meticulously composed, from his smoothly manicured nails to his ageless face, all hiding the monster that lurked beneath his skin.

His pupils were contracted, his eyes flat with disinterest.

She gathered her resonance until she could feel its hum in her fingertips and tempered it faint as spider silk.

She wouldn't manipulate him yet—it was much too early—but the kiss was an opportunity to touch him, to discover what he felt like. And what he *felt* for her. It would give her a starting point.

She slid her arms around his neck, not letting her bare hands touch his skin yet. Her fingers skimmed across the fine dark wool of his coat, pulling him forward.

He smirked as he leaned in, like it was fun.

When their lips were almost touching, she hesitated, almost expecting him to shove his hand straight into her chest and rip her heart out, the way he'd killed Luc's father.

She trembled, and she knew he felt it.

His breath smelled like juniper: peppery, sharp, and fresh-cut.

His eyes were languid again, lashes low as he met her eyes. She wondered what he saw when he looked at her.

Murderers are still men, she told herself. And he was merely a boy.

So she gave him a slow, sweet kiss, the way she could imagine herself kissing someone she was keen on. She didn't try to make it enticing or seductive. She let it be tentative. A first kiss, because it was her first kiss.

As she kissed him, she let her fingertips brush the back of his neck, fingers sliding up through his hair, following the curvature of his skull, and then she let a whisper of her resonance slip beneath his skin.

Ferron was not human.

She knew that the Undying were unnatural, but she hadn't been prepared for how unnatural he would feel.

She could sense him, map him as she might anyone else, the beat of his heart, his nerves, veins, the currents of energy, all the interconnected facets of a body, but it felt wrong. Like trying to touch a mirror's reflection rather than a person.

Ferron was there, physically. And he was alive, technically. But he was immutable in a way that her mind simply refused to comprehend.

She couldn't let herself focus on it. She had to pay attention to what she was supposed to be doing, which was kissing him. Yet she found his physiology far more interesting than his mouth.

She let one of her hands slide down, palm pressed against his face, giving herself more direct contact, pulling him closer. She was losing focus, but his body fascinated her.

How was this possible? She couldn't help but press a little closer.

The tempo of his heartbeat altered and then altered again.

Her mind abruptly recalled the physical reality of what she was doing: Her arm was around his neck, one hand on his face, body arched against his to counter the height disparity.

He jerked away from her.

It startled her, but she dropped her hands immediately, trying not to breathe hard or seem as disoriented as she felt. Had he noticed her resonance? She searched for signs of suspicion or anger in his expression.

His eyes were darker, and he looked significantly less composed with his hair rumpled and falling over his face.

"Well." He blinked and shook his head. "That was certainly—something." He ran a gloved thumb across his mouth.

"You are full of surprises," he added after a moment, voice lower than before.

Helena wasn't sure what to say to that, so she just said the first thing that popped into her head. "Do you say that to every girl?"

He huffed a laugh and ran his hand through his hair to brush it off his face. "No, I can't say I do."

There was a pause.

He'd probably been expecting her to bite him.

Heat rose across her face. She wished she had, but his physiology was so interesting. She couldn't just encounter something like that and ignore it.

He cleared his throat. "I have something for you." He reached into his pocket and tossed an object to her.

She caught it reflexively, studying it. It was a tarnished silver ring; she knew it by both sight and resonance, although her silver resonance was minimal, not high enough for her repertoire to be considered noble. However, this ring was hand-forged rather than transmutationally crafted; she could see the hammer marks that had beaten a scaled, almost geometric pattern onto it.

A bizarre thing for an iron alchemist to have.

"A symbol of our relationship," Ferron said, and when she looked up sharply, he raised his right hand to indicate a matching band on his index finger. "There's a mirrored entanglement in them. If I do anything to mine, you'll feel it. I'll transmute it to warm briefly if I need to meet. Twice if it's urgent. I'd advise coming very quickly if it ever burns twice."

She inspected the ring. Mirrored entanglement was the way her call bracelet from the hospital worked. It was a form of transmutation that was incredibly rare. Few alchemists had the ability to manage it. It made the pieces very valuable, but they were only useful as long as the entangled pieces were accounted for.

The Eternal Flame kept a strict tally of everyone who carried one.

She tried slipping it on the forefinger of her left hand since it was her non-dominant transmutation hand but found it too small. She resigned herself, sliding it down her left ring finger.

"My resonance for silver is only passable, but I think I can manage a temperature shift. Do I call you the same way?" she asked.

"No," he said sharply, his voice startlingly vehement. "*You* don't ever summon me. You burn me, ever, and this deal is off. I'm not a fucking dog. If you want me, you can come here and wait or leave a note, and I'll get around to it when I have time."

The viciousness was startling after all his mocking calm. Crowther was right: Ferron didn't want to be ruled by anyone. It was power he craved.

"Well, I can't always come immediately," she said. "It could be noticed if I'm going out at odd times. Barring emergencies, it'd be better if we stick to a schedule."

"Fine."

"Every Saturnis and Martiday I go out for medical supplies just before daybreak. No one will notice if I come back a little later. Would that work for you? I could do different days, if you'd rather."

He nodded slowly. "That's fine. If I can't make it for some reason, come back again in the evening."

"What if I can't?" Helena asked, not understanding why he was so averse to using the rings for more than basic signalling. The trek to the Outpost was hardly short enough to be worth making unnecessarily.

"I'm sure I can figure it out," he said, lip curling as he looked at her. Then he reached into his coat and pulled out two envelopes, selecting one.

"My first instalment, then," he said as he held it out.

She took it from him. It was addressed to an Aurelia Ingram.

"Crowther has the cipher already," Ferron said as she stood, studying the address. "I trust he has the sense not to use everything at once."

"Your service will be one of the Resistance's most carefully protected secrets. We're not going to do anything that might risk compromising you."

He gave a vague nod. "Then I'll see you on Martiday. Now get out, and make sure you take a different route when you leave."

CHAPTER 26

Februa 1786

"WHAT DO YOU MEAN YOUR RESONANCE FELT wrong?" Crowther said when Helena finished reciting all that had happened. He'd summoned her to his office the moment she'd walked through the gates.

Helena crossed her arms, hugging herself.

"I assume it's because he's Undying. It was different than I expected. I'm not sure if I can transmute him. He looks identical to his student portrait; maybe he can't be changed. He doesn't feel like it's possible, and even if it is, I'm not sure I can do this subtly enough."

"Would a test subject help?"

She stared at him in blank horror. "What? No."

"It would be effective, wouldn't it?"

"No," she said again. "I'm a healer, I've taken oaths—"

"No, you're not," Crowther cut in, a susurration in his voice like the snap of scissors. "Not in this room, not on this assignment. I don't have any use for a healer. I need a vivimancer who will do what is necessary. Heroism is something for others to perform for the masses. Intelligence work—our work—is breaking people open by whatever means necessary to reach their secrets. That is what you are a part of now."

Helena glared at him. "I know how to perform the physiological aspects; it's the regeneration that I'm not sure about. Unless you have one of the Undying on hand, a test subject isn't any use."

Crowther sat back and looked sour. "Not at present, but it's possible if need be." His eyes narrowed. "Did he give you that ring?"

Helena slipped it off, sliding it across the desk. "It's entangled. He intends to use it to summon me in emergencies. He was very specific that the deal's off if I ever use it in reverse. You were right about him, he's incredibly prideful. Just the idea of being called by me practically threw him into a rage."

Crowther scrutinised the ring, rolling it between his fingers. "Is this silver?"

"Yes."

He nodded. "He must have inherited it from his mother. She was a silver alchemist here at the Institute. Minor noble family but passable talent. Atreus was quite taken with her for a time."

"You knew them?" Helena stared curiously at Crowther.

"Of them. The sentiments among the guilds towards sponsored students were no different then. Everyone assumed it was a brief infatuation. A Ferron would hardly stray outside his resonance to that degree. It was a shock when Atreus quietly married her, obviously out of obligation. I can't imagine how an ambitious man like Atreus chafed from his entanglement, but he could hardly afford the social and religious condemnation of putting her aside."

Anyone who studied metallurgy knew that silver and iron were incompatible metals. They couldn't be alloyed. Silver was a noble metal, however, which would have placed the wife above her husband in station if not fortune.

"Kaine was conceived out of wedlock, then?" she asked hesitantly.

Crowther shook his head. "No, he came sometime later. Enid had—difficulties. There were miscarriages, clearly an unfortunate combination of resonance. When Enid was brought to the hospital, pregnant, the doctors had reason to believe her condition showed clear signs of vivimancy in the child. The Ferrons were warned of what she carried, and advised, but Atreus was desperate for an heir. They disappeared to their country estate. A few months later Atreus was caught employing vivimancers to help manage the pregnancy and arrested for several weeks. By the time he was released, Kaine had been born."

Crowther set the ring on his desk.

"They lived *very* quietly at their country estate after that. The birth was said to have been so traumatising for Enid that she never went into society again. Atreus rarely spoke of her. Rumours sprang up among the guilds that Kaine was a Lapse and the family was endeavouring to hide it. Eventually the belief grew so widespread, Atreus had no choice but to present him to guild society, but he was controlling of the boy. Like a dog on a chain. He knew that if there were any signs of vivimancy, the Eternal Flame would act. Atreus had paid so dearly for his heir, he could hardly afford to lose him. It was something of a surprise when Atreus enrolled him in the Institute, but what else could he do? If Kaine couldn't disprove the rumours about his abilities and earn the certification, the family would have lost control of the guilds."

"How do you know all this?" Helena asked, slipping the ring back on.

Crowther raised an eyebrow. "Why do you think I was brought onto the faculty and made Kaine Ferron's academic advisor?"

Helena's eyes went wide. "You were watching him for signs."

Crowther gave a short nod. "Yes, he was one of the students I was asked to observe. Unfortunately, I was reassigned to investigate rumours in the city. If I'd been here, I would have noticed something was amiss when he returned after his father's execution. Everything might have been quite different then."

WHEN HELENA ARRIVED AT THE tenement the next week, she pulled her gloves off and paused, pressing her hand against the door, using her resonance to sense the mechanism inside. Even though the unit looked abandoned both inside and out, she could tell the door contained an intricate lock.

The best locks were a mix of metal and rare compounds, often tailored to the owner's particular resonance, and usually included some inert metals as well, all intended to create blind spots. To unlock it, the alchemist had to know how the movement of the mechanisms was supposed to feel, and which ones to manipulate.

She left her fingers on the panel as she knocked. She was tracking how they spun, so focused on the pattern they followed that she wasn't prepared when a pale hand shot out, catching her by the wrist and dragging her inside.

The door slammed behind her and Ferron had her backed against the wall.

So much for his promise not to touch her.

He leaned in and pressed his palm against the side of her neck, fingertips tracing the ridges of her spine. She forced herself to tilt up her chin as his head dipped forward towards hers.

She started to inhale but couldn't move. Her heart stalled as she registered it.

Ferron drew back, studying her with flat, emotionless eyes.

Her lungs were already starting to burn as she tried to work out exactly what he'd done to her. Experienced as she was as a healer, she'd never had anyone use vivimancy on her.

He tilted his head, holding her upright against the wall by one shoulder. "Do you have any sense of self-preservation? I could have killed you fifty times in this building alone."

Helena couldn't respond. Her eyes were beginning to bulge. Her heart still worked at least; it was racing inside her chest. Her eyes must have looked terror-stricken, because he chuckled.

"Don't worry, I won't take advantage of you," he said softly in her ear.

His fingers just barely moved and the paralysis on her lungs disappeared, but *only* her lungs.

She drew a ragged breath through her teeth because it was the closest she could get to screaming.

She couldn't find a way to untangle her body from his control, couldn't even find her own resonance. He'd caught her completely off guard by making her think he meant to kiss her.

"I'm going to show you something interesting now. I'm told it's one of my special talents." His free hand pressed against her forehead, obscuring her vision.

That was all the warning she got before his resonance pushed into her mind like a large needle puncturing her skull.

Her body jerked.

She could feel him. His resonance hit the forefront of her consciousness like a bolt of lightning, and her memories sprang up before her eyes like a zoetrope.

It was as though she was reliving the moment: her shoulders against the wall, his body leaning in, tilting her face up; then time skipped back and her hand was pressed against the door; then she was finding her way through the tenement and the claustrophobic nearness of the buildings.

Ferron moved deeper into her memory; she watched herself strapping on her medical satchel to head out.

He could *read* her mind.

She couldn't let this happen.

She struggled, trying to get free, to rip her consciousness out of his control.

He delved further.

She was in an empty chymistry lab transmuting several rare compounds into an elixir. She coated his ring with it, careful not to disrupt the mirrored entanglement.

Ferron let go very suddenly, and the paralysis vanished.

Her knees gave out and she slid down the wall, her head throbbing so violently that she could barely see straight.

"What did you do to my ring?" he asked, standing over her.

"What did you do to *me*?" she retorted, her voice tremulous.

"It's a trick I learned from Artemon Bennet," he said, stepping away from her. "He calls it animancy. When we take Resistance fighters alive, it's not unusual for us to examine their memories. So if you're ever captured, there's a chance it'll happen to you. Which makes you a liability for me."

Helena closed her eyes, struggling to compose herself. The Eternal Flame had no idea such a thing could be done. What kind of defence was possible?

"Now, I'll ask again." Ferron's voice was implacably cold. "What did you do to my ring? Where is it?"

She swallowed, forcing herself to speak steadily. "It's an elixir that's bonded to the surface. The coating bends light to make things hard to notice unless you know to look for them."

He crouched and lifted her left hand, his thumb sliding across her fingers until he found the ring by touch. His eyes narrowed. He tilted her hand this way and that.

His eyebrows went up.

She could tell he could see the ring again.

He was silent for a long moment. "I've never heard of anything like this before."

"It was never fully developed."

An eyebrow rose as he met her eyes. "Yours?"

She gave a reluctant nod. "One of my undergraduate projects. Never got it to work well on things much bigger than this, though. The refraction grows irregular."

He stood, pulling her to her feet.

She struggled not to flinch away now that she knew what he could do with that touch.

"I'm not having my cover blown because you're incompetent," Ferron said.

Helena had never been called incompetent in her life, and she bristled. "I wasn't aware that immunity to mind-reading was something you expected from a war prize."

"It's not mind-reading," Ferron said, looking derisive. "What I did was simply a minor manipulation of your brain. It might feel as if I've reached in and seen your thoughts as vividly as if you were reliving them, but unless I'm being exhaustive and replaying them, there's only glimpses; most of it is lost in the noise. It's only the things you focus on that are clear enough to decipher easily. If you're ever caught, don't let your interrogator trick you into thinking they saw more than they have."

"So, what did you see?" she asked, trying to understand.

He smirked. "Mostly your terror. Disorienting you with fear made you vulnerable. You weren't coherent enough to do anything to resist. Then it was a blur. The two clarity points were when you were analysing the door, and the ring. You were so focused on them, you weren't thinking about anything else that would have blurred the memories. The mind is excellent at betraying its priorities."

So an interrogator couldn't see everything, just all the important things. Lovely.

"What do I do, to protect myself?" She hated that she had to ask him. "How are you expecting me to prevent that?"

"An interrogator won't stop until they have valuable information. If you're captured, there's nothing you'll be able to do to stop it, but if they think you're weak they won't look carefully. You have to give up something valuable enough that it seems legitimate as a way to keep the things that matter most hidden."

She considered this, still leaning against the wall because she wasn't sure her legs would hold her.

"Think about it. Choose something. If I'm looking for information about the Eternal Flame or Holdfast, what can you give up that would seem like the biggest secret you have? Using resonance on the mind like that is like setting someone's house on fire. Minds instinctively bolt to protect what's most important to hide. You have to train yourself to do the reverse. Focus on what doesn't matter. And remember, whatever you think they saw, unless you draw attention to it or they're being extremely thorough, they only glimpsed. Don't focus on it."

She nodded slowly. "All right."

"I'm going to test you again next week. Be ready for it."

CHAPTER 27

Februa 1786

When Helena told Crowther what Ferron was capable of, he had her removed from all the Eternal Flame's meetings and cut off from any information regarding Luc's whereabouts.

Everyone assumed it was due to her mysterious "breakdown" which was being whispered about. This was convenient for Crowther but rendered Helena even more of a pariah than usual.

She was relieved when Ferron calmly invited her in the next time rather than accosting her before she'd made it through the door.

The tenement was depressingly drab. Clearly there hadn't been much concern about the workers living in comfort back when the factories had been running.

"Ready?" he asked, stepping towards her and slipping a black leather glove off.

Helena clenched her own bare hands, feeling the texture of the scar across her palm as she nodded.

He didn't paralyse her this time. He simply pressed his palm against her forehead. She couldn't hold back her gasp.

Her eyes rolled back so violently, she could feel the strain down her optic nerves.

Despite knowing what was coming, her mind baulked, panicking, instantly swerving her focus onto things she didn't want to focus on.

Crowther's office. His shadowed face.

She forced her attention away.

Luc.

Crowther had cleared her to use the last Eternal Flame meeting she'd attended as a distraction.

They'd been discussing the new method for taking out the liches and Undying, and what they should do with the talismans they'd retrieved. Luc's unit had brought several back.

The resonance through her mind abruptly stopped, and she stood swaying, trying to force her eyes back into focus, her thoughts swirling.

"Better than I expected," she dimly heard Ferron saying. "Unfortunately, it won't only happen once."

His resonance sliced through her again.

It was worse the second time, like having a wound reopened, ripped larger. It was harder to think.

When Ferron finally let go, Helena felt as though her skull were about to split in two.

Her eyes were welling up with tears, and she bit down savagely on her lip, her chest stuttering as she fought to breathe.

The room swam, threatening to disappear. She swayed, feeling blindly for the wall.

"Drink this." A vial of something was shoved into her hand. "Otherwise you may black out."

She placed it in her mouth, doubting that Ferron would poison her, but if he did, she wasn't sure she'd mind. Her skull throbbed as though there were a drum inside it.

Mouth-numbingly bitter pain relief washed across her tongue. She nearly spat it back into the vial as she realised that he'd given her laudanum for a headache. Did he have any idea how limited opium supplies were in the North?

But it was already in her mouth, so she swallowed.

When she reopened her eyes, the room had a soft luminous quality. She blinked at the way it softened the edges of everything, including Ferron.

"Did this happen to you?" she asked, her tongue sluggish. He was Undying; she didn't know if they got headaches. Or even slept.

"More than once," he said. "My training was rigorous."

She nodded. It was strange how untouched by the war he looked. Yet when she forced herself to look past his appearance, there was an eerie, dangerous stillness about him.

"Why?" she asked.

He stared down his nose at her, eyes growing hard. "To see if I'd be better than my father, or if I'd break under interrogation, too."

She had never thought about what had been done to Atreus Ferron after his arrest. Everyone knew that he'd confessed; she'd always assumed it had been voluntary.

"Was that—before you killed Principate Apollo?"

Ferron stared at her, his mouth twisting. "Are you wanting a confession? Shall I tell you everything I've done?"

She stared into his mocking eyes. "Do you want to?"

There was a flash of surprise that softened his features for an instant. He was lonely.

She'd suspected that he might be. Ever since Crowther had told her about the circumstances of his parents' marriage, she'd re-evaluated her vague memories of Ferron at the Institute. She couldn't remember him having friends. He'd associated with the other guild students, but he hadn't spent much time with any particular individuals. If he had, they would have been inundated with questions and accusations after the murder. The students in their year had all said things like, "I roomed with him last year, but he barely talked," and "We were partners in alloy fusion, but he always did assignments alone."

If he'd been raised on ancestral ambition and little else, always being watched for signs of weakness or vivimancy, he'd probably never had anyone he could risk trusting. Now in war, the stakes had only grown.

He lived among immortal men all consumed by their own desire for power and vengeance. He couldn't possibly risk trusting anyone.

"Why would I want to tell *you* anything?" he asked viciously, stepping away from her.

She didn't press the issue. She didn't need to know.

She only needed him to realise he wanted to tell someone—

—that he wanted to tell her.

That would make her emotionally valuable to him. It would make her interesting enough that he'd begin to let his guard down.

"Did you want to go again?" she asked after a moment, hoping to impress him.

Instead, he stood. "They used to torture me while Bennet did it. Called it practice—in case I got caught." His mouth twisted into a sneer. "But it was an excuse. He enjoys it, how it feels to be inside a mind when it's screaming. If you're ever caught, that's what he'll do to you."

He didn't wait for her to respond, just tossed an envelope too quick for her to catch, walking out before it hit the floor.

HELENA WAS ON SHIFT IN the casualty ward when Ilva Holdfast and Falcon Matias appeared with four girls trailing behind them.

"Healer Marino, we've realised that you're under undue strain as our only healer," Ilva said with a completely unreadable expression while Matias was droning on about sacred duty, pronouncing an invocation, and draping sunstone amulets around the necks of the four girls. "Falcon Matias was divinely led to these four. He has interviewed them extensively to verify the sincerity of their faith and the pure intention of their souls. It will be your sacred duty to guide them as they learn to provide Sol's intercession."

There was a pause; Helena didn't know what to say. When the silence grew painful, she forced herself to nod mutely. Crowther had said there were others who could replace her as healer. She hadn't expected four.

Matias had always overruled the idea of new healers. It seemed Helena's outburst had convinced him that any quantity of healers would be better than Helena.

Although the girls were her trainees, Helena was not expected to do all the teaching. Matron Pace was also assigned to provide the newcomers with basic medical training. Helena refrained from pointing out that this process would create the very same hybrid of medicine and healing that Matias had always objected to Helena openly utilising.

Matron Pace was already reviewing the hospital security protocols with the trainees, stressing that every patient brought in had to be checked for reanimation before they could be treated. It could be difficult to determine in victims that had died recently, but every single one had to be vetted twice, once by the guards upon intake and then by a medic or nurse. Any patients not double-marked with clearance had to be approached with extreme caution; they could be a necrothrall or, even more insidiously, a lich.

Helena tuned out the lecture, resisting the urge to touch the scar on the side of her throat. She'd heard the warning repeated so many times she'd lost count, but every time she did, she wanted to plunge her face into a bucket of ice water and scream.

She knew she should be glad that there'd be more healers, but instead a knot formed in her stomach as she studied each girl.

These were her replacements, because her job as healer was now secondary to her function and purpose as Ferron's possession.

The knowledge sat like a live coal inside her.

One of the trainees stepped forward, extending her hand, then catching sight of Helena's gloved hand, she bobbed in an awkward curtsy instead.

"You're Marino, I know. This is Marta Rumly, Claire Reibeck, and Anne Stoffle. I'm Elain Boyle."

In less than a week, Helena was tired of all her trainees. They did not adapt to their new posts once they began to realise that healing was not an illustrious rank.

Claire and Anne both would barely even try to form a resonance channel. Marta didn't like getting her hands dirty. Elain Boyle was eager to learn but kept trying to heal dead patients.

They were all prone to thinking that just because they could "feel" how to do something that it would naturally be right, and when corrected, rather than seek answers, they acted like baby birds, waiting passively, heads gaping, expecting her to hurry over and stuff the relevant knowledge inside. Being proactive or looking for answers themselves never seemed to occur to them, always waiting to be told what to learn or do.

She couldn't stop thinking resentfully about them when she returned to the Outpost. Ferron seemed to notice her distraction; he caught her chin, tilting her head back so that their eyes met.

She was keyed up in anticipation for his mental invasion, but instead she felt his resonance, a sensation as insubstantial as spider silk, flicker through her nerves. What was he—

His palm was pressed against her forehead, and she scarcely had time to refocus before her mind was split open and it was all she could do to keep her thoughts of the trainees away from him, trying to keep her focus on the repetitive parts of her life that he found unremarkable. For all he knew, she spent her days performing inventory, reviewing medical forms, and washing her hands.

When it was finally over, he studied her with an expression she couldn't place. Rather than step away, he moved closer.

She went stiff, forcing herself to look up at his face so that she wouldn't focus on the physicality of him. His bare fingers touched her chin lightly, tilting her head back so that her throat was bared.

She felt his resonance again.

Was he testing her, trying to see if she could feel it?

"Remind me, what was your repertoire?" he asked softly.

"Broad," she said, knowing not to lie—the Guild Assembly might have access to her immigration records. "That's why the Institute accepted me. There were a few rare compounds that I couldn't pass with, but for the most part, my resonance is broad-spectrum."

He tilted his head to one side, still unnervingly close. "What were you going for?"

"I hadn't decided."

He gripped her chin. "You were two years into your undergraduate studies. How had you not decided?"

"Luc wanted to travel, and he wanted me to go with him. I thought I could choose afterwards."

His hand dropped away, resonance vanishing.

"Of course. You must have thought you were so special, being Holdfast's little pet." He cast her a sidelong look as he withdrew an envelope and held it out. "Look at you now."

The scars on her palm itched as she took it.

The envelope bore the same name as always. "Who's Aurelia Ingram?"

He gave a dismissive shake of his head. "No one." Then he laughed. "Someone my father contracted me to marry when I was—nine. The guild's pushing for it. They're worried about what will happen should I be prematurely consumed by fire."

"But you're—" She hesitated, finding the word bizarre to use in conversation. "—immortal."

"In a way." He rolled his eyes. "But I could still lose my body at some point. They'd like me to have an heir just in case. My betrothed has recently come of age, but I visited her once, and I have no intention of ever doing so again. I keep meaning to write her letters, but somehow," he shook his head, "they all go astray."

CHAPTER 28

Martius 1786

As much as Helena hated it, she had to admit that Ferron's training was doing something, although perhaps not what he'd intended.

His repeated invasions had awakened in her a newfound sense of her own mental landscape. It reminded her of when she'd first realised she was a vivimancer, as if her resonance could suddenly reach something wholly unfamiliar.

Ferron's resonance through her mind made her conscious of an energy there which she could manipulate.

She wasn't sure if she'd always had the ability and simply didn't notice, or if it was the "animancy" Ferron had mentioned. It wasn't as if she could ask.

As far as Ferron was concerned, Helena was only learning to concentrate.

However, she'd realised that she could supplement her focus with her resonance, pushing away her thoughts, rerouting her mind down preferred paths. At first, she practised it simply for their meetings, but she found herself using it constantly at Headquarters, too, pushing away all the thoughts and feelings eating at her.

After another test, Ferron stepped away from her, glancing outside one of the dirty windows. There was barely a view; the Outpost was crowded, but there was a sliver of sky visible in the direction of the islands. He stared towards it. The white, overcast sky was stained with smoke.

He looked at her. "There's always smoke rising from your Headquarters. It's from the crematorium, isn't it?"

Helena said nothing, but his guess was right. They were constantly burning the dead.

"How many soldiers do you have left?"

Helena's mouth went dry. That was one of the Eternal Flame's greatest concerns: that the Undying would realise how exhausted the Resistance ranks were. That one brutal push might be enough to wipe them out entirely.

She said nothing.

Ferron stood silhouetted by the window's pale light. "How much longer do you think you all can keep fighting?"

That, she could answer. "Until there's no one left. There's no surrendering for us."

"Good to know," he said softly, looking back at the smoke.

THE HOSPITAL HAD BEEN RUNNING on fumes for months, so short on supplies that any smuggled in from Novis seemed to instantly evaporate.

"We're completely out of gauze, and we used the last of the opium resin last week," Pace said as she and Helena stood together in the nearly empty supply room. "The Council wants to use the new healers to cover for the shortage, but they're not anywhere near reliable."

Even without a war, opium products were often in short supply. The dual moon tides limited sea trade from the Ortus regions for most of the year, except during the summer ebb, when Lumithia was in Abeyance and the sea separating the continents briefly calmed. The rest of the year, supply caravans had to circumnavigate the sea—a journey which could often take half a year and resulted in prohibitive prices.

The Eternal Flame needed far more than just opium. They needed more food, medicine, clothing, and bandages. Anything not made of metal or transmutable materials was in desperately short supply. If the Resistance couldn't regain control of the ports before the summer trade influx, they'd be starved into submission before the next winter.

"The floodings won't be so bad for a little while," Helena said. "I can find sphagnum outside of the city, and that'll help with the gauze shortage at least. Lots of willow this time of year, too."

Pace nodded, still staring at the empty shelves. "It'd be something, at least."

Without clean, sterile gauze and bandages, injuries would get infected, recovery would be slower, the risk of disease and contagious infections would rise. Even with five healers providing pain relief, their support would come at the cost of other healing they could be doing.

As Helena headed out towards the wetlands in the early morning, she caught sight of Luc and Lila in the commons, armed to the teeth and sparring. She hadn't even heard they were back again.

She'd been sleeping on a camp bed in Pace's office. Pain was often the worst for patients at night.

She paused a moment to watch.

Luc preferred fighting in the traditional Holdfast style that involved an enormous flaming sword that he could transmute into two smaller flaming swords. He was exceptional with fire alchemy. White flames bright as the sun fanned out around him like wings, making his blue eyes glow like sapphires, and even the gauntness of his features somehow made him look more ethereal.

His power really did seem otherworldly.

Helena knew it wasn't; in fact, she probably knew more about how it worked than he did. While Luc had a natural talent for pyromancy, he lacked both patience and interest when it came to the science. As a student, he used to rely on Helena to make sense of the theory sections of his homework.

Pyromancy was more varied than metal transmutation. A pyromancer in combat needed to be able to rapidly improvise without hesitation or miscalculation based on numerous variables—wind, enclosed space, target distances, oxygen levels.

She watched Luc's fingers, mentally calculating which techniques and array sourcing he was using. He was so fast, she could barely keep up.

Because basic projectiles had negligible effect on necrothralls or the Undying, most fighting was either incendiary or close-range.

"Hel!" Luc's voice split the early morning as he stopped short, waving her over.

Luc grinned as she neared. He was all in white, wearing just his amiantos under-armour to keep his clothes from singeing. His face was glistening from the heat. "How was I?"

Her lips pursed.

He laughed. "You can be honest."

Her eyebrows furrowed. "You're overusing oxygen. It's a bad habit. It can be dangerous if you're in an enclosed space," she said.

Luc scrubbed his forehead. "I know, I'm trying to extend the accuracy of my reach, but I can't keep it stable without losing control of how much air it takes."

Helena gnawed on the inside of her lip. "Which formula are you using?"

Luc grimaced. "I don't know, haven't written out an array in ages. Just do it in my head. You know, what feels right."

"You could probably work it out if you actually wrote it down," she said, giving him a pointed look.

He got a sly gleam in his eyes. "Well, maybe I will if you'll look at it. We're about to go on break anyway, and I hear you've got trainees now, which means there's no excuses left. It's next time. Come on. I'll set something on fire if you try to say no."

She exhaled. "I was actually on my way to—"

The sky above them burst into flames with a crackling roar, drowning out her words.

"Sorry, you were saying?" Luc asked.

"You should come, Hel," Lila said as she mopped her face with a towel. "Luc's been going on about this new thing he's doing for weeks, and none of us has any idea what he's talking about."

Helena's heart quickened, and she dared a smile. "I guess I have to help, then."

"You guess," Luc grumbled as he wrapped an arm around her shoulders and pulled her along with them all. "You should be delighted. I'm delightful."

Helena laughed.

She had no idea what had him in such a good mood, but she was glad of it. Kaine Ferron was a small price to pay if it meant there were moments like this again.

"Marino."

Crowther's voice was like a knife through her back.

She flinched, freezing in her tracks.

Crowther was standing behind them in the corridor. "Marino, I need to discuss the hospital inventory sheet you turned in last night," he said, gesturing in the opposite direction.

Luc spoke first, his voice unusually cool. "I'm sure it can wait, Jan. I need Hel for something."

"I apologise, Principate, but it cannot," Crowther said, his voice mild, but his eyes boring a hole through Helena. "It's a matter of some urgency."

Helena started to speak, but Luc squeezed her shoulder and smiled, all teeth. "Sorry. I need her."

Crowther's eyebrows rose. "Are you injured?"

Luc stiffened. "No. She's helping me with something related to pyromancy."

Everything about Crowther seemed to sharpen, like a cat extending its claws, but he bowed. "If you require help with your pyromancy, I would be more than happy to advise. I was personally trained by your family."

"I'll certainly keep that in mind," Luc said in a tone of false civility.

"I am always at the service of the Principate," Crowther said, inclining his head. "And as such, I must insist that Marino come with me. The matter of inventory may sound trivial, but it is of vital importance that the hospital is properly equipped; it can make the difference between life or death for our soldiers." His gaze flicked to Lila, then Soren, then Alister, and onwards, resting on each one of them, as if to insinuate that Luc was choosing Helena's companionship over their lives.

Luc stood silent. Helena could feel his rising resentment, a pressure growing in the air.

A standoff like this could only hurt the Resistance. Ferron's spying would be of little use if Luc disregarded information from Crowther out of dislike.

"He's right, I should go. Sorry, Luc," she said as she stepped away. She looked back. "Next time."

Lila's eyebrows were drawn together, but she didn't speak. It wasn't a paladin's place to speak in situations like this. Soren looked resigned but unsurprised, as Lila noticed; she cast a sharp, interrogative look at her twin.

Luc forced a smile. "Of course. I'm holding you to that."

WHEN THEY'D GONE, LEAVING HELENA alone with Crowther, his vaguely congenial expression vanished as he looked at her.

"You are a known advocate for necromancy with entirely conditional clearance now. Whatever allowances Ilva has permitted in the past, consider them all revoked until you have results that would make the effort of rehabilitating you worth it."

Crowther's words were still ringing in her ears as she set out for the wetlands. There was heavy fog hanging over the river, bringing with it a cold that penetrated to the bones, but there was no smell of blood or miasma, no smoke filling her lungs. Even before the war, being outside within the city never really felt like being outside.

The wetlands were too flooded to traverse, and she was forced to forage along the banks. There was a large copse of willows just below the dam.

Willow bark was best before the sap began to run. While its efficacy paled against laudanum, it could provide some minor pain relief and was also good for reducing inflammation, for managing fevers, and as a disinfectant for wounds. They were getting dangerously low on antiseptic, too.

She harvested ruthlessly, leaving all the stripped branches behind. It was mindless and frigid work.

She had no idea what Crowther expected of her. She didn't know how to make progress with Ferron. She'd expected the mission to be awful but straightforward, but Ferron gave her no opportunities to do anything.

She slit open a thick willow shoot with the tip of her harvesting knife, exposing the white wood beneath and removing the bark with a quick sweep of her arm.

The sound of one of the floodgates opening was almost lost amid the rush of water. A hinge shrieked, startling the marsh birds which burst out of the winter grass.

Helena dropped to the ground on instinct.

Cold mud seeped through her clothes as she peered across the water. The fog was slowly rising with the light, and she could just make out the upper tip of the West Island across the flooded wetlands and river channels. She didn't think she was in danger, but she knew better than to allow herself to be seen.

The floodgates were connected to an intricate tunnel system which led into cavernous flood cathedrals beneath the West Island. As she watched, several necrothralls appeared through the mouth of the open floodgate, dragging a large box by chains.

Behind the necrothralls came several people in black or dark-grey uniforms.

One man waved a hand, and the necrothralls simultaneously pulled long bolts from the top of the box, causing one side to fall open.

Helena watched with fascinated horror as a creature crawled out from inside.

It was larger than a dog, and pinkish like a pig, except its shape was wrong. It had catlike legs and a long, flattened body, but the head was the most grotesque. Reptilian. Flat, with a snout so elongated that the creature struggled to hold it out of the way as it crept forward. There were massive jutting teeth curving out of both the upper and lower jaws.

Helena's mouth went dry. She knew what it was, but it was impossible.

Like homunculi, chimaeras were one of Cetus's prescientific alchemical myths.

But she couldn't deny what she saw with her own eyes.

One of the men in black waved a hand, and a necrothrall stepped into the creature's path.

Teeth flashed as the mutated body lunged, moving impossibly fast.

The necrothrall went down, and the creature used its hooked teeth to peel the greyish skin off the limbs. The necrothrall continued trying to stand until the over-large jaws ripped the head off.

Helena's fingers shook as she buckled the straps of her satchel and began to crawl slowly away, trying to keep hidden.

The men across the water were all in conversation together, watching the monster as it ate the necrothrall. As a group, they turned and reentered the floodgate tunnel, leaving the creature behind, a pale and monstrous sentinel crouched on the bank.

Helena watched from across the water as the monster wandered along the shore with short, disproportionate steps. It struggled to move and stayed out of the water, sticking to the bank.

Helena resumed crawling, not wanting to find out if the chimaera could swim. Her hands had turned purplish grey from the cold. She rubbed them together rapidly, trying clumsily to use her resonance to bring warmth back into her fingertips.

She was just crossing the bridge, able to see the gate and checkpoint, when a searing heat encased her hand, so painfully hot she almost screamed.

The heat instantly faded.

She looked down, realising what it was. The skin around her left ring finger had a red tinge to it, and when she tilted her hand, the ring reappeared for an instant.

It burned again.

She nearly ripped it off. With her hands so cold, the heat was excruciating.

Bastard. There was no reason to make the ring that warm unless he thought she had nerve impairment.

He was probably summoning her to tell her about the chimaera, which she already knew about. Her bag was heavy, and she was freezing, and all she wanted to do was get back to Headquarters.

But Ferron wouldn't know that she already knew. She turned reluctantly and headed for the Outpost.

She arrived first. She'd known she would, but it was still irritating to be so cold and forced to wait. She was barely able to get the door open.

She removed her cloak and then peeled off her jacket, wringing the sleeves so that marsh water trickled out, then she twisted at the extra fabric of her shirtsleeves, trying to make them slightly drier. Her boots squelched every time she moved, and her toes were numb.

The door finally swung open, revealing Ferron, whose eyes instantly narrowed at the sight of Helena.

"What are you doing?" he asked, eyes following the trickle of the muddy water Helena was squeezing onto the floor.

"I was wet."

Irritation flashed across his face, but Helena was beyond caring. She shook her jacket so that it snapped. "So, chimaeras. Is there more than the one?" When he didn't answer, she looked up.

His eyebrows were drawn together. "You're already aware." There was crisp irritation in his voice.

She nodded. "I saw it."

The most indescribable expression passed across his face. "You saw it? How?"

"I was down in the wetlands when they set it loose."

"You were *in* the barrens?"

She'd always hated that name for it.

"Yes. I go there for medical supplies. There's a lot to forage, it's—" She hesitated. "—it's good in a pinch. Is there only one chimaera?"

Ferron refused to return to the matter at hand. "This is something you do often?"

"Well, it's seasonal. There's not much I can get during heavy flooding but—" Helena paused at Ferron's stunned expression.

She sighed impatiently. "I mentioned that I do this every Saturnis and Martiday. I was out today getting some extra."

"No . . ." Ferron said slowly, a dangerous edge to his voice. His posture was still casual, but his tone gave him away. "You said you were getting medical supplies. I assumed that meant meeting a smuggler in the city."

"Why would the Eternal Flame send me to meet a smuggler? I'm getting medicinal plants; it helps stretch the supply."

He flicked his hand towards her. "Alone?"

"Obviously," Helena said. "That's why we can meet after I finish. How have you not realised this? You're constantly crawling through my memories."

"Your mind is considerably less interesting than you imagine. Why would I pay attention to the frivolous things you do on the way here?"

It was almost funny how blindsided he was.

"Tell Crowther to come up with some other excuse for you coming out of the city," he finally said. "You come here, and you go back. I'm not risking my cover having you crawl through a marsh for a few weeds."

Helena stood, stunned with indignation. "You—you can't do that."

His expression hardened and now he moved, finally, stalking her across the room. "Actually, I can. Have you forgotten? I own you."

"Yes," she said, refusing to back down; she'd done enough bending and complying that day. "But you also gave your word not to interfere with my responsibilities to the Eternal Flame. Foraging is part of *my* work. I've been doing it for years. If you want to control everything I do, you can wait until we win."

Ferron stood glaring at her for several seconds, and she was afraid that he'd go over her head, contact Crowther, and force an alternative.

Crowther would do it. She just knew. Anything to make Ferron happy.

Her heart pounded fiercely in her chest, praying he wouldn't call her bluff.

He stepped back, eyes steely. "Fine. Then tell me, how are you protected out there? What weapons do they have you carrying? I want to see if they'll work on the chimaeras."

He held out a gloved hand. Helena stared at it. Despite her still-numb hands, heat crawled across the back of her neck and a lump rose in her throat.

She swallowed. "It's—um, not like that," she said awkwardly, trying to sidle past him.

"Not like what?"

"I don't—have an issued weapon. They pulled me from combat before I qualified. When you only work in Headquarters, you don't—" She gestured at her clothes. "I forage as a civilian."

His eyebrows rose. "You're travelling through the city and out into the barrens alone and unarmed?"

Helena squirmed. It sounded much worse than it was. She had vivimancy, but she couldn't tell him that. It also didn't help that her trips weren't officially sanctioned.

Pace knew. Crowther knew. Matias, her actual superior, did not. Helena didn't want to give him the chance to forbid her from making medicine for some reason.

She tried to make it sound more reasonable. "If I had an issued weapon, that would put me in even more danger if I were apprehended."

"You can't be serious," he said in flat disbelief.

"I have a harvesting knife." She held it up.

He blinked slowly. "And what could you do with that thing?"

She lifted her chin. "We all did the basic combat training at the Institute. I still know the forms; they work with or without transmutation."

He looked her up and down. "And when did you last practise them?"

She averted her eyes. "I don't know, I don't keep track of things like that." She shoved the knife back into her satchel; her fingers stayed wrapped around the handle, its varnish worn away but the wood smooth from use. "I'm rather busy."

"Well, now I know what I'm doing with you next," he said with a sigh. "I thought your mind would be the biggest danger to me, but it turns out you're somehow still a walking liability. I'm not wasting my time training a new contact after all the time I've wasted on you."

Helena sighed. "It's not necessary. No one's ever bothered me."

Ferron raised an eyebrow. "You think there's only going to be one chimaera out there? Bennet's been working on this project for years. Now that he's cracked it, he'll have the barrens and low districts overrun with the creatures. What you saw is one of the early prototypes."

"Tell us how to kill them, then," she said sharply. "We're not going to give up food and medicine because you psychopaths decided to set monsters loose everywhere."

She was already being pulled in so many directions, she couldn't stand to think about having to add combat training.

"Obviously, I'll be working on that," he said through gritted teeth. "That's why I called you here, to let you know to be alert for them. If you're going out there, you have to be trained."

Helena gave an exasperated huff, turning towards the door. "Then I'll drill at Headquarters."

She unlocked the door as he spoke again.

"You don't want me to train you?" His voice had turned slippery and dangerous. "Why not? I'd have thought you'd prefer to fill our time with training rather than with some of the other activities I could demand."

Helena stopped short and looked back. He was cornering her.

He must have realised that she was supposed to seduce him, even if he didn't have any idea of her vivimancy. Damn it all.

"Fine," she snapped. "You can train me."

She knew already that whatever physical training he chose would probably be even worse than the mental training he'd already subjected her to. Combat training hardly seemed the context in which to evoke a sense of obsessive want.

Violent want was more likely.

There was a dull pounding in her head. She could feel Luc being pulled further and further from reach. All light in her life disappearing.

"You look so bitter." Ferron's mocking voice drew her back. His eyes glittered. "You'd think I just demanded you fuck me rather than not. Disappointed?"

Slow rage was seeping through her. "Do you always buy your company?"

It was only a guess, but Ferron seemed the type. Guild families with a tradition of resonance-based marriages had reputations for wandering into the beds of others. Marriage among the guilds was as much a business arrangement as the silk entertainment houses on the West Island.

Ferron's eyes gleamed. "I admit, I enjoy the professionalism," he said with a shrug. "Clear lines. No expectations. And I don't have to pretend I care." His lip curled at the last word, as though caring were the most offensive concept known to man.

"Of course. How very you."

"Quite," he agreed with a thin smile.

She wished she could hurt him, that there was a way for her to do it that counted.

He hurt her so much, without even trying, without needing to know anything about her. He'd simply spoken her name and reduced her to property, his whims locking an iron chain around her throat.

"Do you talk to them, tell them all about the tragic life you've had? Or are you just in and out, quick as you can?" she asked, her voice lilting with the taunt.

His eyes flashed.

"Want me to show you?" His voice was sharp and cold as a splinter of ice.

She met his eyes and raised her chin. "You won't."

His expression hardened. She knew that she could goad him if she kept going.

She'd finally get it over with, stop enduring Crowther and Ilva's search for signs that she'd been ravished or ravaged. Stop lying awake at night, cold with dread, wondering when it would finally happen. She was sick of waiting. Of wondering on and on. Like bracing for a sword to fall.

She kept talking. "It would be too real for you, wouldn't it? If it was someone you knew. I think that's why you haven't. You're afraid I'll mess with those clear lines, so you're making up all these excuses about needing to train me."

The muscle in his jaw rippled.

"Testing me, Marino?" His voice was cool, like the flat side of a knife blade.

She didn't blink. "Yes. I am."

There. She'd done it now.

He walked towards her across that cold, filthy room, and rather than quicken, her heart slowed. Each beat heavy, drawn out as he leaned forward until their eyes were level.

"Strip."

It was all he said.

She couldn't move.

She knew she was supposed to do whatever he wanted. That was the deal she'd made. And she'd wanted it to be over, but now her body wouldn't obey.

She stood frozen. The tenement was nothing but an empty room with a chipped tile floor and a wooden table, and every aspect of Ferron that she could read screamed that he was about to exact a profound degree of cruelty upon her.

"I see now." He smiled like a wolf. All teeth. "It's been killing you, hasn't it? Wondering. You expected me to do this to you right off. The waiting—trying to guess when I might get around to it—that bothers you more than having to fuck me. Well, you have your wish. Take your clothes off, Marino."

She barely managed to swallow. Her ears were ringing until she could scarcely hear herself think.

He wasn't even aroused. She could tell. He was doing it to teach her a lesson.

Crowther was wrong. He was so desperate to get some kind of leverage on Ferron, he'd convinced himself of some kind of slowly germinating obsession, but there wasn't any. Ferron had simply identified what Crowther wanted to believe about him.

The whole mission was pointless.

Her jaw began to tremble uncontrollably. "You don't even want me. Why did you ask for me?"

He laughed. "You're right, I don't want you, but owning you will never get old. *As long as you live.* What a promise to make. I wonder how much I can make you regret it." His teeth flashed again. "Take your clothes off, Marino. It's time to see what I've been paying for."

Her hands trembled as she reached up and began unfastening the top button of her shirt.

"It's power that gets you off, isn't it?" Her voice shook with rage as she forced herself to move down to the next button. "Hurting people is the only way you know how to feel anything. But now even that barely does it for you, so you have to find new ways to do it, make your victims responsible for their pain; making it a choice they made, a vow they consented to. That's what thrills you now. Using what people care about to coerce and enslave them rather than having to do the physical work of hurting." She scoffed in his face. "You think you're better than us because you're immortal, but you're dead inside already."

She said it despite knowing he'd probably enjoy her attempt at bravado, because she wanted to say it at least once. He didn't laugh at her words, though; instead the malice in Ferron's expression vanished.

He stood there staring at her, growing paler and paler.

Then something metal inside the walls of the tenement groaned and the air hummed. Helena could *feel* Ferron's resonance in the room, an uncontrolled surge of energy distorting the room. This was one of the many reasons alchemists were dangerous. When they lost control, their resonance could expand beyond them. It was a combat technique, but without stability and control, it could annihilate anything within their repertoire.

And Ferron was a vivimancer, which meant Helena was within his repertoire. She could feel his resonance in her bones.

Her skin vibrated. A thrum ran through her heart.

Ferron's expression contorted into one of pure rage. "Get out!"

She didn't move, terrified that in an instant she'd be atomised.

He snarled and turned away from her, and the door warped, the sharp sound of metal and mechanisms splintering as it folded in on itself and split apart, writhing as if alive.

"Get out!"

Helena did not need further invitation. She bolted through the door, leaping across the wreckage and fleeing down the stairs so fast, she slammed into the landing wall. She shoved herself back to her feet and fled the Outpost.

CHAPTER 29

Martius 1786

HELENA WAS STILL CATCHING HER BREATH, A stabbing pain in her side, as she was taken to Ilva's office to report on what she'd seen in the wetlands.

Ilva sat across from Helena at her desk, a fountain pen clasped in her fingers as Helena gasped out the information.

"I thought chimaeras were a transmutational impossibility," Ilva said calmly when Helena finished.

"That's what I was taught," Helena said.

"And Ferron says there will be more?" Ilva's expression was difficult to read.

Helena almost flinched at the name but nodded. "It was just the beginning, he said."

Ilva hummed under her breath, her pale eyes distant.

When Luc was at the front lines, he abdicated his other responsibilities as Principate to Ilva, not realising how ruthless she was in making whatever choices protected him alone.

Helena had liked that about her. When Ilva had first taken an interest in Helena, Helena had been flattered, seeing herself and Ilva as kindred in a cause, because they were both fully willing to make hard choices for Luc's sake.

She'd thought they were partners.

"How are things progressing with Ferron?" Ilva asked as Helena started to stand.

Helena stilled, sinking back into the chair, fingernails digging against the punctures in her palm. "He's quite—mercurial."

Ilva just hummed again. The strained expression she'd worn when the offer had been presented had vanished. Ilva seemed at peace with her choice now.

"Hopefully the new healers free you to focus."

Helena's throat closed, her knuckles whitening at the insinuation that the healers were for her benefit.

"I'm sure they will be a great help," she said with a false smile. "Although—the initial training does take up quite a bit of time."

Lines of tension appeared in the wrinkles around Ilva's eyes.

"I'm sure you know about the shortages in the hospital inventory. Usually, when I have time off, I try to help supplement the hospital's inventory—"

"Oh yes, Pace has mentioned it . . ." Ilva said slowly. "Your father had that—little apothecary in the low district, didn't he?"

Helena gave a startled nod. Given that her father's medical licensing hadn't been recognised as legitimate in Paladia, the apothecary hadn't been categorically legal. Medicine, like everything else in Paladia pre-war, was industrialised, modernised, and licensed, which rooted out would-be charlatans but had a tendency to raise prices. An amount considered trivial in the upper districts could be a month's or a year's wages in the water slums.

An unlicensed tincture might not be even half as effective, but it did have the added benefit of not sending the invalid and their family into debtor's prison.

"He was a doctor, though, wasn't he?" Ilva looked sincerely curious.

"Yes. He trained in Khem, manual surgery and medicine. He and my mother ran a surgery and apothecary together in our village before I was born."

Ilva inclined her head. "Is that why you studied so much chymistry? I was on the board approving your scholarship every year. We used to wonder when we reviewed your transcripts. It seemed an odd choice considering your repertoire. You used it to help him during the summers, didn't you?"

Helena froze. Working as an underaged, unlicensed chymist in an illegal apothecary was not within the Institute's student code of conduct.

Ilva waved a dismissive hand. "It's all in the past, Marino. You're not going to be deported right now for a six-year-old violation of labour law. Really, it's an example of Sol's providence that you have all these skills."

Her saliva turned sour; she stared at her hands. "Thank you." She swallowed. "Um, due to the shortages, I've been trying to help where I can. I've been extracting salicin from willow bark; it can act as a stopgap for a few things until Novis sends more." Her voice was stilted. "The thing is, the willow bark is best harvested in early spring. In a few weeks, the snowmelt and Ascendance will have the wetlands flooded, so the more I can process now, the better—but if I was working and got called away, it could spoil the batch. Cost us medical supplies. I was wondering, is there anyone with some chymistry experience who might be willing to help, just help finish up, if I'm called away? Or I could bring them supplies to process themselves."

Ilva's head inclined almost mechanically, her expression growing tight as a demurring smile drew her lips back. "Helena . . ."

"Since it's all we have right now, it seems a shame to waste a resource," Helena added quickly.

Ilva paused, measuring her words. "A few weeks ago, this might have been a very different conversation, but that's hardly something I can ask of anyone now. Our chymists have extensive assignments of their own, and I suspect Falcon Matias is unaware of this supplementing you've been doing. He would have to be informed of anyone assigned to you in an official capacity."

"Of course."

"Actually—" Ilva suddenly sat forward. "I take that back. I just thought of someone who might be interested. Shiseo. I ran into him the other day."

Helena looked up, forehead furrowed. "Who?"

"Oh, he's an Easterner, Far Eastern. All the way from the Empire, in fact. He came to Paladia with a political asylum request after the new Emperor came to power." Ilva tapped her chin. "He's some kind of metallurgist, I think. Apollo was thrilled to have him, always loved foreign alchemy, said that kind of exposure was good for Luc. He's still here. Very educated, I believe. He might enjoy the opportunity to observe Paladian chymiatria."

"Doesn't he work at the forge?" Helena asked in confusion. Metallurgists were a vital resource.

Amusement flickered in Ilva's face. "No. We don't allow an Easterner near the Athanor Furnace, Marino." She nodded to herself. "Yes, I don't think he'd mind at all. You two could work well together."

A Far Eastern metallurgist was not what Helena had in mind. She didn't want another trainee; she wanted help, for something in her life to be marginally less difficult.

"Well, if he's willing, I suppose we could ask."

Ilva hummed, seeming distracted again. "Very good. Well, you can go now, Marino. It would appear I have scouts to dispatch and a Council meeting to call about these chimaeras."

Helena went to her lab and unpacked her satchel, washing and laying out all her willow bark and sphagnum to dry. When she went to her room in the Tower to clean up, the evidence of Lila's return was littered everywhere.

Helena filled the bathtub, sinking in up to her neck. Now that she was alone, she could think about Ferron. Her brazen stupidity and his reaction to it.

He hadn't hurt her.

She hadn't realised how much she'd expected it. She'd assumed that if she ever provoked him, purposely or not, death or severe injury was inevitable.

Everyone knew the Undying were violent and sadistic. There were countless stories about the senseless cruelty they indulged in on the battlefield. Protected with invulnerability, they relished the atrocities they could commit.

Helena had assumed Ferron would be like the rest of them.

Now she wasn't sure what he was.

He'd been so angry. Angrier than she had ever seen anyone, but he had driven her off. He hadn't hurt her at all.

She sank under the water until it covered her face.

Why not? After all, he didn't care about the Eternal Flame. So what held him back? It wasn't as if Ferron was above violence. He'd ripped out a man's heart with his bare hands.

She replayed what she'd said.

The shock on his face, as if he hadn't realised what he was like until she'd told him.

CHAPTER 30

Aprilis 1786

BEFORE THE NEXT MARTIDAY, HELENA SUBMITTED FOR and received a standard-issue alchemical knife. Because of the chimaeras, she skipped foraging and went directly towards the Outpost, casting a wistful glance over the wetlands as she turned towards the dam.

There had been more than ten chimaeras spotted outside the city, mostly wandering the banks of the West Island. There were no deaths reported yet, but many of the people trapped in the city and on the Outpost relied on the river for food. It was only a matter of time.

Several units were being assembled into hunting parties. Predictably, Luc had immediately volunteered his battalion.

Inside the tenement, the door to the unit had been replaced. Helena hoped it was a good sign as she let herself in.

Her cloak and jacket, both abandoned by her flight, were on a table, neatly folded.

Ferron was not there.

She walked around the room, inspecting it. There were remnants of a kitchen, and a far door revealed a filthy bathroom, the sink chipped and stained as if there'd been chemicals poured down it. At least it had a bathroom. Some of the tenements in the low districts were so old, they didn't even have that.

She sat, fingers curling against her palm, using her resonance to tamp down her rising unease and keep her thoughts from anxiously spiralling. It was fine, Ferron was just late.

The minutes dragged on.

She hadn't told Crowther or Ilva what had happened. She'd passed it off as a brief meeting; Ferron had warned of the chimaeras and she'd hurried back, no mention of anything else.

But if Ferron didn't show up, she would have to tell Crowther, explain what had gone wrong. Her chest grew so tight she could barely breathe.

When ten minutes had passed, she forced herself to accept that Ferron was not coming, but as she pulled her satchel up onto her shoulder, the door clicked and he walked in.

He didn't seem at all surprised to find her still waiting there.

He closed the door and stood in front of it, his expression unreadable, body eerily still. It was strange how empty his posture was.

Helena had relied heavily on body language after moving to Paladia. Etras was culturally expressive; words, expressions, gestures were all part of communication. Northerners were canny, and they often communicated more through subtext than their actual words.

That was why Helena had been so drawn to Luc: He wasn't like that; he didn't say things he didn't mean. With other Paladians, Helena had learned to decipher what they meant through their bodies instead of their mouths.

However, Ferron's body said almost nothing. He reminded her of a gambler, hiding his tells. There was nothing about him that indicated his current mood.

"I'm sorry," she said, breaking the tense silence. "I shouldn't have said that last week. I lost my head. I'll do—whatever you want to make it up to you."

Ferron didn't react beyond his eyes flickering briefly.

"It's fine," he said after a moment, his voice void. "When I specified willing, that meant you were allowed to say no. Although, perhaps try saying it next time, instead of provoking me."

Helena looked at him in astonishment. From the moment Ilva and Crowther had told her the terms, she'd assumed her willingness, once given, was irrevocable.

Anything that happened after, she'd already agreed to.

She didn't believe him. He'd mentioned looking forward to her regret. That didn't imply any permission to change her mind or refuse what was demanded. No, he was altering the terms of their agreement because of what she'd said to him.

Her eyes narrowed appraisingly.

Her suspicion seemed to anger him. Irritation flashed across his face.

She averted her eyes; best not to provoke him again. Given time, he'd be sure to change his mind, to redefine the terms to suit his ends, but in this moment, he wanted to believe he had some kind of moral code, that there were things he was above.

She nodded as if she believed him.

"I have an alchemy knife now," she said, hoping the change of subject would distract him.

He held out a gloved hand. "Let me see it."

He took it carefully, his gloves not even grazing her skin. He now seemed overly aware of her.

He inspected the knife, testing the balance. Despite his gloves, the blade morphed, the knife edge spiralling around the inner core.

The purpose was to stab when the blade was flat, transmute, and pull out, leaving a massive wound. The larger a wound, the longer it took the Undying to recover, and the quicker necrothralls were rendered immobile. The blade could also be manipulated into a range of lengths, but that took effort and required familiarity with the idiosyncrasies of the alloy to keep it from being shattered.

Because it was standard-issue, the knife had been forged using lumithium emanations to increase its resonance. That way, alchemists with limited steel resonance could still transmute it. Helena's natural resonance didn't need supplementing—it made the alloy resonance feel uneven—but she was assured that she'd get used to it.

"Are you trained with a knife?" he finally asked.

She'd hoped he wouldn't ask that. "No."

"You'd do better with something longer, then." He flipped it in his hand, catching it deftly; slicing through the air, it morphed into a curving blade. "If anything gets close enough for you to use this, you're already dead."

The Resistance was not going to give a noncombatant anything but a basic weapon. "But . . . anything bigger is more noticeable. I'd be more likely to get stopped."

"Mmm," was all the answer she got as he transmuted the blade back to its base form.

"Any news about the chimaeras?"

He handed back the knife. "Four are already dead. They don't tolerate the cold very well." His mouth twisted with amusement. "Bennet's in high dudgeon."

"Where did the animals come from?" Crowther had told her to ask.

"He's using whatever he can. Domestic animals are the most easily accessed, but larger predators are preferable. I believe there've been a few hunting trips into the mountains. There was also the zoo."

"It seems a lot of work just to have them die in the wetlands."

Ferron gave an absent shrug. His eyes avoided her, instead looking almost anywhere else in the room. "There's not much else that they're good for. They're not manageable. There are rumours the High Necromancer feels misled about the project's potential and the resources involved."

He pulled out an envelope, but rather than handing it over, he set it on the table and left without another word.

It was the same routine for the next several times. Ferron would arrive, occasionally answer a few questions, and then leave. Sometimes he was there for less than five minutes.

There was no more mention of any training. Each time, Helena had to admit to Crowther that she had no progress to report. Ferron's information continued to be good, but Helena was little more than a glorified mail carrier.

She kept training the other healers, and working in her lab, where she now had an unofficial assistant. Shiseo was a small, balding man with dark eyes. He could read and understand Northern dialect fluently but spoke very little.

He caught on to the techniques of chymiatria quickly but kept to himself, shadowing Helena at a conscientious arm's length. Helena knew she should appreciate him—after all, she had asked for help—but with the trainees and now a lab assistant, there was nowhere left for her to go where she wasn't reminded that the accommodations were there because her priority was supposed to be Ferron.

Everything else was theatre now, a cover for a mission she was failing.

FERRON WAS LATE AGAIN. HE was often late, but he'd never left her waiting this long. She dreaded the thought of going back empty-handed, but at least the trip hadn't been a complete waste of her time.

She'd resumed foraging. The chimaeras had mostly died, and it felt criminal to miss the entire spring harvest. The river was rising, the floodwalls were marked to track the steady creep of Lumithia's Ascendant phase, and the mountain wind was losing its icy edge, which meant that soon the snowmelt would come rushing into the basin and the wetlands would be left underwater until nearly summer.

She opened her satchel and started sorting her harvest, blinking to concentrate.

She'd been so tired lately. Hospital shifts sometimes left her so exhausted, she could barely make it to her room.

She knew it was a sign she was over-expending herself healing, but she'd always healed that way, and it had never bothered her before. She couldn't understand it. The Toll wasn't supposed to take effect so suddenly, but she couldn't think of what else it could be.

She stared stupidly at the bundles of gathered herbs. Eventually, she leaned forward, resting her head on her arms. Her eyes fluttered shut.

The mechanism in the door startled her awake. She jolted upright. How long had she been asleep?

A gear in the door spun, but the lock didn't click and the door didn't open. There was a pause.

Helena shot to her feet as she heard the gear begin moving again, grinding slowly, as if the lock were being picked.

She fumbled for her satchel, digging for her knife. As her fingers wrapped around the hilt, the door swung inward. A stripe of red ran down the centre of it, topped with a scarlet handprint.

Ferron stood, swaying in the doorway.

His face deathly pale, his eyes out of focus.

The knife slipped from her fingers. "What happened?"

He looked at her as if confused to find her there. "Ss-nothing." He waved her off with his right hand as he got clear of the door, more blood spattering on the floor. There was a trail running down the hallway.

"You're . . . you're injured?" It was half a question. She didn't know he *could* be injured. Wasn't he supposed to be instantly regenerative? How could he be bleeding like this?

She started reaching for the clasp on his cloak, trying to see the extent of the wound.

He shoved her away, recoiling. "What are you doing?" No pride now, he moved like a stray expecting to be beaten, the whites of his eyes glaring.

Her fingers where she'd touched him were wet with blood. "You're hurt."

He slumped, looking down slowly. "Be fine—" His words slurred. "Jsst—need a minute . . ."

He slumped against the wall. Blood was trickling in a constant stream from his left sleeve, forming a pool on the floor. Just the sight of it threatened to send Helena into a frenzy.

Blood loss was dangerous. The Resistance lost more people from exsanguination than anything else. Staunching a bleed was something everyone was expected to know how to do properly and efficiently. Too much blood loss and even plasma expanders and saline wouldn't be enough.

How much blood could Ferron lose? Immortal or not, surely it couldn't be infinite.

She held her hands apart, palms showing, her voice placating. "I'm a—medic, Ferron. Let me help."

He stared at her, dazed, as if he needed time to process the information.

"What happened?" she asked, risking a step closer.

Blood was still flowing at an impossible rate.

Finally, he shook his head. "Just lost my arm."

As if to prove it, he unclasped his cloak. Both it and his grey coat fell off, revealing that there was nothing but scraps of burned fabric beneath, and a haemorrhage of blood where his left arm should have been.

He swayed, his eyes losing focus. "It'll grow back. But it's—taking a while."

Helena had never seen the Undying regenerate in person. Combatants described it as nightmarish and rapid, bones shooting out, muscles and tendons wrapping around, and then pale skin emerging from the raw tissue like mould.

All her time in the hospital testing the bounds of regenerated tissue, it was hard for her to believe that anyone could regrow an entire limb.

She'd tried growing back fingers once, but the amount of spontaneous regeneration it required was simply too much. Healing had hard limits. The Undying seemingly did not.

Ferron's arm looked as if it had been torn off. She stepped towards him, but he tensed again. She halted, mind spinning. Maybe she'd try talking again first. He seemed responsive to questions.

"I thought regeneration happened right away."

"Sometimes—takes longer," he said through gritted teeth, walking over and dropping into a chair. His head lolled back. "Lot of damage . . ."

"There was more?"

His face, tight with pain, pulled into a taut smile as he looked at her. "I have command of a new district . . ."

His voice trailed off. He straightened as if trying to rouse himself, blinking several times. "Previous commander—rather attached to it." He gave a lopsided shrug. "Insulted his mother—few times. Insinuated some unfavourable things about his wife and a certain horse." His head lolled back again. "Didn't like that. Duelled to the death. Well—close as we can get. I won, so now I get his command posts."

The last words were garbled. He was mostly talking inside his mouth.

He gave a barking laugh so abrupt that Helena jumped.

"He was a pyromancer, though. The arm's nothing compared with the burns. They were—worse. Gone now. Usually I can—" He gestured at himself. "But I'm—"

Whatever he was, his voice trailed off before he could specify.

She never would have thought that pain and chronic blood loss would be the trick for making Ferron talkative, but that was far more words in succession than she'd heard from him in weeks.

His eyes went out of focus. His breathing had grown shallow, almost stopping. He was going into shock.

"Why are you here? You didn't have to come." She stepped tentatively closer, prepared to be shoved away again.

He blinked slowly, staring up at her. His pupils had dilated so much, the black nearly swallowed the irises.

"Marino . . ." He sighed, as if it were obvious. He was still talking inside his mouth, lips barely moving. "Once I'm done here, I intend to drink so much I won't remember my own name for the next three days. I have a map—somewhere." He patted awkwardly at himself with his remaining arm and only then seemed to realise that his clothes were ashen scraps. "Fuck . . ."

Helena steeled herself and stepped closer.

"Ferron," she said gently but firmly, "I have medical experience. I'm going to check you and see if there's anything I can do to help."

He didn't seem to hear her, and didn't resist as she pressed fingers against his neck under the pretence of taking his pulse, cautiously using her resonance to find out what was wrong with him.

However unnatural he had felt the first time she'd used her resonance on him, it was a thousand times stranger this time. He was losing so much blood, he should be dead, but somewhere in his chest, a power source like a beacon was radiating out, regenerating him faster than he could die.

The lumithium talisman. That must be it. The source of the Undying's power.

Nonetheless, his body was trying very hard to die anyway.

Helena could recognise newly regenerated tissue, and he was covered in it. Most of his torso and face had been regenerated all the way down to the bones. Several of his organs seemed new as well.

However, it was the nonstop blood loss that was the problem. The body was not made to produce blood at even a fraction of the rate he was losing it. It was stripping him of resources to pull blood out of nowhere, all so that he could dump it out on the floor. A nonstop destructive loop. His body was so preoccupied with making more blood, it couldn't expend the resources necessary to regrow his arm and thereby end the blood loss.

Apparently somewhere in his anomalous regenerative abilities, the concept of blood clotting had been lost.

Helena drew a careful breath and spoke with as much assurance as she could manage.

"Admittedly, you're the first immortal person that I've treated, but you really need to stop bleeding this much." She pulled at the remaining tatters of his shirt. It crumbled away.

She didn't think that staunching the blood loss would cause regeneration issues.

"Let's get you onto the table," she said, pulling his existent arm over her shoulder and dragging him to his feet. It was fortunate that he was all limbs, because he was a deadweight to get up and onto his back. His eyes had fluttered closed, and he was nonresponsive, his chest barely rising.

She doubted he was conscious, but she maintained the charade of being a medic just to be sure. Using the heels of both hands, she pressed down on his shoulder to conceal her resonance as she constricted the veins and arteries in his arm.

It was remarkable how quickly that alone stabilised him.

Once he was no longer bleeding to death, his arm immediately started regenerating. She watched, mesmerised, as the bone burst out, expanding, muscles wrapping around it, regenerating his biceps, the elbow, the radius, and the ulna.

She couldn't help but release her resonance a bit more as she watched, trying to get a feel for—whatever he was. Wanting to understand how it worked. His body had already stopped feeling like it was on the verge of death.

The bones in his hand unfurled, and the veins and muscle tissue wove around them, and by the time it was done, she would never have known he'd lost the arm.

She eased the pressure of her hands off his shoulder as she reopened the arteries and veins, letting the blood rush through all the new tissue. The muscles in Ferron's arm rapidly evolved into established tissue.

She'd never considered regenerating more than new tissue, but as she felt Ferron's body reverting itself to its former state, she wondered if she could. There was no reason she had to stop there at basic regeneration.

The power radiating from inside Ferron's chest faded until it was barely discernible. A vague knot of energy and lumithium. It felt tiny for something with so much power.

She didn't dare push deeper, but she didn't pull her hands away.

Of all the contexts in which she'd imagined Ferron half naked in her presence, healing or medical care had not crossed her mind, although it was infinitely preferable to kissing him.

She was comfortable with this kind of physical contact.

She studied him as his heartbeat finally dropped to a steady rhythm, colour slowly leaching back into his body as the blood loss faded away.

He was—even in the most generous terms—gangly. There was hardly a trace of body fat on him. She could see his ribs, the jut of his sternum, bony shoulders. He had long limbs and knobby elbows. Stripped down, he looked so young.

It was no wonder Ferron wore a good three layers of uniform in an effort not to look so overtly juvenile.

Her fingers traced absently across his now unmarred skin.

She couldn't imagine being trapped in the body of a sixteen-year-old for eternity.

"Do you leer at and fondle all your unconscious patients, or am I special?" Ferron's voice was as unexpected as a bucket of ice water.

Helena started, her heart slamming into her throat as she snatched her hands away, her face scorching hot.

"I was not," she said, her voice tight and rising, even though she had no excuse for touching him that way. "I was just wondering about your body fat ratio."

"Of course you were," he said, sitting up with a suggestive smirk.

She could probably heat the entire tenement with the amount she was blushing.

"I wasn't leering at you," she said forcefully. "You look scarcely grown. I don't fancy boys."

The smirk vanished. He stared at her for a painfully long moment and stood up. "As I recall," he finally said, his voice clipped, "I never asked you to look at all."

He went over and picked up his cloak, which was the only part of his clothing that wasn't nearly burned to ashes, and pulled it on. It smeared him all over with blood.

"Sorry, I didn't mean to—"

"Your meaning was incredibly clear," he said in a cool voice, his jaw set.

"Ferron," she said, the idea abruptly occurring to her, and she wondered why she'd never thought to ask before. "Was it a punishment for you—being made Undying?"

He glanced at her, his face empty. "How could immortality be a punishment? It's what everyone wants."

HELENA FELT HAUNTED BY FERRON when she returned to Headquarters—not only by his answer, but by everything about the interaction.

For months, he'd been something bloodless and soulless. Not a person, but an evil to endure and an obstacle to overcome. Seeing him injured, stripped of the shell of a uniform that he hid inside, had altered her perception of him.

There was a fragility that she had been unprepared for.

He'd seemed so human, and she didn't like thinking of him as human.

Undying. Murderer. Spy. Target. Tool.

That was how she needed to view Ferron.

Not as someone who could be hurt. Not as someone who didn't understand blood loss and who rambled explanations. Not as someone who assumed a hand extended was meant to hurt him.

For so long, all she'd seen was his pride and anger. Now she couldn't help but feel that there was something terribly tragic about him, straining beneath the surface.

She felt an urgent need to smother that feeling.

Kaine Ferron was the enemy. The war was his fault. He'd murdered Luc's father.

She washed his blood off her hands, getting ready for her shift in the hospital before remembering that she was off that day. She sat on her bed, staring at her notes, trying to make sense of the tangled contradictory emotions inside her.

The door opened, and Lila strode in, decked out in practice armour. She stopped short at the sight of Helena.

"You're here."

Helena closed her notebook. "Pace is having one of my trainees cover my shift today. She wants to see how they'll perform on their own." Her lips pursed. "I'm not allowed to be there because apparently I glare and it makes people nervous."

Lila nodded, propping her weapon against the wall and then straightening her braid and cracking her neck in both directions as Helena winced.

"You do glare," Lila said, unclasping her armour. "You're going to get loads of wrinkles right here." She touched the spot between her eyebrows.

Helena rolled her eyes and dropped her notebook casually into her trunk, her fingers bumping against the amulet. It felt strangely warm. A familiar solace. She almost picked it up but then turned her hand, staring at the scars on her palm instead.

"Not really something I worry about," she said quietly.

"Hel . . . you all right?"

Her head shot up. "Yes. Why?"

Lila shifted, her unfastened armour clanking. She was always in armour. She even slept in a light mesh set, saying she felt naked without it, but Helena knew she was afraid of making the mistake her uncle Sebastian had as Principate Apollo's paladin, of believing that anywhere was safe for Luc.

"You've seemed off lately. I thought you'd be glad about the new healers, might relax a little bit, but you seem—" Lila hesitated. "Withdrawn. You're always disappearing. Luc's noticed."

"I just worry, is all," Helena said. "Any luck killing the chimaeras?"

"No. We did go out yesterday, but they're freakishly fast. I had one almost cornered, but it smelled atrocious. Worse than the greys. I could have killed it, but my gods, I couldn't even see straight and then—" She shook her head abruptly. "Why are we talking about chimaeras?"

Helena averted her eyes.

"Screw you." Lila gave a huff of exasperation. "Don't distract me by changing the subject. I don't want to talk about chimaeras." She walked over, her right leg clicking with each step until she was standing over Helena. "You've been off *and* you haven't been in meetings lately. I finally pried what happened out of Soren yesterday. So good job to you all, that was an impressive amount of secret keeping."

Helena went tense. "Does Luc know, too?"

"No."

Helena released a breath. "I don't want to talk about it."

Lila said nothing for a moment. "Couldn't help but notice you picked a day when Luc and I weren't there."

"I would have said it anyway," Helena said, picking at her cuticles. The skin around her nails was cracked and ragged from constant washing, and there were still traces of Ferron's blood under them. "But I was glad Luc wasn't there. I didn't want him trapped in the middle of something. I knew they'd say no. I just—I needed to say it. Soren said that was a good battle for all of you, but in the hospital—we ran out of everything. Beds, bandages, laudanum, and antiseptic. And bodies kept coming, and I couldn't—I couldn't make up the difference."

Lila sat on the edge of Helena's bed. "Are you—" Lila wasn't looking at Helena and seemed to be choosing her words carefully. "Are you not all right anymore? Is that why you spoke and why there's all the trainees now?"

There was a pause. Helena looked sharply at Lila, but Lila was focused on unfastening a buckle and didn't meet her stare. It had never occurred to Helena that Lila might know of the Toll.

It was more than she could handle thinking about just then.

"No. I'm fine. The trainees are because Matias hopes to get rid of me."

"Oh, good. I mean, not good, but that makes sense," Lila said, and cleared her throat. "I can see why you're not thrilled about them, then."

Helena forced a laugh. But the tension, the new undercurrent between them lingered. It was Lila who spoke next.

"You know, you can talk about—anything with me, if you want."

"No," Helena said. "I don't need to talk. There's—no point in talking, and as I have now been reminded publicly, I'm not a fighter. I don't know anything about what war really is. So—what would I even have to say?"

Lila's prosthetic leg clicked as she shifted and then said, "I think the hospital's worse than the battlefield."

Helena went very still.

"I realised it when I was in there for my leg." Lila's gaze was faraway, eyebrows furrowing. "At the front—everything's so focused, you know. The rules are simple. We win some. We lose some. You get hit sometimes. You hit back. You get days to recover if it's bad. But—" She looked down, her fingers tapping absently along the place where her prosthetic was joined to her thigh. "—in the hospital, every battle looks like losing. I can't imagine what that's like." She looked at Helena. "All you see in there is the worst of it."

Helena said nothing.

Lila sighed and unclasped more pieces of her armour, leaving them all over Helena's bed. "When Soren told me what you said—I don't agree, but I get it."

Helena didn't answer.

Lila nudged her with her elbow and stood. "Even if the trainees are just because of Matias's meddling, I'm glad you're getting more time off. I think you've needed that—some space from it all."

CHAPTER 31

Aprilis 1786

FERRON WAS WAITING FOR HELENA WHEN SHE opened the door. The room had been cleaned, the floor, table, chairs, all spotless. Not even a trace of blood.

His mouth was set in a taut line as she walked in.

As she closed the door, he shrugged off his cloak. "Let's see how you fight, Marino."

He lunged so fast, his body blurred.

There was no time for Helena to go for her knife. She swung her satchel at his head.

It bought her a split second, but he snatched it out of midair, ripping the strap from her fingers, and threw it across the room.

She heard the glass vials shatter as she scrambled away. There was nowhere to run.

The door was too complicated to unlock.

She managed to get to the other side of the table, trying to create a barrier between them.

He kicked the table. The legs screamed across the tiles as it flew towards her. She dove. The table struck the wall so hard, the top split.

She hit the floor, her left hand bending the wrong way, a bone in her wrist cracking against the stone. Pain exploded up her arm.

She cradled it against her chest, trying to scramble to her feet.

"Ferron, stop!"

He didn't stop. He grabbed her by the throat and shoved her against the wall, squeezing. His expression was void of emotion.

She clawed at his grip with her uninjured hand, fingernails carving grooves into his skin. She tried to knee him in the groin, and he kicked her foot out from under her and brought her to the floor.

The force knocked her breath out. She saw stars.

He pressed his knee into the middle of her chest, bearing down enough to make the bones strain. "Anything?"

She couldn't breathe, her lungs spasming. She writhed, trying to twist out from beneath him, scrabbling at every part of him that she could reach.

He grabbed her hand in his, his eyes glinting. She tried to pull away, but he squeezed tighter. Pain shot down her right arm, the metacarpals grinding against one another.

"Don't break my hand! You can't—hurt my hands!" She screamed the words at him in pure panic.

He leaned closer. "Then *fight* me off."

Both of her arms were on fire. She could barely breathe. He was seconds from caving her chest in. Struggle again and she was certain all the bones in her right hand would snap.

She went limp.

He held her for several more seconds, as if expecting her to suddenly spring into action. Confusion flashed across his face for a moment as he exhaled, then his expression hardened again.

"You're pathetic," he said, adding more weight to her chest. Her eyes watered but she didn't make a sound. "I could do anything I wanted to you, hurt you in ways you cannot even imagine, and you couldn't do anything to stop me. I wouldn't even need my resonance. I could do it with my bare hands. That's how *weak* you are."

He sneered and let go. His hands were streaked with blood, but the marks she'd gouged were already gone. He stood, pulling out a handkerchief to wipe the blood, straightening his clothes.

Helena remained gasping on the floor. Her spine and the back of her head throbbed. When she tried to brace herself into a sitting position with her right hand, she nearly cried.

Pain was radiating through her hands. There was blood and skin under her fingernails, staining her fingertips.

Her left wrist was beginning to swell. Her right hand was hardly better: When she tried to curl her fingers into a fist, pain burst like a halo up to her elbow.

"For the record," she said, struggling to keep her voice steady, "this qualifies as interfering with my work. If you want to hurt me"—her jaw trembled uncontrollably—"it can't be my hands."

So much for claiming she could say no to things.

Ferron said nothing, just walked over and pulled his cloak back on without looking at her again.

Helena stayed where she was. She'd known this was a possibility, but he'd lulled her into a false sense of security, waiting until she let her guard down to finally hurt her.

It was crueller than if he'd done it from the start.

"Do I get to know why?" she asked, still staring dully at the floor, ribs aching with every breath. "Did I—did I d-do something?"

"You exist, Marino. I think that's reason enough."

She had no response to that. She got up slowly. "Do you have any information today?"

He gave a thin smile. "No. That was all."

She retrieved her satchel without a word, gingerly hooking an arm through the strap. She couldn't get it up to her shoulder. Broken glass tinkled inside.

She'd added an emergency kit after last week, thinking that if Ferron was ever hurt again, she would come prepared. The waste of medicine it represented was almost as painful as her ribs, and the broken glass and contents would have contaminated everything she'd foraged that day. Hours wasted.

She went to the door and tried to flex her fingers enough to open it, but all she could feel was pain.

"Will you"—her voice finally betrayed her and shook—"will you let me out?"

IF SHE'D HURT ANYTHING BUT her hands, it would have been easy to follow Crowther's instructions and hide the bruises before she returned to Headquarters, but there hadn't been any contingency plans made beyond that.

Once she was off the Outpost, Helena wandered up and down along the dam. She was functionally useless without her hands. If she tried to get back to Headquarters looking as bruised as she was, there could be questions that she couldn't answer.

Finally, in desperation, she scrambled down the embankment towards the marshes. Without her hands, she was clumsy, quickly covered with dirt. She crawled back to the firm ground, drenched and muddy, smearing at her face and throat so that any bruises would be covered.

At the checkpoint, they recognised her and pitied her enough that they didn't ask many questions. When she reached Headquarters, she was forced to go to the hospital because she couldn't use the lift.

"What happened?" Matron Pace came to meet Helena as she arrived at the doors.

"I fell in the marsh," Helena said without meeting her eyes. "Sprained my wrists."

"Both of them?"

Helena didn't look up as she nodded.

Pace didn't move for a moment but then recovered. "Let's get you out of these muddy clothes and see what needs to be done." She led Helena towards one of the private rooms usually reserved for the high-ranked members of the Eternal Flame, shooing away anyone who came towards them.

Helena had always appreciated how professional Pace was. No matter the circumstances, she was unflappable. Helena's hands were too swollen and cold to manage buttons or clasps. Pace didn't say a word about all the mud that spread to her apron and sleeves and hands as she helped Helena undress.

"It's a novelty after all the blood," she said dismissively when Helena tried to apologise, squeezing out a wet cloth. "Now let's get you clean, and see what the damage is. Elain will be the best choice for your hands."

Helena tensed, but there was nothing to be done. Once the bruises were visible, Pace would realise that Helena had not sprained her wrists by tripping, and Elain, while the most competent trainee, was a terrible gossip.

Pace paused the instant Helena's throat was clean enough to make the bruises ringing it unmistakable. Before Helena could think of anything to say, there was a knock on the door.

Pace pressed her lips together and went to answer, her body blocking out the hospital ward beyond.

"What is it, Purnell?" Pace said.

A hushed voice replied, "Message for you. Said it was urgent."

Pace took something and then shut the door. She unfolded, read, and then ripped up a slip of paper as she walked back to Helena.

"I have instructions to send you to your room. Immediately," Pace said, her cheeks a furious red. "But I think I can get you a little cleaner first."

Once she was clean, Helena was bundled up as though she were hypothermic, and Pace accompanied her to the Alchemy Tower. Crowther was waiting as they exited the skybridge. Pace stiffened at the sight of him.

"Matron Pace," he said. "What can I do for you?"

Broken blood vessels stained Pace's cheeks. "I came to be sure that Marino is being looked after."

Crowther's eye twitched. "Of course." He looked at Helena. "I presume, then, that you're in a condition that requires healing?"

Helena had been considering the question. "If I have my left hand treated, I think I can manage the rest after that."

"I'll send for someone. Stay out of sight until then. Matron, you're dismissed." He turned and walked away without another word.

Pace didn't return to the hospital; instead she went with Helena to her room, and stayed even after Helena was in her bed.

"You know, I knew a few healers when I was a midwife," Pace finally said, sitting down at the foot of Helena's bed and looking around the room. "City-trained doctors didn't care much for working in the mountain villages. The ones I knew didn't always call themselves healers, they just thought it was intuition. They were mostly older women who'd thought for a long time that they had a good sense for bodies. When I was told there was a healer coming from the mountains, I expected someone my age." She finally looked over at Helena. "You're so young. You don't even know how young you are. You're sacrificing things you don't even comprehend the value of."

Helena's emotions were a tangle inside her. "No one's forcing me to do anything I didn't—agree to."

"What have you ever said no to?" Pace asked. Before Helena could reply, she continued, "You think a man like Crowther hasn't noticed that?"

Pace might have said more, but the door opened, revealing Crowther with a young girl beside him.

"You may return to the hospital, Matron," Crowther said pointedly, holding the door.

Pace patted Helena on the knee and stood, glaring at Crowther as she passed. Crowther closed the door firmly before turning to Helena.

"This is Ivy; she'll do as instructed to get your left hand working."

The girl stepped forward. She moved haltingly, like a deer, but her eyes were sharp and foxlike. She was perhaps fifteen, but Helena doubted she was even that. She'd never heard of a vivimancer so young. As Pace had said, typically it manifested later in life.

The war had prematurely aged people in all kinds of ways.

Ivy didn't say a word as Helena gestured at her left wrist and explained in the simplest terms what she thought was wrong with it, what needed to be done, and what to be careful of. Helena had never been healed by anyone except herself, and she shot several panicked looks at Crowther as Ivy reached out and touched her arm.

The girl was startlingly adept with her vivimancy, but her resonance was not subtle at all.

The pain and swelling in Helena's wrist and fingers rapidly vanished, and Ivy searched for the fracture in Helena's wrist. In a matter of minutes, Helena could move her fingers again without much pain and begin to feel her resonance.

"Thank you," she said, drawing her hand away as quickly as she could.

Ivy's hand dropped to her side. She watched Helena, an uncanny look of curiosity in her eyes. "My sister likes you."

"Oh. Does she work in the hospital?"

"Ivy," Crowther said sharply, "out now. And not a word about this to anyone."

Ivy gave a careless nod as she left.

Crowther closed the door again. Helena wanted to ask who the girl was, but she dreaded the conversation and turned her attention to her right hand. She blocked the nerves at the elbow and began a cautious examination.

"What happened?"

"I think Ferron was upset about last week," she said, glad she had something to focus on so she didn't have to look at Crowther. "You know how prideful he is. I don't think he liked that I'd helped him. I barely arrived and he said he wanted to see me fight."

She glanced up in time to see Crowther's lips disappear into a thin line.

"Did you reveal your vivimancy?"

"No."

"Are you sure?"

"I'm sure."

Crowther nodded, still looking sceptical.

"Who was that girl?" Helena asked.

"Orphan," Crowther said. "Found her in the slums." He made a sound of irritation. "You'll say you caught a cold. You can have a few days off. But you can't be seen returning to Headquarters like this again. There's a drop location a little way away; it's kept stocked with clothes, basic supplies. In the future, you'll go there for things like this. If you don't turn up here, that's where you'll be looked for."

Helena gave a dull nod as the swelling in her right hand was finally reduced to the point that she could use it to examine Ivy's work on her left hand.

She had nothing to do while her hands finished recovering. Having days off was overly cautious, but better to be safe. If she ended up with nerve damage in her hands, she'd be rendered almost useless.

She preoccupied herself by sorting through the contents of her trunk. There wasn't much inside it but old notebooks from her classes at the Institute. Most of her possessions had been left behind in Etras because the Institute had small dorms and strict dress codes. Inside a small box lay a tintype of Helena with her father just before she'd begun at the Institute. Ten years old and in uniform, her expression so eager. Her father had worn his white medical coat for the picture, even though he wasn't licensed in Paladia. He'd wanted to look professional when he brought her.

She closed the box and picked up the amulet, letting the rays align with the scars in her palm.

She went over to the window, still holding it, as she clambered out onto the roof. It had been Luc who'd shown her how to climb from the windows and onto the gently sloping roof below the Tower beacon.

The fires of the Eternal Flame glowed overhead as she stood there alone, a low iron railing the only barrier between her and the lethal drop.

She wished she could shut her mind off for a little while. The redirection technique could only create a little space, but her misery just kept seeping back.

She stared at the suncrest as the white flames overhead glittered across its surface. She almost let it drop off the edge, wanting to watch it fall until it vanished.

She felt ashamed every time she looked at it, embarrassed by how much meaning she'd thought it had.

She let the chain slip through her fingers but stopped.

No. This amulet didn't represent Ilva, it stood for Luc. Ilva had exploited that, but it wasn't Luc's fault. Helena was doing this for him, and he was worth it.

She pulled the chain back over her neck, hiding it beneath her clothes, and sat staring across the city as the gold grew warm against her heart.

WHEN SHE WENT BACK TO the Outpost the following week, there were contingencies in place. The drop point in an abandoned basement would function as a makeshift safe house. If injured beyond her healing abilities, Helena would go there. There were basic medical supplies and a shortwave radio. A coded message would have Ivy dispatched.

Ferron was late. Again. He was often late, but she was too anxious to wait this time. She was pulling her satchel onto her shoulder just as the door opened.

She flinched when he stepped into the room, closing the door behind him. Her heart lurched when she heard it click and lock.

"I'm late," he said.

Helena had to focus and make herself breathe before she could speak. "Are we—t-training again this week?"

"No," he said quickly. "No. I won't do that to you again."

She gave a short nod, but she knew better than to believe him now. He'd redefine the terms of the deal every time it was convenient to him.

She watched him warily.

He started to open his mouth but then stopped, his hand curling into a fist.

"What?" she snapped, glaring at him, sick of waiting for what he'd do next.

He avoided her eyes, looking at the floor.

"I didn't mean to hurt you," he said.

She gave a brittle laugh. "Well, I always expected you would."

Anger flashed in his eyes as he looked up at her.

She was beginning to make sense of him now. He thought he was better than the other Undying. He resented anything that lumped him in with them. That was why he'd backtracked and tried to pretend that she had autonomy in the arrangement. But no matter what he wanted to tell himself, he was cut from the same cloth as all the rest of them.

She glared at him. "If anyone had died last week because I was too injured to work, that would have been on your head."

He scoffed. "Is that supposed to matter to me?"

"It would, if you were human."

His jaw clenched. "Well, if we're being honest today, you're pathetic at self-defence. Worse than I expected. Which is saying something, because I have a very low opinion of you. I assumed they'd keep all their medics somewhat combat-ready."

"The hospital is protected. That's more practical than expecting the medical staff to be trained and practising for combat situations."

She could tell Ferron disagreed.

"Well, you're not in the hospital right now." He walked around her slowly. "You're too scrawny. No muscle at all. I don't think I can even do anything with you in this state. I'm going to need to start you with calisthenics before I can even get anywhere with you."

Helena's least favourite class at the Institute had been callisthenics. "Even if I exercise, you can't train me in anything that could hurt my hands."

He paused. "If you get hurt, I'll fix it."

Helena's head swam. It hadn't occurred to her that if he wanted to, he could hurt her, heal her, and hurt her again, leaving no trace.

He pulled out an envelope, extending it, but when she tried to take it, he held on, studying her. "Are there food shortages?"

She said nothing, just held on to the envelope, waiting for him to let go. Crowther had been clear that Ferron should glean no intelligence from her.

His mouth hardened into a flat line. "The transport information I included for the southern quarter is likely food supplies. If they manage to seize them, tell Crowther to increase whatever your rations are."

A WEEK LATER, ONE OF the scouting teams managed to capture and kill a chimaera, although they admitted it had already been nearly dead when they cornered it.

The corpse had been brought back for analysis, and after some debate, Helena was assigned the job of dissecting it.

The chimaeras were made with vivimancy, therefore a vivimancer would be needed to understand the process. It was the duty of the Eternal Flame to study the practices of their enemies.

The remains already smelled terrible, as though the chimaera had been in an early stage of decomposition when it died. In the process of creation it had been flensed and vivisected, its muscles filleted and intermingled with the parts of other creatures. Several of the organs had been replaced. It had the skull of a reptile, but part had been hollowed out and made to accommodate a larger mammalian brain.

It wasn't created using necromancy; reanimating animals had been attempted many times in the past and never worked. The chimaera had been alive when it was made, but Helena couldn't imagine how it had been kept alive.

Shiseo was on standby as she worked, handing her tools as she needed them. She didn't understand why he worked with her as an assistant. He was too educated for it; the breadth of his metallurgical knowledge would have put many grandmasters to shame. Ilva's request was an insult.

While she was writing up the report, Shiseo busied himself with sketching compound arrays for the metal-infused tinctures they'd been discussing. Silver and copper and iron all had medicinal uses and could boost the efficacy of certain extracts.

"Shiseo," she said, looking up, "do you have a workspace of your own?"

He paused. "No. I was meant to perhaps teach at the Institute, but—" He shook his head.

She shifted, feeling awkward about how long it had taken for her to realise why he'd taken the post. "I should have said something sooner. If you want to work on your own projects, you're welcome to use this space."

He gave a vague smile, inclining his head, but she could tell immediately that he wouldn't take her up on the offer.

Perhaps she was wrong. Had Ilva guilted him into the position? Of course. He'd come seeking political asylum, and Ilva had called in that debt. It would explain why he was so carefully inoffensive. She felt guilty, but she did need him.

"I should warn you, I technically stole this lab," she said, looking up. "I mean, obviously it's always been here, and no one was using it, but I did just move in and start making things without permission." She shrugged. "Everyone just assumes someone else must have approved it. So if you don't like—ill-gotten laboratories, I understand, but you are welcome to use the space for whatever you're interested in."

He looked at her with his impassive, guarded face, and then the corners of his eyes crinkled. "Perhaps there are a few things."

IN THE WEEKS THAT FOLLOWED, Ferron's liaising grew sporadic. Helena dutifully performed callisthenics, per his instructions, but he often failed to appear. Sometimes there'd be an envelope left on the table; other times, Helena would wait and eventually leave empty-handed. Her ring would burn at odd hours, and she would be forced to hurry to the Outpost, only to find a letter or map left, Ferron having already moved on.

The information seemed useful, but she could tell that Crowther was giving up on her, treating her as a write-off.

She was startled when she opened the door of the tenement and found Ferron waiting for her again.

He was sitting at the table with a silver coin in his hand, spinning and flipping it idly when she entered.

There was a long silence before he spoke without looking over at her. "The High Necromancer will be out of the country for the next week. He's travelling into Hevgoss. There have been extensive preparations made for it. Nearly a third of the Undying will be travelling with him. The trip has been kept secret; only a few know."

There was a pause.

Ferron pocketed the coin. "He's never left like this before. If the Resistance has been waiting for an opening, this would be the time. The Undying are unlikely to coordinate well because they'll all want the credit and glory for themselves."

"And I assume you're among those going," she said, because of course he'd leave the city to burn, and for the blame to fall, and only come back to reap the rewards.

This was what he'd been working towards from the beginning. His long game. The Resistance was playing right into his hands, and there wasn't anything Helena could do about that, because they had to seize an opportunity like this, or they might as well surrender now. They wouldn't last to the end of the year.

He said nothing.

"Anything else?"

He shook his head as he stood and walked to the door, pausing just before he opened it. "I think we might as well plan to skip the next few weeks. I don't expect to make it."

CHAPTER 32

Maius 1786

THE NEWS THAT MORROUGH WOULD BE GONE along with so many of the Undying was the opportunity the Eternal Flame had been waiting for. Like a machine springing into action, the Resistance rapidly began preparing to attack.

Crowther had been disseminating Ferron's intelligence over the last several months, attributing to various sources his maps, the information about patrols and rotations, chains of command and the hierarchies of who'd be called on first, and how they'd counterstrike if the Resistance attacked.

The battalions were raring for the fight.

However, a relentless sense of dread lurked beneath Helena's skin, growing with each passing moment. What if it was a trap? What if Ferron had lied, hidden a noose within his information? She kept thinking about how strange he'd seemed.

The hospital waited, tense, strangled between hope and dread. Then the sirens started, and the lorries began to arrive, bodies flooding in, filling the hospital and lining the halls. There wasn't room for all the wounded.

Helena had no opportunity to more than register her despairing guilt as the fallout of the battle filled the hospital. She had to work.

Your fault. You should have known. Ferron's a monster. A born traitor, just like his father. She had never done so much healing, working in such a frenzy that the amulet around her neck almost burned against her skin. Two of the trainee healers collapsed, their resonance shot from burnout.

It was more than a day before someone told her they hadn't lost. The attack was not a failure but a spectacular success. The Resistance had the ports; they'd retaken most of the East Island. Battles were still raging in the south-west corner, but they expected to retake the entire island.

Even once it was confirmed, Helena still barely believed it. The injuries just kept coming.

The Resistance found prisons filled with dissidents. One of the largest buildings near the ports had been a laboratory. The Resistance brought back lorries filled with medical supplies and tools that Helena had not laid eyes on in years. Real anaesthetic and antiseptics. Cases upon cases of opium resin. Gauze and fresh bandages.

But the elation that filled the hospital as all the supplies poured in vanished as the victims from the laboratory began to arrive. Medics and nurses who'd worked unflinchingly for years had breakdowns over the victims and had to be excused.

The laboratory had not only been making chimaeras with animals. The victims arriving were nearly unrecognisable, experimented on in ways that defied reason. Bodies methodically dismembered and reassembled. There were so many.

Attempts to treat them fell to Helena. The surgeons were at a loss, and the trainees couldn't take it. There was nothing Helena could do, either. No matter what she tried, they all died.

For their combat forces, the Retaking was over quickly. What the Undying had spent years slowly carving into, recovered in one coordinated sweep. It was regarded as a military triumph for the ages.

For the hospital it was an unending nightmare.

Reports that Morrough had returned were followed by rumours of extreme upheaval among the ranks as blame fell. Then came the counterattacks and attempts to retake the ports.

It took weeks before things finally calmed, the hospital shifts slowly resumed the normal rotation, and more trainee healers were brought in. Crowther and Ilva somehow knew exactly who possessed the latent resonance for it, even when the girls themselves did not.

Helena was so exhausted by the end that she could barely talk for several days. As if she'd forgotten how to be human anymore.

Pace kicked her out of the hospital when she found her in the supply room, mechanically taking inventory, saying that barring an emergency Helena was not to come back for four days at least.

Helena didn't know what to do but resume her old schedule, and so when Martiday arrived, she rose with the dawn, took her satchel, and went out of the city. The spring flooding had ebbed, and the wetlands had come into bloom.

There were flurries of insects dancing in swarms, light glistening on their wings. Sun limned the eastern stretch of the mountains, turning their ridges gold. The wind no longer rattled the dead reeds but whispered through marsh grass. The air was filled with warbling birdcalls. The wetlands were lush with new growth, brimming with life. Helena could have harvested for hours and still left plenty behind. She took only what she thought was most valuable before she washed her hands in an alga-green pond and headed to the Outpost.

She'd barely had time to think about Ferron, but she figured she should at least check and see if he'd left any messages. She'd received no instructions from Crowther since the attack.

She caught sight of him the instant the door opened. He was leaning his hip against the table. His shoulders were stooped, arms hanging limply at his sides.

"You look awful," he said as she came through the door.

She stopped short. "You look worse."

He gave a strained laugh. "Do I?"

She was too shocked to reply.

His face had grown gaunt, as if he'd lost almost all his remaining weight, the bones of his skull jutting starkly through his skin.

He looked—

—like a corpse.

Her heart lurched into her throat.

His skin was grey and papery, eyes sunken. His dark hair hung limp around his face. Dirty and uncombed.

He didn't appear to have eaten, slept, or bathed in all the weeks since Helena had last seen him.

"Are you—are you a—are you dead?" she forced herself to ask. Could he be killed and then made into a lich using his own body? Was that possible?

He cracked a smile that made his lower lip split, a trickle of red blood running down his chin. It healed instantly. "You'd think that, wouldn't you? No. Still—alive."

"What happened?"

She went forward but was afraid to touch him. He looked like he might crumble into dust.

He drew a shallow breath. "Well, you may have noticed, the High Necromancer wasn't pleased about the ports." He drooped, his head dipping, but then he jerked up sharply, face contorting in pain. "Bad luck—for the commander in charge."

Helena's head went light. No . . . that wasn't possible. He'd been gone, with Morrough and the others to Hevgoss.

She shook her head. "But you're not in command there. It's—they were commanded by—by—"

She couldn't remember the name, but it was someone else. She would have remembered if Ferron had been the one in charge. He wasn't ranked high enough for a position like that.

"It was a recent change in leadership," he said. There was hoarseness to his voice. "Doesn't matter. Did it work? The attack? Obviously you got the island, but—" He swallowed. "—you'll keep it? You have enough men for that still?"

She wasn't supposed to tell him anything, but he was so clearly in pain, she couldn't help herself.

"More than we hoped," she said.

He swallowed and gave the barest nod. "Good." His eyes fluttered closed for a moment. "That's something, I guess."

He drew an unsteady breath. "I should go. Just—wanted to know . . . Won't be making this trip again."

He tried to straighten but collapsed. He caught the chair and fell onto it. A low, almost screaming gasp escaped him. He tried to stand again but couldn't seem to put weight on his arms. His breathing was growing increasingly ragged.

"Ferron, what's happened to you? What's wrong?" Her voice rose sharply as she hovered, not sure what to do.

His eyes shut. He was breathing shallowly. "F-Fuck off, Marino."

She approached like he was an injured animal, her hands outstretched and visible.

"Ferron—I know you're hurt. Maybe I can help," she said as gently as she could.

He gave a rasping laugh. "There's *nothing* you can do."

"Let me try." She was close enough now to see the veins beneath his skin along his neck, not blue but almost black like poison. "I'm not going to hurt you."

His eyes snapped open, anger lighting his face.

"Don't pretend to care," he spat. "You expect me to believe you didn't know this would happen?"

She shook her head. "I didn't. I would have come back sooner if I'd known."

Based on his appearance, this was not quick deterioration he was suffering from. He'd reached this point slowly, over the course of weeks.

If he was telling the truth, if he'd been in command at the ports during the attack, then all the information he'd passed on would have been to his knowing detriment.

"Please." She held out her hand. "Let me try to help."

"Your marsh herbs aren't going to fix this," he said, grimacing as he tried to stand again. "A medic like you can do fuck all."

She swallowed hard.

"That'd be true if I actually was a medic." She touched his cheek with her fingertips, and didn't hide her resonance.

She knew that she was sabotaging her mission, but that wouldn't matter if he died; the mission was already a failure on every level. When her resonance connected with his body, she almost snatched her hand back. The talisman in his chest was emitting so much power, it threatened to burn her nerves touching him. Every cell in his body was singed from it.

He was dying. Over and over. His body pushed so far over the edge that it failed, only to be instantly regenerated, and fail again. He was simultaneously dead and alive because it was a sort of repeating cascade of regenerative failure.

Ferron jerked away as if he were the one burned. "You conniving little bitch. I knew I felt your resonance when I lost my arm."

She let her hand drop, avoiding his accusing glare. "I was ordered not to tell you."

"And now?" His eyes were narrowed into slits.

"I don't think it matters. If I don't do something, you're going to die."

"I doubt I'm fortunate enough to manage that," he said in a dull voice.

She reached out, just barely touching his arm. "Ferron, what's happened to your back?"

His eyes fluttered closed as if he was too exhausted for the conversation. She could see the black veins even in his eyelids.

"See for yourself," he finally said, "since you're so determined."

Very slowly and carefully she unfastened his cloak and lifted it off. He flinched but didn't utter a sound. The miasma of old, fetid wounds filled the air as she unfastened the buttons of his shirt. Stepping behind him as gently as she could, she drew the clothing off his shoulders.

There were no bandages underneath. His entire back was a rotting wound, lacerated surgically from his shoulders down past his ribs.

There was an alchemical array carved into his skin.

He inhaled and she could see the white of his ribs, scored with grooves.

The incisions over his shoulders were the worst of it. Not merely cutting to the bone but *into* the bone, carving into his shoulder blades, a lumithium alloy welded in, bonded with the bone to keep the array intact and activated.

Whatever regenerative abilities Ferron had, it was not enough to counter an injury of this magnitude.

Arrays could be simply illustrative, to record or visually calculate a process, but they were also used for transmutation or alchemisation when the process was too complex for simple resonance manipulation, or when working with organically derived compounds that tended to be volatile. Drawn with chalk or charcoal, or etched into a surface with a stylus. But Helena had never seen anything like what had been done to Ferron.

"Why—" Her voice failed. "—why would they do this to you?"

"Well . . ." Ferron said slowly, his voice far away. "There were lots of ideas about what to do with me—all manner of punishments were discussed for my—failure. Bennet was put out over losing his lab, all those subjects and experiments of his. He's been wanting to experiment on one of the Undying. He said that as the one who'd suffered the greatest loss, he should be allowed to punish me."

He was silent for a moment and added, "The High Necromancer says if I survive, I'll be forgiven."

Helena couldn't tear her eyes away from the wound. The skin around the incisions showed signs of septicaemia. Tendrils of infection were spreading beneath his skin, leaching into his blood.

Too afraid to touch near the array, she placed her hand on his arm. He flinched at the contact. His body was still trying to regenerate, to heal the wounds that made up the array. The nerves were all intact. He had to be in an incomprehensible amount of pain.

She didn't know where to begin, but she couldn't just stand there looking at it. She tried to numb the area, to work inwards, but it didn't last. Anywhere with enough living tissue to numb, his regeneration reversed it. She couldn't even spare him the pain.

Working as close as she dared, she could feel the metal welded into his shoulders was a lumithium-titanium alloy, its resonance so sharp that Helena could feel it in her teeth. She had no idea how Ferron was even sane while having it adhered to his body.

This was beyond the scope of her abilities, more than anything had ever been before.

"I'm sorry, I can't heal this."

He gave a dry laugh. "I know."

"But—" She swallowed hard, still thinking. "—I think I could help contain it, and reduce the strain it's putting on you. It might—give you a chance of surviving. That's the condition, right? If you survive, they won't do anything else to you."

Ferron gave no response.

Starting on his left shoulder, she followed the veins with her resonance, her fingertips a breath away from his skin, drawing the blood poisoning back to the incision. Pus and blood that was nearly black trickled down across his back. She used the corner of a handkerchief to wipe it away as gently as she could, to keep it from getting into the other wounds.

Ferron's whole body shook, and he gave a soundless rasp.

"What are you doing?" he ground out through his teeth.

"These incisions are poisoning you. You've been dying and your body is pulling resources from everywhere it can to regenerate and revive you, but it's running out of places to draw from. This is like when you lost your arm. You couldn't regenerate until you stopped bleeding. If you want to recover, we have to deal with this infection and work backwards from there."

He dropped his head, exhaling unevenly. "How fortunate that you got such a thorough overview of my physiology while I was passed out."

"Yes, it is," she said curtly, and pulled out more poison.

He moaned through his teeth, his hands spasming repeatedly when the handkerchief brushed his back again.

He hadn't even made a sound with his arm ripped off.

She paused, hands hovering.

"Would a sedative work on you?"

"No," he said dully. "Everything wears off. I can barely get properly drunk."

She tentatively touched the base of his skull.

"I usually work locally when blocking pain, but there's a place here in your brain. If I stimulate it, it'll put you to sleep. You won't feel anything.

Your body shouldn't interpret that as tampering since I'm not blocking anything. Do you want me to try?"

"You can—" His voice caught. "You can do that?"

"Yes. I think so."

He was silent. She watched the flutter of his ribs as he breathed unsteadily.

"Try, then, I suppose," he said. "It's not like there's ever been anything stopping you from killing me."

She ignored the comment. "You should lie down, then."

The table was cracked down the middle, but still stable enough, so she assembled it into a makeshift bed, spreading out his cloak. His hands trembled, gripping her shoulder as she helped him stand, and he groaned under his breath as he leaned his weight on her. His whole body was shaking violently as he nearly collapsed onto the table.

She laced her fingers through his hair until she found the dip at the base of his skull just below the occipital protuberance.

It required only a little shift in the energy until she felt the peace of numbness flood through his body as he slipped unconscious.

She could work more easily now that Ferron wouldn't flinch every time she touched him. She drew out the infection, wiping it away, but all she could think about was how old the injury must be.

She should have come back sooner. This was her fault: She'd assumed he'd leave the city to burn, and she'd pushed him from her mind.

She'd been so terrified he would betray them that she'd never stopped to consider what would happen if he didn't.

Her hands trembled, hovering over the now clean wounds, as she debated what to do. She wanted to pry the metal out of his bones, but the titanium had bonded.

She gripped her amulet, desperate for any sense of reassurance.

The injury was more than merely incisions and metal transmutation. The array was active; she could feel the hum of resonance moving through it. Altering an active array was extremely dangerous. The kind of thing that cost limbs.

Attempting it might kill them both.

She had to figure out a way to make Ferron survive it, but it was rooted into him and drawing on the energy emanating from the talisman, diverting what should have been regenerating him and instead sending that power along the pathways of the array.

There was no containment circle to limit it. It was activated constantly, the symbols not acting on an external target as they would in a lab, but *on* Ferron. The power was being diverted, mutated, and then fed back into him in a closed loop.

That would kill a normal human, but Ferron didn't die so easily—yet he also couldn't change. Helena was beginning to understand how the Undying were "immortal." He was not ageless; his body was trapped in time, his regeneration keeping him exactly as he was. It did not let him change, not with age or injury. But the array was designed to change him. The mutated power existed for the sole purpose of alteration, and that contradiction was killing him in a way far more profound than the mutilation of his back.

He was in a crucible, and he *was* the crucible, and he would either die terribly or be wholly alchemised into something that could survive the paradox.

She studied the symbols, trying to understand what they were intended to do.

She'd never seen an array intended to act on a person, but she was well versed in alchemical notation.

The fundamental design was a classical celestial star correlating to the eight planets. Paladians loved things in sets of five or eight. The only exception she knew was pyromancy, which the Holdfast Suncrest was modelled after. Which used seven.

The use of the notation carved into Ferron's skin was like using an alchemical formula to express a literary concept. It wasn't unheard of for alchemists to write with alchemical symbolism and symbols, particularly in textbooks as a way of restricting information to the educated, but Helena had never seen the method applied to a functioning array. Each of the eight points had a distinct concept using combinations of symbols. Helena parsed the meaning slowly.

Calculating, Cunning, Devoted, Determined, Ruthless, Unfailing, Unhesitating, and Unyielding.

It made sense that an array on a person couldn't be a typical transmutation formula, but the idea of forging traits into a human was horrific. If it worked, it would carve Ferron down into these eight compounding qualities, potentially erasing everything else about him.

He would have kept healing at least until the metal had been welded into place. The lacerations were all interconnected to make the array continuous. Given the way Ferron reacted when she offered to knock him out, he'd probably been conscious the entire time.

Her fingers trembled, and she laid her hand over his. His skin was cold and papery thin.

She wanted to close the wounds, but there was too much interference channelled through the incisions. It would kill any new tissue.

If she could get him healthy again, then his body might work with her to close them, but that would take time. As much as it had taken for him to reach that point.

She used her vivimancy to remove the dead tissue and then went to her satchel, rummaging through her supplies for the little medical kit she'd repacked. She debated running to Headquarters, but it would take too long.

She sorted through what she'd foraged that morning, trying to think of what would be useful.

Sedatives and transmutational interference didn't work, but topical treatments might still have an effect. They would at least prevent infection. She'd make a transdermal salve with a prolonged release. Shiseo would be sure to have ideas.

She gnawed her lip as she pulled out a salve she'd made with her willow bark, tapping her fingers on the lid, wishing she had something with opium in it. It would do for now and keep the wounds clean until she came back.

She coated the incisions with the analgesic, emptying the entire jar, and then placed gauze over each one, sprinkling dried sphagnum over them to keep the wounds acidic and prevent infection, before swathing his back in bandages.

She knew she should wake him, but he was exhausted. He could use the rest.

Reaching out tentatively, she tucked his dark hair back from his face. His features were sunken, hollows in his cheeks, temples, and eyes, all that eerie youth gone.

He looked broken.

She fidgeted with her nails, wishing there was something else to do, as she fought back the storm of emotions in her chest. She was so accustomed to resenting him, to seeing him as a threat to her and everyone else.

She thought of him flipping that silver coin and telling her what the Eternal Flame needed for the attack. He'd known he'd be punished.

His rambling, barely conscious comments about purposefully provoking another commander to gain control of a new district: She'd brushed them off, attributing them to ego and stupidity. He'd been building up to this all along.

He could have made it a trap. He could have spent the last several months drip-feeding the Eternal Flame inaccurate information to execute a perfect sabotage. Instead he'd given them more than they'd dreamed they could achieve in a year, knowing he'd pay the price.

And he'd thought she'd known. The thought gutted her. That he'd thought she knew and had abandoned him to this.

She touched his temple, leaning closer, searching his face. "Why are you doing this?"

When she couldn't justify keeping him unconscious for any longer, she laced her fingers through his hair and woke him as slowly as she could so that the pain wouldn't hit immediately.

As he was regaining consciousness, she took his nearest hand, careful not to shift his shoulder as she started massaging the palm and worked slowly to his fingertips, knuckle by knuckle, her resonance seeking out every bit of tension and knotted muscles.

Her father used to massage her hands like that, even before Paladia. Every night. An alchemist's hands were like a surgeon's, he'd said, they had to be taken care of.

She knew Ferron didn't need it. It was only meaningful to her, but it was all she could do.

The instant he became conscious, she could feel the tension radiate across his body. His eyes snapped open, his pupils contracting with pain. His fingers spasmed against hers, but he lay there unmoving, and so she kept working along his fingers.

His eyes weren't quite focused yet.

"What did you do?" he finally asked.

Helena wet her lips. "I drew out all the infected blood and removed the dead tissue, then applied an analgesic salve to the incisions and got you bandaged. It's not the most effective treatment, but I think it'll help until I can make something better back at Headquarters. I—I can't close the incisions yet, but I might be able to eventually, once you're stronger. If you can recover some first."

He pulled his hand away and slowly got up as she was speaking. It had to be agony to move, but he didn't make a sound, although he wavered as if on the verge of fainting as he pushed himself off the table.

"It doesn't matter," he said, reaching for his shirt. "Healing me isn't your job."

"Your wounds need to be monitored and watched for infection or further deterioration. And the bandages should be changed at least once a day," she said, stepping forward and blocking him.

"Unfortunate," was all he said.

"Ferron." She took his shirt away from him. "I know you're not used to it, but you need medical care. If you leave things as they are, you'll probably die—or maybe something worse."

He gave a rasping laugh. "Marino, that is the point. You think Bennet did this expecting it to work?"

"But I can help you," she said desperately, helping him slip his shirt on, trying to prove how useful she could be. "Listen. I have a laboratory. I'm good at chymiatria. I'll make a salve for you, it'll be topical so it'll work on the incisions. I'll come every day to change your bandages and make sure nothing goes wrong."

"Really, you have time for all that?" His expression was scathing.

"I'll make time. I'll come every day. Please."

He seemed caught off guard. "Fine," he said, looking away from her. "Eight o'clock in the evening. But if you make me come here, and you don't show up, I won't come back again."

"I'll come," she promised. "Every evening at eight."

She might need new papers to get permission, but she'd make Crowther give them to her. Or forge them herself.

She buttoned his shirt, pausing when her fingers were just below the dip of his throat. His bones showed through his skin, the dark-coloured veins still visible. "I'm so sorry, Kaine."

His expression was almost blank with exhaustion, but he quirked an eyebrow. It had less of an effect when she could see all the effort it took.

"If I'd known healing would make you so familiar, I would have said no." He almost sounded like himself.

She shrugged and picked up his cloak, doubtful about the added weight on his back. "Should I not call you Kaine? It seems odd to keep going by surnames. We're going to be around each other for the rest of our lives, you know."

He looked heavenwards and sighed. "I don't care what you call me, but I'm not changing anything."

"Good. Then it's Kaine now."

She needed to make herself think about him differently. She'd made too many wrong assumptions while seeing him as Ferron.

"I'm a bit out of the loop at the moment, but I do know where Bennet's new lab is." He gave a strained smile. "He likes them near the water. One of the warehouses near the West Island shipyard. I'll bring a map next time."

CHAPTER 33

Junius 1786

Helena set out early in the evening to ensure she wasn't late, carrying new travel papers that claimed she was going to the Outpost to deliver medical relief.

She felt guilty that it wasn't the real purpose of her trip. The Outpost had grown crowded, but the Resistance couldn't afford to reduce their limited supplies by distributing anything.

When she reached the tenement, there were dozens of people inside, clustered around a fire.

She stopped short, not sure what to do.

With his injury, Ferron couldn't possibly get there without being noticed. Someone might recognise him. She wasn't even sure how he managed it normally.

As she stood, trying to find a path to the stairs around the huddled group, a figure crumpled against a nearby wall stood up. The hood covering the face slipped back for a moment, just long enough to reveal the waxy features of a necrothrall.

Helena started back.

It had been a man. A tangled beard covered half his face, with thick eyebrows almost hiding the milky white of his eyes. He'd been expertly reanimated. He showed no signs of decay other than the sheen on his skin and the clouding of his eyes.

She was so used to hearing of necrothralls being aggressive, she hadn't considered that they could be concealed, waiting.

It came towards her, and her heart lurched into her throat. A pulse in her temples began, throbbing like a drum, a burn of pain across the side of her neck—

Don't think about it.

The necrothrall paused and pulled up his sleeve. Painted onto his arm was the same stylised symbol for iron that was on the doorway of the tenement.

This necrothrall belonged to Ferron. She'd almost forgotten that he was a necromancer. The sleeve slipped back down as the necrothrall gestured to the left.

Knowing the necrothrall was Ferron's didn't make it easier to voluntarily follow into the bowels of the Outpost.

Her heart was pounding inside her chest as they reached a door that blended into the wall. The necrothrall produced a small key and unlocked it, revealing metal stairs that descended into the belly of one of the factories.

There were dim electric lights that flickered unsteadily overhead. They entered a boiler room—the passage was cramped—then went through another locked door into a more spacious hallway. There was a large door, and as they approached, it swung open from the inside. The door was thicker than the length of her forearm, as though it were a bank vault.

Through the doorway was a large room filled with decadent furniture, chandeliers with glittery prisms dangling, and Ferron—drinking.

The indulgence in the room felt grotesque.

The walls were covered in heavy luxuriant drapes and murals. There were rows of decanters and bottles lining a wall. One section of the room had a seating area with ornate side tables, a large sofa, and chairs. On the other end was a mahogany desk and chaise. Everything was ornate, with the kind of craftsmanship that cost a fortune.

"There you are," Ferron said, drawing her attention away. He was wearing only trousers and a white shirt with half the buttons undone.

She was used to seeing him always fully dressed, layered in his defensive shell of a uniform, and while she'd stripped him to the waist twice now, both occasions had been for medical purposes.

The room they were standing in did not feel professional. Despite his haggard state, Ferron—Kaine, she mentally corrected—looked oddly striking, as if she'd never seen him in the proper environment before.

"What is this?" she asked, stepping cautiously into the room.

The necrothrall didn't enter, instead stepping back and closing the door, which sealed with a heavy reinforced thud.

"A panic room," Ferron said. "My grandfather had it built during a strike a few decades ago. In case of emergencies."

"I can't imagine why they'd want to hurt your grandfather when he clearly spent his money on such reasonable things," she said, glancing at the three crystal chandeliers hanging overhead.

"A mystery indeed." There were several fingers of liquid in his tumbler, but he knocked it all back in one gulp.

She looked at him sidelong. "You know, you could take pain relief in those quantities, if you're going for numbness."

"No fun in that," he said, hand trembling as he poured himself more. "Alcohol only dulls things for a few minutes. I prefer poison when I really want to feel intoxicated. Generally, it lasts longer, and some poisons have very interesting side effects. I thought you might disapprove, though." He sighed. "Given the current atmosphere in the Outpost and the fact that I have no desire to lie upon a kitchen table ever again, I thought this location made more sense."

Helena nodded, not sure if she was offended or grateful that this was not where they usually met. She probably would have panicked if she'd initially arrived in a place like this.

She dragged one of the spindly-legged side tables over and refused to worry about scratching the polished surface as she pulled out her supplies.

Ferron knocked back the contents of his second drink and straddled a chair backwards, unbuttoning his shirt. Before she could help him, he twisted his shoulders to pull it off, stifling a low gasp of pain.

"Did you feel any better?" she asked, placing her bare hand against his arm. He flinched away. His skin was unnaturally cold. No fever, though, which she hoped was a good sign.

He didn't answer.

She cleaned her hands with a dilution of carbolic acid and unwrapped the bandages as carefully as she could until there was only the gauze over the wounds. She used a saline irrigation and tried to lift one, but it stuck. Kaine jerked, his body shuddering.

"Fuck! Don't—!" His knuckles were white where he was gripping the back of the chair.

She snatched her hand back. "I have to get the gauze off."

"Do you really?" He pressed his forehead against the chair back, breathing raggedly.

She felt that the answer was obvious.

He shuddered again. "Fuck."

"I'm sorry."

"Shut up!"

She stood silently, waiting until his breathing slowed.

"Fine," he bit out. "Go on."

"Do you want me to knock you out again?" she asked.

He lifted his head and looked at her. His eyes were empty. His face bruised with exhaustion. "Is there really a point to this?"

Helena met his stare. She could fix this. She wasn't going to let him suffer and die for finally doing something good in his life.

"Please, let me try."

Something incredulous flickered in his eyes. His lips started to move, but then he turned away, forehead pressed against the back of the chair.

"Fine," he said, sounding resigned.

She slid her fingers against the base of his skull. It took only a few seconds, and he went limp.

She removed the gauze and cleaned the wounds, washing his entire back with saline and then a carbolic dilution. At least the Resistance had enough supplies now that she could treat him properly.

She examined him with her resonance, working slowly to better understand what the array was doing to him. When she'd finished in the lab, she'd gone to the library and researched arrays, trying to find any information that might be relevant. There was nothing. No one had ever carved an active array into a human before.

She could feel it in her resonance that his body was dying. Tiny flashes of that horrible dissipating coldness, over and over. The array was not only draining the energy from the talisman, but also stripping his body of every resource he had.

Ferron didn't have the physiological resources to counterbalance the deterioration, so it grew worse with every passing moment.

She pressed a hand on his arm, using her resonance to try to warm him. If she'd known sooner, if he'd summoned her, maybe she could have done something more—

She was so late.

She stood staring at him, throat too tight to swallow. She'd reported the injury to Crowther, and he hadn't seemed to care, either that Kaine was hurt or that Helena had revealed her vivimancy. He'd provided her with the papers and instructed her to do what she could to get any further information from Ferron, adding that if he was beyond hope of recovery, she should bring back the talisman. They had no use for Ferron as a lich.

Save him or kill him.

She stood, staring at the array, gripping her amulet through her shirt, feeling its points prick the scars in her palm.

She couldn't kill him. Not after he'd trusted her. Not after he'd helped them.

A month ago, perhaps, but not now.

The Resistance needed him. All the advantages and territory they'd retaken was because of Kaine, and the war was still not won. She had to save him.

She pulled the amulet off, rubbing her thumbs across the surface.

She'd realised after she started wearing it again that she'd stopped feeling so tired, so physically strained by her vivimancy.

She knew the sunstone amulets were supposed to be special, to hold some of Sol's light and strength within them, but she hadn't realised what a difference it had been making all these years. Buying her time. Getting her to this moment.

If it could do that, maybe it could save Kaine, tilt things into balance and give him a chance.

If he died, it didn't really matter what happened to her. There were other healers now, and with the ports back, her medicine wasn't needed anymore, either.

She was replaceable. Ferron wasn't.

She'd never had much resonance for gold, but she tried to use it to bend down the golden rays on the amulet. Kaine would never agree to wear the Holdfast crest, but if it looked a bit more ordinary—

The setting bent, and the sunstone slipped, plummeting to the floor.

It hit the ground and shattered.

Helena stared in horror as red shards scattered everywhere, and on the ground all that remained was something silvery white.

She knelt down, reaching towards it. It was like quicksilver, a puddle of liquid metal on the ground, but the gleam was pearlescent, sort of glowing. When she touched it, it turned solid and cold.

She picked it up and it melted again. Without using her resonance, she could feel a warm hum of energy coming from it, seeming to seep through her skin. The feeling faded when it moved, turning solid like a stone.

She watched, mesmerised. The hum seemed to grow as though she were in a dream. Things were almost real, but the details blurred when she focused on them.

Raw and exposed, it had a burn to it almost like the talisman inside Ferron's chest, but softer, more familiar somehow. Like an old friend.

She'd always dismissed the claims of a healer's intuition, the idea that vivimancy endowed any kind of fundamental understanding of human physiology that was divine or intuitive, but she was certain that the object in her hand could heal Ferron. It would.

She went over to him, carrying it. Very carefully with her free hand, she pulled him back, trying not to put pressure on the lacerations.

She tilted her hand against his chest, near the talisman, and the liquid turned solid and rolled. When it touched his skin, rather than melt again, it stayed solid, only warm and liquid against Helena's palm.

She pressed her hand flat over Kaine's heart and used her resonance. It was like plunging her hand into scalding water. Heat ran up her nerves.

The stone was solid, but as her resonance pushed through towards Kaine, it flushed warm beneath her palm and vanished.

She snatched her hand back in time to see the silver brightness disappear through Kaine's skin.

For a moment, his body was illuminated from the inside out.

She could see the shadows of his bones and veins and heart as it shone inside him and then disappeared.

Helena blinked as if she'd just woken from a daze. The humming was gone, the room still, and all that remained was the disfigured shape of the suncrest and the broken red glass on the floor.

She touched Ferron's chest, tentatively, wondering if she'd just hallucinated. It didn't feel like anything in the last several minutes had been real.

She reached out with her resonance, not sure what she'd just done. He felt the same, a dissonant sense of deadness and energy. There was no apparent change—except maybe he was a little warmer?

She leaned him forward in the chair, and her fingers trembled as she looked around. She swept up the glass with a calm she did not feel, pouring it into an empty glass vial and tucking it into her satchel, warring between trying to convince herself that it had happened and telling herself that it hadn't. Neither option felt fully plausible.

She went back and examined Ferron again as she would any patient. To her resonance, there seemed nothing distinctly different except that he was warmer now; the flashes of coldness didn't tear at her resonance so intensely when she touched him. But there was nothing inside him except the talisman, still burning and glowing near his heart, and the lumithium alloy on his back.

She closed her eyes for a moment, reaching up out of habit to grip the amulet before remembering that it was gone. She'd just have to wait and see what happened.

She began applying the salve she'd made with Shiseo. They'd used morphine as the numbing agent, bonded in various forms of petroleum jelly and beeswax for prolonged release, along with copper and honey to prevent infection.

Then she bandaged him before putting her amulet back on, trying to flatten the empty setting before hiding it beneath her shirt. The gold was cool against her skin.

As she woke Kaine, she took his hand again, rigid with tension, working it slowly, coaxing it to relax. She felt him regain consciousness, but he didn't move or speak for several minutes. Finally, he slipped his hand away and stood, reaching wordlessly for his shirt.

She helped him dress, feeling his eyes on her as she fastened each button. She tried not to stare at the place where the stone had vanished.

She only looked up when she reached his throat. His eyes seemed clearer. More alert, but she suspected that was only because he was sober again.

"I'll come back tomorrow night," she said.

The next night, Ferron's skin was no longer so visibly grey-tinged. He still looked skeletal, his face tight from pain, but along with his colour, his skin was a touch warmer. He refused to be knocked out again. She could tell he was suspicious of her and wanted to know exactly what she did, but he wouldn't ask, and she wasn't about to volunteer what had happened.

He wasn't healing or regenerating; he just wasn't dying so aggressively. There was still a long journey ahead that relied on his body somehow adapting to the array.

She tried to be gentle, but he shuddered, gripping the back of the chair until his knuckles turned white as she washed and cleaned the wounds. She worked quickly, warning him each time she touched him, explaining each step, trying to help keep the end in sight.

He still flinched every time she touched him.

Every night she came back to the Outpost, following the same routine. Most nights, Kaine didn't speak to her at all. He was always slightly drunk and somehow seemed annoyed that she kept coming back. After five days, the talisman stopped radiating energy as if it were a leaking battery, and she could feel the aggressive decay from overstrain slowing.

After more than a week of wordless treatment, he spoke abruptly when she was washing her hands. "The High Necromancer wants someone."

She paused. "Who?"

"A guard from one of the Hevgoss's prison complexes."

"Why?"

"I'm still persona non grata, so I don't know all the details of what's going on. Apparently at some point, Morrough promised the Hevgotian militocrats the key to immortality. It's been decades, and he hasn't produced the version of it that they want. The reason they're supporting the Guild Assembly is because the High Necromancer somehow convinced them that he can develop it if he can take Paladia. The alliance soured with the latest setback, and now Morrough's suddenly concerned with getting his hands on this guard without Hevgoss knowing. A few aspirants are going in quietly, trying to track him down. If the Eternal Flame wants more details, they should send someone after them."

"Why not send the Undying?" she asked.

"It's more complicated to send us. It takes special preparations, and there's limits to how long we can go."

She paused. "Why?"

She could feel his annoyance at the question. "Because we're bound to Morrough."

Her hands froze. "Do you mean like"—there was no polite way to phrase it—"are you like—the necrothralls?"

He glared from the corner of his eye.

It was well known that necrothralls could go only so far from their necromancer or else they'd "die" again. Most necromancers could manage a few miles at most. The Undying's reanimations were particularly powerful; the necrothralls in Paladia moved so freely, no one was sure of their limits, but they were assumed to be somewhere within Paladia's borders.

That a limitation of distance applied to the Undying indicated parallels between the two.

"Yes," Kaine said, his tone begrudging.

"But Morrough left, and he didn't take everyone. You were still here. How did that work?" she asked as she began applying the salve to lacerations that were still fresh and raw.

"We're not always bound to him exactly." He sighed. "We're—he uses his bones, pieces of them, when we're made. Part of the outer bone of his right arm was used on me. He calls them phylacteries. It's what creates our physical immutability. A part of that is used to make the talismans." He gestured at his chest. "He takes the phylacteries out sometimes and either grows a new bone or takes a spare from some necrothrall. That's what he did when travelling, so he could leave some of us behind during his trip. He doesn't like to do it often, but if he travelled without leaving the phylacteries, the connection would sever, and we'd—die."

"His bones?" Helena was stuck on that point.

He nodded. "Yes. He shares a piece of himself with us, and we give all of ourselves to him."

He was silent, and Helena just kept working, her mind churning, until he spoke again.

"A few tried to run, back when the war started. When they realised it wouldn't be a tidy little coup to depose the Holdfasts. The High Necromancer had the corpses brought back. He'd made new talismans from each of the phylacteries and put them into the corpses. I believe you call them liches when they're dead like that. That was when we began to realise what being 'Undying' meant."

"What would happen if you stole your phylactery?"

He laughed under his breath. "You've never been anywhere near Morrough if you think that's doable. He can fill rooms with his resonance. But even if it were possible to steal from him, they start crumbling after a while. That deterioration doesn't kill the Undying, but—their minds start to go."

Well, that explained why Ferron needed the Eternal Flame; he was dependent on them defeating Morrough for him.

"I'll let Crowther know," she said as she finished.

HELENA PAUSED HALFWAY ACROSS THE bridge to the East Island, looking back towards the dam and mountains. Lumithia was a waning crescent, approaching the summer Abeyance, but still her light gilded everything.

A few more weeks and the summer tides would fully ebb, making passage across the seas possible, and the month-long deluge of trade would pour across the sea, hurrying inland. The Resistance had secured the ports just in time for the annual trade season.

Helena stood, studying the stark world around her, cast in black and silver.

She felt lost. Kaine's injury was eating into her detachment. She could feel herself losing focus. Now that he was showing signs of recovery, she couldn't let herself forget her task.

Hold his attention. Make him loyal. Or obsessed. Whichever came more readily. As vital as his information was, he remained a liability if his service was solely at his own discretion.

Undying. Murderer. Spy. Target. Tool.

She repeated the list to herself, but her conviction in them rang hollow.

The motives Crowther attributed to Kaine felt like an ill-fitted façade, something that Kaine hid behind. Helena was an alchemist; she was not in the habit of manipulating or altering things until she understood their nature.

She crossed the bridge, heading towards Headquarters, but a rain garden caught her eye. She'd passed it countless times but never stopped. Tonight something drew her. It had probably been pretty once but was neglected now. In the middle of the stream sat a shrine to the goddess Luna.

Acknowledgements of Luna were a rare thing in Paladia. Outright snubbing one of the gods was regarded as dangerous, but she was rarely recognised except as part of the Quintessence.

In Paladia, Luna was regarded as fickle and vain, treacherous as the tides. According to the Faith, it was because of Luna's inconstant nature that Sol had birthed Lumithia from his own heart, placing her in the night sky so that mankind would not fear the dark. Luna, envious of

Lumithia's greater brilliance, had sought to drown the world in retribution. Lumithia had faced Luna in a celestial battle so devastating, it had rained fire across the earth. After the battle, Lumithia settled in the sky and—to repair the destruction caused by the Great Disaster—bestowed the gifts of alchemy upon mankind. Meanwhile Luna, remorseless even in defeat, continued to express her fury by keeping the ocean and sea frothing with her endless jealousy, only calming when she ruled the skies alone.

Millennia later and Luna remained reviled, small and insignificant compared with Lumithia's brilliant beauty and power.

The statue of Luna was worn featureless, leaving little more than a vague figure behind.

The Paladian treatment of Luna had been a shock when Helena first arrived. She'd known of Paladia's great devotion to Sol and Lumithia, but the very concept of religion was different.

The islands of Etras had little metal for alchemy, and being in constant proximity to the sea meant that Etrasians regarded Lumithia as the one responsible for the severe tidal shifts that ruled them. In their myths, Lumithia was a violent interloper who'd sought to destroy the earth, and Luna had thrown herself into Lumithia's path. The act had left Luna so grievously wounded, she nearly fell from the sky, and the seas had tried to rise from their beds to catch her. Lumithia, chastened by this act of self-sacrifice, was quieted from her violence and came to share Luna's vigil over the night sky. But the seas did not forget: They still rose in rage when Lumithia waxed full, only quieting in her absence.

Because of this, in Etras, Luna did not merely rule the seas; she was also regarded as the patron goddess of protection, an intercessor. A mother.

Helena picked up a smooth stone from the creek.

In Etras, to pray to Luna, they'd balanced rocks in stacks along the beach, each stone a prayer for the tides to carry to her.

There would be no tides here to wash it away, but Helena had always loved the meditative focus of the ritual. She made a neat stack, the first stone Luc, then Lila, and Soren, Matron Pace, the medics and nurses and trainees in the hospital, Shiseo, Ilva (begrudgingly), the Eternal Flame, and the Resistance.

The tower grew until it wobbled dangerously.

Helena held one last stone. She hesitated.

If she knocked the tower down while building it, it would be for naught. She almost put the stone back.

She placed it.

Don't make me responsible for Kaine Ferron's death.

The stack wobbled, threatening collapse. Then it settled.

Her throat thickened, and a weight in her chest lifted, as if the universe was telling her it was possible.

A southern ritual had no place in the North, but she'd given everything for the war, and it had not been enough.

Superstition was all she had left.

CHAPTER 34

Julius 1786

SHE NOTICED THE STREAKS OF SILVER WHILE treating Kaine's back. They were just barely visible at his temple, glimmers of silver-white threaded through his dark hair.

She stopped and leaned closer, inspecting them. "Did this just start?"

He reached up, brushing the spot with his fingers. "I noticed it this morning."

"I thought you couldn't change."

"Well, I am an experiment now," he said dryly. "It's not as if anyone knows what will happen. That's why people perform experiments."

She leaned in closer, trying to convince herself that he was simply going grey, and that it was *not* the exact shade of silver-white the stone had been.

He swivelled his head to face her, their faces a breath apart. "Do you mind?"

She blushed, drawing back quickly. "Sorry."

He spoke again as she was applying the bandages. "Apparently I'm being gifted a chimaera."

"Gifted?"

The casual way he said it made it sound like he'd been given an unwanted house pet rather than a rabid monster that had a tendency towards decomposing while still alive.

"So far, they've all been savage, but a tameable chimaera would be ideal." He stood up. "Those of us with the 'resources' to raise one are being 'given' a chimaera to train. It's a test, obviously."

She stepped around him, helping him put his shirt on. The haggard bruising under his eyes had almost faded entirely. "But you're injured. It's not fair to expect you to tame something like that when you can't heal properly or raise your arms."

He looked condescendingly down at her. "Marino, this may be a shocking revelation for you, but the High Necromancer does not care about fairness. It's his opinion that anyone without the wits and will to survive deserves to suffer and die. Ideally for his amusement."

She could tell he was baiting her. "Do you know what kind of chimaera it will be?"

"Well, given the use of the word 'train,' I imagine it will be at least part dog. But I'm not Bennet's favourite person. Whatever it is, I'm sure to get the worst one."

The idea of a chimaera that could be trained was horrifying. More and more of them kept appearing. They died quickly, but the deaths associated with them were slowly increasing.

"Could you—kill it?"

He raised an eyebrow. "You think I should kill my gift that I'm being tested with?"

She went hot and cold all over, not sure how to reply.

He was already injured. If the chimaera he was entrusted with were to die, he'd undoubtedly be punished, but—

He caught her chin, tilting her head back until her eyes met his. There was a vaguely silver gleam in them. "If you were me, what would you do?"

"I—" she stammered. "I would see if I could make it loyal."

"And if you couldn't? If a monster can't be made loyal, what would you do then?"

Their faces were close. Helena's throat tightened, her heart beating too fast.

"I'd look for flaws in the transmutation," she said. "The splicing isn't very good, so there are mistakes that could be aggravated to accelerate deterioration. You wouldn't have to kill it outright, you'd just—speed up the inevitable."

He leaned forward, so close she could feel his breath. For a moment she thought he was going to kiss her.

"You're so pragmatic." The words brushed against her lips.

He released her chin abruptly and stepped away, eyes glittering.

Her cheeks were still hot as she packed up all her supplies, refusing to look at him again.

He spoke just as she was leaving.

"Don't die, Marino. I might miss you."

VANYA GETTLICH WAS A STUBBY-LIMBED spinster with small eyes, a large round nose, and sharp ears. The combination, she'd always said, that was the secret to her success as one of the best scouts in the Resistance. No one ever noticed a homely woman.

Generally, scouts didn't live very long. Months was considered impressive. For many it was far less. Vanya had been a scout for years, crossing in and out of enemy territory collecting intelligence and information that no one else dared obtain.

But when she vanished, everyone knew that she wouldn't come back. She was marked missing for two weeks before being listed among the presumed dead.

It was a shock when Helena received an emergency summons to the gatehouse after one of the patrols radioed in, claiming to have found her. Gettlich was grievously wounded. They'd verified that she wasn't a necrothrall, but it was harder to be sure that it wasn't a lich trying to infiltrate Headquarters using her wounded corpse.

When she was checked for any signs of a talisman, they'd found anomalous forms of metal distributed through her body, including detectable lumithium.

There were no exceptions to the rules. Anyone found with lumithium inside their body could not enter Headquarters without full restraints.

They strapped Gettlich down while she screamed, begging them not to, promising it was her, but Helena was not allowed to treat her otherwise.

Helena had just stepped forward when the doors burst open and Luc entered, threatening to put his own guards in the ground if they tried to stop him.

Lila stood beside him, weapons ready, conflict written across her face as Luc leaned over Gettlich, indifferent to the danger.

"Gettlich," he said, his voice hoarse. "I'm so sorry."

Gettlich calmed then. Luc had that effect on people. She hushed his apologies, called him a silly boy. While Helena worked, unnoticed, she gave her final report.

She'd been caught while investigating the new lab near the West Port. The Undying had used her as a test subject there, trying to suppress her alchemy. They'd injected her with metal over the course of days. The experiment was deemed a failure when her organs started to shut down.

The guards ordered to dispose of her had decided to make use of the dying prisoner. They'd taken her out of the building for privacy and left her for dead once they were done.

As Gettlich told Luc all this, Helena verified it. The metal in the blood interfered with Helena's own resonance, making it blur like static. Her arms and legs were mottled with old bruises from restraints. She was slick with blood from the waist down. She would have died from metal poisoning her blood, but the internal damage was going to kill her first.

All the metal interfered with Helena's vivimancy too much for her to do anything. She had to keep shaking her head each time Luc begged.

Laudanum was all Helena could offer. Relief until it was over.

Gettlich's heart kept trying to rally whenever Luc spoke, promising that the Eternal Flame would never forget her, that he'd find everyone who'd hurt her. He'd make them all pay.

The Council had to lock Luc in his quarters to keep him from trying to take his battalion and find the lab. The Gettlichs were an old family. Luc had known Vanya his entire life.

Because of the circumstances of the death, the traditional mourning and cremation processes were suspended. The body was placed in a secure room, still strapped to the gurney, covered with a sheet.

Helena was summoned to Falcon Matias's office, a drab little room with no decorations except one very large painting of the sun. She always felt cold in any room that Matias occupied.

"The Council has determined that an autopsy on Gettlich is necessary," Matias said without preamble, his face puckering as he looked at Helena. "You have been selected to perform it."

"I'm not trained—"

"There are books on the matter. You can ask Surgeon Maier for them," Matias said, waving his hand.

"Then shouldn't Maier be the one to—"

"I am told the state of Gettlich is deeply disturbing. You have already seen it, it will do you no harm to see it again," he said, cutting her off once more. "You will be observed throughout to ensure you take no untoward actions." His watery blue eyes narrowed. "If you are suspected of any violation of that body, I will have your hands cut off and your soul cursed to sink into the dark fires of the earth. Do I make myself clear?"

He glared at her, sticky strings of saliva visible in his mouth as he spoke. He only imbibed enough water to survive, considering the demands of the flesh as something to conquer. It was a common idea among those of faith, although Matias took it further than anyone else Helena had ever met.

Helena stood, her stomach knotted in dread. She'd never performed an autopsy.

Gettlich had taught introductory alchemy, one of Helena's first instructors. She knew her.

But nothing from Matias was ever a request. His word was law for Helena.

She gave a slow nod.

"The procedure will take place tomorrow, when Sol is at his zenith." Matias's tongue smacked again. "Go purify yourself in preparation."

Helena left, her head hollow, but there was nothing she could do. She couldn't bring Luc into this. He was already shattered by the death and wouldn't want an autopsy at all, but the Council was right: They needed to know what had been done.

She spent her evening researching autopsy methods until it was time to head to the Outpost. She felt almost comatose with dread and was grateful for a routine to escape to.

Ferron was in his usual place, a tumbler dangling from his fingers, but the furniture in the room had all been shoved to one side. His expression was languorous, eyelids lowered, but a sharp, almost silver gleam glittered beneath his lashes.

Helena didn't ask. She had her own preoccupations.

It was undeniable that he was in one of his moods. There was an edge to him, a strange quality in the way his eyes landed on her when she arrived. Not his typical resentment.

Helena feigned obliviousness, removing the bandages without a word and studying the wounds. His colouring was almost back to normal, and there was no sign of rot or infection anywhere. Only tiny traces of dead tissue in the immediate area around the symbols.

In a week or so, she might try closing the incisions. Survivable or not, it wasn't sustainable for him to have a perpetually open injury. As much as he tried to hide behind a routine, she knew he could barely move without excruciating pain. She didn't trust Crowther's or Ilva's charity lasting much longer if Kaine was unable to resume spying.

She rested her hand briefly on his shoulder. He shifted but didn't flinch at all.

"You're done," she said quietly as she finished wrapping the bandages and helped him with his shirt.

He said nothing, just stood and poured himself another drink.

She packed up her bag, heading for the door. Usually the necrothrall opened it as soon as she was near, but tonight it remained closed.

She stood waiting for a moment before finally looking back towards Kaine, standing by the bar. "I never got around to training you, did I, Marino?"

Her mouth went dry. The room around her was suddenly very present.

She'd known that once Kaine began to feel better, he'd find it necessary to remind her that *he* was in charge. He so obviously hated feeling vulnerable around anyone. He'd feel the need to put her back in her place.

She'd known, and filed it away as a future concern.

She took a step back.

"Come here."

She shook her head. "I have—I have a procedure tomorrow. You can't hurt me t-tonight."

He stilled, and then his knuckles gripped the tumbler, turning white as his expression darkened. "I realise you consider me a complete monster," he bit out. "But I do generally keep my word. I'm not planning to hurt you. Come here. I want you to try attacking me, so I can see what you know."

"What?" She stared at him, incredulous.

"You're travelling at night, outside of Resistance territory." He was speaking through clenched teeth. "We've already established you're shit at defence. Let's see your offence. Come. Here."

She glanced around the cleared space in disbelief. "I'm not going to attack you when you're injured."

He stared at her in confusion. "It's not like I can die."

She wanted to tell him he was insane but tried to be tactful about it. "Look, Ferron—Kaine—I appreciate the concern, but I'm a vivimancer. I'll be fine."

"Will you?"

She gave a sharp nod. "Yes. I might not be the best at defence, but I've always got that. So my fighting abilities aren't something you need to worry about. But"—she drew a deep breath—"I appreciate that you did."

"I suppose you have a point," he said slowly, his eyes sliding out of focus.

She heard the door behind her open and gave him one last nod as she turned to go.

In the doorway, instead of the one necrothrall waiting for her, the passage was crowded with them. There were a dozen at least, some old and grey, others new, their wounds still red.

The blood drained from her head.

"Don't worry, they're all mine," she dimly heard Ferron say. "Now then, let's see you fight with vivimancy."

He said something else but she couldn't hear him anymore. Her eyes were trapped on the necrothralls that were all shuffling into the room towards her. Their faces blank.

There were so many.

They crowded towards her. She was trapped. Trapped with them. She couldn't escape.

They'd all close in.

"You call yourself a vivimancer. Show me."

She barely heard his words.

It's not the hospital. You're not in the hospital, she told herself, but every time she tried to breathe, her chest clenched tighter. She managed to step back.

She held one hand out, to ward them off, but it shook violently.

"Marino." Kaine's voice was annoyed. "Are you more afraid of thralls than you are of me? I'm actually offended."

"F-Ferron, call them off," she said, a tremor in her voice. She couldn't tear her eyes away from the necrothralls.

"No. I want to see you fight."

"I don't want to fight," she said, backing away farther. "Stop it. You said I could say no to things. I'm saying no."

Her voice was rising.

"They're corpses. You said you can protect yourself. Show me!"

Her stomach clenched, her legs threatening to give out.

"Let them go." Her voice shook.

"You take any out, and I'll burn them." His tone was sardonic, as if the whole thing were funny. "Come on now. Show me what you've got."

The necrothralls fanned out, backing her into the corner. Her shoulders hit a wall.

"Ferron!" Her voice was sharp, a note of hysteria in it. "Call them off. I don't want to do this!"

"This is war." His voice came from somewhere beyond the bodies crowding around her. "You don't get to want; you get to live or die."

She shrank back, making herself as small as she could. Her throat was closing, as if fingers were already wrapped around it. They'd slit her wide open.

She screamed and shoved her hands out.

Everything turned red.

Everything.

She blinked and couldn't see anything but the dark coagulating blood dripping down her face. It covered her skin, sticking to her lashes. There were no necrothralls now, just bits and pieces of bodies.

Her knees gave out, and she slid down the wall to the floor, gripping the strap of her satchel.

She could taste the blood in her mouth. The scent of decomposition was thick in the air. She was still suffocating, choking on blood and viscera as she tried to breathe.

Two hard hands gripped her shoulders.

She shoved outwards with her resonance, but it was met and shoved back in so violently that it was like a cannon going off inside her head.

Her vision went white, and when it returned Ferron's face swam before her, except he was glowing. His eyes had gone bright silver.

"What the fuck, Marino?"

Her head was ringing, and she couldn't form words. She just knelt there, staring at his living face.

"I told you—I didn't want to," she finally said. Then her face crumpled, and she burst into tears.

There was a pause.

"Perhaps I did slightly underestimate you." He pulled a handkerchief out and wiped her face until there was no more blood clotted in her lashes.

She sat, numb, until he dragged her up from the floor, his arms nearly giving out as he pulled her along to the bathroom.

He pushed her in, twisting a tap to turn on the shower before opening a cabinet and pulling out several towels and some fresh clothes.

"Clean up," he said.

Helena looked down at herself. She was covered in viscera. It smelled worse than the hospital. All the decomposition. Her throat convulsed.

She stepped into the shower with her clothes on, fingers trembling as she forced herself to remove them, peeling off the wet layers like skin.

It was as if Ferron had found a festering wound and jabbed his fingers into it. Cocooned under the water, she could barely bring herself to step out.

She knew she was only delaying the inevitable as she slowly dried and rebraided her hair, pinning it carefully back into place before looking at the clothes Ferron had left. They were his. Trousers and a shirt.

Did he live here? She pulled them on slowly.

As she stood, carefully fastening the familiar buttons, her shock thinned, her mind resurfacing raw with anger.

When she emerged from the bathroom, she braced herself for the nightmare of blood and gore, but the room had been cleaned. She'd been in the bathroom longer than she'd realised.

The floor had been mopped. Even the furniture had been put back. The scent lingered, but visual traces were all gone.

Ferron was seated backwards on the chair, the fingers of one hand pressed against his forehead as if he was dealing with an intense migraine.

She hoped he was.

He looked up, hand dropping languidly away.

"Well," he said slowly, his enunciation precise. His eyes still had a strange silver gleam to them. "You really are full of surprises."

The sight of him so unapologetic only added to her brewing rage.

She went over to the bar, pouring herself a generous amount of something from a very fancy-looking bottle.

She sipped it. It was sharp and bitter. She wished she'd chosen something else; she'd always preferred wine, but Ferron didn't appear to keep any. Likely not strong enough for his taste.

She braced herself and gulped it, not caring at all about the way it curdled her tongue, burning down her throat and into her empty stomach.

She squeezed her eyes shut and then poured more, drinking it almost as quickly.

She wanted to get drunk as fast as possible. She swirled her fingers, feeling her own body with her resonance, prompting her digestive system to absorb the alcohol a little faster, to get it into her blood before she did something like throwing every single bottle on the wall at Ferron's head.

She closed her eyes, sinking hard into the warm, blurring relief.

She rarely drank alcohol, and now she was reminded why. It felt so much better to feel like this than the way she actually felt all the time: like a raw nerve.

She gripped the glass, pouring herself a bit more.

"I think that's enough," Ferron said behind her. "I don't believe your liver regenerates."

She'd only intended to add a little, but at those words she upended the bottle, pouring all the rest into her glass. It sloshed over the side, spilling onto the rug.

"Fuck off," she said.

"I didn't know you could swear." He sounded amused.

Her jaw clenched, and she turned and told him to fuck off in three more languages.

He arched an eyebrow. "Am I supposed to take you more seriously now?"

"I hate you."

He gave a strained laugh. "I am aware."

She looked down at the drink. She wanted to leave—she was tired, jittery, and knocked completely off kilter—but the door was closed again. Ferron clearly intended to keep her. She went over and curled up at the end of the sofa, as far from him as she could get.

"I hate you," she said again.

"I hate you, too."

The alcohol had set her tongue loose. "This war is your fault. Everyone who's died. It's on your head. And now, because of you, even when it's over, I'll still have nothing."

"Am I supposed to care? Do you think that ruining your life is the worst thing I've ever done?"

She looked away.

"When did you find out you were a vivimancer?" he asked.

She was not drunk enough for that conversation. She gulped more of her drink. She was going to have the most blistering hangover tomorrow.

"I should've wondered that sooner, shouldn't I?"

She said nothing so he kept talking.

"Vivimancy is often a late-onset ability. Mid to late adulthood. Young people tend to manifest it as a reaction to a traumatic event. You weren't surprised at what you did to those thralls, which tells me that wasn't the first time you've done that. So what did it? What happened to set you off like a bomb?"

Helena tilted her head back, staring at the ceiling. Everything inside her went soft when she was this drunk.

"We thought at the beginning that the usual rules of war would apply. We set up field hospitals so that people wouldn't have to travel through combat zones to reach a hospital."

"The massacres."

She nodded.

The hospital massacres had been the first major atrocity in the war. Apollo's assassination had been devastating, but the massacres were when it all became irrevocably real.

The Undying followed no rules. It was not an "honourable" war. Morrough wanted people to be afraid or dead.

The Guild Assembly defended the attacks, saying that the hospitals were run by the Eternal Flame as covers for military bases, and the surrounding countries swallowed the lie, because it was easier than involving themselves in Paladia's conflict.

"My father was a Khemish surgeon. Here in Paladia, manual surgery is considered antiquated, so he didn't have much luck getting a job." Helena swallowed hard, staring across the room. "When the war started, he wanted to go back to Etras, but I'd promised Luc that I'd stay. When I wouldn't go, he didn't, either. The Resistance was setting up the field hospitals. It was my idea—him working there. I thought he'd be safe, and if the people saw how talented he was, he'd have opportunities—afterwards."

She gulped more from her drink. The room was swaying.

"I was going to be a combat medic, so I'd volunteer at the hospital while we were training for dispatch. That day—we thought it was poison.

All these people came in with fevers. We couldn't bring them down. One of them, he kept getting hotter and hotter, screaming, 'Get him out'—and he got violent. My father sent me to look for someone, and the patient was dead when I got back. They were trying to find a cause of death, and the patient suddenly sat up." She hiccoughed. "We knew about the Undying regenerating, but we didn't know about the liches then."

Her voice was barely more than a whisper.

"They blocked the doors and started killing and reanimating everyone. The necrothralls they made helped them kill faster." She swallowed. "The hospital wasn't equipped. My father—he'd never—he'd only heard about necrothralls. These were colleagues. Patients. I told him they weren't people anymore, but he still didn't fight back when they caught him."

She reached up, pressing her palm against her throat for a moment, her fingers curled, following the thin scar just below her left ear that swept towards her throat.

"He was so gentle. He had this deep voice that would rumble in your chest when he hugged you. He would never have hurt me . . ."

"The reports said there were no survivors." Ferron's voice seemed to come from somewhere far off.

"They didn't find me right away," she said dully.

She squeezed the glass in her hand. "All the field hospitals. In one day. They killed everyone, nurses, doctors, surgeons, all the patients. And we found out about the liches. And what I was."

"The liches who infiltrated the hospitals were a failed experiment, I'm told," Ferron said quietly. "Morrough and Bennet were trying to see if placing talismans inside other living bodies would let the Undying take over and remain alive. But the host bodies always went into shock."

"Oh," was all Helena could think to say. Her intoxication had struck; even stringing words together felt arduous, but she struggled through, Gettlich's face floating in her mind. "Do you know what they're working on now?"

His eyes narrowed. "I don't hear much beyond rumours presently. Why?"

She looked away. "No reason."

"Why'd they make you a healer?"

She blinked. "Healing's efficient. Things that can take weeks or months to recover from, can be fixed in minutes or hours with vivimancy. They needed someone who could save people."

Ferron gave a derisive scoff.

Her anger reignited. "You have no idea how hard it is to save someone, to fix all the ways the people like you break them." She glared at him. "I hope someday you have to try. See how little you think of it then."

He looked away.

She felt an odd spark of satisfaction.

There was a long silence. Ferron seemed completely lost in his thoughts, and Helena was so drunk she could barely see straight. She closed her eyes, drifting. When she reopened them, he was staring at her.

She looked back and couldn't help but think he looked different now. Older. Or perhaps she was incredibly intoxicated.

"Can I ask you a question?" she asked, struggling against dizziness. "Do you feel the array? Can you tell it's affecting you?"

"Yes," he said with a faint nod. "I didn't think I could change, but it's like being cold-forged. I'm gradually being beaten into a new iteration of myself. It doesn't countermand who I am, but I feel certain things less than I did. It's easier to be ruthless and focused, harder to dissuade myself from impulses that align with what I want."

She squinted at him. "Why that design? What was Bennet trying to turn you into?"

"I designed it," he said quietly.

That information was shocking enough to sober Helena. She sat up.

"It was my punishment," he said. "I expected it would kill me, but if I survived, I didn't want them to choose what I became. So I asked to design it, as proof of my penance."

She sat forward, studying him. She wasn't imagining it; he was different. It was like witnessing a slow metamorphosis. The effect of the array was likely exacerbated by the delay in healing, the deterioration making him more malleable.

His features had grown more defined, still gaunt from sickness, but it had carved the boyishness from his face. He actually looked like an adult now.

She tilted her head to the side. If she saw him, without the context of who he was, she might find him rather handsome.

The thought made her blink so hard, the room went out of focus.

She stood quickly. "I need to go back; the checkpoints close soon."

CHAPTER 35

Julius 1786

HELENA HAD THE MOST BLISTERING HANGOVER THE next morning and lay in bed, so nauseous she didn't even feel guilty for sleeping in until someone was sent to remind her that she was due to perform an autopsy.

She almost threw up upon being reminded, but there was no delaying. She spent several minutes transmuting her own body until she didn't feel sick from standing upright.

The autopsy would take place in the Alchemy Tower's operating theatre so that Falcon Matias and several of the Flame Keepers who managed the crematorium could observe to ensure she did nothing to violate the sanctity of the body.

Helena's mouth was dry as she stood before the covered gurney, the metal instruments laid out on a tray, gleaming under a bright light that illuminated her and Gettlich, leaving her audience in the shadows.

She felt disconnected from her body as she pulled the sheet back.

"May I begin?" she said to the darkness.

"Begin," came Matias's voice.

There was something particularly horrible about having to cut open the body of someone she'd known, removing the organs and examining the body in components while narrating in detail the kinds of abuse she found evidence of. What she could and couldn't feel through resonance about the experimentation.

She wished she could cover the face, so she didn't have to look at it while she was working, but the dead had to be respected.

When it was over, two of the Flame Keepers emerged from the darkness and took the body carefully away. It was important for every part to be burned, to ensure that no earthly remains could hold back the soul's ascent.

In the war room, Helena listened as the guard reported on how Gettlich had been found and what she'd said. Then Luc recited in an empty voice everything that she'd told him.

General Althorne showed the location of the West Port Lab. Ferron's contribution. It was better protected than the previous lab had been, the building extensively reinforced to repel an assault. It would be difficult to reach, and they risked too many combatants if they went that far into enemy territory.

"The Council recognises Healer Marino," Matias said. It was the first time Helena had spoken before the Eternal Flame since her "hysterical outburst." She hadn't known that she'd be called on. Matias could give the report himself.

Ilva's eyes flicked to Crowther as Helena stepped forward.

She wet her lips. "Based on my—examination, the information Gettlich gave Luc—the Principate, appears accurate. It was likely an unsuccessful attempt to neutralise her resonance. There were multiple injection sites throughout the body, some near the brain but most along the arms. It was a variety of metals reduced to microparticles and injected with a carrier fluid into the muscles. I couldn't accurately analyse it through resonance; there seemed to be some compounds beyond my repertoire. I extracted what I could and turned the samples over to the metallurgists. It wasn't possible to determine whether the method was successful in suppressing alchemical abilities, although prior to her death, I did have difficulty offering relief through healing."

"How would such a thing work?" Ilva asked, her fingertips drawing absentminded circles on the table in front of her.

Helena inhaled, hoping that they would not punish the messenger. "My theory is that the injections were intended to create an internal interference with Gettlich's resonance. By placing the microparticles inside the body near the brain and hands, they thought to obscure Gettlich's ability to sense metal outside her body. Based on the number of injections, I believe they kept dosing her until she couldn't resonate anymore, but the quantity of metal was toxic at that point."

"What are the odds they succeeded?" Althorne asked in his deep voice.

"I couldn't say," Helena said.

"What I wish to know," Falcon Matias said from his seat beside Ilva, "is what the purpose of this experiment is. What use would they have for suppressing resonance?"

"I don't know," she said.

"You're a vivimancer," he said pointedly. "Surely you have some idea of how it could be useful for your kind."

Luc, who'd been slumped in his seat ever since Althorne overruled any possibility of raiding the lab, suddenly straightened. "What's that supposed to mean?"

Matias smacked his tongue, pressing a handkerchief beneath his narrow nostrils. "It is a relevant question. Healer Marino"—he said the title as if it were an insult—"has the same abilities as those responsible. Because of that, she may have ideas that would not occur to the rest of us."

Luc's eyes flashed dangerously. "Helena is a healer. She has devoted her life to our cause. She's as loyal as anyone. She's nothing like those responsible."

Rather than answer Luc, Falcon Matias turned his gaze back to Helena. "Healer Marino, prior to this autopsy, you performed a transmutational dissection, did you not?"

Helena nodded, fingers flexing inside her gloves. "At the Council's request—"

"That was a yes or no question," Matias said sharply.

"Yes."

"And during that dissection, you used transmutational abilities to examine and reverse the creation of the chimaera in ways that any other medical personnel would have been incapable of, did you not?"

"I was instructed to—"

"Yes or no?"

"Yes."

Matias turned his attention triumphantly back to Luc. "Then my question stands. Healer Marino, as a vivimancer, what would you consider the potential use of people with suppressed alchemy?"

The room faded from view, and all Helena could see was Gettlich, cut open, her arms with the skin purpled and greyish around the injection sites, the holes left behind from the syringes, and her own subconscious puzzling out the methodology, trying to understand the intent and technique, unable to keep from noticing avenues of improvement because that was how she'd been trained to perceive all forms of alchemy. Even torture.

If she admitted those theories, it would be proof of what she was. If she refused, she might endanger the Eternal Flame by withholding imperative information.

"It would control prisoners," Crowther said before she could answer, "or they may endeavour to weaponise it. Or use it to make human subjects easier to manage during their experimentation. There are many possibilities, Falcon."

Matias glanced scathingly towards Crowther. There were mutters in the audience. Crowther almost never spoke during meetings.

Helena gave a stilted nod. "There may be a number of potential uses for suppressing alchemy, but there's currently no evidence that they've discovered a reliable means of doing so, only that they're attempting it."

"We should prepare for the possibility, but keep the information away from the general population," Ilva said. "We have no need for fearmongering over something that may never come to pass. And Matias." She turned imperiously to gaze at the Falcon. "Need I remind this Council that Healer Marino's work and title come with the blessing of the Faith and the Principate?"

Matias nodded sourly as Helena went back to her seat.

It was both unsurprising and undeniable that Falcon Matias wanted Helena removed from the Eternal Flame, possibly the Resistance. With all the trainee healers, Helena was no longer the necessity she'd once been. Luc might be the only obstacle to that.

The Council was supposed to be five equal votes, but Luc had greater sway than the other four members combined. They could outvote him, but they'd never dared to veto him openly.

They preferred to simply keep him in the dark.

Luc had an overpowering sense of what was right, his decisions ruled by conscience, but as a result, he was left out of many of the Council's deliberations, nudged to spend his time at the front where choices did not involve such delicate politics.

Helena watched him sitting among the Council, Ilva and Matias on one side and Althorne and Crowther on the other, like a marionette unaware of its strings.

Helena wished she could save him from it, but she knew that left to his own devices he would blindly sacrifice himself at the first opportunity.

CROWTHER GESTURED TO HELENA TO follow him when the meeting ended.

"Is Matias going to be a problem for me?" she asked once they were alone.

"Yes," he said as they walked across the skybridge into the Alchemy Tower.

They entered the lift, but rather than ascend to his office, he inserted a key and the lift went down.

"He wants you gone, and now he's begun taking steps to achieve it."

Helena swallowed hard. "Is that something you'll allow?"

He glanced towards her. "Are you doing anything that would make interfering worth the effort? Insofar as I'm aware, the only thing you've done for the last several weeks is waste our limited opium supplies on Ferron."

The lift was still descending. They passed the ground floor. Helena's stomach seemed to drop with it.

"Where are you taking me?" she asked.

"To see how useful you can be," was all Crowther said as the lift lurched to a stop and the doors opened, revealing a dark passage.

Helena knew there were places underground. She'd been down here a few times to retrieve things from the storage rooms. The plateau where the Tower was built was stone and had been extensively excavated over the centuries. She had no idea why Crowther would bring her here.

He led the way, picking up an electric torch from a ledge, clicking it on, and wedging it into the space between where his body and his paralysed arm were strapped together so he could unlock a heavy door. Instead of revealing a room, it revealed a flight of stairs that led down into pitch blackness. The scent of mildew rose from the darkness.

Helena stalled. "Where are we going?"

"On occasion I have—special prisoners who require medical attention. Ivy doesn't always possess the finesse needed. Come, Marino, show me how much effort you're worth."

HELENA DIDN'T KNOW MUCH ABOUT the Resistance's prisoners, but she did know they weren't supposed to be kept in what amounted to a hole underground. There were ruins beneath the Tower, tunnels and underground rooms, too elaborate to have been made just for Institute storage. Most of them had been transformed into cells filled with unfamiliar prisoners.

She also knew that burn injuries were common in the war, but combat pyromancy was a blunt weapon. It left large burns, not wounds targeted precisely at areas of the body with the highest concentrations of nerve endings.

The person would need to be restrained, and the pyromancer very experienced.

Helena lost track of how long she was down in the dark, eyes straining to pick out details from the unsteady sweep of Crowther's electric torch that gave her only glimpses of filthy bodies and charred flesh. She healed by touch, reaching out and finding bodies in the darkness.

It felt criminal. Relief, but for what? Further atrocity?

She debrided, regenerated the tissue, closed the open sores, healed fractures, and found many hands with every bone meticulously broken.

Which threat was Crowther making by bringing her here?

"I'll—I can have Ferron healed by next week," she said in the lift afterwards, trying to keep her voice from shaking. She was cold all over, and the light hurt her eyes. Complicit. Complicit. Complicit. The word rang through her head. "I'll get it done."

Crowther said nothing, his thin, spider-like fingers tapping absently along his paralysed forearm.

She pressed on, speaking quickly. "He's—I think he's starting to regenerate normally again. The array will be difficult to work with, but I can do it. I think it could be an advantage in the long run. The injury has made him more emotionally vulnerable than he would have been otherwise."

Crowther's fingers stilled. "Don't mistake that for loyalty."

Dread shivered in her lungs.

"I don't. I realise that it's not necessarily leverage yet, but—the array affects him. He mentioned that it's become harder to dissuade himself from what he wants. I can take advantage of that."

"You're deluding yourself."

Why was he suddenly sceptical when this was the mission *he'd* given her?

He looked over. "Kaine Ferron remains the youngest of the Undying. In all this time, there has never been another so young." He was standing near enough in the lift that she could see the metal fillings in his back molars as he spoke. "He should have been taken advantage of immediately—a boy of immense fortune, not yet a man, fatherless in a war. And yet he has climbed rank. He has no friends, no lovers, not even a particular whore he favours. He is calculating and mercurial and takes risks that anyone else would consider insane."

"I kno—"

"No, you don't. If you did, you'd realise the error in your strategy. He is not a person, he's not human, and you are not creating a relationship of trust with him. He is an animal."

Helena stared at Crowther in bewilderment. The lift stopped, the doors opened, and she almost tripped stepping out. "But you told me to—"

"I told you to use *vivimancy,*" Crowther snarled. "And instead, you offered endless excuses about needing the right opportunities, that it would be too obvious, and now you think the array, this injury, is the solution to your failures."

"You said to take priority over his original goals. I'm doing that."

Crowther's eyebrows dipped into a sharp frown, and he seized her by the elbow and dragged her towards his office, not answering until they were behind closed doors.

"I told you to enthral him with vivimancy." Crowther's voice had grown icy. "What you are doing is making him depend on you, to consider you someone he needs. That is entirely different. Can you turn this array off? Control the intensity of its effect? No, you cannot. I did not ask for something irreversible, I asked for a vivimancy-controlled obsession."

"Well, that's not how vivimancy works," she snapped back. "You can't just turn human emotions on or off, not in a way that gives you the kind of leverage you're wanting. It's not magic."

He glared at her as he seated himself at his desk. "I have no use for tools I cannot control. If you manage to succeed in this manner, you're more likely to destroy the Eternal Flame than save it. The Ferron family is fuelled by their ambitions. They have always resented the noble families. Now Paladia is built with their steel, and they think that means it belongs to them, whether to seize or ruin. They do not share. They are *obsessive* about what they regard to be theirs. You do this and Kaine Ferron will never let you go, and he will not be content with being secondary to *anyone.*"

Terror ran through Helena like a knife, but she squared her shoulders, meeting Crowther's glare, refusing to back down because she had nowhere to go. Her every bridge was burned. He'd seen to that.

"You gave me to him," she said, her voice full of fury. "Now, and after the war. Those were the terms. You said it was Ferron or lose, and so I chose him. When was he ever expected to let me go?"

She drew a shaky breath. "You said to make myself the mission for him. He is changeable right now, and this may be the only moment in which he ever will be. If you think what I'm doing is too dangerous, then give me a different option, because this is the only way I can give you what you asked for."

She could see anger in Crowther's eyes, but he said nothing.

What had he expected her to do? Had he really believed that vivimancy could create obsession in Ferron without a sense of need? That it was a faucet she could turn on and off? Did no one understand what vivimancy was?

Crowther sat staring at her, and she could almost see the pieces moving as he adjusted his strategy, weighing what to do. When he said nothing for several minutes, she eventually turned to leave.

The corridors of the Tower felt too warm and enclosed in the summer heat. Helena could barely breathe.

She went out onto a skybridge.

Down below, Luc and Lila were sparring against their unit while Soren was calling out critiques of their forms. A small crowd was gathered to watch.

Knowing Ilva, she'd probably told Soren or Lila to do something to preoccupy Luc and keep him from fretting over the West Port Lab.

Combat alchemy could be so beautiful, it was almost hard to remember the violence of its purpose, and the ceaseless ugliness left in its wake.

Helena watched, listening to the cheers below, heart aching.

She'd always thought that she could do anything for her friends. She didn't need recognition, just the comfort of knowing she'd done what was necessary. Pragmatism had stolen away any lustre of heroism from her, and she kept telling herself it was all right . . .

But she was so lonely.

Her fingers wrapped around the empty amulet, the points catching on her palm. There was a dull sense of emptiness that never went away now, a slowly growing wound that she couldn't heal.

She couldn't fix herself anymore, and no one else seemed inclined to even notice she was breaking.

You are all alone, and when the war is over, you will still be alone.

She blinked as the figures below blurred into halos of gold and silver.

THAT NIGHT, SHE STUDIED THE array with a renewed sense of urgency. It had become a familiar sight, but when she paused to take it in, it was horrifically stunning. Designing it had required the work of a meticulous alchemist.

Which Ferron had been, prior to becoming an assassin.

She couldn't imagine designing something so intricate, knowing that every line drawn would be an incision into her own skin.

"I think I can close the wounds soon," she said.

He was silent for a strangely long time. "Really?"

His voice was so toneless, she couldn't read his reaction.

"It will be experimental, the procedure," she said as she applied ointment. "But I'm familiar with how your regeneration works now, and how it intersects with my resonance. There's only one thing . . ."

He tensed. She watched the subtle ripple of his back, incisions widening.

"What?"

"The Abeyance. Resonance will be at its lowest ebb. It would make working with the lumithium in the alloy on your shoulders easier, but I'm not sure if completing the array with its effects reduced is safe or not."

"It shouldn't matter, but with low ebb, I'll regenerate slower."

"That's fine. Preferable actually."

She was at the door when he spoke up behind her. "Marino."

She looked back.

"There's a rumour Bennet's experimenting with alchemy suppression."

"Why?" she asked, hoping he knew something, that she'd be able to take new information back to Crowther, proof of Kaine's continued usefulness.

Kaine didn't shrug, but his expression shifted to communicate that he would if he could. "Who knows."

She stepped away from the door. "You mentioned once that Morrough thinks Paladia is key to the immortality Hevgoss wants. Do you think he could be looking for the Stone of the Heavens?"

He set down the drink he was pouring. "You think the High Necromancer came here to steal a magical orb that doesn't exist?"

She flushed. The stone was a fairy tale. The belief that Sol's blessing was a physical object was a misinterpretation of the early artistic renderings of Orion Holdfast. The region had been prescientific and illiterate at the time; the imagery was all that many people knew.

While the historical records had been corrected, the myths had endured. Helena had believed there was a real stone for years until Luc awkwardly corrected her.

"No," she said quickly. "I know it's not real. I just thought maybe Morrough heard the stories and came here thinking it was. It's not like there's any reason Sol couldn't have made it a stone."

Ferron scoffed. "You believe in Sol?"

She shifted, gripping the strap of her satchel. "Yes, well, maybe not exactly the way people here do, but—you don't? Not—not at all?"

Kaine's lip curled. "Not at all."

CHAPTER 36

Julius 1786

KNOWING THAT HER DAILY HEALING PILGRIMAGE WAS coming to an end, Helena found herself taking a sense of proprietary pride in her work. She hadn't been sure a full recovery was possible, but now the wasted, skeletal version of Kaine had vanished completely. When he was dressed, a person might not even realise he'd been injured.

When the Abeyance arrived, Crowther still had not sent word or issued orders. The choice to heal Kaine, and whatever consequences arose from it, would rest entirely upon her.

Helena packed her satchel in preparation, and she was applying the finishing touches on what she hoped would be the last batch of numbing salve when there was a knock at the door.

She turned just as Luc entered.

"I didn't know you had a lab," he said, pausing and looking around the small room. What had once been a ramshackle workstation had been transformed into a true alchemist's workshop, filled with crucibles, flasks, and shelves stocked with a variety of alembics and cucurbits.

"I wanted to help make ends meet during the supply shortages in the hospital," she said, eyes darting past him to see if there was anyone else with him.

She used to dream about Luc visiting her lab, seeing her work, and realising everything she was doing for him, but instead of elation, all she felt was worry.

She couldn't be late tonight.

Luc smiled, but it was one of the broad ones he made when performing. "Sol always provides, doesn't he? Why didn't you tell me?"

"It just—never came up, I guess," she said, twisting the jar of salve in her hands.

His smile vanished. "Well, I guess there's a lot I don't know, isn't there?"

Her spine went rigid.

He wasn't looking at her. "I went to see Falcon Matias. I wanted to tell him that he shouldn't have talked about you like that in the meeting, that you'd only done what you'd been asked. And he told me that you were censured, months ago, and that's why he doesn't trust you, and why there are new healers. Because you proposed using necromancy on our dead soldiers."

He gave a dry laugh. "Apparently *everyone* knew about it except me."

Helena's mouth went dry. "Don't be mad at Lila," she said. "She wasn't there, either."

Luc's jaw clenched. "I know she wasn't. But she still found out. Soren told her, but no one told me. You could have told me."

She blinked hard. "I was afraid you'd think it meant I didn't believe in you, and I do, I just—want this to be over."

"Hel . . ." He looked down, fidgeting with the ignition rings on his fingers. "This isn't your war."

She flinched. "What do you mean, it's not my war? I've been here from the start. I promised you—" She shook her head. "You'd never say this to Lila. To anyone else."

He looked pained as he shook his head. "No, I wouldn't, because everyone else knows that in the battle between good and evil, it gets worse before it gets better. That it's our job to stay the path and not give into the temptation of doing what's easy."

Her throat closed, and she stepped back, her eyes burning with hurt. Easy?

"Look, I know you meant well, you were just trying to help, and to you it seems like there's a solution right there that we're wasting, but we're—*I'm* held to a different standard than that. Sol expects more. And—if you want to be a part of this, you have to believe that."

She could see Matias's plan now, making Luc think it would be better and kinder to send her away. That she didn't belong, someone like her couldn't understand the Northern Faith and Northern ways. Then Luc would see it as a sacrifice, as giving her up, not punishing her, if he sent her away.

"I'm sorry," she said. "I was wrong, I know that now. It won't happen again. I promise."

He exhaled. "No, I'm the one who's sorry. This is all my fault. I leave you here alone all the time and assume you'll be fine, but that's not fair. I'm going to fix this." He nodded. "Starting tonight. The unit's on reserve because of the Abeyance. How about I show you that array? We can catch up and do—anything you want. You can show me what mad genius things you're up to in here." He smiled his crooked smile. "What do you say?"

He held out his hand.

"I have work tonight," she said, her voice painfully small. "Abeyance is alchemically significant for—things."

"Oh. Right . . . well," he forced a smile, "next time, then."

She managed a nod and a tight smile back. Her eyes returned to the clock, gauging the distance to the Outpost, the fastest she could get there. Even if she ran the whole way, even if the checkpoint had no line, she wasn't going to make it in time.

Luc was still standing there, clearly hoping she'd change her mind.

She turned away awkwardly and started measuring things, pretending she'd forgotten him, but it took more than a minute of painful silence before he quietly left.

Before the door shut, she heard Lila's voice say, "I'm sorry, Luc."

Helena's hands went still, and she waited, trying to guess how long it would take for them to reach the stairs or the lifts so that they wouldn't see her leaving. While she waited, she pushed the conversation away, down within her mind and memory, trying to make it stop clawing her heart open.

Helena ran once she reached the bridge. She was still ten minutes late.

Kaine raised an eyebrow when she burst in, so breathless she doubled over.

"I thought you were finally standing me up," he said.

She braced her hands on her knees, catching her breath. "Someone—wanted to talk. Couldn't—rush off."

There was an atrocious stitch in her side. She pressed her hand against it, trying to soothe the ligaments. Her lungs were burning.

Still winded, she got to work, pulling out all her supplies from the medical satchel strapped over her shoulder and belted at the waist.

"Do you always carry this much in that bag of yours?" Kaine asked as he watched.

"Usually it's empty, so I can fill it up in the wetlands." She looked at him more closely. "How do you feel?"

He tilted his head, considering. "My regeneration is slower right now, and the array doesn't feel like a screw being twisted through my consciousness. It's lovely."

He took a sip of something amber, swaying, and she realised that he was slightly drunk. Slower regeneration indeed.

"That's good, because I think it's best if I keep you conscious for this," she said. "I'll need you to move as I work, to make sure the new tissue won't tear or heal rigid, because it might keep regenerating that way." She drew a deep breath. "This is probably going to hurt a lot."

"You wouldn't believe how often people say that to me."

"I'm serious." She sterilised her hands. "Drinking is probably for the best tonight."

Beginning on his left shoulder, she pressed two fingers very close to one of the incisions. He tensed, but it had been a long time now since he'd flinched at her touch.

The edges of the wound looked freshly cut. The effect of the lumithium was weaker because of the Abeyance.

Extrapolating heavily on the way he'd regenerated when he lost his arm, she believed her vivimancy could guide his regeneration back on track, but she had to proceed cautiously. Make a mistake and he might be stuck with it.

She applied a thick layer of topical opium to the area she wasn't working on.

"Ready?"

He nodded.

She began with a small section where the titanium-lumithium alloy had been fused into the bone, regenerating enough tissue to close the incision over the metal. Not too much scar tissue, but not too little.

Once formed, the tissue stayed alive. Ferron's regenerative abilities were finally strong enough to withstand the array's energy.

She made him fully rotate, extend, arch, and stretch his shoulder. The other incisions began to bleed. Helena winced.

The new scar tissue pulled, threatening to tear. She tried altering the tissue composition to increase its elasticity, but the regeneration was stubborn.

She used a scalpel to cut it away, and as she'd feared, it began regenerating back. She had to use her own resonance to suppress his regeneration as she sliced the healed tissue open and started again.

Kaine said nothing, but his breathing was shallow, and his resonance hummed through the air.

When she finished with the first array point, she could no longer feel the lumithium there, as if he'd internalised it.

She completed a second one before Kaine finally broke.

"I need a minute." His voice was shaking as he stood and walked over to the bar. He grabbed the closest bottle and drank straight out of it.

She wiped her forehead with a cloth, realising only then how hard her heart was pounding.

Kaine returned, gripping one bottle by the neck and two more laced in the fingers of his other hand, dropping onto the chair and pressing his forehead against the back of it.

He drank steadily through the rest of the night until there was an accumulation of bottles littered around him. It was enough alcohol to kill most people. Helena's hands began to cramp. Every time she had to pause to massage them and force her fingers back into compliance, Kaine would go and retrieve another bottle.

When it was finally over, she wiped away the remaining blood and applied a copper-based ointment.

The scars were all an angry, agitated red, but every incision was finally closed.

"There." She felt lightheaded, as if she were high in the mountains, the air turned thin.

Kaine said nothing, finishing the bottle in his hand.

She turned, wincing at the mess of bloodstained linen and all the dirty instruments. Even with the ports open, they were always short on bandages.

She wiped the tools clean and packed everything away. When she turned back, Kaine had stood. His shoulders were twisting and contorting as he moved. Small movements at first, but they progressed until his arms were overhead, his back arched like a strung bow. He gave the most indecent-sounding moan, his face slack with relief.

His arms dropped to his sides as he drew a deep breath, shoulders still rotating, giving a low shuddering sigh that Helena felt through her own nerves.

She snatched up her satchel, lightheaded with exhaustion and relief. "Well, I'll be off now."

He turned instantly. His eyes were dark, but there was that silvery sheen to them she'd noticed a few times before.

His movements were loose and languid, the way he used to move, except now he looked entirely different from the boy he'd been a few months ago. Not just because of the silver threading at his temples, or because pain had reset his expression into something much harder. He'd aged, his body seemingly lurching through time.

"Why so eager to be off?" he said.

She felt like a cornered animal. She hadn't realised *how* accustomed she'd grown to his injury, to the energy he devoted to tolerating the pain.

His full attention was blistering.

"Got someone waiting for you?" he asked when she tried to sidle towards the door.

The question caught her off guard. She blinked, a lump rising in her throat.

"No," she said.

He grinned. "Nor I. Let's drink in celebration. What do you want?"

He went to the bar, scanning the remaining bottles.

"I think the once was enough—"

He picked up a bottle, sniffing it and holding it up in the light. "This one."

He came over, decanter in hand, and Helena was nearly overcome with the instinct to bolt. He was intoxicated. Properly drunk, from the combination of alcohol and the euphoria of being healed.

The way he moved reminded her of a panther she'd once seen in the zoo. No bandages, no shirt. There was so much bare skin and now that she was not healing it, it was simply there.

She backed into the wall. "I'm not sure—"

"Stay," he said softly, and his head dipped so close she felt his breath in her hair. "You know, there's something about you, Marino, that inspires the most terrible decisions from me. I'll know better, but then I'll still . . ."

His voice trailed off as he tucked a stray curl behind her ear, finger running along her jaw.

She knew she should stay. For the purpose of her mission, staying during moments like this was her job. The point of healing him. But he was so hard to predict; he was in a good mood now, but there was no knowing how long it would last.

What kind of person was Kaine Ferron without inhibition?

Her throat closed, threatening to choke her. She wanted to leave.

His thumb tilted her chin up as he stared at her through darkening eyes.

"You have such a singular mind. Even when I'm not inside it, I can still see it churning away behind those eyes of yours."

Helena's pulse thrummed. He pressed the decanter into her hands, and when she looked down and tried to hand it back, he took her face in both hands, tilting it up so she had to meet his stare.

His hazel-grey eyes were gone, replaced by a silver-bright glow.

This was no mere transmutation; Kaine Ferron was becoming something altogether new. She had finalised the process with her bare hands, drawn into completion something that he alone knew the entire purpose of.

"Stay," he said, his voice coaxing, pleasure-soaked, his face so close to hers. "Have a drink with me."

Instead of perpetually ice-sharp and guarded, he felt like something she might drown in.

"Just—one drink," she said, her voice barely wavering.

He smiled. The first real smile she'd ever seen from him.

"One drink," he said.

He pressed a finger beneath the decanter she held, lifting it up, and watching as she brought it to her lips.

CHAPTER 37

Julius 1786

THE ALCOHOL BURNED DOWN HELENA'S THROAT, BRIGHT and smooth, leaving an aftertaste like wood smoke on her tongue.

She handed the decanter back, not sure why they were passing something so unwieldy.

One sip and she could already feel the alcohol loosening her insides as he gestured towards the sofa. She curled up nervously on the far end.

He pushed the bottle towards her and when she tried to demur, he slid closer, his body closing in, sending her heart skyrocketing.

"You need to catch up."

"I don't have a regenerative liver," she said in protest, looking dubiously at the amount inside and realising only then that the entire bottle was the "one drink" she'd agreed to.

The sofa was long enough that there was no reason for him to be so close, but there were barely inches between them. She took another sip and tried to return it, but he refused to take it, watching her like a curious cat before it springs.

"You're going to regret this if I start crying." She could already feel the alcohol in her face. "I get emotional when I'm drunk."

His eyebrows furrowed. "Is there a reason to cry?"

She looked down, rubbing her thumb over the etched pattern on the decanter. "There's always a reason."

Kaine shifted, rubbing his shoulders against the sofa like a cat marking its territory. His eyes fluttered shut as he moaned. "I never realised how much I enjoy leaning against things."

"Should I give you and the sofa some privacy?" she asked, trying to scoot farther into the corner.

He stilled, eyes instantly opening, and reached towards her. "Don't go."

Heat rose all the way to the roots of her hair. She looked away, drinking more.

"I know you feel a lot better, but you need to be careful for the next few days," she said between sips. "I think I did everything right so the scar tissue won't tear, but once the Abeyance is over, things might change. If it feels off, at all, you can call me. I can keep coming to make sure."

He shook his head in disbelief. "Is there anyone you don't feel responsible for?"

She looked away, trying to stifle Luc's voice in her head calling her choices easy. "It's my job," she said quietly.

"Thank you, Marino."

She swallowed, lifting her gaze. "Still not Helena?"

He exhaled, avoiding her eyes.

"Helena." He said it slowly, drawing it out, as if he was testing the way it sounded.

She smiled at him. "See? Not so hard."

He stared at her without smiling back, and she tried not to be distracted but he was so close, and still without a shirt on. Her eyes kept dropping involuntarily. She was trying not to look, but ordinarily when she saw people without their clothes on, it was because they were dying.

He was—very alive.

Her breath grew short. She tore her eyes away, not wanting to be accused of leering again, but he didn't seem to have noticed this time. He was still studying her.

She couldn't tell how intoxicated he was, but she was beginning to feel very drunk. Her head was growing heavy, and she had an overwhelming desire to laugh and cry simultaneously.

"You should put a shirt on," she said, her voice jumping. "You must be cold."

Faster than she could blink, her hand was in his, and he pressed her fingers against his chest.

"Do I feel cold?"

She shook her head, speechless, his skin warm against her palm. He didn't flinch when she touched him now, instead leaning into it.

"You can use your resonance, if you don't believe me."

A shiver ran down her spine.

"I guess you're all right," she said, her fingers brushing against his skin.

He inhaled unsteadily, and she felt the shudder under her palm. His hand was still over hers, but he wasn't holding it in place any longer.

She looked up and realised she found him handsome.

Before, he'd been too young and vicious, like a newly hatched viper striking at anything that moved. Then gaunt and dying and perpetually furious looking.

Now there was something still about him. His features had filled out. The threads of silver-white in his dark hair made him look even older than she was.

The coldness she associated with him had become a distant memory; his skin was warm, and his breath where it touched her cheek was warm. Drunk and feeling his heartbeat beneath her fingers, she couldn't remember when she'd stopped being afraid of him.

"I must admit," he said in a low voice as though making a confession, "if anyone had told me you'd become so lovely, I would never have come near you. I was rather blindsided when I saw you again."

Her eyebrows furrowed in confusion.

"You're like a rose in a graveyard," he said, and his lips twisted into a bitter smile. "I wonder what you could have turned into without the war."

"I—never thought about it."

He nodded. "That doesn't surprise me." He reached out and captured the loose curl behind her ear. "I remember your hair. Is it still the same?"

She flushed. He would remember that, of all things.

"Unfortunately," she said.

"Like you, then," he said, twisting the curl so it wrapped around his fingertip, "trapped in place, but still the same somewhere underneath."

She stared at him, startled by the remark, and then tears welled up and streamed down her cheeks. His eyes widened.

"Gods, Marino, don't cry," he said hastily.

"Sorry," she said, pulling her hand free and scrubbing her face. "I'm just—really drunk."

The moment vanished like mist in sunlight. She wiped her eyes several times, suddenly feeling so raw.

When she glanced up, he'd looked away, eyebrows knitting together.

She'd never seen him so casually expressive before. As they sat there, she felt as if she were finally seeing the real him. He looked so sad at first; but as she watched, an empty look of bitterness filled his eyes, darkness spreading across his face.

She reached towards him, not sure what she was doing but wanting to pull him back from wherever his thoughts were taking him. She caught his left hand in hers, and when he didn't resist, she pressed her thumbs up across the palm until his fingers flexed and began massaging it from the wrist to the fingertips.

"Why do you do that?" he asked after a minute.

"My father used to do this for me," she said without looking up. "He said alchemists were like surgeons, so we have to take care of our hands."

"But why are *you* doing it for me?"

Her fingers stilled briefly; she stared at the lines of his palm. "My mother died when I was seven. She'd been sick for a long time. All my life actually. One day I went to wake her, and she was—cold. She'd slipped away in the night, no warning, no goodbyes. After that, I was afraid to go to sleep. I wasn't scared of being dead, but I was worried my father or I might slip away like that and leave the other all alone. So he'd hold my hand until I fell asleep, so I'd know he was there. You looked lonely just now, so I thought . . ." She shook her head and let go. "I don't know. It's nothing. Sorry."

She sat awkwardly fidgeting with her fingers. If she stayed much longer, the checkpoint would close and she'd be trapped outside the city overnight. As she opened her mouth to excuse herself, he spoke.

"Would you do something for me?" The question was quiet.

She looked up. His expression had relaxed again, and his hair had fallen across his forehead, softening his features.

She scanned him quickly. "What do you want?"

He tilted his head. "Will you take your hair down? I want to see it."

She blinked in surprise. "Really?"

He just gave a short nod, watching her.

She reached up awkwardly and pulled the pins out. The two braids tumbled down, and she removed the ties, running her fingers through the strands to unbraid them, feeling the tension in her scalp release as she dropped her hands into her lap, not wanting to see his reaction, heat already scalding her face and neck.

"There. My mane."

He stared in silence, as if he needed time to take it in. "I didn't realise it was so long."

She squeezed the pins, daring to glance up. "The weight makes it more manageable."

He said nothing else, just staring as if mesmerised.

She flushed. Having her hair loose felt as if she was revealing something deeply intimate about herself, something she was accustomed to keeping carefully put away because it was so often treated as either unacceptable or pitiable. She wasn't prepared for this kind of reaction.

He leaned forward, lacing his fingers into her hair along her temple, running his fingers through it. His expression curious. She shivered at the sensation, at the nearness of him.

"It's softer than I expected," he said. His eyes were fascinated.

She didn't know what to say.

His hand slid up her neck and tangled with the curls at the base of her skull. His breathing had grown shallow.

He wasn't looking at her hair anymore; his eyes were on her face, on her lips, that silver gleam lighting them again as he shifted closer.

"If you don't want me to kiss you, you should say so now," he said.

He was so near, she could taste his breath, the burn of alcohol on it.

Everything had become blurred and dreamlike, except him.

She could feel the weight of her life bearing down, crushing her day by day, always taking more than she could spare, but she could also feel Kaine, the warmth of him and his fingers laced through her hair.

He was gentler than she thought he could be. He looked at her like he saw her.

And he was asking.

She kissed him.

A real kiss this time.

The instant her lips met his, he took control. As if she'd sprung something loose in him, his arm was around her waist, drawing her towards him, pulling her close until their bodies pressed together, and she was on his lap.

Her hands were on his shoulders, fingertips brushing across the outermost point of the array while he deepened the kiss as if wanting to consume her. When his lips left hers, he arched her neck back, his breath and tongue hot on her bared throat.

He seemed to be mapping her with the span of his fingers, a topographer exploring the curve of her clavicles, every dip and rise of bone and flesh.

He pulled her so close that she could feel the barrier of her clothing between them, her skirts around her hips. His hands gripped her waist, thumbs tracing her ribs.

She ran a hand along his jaw, and when her palm grazed his cheek, he pressed his face into it, eyes fluttering shut, a breath escaping him, as if he were starved of touch.

His hands slid up her back, following the length of her spine, and she arched like a cat, leaning into him. His touch sent a heady rush through her, her mind tumbling as if caught in a wave.

She hadn't realised how much she'd wanted to be touched. That she was starved of it, too.

She wrapped her arms around his shoulders, clinging to him, her heart pounding so violently she could hear it. A bruising pleasure rippled through her at his touch, making her chest clench. His fingers on the buttons of her shirt, unfastening them one by one. The layers between them slipping away.

She had not comprehended her stark lack of intimacy until this moment. Now awakened, it seemed to claw out from under her skin, a need that she'd only ever known as an absence.

She knew that people enjoyed sex, but she had always thought it was an indulgence. She had not known it was a hunger.

Or that she was starving.

She pressed closer, wanting to erase every sliver of space between them, so tired of being always alone. A thing apart, reduced to her functions. Healer. Chymist. Liaison. Tool.

Whore.

Her eyes burned and she closed them, trying to slip free and lose herself in a place where her thoughts couldn't catch up, but they chased her down, insinuating themselves beneath her skin where Kaine's fingers didn't reach. Whispering through her skull, like a damning, mocking chorus.

This was a mission. A job. What she'd been sent to do. What did it say about her, that she was so eager? So hungry for this feeling of being wanted?

Kaine's teeth scraped along the curving bone of her jaw, his touch evoking an ache that nearly split her open.

When he bit down on the side of her neck, she shuddered with a gasping moan, fingers grasping, digging into his skin, and he turned her until she was beneath him on the sofa, his warmth and weight surrounding her, pressed against her.

It was happening so fast. Why would he so suddenly want her like this?

Reality caught up like a blow to her chest: He didn't.

He was intoxicated. And no longer injured.

After months of agony, he was ravenous for pleasure and physical release.

And she was here. Drunk and compliant, ready to be consumed.

A starved wolf would sate itself on anything.

She stared at him, her ribs clenching around her lungs until she couldn't breathe. Shame burning trails down her temples as she recoiled.

Kaine went still, then lifted his head. He looked at her for only a moment, then pulled his hands away and himself off.

"I think it's time you go," he said.

CHAPTER 38

Julius 1786

HELENA SAT UP BUT DIDN'T MOVE TO leave. She just sat beside him on the sofa, trembling as she fought back tears. She looked over at the clock and a wave of despair washed over her.

"The checkpoints are closed now," she said. "I can't get into the city until morning."

He sighed, sitting back and looking away from her.

She wrapped her arms around herself, pulling her shirt closed, fumbling at the buttons, her chest hitching as she tried not to cry.

"Why are you crying?" he finally asked.

She smeared at her cheeks with her hand. "Because I'm lonely, and kissing you, and you don't even like me."

He looked at her and then tilted his head back and stared at the ceiling for a full minute.

"Why do you think I was kissing you?" he finally asked in a tight voice.

"Because I'm here."

He looked at her again. "Why'd you kiss me?"

She stared across the room at a tapestry of Tellus, spinning the earth into being.

"You made me feel like the parts of me that aren't useful still deserve to exist. Like I'm not just all the things I can do."

The decanter was on the floor, abandoned. Helena snatched it up. There was only a little left. She had a lingering hope that if she finished it, she might reach the point of inebriation beyond feeling.

He watched her drink and then leaned back, slinging an arm over his eyes. When she glanced over, his arm had slipped down, and he was asleep.

She stared at him for a long time, studying his features, trying to pinpoint the changes in his face, but her own eyes were heavy.

She should get up. Move to the chaise over by the desk.

Her vision dimmed. She'd let her eyes rest, just for a moment. Then she'd go . . .

WHEN SHE WOKE, SHE WAS still on the sofa, and so was Kaine, except somehow they'd ended up tangled together. Her face was crushed against his chest, his elbow prodding her ribs, and his chin was digging into the top of her head.

It was a miracle that neither of them had fallen off the sofa.

Helena didn't move immediately; her head was on the verge of cracking open. She suspected that any sudden movements would result in a lot of smoky, overly expensive whisky coming back up.

She managed to slip a hand up to her face, using her vivimancy to alleviate some of her nausea before slowly extricating herself.

Kaine didn't even twitch. He was insensate. He probably hadn't slept properly since spring.

She gripped her satchel and went to the heavy door, prying it slowly open, and fled without looking back.

She threw up over the dam, and again crossing the bridge, retching into the river. Rather than feel better, she felt worse.

She made her way slowly back towards Headquarters, wanting to kick herself. She'd kissed Kaine Ferron. Not a fake, strategic kiss but a real one, and he'd returned it, and it would have been the perfect opportunity to take the next step, but she'd blown it.

Kaine had handed himself to her on a platter, gone above and beyond what Crowther and Ilva had ever hoped, and Helena had sabotaged herself because it wasn't real and she'd wished it was.

She'd let herself become wrapped up in her feelings at being compared to a rose and called lovely, at having aspects of herself that no one had ever liked treated as a source of desire.

Apparently that was all it took for Ferron to seduce her.

Just thinking about it left her cold, a pit of nauseous shame threatening to choke her.

"Hel." Soren's voice broke into her thoughts as she came through the gatehouse into Headquarters. He was sitting with a group of the guards.

She stared at him, dazed by her own thoughts, too hungover to speak.

"Are you all right?" he asked. "What happened to your hair?"

She didn't understand the question until she reached up and remembered it was loose, tangling around her shoulders.

"Brambles," she lied promptly.

His eyebrows knit together, studying her with his deep-set eyes. "You should be careful out there, especially during the Abeyance."

"I only went out after light," she said, trying to slip past. "Just a bit of harvesting. I need to process it."

Soren was still watching her. "You know, I forgot your hair looked like that. It's pretty, the way you braid it now."

"Yes," she said, forcing a smile, her eyes burning. "It's best when I keep it braided. I hardly know what to do with myself when it's like this."

She went straight to her room and into the shower, scrubbing herself violently, trying to erase the physical memory of Kaine's hands. The water was hot, and she turned it up until it was scalding on her skin, standing under the spray until she was raw from the heat.

She wasn't crying. It was just the spray of the shower. It was just water on her face.

She barely towelled off before quickly pulling her hair into two braids so taut they tugged at her face. She coiled them at the nape of her neck, letting the pins scrape across her skin as she lodged them into place.

She didn't let herself look in the mirror until she was done, until there was not a stray curl to be seen.

SHE WAS RESTOCKING THE HOSPITAL inventory when one of the orderlies materialised beside her, placing several bottles of plasma expanders in a box.

"Crowther wants you to meet him at the lifts, right away," the girl said without looking at Helena.

Helena turned sharply. The girl was soft-featured with soulful eyes, and Helena was certain she'd seen her before, but the girl was unobtrusive enough that she only flickered on the edge of Helena's memory.

Of course Crowther would have eyes everywhere, including the hospital. Still, it set Helena on edge.

"Who are you?" Helena said as the girl seemed about to slip away.

"No one."

"What's your name?" Helena wanted to know who to look out for on the roster.

The girl glanced up, seeming flattered at the question. "Purnell."

Purnell. She felt she'd heard the name before. She nodded absently. "All right, you can go."

The orderly hurried off.

Helena finished restocking and headed reluctantly towards the Tower.

Crowther was waiting for her. The lift went down.

In the tunnels, there was a young boy crouched beside the door. Helena blinked and realised it was Ivy, Crowther's other vivimancer, her hair tucked up under a cap. She looked like a street urchin.

Ivy stood up and threw open the door. The room contained a single figure restrained in a chair, head slumped forward, breathing shallowly.

"Who is this?" Helena asked, wanting to bolt. The smell of old blood and dampness underground made her sick.

"One of the Aspirants sent to Hevgoss," Crowther said. "Intercepted and brought back, but he's proving difficult. He's quite desperate for a taste of eternal life. He's requiring more persuasion than he can currently survive."

Helena expected severe burns but found vivimancy instead.

There were no visible signs of torture. No cuts or any external wounds. Instead the corticospinal tract in his spine had been pinched, paralysing him but leaving his sensory nerves intact.

That way, he would feel everything.

Beneath his skin, Ivy had flayed him, using vivimancy to sever the individual layers of skin. Blood had pooled between each one. In some areas, he was flensed down to the muscle.

It was one thing to heal people injured in battle, but healing torture was a different kind of horror.

Crowther did not seem to think that any physical violation went too far in the war against necromancy, so long as the soul was not violated. Based on the tenets of the Faith and the Eternal Flame, there was nothing wrong with the torture of necromancers or aspiring necromancers; flesh was an inferior substance to eventually be consumed by fire anyway. What these people were willing to do to civilians and the Resistance was far worse than anything Crowther did to them.

The prisoner regained consciousness while she was working on his feet.

"I know you," he said, raising his head. His Northern dialect was thick, the kind that pulled hard on the consonants.

She glanced up. He had wheat-coloured hair and thick stubble across his face.

"You're Holdfast's little foreign bitch."

She looked away again, ignoring him, determined to finish without speaking. She felt marginally less sorry for him now.

"I'm going to tell you a secret," he muttered while she was finishing his hands. "You're going to lose this war. No one can stop the Undying. They're the new gods. Someday I'm going to be one of them. People are going to know the Lancasters."

She looked up again. Now she remembered him; he'd been at the Institute and left after receiving his certification. A guild family. Nickel, she thought it was.

"Once I'm Undying, I'm going to kill that little bitch so slowly she'll beg me for it. Everything she does to me, she'll get it tenfold. And then I'm going to bring her back." His teeth bared gruesomely.

Helena's jaw tensed, and she fought to stay focused. She was supposed to leave patients conscious. Crowther didn't want them waking and finding themselves healed, he wanted them dreading, thinking about what would happen to them once she was done.

Once she finished, she stood and left without a word.

Ivy and Crowther reentered the room together, the door shutting. Screaming began vibrating through the door, echoing down the underground corridor.

Helena walked farther, trying to escape it, but it followed her.

She wandered blindly through the tunnels, not caring if she became lost amid them. They turned and twisted, opening into a large room lit by green glass sconces. There were dozens of tunnels leading into it. The walls were covered with intricate but faded murals. It looked almost like an abandoned church.

She'd had no idea any of it existed, buried beneath the Institute. The screaming seemed to carry along all the tunnels, magnifying and concentrating in the room. The place had a sick, eerie feeling about it.

She entered another tunnel, trying to get away, but no matter which one she took, or which way she turned, they all seemed to lead back to the same room. As if to mockingly remind her that she could not escape herself, and what she had become. This was what the war had made her.

Finally she turned slowly back, walking towards the screaming, tired of running from herself.

She'd climb over tortured bodies, sell herself, and tear out Kaine Ferron's heart if that was what it took to win.

SHE WAS CALLED IN TWO more times before Lancaster finally broke. By the third time, Helena didn't think he was still sane.

Waiting in the underground passages, ears plugged to try to keep from hearing what was happening in the next room, she'd reevaluated her assessment of the previous night.

Now that it was a little less fresh, her missteps felt less disastrous.

Kaine did feel some sort of partiality towards her. After all, he'd wanted *her* to stay.

However, whatever flicker of desire or fondness he felt was barely kindled. Too much fuel too fast would smother it. It was for the best they'd stopped when they did. That he was left wondering what could have happened.

She suspected he burned for things more deeply than he knew. Therefore, the key would lie in cultivating that spark into something beyond his control.

He was too calculating for anything else to be effective. It was all or nothing. Leave him as the threat he was, knowing that he was now infinitely more enabled by her to achieve his desires, or try to redirect his ambition and obsessive nature onto her.

People always said there was no greater temptation than the forbidden.

As for the fact that she wanted him back . . . that she was so willing.

She chewed anxiously on her thumbnail.

It was for the best. Everyone had always said she was a terrible liar.

The door opened, and Ivy came out. Helena looked over at her. "Again?"

Ivy shook her head, shutting the door. "Crowther's still working on him."

Ivy crouched down next to Helena, drawing a finger idly through the dirt on the ground. Helena watched her in silence, trying to ignore the smell of burned meat beginning to permeate the air.

"You know," Helena couldn't help but say, "there's other ways to get information out of people. You don't have to torture them."

Ivy looked up with her sharp eyes glittering. "I like hurting them. It's the best part of the job. The rest is boring."

"Oh."

There was a long silence. Finally Ivy spoke up. "Can vivimancy get rid of memories? Make someone forget something so they'd never remember it?"

Helena watched her curiously. "Is there something you want to forget?"

Ivy shook her head, staring down the tunnel, and her face twitched oddly. "My sister, she doesn't remember things. Matron said it's called a fugue—her not remembering—but it might all come back someday."

"Don't you want her to remember?" Helena asked.

Ivy gave a sharp shake of her head. "No." She looked up at Helena and laughed. "You think I'm bad. If she ever remembers, she'd go completely mad."

The door opened, and the stench of burned meat wafted out. "Marino. We're done now."

Crowther had drugged Lancaster with something synthetic. He was hallucinating wildly. He'd nearly bitten through his tongue, and Helena had to paralyse him to reattach it. His skin was charred all over, although Crowther was always careful never to burn deep enough to kill the nerves.

Lancaster was babbling. It seemed Helena and Ivy had converged in his mind. One moment he'd struggle violently, nearly biting her hands when they were near him, threatening to pour molten metal through her veins until her eyes burst like grapes, and the next he'd be trying to lean towards her and drawing deep rasping breaths, crooning that she was a sweet thing, how once he was Undying, he'd keep her as a pet with a collar and chain, just like Holdfast.

Then he'd think she was Ivy again, and he'd threaten to eat her. Cut her into pieces. Put her back together wrong. Violate her in every way imaginable.

When she was done, she wanted to peel the skin off every place he'd touched her.

"Why don't you kill him?" she asked Crowther when she got out of the room. Her skin was still crawling.

He seemed amused by this. "Why?"

"You have what you want. He's a waste of rations."

He shook his head. "Until we've found the guard he was looking for, we'll keep him. Morrough's determination to unearth this Wagner in Hevgoss indicates a significant degree of importance. Lancaster is a uniquely devoted Aspirant. He could be useful as evidence if we are ever in contact with Hevgoss. Don't worry about him. I've never lost a prisoner."

"Can I go, then?" she said dully. Her clothes were stained with Lancaster's blood.

"Yes, I'll escort you," he said. "You healed Ferron? Was it a success?"

She gave an idle nod without looking at him. Whether he was pleased or disappointed by this, she had no energy to care. "Yes. The procedure was a success."

There was a pause as they ascended the stairs. Crowther blocked the exit, his eyes skimming across her. "I hear you were out all night and returned—dishevelled."

Her stomach clenched. "It took longer than expected. The checkpoints were closed for curfew. I had to sleep there."

Crowther waited but she volunteered nothing else.

His eyes narrowed. "Carry on, then."

CHAPTER 39

Julius 1786

Helena returned to the Outpost that evening, but found the door in the factory wall locked, the necrothrall that usually appeared with the key nowhere in sight.

She went to the tenement, but the unit was cold and empty, too. She lingered for a little while, just to be sure.

The next evening was the same.

She told herself it was a good sign. The healing was a success. Still, it felt abrupt to suddenly have her evenings again.

Helena hadn't realised how much time she'd spent making salves and journeying back and forth until all those hours were at her disposal once more.

On Martiday, she went foraging and then headed towards the tenements.

She wasn't even halfway there when a necrothrall stepped out of the shadows, intercepting her. Helena's stomach clenched. It wasn't the normal man, but a woman. She showed an iron symbol on her pallid inner wrist and then held out an envelope.

Helena took it, and the necrothrall turned and walked away.

Helena didn't usually open the missives, but this time she broke the seal and pulled out the contents, looking for instructions or a message.

It was just an encoded intelligence report.

On Saturnis it happened again.

She hadn't considered that Kaine could do that, but there was nothing about the way his information was passed on that required the in-person meetings.

She spent her newfound free time in the laboratory experimenting with Shiseo, who had become a collegial companion and collaborator.

Because healing was considered separate from medicine and medical care, the two did not always complement each other. Many sedatives inhibited vivimancy, requiring countering or workarounds in ways that made the healing process unnecessarily complicated. Healing Kaine, far from Matias's purview, had allowed her to begin considering the possibilities of chymiatria designed for vivimancy.

She began with tonics to support things like blood regeneration and bone repair, but her primary interest was developing something that would maintain vivimancy's effects by controlling the body's inner chymistry. She and Shiseo synthesised a glycoside from foxglove and extracted alkaloids from nightshade, working piece by piece.

Creating a niche for herself was a consolation because Elain Boyle was becoming widely preferred as a healer. Helena tried to tell herself it was a good thing to have a healer so naturally likeable. No one ever jumped or even batted an eye when Elain forgot her gloves, but Elain's social strengths also undermined her as a healer. She was too much of a people pleaser, and it affected her methods. She had a relentless tendency towards prioritising her intuition over her training and healing symptoms rather than causes.

A necessary fever never ran its course when Elain was on shift. People *felt* better but developed infections more often and recovered slower.

In late Augustus, Basilius Blackthorne tried to retake the southern tip of the East Island. Blackthorne was one of the Undying that everyone feared. He didn't wear a helmet as most of the Undying did, making no effort to hide his identity. Whether he won or lost his battles, the devastation he left behind was terrible. He was known for eating his victims on the battlefield.

After days of fighting, when it was clear the attack was a failure, Blackthorne set his own army on fire and sent them as far into Resistance territory as they could get. The rainy season hadn't begun; everything was unusually dry. The flames spread fast, jumping across the tributary between the East and West islands and consuming a large swath of the city. The sky to the south glowed red as an ember.

The hospital was flooded with burn injuries and lung damage, combatants and civilians alike.

The healers were on duty in the hospital for so long, Helena lost track of the days. She didn't realise how tired she'd become until she was in the war room, listening to reports, and Ilva made a comment that they were unlikely to have an estimate on enemy losses for another day.

She'd already missed more than a week. She had to go.

When she got up the next morning, the room tilted. Lila was sound asleep, a lump under the blankets on her bed. The battalion had returned black with smoke. Luc had kept the fire from advancing on Headquarters, but even his pyromancy had limits against an inferno.

Helena's head was hollow, throbbing from exhaustion as she dressed and headed out.

Everything was eerily quiet, as if even the birds were afraid to sing. The smoke hung like a shroud over the city.

Even the Outpost was quiet, but Helena paid no attention, just looking for the necrothrall so she could get Kaine's missive and head back.

She came around a corner and found four of them. She was so tired, she stopped and stood staring stupidly for several moments, trying to understand why Kaine would send four.

Then it dawned on her that they were not his. These were ordinary combat necrothralls.

She immediately began backtracking, noticing only then that the encampments that covered the Outpost were torn apart. The Undying had retaken the Outpost, and she had walked straight into it.

She turned and fled, only to run into another group of necrothralls.

She had to retreat again, winding through the maze of buildings and factories. She tripped over a body, not reanimated.

Every time she escaped one group, she stumbled across another.

Necrothralls didn't generally move fast, but they didn't need to. They were herding her away from the gate, from the bridge, from the only way off the Outpost.

She ripped her gloves off as she was cornered in a tight alley and backed away until she hit the wall. It was narrow enough that they could only enter a few at a time.

They shuffled forward.

A few carried weapons. It was hard to say what was worse.

When they got in range, she shoved her hands towards them, forcing her resonance outwards, closing her eyes instinctively.

Her resonance flared for a moment and then burned out like a lightbulb filament.

She opened her eyes, barely seeing the remaining necrothralls approaching because of how raw and wounded she felt inside, as if she'd ripped out a vein.

Burnout was common for defence alchemists, who frequently strained the limits of their range and abilities. It also happened to healers. Once it started happening a lot—

She forced herself to focus.

There was blood everywhere, but two of the necrothralls were still coming towards her.

She fumbled for her knife, lost in the bottom of her satchel, barely managing to grasp it in time.

She aimed for the nearest necrothrall's throat. Straight through to the spinal cord. With her resonance burned out, she couldn't transmute the blade, but she twisted it and jerked left. The head toppled off with a grotesque squelch, body following as fiery, white-hot pain exploded up her leg.

When she'd lunged towards one, the other necrothrall had tried to stab at her with a metal spike.

It had missed her torso and gone through her calf.

Helena nearly collapsed, slashing clumsily. She barely managed to sever enough fingers that it couldn't jerk the spike back out.

Her brain clamoured to pull out the spike, as her calf muscles tore around it, but she knew she'd bleed out if she did. The rough metal shifted, and she bit through the sleeve of her shirt to keep from screaming.

The necrothrall was still coming. Most of the fingers on one hand were gone, but it could still bludgeon her, and she knew the most dangerous part of necrothralls was often their teeth.

She gripped the knife tighter, forced to wait until it reached for her. As soon as it was in range, she grabbed its outstretched hand, her absent resonance like a hole inside her. Teeth swung towards her face, and she shoved her knife straight through the V of the jaw.

Something slammed into the side of her head, sending her stumbling.

The arm was wrenched free of her grasp. Broken fingernails clawed at her skin.

There was thick old blood in her eyes.

She lurched forward. Her left leg failed, but it gave her enough momentum to drive the knife through the top of the skull. Purple blood spurted across her face as the necrothrall collapsed.

Helena stood dazed and gasping for breath, scrubbing at her face. The blood was all she could smell.

She tried to make out where she was using the towers of the city to orient herself. The bridge was on the far side from her, but the tenement was nearby.

She'd hide there first, and then make a plan. She leaned against the wall, trying to keep from putting weight on her left leg. Even dragging it was agony.

She reached the tenement building and crawled up the steps, but it was only as she reached the landing that she remembered that door had a resonance lock. She couldn't get inside.

She crawled over and pressed her hand against it anyway, as if her resonance were a well and there were some final drops she could plumb, even though she knew burnout often took days to come back from.

She sat back, cursing herself for being so accustomed to the routine to be this careless. Her head was swimming, although she didn't know if it was from exhaustion or blood loss.

She found the cleanest spot in the corridor and forced herself to look at her leg. Blood had coated her calf and foot, leaving an obvious trail. Fortunately, necrothralls weren't generally aware enough to notice anything that didn't move.

Her vision blurred, the pain seeming to crush her ability to think down into a funnel.

No artery, she didn't think. She debated pulling out the spike, but she didn't have enough supplies to pack a wound that large.

If she could reach the checkpoint, they'd get her to Headquarters, but no one was going to come looking for her on the Outpost.

She fumbled through her satchel.

The priority was stabilising the spike, and applying pressure to reduce the bleeding. Then she'd plan.

She chewed on an abandoned sprig of yarrow as she wrapped bandages around her leg.

Blood was already seeping through before she'd finished, and her mind had gone sluggish.

She tried harder to focus, head lolling as she struggled to stay alert.

Stay awake. You have to stay awake.

Her vision lengthened. Her legs seemed far away, all the way down a tunnel, and then everything faded away.

"What are you doing?"

Helena started, her leg jerking reflexively, pain bursting through her.

Kaine was standing over her, seemingly having appeared out of thin air.

At least, she thought it was Kaine. Her vision was blurry, and his presence seemed to swallow the space. As his face swam into focus, he was glaring at her icily.

Her heart lurched at the sight of it.

"It's Martiday," she managed to say.

"What happened?"

She gestured limply at the metal spike still running through her calf.

He barely glanced at it. "Yes, I noticed. I'll admit, your commitment to the bit is impressive. I can't say I expected you to go this far."

She stared at him, not understanding.

"Tell Crowther I have no time for his tricks. Pull something like this again, and he can consider the deal off." Kaine turned, walking away.

Her chest felt hollow as she watched him leave, realising that he thought she'd injured herself on purpose.

He paused at the top of the stairs, staring at the trail of blood before looking back at her.

"Get up." He was speaking through clenched teeth.

She shook her head. "I'm waiting for my resonance to come back."

His head jerked sharply. "What?"

She looked down. "The fires . . . there were a lot—I was too tired today. I didn't realise—never burned out before. So I'm—waiting."

Kaine walked back over and crouched in front of her, his eyes narrowed. His hair was so much more silver now.

"Marino, what kind of vivimancy do they have you doing in the hospital?"

"Depends who's injured." Her head was very light; her consciousness was threatening to rise through the top of her head and float away.

Fingers snapped sharply in front of her face.

"Focus," he said. "Describe the healing you do. Are you just transmuting physical injuries away or are you using your vitality to keep people alive?"

"Depends . . ." she said again. She was having trouble making her eyes focus. His own eyes shone, and she stared at them, mesmerised. "We use triage protocol. Can't afford to lose our combatants. Especially not alchemists."

His jaw tensed. "I assumed they'd save that for the likes of Holdfast."

The corridor had stretched into a tunnel once more.

"Luc can't win by himself," she said.

Ferron was suddenly very close, reaching towards her. He pulled her up off the ground, sending an inferno of pain through her body. She screamed and fainted.

When her eyes opened again, she was in the tenement unit, lying on her back, her injured leg elevated with a chair. She felt simultaneously better and worse.

She was overwhelmingly thirsty.

Kaine was studying her calf where the spike ran through it.

"How do I heal this?"

She blinked sluggishly, the ceiling swirling overhead.

Think, Helena, you've taught healing before. "Numbing the area is the first step, but I don't have enough blood to . . ."

Her words slurred away. Explaining the lack of saline and plasma expanders was too many words to string together. Did he even know how to numb? With the new healers, she'd use her resonance at the same time and guide them, so that they'd know what to look for.

She was so thirsty.

She shook her head. "I don't think . . . It's . . . tricky for beginners . . . nerves."

Annoyance flashed across his face. "I did paralyse you once. I'm familiar with nerves." His bare hand pressed just below her knee. "Here?"

She nodded and barely felt his resonance before her leg went numb. She drew several deep breaths, feeling less shaky now that she wasn't distracted by pain.

"Um," she said, swallowing, "you need to identify what's damaged before you pull the spike out. Nerves, veins—I don't think it went through the artery, but you should check. Might've fractured the bone. Blood flow's easy to sense. Close the veins and arteries temporarily—not too long."

Kaine was silent, his bare fingers pressed against her calf, and his eyes went out of focus. She couldn't feel what he was doing, which would normally bother her, but right now she was not lucid enough to care properly.

He placed his hand on the spike. Despite being numb, she tensed, bracing herself for the grind of metal against tissue.

Rather than pull it out, he transmuted it. The metal rippled in his hand, shrinking out of the wound so that it didn't drag or tear. Only a little blood spattered on the floor. He dropped the bar, studying the puncture with a critical eye.

"I don't feel any trace metals left. Do I clean it?"

She nodded, starting to tremble even though the spike was out and the pain was gone. "There's leftover carbolic dilution in my satchel."

He rummaged through it and found the vial.

"Lucky I healed you," she said as he wordlessly unscrewed it and poured the contents over the wound. It looked like water trickling through and joining the puddle of blood on the floor.

Then he began closing the puncture. She warned him to only perform the most basic regeneration, because she didn't have the physical resources for more.

Gradually the hole in her leg was gone, replaced with delicate, extremely inflamed new tissue, and he partially removed the block on her nerves. Pain rolled through her like a wave. She'd need more healing, but this was enough to get her back.

She tried to rotate her foot, but the muscles weren't intact enough. She could limp, though.

"Thank you."

He didn't acknowledge her, wiping his hands off on a handkerchief and pulling his gloves back on. He radiated impatience as she got up, favouring her left leg. There was a new sort of hardness about him.

Her head was light, but she felt less wobbly.

She touched the door, but her resonance was still just a gap, like a lost tooth. Her fingers skittered across the surface. Before she could say anything, she heard the mechanisms inside move, and the door clicked open.

She looked back, expecting to find Ferron behind her, but he was still across the room.

CHAPTER 40

Septembris 1786

Despite the Outpost being retaken, Helena returned the following week. Even with necrothralls patrolling, there was no better place to meet. Anywhere else in the city would have checkpoints maintained with living guards with long-term memories who'd inspect her papers every time she passed through. Helena was too memorably foreign looking to safely move in and out of enemy territory.

The Outpost, although Undying territory, was only being minimally patrolled by the necrothralls, something Helena would have known if she hadn't been half asleep during the meeting.

Her leg still ached when she walked on it, a side effect of not being able to heal herself for the several days it took for her resonance to return. Regenerated muscle took time to fully reintegrate, but the injury wasn't anything permanent.

She navigated the Outpost cautiously, her knife gripped tightly in her hand, but she only saw a few necrothralls at a distance. No solitary necrothralls approached her with missives. She wondered if Kaine had gotten the memo about still using the Outpost.

She was about to leave when her ring burned. She headed for the tenement.

He was seated at the table, waiting, when she arrived. She'd grown so used to seeing him always straddling chairs, it was surprising to see him seated on one properly.

His eyes swept from head to toe, as if expecting her to be bleeding from somewhere again.

"I think it's time I trained you," he said as the door shut behind her.

She said nothing. She felt too many emotions to even begin to make sense of them all.

So he was back, no explanation for his month-long disappearance, while she'd been left to endure being written off as a failure and castigated for wasting critical resources on a gamble that had failed to pay off.

Crowther had been scathing, because although the missives had still arrived every four days, Kaine passed on only the information he chose to. They could not ask for anything. Everything they received was at his discretion, for only as long as he chose to provide it.

Relying on Kaine Ferron was like walking on black ice, knowing that at any moment it might break beneath their feet.

Her fingers curled into a fist, feeling the punctures in her palm, not trusting herself to speak.

He tilted his head back. His dark hair was threaded through with silver so that it almost gleamed. "How long have you been healing?"

She paused, calculating. "Little more than five years now."

There was an almost charring intensity in the way he was looking at her. "I assume you're aware of the Toll."

She nodded.

"Have you burned out like that before?"

She shook her head. "No, it was the first time." Her fingers bumped absently against her chest where the empty amulet hung beneath her clothes. "I used to—handle it better."

"Well, that's something at least." He stood up. "How was it explained to you? I assume that Falcon or the Holdfasts told you about it."

She looked away, staring out the window. "Vivimancy is a corruption of resonance that can use vitality as well as the energy of resonance. It's caused when an unviable soul sustains itself by stealing life from another. Souls like that can only be purified through a life of self-sacrifice. The toll is—penance. It's giving up what was stolen."

His mouth twisted into a sardonic smile. "Right. You mentioned that your mother died when you were young."

She nodded wordlessly, cold all over. She'd still been in shock from her father's death when Ilva had her sent away to Matias, a Shrike at the time.

He had been the one to tell her that she was the reason both her parents were dead.

Her mother's mysterious sickness, diagnosed as a kind of consumption, was the Toll. Not because her mother had been a vivimancer, but because from the moment of conception, Helena's defective, corrupt self had leached her mother of life from within her womb, stealing all but those seven years away. That vivimancers were parasites by nature, and they would rot and burn in the bowels of the earth for an eternity if they did not repent and purify themselves by giving up every drop of the vitality they'd taken.

Just thinking about it made Helena's head throb. All the years she'd spent hovering over her mother, watching her father attempt cure after cure, running them into debt buying expensive ingredients, and it was Helena who'd been the cause.

"So . . ." Ferron said slowly, moving idly towards her, "you use your vitality to save—anyone you're told to save, as penance?"

She wished he'd stop talking.

"I want to show you something." He was in front of her. "Give me your hand."

She extended her left hand reluctantly.

He took it and she had barely time to brace herself before his resonance shot down her arm into her chest, and she felt a hard yank.

It was like being wrenched forward on a cellular level. Her whole body lurched as if his resonance were hooked inside her, trying to rip her soul out, but before it could budge, a rebound of energy severed it, and Ferron's resonance slammed back into him with bone-charring speed.

She felt it scorch his fingers as he let go. She almost fell backwards.

"What'd you do—" Her tongue scarcely worked. She doubled over and nearly threw up.

He flexed his hand as if burned. "I just tried to take your vitality by force. Notice anything?"

Helena's hand pressed against her chest, trying to erase that awful pulling sensation that seemed diffused through her entire body. "It—hurt?"

"It didn't work," he said. "It's not possible to take it by force like that. If it was that easy—" He scoffed. "—Morrough wouldn't be bothering with most of this. Try it yourself now."

Helena drew away from his proffered hand. "No, thank you. I get the idea."

His expression hardened. "I don't need you to get it, I need you to believe it. You're being driven by the guilt over crimes you never committed, that you think you deserve to suffer for, and that's making you a liability for me."

Of course this was all self-interest on his part. As usual.

"Take my hand," he said.

She grasped his hand limply.

"You know what your vitality feels like when you use it; feel for mine."

She shot him a look. "You're not exactly normal."

She focused on reaching with her resonance, not merely trying to get a read on his physiology but searching for the actual spark of life within him. Except it was not so much a spark as a small sun.

It was like being flung bodily into the face of Lumithia at full Ascendance, a cold searing burn that etched itself into her teeth and bones.

She tried to ignore it. Pull. She had no idea how to do that. Healing, when it required the use of vitality, worked in the opposite direction, pushing in, giving, but she knew what it felt like when Ferron did it, so she tried to imitate the feeling.

She reached with her resonance towards the overwhelming burn and tried to tug at it. It prompted an instant recoil.

Her resonance rebounded like a rubber band snapping her fingertips. An odd look of amusement flickered on Kaine's face as she let go.

She swallowed, blinking hard. "But if that's—if that's true, then why did my mother die? If I didn't take it?"

He exhaled. "My father sought treatment for my mother prior to my birth. A vivimancer they employed believed she likely possessed a latent degree of vivimancy, and didn't realise that using her vitality wasn't necessary." He wasn't looking at her. "Perhaps it was similar for yours."

Hearing those words, Helena felt like an immense weight had been partly lifted from her. It was possible that her mother's death, while still her fault, had at least not been her doing. She drew a shaky breath, not sure if she could believe it. Why would Kaine tell her this? Why would he care about her guilt?

"Vitality is a strange thing," he said, stepping away. "It doesn't take much to do things like necromancy or healing. If it did, necromancers would hardly be a threat, and you would've been dead in a week as a healer. Here's what's interesting, though: If I were a necrothrall, you could have ripped out my vitality. Reanimation doesn't fully bond with other bodies, it just reactivates a corpse. Bennet would give almost anything to be able to transfer souls between living bodies, but it always kills them instead." He arched an eyebrow. "Do you see where I'm going with this?"

"No."

He waved a hand, and despite being halfway across the room, the lock turned and the door opened. Helena was horrified as a necrothrall entered the unit.

"Ferron!" she said sharply, backing away, but she ran into something solid. He'd moved behind her, and when she tried to escape the approaching necrothrall, he gripped her by the shoulders, trapping her in place.

She tried to kick him, her heart racing. "Let go! Let go of me."

"You're not going to blast it apart, and you're not going to attack. When it reaches you, you're going to take the vitality reanimating it."

"Are you insane?" She tried again to twist away, but he took her by the wrist and pushed it forwards, firmly, so that her hand pressed against the necrothrall's chest.

It was a man. He looked as if he'd been around forty. He'd been dead for a few days at least before being reanimated. She couldn't see a visible cause of death, but she could smell it. It was probably hidden somewhere beneath his clothes. His eyes were empty, the whites yellow-stained, the skin taut.

"Feel the energy," Ferron said softly. His hands were warm on her shoulders, simultaneously bracing and trapping her.

She'd never touched a necrothrall with resonance like this, never experienced the dissonance of life and death entwined. There was a heart beating sluggishly, oxygen-deprived blood crawling through the veins. There was no life; it was just energy.

The living had a vibrancy, but the necrothrall was dead. It was like a perpetual electric shock on an animal corpse to make the systems function.

"Do you feel it?" Ferron asked.

She gave a shaky nod.

"Then take it."

She squeezed her eyes shut and pulled. It was like a plant in loose soil. The energy came loose, and a shock of power ran up her arm.

The world went silver-white, as if she'd exploded in place and then instantly reconstituted.

She dimly heard the muffled thud as the necrothrall hit the ground.

She blinked to find Kaine kneeling beside the corpse.

He touched the hand for only a moment, and the dead man sat up, standing and walking back out.

Kaine looked at her. "If you're ever attacked by necrothralls again, don't waste your energy obliterating them. Just rip out the reanimation." He looked away. "It's possible it may keep the Toll at bay for you."

Helena said nothing. Beneath her skin, her nerves were still buzzing.

"I didn't know that was something vivimancers could do," she said, trying to get her thoughts straight.

"I don't think that most can," Kaine said, straightening. "It's something only animancers are capable of."

He said it so casually that it took Helena a moment to process his words. She looked at him sharply.

"How'd you realise?" she said.

A thin smile curved across his face. "It was just a guess."

She flushed.

"I did think you were rather quick to catch on with the memory trick." He straightened. "Now that you're not at risk of keeling over from performing a bit of basic transmutation, I want to see your combat forms."

Her stomach sank. She could already feel his impending judgement.

"It's been a while," she said, digging for her knife from her satchel. It had fallen to the bottom, and she had to dig out several bundles of herbs and sphagnum moss to find it. "I wasn't very advanced. Academic track, you know."

"So was I," he said, watching her through insolently lidded eyes, but she could see a gleam of silver beneath his lashes. "You should be wearing that knife. You can't afford to waste time fumbling through that bag of yours, and you should have at least two of them."

"Two knives would get in the way of my vivimancy."

He raised his eyebrows. "With thralls, yes, but not if you're fighting the Undying. Or a chimaera."

She looked up. "Couldn't I still use vivimancy?"

"If *you're* close enough to touch them, they'll have already killed you. You don't regenerate. To survive, you need distance."

She looked down at the knife in her hand. It was annoyingly hefty, but everything standard-issue was. "A knife isn't going to give me much more reach than I already have, and if I'm walking around armed, I'm more likely to be noticed. It's safer to be mistaken for a civilian. Necrothralls usually leave them alone."

"Not anymore. With the losses incurred this year, now that the Eternal Flame controls the entire East Island, there are no civilians any longer. Anyone on the East Island, or elsewhere without the right papers, is an enemy, and may be treated as such."

Helena's mouth went dry. "Anyone?"

"Man, woman, or child. When the Eternal Flame was constantly losing territory, the Undying could afford to be magnanimous, but the goal is eradication now."

HELENA KNEW ABOUT COMBAT FORMS. Academically.

She had also practised them, but it had been a very long time.

Kaine seemed to think she was the most incompetent combatant he'd ever seen. After only brief observation, he started her all the way back with first-year forms, drilling them on and on until they were perfect.

After he was relatively civil about the animancy, she wasn't prepared for how merciless he'd be about combat. He was completely vicious. It was only marginally preferable to being chased around the room having furniture thrown at her.

"I doubt this is going to save me from anyone," she said after a week, growing uncomfortably sweaty. Her arm trembled as she raised the knife over her head for the hundredth time and channelled her resonance, altering the length and curve of the blade.

"If you can't master the basics, you're not going to survive anything." A boot collided with the small of her back.

She gave a startled scream and barely managed to keep herself from ramming face-first into the wall by getting one foot out to catch her momentum, her knife curving instinctively as she spun around to face him.

Her spine was throbbing. A little harder and he might have broken it.

"What the fuck, Ferron?"

"Ah, back to surnames, I see," he said coolly.

"That. Hurt," she said through gritted teeth, touching her back gingerly, her resonance preventing the swelling before it could start.

"Then keep your guard up." His eyes flashed. "I'm not training you to take a test. Do you think combat is for standing around seeing who transmutes best? You'll never know what's coming. You use your resonance to predict attacks. If you let me close enough to hit you, I will. Now keep going."

She shook her head, refusing to move.

His expression darkened. "I said, keep going."

"I'm *not* like you," she said venomously. "If you hurt me to teach me a lesson, I need time to recover. And when I'm exhausted, I just make more mistakes. I'm not staying here to see how much you have to hurt me before you manage to remember that a trivial injury for you can paralyse me. You're lucky you didn't just now."

His lips turned white. She turned away, sheathing the knife and shoving it into her satchel.

"This isn't combat training," he said when she was at the door. "You're going to get killed if you don't learn how to defend yourself. That's the only way to survive."

"Well, whatever it is, you're a terrible teacher," she said as she opened the door and slammed it behind her.

CHAPTER 41

Octobris 1786

THE WAR HAD ALWAYS MOVED SLOWLY, BUT as autumn set in, it slowed to a crawl. The two sides held almost equal territory. The ports had made a significant difference in the Eternal Flame's strength, but they lacked any clear path to victory. The West Island was even more vertical than the East. The way the towers and buildings interlocked and intersected made it almost impossible to retake without risking mass casualties.

The current balance was thanks to Kaine, but it was a tenuous stalemate because they had no idea when he might someday stop or, worse, betray them.

At his reappearance, the pressure from Ilva and Crowther resumed tenfold, but Helena had no idea how to make progress. Kaine was angry and perpetually on his guard around her, and his methods of training offered few openings, although he was noticeably careful not to hurt her again.

Under his exacting eyes, she learned to key up her resonance until it filled the air around her, sensing attacks coming before they hit.

"Finally," he said after she at last managed to block a light-speed blow without breaking form at all and immediately followed it with an attack.

It was the closest thing to praise she'd earned.

She slumped against the wall, breathing hard. The muscles in her forearms and biceps felt raw and coppery from all the metal transmutations she'd done over and over. Her resonance ached inside her nerves, brain buzzing, a hum that made her teeth itch.

It was no wonder Lila was always jittery when she came back.

Helena flexed her hands.

"You need a better knife; that alloy's wrong. It's slowing you."

She looked away. It was raining outside, water streaming across the windows. She was so hot that she wanted to walk out and douse herself in the fresh autumn rainfall.

"I don't have the rank for anything else," she said.

The Resistance metallurgists had years' worth of projects on their dockets: tools, base weapons, rappelling harness gear, armour, prosthetics, not to mention the expectation that they'd invent new weaponry as the war progressed. Without the Institute being able to train new metallurgists, those they had were a critical resource. The generation who should be learning the craftsmanship were all either in combat or dead. Standard-issue was what everyone in the Resistance got. If they couldn't fight with that, they couldn't fight as alchemists.

To obtain bespoke weaponry was something combat alchemists dreamed of: weapons forged to perfectly match the owner's specific resonance strengths and combat style. They were versatile, felt impossibly light, and took almost no effort to transmute. They were also much harder to defend against.

"What do you mean you don't have the rank? Aren't you a member of the Eternal Flame?"

"Yes," she said quietly.

"I thought that was part of the package deal: You swear your life to a set of asinine religious ideals and get a valuable weapon in compensation."

She stared at her shoes.

It was traditionally a part of joining the Order of the Eternal Flame.

They were issued following a vow ceremony, a weapon to defend the ideals they'd sworn to uphold. They were deeply symbolic.

But when Helena joined, it was just after Principate Apollo's death. Many people had joined at the time. She'd been sixteen, just starting basic training. New members going immediately into combat had greater need. Helena didn't even know what type of weapon would be suitable.

The matter had been forgotten when she became a healer. Weapons were for those in combat. She was not, and never would be.

"There are more immediate needs than making me a special weapon that I'd barely use," she said.

"Consider it an immediate need now. After six years, surely there's been time," he said. "How many swords and suits of armour does Holdfast have?"

She bristled. "Luc fights at the front lines."

Kaine scoffed, his lip curling. "With fire. Get a better knife."

SHE RETURNED WITH THE SAME knife.

Kaine was across the room the instant she pulled it out. Moving impossibly, terrifyingly fast, he was right in front of her. He ripped it from her hand.

"Why do you still have this?" he hissed. "I told you to get a new one."

She tried to snatch it back. "I can't just show up on the docket like that. People know weeks out before they're up for testing. It'd be noticeable if I'm suddenly prioritised." She tilted her head back, meeting his eyes, and recited verbatim, "'Your request has been declined. It would raise too many questions.'"

Ferron looked like he wanted to strangle her. He raised his hand as if to fling the knife out the window but then drew a measured breath.

"Give me your resonance alloy, then," he said, slamming the knife onto the table.

"What?"

His eyes turned flinty. "Surely you can manage that at least?"

"Yes—but—" She was flabbergasted.

"What?"

Outside of the Eternal Flame, bespoke weaponry was prohibitively expensive. That was why the weapons were such an honour. Especially during the war, most of the metallurgists who hadn't joined the war effort on one side or the other had fled Paladia altogether and taken their valuable talents to safer countries.

She kept staring wordlessly at him until he looked away. "You can consider it thanks for healing my back."

She seized the opportunity. "Did it—did the scar tissue set properly? I came back to check—but you—"

"It's fine," he said in a stiff voice, his posture rigid. His head was turned so that she could see only his jaw. "I hardly feel it."

She exhaled. "Good. I was afraid that maybe something had gone wrong and that's why you didn't come—"

He whirled on her. "It's not any of your fucking business."

She started back. "I just meant—"

"Fuck off, Marino." His voice was deadly soft. "I'm not your pet. I don't need you."

Before she could reply, he ripped an envelope out from an inner pocket and slammed it down on the table beside the knife, before stalking out.

Helena stashed her knife in the outer pocket of her satchel and set out, vigilant until she passed the first checkpoint; then she let her footsteps slow, ignoring the rain.

What was it he'd said about the array? That it didn't countermand his behaviour but wrote in new aspects. That it was easier for him to be ruthless, and harder to resist impulses and what he wanted.

She'd spent so many evenings staring at it, she could still see it when she closed her eyes.

Calculating, Cunning, Devoted, Determined, Ruthless, Unfailing, Unhesitating, and Unyielding.

What Kaine was driven to do was unstated and thus left to his discretion. No doubt he'd thought himself clever, leaving himself that loophole.

Except Helena was the one who'd exploited it.

The decision to refuse Kaine's demand for a weapon had been a gamble. Ilva and Crowther wanted to see what Kaine would do if he was told no. Their excuse was within reason, but the choice itself had been a test. They were forcing him to show his hand, and he had.

Helena was making progress.

She should be proud of that, but all she felt was the treachery and danger of it.

She blinked and found she'd wandered to the rain garden. The creek was swollen, overflowing its banks. The water streamed around Luna's pedestal, but despite it, even after months, the prayer tower she'd built still stood. All Helena's prayers were rejected.

She reached out and almost toppled them herself.

She looked up at the buildings looming above, the rain splattering her face. It still startled her sometimes how beautiful the city could be.

Even in the downpour, the buildings gleamed.

She looked at the abandoned shrine again.

Survive, Kaine kept saying. The only goal. She was learning to fight not to win, but to escape. As if she were a prey animal.

She knew very well that if it ever came down to her and Kaine, she would die. No matter how similar their abilities, murder was exclusively within his purview.

She smiled bitterly at the difference between them.

Her death count was the numerical representation of her failures. All the lives she hadn't saved, the ways she fell short.

For Kaine, it was a mark of power. His victims, even Principate Apollo, all represented what made him so valuable.

They were the inverse and counter to each other.

A healer and killer, circling slowly, the push and pull inexorable.

As THE RESISTANCE RE-ESTABLISHED CONTROL of the island, their base of operations broadened. Headquarters remained most defensible, but forcing combat units and supply dispatches to travel the island from end to end was a waste of time and resources. There was now a secondary base of command near the ports, with a secondary hospital there. Matron Pace was currently stationed there to get it up and running.

It meant that Luc came back less. Even Crowther was often gone.

She took her report to Ilva, who never left Headquarters.

"Well?" Ilva asked when Helena entered her office.

"He's asked for my alloy," Helena said, sitting down in front of the desk and handing over the envelope. "He said he'll take care of it."

Ilva looked up, a gleam like sunlight in her pale-blue eyes. "Did he?"

Helena looked down at her nails. The nail beds were all stained with dirt, and her skin was tinged green from cuttings. "He said it's thanks for healing him."

"I'm sure." There was a melodic note of sarcasm in Ilva's tone.

Helena bit her lip. She hated debriefings like this, disclosing all her conversations and interactions, laying out Kaine's words, his tells, his lack of tells. Letting Ilva or Crowther dissect him as if performing a kind of emotional vivisection, identifying his weaknesses and vulnerabilities so that Helena could be sent back to try to exploit them with greater precision.

"Anything else?"

She looked up to find Ilva studying her closely. The brusqueness had thawed after Kaine had resumed training her. Now that Helena had potential use, she was worth their time again.

"With the way things are going, I don't think we should discount the possibility that Ferron may kill me."

Ilva straightened, her thin lips vanishing. "Are you asking to be pulled out, Marino?"

There was a sudden intensity in her voice.

Helena's chest tightened as she shook her head.

"No. We need the information. I just—I want to know what I should prioritise. Elain is probably best suited as my replacement, but there's still a lot of basic medical knowledge she needs to learn, and that's not even considering some of the more advanced healing techniques that she's been afraid to do. She's not as driven. I think the Council will need to officially designate her as my alternate so I can push her harder."

"I'll speak with Jan and look over the hospital's reports. If you could make a list of which areas would have the least redundancy, that would be useful."

"All right." Helena's voice came out stilted and mechanical. A thought occurred to her. "Shiseo—he's a metallurgist. Could I ask him to test my resonance for my alloy?"

Ilva coughed. "If you'd like."

Helena stood to leave.

"Helena," Ilva called softly just as she reached the door.

She paused, looking back. Ilva's expression was unreadable.

"Tell me, what's your strategy with Ferron now?"

Helena paused, feeling tired. She couldn't rightly remember the last time she hadn't been tired. She leaned against the door, letting it brace her.

"I think . . . he wants me. Treating the array changed things between us, but he knows what I'm doing." She swallowed hard. "He's very obsessive about things. I think he always has been, but the array makes it worse. If things go according to plan, that'll be good for us. I don't think he'll ever abandon the Eternal Flame then. Willingness seems critical with him, and he knows mine is conditional on the Eternal Flame's survival. But—given how far he's willing to go for things, I'd say there's a chance he'd destroy anything that stood in his way. That might include me."

Ilva was silent, still watching Helena.

Helena felt raw, as if she'd been flayed and was now being kept under observation. "Maybe I'm just overthinking it."

Ilva looked down at her desk, picking up a glass paperweight and rolling it in her hands. "You've done much more than I expected."

Was that supposed to make her feel better?

Standing there, Helena thought she should feel something, but instead her heart seemed to be compacting inside her chest, growing smaller and harder day by day. She used to think she had so much to give that she could never run out; now she felt like an upended pitcher, with an impatient cup waiting for the last drop.

"I'm not—" she started, and then paused. She twisted at the ring around her finger. "I think he's lonely."

Ilva straightened, rising several inches in her seat. "I hope you're not getting attached, Helena. The Eternal Flame is depending on you to stay on mission. If you're compromised, you should say so."

Helena shook her head, regretting the comment. "Never. My loyalty will always be to the Eternal Flame."

Ilva's expression remained wary. "You know," she said slowly, "I can only keep Luc and his unit away from the worst fights if we know which ones they'll be."

Helena's heart slammed into her throat. "I know." Her voice was tight. "I'm doing everything I can. I'll never do anything that could risk Luc."

Ilva's posture softened. "All right, then. You can go." She waved her hand in dismissal, returning to her files.

Helena turned, then gave a brittle laugh. "You know, I just realised, if I succeed, you'll control Ferron the same way you use Luc to control me. It makes me feel rather sorry for him."

Ilva didn't look at her. "Well, he'll deserve it more than you do."

CHAPTER 42

Octobris 1786

When Helena asked Shiseo if he could test her resonance for a weapon alloy, he'd seemed surprised by the request.

"You don't know?" he asked, looking up as he adjusted the temperature under an alembic.

"I never got around to it," she said, trying to make the request seem casual. Shiseo was an excellent collaborator, but he was excruciatingly private. He never spoke of himself or the Eastern Empire except in ways specific to their work.

"It's all right if you don't have time," she said. "It's mostly curiosity."

Shiseo blinked slowly. His expressions were even more unreadable than Kaine's. "Remind me, what part are you from?"

Helena exhaled, fingers skittering across the medical textbook she was reading. She'd had an idea for an injected drug for emergency situations where a heart needed intense stimulation, but she was uncertain about the composition she'd developed.

"Etras. It's south. Out in the sea. The crescent of islands between the two continents. Not many alchemists there, since there isn't much metal, and no lumithium."

"Is that why you came to Paladia?"

She nodded without looking up. "My father thought my repertoire was too special to be—wasted there."

Shiseo gave a mysterious little hum and nodded. "I will bring my set to test you, but I would like to ask a favour, if I may."

She straightened, and now she was looking at him curiously. "Of course."

"The metals from that woman's blood some months ago. I heard about them. May I try identifying them?"

Helena's mouth went dry at this casual mention of Gettlich. She'd had no idea Shiseo was even aware of the event, much less knowledgeable enough to have picked up on the fact that there was anything unusual retrieved from the body. Several metallurgists had tried to identify all the trace metals and compounds found in the blood samples without success.

Shiseo's expression had not changed; he wore the same mild look he always did. "I heard that some are not identified."

"I'll ask for a sample."

When Shiseo returned to Helena's lab, he brought a little case that was filled with glass vials, each with pure compounds and metals inside, labelled in a script that Helena couldn't read.

He arranged them in rows. "These"—he pointed to the closest—"are common Paladian metals. These"—he pointed to the second and third rows of compounds—"are a little more rare. We will see."

He removed them one by one, and Helena used her resonance to manipulate them into hollow spheres while he timed her. Then he used his own remarkably wide repertoire to slice them into quarters and examine the evenness of her distribution, the orderliness of the structure, grading each aspect on a chart.

If some were graded lower than others, there was a mathematical formula to calculate the level of lumithium emanations necessary to balance the potential alloy's resonance to match the alchemist's base level.

"You have an interesting repertoire," he said in his quiet voice as they moved into the third row of vials. "Very unusual. Good attention to detail. I am surprised you are not a metallurgist."

"I wasn't sure what to do," she said, handing another metal back for grading. "It felt like whatever I chose, someone was disappointed. Everyone—" She fluttered her fingers but, catching herself gesturing, folded them in her lap. "Everyone wanted a lot for me, and I'm not sure I ever knew what I wanted." She shrugged. "Probably good that I didn't, since it didn't matter in the end."

Shiseo didn't reply. He was studying the notes he'd taken, then he looked at her, staring at her folded hands. "I don't think a steel weapon would suit you."

"What?" Her resonance for both steel and iron were excellent. There was no reason why she wouldn't be perfectly suited for a steel alloy, it was what most metallurgists were specialised in. Almost all the weapons in Paladia were steel.

"You are exceptional with titanium. I met the titanium guildmaster once, and even his work was not so perfect." Then he picked up a piece of her nickel work, studying it as well. "Have you ever tried nickel-titanium alloy?"

She shook her head.

"It would make a better weapon for you. Very light. You'd waste your strength with steel."

"This isn't for a weapon," Helena said quickly. "It's just—curiosity."

Shiseo just made a little click with his tongue. "Well . . . if you wanted a weapon, I would advise you to use nickel and titanium. Don't limit yourself to what Paladians do."

She couldn't imagine giving Kaine Ferron, heir of the iron guild, a resonance alloy without any iron in it. Titanium and nickel might not even be in his repertoire. She'd be asking for a weapon he couldn't sense or transmute. It would seem like a threat.

After some pleading, Shiseo finally consented to writing a steel alloy, too.

She almost threw the titanium alloy away, but Crowther instructed her to include it. He wanted to see what Kaine would do.

ELAIN DID NOT UNDERGO ANY new training.

When Helena had tried to add the additional training sessions and one weekly foraging trip, Elain had filed a formal complaint with Falcon Matias that she was being overworked and had never agreed to be an apothecary, and of course, not only did Matias side with Elain, but he'd wanted to know how and why Helena was an apothecary, and who had approved it.

A moratorium was placed on Helena's lab work, and the next thing she knew, it was not her lab at all but Shiseo's, and Ilva had Helena passed off as the lab assistant, tasked with running errands and fetching supplies from the wetlands for him.

It was all technicalities, and better than being banned from chymiatria, but it still felt like a blow.

Her only solace was anticipating a bespoke knife. She'd given the alloy slip to Kaine, and he'd taken it without comment.

It was hard to temper her expectations. Whenever she used any kind of tool or weapon, she'd wonder what it would feel like to hold something made to resonate with her. Lila treated her weapons like they were children, naming them, coddling them, spending hours caring for them, ensuring they were in perfect condition. It was the same with her prosthetic and armour. They were so intrinsically customised, it made them an extension of herself.

However, Kaine made no references to the knife. Helena began to habitually push the thought down so she wouldn't experience a pang of disappointment every time she saw him.

He finally decided she was "passable" at the forms and moved on to attacks and techniques specific to her abilities.

"You're still doing it wrong," he said, standing and stalking over to her. "The idea is to target the tendons. You start low. Left Achilles, then the inside of the right thigh; they fall, and your blade is there to catch them through the throat and into the skull. That is when you'll punch your fist into their chest and rip out the talisman."

He demonstrated again, but she kept dropping the knife. The attack wasn't complicated, but the knife-work had to be done with her off hand, so that her right hand could perform the human transmutation at the end.

Three transmutational shapes in seconds while using her non-dominant hand tested the limits of her coordination.

He stepped behind her. Not being able to see him made her keenly aware of how close he was.

There was a pause before his hands wrapped around hers, fingers brushing across the inside of her wrists, her back against his chest.

She could feel him through her resonance, and even though she wasn't directly touching him, she was so keyed up from her constantly flowing resonance that it formed a torus of energy around her. She tried to block him out, but she was too frayed to only attenuate on her knife.

His arms ran against the length of hers as he guided her down into a low lunge, her left hand angling to catch a tendon, transmuting her knife into a curve, then—with a quick flick of the wrist upwards—using a straight-edged blade to take out the hamstring of the opposite leg. In this same upwards movement, the blade widened into a brutal spike intended to maximise brain damage.

Then he drove her other hand forward in a brutal punch into empty air. With her resonance behind it, she'd go straight through the bone and find a talisman.

"It's one movement," he said, his voice near her ear. A shiver ran through her gut. Helena could barely hear his words over her own heartbeat. "You go quick. Hit as many points as you can. Tendons are the best way to slow them. A blade through the brain will knock them out for a few seconds, at least, and keep them disoriented for longer. Even if you miss the talisman, they won't recover immediately. The regeneration will focus on the brain. But miss that blow and you're dead."

He took her through the movement one more time slowly, and then faster to demonstrate the upward lunge of a counterstrike intended to be fluid and quick as lightning.

"Do you *feel* it now?" he asked, his voice low, the heat of his breath near her ear, brushing through her hair, making it impossible to focus.

She didn't think he was helping at all. There was an intense pressure that grew inside her whenever he was close, a sort of frantic desperation, like swimming up towards the surface yet never reaching it.

She nodded shakily, and his hands slipped away from her wrists.

"Go again."

WHEN THE TOWER BELL WENT off, the air vibrated. An attack warning, or else a call to be ready. For fighters to go out, and for the hospital to prepare.

The sirens in the hallway began blaring loud enough to split her skull as Helena hurried towards the hospital.

"What do we know?" she asked as she tied on her apron, stripping her gloves off to wash and sterilise her hands.

Whatever had happened did so without warning. Normally as soon as significant fighting started anywhere, messages to Headquarters were dispatched and the hospital was prepped. This time the sirens had gone straight to full alert.

"Nothing yet," Pace said as she directed medics. She'd only returned from the other hospital a few days ago, worn to the bone, but she never stopped working.

Orderlies and nurses rushed around, making sure everything was ready.

The bell was still sounding.

"I'm going to the main gates to find out what's happening," Helena finally said.

Out in the courtyard, without the walls acting as a barrier for the sound, she could feel the Tower bell's ringing in her teeth, its low cadence a vibration in her stomach.

The noise finally cut off as she reached the gates. There were dozens of soldiers and guards, all awaiting orders. Even Crowther was lurking, curious as everyone else.

"Do you know what's happened?" Helena asked a guard.

"Ambush," he said, his eyes locked out towards the street. "Don't know much more than that. Two teams went out. That's all I know. We've heard nothing else."

There was a commotion beyond the gates.

Then she heard Luc, his voice pure rage. "Let go. Let me go!"

Then there were other voices. Shouts of "Watch out!" and "Hold him!" and a scorching whoosh of flames.

"Let me go!"

Helena went forward instinctively, along with a dozen others.

There was an explosion of fire as she emerged from the gatehouse to the sight of nearly a dozen people trying to drag and wrestle Luc towards Headquarters. Soren, Sebastian, Althorne, and several others from Luc's unit had him by the arms and legs, trying to pin him to the ground.

Luc had been disarmed, but they couldn't pry his ignition rings off his fingers. Fire sparked but suddenly vanished as Crowther darted forward. His left hand swept through the air and extinguished the flames as he clenched his fist.

"Marino, put him down!" Crowther snapped.

"You left her! *Let me go!*" White fire exploded off Luc, flame tearing in all directions, violent and uncontrolled, fuelled by rage. Luc lurched to his feet.

A tongue of metal shot out, Althorne's arm jerked back, Luc hit the ground, and there were several people on him again. Fire erupted and vanished.

"Marino!" Crowther snarled.

Luc lunged violently, ripping one hand free, and a wall of fire shot in all directions. It slammed into Crowther, and he hit a wall with a sickening crunch.

Everyone froze, including Luc.

"I didn't mean to—" He was still trying to get free. "Just let me go—"

Helena reached out towards him.

"They got Lila," he said, taking her hand without hesitation.

She squeezed tight, resonance shooting along his arm. Betrayal flashed in his eyes, and then he was unconscious.

The men pinning Luc down let go cautiously. Helena sank to her knees, kneeling over him, her fingers slipping into the occipital dip of his skull to ensure he would not wake.

He was bruised and covered in blood. Half his fingernails were missing.

Soren didn't get up; he was slumped next to Helena. One of his eyes was black.

"Get him inside and keep him unconscious," Althorne was saying. "I don't want that boy awake until we know what's happened to Bayard. Someone get Crowther to the hospital."

There was heavy bruising on one side of Althorne's face, a gouge across his cheek as if he'd been clawed at. Several soldiers picked Luc up gently and started carrying him inside.

Helena was still kneeling on the ground.

Lila had been taken. Whatever happened next, the implications were horrifying.

Lila as a necrothrall, all her proficiency in combat now targeted at the Eternal Flame. At Luc. Or Lila in a laboratory, being used for experimentation.

"May I be dismissed?" Soren said, his voice muted but wavering with emotion. He was looking to Althorne with an expression as if something had been carved out from inside him.

Althorne rested a large hand on Soren's narrow shoulder. "Until we recover Lila, you're paladin primary. We can't lose you, too."

"They took my twin," Soren said, looking out towards the rest of the island. "I have to bring her body back."

"There are three teams in pursuit. If she can be saved or recovered, she will be. We need to debrief and prepare. And you need to protect your Principate. You know where your sister would want you."

A stretcher arrived for Crowther, and Helena followed it.

In the hospital, Elain was already hovering over Luc, healing his minor injuries, and asking if she could wake him up. She was sternly forbidden.

Helena focused on Crowther. That soft-faced orderly, Purnell, hurried over to assist. He had a gash on his face, but his paralysed arm had taken the brunt of the injury, broken at the elbow.

As Helena began with her habitual block of the nerves, she found why his arm was paralysed. There was an old break of the humerus, and back when it had broken, the radial nerve had been severed. The gap was tiny; any healer could have fixed it.

The injury was old now, and the nerve's connection to the muscle had died off. Helena wasn't sure how much dexterity could be recovered, but surely some was better than nothing. If the day had proven anything, it was that the Resistance desperately needed flame alchemists.

She fixed the severed nerve along with the broken elbow.

She'd just finished when she heard shouting.

"They got her! Bayard. They're bringing her in!"

A combat group practically ran into the hospital with the stretcher. There was a flash of bloodstained blond hair. Pace's voice rose above the chaos.

Helena barely heard the voices. She moved towards Lila on instinct as the medics transferred her from the stretcher to a hospital bed. One of them was holding gauze firmly against the side of Lila's neck.

Other injuries.

Priority.

Marino, get her healed. Whatever it takes.

She wasn't sure who gave that final order. It didn't really matter. She didn't need to be told.

Lila was covered in blood, and even before Helena touched her, she could see the broken bones. There were huge punctures all over the right side of her chest, straight through her armour.

The moment Helena's resonance touched her, she could feel it.

Lila was going to die unless someone cheated death, and fast.

Her right lung had been repeatedly punctured by bites. There was blood pooling in the chest cavity. There was kidney damage, and her liver was punctured. Her ribs were shattered. She'd lost so much blood.

It was a miracle she was alive.

Helena didn't have time to be delicate with her resonance. It was a cascade of internal failures that she was staunching, but it was all happening too fast and there were too many things that had to be done at once. The medics were cutting off her wrecked armour as quickly as they could, everyone trying to work around one another without getting in the way.

The recovery team had been badly injured.

"It was Blackthorne in command," someone said. "That fucking psychopath."

Helena could hear the flurry behind her, but she couldn't worry about anyone but Lila.

If Lila died, so would Luc. Maybe not immediately; if he never saw combat again, physically he'd live, but every day, bit by bit, the guilt and grief would kill him.

"Don't you dare die," she said, shoving her vitality down through her resonance, in a wild attempt to keep Lila from slipping away, forcing the feeble heartbeat to keep going. "Don't you dare! Elain. I need Elain! And a medic! Where is everyone?"

Elain appeared, her hands bloody. "I'm already—"

"I don't care," Helena cut in. "Stand near her head. I need you to keep her breathing, and don't let her heart stop! Do you understand? I need both hands to heal, and I need to know she's breathing and her heart is beating while I work."

She waited until she felt Elain's tentative resonance assume the rhythm of Lila's heartbeat, the laborious in and out of her breath, as the last of Lila's armour was finally out of Helena's way and she worked easily.

A medic appeared at her elbow. Helena acknowledged her with a jerk of her head.

"I need four vials of that blood-supplementing tonic in the cabinet. You have to administer them without letting her choke."

"We're not supposed to—"

"I need more blood! If I can't regenerate more, this healing will kill her, and if I do it without the tonics, it's going to make something else fail. I don't have enough hands. Do it now!"

It was intense, delicate work. Helena's vision was blurring, and her resonance had singed the inside of her bones as she fought to get Lila stabilised. Elain was saying something about a hand cramp. Helena told her to shut up.

When Lila finally stopped feeling on the verge of death, Helena wanted to cry with relief. It had been so close. She could never tell anyone how close.

She leaned over Lila, her hands covered in blood, and touched her cheek for a moment.

"You can stop," she finally remembered to say to Elain.

The punctures covering Lila's chest were roughly transmuted skin. They'd scar, because Lila's body would be focused on vital recovery, but she would live. Elain disappeared so the nurses and orderlies could take over.

Helena's fingers trembled uncontrollably as she squeezed Lila's hand. "Idiot. You know you're not allowed to die."

Her knees gave out. She sank to the floor, her head resting against the mattress of the hospital bed. Lila still had at least twenty broken bones, fractures in both legs. Half her fingers were broken, but Helena's heart was pounding too violently to think straight.

"Marino, can you—" Pace was calling to her from another bed.

She tried to lift her head but couldn't move. Her whole body was leaden. Why was it so heavy?

"Pace, check Marino."

Was that Crowther's voice?

She tried to look up, but instead the world tipped sideways. She could see feet moving under the rows and rows of hospital beds. Bloodstains on the floor.

She was rising upwards.

"Come on, Marino, no napping here," Pace was saying as she pulled her to her feet. Someone was on the other side as well. Her head lolled, and she saw Crowther watching her from one of the hospital beds.

They passed through a door into the records closet that Pace used as an office.

"Just here, Sofia. Thank you, I can manage from here," Pace was saying as Helena was lowered onto a camp bed.

Helena knew, dimly, that she'd gone too far.

She was normally careful, but there hadn't been any choice this time.

She was so cold and tired. Blankets were pulled up and tucked around her. She heard Pace's voice, calling her a fool girl with no sense.

Helena just wanted to sleep for a few years.

She felt a needle in her arm. It made her skin itch, and when she tried to transmute it out, her hand was smacked away.

"Worst patient I've ever had."

Thick velvet darkness swallowed the world.

CHAPTER 43

Octobris 1786

The hospital had grown quiet when Helena woke. She felt weak as a kitten. She lay unmoving until Pace entered.

"How's Lila?" she asked, her voice barely more than a whisper.

"Recovering," Pace said in a tart voice. "Quite a miracle that she survived. All thanks to the recovery team's quick thinking and daring rescue." She cleared her throat. "They'll all be medalled for bravery, and there were several Ember Services called, to devote prayers of thanks to Sol for his—grace in saving her."

Helena stared up at the ceiling. "How long have I been asleep?"

"Three days." Pace went over to her desk, sorting loudly through a drawer without removing anything. "I said you were quarantined. All that foraging exposes you to the elements too much, I think."

Helena's eyes threatened to slide closed again. "Thank you."

"I do what I can. Crowther wants to see you when you're up again," Pace said. She started to leave, but then paused. "Lila Bayard is not the only person that the Resistance would suffer greatly for losing. I've told Ilva, Crowther, and Matias as much time and again, though I can't say they listen, but maybe you will. There are rare talents that shouldn't be squandered even if they are overlooked."

When Helena went out, Luc was sitting beside Lila, who lay so still she scarcely seemed to be breathing. Lila was taller than most people, but she looked shrunken without her armour. She was swathed in neat bandages that had been packed with salves to ease the pain and sensitivity from the new tissue. Her breathing was slow and laboured, but Helena had only to brush her fingers against Lila's hand to feel that her vital signs were stable.

She stood beside the bed, fingers just barely touching Lila's.

Luc was staring at Lila's face. His eyes were huge, purple-blue circles bruised under them as he held his paladin's hand in both of his. Soren was across the hospital, stationed near the doors.

Paladins were as intrinsic as the Holdfasts in the history and tapestry of the nation. The country was named for them, in acknowledgement of their vital role in the first Necromancy War. As the centuries passed, the role had gradually become mostly ceremonial.

Lila had been something altogether new, though, a once-in-a-lifetime talent. Her parents had wanted her to have all the chance for the greatness traditionally limited to sons. Lila was placed solely in the combat track, training to join the crusades to experience real combat when she was only fifteen, while Soren was double-track at the Institute, like Luc. Soren would have been considered an excellent combat alchemist if his twin sister wasn't his competition, but no one compared to Lila.

There'd been a procession when Lila came back after a year crusading. Helena hadn't really known Lila then, aside from her being Soren's sister.

She'd dismounted from a charger, pulled off her helmet, and stood resplendent, like a goddess stepped out of myth. Her pale hair was wrapped around her head like a crown, and she presented her weapons to Luc, who had stood, looking as if he'd been struck by lightning until Soren kicked him in the ankle.

Luc, who'd always been a bit of a larker about combat training and dismissive of the idea of a paladin, developed a passion for it overnight. He'd started constantly disappearing from study sessions and social events to practise with Lila.

His interest had been so painfully obvious that Helena and Soren were embarrassed just witnessing it, but before anything could happen, Principate Apollo was dead.

Lila had spent her whole life training to be a paladin. Soren was not remotely prepared, and Sebastian Bayard, able as he was, had just failed in his own vows by having been absent when Apollo was murdered.

Lila took the vows. To protect Luc with her life, to die for him. Luc had no choice but to accept them. Whatever had or hadn't briefly existed between them was buried beneath the weight of those vows.

"I'm sorry . . ." Luc said, his voice barely more than a whisper. "I lost my head when I saw it take her."

His expression was dazed, and his blue eyes didn't seem to see the room around them. Helena knew the look. He was back in the moment, reliving it over and over, dissecting it into every instant when he could have done things differently.

"It was after me. The chimaera. I couldn't get my sword out in time. Should have just used fire." He shook his head. "Don't know why I didn't. It was so fast. Lila threw herself in front of me and I heard the sound when it bit her—"

His voice died.

People were often like this in the hospital; their failures poured out of them.

"There was blood coming from her mouth, but she didn't scream—she told Soren to hold me back. It ran with her and I—I should have just used fire—" he choked out. "Soren wouldn't let go and I—"

"She's going to be all right, Luc," Helena said. "All her vital signs are stable. No lasting injuries."

He nodded jerkily, his eyes still fastened on Lila's face.

"When I was a kid," he said, his words rough, "I used to think it wasn't fair that all the real wars were over before I was born. Used to be afraid I'd be one of the Principates everyone forgot, because nothing happened." He looked down; he was ripping at his nails, all his fingers bleeding. "I'd do anything to have that now. I can't taste anything now except blood and smoke, and I don't feel anything except when I'm on fire. The stories made it sound so good. Fighting for a cause. Being a hero." He shook his head. "Why does everyone pretend it's anything like that?"

Helena reached out, fingers brushing against his shoulder, not sure what to say, how to comfort him.

"Maybe that's what they had to tell themselves, to live with it. Maybe it's all they let themselves remember," Helena said, but she, too, wondered that anyone who'd seen war's true face would let it be so gilded.

THE DEBRIEFING THAT OCCURRED ONCE Lila woke and was declared out of danger was tense. It was the first time Luc would leave the hospital.

Matias, Ilva, Althorne, and Crowther all stared down at Luc from the dais while he glared defiantly back at them. All his penitence seemed to have vanished.

"Lucien," Ilva said after a long silence, "Lila Bayard is your paladin. It is her sworn duty to protect you, be it at the cost of her own life. You endangered your entire unit, injured a dozen of your own men and Council member Jan Crowther, and violated your vows as well as the orders of General Althorne. You have been summoned for censure."

Luc lifted his chin. "I'm sworn to protect this country and represent the values of the Eternal Flame which my forefathers established. Neither of those vows will be fulfilled if I let people die for me when I can save them."

"You are the heart of the Resistance. A symbol of hope and light and goodness. You do not get to choose one person's life over that. You betrayed the people who follow you, and you betrayed your paladins, particularly Lila, who knew her oaths and was prepared to do as she had sworn. Your selfishness nearly rendered her sacrifice worthless."

"I'm not a symbol," Luc snapped, "or a heart. I'm Principate. We lead by our actions, not our commands."

The argument was all theatre. The Council had to censure him, and Luc stood there like a figure of myth, inexorable and resolute.

Ilva sat, gaze like a serpent as she stared down at her great-nephew. "That is not your choice. If you cannot follow orders and protocol in the presence of your *friends*"—she emphasised the word carefully, the insinuation crystal-clear—"then you will be reassigned to a different unit and provided with new soldiers to act as your paladins. Although, in keeping with tradition, we will allow you to retain Soren Bayard."

Luc's mouth snapped shut like a sprung trap, his face losing a shade of colour.

"The choice is yours," Ilva said, seeming satisfied by his silence. "Choose carefully."

Luc stood a moment longer, radiating fury. Soren was just behind him, standing to his right, still acting as primary while Lila recovered. There was a new gauntness to his face.

"I will uphold my vows and those which I have accepted." Luc's voice was hollow and defeated.

"Good," Ilva said, but her voice was still cold, disapproving at how long it had taken Luc to choose. "The recovery team managed to kill the chimaera before it escaped the East Island. A wall was found breached. There will be an investigation into how that happened. Given the behaviour of the creature, we must assume that they're capable of more than we realised. Based on reports, it appears likely they wanted Luc taken alive, and the animal was capable of targeted hunting. Althorne, you have the floor."

HELENA PUT OFF THE MEETING with Crowther for as long as she could, but eventually she ran out of excuses. In retrospect, her decision to restore the nerves in his arm had been impulsive. It hadn't been an emergency; she could have waited for him to regain consciousness and asked if he wanted it done.

It had been a reactive choice. She'd seen the danger Luc represented to everyone and acted based solely on that. Now she regretted it. Crowther was more likely to use two hands for torture than to ever use them to protect Luc from himself again.

Crowther was putting away a chess set as Helena entered, using his right hand to slowly grasp each piece and place it in a box.

"Marino."

Helena just stood there, not sure what to expect. Crowther paused in his work, staring at his hand, opening and closing it slowly. It was barely more than skin and bone.

"I understand that I have you to thank for this."

She wasn't sure if he meant it sarcastically or not.

"I should have asked," she said. "I just—after Luc, I was worried about what would have happened if you hadn't been there."

She couldn't read his expression, but he nodded slowly.

"You have an interesting intuition. I may have underestimated it," he finally said. "I can't say I've ever thought much of vivimancy. However—you do the Eternal Flame credit."

WINTER BORE DOWN ON PALADIA. Icy mountain wind whipped across the river basin, leaving the buildings and windows brilliant with frost. With nothing left to forage, Helena had long hours to work in the lab.

Shiseo had done what no one else could and identified the remaining compounds of the alloy which had been injected into Vanya Gettlich all those months ago.

The final compound in question had evaded analysis.

Shiseo and Helena had worked manually using old chymistry techniques to determine, as the other metallurgists had, that it was not a natural compound but a synthetic fusion of lumithium and something that Helena had never encountered.

When Shiseo checked his work several times, his hands trembled.

"I don't know how they have this," he finally said. "This should not be here."

"What is it?"

He was silent for a long time.

"In the East, there is a rare metal found deep in the mountains. It is—rarer than gold. Only the Emperor himself is permitted to possess it. We called it mo'lian'shi. It—creates inertia."

Helena had never heard of such a thing. There were metals and substances which were inert in their natural, raw state, and there was lumithium and its emanations which could reverse inertia to create resonance. Iron was often inert, but once it was processed into steel, even without emanations, it developed a low resonance.

The Irreversibility of Resonance had been established by Cetus about the nature of alchemy. One of his few principles to stand the test of time and scientific interrogation.

Nothing could be *made* inert.

"I've never heard of that," Helena said.

He shook his head, his eyebrows drawn together.

"You wouldn't have. It is a part of the Emperor's power. As lumithium can create resonance, mo'lian'shi takes it back. What this is—" He looked down and seemed deeply troubled. "This is mo'lian'shi fused with lumithium. The simultaneous effect of both together creates a resonance haze."

He looked at his notes again. "It is unstable. The fusion is deteriorating, but they may perfect their methods in the future. This was probably only a first attempt. But . . ." His voice trailed off. "I don't know how they have this."

He fell silent and did not elaborate for a long time, but finally said, "When the new Emperor came to power, there were questions, mysteries about how he found the wealth to pay his armies."

Since working with Shiseo, Helena had heard a few rumours about what had brought him to Paladia. That he'd been a eunuch who'd served the previous Emperor, or the illegitimate child of someone in the court.

Helena stared at Shiseo, wondering just who he was. Exceptionally educated was one thing, but knowledgeable about a secret imperial metal was another.

"Perhaps the Undying bought it from the black market," she said, but she was already thinking about how Crowther and Ilva would interpret this. If Morrough had an alliance with Hevgoss and secret trade connections with the Eastern Empire, the threat that loomed over Paladia had just grown by magnitudes.

If the new Emperor had obtained his throne selling something of imperial value, that was a violation of his own trade laws.

Shiseo shook his head. "You don't understand how carefully mo'lian'shi is protected. It is a rare and delicate thing. Once mined, it must be carefully processed to bring out the effects. It is often immediately alloyed to prevent it from degrading. But this—" He touched the vial lightly. "—this was made from pure mo'lian'shi. Only someone of royal birth, with an Emperor's seal, could access it."

"And *you* know of it," she said slowly.

Shiseo met her eyes briefly before they slid away. "And I know of it."

Now Helena was silent.

"Did you suspect this?" she finally asked. "Is that why you asked for a chance to analyse it?"

He looked absently around the lab. "When I heard of the struggle the metallurgists had, I thought it was a new variety. But this, I am sure, is the Emperor's. They would not have an identical refining technique."

Helena felt as though she stood upon a political landmine. In their hands was proof of a deal not merely between Morrough and another country, but of a treachery between a ruler and his own empire. The information was dangerous and raised more questions than it answered. If the Emperor was in debt, how would Morrough have gotten the money to involve himself?

Shiseo was probably the only person who could have discovered it. When the deal was made, it had most likely been done under the assumption that no one could ever connect it to the East.

"Officially, we can call it a synthetic fused metal, using lumithium and an unknown compound," she said slowly, trying to gauge his reaction. "In the future, if it seems necessary to reveal the Empire's potential involvement, perhaps we can—discover it, then."

Shiseo nodded slowly.

"We will have to tell Ilva and Crowther at least. They'll need to know about this."

"KAINE," HELENA SAID QUIETLY. SHE was seated on the floor, trying to relieve the raw sensation in her resonance. "Do you think the Eternal Flame can win the war?"

He was leaning against the wall. "Does it matter what I think?"

"I live among idealists, but all I see are bodies. I'd like the opinion of someone who doesn't believe that optimism somehow improves the odds."

He glanced at her. "Does the Eternal Flame have a strategy to win?"

She looked down. As far as she knew, the plan was to reclaim lost territory, drive the Undying back, and burn as many of the dead as possible. The same method that the Eternal Flame had followed in all the Necromancy Wars in the past.

She gave an awkward half nod.

"The High Necromancer will do whatever it takes to win. The method doesn't matter. He wants Paladia, ideally with the city intact, but if he can't get it, he'll raze it instead. You're fighting someone whose only objection to genocide is the waste of potential resources. Even a genocide is acceptable if it leaves him with the materials for more necrothralls. And you're trying to win by—what? Waiting for Sol's intervention? Is there *any* plan that doesn't hinge on the inherent superiority of goodness?"

Not that she was aware of.

"Why aid us, then?" she asked. "If you don't think we can win."

His expression grew mocking. "Don't you think you're worth it?"

"Oh yes, your rose in a graveyard," she said, lip curling. "Was the array for me, too?"

"Who else?" he asked, his voice empty, just a touch of irony in it.

"Aurelia, perhaps."

He smiled. "Right. Quite forgot about her."

"Why are you helping us, Kaine?"

He looked over at her. His features had grown markedly different in recent months. He'd lost all trace of juvenile ungainliness; there was a hardness to his features now that felt more accurate to who he was. His hair more silver every time she saw him. There was no hazel left in his eyes.

He looked a world apart from the dark-haired, insolent boy he'd been when she'd first come to the Outpost. There was an unearthliness to him now.

Touch him and she'd bleed, and yet she could not escape the allure of it.

Their eyes met, and a wave of bitterness swept across his face.

"It doesn't matter," he said, looking away.

She opened her mouth to argue, but anything she said would be a lie. Whatever his motive was, he didn't trust the Eternal Flame not to use it against him. They both knew Crowther would.

"I suppose not," she said, pulling on the thick green pullover to keep out the cold. When she reached the door, she looked back.

Kaine's gaze flicked away as she turned, as if he hadn't been watching her go.

There was something haunted about him.

"Don't die, Kaine," she said. The line he walked frightened her. If the array was the punishment for a failure, what would the price of betrayal be?

A smirk twisted his mouth as he looked at her. "There are far worse fates than dying, Marino."

She nodded. "I know. But that one you don't come back from."

He gave a bitter laugh. "All right, then, but only because you asked."

CHAPTER 44

Decembris 1786

THE WAR FROZE ALONG WITH PALADIA. THE tension between the two sides endlessly strung out. A fragile balance that might be lost at any moment. Every battle was sudden, without warning and with terrible casualties.

The tension between Helena and Kaine felt similar.

There was a new sharpness to him that had not been there before, as though he were being ground down like the edge of a blade on a whetstone.

He'd show up sometimes badly injured, healing very slowly, and snap savagely at her when she offered to help him.

Normally he'd recover by the time she left, but she wasn't sure how he was being hurt at all. As if this was the consequence of her request that he not die, she was instead forced to witness the misery of his inability to. She worried there was a defect in the array.

One minute he was lounging in a chair, watching her train; the next his eyes rolled back in his head and he toppled onto the floor.

There was a bloodstain under him when she got him on his back. His clothes were soaked with it.

Beneath his uniform, he was heavily bandaged, but his blood wasn't clotting, and the wound wasn't healing. When Helena tried to find it, her resonance seemed to fail.

She peeled the bandages off in terror and found a stab wound.

The injury had missed his organs, but whatever had been used had broken off, and there were pieces of it left inside him.

It wasn't a lot of metal, but he wasn't healing.

Maier usually handled shrapnel injuries; their treatment wasn't suited for vivimancy.

Helena's resonance faded, distorting when she tried to appraise the injury and gauge how much metal was inside the wound.

She didn't have tools for surgery. She washed her hands and stuck a finger into the wound, catching a piece and pulling it out.

Holding it, she could feel it as a physical, tangible object, but when she channelled her resonance towards it, it felt drawn in towards the metal but then—static. Her sense of resonance told her there wasn't anything there. It began crumbling in her fingers, as though rusting, little bits and grit, corroding in Kaine's blood.

This was the alloy. The lumithium and mo'lian'shi. Kaine had been stabbed with it, and it had been left inside his body.

"You idiot," she said to Kaine, even though she knew he was insensate.

She put the shard on a piece of gauze, wiping her fingers. If it distributed through his blood, she wasn't sure what would happen.

His body was stubborn when it came to its immutability, but based on the way the alloying was interfering with regeneration, the Undying's progress in blocking resonance seemed much closer to success than the Eternal Flame had expected.

She ran her hands across Kaine's skin, trying to get as clear a sense as she could of the internal wound, her resonance flickering in and out as if it was riddled with holes.

She retrieved her satchel; she'd put together a full kit of medicines and materials for healing him on the off chance he ever allowed it. She spread a salve around the wound to slow the blood loss as she tried to figure out what to do. If she had the stimulant injection she'd been working on, it might help, but she was still working out the right balance of epinephrine.

If she couldn't use resonance to remove the shards, she'd have to do it with old-fashioned surgery.

Alchemical surgery was much less invasive. Most of the hospitals in the North exclusively employed alchemists, while manual surgery was viewed as archaic and brutal with its large incisions and scars.

She took her alchemy knife and muttered an apology to it as she broke the components apart. A transmutational weapon was complicated to reassemble. It would be near impossible once she was done with it.

She tried not to think about the potential consequences of destroying an issued weapon as she manipulated the metal into a long set of basic manual clamps, using part of the blade to make herself a scalpel. She hoped the clamps would be enough.

She washed, heated, and cooled the metal, trying to get the pieces sterile.

Growing up, she had watched her father perform surgery. After her mother died, she'd preferred it to being alone.

She used her resonance in reverse, identifying the location of the shrapnel bits by the negative space they created. The pieces were delicate, and they crumbled easily. She had to work slowly. She pulled them out, depositing each one on a cloth.

Once she'd removed most of them, Kaine's body seemed to remember how to heal itself, and the wound began to close while there were still pieces inside. She had to use the scalpel, making the incision over and over until she had all the pieces out and had irrigated the wound as best she could. She checked using her resonance several times to ensure that there was nothing left. There was still a slight hum of interference but nothing large; hopefully, his body could handle it.

She washed her hands and stashed half of the shrapnel pieces in a bottle, which she hid in the depths of her satchel, and then placed the rest in another more obvious bottle, in case Kaine demanded she give them back.

The wound left a scar that didn't fully fade away. Looking him over, it wasn't the only one.

She placed her hand in the centre of his chest, letting her resonance seep through. He was still weak with blood loss; the residual metal was impacting his blood regeneration. She propped his head on her lap and very cautiously poured an elixir down his throat, using her resonance to ensure it ended up in his stomach and not his lungs. Even unconscious, his expression was tense, as if braced for a blow.

She brushed his hair back from his forehead, trying to smooth the tense furrow between his eyebrows, and just sat with him for a while. When he felt closer to normal, she leaned forward, her fingers touching the back of his head to help him wake.

His eyes shot open.

Faster than she could move, his hand was around her throat, jerking her down as he jolted upright, his expression panicked fury.

He recognised her, catching her an instant before the back of her head slammed into the ground. Her neck snapped back, and her vision went white, pain shooting through her skull.

"What?" He still sounded dazed.

She felt his hands along her neck, resonance along her spine, as her vision swam back into focus. He was kneeling over her, the back of her neck cradled in his hands. Her heart was in her throat, pounding with such shock she could barely breathe.

Kaine was also breathing hard. "What the fuck, Marino?"

"You—passed out," she managed to say.

He looked at himself, only then realising he wasn't wearing a shirt and that the wound was gone. She thought he'd relax once he understood, but he looked angrier.

"I nearly killed you."

"You were hurt," she said, releasing a shaky breath. "Badly. Even by your standards." She sat up and winced, touching the side of her neck gingerly. "As previously established, it's my job to keep the Eternal Flame's assets alive. You're one of them."

"I wasn't going to die," he said scathingly, but he leaned towards her.

She almost drew back, but he reached out tentatively and she made herself hold still.

He pulled her hand away from her neck, his eyes fastened on her throat, his fingers moving slowly down the length of it. She felt his resonance under her skin, warm along her spine. Another crack in his façade of indifference.

"Were you not supposed to be healed?" she asked, suppressing a shiver as his finger brushed along her neck. "I can—cut you open and put it all back in if you want."

His fingers stilled, and he glared at her. "I'm not your patient."

He might have been intimidating if he wasn't sitting on the floor, both hands cradling her neck, tilting her head slowly from side to side. He'd clearly come around to taking spinal injuries very seriously.

Her heart was beating even harder now, remembering his fingers in her hair, pulling her towards him. When she was alone, she often went back to that memory, wondering what could have happened.

She drew a shivering breath and reached up, her fingers wrapping around his wrist. "I can't let you die."

He stilled. She felt his pulse against her fingers. She watched his eyes darken, the slow shift of black expanding as the heat of his hands bled into her skin.

He shook his head. "They don't let me die."

She squeezed his wrist tighter. "Are they—is Bennet still experimenting on you? I thought if you survived the array, then he couldn't—"

He pulled his hand free. "I have this habit of surviving against all odds. Deserves to be studied, apparently."

Without thinking, she reached out, touching his cheek. "I'm so sorry, Kaine."

He looked startled, and it made his expression turn so young and scared, as if a part of him was still that sixteen-year-old. Then he went rigid, wrenching himself away from her touch, and when he looked at her again, he'd turned vicious. He shook his head as if in disbelief.

"You are unbelievable," he said. "Truly."

She didn't know what he meant.

He shook his head. "When you first showed up here, I didn't think you'd have it in you, but you are truly something else."

Her gut twisted into a hard knot. "What do you mean?"

"You will do anything for that family, won't you? But someday, Holdfast will realise you don't belong in his kingdom of gold and purity. I wonder what he'll do with you then."

She knew he was trying to hurt her, but it was something she had thought about so much, the sting of it had worn away.

"He won't have to do anything; you took care of that for him." She gave a tight-lipped smile. "But even if you hadn't, I knew I'd be expendable from the moment I became a healer."

She thought that would silence him, but he laughed.

"You think it started then? You've always been expendable. Do you really think this war is about necromancy? That any of the wars have ever actually been about necromancy?"

She shook her head warily. "No. It's always about power. And what people will do without caring about the cost."

He tilted his head, studying her. "Have you never wondered why it was so easy for the High Necromancer to recruit the guild families? After all, plenty of them were devout, or owed their fortunes to the Institute."

She shrugged. "Because you're jealous and petty and wanted more than the plenty you already had."

He raised an eyebrow as he pulled his blood-drenched clothes back on. "Well, I suppose that was a part of it, but no, what Morrough did was widen a crack that the Holdfasts have been growing for centuries. Since the moment they founded this city, they set themselves up as kings while claiming not to be. They weren't the lowly sort who'd 'pursue' power; no, they were divinely destined for it. Called, you might say."

"That's because they didn't want to rule," she said fiercely. "Luc certainly never did, and Apollo always cared most for the Institute. He hated politics."

Kaine's mouth twisted. "Yes. Funny how often people in power hate politics, as if what they really want is to do as they please and be praised for it, and if they aren't, then it's all beneath them. Considering how much they despised it, they certainly were unwilling to part with it. Only handed the minutiae of governance over to those of faith, let the Falcons and Kestrels and Shrikes manage all that tedium. The Institute was founded on the idea of pursuing the heights of alchemy, but that began to crumble the moment the science began contradicting the Faith. You should have seen the crisis when new metals were first discovered. The Faith spent years insisting there could be only eight, calling them compounds or alloys, and refusing to formally acknowledge those guilds because religiously, celestially, the number was limited to eight. So much for all those ideals of uniting the world through the study of alchemy."

He eyed Helena. "Of course, they couldn't go back on all those promises completely, Orion's legacy had to endure, so they'd import someone from time to time. Some prodigy from a distant land that they could show off as proof of their magnanimity, to serve their ends while beholden to the Principate."

Fury rose in Helena like a volcano. "That's not what they did!"

He flicked his eyes over her derisively. "You were a desperate scholarship student who nearly cried every year when your exam scores were listed because it bought you one more year of education, and your father lived near the water slums because he couldn't get a job."

"Yes, but if they'd been any more generous, you guilds would have thrown fits about it."

"Why would that have mattered? We already hated you. It would have cost the Holdfasts a pittance to find your father some menial job, but if you'd ever been able to stop struggling, you might have realised what a web they had you trapped in. I hear Ilva Holdfast was particularly talented at that kind of thing. Always knew just how much pressure a person could take."

A sick feeling swept through her, but she shook her head.

"So all you guild students were just—what? Playing along?" she said scathingly.

He laughed. "No. We did hate you. Consider it from our perspective: You were the line the Holdfasts drew between the Eternal Flame and all the rest of us. Some little nobody plucked from obscurity and given the attention and praise that none of the guilds could ever earn. We built ourselves from the dirt and emptied our pocketbooks annually buying certification and lumithium from a family that could make wealth from nothing, and we were expected to be grateful to do so. When we looked up at what we wanted, *you* were the first thing in the way."

A chill ran down her spine.

Kaine looked across the room. "When Morrough came here, he didn't even have to offer immortality or riches. He just offered to remove those who would never let us rise further. With the Holdfasts gone, the Faith's grip on Paladia was supposed to crumble. An easy takeover. The city should have barely been affected. Even the Institute was intended to be left intact."

"But then your father was arrested."

He nodded, his eyes flat. "But then my father was arrested, and it was all a lie anyway, but by the time those who'd object realised that, it was too late for them."

"There were Undying who objected?" Her pulse sped up, thinking about potential sympathisers. This was critical information. This could change everything.

He nodded idly.

"Who?" She leaned in. "Who objected?"

"You really want to know?"

She nodded, fervently.

He reached out, fingers wrapping around her throat, and pulled her close. "Basilius Blackthorne. Recognise that name?"

Her blood ran cold. Yes, she knew it.

"Blackthorne was—?"

"Quite the monster now, isn't he? I told you about the phylacteries, remember?" His fingers around her throat tightened. She gave a small nod, heart rising.

"After I killed Principate Apollo, Basilius said he'd never agreed to such methods and bloodshed. Morrough—he still went by Morrough back then—pretended to give this some consideration. He called a meeting of us all. We hadn't known our numbers until that night. Morrough said he wanted us all there, to see him change Basilius's mind. He brought out Basilius's phylactery in a box and reminded us that we had all entrusted ourselves to him, and then he began carving into it using a talon ring. Basilius began to scream and tear at his own body, until there were pieces of him all over the floor, but it never stopped, he just kept regenerating. Over and over until the floor was covered. When Morrough was finally done, I'm told Basilius went home and ate his wife alive in their marriage bed. I believe he had children, too. All gone."

Kaine described it without emotion, his fingers still wrapped around her throat.

"We are all expendable to Morrough. So you see, I am intimately acquainted with the illusion of choice." He smiled, slow and cruel. "That's why I recognise it."

She shook her head, and he gripped her tighter, until she could feel her pulse against his palm. Her heart was pounding in her chest. He leaned in, looming over her, and she could tell he wanted her to be afraid of him. But she wasn't. Not anymore.

"Luc isn't like that," she said. "The reason I remain loyal to him is because I know he'd do the same for me."

His eyes turned black. "Really?"

His thumb had found the curve of her jaw. There was faint colour in the pale hollows of his cheeks. His eyes darted down to her lips, and she felt the draw between them. A feeling like a string instrument, stretched taut and ready to vibrate.

He drew her closer until their faces were nearly touching, and everything around them seemed to fade away. She watched his lips part, hesitating, so close she could taste his breath. He inhaled.

"And what would your dear Luc say if he learned how you let his father's killer buy you like a whore?" As he spoke, his free hand found her waist and he pulled her close, hand sliding up her body, groping her as if he were about to push her down and ravish her there on the bare floor.

But his eyes were cold.

There was no desire. It was a pantomime of their kiss, now performed with rough indifference, as he reminded her of who it was she'd willingly given herself to.

She jerked away, skittering across the floor until she was out of reach.

He just laughed.

Her cheekbones ached, body going hot and cold as she curled inward, trying to compose herself. As if there was any point. What a grotesque and pathetic creature she was.

Property. No, not even that.

She was a trinket. Something he'd thrown into his demands. So insignificant that Ilva and Crowther had looked at her and seen no reason to refuse.

He could talk all he wanted about how her education was to leverage her, how the Holdfasts were to blame. But he was the one who'd turned her into a whore.

Sometimes she wished she'd died in the hospital with her father, to be remembered and mourned for her possibilities, rather than live day by day growing ever lesser. Now it didn't matter if she'd been an alchemist, or a healer, or anything else. To anyone who ever learned of it, she would only be that one thing. Women were always defined by the lowliest thing they could be called.

But worse still was knowing all that and still craving those rare moments in which he was gentle. Because that was all she had left.

"I have to go," she finally forced out. "Do you have—do you have any information this week?"

It was almost ironic to ask that question right then.

He reached into his discarded coat, pulling out an envelope, its edges bloodstained.

He tossed it, letting it land on the floor between them.

Helena was outwardly calm when she returned to Headquarters, but her hands were shaking as she presented the shards to Crowther and received instructions to have Shiseo analyse them. She took them to the lab and went down to the hospital for her shift.

She wished it wasn't such a quiet day. She couldn't stop thinking.

She returned to the empty lab after curfew and sat, left alone with herself.

It was nearly the winter solstice. The North had many feasting traditions from back when they'd slaughter the animals they couldn't feed through the winter before the new year set in, sharing supplies so that everyone would survive until spring.

In modern times, supplies had been replaced with gifts: books, crafts, puzzles, things to while away the dark hours of the long Northern winters.

Helena had never been very good at gifts.

Her singular success had been a map she'd given Luc, upon which she'd marked a route to all the places they'd travel someday.

She hadn't given anything last year, but this year she'd thought of making medicine kits, with some basics that were good to have on hand in case the field medics weren't nearby. But Ilva had made no mention this year of her seeing Luc or anyone else for solstice, so she'd discarded the idea.

After a few minutes, she went over and opened a cabinet, pulling out vials from various shelves, laying them out on a strip of waxed canvas, making marks on the fabric as she arranged everything to fit, blinking hard every few minutes.

She had a job. She had to do it.

THE ICY, MISTING RAIN MADE it hard to see when Helena crossed the bridge the next week. She gripped her foraging knife close as she walked through the Outpost. It couldn't be transmuted without losing its edge, but it was still serviceable.

It was going to be a while before she had an alchemy knife again.

A person couldn't lose an alchemical weapon and expect to get a new one without an explanation. If Helena said she lost it, she'd be subject to discipline and, as a noncombatant, be placed at the bottom of the wait list. If she attributed the loss to an attack, she would have to specify which attack.

Until Ilva or Crowther could find an unaccounted-for alchemy knife, Helena would have to make do.

The tenement was so cold that day, her breath condensed into a wisping cloud in the room. Kaine entered a minute later, shoving a hood back from his face. She looked away but couldn't help but notice his black uniform was drenched.

"Where is your knife?"

Her heart sank. She'd hoped he wouldn't notice immediately.

"Oh." Her voice lifted in an awkward attempt at casualness. "Well—" She swallowed. "I lost it."

"You—lost it?" He said it slowly, and she could hear the implied use of the word *idiot* punctuating each word. "When?"

She was still staring at the floor, watching his feet. He moved lightly, almost like a cat, making very little noise.

"Last week."

His feet stilled. "You were attacked?"

He came towards her very quickly, and his eyes had that intense gleam to them, looking her up and down.

She shook her head. "No, I broke it. I needed tools for surgery when you wouldn't wake up. So I made them."

She risked glancing up then to gauge his expression, and rather enjoyed the stupefied look on his face.

"I'll get a new one," she added hurriedly. "There's just some—logistical delays. Anyway, I brought you a present," she said, forcing her voice to be bright.

She rummaged through her satchel, finding the wax-cloth case, and hurriedly held it out.

"It's—it's an, um—it's an emergency healing kit," she said, trying to explain herself quickly before he could refuse it. "I made it with things that will work with your regeneration."

This seemed to catch him fully off guard. He stopped short and took it, then—realising that she was waiting expectantly—he sighed and flipped it open. "You realise I can *buy* medicine, and I don't particularly need it."

"Not these. I developed them. They're designed to work with vivimancy—or regeneration in your case."

She took a hesitant step closer, pointing at the various vials.

"They're all labelled, and I added notes about exactly how to use them on the waxed paper here. These are made to support transmutational healing. Traditional medicine can interfere, so I've been developing things that complement a regenerative healing process."

She pointed to the nearest vial. "This is yarrow powder infused with copper, to slow bleeding. You pack it around the wound before bandaging. I know you're used to just letting yourself regenerate, but slowing blood loss is still a good idea. This"—she tapped a blue-green bottle—"will support blood regeneration; it has a high concentration of the components your body needs, so you're not giving yourself a deficit of crucial minerals and other things your body requires to function. This is the salve I developed for your back, for topical pain. If you have a wound that doesn't heal, you can at least numb the area until—"

"Until what?" He looked sharply at her then.

She knew he expected her to say something like, *Until you can come to me, and I'll tenderly nurse you to health.*

"That's the other part of your present," she said, meeting his eyes. "I thought I could show you some healing techniques, so you can do them yourself. I know most of the time you don't need it, but if you're strategic and direct the way your body regenerates, you'll recover faster."

She reached towards him slowly. "May I?"

He gave the barest nod.

She took his hand and set it on her own arm, then rested her fingers over his. She ran her resonance through his fingers, into her own body, the sensation creating an almost ghostly feeling under her skin.

"Of course, my body isn't the same as yours, but—most of the anatomy is, and you do regenerate according to the same basic rules." She spoke in the efficient way that she'd taught the trainees. She was grateful now for the practice. "You've mentioned that regeneration starts with the most vital parts of the body: brain, organs, limbs. When you lost your arm, the reason it didn't regenerate was because you'd been bleeding too long, and you'd already had to heal from extensive burns. Just because you have the vitality to regenerate doesn't mean that you necessarily have the physical resources for it. Those have to come from somewhere. If you're badly injured, you might not have a resonance stable enough to heal yourself, but you can guide it, and the kit can provide support."

She ploughed through as much information as she could. Showing him all the different systems in the body, how they interacted, how a disruption in one place could have effects elsewhere.

She kept rattling off tips for as long as she could, working through all the major systems as quickly as possible.

"Eyes are awful. I mean, hopefully if you ever lost one, it would just grow back, but if not . . ." She exhaled. "The tissue doesn't matrice the same way. It's very tedious work, and nerve-racking. You should—probably come to me for that. Well, I mean—"

She stammered.

"The High Necromancer doesn't have eyes," he said.

She stopped short and looked up. "What?"

She'd never seen Morrough, but she'd heard that during his rare appearances, he wore a golden mask—a large crescent that obscured most of his face and fanned out like horns on each side of his head. An eclipsing sun.

"It's rather gory to look at, but he doesn't seem to mind." He pulled his hand free, clearly done with the lecturing. "It's like someone burned them out. He uses his resonance to see."

"I didn't know that was possible." She rubbed her hands on her skirt. "Well, that's the basics. If there's anything you'd want added to the kit, or ideas you have, I can try to make them."

"The basics?" He pulled a watch out of his pocket. "You've been talking for over an hour."

She fumbled for her own watch, certain he was mistaken. No, he wasn't. She was going to be late for her shift if she didn't leave.

"I mean . . . it was still only the basics," she said defensively, but she added, "I should go. Happy solstice. I hope your days grow brighter."

He did not return the season's greeting but then spoke as she reached the door.

"Marino."

She tensed, looking back. He was still standing where she'd left him, irritation evident in the sweep of his eyes. He looked her up and down as if debating something.

"I have—something for you," he finally said, as if having a tooth extracted. He pulled out something rolled up in an oilcloth and held it towards her.

Inside lay a set of beautiful daggers, sheathed in mesh holsters. Helena felt her resonance respond before she even touched them.

"The longer one goes on your back, the smaller one on your forearm," Kaine said when she was silent. "They're sized for you. Titanium and nickel is a mnemonic alloy, which will allow you to transmute them further than most weapons; they'll still return to form. It has three memory shapes depending on the resonance phase you use, and you can alter them if you wish. That's why the sheaths are malleable."

She picked up the larger dagger.

After the months of training with a steel weapon, the dagger hardly weighed anything. She slipped it from the sheath, and it sang in her fingers. She barely had to focus her resonance before it morphed, maintaining its razor edge but changing shape and length entirely, unfurling like a ribbon into a long, flexible whiplike blade. She altered the timbre of her resonance just slightly, and without her even needing to guide the metal, the blade morphed back into a perfect dagger.

She let out an unsteady breath, hardly able to believe that anything could be so easy to transmute. It was as effortless as moving her own fingers, and it weighed nothing.

She couldn't stop turning them over, taking in every detail, the weight and texture, the incredible sharpness of the blades. There were elegant curving details like vines on the hilts that made the grip more secure.

She didn't know what to say. *Thank you* felt entirely insufficient.

Kaine was watching her, his eyes intent, but the expression vanished the instant she looked up. His eyebrows drew down. "You are not ever allowed to take these apart or turn them into medical instruments. Not for anyone."

She flushed. "I thought you said the shapes were programmable."

"Not enough to be entirely deconstructed. Are we clear, Marino?" His voice was icy.

"All right. I promise," she said, rolling her eyes. Trust Kaine to ruin any moment.

After a pause she looked at him again. "Thank you. I don't even know what to say. They're beautiful."

He avoided meeting her eyes. "It's nothing." He cleared his throat. "I'm glad you like them, though, because I expect you to wear both every time you set foot outside of Headquarters. Actually—you should always be wearing them. They shouldn't come off unless you're asleep. These do not belong in the bottom of your satchel. When you arrive here, I will expect to see them already on you, every time. Are we clear?"

"Yes, I'll wear them," she said as if it were a concession. She didn't ever want to put them down.

"Good." He shifted. "Well, this has been delightful. I can't even remember how many times I've wished someone would lecture me on the systems of the human body."

She looked up, and he smiled insincerely at her.

He started turning to leave and then paused. "Now that you have a decent weapon, I think we'll move on to training that's a bit more intense. Be ready for that next week." He held out an envelope. "My latest instalment."

As she reached to take it, he held on until she met his eyes.

"I must say, Marino, you've ended up being quite expensive."

CHAPTER 45

Decembris 1786

Crowther was still absent from Headquarters, so Helena had no choice but to take her report to Ilva.

As she ascended the floors to Ilva's office in the main building, she kept thinking about all the things Ilva knew about her. She'd been on the board that had approved Helena's scholarship each year, and likely the admissions board, too.

The particular interest Ilva had personally taken in her since her father's death felt much less warming now.

Ilva was staring down at a report, a pen dangling from one hand as she read, and didn't look up when the guard let Helena in.

"Marino," she said, her voice cool. "Sit. I'll be with you in a moment."

Helena waited, fingers flexing.

"How is your work on the nullium with Shiseo progressing?" Ilva asked, flipping the file closed and looking up.

The Council had named the lumithium-mo'lian'shi alloy *nullium* for the sake of convenience. While the knowledge of the alloy was not widespread, several metallurgists and chymists were all experimenting with it.

The question caught Helena off guard; she'd expected enquiries about Kaine.

"Good. We've finished synthesising the chelating agent using the samples I took from Ferron. If any of our combatants are injured by it, hopefully it will be able to capture and remove the traces of metal in the blood."

The shrapnel samples Helena had retrieved could not make a sturdy weapon, but the alloy wasn't supposed to. The fusion was intentionally unstable; it shattered on impact and the shards tended to deteriorate quickly when exposed to blood, dissolving like a poison blade targeting resonance. Helena and Shiseo had been instructed to pursue potential treatment methods.

Because metal toxicity could happen frequently in certain fields of alchemy, chelators were already commonplace.

Ilva nodded. "What does Shiseo think?"

"He doesn't think that true alchemy suppression is possible with the method they're using. While it does prevent healing and alchemical surgery, it's of limited use for combat, but that could change if they re-configure the ratio and composition."

Ilva's eyes narrowed. "Is there an alternative method that you and Shiseo have in mind?"

Helena swallowed, trying not to squirm. "We have an idea, but it's purely theoretical. We don't have enough nullium to test it."

"And it is . . ."

Helena's stomach knotted. She hated these kinds of conversations.

"Given the alloy's behaviour and how resonance is used, making it into a weapon or injecting nullium into the blood is less effective than simply targeting the limbs with it. If that kind of interference was focused near the hands, it would be almost impossible for an alchemist to accurately sense their resonance. Shiseo thinks that if the alloy was paired with something that has a high, sharp resonance point—like copper processed with a high level of lumithium emanations—that could create a type of interference that would suppress most kinds of resonance regardless of the alchemist's repertoire."

"How would we counter that?" Ilva leaned forward with interest.

"Well, any good metallurgist could, if they were comfortable working without resonance. But that's not something most Paladian metallurgists have ever had to worry about."

"Fortunate, then, that you fished those shards out of Ferron," Ilva said, although the sentiment was hardly reflected by her tone.

Helena gave a tight nod. "Here's his report," she said, pushing the envelope across the table.

Ilva plucked it up and dropped it into a drawer.

"And I—" Helena hesitated, heat rising to her hairline and the tips of her ears. "He gave me a set of daggers as a solstice gift, using the titanium-nickel alloy."

She pulled out the oilcloth and opened it on the desk for Ilva's inspection. Ilva raised an eyebrow, glancing for a moment before flicking the cloth to cover them as if she found the mere sight distasteful.

Helena's stomach dropped and she wrapped them up quickly, wishing she hadn't shown them without being asked. "It's a good sign, isn't it?"

Ilva tilted her head, studying Helena for a moment. "Ferron's climbing rank," she said as she reached into a drawer and pulled out a file, dropping it onto the desk. "Did you know?"

Helena's heart stalled. She had noticed his uniform was darker.

"It seems he's already surpassed everything he'd ever achieved prior to that injury of his. He controls several extremely valuable districts. Recently he's taken over the factory Outpost where you've been visiting him, consolidating power at a remarkable speed. It seems all our recent successes have benefitted him greatly."

Ilva tapped a fingernail on the desk, looking up at Helena with a cold smile.

"I didn't know," Helena said.

Ilva shook her head. "No, I didn't imagine so. I'm beginning to worry whether you remember what he is."

Helena's breath caught, but Ilva continued, flipping through page after page in the file before her.

"There have been rumours for months that Morrough has a new weapon. We thought it was a chimaera, like the one that nearly killed

Lila, or the nullium, but no. It's neither of those things, is it?" Ilva folded her hands, looking squarely at Helena. "How is it that he's still alive?"

"Crowther told me to do what I could."

Ilva's eyes flicked down from Helena's face to her neck, where the chain of her necklace was barely visible beneath her collar. Helena went very still.

"You know, Ferron's not our only spy," Ilva said. "We have a number of informants. Based on their reports, following the recovery of the ports, he was punished. Extensively. He was dying. I was *assured* of that."

"You knew?" Helena asked, her voice shaking. "You knew what they did to him, and you—you didn't tell me?"

Ilva stared piercingly at her. "Why would we have told you?"

Helena could hardly speak. "Is that why the attack was so elaborate and used so much of the intelligence? Because you expected he'd be killed for it. Because you *wanted* him killed for it."

Ilva said nothing, but now Kaine's resentment and disbelief when Helena kept coming back began to make sense.

"Why didn't you tell me?" Helena's voice trembled with rage.

Ilva's lips pursed, her eyes flicking across Helena's face. "You've always been—remarkably forthright." A smile stretched across her lips. "That's why Luc trusts you so much. If we'd told you the plan, do you really think you could have gone, knowing, without giving any sign to Ferron?"

Helena began to tremble. She gripped the arms of her chair as the room blurred.

"We assumed you'd realise it," Ilva added. "When it became clear that you hadn't—that you felt some sort of obligation to him—we agreed to let you try to heal him in the hope that once you realised the futility of it, you'd be able to bring his talisman back."

Ilva cleared her throat. "So you can imagine our surprise that he has not only survived but become more dangerous than ever before, that treacherous spy of ours. How did you do it?"

Helena swallowed hard. "We were losing, and it was only because of him that we could retake the ports. He did that for us. You didn't see him the day I went back. He knew he'd be punished; he expected to die." She gave a panicked breath. "If you wanted him dead, you should have told me. Crowther said to do what I could."

"What did you do?" Ilva had become impossibly more tense. "Did you—" Her lips thinned, her eyes flickering to the chain around Helena's neck once more. "Did you use something to manage it?"

Helena squeezed her hand into a fist. "I assumed that if you had to choose between the two of us, you'd want him."

Ilva's face went white.

"So I used the amulet you gave me, I thought it—"

"You gave the amulet to him?" The question was almost a shriek.

Helena had never heard Ilva raise her voice. "No, I—"

"Do you still have it or not?"

Helena's stomach twisted into a tight knot as she reached up, pulling the chain over her head. "I have the amulet, but the sunstone is gone."

Ilva snatched it from her so quickly, the chain ripped open Helena's kidskin glove. Ilva pressed her thumb against the centre where the stone was missing, staring in horror before looking at her. "What did you do?"

Helena swallowed nervously. "It broke and this—substance came out. Like quicksilver, and—it—it fused with Ferron."

There was a ghastly silence. Ilva looked so stunned she said nothing, just looked at the amulet again, as if the stone could magically rematerialise. Finally, Helena couldn't bear it anymore.

"If you didn't want him healed, you should have told me."

Ilva didn't reply, just stared at the amulet in her hand. "Do you know the story of the Stone of the Heavens?" she finally said, still running her thumb over the empty setting.

Dread swept through Helena like a tidal wave.

"No," she said, shaking her head. "It's a myth. Everyone knows that was a misinterpretation. Luc said it wasn't real."

"Every choice I have made was to protect Luc," Ilva said. She wasn't talking to Helena so much as speaking aloud or perhaps to the amulet in her hand. "I was never trained to be a steward, to bear the weight of this legacy. I was happy with my role, but Luc was too young for all this. I've tried to make the best choices I could."

Ilva looked up at Helena. "When your—vivimancy made its appearance, I thought I'd been given my way forward. That Sol had provided a fail-safe so that I could protect him. Of course there was still the politics of it to contend with. Matias did not make it easy. With all the concessions he demanded, I was concerned about the Toll taking you too prematurely. That amulet had been locked away for centuries, lying idle as generations of Holdfasts protected it. I'd hoped this war might rouse it to do something."

"What was it?" Helena asked.

Ilva stood, seizing her cane so tightly that her swollen knuckles showed white as she walked past Helena to the window, looking out towards the Alchemy Tower.

"My family built this Institute and this city to ensure that necromancy would never come to power again. They gave their lives to that cause and kept countless secrets to that end."

Ilva fell silent for a long time. Helena didn't dare speak.

"Have you heard the stories of Rivertide?"

Rivertide was the name of Paladia back before the first Necromancy War. It had been wiped out by a plague, and when the Necromancer found it, he'd used the corpses for his army.

"There was no plague," Ilva said, still not looking back. "Orion called it a plague because it was kinder than immortalising what truly happened to them all." She pressed her hand, still clutching the amulet, against her chest. "The Necromancer realised the alchemical potential of the area and came to Rivertide specifically because of the people living here."

"He killed them?" Helena couldn't understand the purpose of that secret. That the Necromancer massacred Rivertide was even more believable than a story of finding a convenient town of corpses.

Ilva shook her head. "No, they're still alive, to this day."

Helena stared at her, not understanding.

"The Necromancer was a vivimancer, just like you, but the ability was even more mythical back then. He came to Rivertide performing miracles. They thought he was a god. They built him a temple on the plateau, gave him everything he asked for, and he promised them immortality if they only had the faith for it. Then one day, he brought them all together in a great assembly, in a secret place he'd carved underground, and declared that if they trusted him fully, utterly, he could make them live forever. I'm not sure of the process, but afterwards, his temple was full of corpses, and their souls were bound together, synthesised into this—substance. He used it, the power, to reanimate them all."

Ilva began to pace, her steps jerky, her cane trembling in her hand; she was too agitated to be still. "When Orion fought the Necromancer, the souls were still conscious, aware of the betrayal exacted upon them—that the gift of 'immortality' came at the price of eternal enslavement. During the battle, the Necromancer's control slipped, and the Stone turned on him. There was a light as bright as the sun. It filled the valley, destroying the Necromancer and all the necrothralls in a wave of fire. When it was over, Orion and his followers were all that remained." Ilva shook her head. "If the truth of the Stone's nature were known, Orion feared that others might be inspired to rediscover the methods, and so, when those who'd witnessed the battle called the Stone a gift from Sol, Orion had no choice but to let them believe it."

Ilva paused, her expression mournful.

"It's all a lie?"

Ilva whirled on her, looking furious. "What else could he do?"

Helena stood up, ready to ignite. "Tell the truth! You don't get to make up history to suit your preferences. Do you realise what you've done? Luc thinks he's supposed to be earning a miracle. That the reason he hasn't already won this war is because he hasn't suffered or been enough like Orion to earn it, and that's his fault. But there will never be a miracle that will save us. You're torturing him to death on a lie."

"That's why I am *making* him miracles," Ilva snapped back. She looked equally incensed, as if Helena were the traitor. "You think I want him to suffer? I want to tell him, but when is there time for that?" She swept her arm out. "Apollo should have been the one to tell him—when he was old enough, and ready for it all. There's a process to it, but all that was destroyed when Ferron murdered Apollo and brought this war upon us. All I can do is try to make that faith real and keep him from losing hope."

The whole city, the Principate, the Faith, the history, every mural, every amulet. All lies.

"You have to tell Luc the truth. You can't keep doing this to him."

"And what do you think would happen if he knows that no help is coming? What will he have then?" Ilva glared at her. "That is too great a risk, but now thanks to you, I am left with nothing but terrible choices."

Helena set her jaw, too angry to accept the fault. "Why would you give me something like that without explaining what it was?"

Ilva's eyes flashed. "Because I was trying to save you, spare you. I thought maybe the damned thing could manage that much, and it seemed that it did. But when Ferron made his offer, Crowther said it was the only chance we had left. I considered taking it back that night. I could have, after what you'd said before the Council, but I remembered your face when I first put it on you. I thought you treasured it enough to have sense. You stupid, stupid girl." All the strength seemed to suddenly leave Ilva, and she nearly collapsed into a seat.

"You don't get to lie to me and then get angry when I make the mistake of believing you," Helena said. "If the Stone's that special, why not let Luc use it."

Ilva's expression twisted bitterly. "It doesn't serve the Holdfasts." She looked away from Helena, jaw set. "Even in Orion's own hands, it was hard and cold, never bestowing its power or favour upon anyone of the Holdfast line. There have been a few whom it would warm to, but it always went cold eventually. And you of all people had it. You could have done *anything,* and you healed Ferron with it."

"So sorry I wasn't the puppet you wanted," Helena said bitterly, standing. She felt as if the entire world had dropped out from beneath her feet; she had no idea how to navigate this newfound reality. After so much time being maligned for her lack of faith, it was all an invention. She wasn't sure what was real. Even being given to Kaine had been an elaborate con.

It had never been about securing Kaine's loyalty, but simply about giving the earnest appearance that she was trying to.

And Luc. Her heart ached. What would he do if he learned the truth?

Could she tell him this? After all she'd omitted over the years, was she going to come clean by destroying everything he believed in?

She couldn't. There was too much at stake, and Ilva knew that.

Helena paused as she reached the door. "In the future, perhaps tell me what you want instead of expecting me to fail where it's convenient to you. Maybe then we'll both end up less disappointed in each other."

"You want honesty?" Ilva's voice was viperous. "I want you to kill Kaine Ferron."

Helena froze, turning slowly back.

Ilva met her eyes. She was composed again, chilly as a lake. "He was always going to die, but I want you to do it. You created this new threat to Luc, so you will put an end to it."

"He hasn't done anything to betray us."

"He murdered my nephew." Ilva's voice cracked like a whip, and Helena saw the fury and hatred that the woman kept so carefully concealed. It rose like a beast from inside her. "You want to what? To wait and see who he'll kill next? Whose life are you prepared to gamble on that?"

Her chest clenched. "You can't ask me to betray—"

"Why not? What has he done for you, Marino, except play you like the fool you are? Are a few trinkets all your loyalty costs?" Ilva's eyes flicked derisively to the oilcloth still clutched in Helena's hand. "If Ferron wanted you, he would have taken you by now. You're just a toy; he winds you up and watches you spin."

"No. I'm making progress. A little more time and I'll have him just the way Crowther wants him."

Ilva gave a disbelieving laugh. "Crowther was delusional, thinking to use you to tame Ferron. You cannot bring a mad dog to heel." She shook her head. "But very well, you're welcome to refuse; it doesn't matter, we have more than enough evidence of his treachery. Jan has been assembling a comprehensive package. It would be a trivial matter to send along to the Undying. I suppose you could say the case is ironclad. Do you prefer that? Do you think they'll kill him this time?"

Helena's chest felt as if it had been punched through. "You can't do that to him."

Ilva was unmoved. "Why not? It would be fitting, no? After everything he's done. I'd say he more than deserves it."

Helena realised then what she should have realised long before, that Ilva had always wanted revenge. Crowther looked at the civil war and saw all the political machinations of the surrounding countries; Ilva's game of war was equally intricate, but hers was wholly personal. It was about Luc, it was about her family's legacy, and it was about revenge.

Crowther had been the ambitious one who'd wanted Helena to make Kaine loyal, something utilised in the long term. That had never been Ilva's goal.

"We need him, though. We've only come this far because of him. If we lose him, if things start falling apart again, people will blame Luc for that."

Ilva gave a thin smile. "Fortunately for us, Ferron has made himself quite the integral figure among the Undying in recent months. With him suddenly gone, the destabilisation will be widespread."

"You can't do this," Helena said.

"I am trying to save everyone, Marino." Her voice crackled with intensity. "That includes you. No matter how you've romanticised him, Kaine Ferron is not a person. He is a monster." Ilva pressed her hand over her heart, a gesture many people made when alluding to Apollo. "He and his family should have been dealt with long ago, but Pol worried about how the guilds might react. He let that boy attend the Institute despite the suspicions surrounding his birth, and look how that kindness was repaid. I will not make that mistake with Luc."

"Please, Ilva, I can make him loyal. I just need more time."

Ilva stared at her. "Are you choosing Ferron over Luc? Over all the vows you made?"

The question stopped her cold.

"No," Helena said quickly. "No," she said again, her voice breaking. "I am loyal. But"—her throat worked several times—"if I had proof that *he* was loyal, that he'd do whatever you wanted, would you let him live? I swear, if I can't, I will—I will kill him. But if he was loyal, he could be useful.

"Please, Ilva." Her voice shook.

Ilva gave a small sigh and looked tired. "If you can present Ferron on his knees, crawling, willing to do anything, within a month, I'll let you keep him." Then she shook her head. "But be honest with yourself. There's no such thing as loyalty in his kind. The Ferrons are as corruptible as their resonance."

There was pressure in her throat like a stone, but Helena forced herself to speak. "I'll do it. One way or another. *I'll* finish it. Don't let Crowther send what he has."

Ilva had leaned forward on her desk, the chain from the empty amulet dangling between her fingers. "One month, Marino."

CHAPTER 46

Decembris 1786

A MONTH. THE DAYS FELT BRANDED INTO HER bones. Helena couldn't sleep that night. The future haunted her. There was an Ember Service before first light as Falcon Matias consecrated the coming year to Sol's guidance, and then Helena began her hospital shift.

She felt cornered, as if the world were closing in, and there was no escape. No one to turn to.

She tried to push her dread down using animancy, but it consumed her utterly; every thought led to the same despair.

When her shift was over, she went to the desk to see if she could perhaps stay on for the next one. Surely someone would rather celebrate solstice, and Helena could keep busy.

Purnell was on duty at the hospital desk, wearing a pin with SOFIA P etched into it. Helena tensed at the sight of her, and before she could speak, Purnell held out a slip of paper.

"The steward said to give you this when your shift was over."

Helena hesitated a moment before reading it.

There were only a few words. As thanks for all her hard work, Ilva had ensured Helena could have a few hours off to attend the solstice celebrations at Solis Splendour. Luc would be present and happy to see her. Rhea was expecting her.

Helena stared dully at the obvious manipulation.

Ilva was losing her touch. Or perhaps Helena was finally getting wise to her.

She put on the green wool pullover that Rhea had gifted her over her uniform and made her way to Solis Splendour. It was already dark, the year and the sun both preparing for rebirth.

In four weeks, Kaine would be dead.

She barely knocked on the door, but it swung immediately open, and warmth and light, music and laughter all spilled out. She squinted, dazed. Had she knocked at the wrong house?

"Marino? I didn't know you were coming." It was Alister, one of the boys from Luc's unit. He held the door for her. "Come in. We've got loads of food."

Helena entered, feeling as if she'd somehow stepped out of reality into a dreamlike version of Solis Splendour. The house was lively, decorated with tinsel and streamers and bits of evergreen, and the children ran through like a pack of feral puppies.

She knew the faces, recognised people, but everything felt different. Wrong.

Why was everyone so happy?

There was music from a gramophone and drunken laughter filling the next room. A mug of mulled wine was shoved into her hands before she'd gotten across the room, and she sipped it on instinct. It was warm and sweet, instead of sour and watery from being stretched.

The signs of their access to the ports and river trade were everywhere, but all she could think was *Kaine did this,* remembering the wounds lacerating his back, the dead tissue rotting and poisoning him. He'd been gaunt and grey, paper-thin, and he'd just wanted to know if it worked.

The room blurred. She wandered in a daze until she caught sight of Titus Bayard sitting cross-legged on the floor, peeling oranges. They must have come all the way from the southern coast. There was a small mountain of peeled fruit on the table beside him.

Helena searched for other familiar faces.

Lila was sitting crammed in an armchair with Soren, who was wearing the expression of a beleaguered cat.

Ever since her injury, Soren let her get away with anything. Lila had made a complete, and stunningly rapid, recovery and acted as if the entire thing had been overblown. When she'd learned about Luc's attempts to disregard orders, they'd had an explosive argument. Helena had only heard gossip, but it had been bad enough that the entire unit had been held on reserve for several weeks until things simmered down.

Things seemed better now but Helena couldn't help but feel that somehow Soren was the one most irrevocably damaged by the attack.

One of the unavoidable bits of Bayard lore that Helena had heard many times over the years was the fact that Soren was older than Lila. Twenty minutes the elder twin. The disparity of age was treated as gravely significant in matters of hierarchy in times past.

It was mostly a joke, but Helena suspected that Soren took it more seriously than he let on. Paladin primary or not, Lila wasn't only his twin, she was his younger sister.

Luc was playing cards with a group of convalescent soldiers, and Lila and Soren both watched him, Lila's leg swinging back and forth, the gears making a soft click, click, click.

Helena knelt down next to Titus, trying to complete her list of obligations quickly so she could leave. The mood of the house was so dissonant it made her feel ill.

"Hello, Titus," Helena said, following the script she always did. "Do you mind if I look inside your head a little bit?"

He didn't react. She slipped a glove off, touching the scar along his temple. She closed her eyes as she reached with her resonance, and it was all the same except Helena was not the same. Her techniques and understanding of the mind had changed in a year. There were patterns of energy that she had not understood the intricacies of before.

Now she could sense where her errors lay. She had transmuted tissue without knowing how to follow the currents of energy that carried the mind through the brain matter.

Of course, Titus was often unresponsive, his mind limited; she'd hemmed him inside his own consciousness.

The connection between them snapped as Titus suddenly shoved her hand away. His face was contorted, the orange in his hand crushed into pulp. He shook his head several times as if trying to clear it.

Helena stared at him, her eyes searching as he scooted away from her, his expression unsettled. She pulled her glove back on automatically.

Was it possible that she could cure him? She was almost afraid to think it. She had to be certain before she brought the possibility to Rhea. She couldn't break her heart again.

She was startled from her thoughts at a burst of laughter.

She slipped into another room that was quieter and less crowded, trying to collect herself in a window alcove that was cooler, the drapes creating a barrier from all the noise.

"Helena."

She looked up to see Penny Fabien slipping into the alcove with her.

"I thought it was you slipping in here," Penny said. "Are you all right? You looked upset."

Penny was a year older. She'd been the dorm monitor for Helena's room during their Institute days.

"Just a bit close in there," Helena said, looking away. "Did something happen?"

Penny looked at her. "What do you mean?"

"Why is everyone so happy?"

Penny blinked with surprise. "We're happy because the war's almost over."

Helena stared at her in bewilderment.

The war wasn't almost over. They didn't even have a plan to win. Six years of fighting for survival while waiting for a miracle that would never come.

"Weren't you at the Ember Service?" Penny asked. "Falcon Matias was talking about the stages of transmutation, how each one correlates to a period in the war, and how we're nearly at the final transformation where the soul becomes truly purified. Think about it. A year ago, we were hemmed in around Headquarters, no supplies, barely enough rations to keep fighting, and now we've retaken the entire East Island. The ports. All because we had faith."

Helena had not paid any attention to Matias during the service. All she'd heard was Ilva's voice in her ears, saying *a month* over and over.

"What?" Helena's voice came out strangled.

A look of sympathy swept across Penny's face. "I guess you're not really out there at the front, are you? You must not have any idea. Things have been going so well this year." Penny's face was alight. "It's because we passed the test. We held firm and didn't let our fears corrupt us, and now Sol is bestowing his favour. We can't lose now."

Helena flinched as if she'd been struck and stared at Penny in such abject shock that Penny's smile faded, and a look of comprehension and discomfort suddenly swept across her face.

"Oh, right . . ." Penny said, wringing her hands. "I heard about what happened with you and the Council. I'm sorry, I didn't mean to imply anything about your soul—"

Helena's jaw started trembling uncontrollably, and then it spread until her whole body was shaking.

Penny stepped towards her, stroking her arm. "Don't feel bad. I'm sure you—meant well. We've all hit points when we think anything would be worth it to make it all stop. Just think of how much things turned around after that. Maybe you were—a final test for us."

Helena was going insane. She was about to start screaming right there in the alcove. She had never imagined this possibility.

They thought the war was being won because her proposal of necromancy had been so sharply reprimanded that the Resistance passed some final spiritual test, and all the success of the last year was a reward for it?

Without even realising it, she'd proven their mythos. No matter what happened now, no one would ever listen to her. She was cast forever into the role of doubter, of tempter. Standing there, she suddenly remembered the odd expression in Ilva's and Crowther's eyes as she was censured and dismissed. What a perfect opportunity she'd given them in that moment.

No wonder Ilva had told her the truth about Orion. She knew that no one would ever believe Helena's claims.

Now Ilva wanted one last trick.

Kill Kaine. Bury the evidence, the true means of their success. Create one more miracle.

Helena forced herself to breathe. It came out as a choking gasp. Penny pulled her suddenly into a tight hug.

"It's all right," Penny was saying, as if Helena were a child who needed soothing. "We all make mistakes. Don't feel bad, it's all right now." Penny patted her back. "You know what, the real trouble is that you're too isolated. With everyone at the front and you always in the hospital, you never get to see how it really is."

"I guess so," Helena said dully. "That must be it."

Penny was nodding as she stepped back. "It's all right. You just stay with me. I'll make sure no one bothers you."

Helena was too dazed to resist as Penny pulled her out of the alcove into another room, where Alister was currently playing the piano. Soren was now playing a card game in the corner, and Lila had disappeared. Several people, including Luc, were crowded around the piano singing. Penny installed Helena on a sofa and then, after trying to coax her into joining, went over to the piano, too.

Helena sat tense, waiting for Penny to grow distracted so she could slip away, but before she could, Luc caught sight of her and immediately left the group.

He dropped onto the seat next to her. "I'm glad you're still here. I was afraid you'd snuck out already."

She gave a mute shake of her head.

"You all right?" he asked.

"Tired is all."

He leaned forward. "Your trainees not pulling their weight?"

"No, they're fine. Just—always seems to be something new to do."

"I don't know, I think you like being busy." There was a teasing note in his voice.

Helena's stomach clenched into a hard knot. "Maybe so," she managed to say.

Soren slunk over and slid across the arm of the sofa into the space on the other side of Helena. "You two have to hide me. Someone told Mum we were gambling."

"You're dead," Luc said with a laugh. "Did you manage to win at least?"

Soren shook his head mournfully. "Fuck me, why's Lila coming over here?"

"Language in your mother's house," Luc tsked, "and as your precious sister approaches."

"Fuck off."

Lila was headed in their direction with a large, intricate box hanging from her neck. She stopped in front of them. "Mum has me on photo duty." She tapped the contraption.

Soren groaned.

"Sit up and hold still. This thing is finicky." Lila was peering into the apparatus, adjusting lenses, shifting back and forth. "Soren, don't you have a spine somewhere? How do you manage to slouch in armour? You're folded up behind Helena like a wet noodle. Luc, poke him, would you?"

Luc reached behind Helena and obliged.

"Much better." Lila grinned, and Luc instantly did, too. "Right. No serious faces, it's solstice. Be cheery."

They stared at the contraption, and just before the click, Luc's arm wrapped around Helena's shoulders, squeezing tight. Helena tried to force the corners of her mouth up as the camera flashed.

Luc moaned, shielding his eyes. "Sol's light, I think I'm going blind."

"Soren, Mum wants a picture of you and Dad." Lila peeled a reluctant Soren off the sofa and dragged him into the next room.

Helena watched them go and felt as though her chest were being crushed. Her hands were clenched into fists so tight, the leather bit at her knuckles.

"Are you thinking about your father?" Luc asked quietly.

She hadn't been, but perhaps that was what was wrong with her. She should think more about all the people who were dead, whose common trait was the way their life had overlapped with hers.

Whether or not vivimancy was a curse, she was becoming quite sure that *she* was one.

"Hel, what's wrong?" Luc touched her arm.

She looked at him and realised that she was being forced to choose. Luc or Kaine? She could only save one. She had to choose Luc, but it was going to kill her to do it.

"I have to go." She started to stand.

"No, you don't." He wrapped his fingers around her hand. "You always say that, but I'm not letting up this time. Stay with us."

He gave a teasing, pleading smile.

He'd always had a terrible talent for persistence. From the very start, when he'd found her crying after her first class because the lecturer's Northern dialect was thick and spoken so quickly.

He'd coaxed the whole thing out of her in a dusty corner of the library. The next week, the lecturer had talked slower and wrote all the key terms on the board so Helena could copy them down and look them up. Having Luc in her life had always felt like magic.

There'd been no reason for him to go out of his way for her, but he had, and then he kept doing it. He'd just picked her out on that first day and decided she was the friend he wanted. And if that required sitting for hours in the library while she did homework, even though he hated homework, that was what he'd do.

She couldn't imagine her time at the Institute without him. It was like imagining the world without the sun in it.

"Come on now, what's wrong?" he asked, leaning in so their heads were together.

Everything. Everything was wrong and it was going to be wrong forever, and it wasn't their fault but they were paying for it. She couldn't tell him that; it would be too cruel to rip everything away, to expose the lie that was his whole life when it was all he had.

"Everyone seems so happy," she finally said. "It makes me afraid."

He nodded slowly, his worry clearing. "I know, it's hard to believe it might be over soon. Doesn't feel real." He nudged her with his shoulder. "That's why it's so important to have people that ground you." He glanced towards the next room where Lila and Soren were kneeling beside their father as Rhea snapped a photo. "When it doesn't seem possible, it helps to think about everything I'm waiting for."

Helena's chest clenched, wondering what fantasy Luc had spun for himself to get up each day.

When she said nothing, he gave her a sidelong grin. "We'll finally go on our trip. Once everything's over and settled, Ilva can manage a bit longer. It won't be the big trip like we said, but if we wait for the Abeyance, we could take a fast ship to Etras and spend at least a week there before the tides come back. I've always wanted to see the lost cities. I've still got your map on the wall."

"That's not going to happen, Luc," she said, her voice low. Even if he had to believe in this lie, she couldn't be a part of it. She couldn't live as a prop in this deceit.

"What?"

She looked down at her gloved hands, as emptiness hollowed her lungs.

She swallowed hard. "When this is all over, I don't want you to think of us as friends anymore. I think it will be better that way for both of us."

"Why?" He looked horrified.

"Because I'm not your friend anymore. Your friend Helena Marino died in a field hospital six years ago. She doesn't exist anymore. I need you to let her go."

He didn't, though. Luc caught her hand again. His face was stricken, and he was so beautiful.

Even in the depth of winter, he looked limned in sunlight. Divine or not, the Holdfasts had a look as if they were born to be immortalised in marble. Like the sun, born for eternity.

Helena was not a planet or any celestial thing. She was just a human bound tight to the present, to the brevity of existence, and she could feel time running out.

"No. I won't let you go," he said. "I can't. Hel, just tell me what's wrong, and I'll fix it. You and me, we're friends forever."

She pulled away from him, shaking her head.

All Luc knew was Paladia, alchemy, and the Eternal Flame, with their ideals about the refinement of fire, of trials and sacrifice, the purity of suffering. That it would be worthwhile eventually, in the next life if not this one.

Maybe if Helena were at the front, she could believe in all that, too. But she'd spent every day of the last six years watching people die. She lived in the aftermath of every battle, breathed in the devastation until she was drowning in it. Nothing and no one would ever convince her that anything noble or purifying could come from this scale of suffering. That any rewards could ever be worth it.

To trick people into embracing it was cruelty. But how could she tell Luc that? That none of it had ever meant anything. That the miracles he believed in were mere sleights of hand, bought and paid for with betrayal. She couldn't.

"If I was ever your friend, let me go now." She jerked her hand free and fled the house.

Her heart was beating so hard, it hurt. The blood pounded in her ears until she could barely hear the wind, the cold slicing across her cheeks.

Snowflakes fell, spiralling onto the street.

She paused and looked up at the sky.

It was supposed to be good luck, snow on the solstice. A brightening of the longest night.

She stood watching it fall until her hands and feet were numb with cold. She wanted to stay there and freeze to death. She'd read it was a gentle way to go, like falling asleep.

The beacon of the Eternal Flame burned overhead. She turned, putting her back to it, wandering without destination. There was nowhere to go. Her life was so small. Beyond the gates of the Institute, she was homeless.

She followed the only route she knew by heart.

It was eerily still on the Outpost. The snow-heavy clouds had a dim silver glow from the moons. She'd always found the Outpost so ugly next to the elegant, natural lines of the islands' architecture, but now she found the brutality of the towering steel, concrete walls, and jutting smokestacks fitting. She didn't want to be somewhere beautiful.

There was no pretence on the Outpost, no ornamentation to distract the eye; it didn't hide what it was. Which was more than she could say about the city or Institute.

A lie. All of it a lie, the celestial emblems that decorated the island, all those murals and paintings of the Holdfasts, the sun always rising with them. All lies.

Her face grew numb, but she couldn't bring herself to turn back. She went towards the tenement.

The door unlocked easily even though her fingers were stiff. The wind rattled the windows.

She sat at the table, resting her head on the edge, and closed her eyes.

The door banged open.

Her head shot up, and she stared in astonishment at the sight of Kaine in the doorway.

There was ice flecking his hair, lashes, and eyebrows, as if he'd come through a blizzard.

His eyes found her instantly, scanning her from head to toe. She stared back at him, a feeling like hunger rising inside her.

"What is it?" he asked as the door closed behind him. "Did something happen?"

"How did you know I was here?"

He levelled her with a hard stare. "I keep an eye on this place."

Of course. Just because she hadn't seen necrothralls didn't mean they hadn't seen her.

"Why are you here?" he asked again, scanning her from head to toe once more. "And unarmed, I might add."

She'd hidden the knives in the lab. It would raise more questions than she could possibly answer if anyone saw them, and after Ilva's reaction, they felt too personal to let anyone see them.

"I—didn't know I was coming here. I didn't have anywhere else to go."

"If it wasn't on Resistance business, you shouldn't have come."

She nodded jerkily. Of course he was right. She should have just gone to the bridge.

And jumped.

No. She blinked the thought away. The whole reason Ilva and Crowther had lied to her for so long was because they knew Kaine would see straight through her. Her feelings were always stamped right on her face.

"You're right. Sorry," she said, her voice so hoarse it was barely more than a whisper. "I'll go."

She moved slowly, careful not to look at him, but as she passed, his fingers hooked her arm, swinging her around. Her back was against the wall as he stared her square in the face.

"What's wrong?"

"Nothing." She looked down quickly. His gaze was like a brand on the top of her head. "I just came because I was—worried about you."

He scoffed. "Since when have you worried about me?"

She looked up without thinking.

His expression was hard. Defensive. The ice in his hair had melted into tiny droplets of water that trembled, glittering like stars on his face.

"I don't know," she confessed. The habit had crept up on her without her realising.

He scoffed. "And now—what? You suddenly can't help yourself?"

"I came because I wanted to see you." She realised only as she said it that it was the truth. That was why she'd come.

His throat dipped. "Why?"

Her chest tightened. "I'm afraid that someday I'll come, and you—you won't be here."

He went still, his eyes darting across her face. His expression wavered, something she couldn't decipher flickering in his eyes. He gave a low laugh. "Is this goodbye, then, Marino?"

The question jolted through her, and she reached out, grabbing hold of him. "No! No."

A month.

She swallowed hard. "I got worried, and I—didn't have anywhere else to go."

She'd said that already. She felt so stupid, so blindly trusting. And she was too late, too slow; there wasn't enough time left.

His right hand rested on her shoulder, heat seeping through her. She bit down on her lip, swallowing hard.

"You always have to come back," she said. "All right? Don't die. Promise—"

Her voice failed.

"Marino, what's wrong?" He tried to step back, but she wouldn't let go.

"Nothing! I just spent a lot of time making that medical kit for you, and I did spend an hour teaching you how t-to use it, so—I think it would be really ungrateful if you—d-died."

He gave a hollow laugh and stepped closer so that his chin grazed the top of her head. His sigh was almost despairing.

"All right . . ." he said, "but only because you asked."

The words ran through her like a knife through the chest.

She'd thought for so long that she could do anything. For the war. For Luc. That she had it within her to pay any price. Now she'd found her limit.

Kaine wasn't innocent, but he wouldn't deserve what would happen to him if he was caught. Even if she could rip out his talisman and take it back with her, he wouldn't be dead. He'd just be in some cursed limbo inside Morrough.

His hand slipped away from her shoulder. He stepped back, and there was a strained look in his eyes.

"You shouldn't have come here," he said. "I thought there was an emergency. If you show up like this for no reason, you risk my cover. I have to guess whether or not I need to respond."

It wasn't until he'd told her about Blackthorne that she'd even begun to consider the magnitude of the risk Kaine was taking. Crowther and Ilva had kept her so focused on the danger that Kaine represented to them, she'd never considered the threat they were to him.

The blood drained from her head. She'd always thought of him as so much safer than her, that she was the one taking all the risks, venturing out into enemy territory, mortal as could be. That wasn't an accurate way to view it at all. The Resistance spies and scouts often carried cyanide pills to escape interrogation if their capture was inevitable. That wasn't an option for him.

Even if he ran, hid, it wouldn't matter, because Morrough had the phylactery. He'd be far safer if he only ever sent the necrothralls, but he was here right now. He'd come because she had.

Why couldn't Ilva see the significance of that?

"I'm sorry," she said. "I won't do it again."

He looked doubtful.

"I swear," she said. "If I ever come back, it'll be legitimate."

He gave a sharp nod. "You've given your word. I'll trust you to keep it."

Her stomach clenched. *Don't trust me. Don't trust the Eternal Flame. We're all liars.*

She gave a small nod.

When he was gone, Helena stood alone. The windows were rattled by the wind, but she lingered, growing colder and colder, wondering what to do.

CHAPTER 47

Janua 1787

WHEN HELENA RETURNED TO THE OUTPOST THE next week, the room was covered in some kind of thick drop cloth that padded the floor and bunched up around the door when she tried to push it open.

Ferron was already there, his cloak and coat stripped off, dressed down, and his shirtsleeves were rolled past the elbows. She froze.

Northerners were all so pale that they nearly glowed in the wintertime, while Helena turned sallow and sickly looking without sunlight. She missed the warm southern sun so much, sometimes her skin ached for it.

"I'm not training you for a battlefield," Kaine said. "The point of all this is to ensure you have the skills to get away. At this point, you should be fine around necrothralls as long as there aren't too many, but if you run into one of the Undying, they will pursue, and you'll be lucky if they only kill you."

She gave a stiff nod.

"Your reflexes are passable now, but an actual fight is different. There are no rules; it's close and dirty. Every second it takes you to attack or to get into position is a point against you. Time will never be on your side. Your sole advantage is that they'll underestimate you, but you'll only get that advantage once."

Why was it that every time he uttered anything vaguely complimentary, he had to couch it with six criticisms?

"Right."

He looked at her sidelong. "You're hardly built for combat or particularly strong, but you can use that to your advantage. Looking at you, no one will see you as a threat. They're likely to send thralls after you first, but if they see your abilities, you'll be in real danger." He gave her a once-over. "I don't particularly fancy being extensively stabbed today, so we'll be using practice daggers."

He picked up a set from the table, tossing them.

Helena fumbled but caught them. They were light, about the same size and weight as her set, but wooden. She squeezed. It was strange, not having any resonance.

"Your goal is to either escape and knock on the wall three times—we'll count that as getting away—or else contact enough to form a resonance channel. We'll consider that a hit. You know what to do after that."

It sounded overly simple, but it was the first time they were properly sparring. He probably wanted to start easy.

"Now, imagine you're out in that bog you're so partial to. The terrain is terrible, and while you were up to your knees in mud gathering frogs or something, a few necrothralls spotted you. Since you don't have a combat partner to cover you, while you were dealing with them, you didn't notice the Undying approaching. He's seen you're a vivimancer, and his guard's up, but he knows he'll be rewarded for getting you alive." He stepped towards her until their bodies were touching. "What would you do now?"

Helena went for his chest, but rather than dodge or parry, the flat side of his hand struck her wrist. The blow was so sudden that her grip failed, and the wooden knife plummeted towards the floor. He caught it in midair.

Helena tried to jump back and regroup into a better defensive position, but the cloths on the floor slowed her. Bad terrain. Kaine's empty hand closed around her wrist, jerking her back.

The knife, now in his hand, sliced through the air towards her throat. She managed to block it with her second knife, but he caught the tip of the handguard, ripping it from her fingers.

It thumped to the floor.

"Five seconds and you've already lost both knives." He pulled her closer until she could feel his breath on her skin.

She tried to shove at him. A resonance touch, that was all she needed. Forget the knives.

His left hand, which she'd sworn had a knife in it a split second prior, was suddenly empty, and it closed around her wrist before she could lay a finger on him. She tried to wrench herself free, but his grip was iron.

"Now I have both hands captured," he narrated, as if she hadn't noticed.

She threw herself backwards, trying to wrench free.

"A word of advice," he said conversationally, not even swaying as she used all her strength and weight trying to break his grip. "Don't leave your wrists open. Once I have you by the wrists, I can do practically anything to you. This is much easier for me to maintain than for you to escape from. That rule also applies to feet. Be careful kicking above the knee. If I get you by the ankle, you'll be on the ground in seconds. Most of the Undying are guild; they weigh twice what you do. Even if you manage to kill them, you'll be trapped. Stomping or kneeing is much better than kicking. Stomping uses your weight, rather than relying on your momentum. Stomp hard and go for the ankles or the sides of the knees. Disabling is key; dislocating the knee will take longer for them to regenerate than a stab wound. A knee to the groin works, too." He grinned. "Even the liches hate that."

Helena promptly tried to knee him, but he effortlessly sidestepped.

"See? It's dangerous to lose your arms."

His lecture was getting annoying.

Helena stomped on his foot and kicked him in the shin.

He grunted. "Better, but if I were trying to capture you, I would have already drowned you in the marsh until you passed out. Or taken you by the neck and rammed your head into my knee. You need to fight dirty. Forget every word you've ever heard about honour in combat. The honour is surviving."

He let go, and she stumbled back, winded already.

He watched her, his gaze as intent as a predator. A shiver ran down her spine.

"If you're ever attacked, you will be outnumbered, and even if you aren't outnumbered, you will never be as strong or resilient as the Undying. We don't tire. We can keep fighting for hours, and any injury you inflict, we will recover from in minutes if not seconds. If they hurt you enough to slow you, you're worse than dead."

"I know," she said, her voice hollow.

"Do whatever you have to to get away."

Helena nodded.

"Be devious. When your opponent is stronger than you, it's crucial to use that against them. They will underestimate you, and they'll be angry if you manage to injure or evade them. There's risk and advantage to that. If they're angry, they will try harder to hurt you, but they'll also stop thinking clearly; that'll make their attacks predictable. In combat, there's no difference between an angry person and a stupid one."

He let her pick up her knife and pulled the other from his pocket, tossing it back to her.

He attacked her again. And again. And again. Winning every time. Despite that, he was in a bizarrely good mood. She couldn't for the life of her figure out why, because usually he treated her mistakes like they were personal insults.

All she needed to do to "win" a round was to get stable contact once. Anywhere. One touch. Or else reach a wall with a few seconds before he caught her.

Both were impossible. Kaine could disarm her without effort, ripping the knives out of her hands, tripping her, dodging her blows, and sidestepping. Then she'd make a mistake, leave herself open for an instant, and that was all he needed. He wasn't armed or using his resonance. He didn't need to. He'd get her by one arm and twist it up behind her back or into some other helpless position, all while relentlessly criticising her, telling her all the ways she was doing things wrong, all the advantages her incompetence gave him.

Helena grew progressively more and more enraged, which he also noticed and seemed amused by.

"You should be using your resonance," he said as he attacked her the twentieth time, knocking her off balance by dodging a blow.

With a quick sweep of his boot, he sent her to the floor. She tried to jump back to her feet, but he caught her by the ankle, dragging her along. When she tried to stab him, he managed to catch both her wrists in one hand.

He pinned her wrists over her head, forcing her knives to fall from her fingers, and then he proceeded to sit on her hips.

"If I were Blackthorne, I'd slit you open and eat your organs while your heart was still beating," he said, leaning over her. His weight had her wrists so firmly pinned down, she could feel the tiles beneath all the fabric on the floor. His fingers ghosted across her stomach.

A shiver ran through her gut, heat rolling through her like a wave.

"You're terrible at hand-to-hand combat. I thought your stance-work was awful, but you're even worse at this," he said, but his eyes were following his fingers.

"Well, I've never done this before," Helena said mutinously as she tried to wriggle free. Her heart was pounding. "I thought we'd both be fighting with weapons."

He laughed. "Why would I need a weapon? You can't even beat me when I'm empty-handed."

She frowned at him. "Why are you in such a good mood?"

He quirked an eyebrow and stood, extending a hand to help her up. "Do you prefer me angry?"

She ignored the question but watched him warily. He still seemed bizarrely cheerful, despite the endless criticisms and warnings about all the ways she could be killed.

It should have come as a relief—she'd grown so used to his anger—but instead she felt on the verge of a breakdown just looking at him. She was running out of time.

Even if she could manipulate him to some degree, by taking advantage of how contrary he was, it wouldn't be reliable. That wouldn't meet Ilva's demands.

She picked up the knives. There was a throbbing pressure inside her skull. She'd barely slept since the solstice. She kept dreaming of him going mad, ripping himself apart like Bașilius did but then consuming it all, eating himself endlessly like the dragon in the Ferron crest.

His voice broke her from her thoughts. "Don't be afraid to use your elbows. When you're fending off a close-range attack, elbows work well. You're more likely to break something with your elbow than your fist."

He lunged at her.

Rather than bolt, she moved towards him, sidestepping at the last minute. He pivoted, but she'd already gotten him in the leg with one of her knives. With a real knife, she would have severed a tendon and artery, enough to hobble him for a minute.

She tried to leap back for the next attack, but he used his remaining leg as leverage to tackle her, dragging her to the ground. She tried to roll but his weight trapped her. Helena kicked and snarled as she tried to fight free, but his grip was relentless, blocking her hand.

"If this were a real fight, I'd be very angry by now," he said, his voice low as he slithered up her body, pinning her wrists to the floor, his torso moulded against hers. His mouth reached the base of her neck, breath running hot across her skin.

She kept twisting and bucking her hips to try to break free. Kaine abruptly let go of her, shoving himself off.

The muscle in his jaw rippled, and his eyes were dark as he stood up, breathing heavily, a low flush in his cheeks.

"If you're ever pinned down like that, I would not recommend trying to escape that way," he said in a tight voice, turning as if catching his breath.

Helena was so tired, she lay there on the floor a moment longer. "How should I do it?"

"Like I said," he said without turning, "elbows. Target the nose and eye sockets. Or go limp long enough that they get careless and let go of your wrists. Once you have a hand free, do whatever you want, liquefy their brain. Just don't—squirm."

She was following now.

She immediately sat up. "Noted."

"Again." He'd turned back and attacked her before she'd gotten her knives back.

When she left the Outpost, her whole body was aching. She paused on the bridge to heal the bruises so that she could walk normally before reaching a checkpoint.

She found a few books on hand-to-hand combat in the library and read them diligently. She reviewed all her notes about Kaine, their interactions, his words, his tells, the things he said and all the things he didn't, trying to understand him. All the time she'd spent with Crowther, dissecting his behaviour, and yet she still had no idea what any of it meant. What could Kaine possibly want that could ever be worth this much risk? She didn't see the ambition or hunger for power that Crowther and Ilva were so convinced he possessed, but she had no alternative explanation for his choices.

Everyone who'd returned to Headquarters for solstice had gone again, the heroes off to reclaim more of their city. There was no one to notice the strange hours Helena spent flitting between the hospital and the lab like a ghost.

Each time she went back to the Outpost, they continued with hand-to-hand combat, her armed and him empty-handed, as he demonstrated technique after technique for disabling and killing the Undying. She wished he'd stop.

"Is there any point in training you if you aren't even paying attention?" he said, irritated at last after he'd disarmed her for the tenth time without effort.

Helena retrieved the wooden knife from the floor automatically. "I just don't see the point, if I'm being honest. If I'm attacked by one of the Undying, I doubt I'll survive it. If I do, I'll probably be so badly injured there won't be any point in it."

He shifted his stance, eyes narrowing. "What's wrong?"

"I'm tired," she said, staring at the floor. "I'm tired of this war. I'm tired of trying to save people and watching them die anyway, or saving them only to watch them die later—in a worse way. It's the same cycle, over and over. I don't know how to get out, and I don't know how to keep going, either."

"I thought you'd do anything for Holdfast." He was pacing the room.

"The price keeps getting higher," she said quietly. "I don't know if I can keep paying it."

He stilled. "I suppose even martyrs have limits."

She glanced up, glimpsing for a moment the intent way that he watched her when she wasn't looking.

She wasn't imagining it. It was there, just below the surface. There was a want in him that practically shone in his eyes. But he refused to give in. Whenever she tried to beckon, to tempt him across the line he'd drawn, his malice surfaced, vicious as a serrated blade.

He was always cruellest when he was vulnerable.

Lately he'd hardly been cruel at all, which told her everything about her chances now.

Perhaps if she'd been more dogged, she would have found a way to push through the pain, but he always seemed to know how to hurt her most.

She had to do this, though.

She drew a deep breath, shaking her head, trying to focus. "Just an off day," she said. "I'm fine now."

She retrieved her knife, and he lunged without warning. She sidestepped, using her free hand to try shoving him past her, but he easily evaded her. With lightning speed his hand caught her wrist. Her first knife dropped. She pulled out the second, managing to elbow him in the ribs, and wrench herself free.

She snatched the larger knife up off the ground as she got back into a defensive position, ready as he closed in again. He grabbed her by the arm when she stabbed at him, ripping the larger knife out of her grip again. She attempted to hook her foot behind his ankle, but he swept back and dodged, getting her arm twisted behind her back. He liked that trick, it was almost predictable, and his hold always just marginally loosened as his grip rotated.

She lunged, breaking free, experiencing a flash of triumph before realising he'd let her go.

Using the momentum of her escape, he spun her, caught her ankle with his boot, and slammed her to the floor. The wind was knocked from her lungs, and she lay gasping.

He knelt over her. "You're still trying to win by being quick rather than clever. *Use* that brain of yours. Again."

Helena was tiring, but she managed to last longer. She could tell she was getting the hang of it; starting to see the patterns, the openings, to begin spotting weaknesses and opportunities. She wasn't fast enough to exploit them, but with time, she could get there.

She managed to knock him down twice, but he always evaded. He tried to pin her down, and she spun to the side, using his momentum. They fell, tumbling across the floor until he hit the wall, and she pinned him there. His left hand was wrapped around her throat, but she had a knife across his, and her other palm was pressed flat against his chest, her resonance humming through him.

She could feel his heartbeat as though it were cradled in her palm.

She gave a startled laugh as they both went still. Their faces were so close, they were almost touching.

"Just like that," he said, panting. "Just push in. It's right there."

She looked up sharply. He was watching her, making no move to stop her. Waiting.

Her smile fell, and she stared at him in horror.

That bitterness in his eyes—she finally understood it. He had been waiting for her betrayal.

This was what held him back.

He'd known from the beginning, before the possibility had ever occurred to her, and he'd trained her anyway.

She didn't need a book or Crowther to tell her what the expression on his face meant. She could feel it.

His hand was warm against her throat, and his thumb ran slowly along the scar below her jaw.

She leaned closer, her hand sliding up from his chest to his shoulder to pull him forward and kiss him.

It was not a slow, sweet kiss. It was not a kiss caused by alcohol or insecurity.

It was born of rage, despair, and desire so hot, it threatened to burn her into oblivion.

It was possibly a kiss goodbye.

She wanted him to know. It was real. For her, it had always been real.

He froze when their lips met. She felt his hand on her shoulder and braced herself to be pushed away even as she deepened the kiss, gripping the fabric of his shirt tighter, her lips frantic.

He wavered a moment and then something broke inside him, like a dam bursting, and Helena was drowning in him.

He wrapped his arms around her and kissed her savagely.

The heat was like wildfire.

The tension, the waiting. Months of expectations. After being told this was what she was sent for, why she was wanted. All a ruse. A feint to conceal his true motive. Demanding her had been the same trick of misdirection he taught her to use to protect her memories.

A lie, until it wasn't.

Somehow she'd shifted in his estimation, manipulated her way into becoming the very obsession he'd pretended she was. His palm pressed against the side of her neck before he slid his fingers up under the braids and anchored her in place as he kissed her, twisting so that she was under him on the floor.

Her fingers slipped beneath the collar of his shirt, following the dip of his collarbones, the curve of his neck.

She ran her fingers through his hair, wanting to lose herself completely in the nearness. Her fingernails bit into his shoulders. She could feel the scars on his back, the thrum of energy inside them.

Despite how cold he often was, a dragon was an apt sigil for the Ferrons. He kept walls of ice around himself, but there was fire in his heart.

Her shirt ripped as he tore it out of the way. She pulled him close, tight against her body until she could feel his skin on hers. She bit him without thinking. There was a hunger inside her that she couldn't explain, a pit of want to taste and feel and hold and not be always, always empty. She wanted to curl up so tight alongside him that she vanished.

Her clothes were slipping out of the way as he ran his hands along her ribs and waist, kissing across her breasts, body pressed between her legs. Her skirts sliding up as his hand trailed along her thigh.

It happened so fast. She'd never thought it would be something soft or slow, but it was more like a collision, like breaking across each other. The rush of skin and teeth as she let herself be consumed.

He sank into her, and her heart stopped, eyes going wide. She bit down on her tongue so hard she tasted blood, her eyes squeezed shut. He paused and kissed her, his lips so searing she felt it in her bones, and she nuzzled her face against his, but it hurt.

She'd known it might hurt if not done slowly, but she was glad it did.

Certain things were meant to hurt. She'd seduced Kaine when it was abundantly clear that this was a line he had no desire to cross. She had pushed and persisted and done it anyway, because she was desperate.

That *should* hurt.

His frame practically enveloped her, his lips nipping at her hairline. His arms wrapped around her shoulders, holding her tight against himself. She forced her eyes open, wanting a glimpse of what he felt in that moment.

Even now, his jaw was tense. His expression guarded. His mouth held in that hard, flat line.

But his eyes . . .

She could tell—

He was hers.

The realisation broke her heart.

Kaine dropped his head against her shoulder, moaning into her skin, pulling her closer, and then suddenly, it wasn't merely a pleasure he was taking in her. Heat came to life inside her, her sense of control untethering as it threatened to engulf her. But shame and guilt rose equally quick, cold and bitter as seawater, until she was on the verge of sundering.

His body shook. He gave a low groan, slumping, arms still around her. His breath dragged across her skin as he panted, pressing a kiss on her bare shoulder.

Helena lay still, the weight of his body against her, suddenly aware of the cold radiating from the floor. The dirt and gravel and rough cloths that bit against her skin, rubbing it raw.

The only thing she could think of was how relieved she was that it was over before anything else had happened.

Even whores were not so low as to find pleasure in their work the way she nearly had.

She tried to lie still and not tremble. Kaine's body and breath were the only warmth in that cold place. Then he went rigid and shoved himself away. His expression was drawn, and he didn't even look at her as he scrambled off, pulling his clothes back on.

Helena slowly sat up, watching him because she didn't know what else she was supposed to do.

He was growing paler and paler as he re-dressed. His expression disbelieving.

"Fuck—" he muttered, dragging a hand through his hair before he pulled his shirt back on.

His breathing was growing unsteady. When his shirt was on, he fumbled for the buttons, and when he found some missing, he seemed blindsided.

He clamped a hand over his mouth as if he were about to be sick. His throat dipped, and he closed his eyes. He drew a deep breath before he turned to face her, his expression cold. He only looked at her face for an instant before his eyes dropped down, and the little colour remaining in his face vanished.

"You—were you a virgin?"

Helena looked down. There was blood smeared at the top of her inner thigh. No wonder it had hurt.

She pressed her knees together instantly and shoved her skirts farther. "It was assumed that was how you'd want me," she said, trying not to think about everything the question insinuated.

For a respectable girl to lose her virginity was to give up everything, a career, education, alchemy. Only virgins were given Lumithia's grace. If Helena were somebody of note, Kaine would be expected to marry her now. An indiscretion like this was the reason for his parents' marriage after all.

Clearly he'd never considered her as belonging in that category. Her lungs shrivelled inside her chest.

"I—" His voice failed him. "I—I would have been gentler—if I'd known."

She drew her legs closer, as if being smaller would shield her from being so seen.

"I didn't really want you to be," she said quietly. Her hands shook as she tried to get her clothes back on.

His mouth closed then, and the room went still. She could feel the change in the air between them. But she didn't understand why it mattered, why this was the line he'd drawn.

The array must be part of it. Just after he was healed and fully internalising its effects, he'd kissed her. Wanted her. It had created a crossroads for him; that was why he'd stayed away for so long after that. Perhaps giving in, even once, was enough to tip the scales. Perhaps he couldn't change course now; he'd made his choice.

Obsessive and possessive.

She had him. If she was smart enough to leverage it.

On his knees, ready to do anything, Ilva had said.

She still didn't know how to do that, though. It wasn't as if Ilva or Crowther would see any significance in the fact Kaine had finally slept with her; that was what they'd expected him to do from the start.

She was torn between the desire to laugh and cry, her mouth twisting in a grimacing smile.

"Well, you seem pleased," he said in a bitter voice, his lip curling, "to have finally whored yourself."

Her fingers froze, and the room went out of focus.

"That was my job," she said. "You had to have known it was my mission."

"Of course," he said tonelessly, looking around the room as if he couldn't quite believe he was there. His arms were hanging limp at his sides. "I just—I never thought you'd actually succeed."

There was a pause while Helena finished dressing.

"I wasn't going to betray the Resistance," he finally said. "I was never going to. You were already losing when I made the offer, and you're probably still going to lose now, but I never cared. I just wanted to avenge my mother."

He pressed his lips into a tight line and looked down at the floor. "Unfortunately, by the time I had an opportunity to offer my services, she'd been dead too long and there was the coroner's report saying she'd died of natural causes. What could I possibly have to avenge?" The bitterness in his voice and on his face was unadulterated. "I knew Crowther well enough to know he'd only consider me as valuable as the strings he could pull, so I thought I'd give him a dead end to dig himself into."

Then his expression turned vicious and disdainful. "I tried to think what could I possibly want from the Eternal Flame. A pardon, because it was as ridiculous as it was obvious. But the Resistance was losing, everyone knew you were losing. I knew I'd need a contact, someone who could retrieve messages for me and come when called. I didn't want Crowther choosing one of his rats, and I thought demanding someone specific would play into—what they expected of me."

He swallowed. "But the Eternal Flame's noble families are too precious, I had to want someone they'd consider disposable, and Crowther was standing there, waiting for an answer. I had to come up with something. I remembered your name, on the exam lists. When I said Helena Marino, Crowther got this look in his eyes, and I knew he'd taken the bait."

He sneered. "As if I would betray the High Necromancer for you. I knew they'd send you with instructions to try to play up the obsession I was supposed to have—to ensure I wouldn't get bored or change my mind—but I wasn't worried. You were no one, just an awkward shadow behind Holdfast, following him like a dog. I thought it would be funny, watching you try."

He looked away from her then, his face twisting. "But you—you—" He shook his head. "It doesn't really matter. You outmanoeuvred me. Or maybe I'm just too tired and grieving to keep pushing you away. You won." He met her eyes for a moment, his expression bitter and derisive. "Well done."

Then he went and leaned against the wall, shutting his eyes.

Helena watched him sceptically. She wasn't sure what angle he was trying to play with this confession.

What he said about her was believable enough. It aligned with their inconsistent interactions, but to claim that avenging his mother was his true impetus? Avenging her for what?

"You switched sides because your mother died of a heart attack?" She gave a loud scoff, standing up, hiding a wince. "Her death wasn't anyone's fault, and even if it was, did you murder Principate Apollo by ripping out his heart by accident? Ran off with it and joined the Undying for three years, saw her die, kept going, and then what? You got so melancholy because you can't get drunk that you decided to turn spy?"

She was baiting him. She knew it would enrage him. She hoped that if she goaded him enough, he'd finally tell the truth.

His eyes snapped open. They'd turned silver, and two splotches of colour flushed in the hollows of his cheeks. "Fuck you."

She flinched but spat back, "You already did."

Her back felt bruised, the skin rubbed raw from the floor, and her lower abdomen ached as if she'd been punched low in the pelvis. She'd never felt so cold as she did then, standing there, but she was so angry, and finally it was all out in the open. No more of this game.

"You are a monster," she said, crossing her arms. "Do you expect me to forget what you've done? To think you became so high-ranking because of that delightful personality of yours? You think invoking your mother's death can erase all that? Everyone has lost someone, and most of them, more than you ever could. If you want to blame her death on Morrough, then maybe you shouldn't have spent all that extra time supporting him after she was gone. After you started this war. And *chose* to become Undying."

He was so angry that she could feel his resonance humming in the air, pushing at her skin. He would probably flay her if she didn't use her own resonance to push back.

"Do you want to know why I'm like this?" he asked slowly, his teeth flashing like fangs. "You asked once if it was a punishment, and I was honest when I said it wasn't. It was the bargain I made."

He walked towards her, rage radiating off him until she could feel the room warp.

"After my father's failure, after he revealed Morrough's plans, do you think the High Necromancer was understanding?"

Helena stared at him, frozen in place.

"I was still at the Institute, finishing up the year. Who do you imagine was alone with him when word came that my father had been caught and confessed to treason?" Kaine's expression contorted with grief. "He had my mother in a cage when I got home. He'd been torturing her for weeks."

His breathing grew ragged and uneven. "You sold yourself to save the person you care about. Well, so did I. What was I supposed to do, fail to kill Principate Apollo knowing I wouldn't be the one who'd suffer for it? This"—he gestured towards himself—"this was how I proved I'd be loyal, how I got him t—" His breath caught. "—to stop hurting her."

Helena's head had grown light. "We—I didn't know."

His lip curled up in a snarl, but then he turned away and his voice grew thick. "She never recovered. Morrough and Bennet were short on subjects at the time. They liked to experiment together. I'd hear her screaming for hours sometimes. They'd do things to her and then reverse them, so there were no traces after."

He shoved his hair away from his face, his throat working. "The whole summer. I couldn't—do anything but tell her I was sorry. That I'd do it and come back for her. That I wouldn't fail."

He braced against the wall as if he were about to fall. The words, so furious at first, were turning into a tidal wave of grief that seemed to pour from him.

"When the Principate was dead and I brought the heart back, the High Necromancer let her out and made us leave with him before the Eternal Flame came for me. Even before that, my mother—she was never very strong. When she was pregnant, she wouldn't listen when the doctors warned her what I'd cost her. She was always fragile after that. My father always said I had to take care of her. That I was—responsible. He used to make me swear again and again, growing up, that I'd always take care of her. I tried to make her flee. I got it all arranged but—she wouldn't go. Not without me. Said she couldn't leave me here."

He pressed the heels of his hands against his eyes. "I was trying to figure out if there was a way, and there were these parties they'd hold, the Undying. She said I should go, thought if I had friends, I'd be—protected. But that wasn't why I'd been invited. They thought it would be interesting to find ways to make an injury that would last on one of us, and I was the youngest. Automatic short straw . . ." He blinked as if he wasn't seeing the room anymore. "I thought she'd be in bed when I got back, but she'd waited up for me. She was by the door, and when she saw me, she started screaming. I kept trying to tell her that it would heal, but she kept saying it was all her fault, and her heart stopped, and I—couldn't—"

His voice broke and he slid down the wall, shuddering as if he were about to split open. When he spoke again, his voice had deadened.

"After she died, I was being watched. Morrough knew I'd joined for her. I had to earn back trust before I could risk doing anything. I'm not one of your fucking idiots who thinks one moment of self-sacrifice can change everything. If I wanted my betrayal to matter, he couldn't see it coming."

Helena stood frozen in horror. How had no one known this?

"I am so sorry." She felt faint with shock.

"I don't need your false sympathy, Marino," he snarled, but his voice was shaking.

He'd probably never told anyone what happened. His mother's death had been dismissed by everyone. Why would a heart attack matter, when people were dying in battle.

But Helena knew the kind of torture a vivimancer could perform and fix without leaving a trace. She could imagine what that would do to a heart over time. Kaine had been carrying that guilt for years, trying to make amends as best he could, trying to exact some form of revenge for her, knowing the indescribable punishment that awaited him.

"I'm not lying," she said. "I'm sorry. I am truly sorry for what happened to her."

She drew closer to him. He looked so utterly broken, as if he were about to collapse into himself.

She placed a tentative hand on his arm, half expecting him to fling her across the room, but his shoulders trembled and he dropped his head onto her shoulder. She pulled him into her arms; he gripped her close and sobbed.

"I can't—I can't—" he kept saying over and over.

Helena didn't know what to do. She ran her fingers through his hair and just held him.

"I can't—I can't do this again—" he finally gasped out. "I can't care for someone again. I can't take it."

She blindly found his face, pressing her hand against his cheek, felt tears slide along her palm and down her wrist.

"I'm sorry. I'm so sorry, Kaine." She said it again and again.

She was apologising for everything.

For the first time, Kaine Ferron was fully human to her. She'd slipped through his walls and peeled away the defensive layers of malice and cruelty, and found that there he carried a broken heart.

She could use that.

CHAPTER 48

Janua 1787

When Kaine stopped crying, Helena sat back, studying him soberly.

His expression turned guarded and embittered, as if he'd wept out all his softness and once again only his venom remained.

She had him, she could feel it. She'd followed orders, done what she'd been instructed to do, but she *still* didn't know how to prove that. The right way to leverage it into demonstrable loyalty.

Ilva would not lend any credence to a feeling Helena had. Caring about Helena didn't make Kaine a dog she could command.

"If you really want the Eternal Flame to win, why keep climbing rank? What are you doing?" she asked.

His eyes shone like mirrors. She could almost see herself in their reflection. His mouth twisted into a mocking smile. If his face weren't still wet, she'd never have known he'd been crying.

"It was obvious that my offer was only accepted out of desperation. The Eternal Flame may claim to be honourable, but Crowther is a snake. Ilva Holdfast can promise whatever she wants; she's only a steward, and a Lapse at that. She knows full well that if they win, the Eternal

Flame will pick and choose which of her actions were legitimate. Anything Holdfast doesn't like will vanish like smoke. I assumed that once I'd outlived my usefulness, you'd blow my cover to take advantage of the instability it would cause. So." His teeth flashed. "I tried to position myself to maximise that fallout."

Helena furrowed her eyebrows, studying him. That seemed a bit too selfless for him. He might want to avenge his mother, but he had no fondness for the Eternal Flame. They were merely a means to an end.

"Why kiss me?" he abruptly asked. "What was the point—in all this?"

She looked down, not sure she had an answer. "I didn't know you were supposed to die after we retook the ports. Apparently it was obvious, but I didn't realise."

Kaine gave a deadened laugh.

She couldn't meet his eyes as she spoke. "They expected you to die from the array, and they were—waiting for that. When they realised you've been climbing rank, they assumed you've been playing the two sides against each other, so you'll be the one who comes out on top in the end."

"Did you think that?" he asked softly.

She swallowed hard, still not meeting his eyes. "No, but it doesn't really matter what I think. They said just before solstice that I had a month to"—her voice dropped, lower than a whisper—"*make you crawl* or kill you, or they'd let Morrough do it instead."

He laughed again. "One more meeting to go, then. So this was a goodbye fuck? Final payment for services rendered?"

A tremor ran through Helena. "No. I—I just—"

Her throat closed. She leaned forward, gripping his shirt, wanting to shake him. She hated the way he'd switch, one moment vulnerable and the next so bitterly cruel.

"I just have to prove that you'll do what I ask. If I can—they won't kill you." She studied his face desperately.

His eyebrows rose mockingly. "Really? Is that all? Just servitude and I'll get to continue this delightful existence of mine so long as I'm more useful alive than dead? That's so generous. How could I possibly refuse?"

Her grip loosened, and she gave a disbelieving laugh.

He didn't want to be saved. Her efforts had only made things worse. All because Ilva and Crowther hadn't told her, they'd made her believe it was all real, but it didn't matter—it had never mattered whether she believed it—because Kaine had always known.

She drew a slow breath trying to reorient herself, but her mind wouldn't comprehend it.

It couldn't end like this. She'd done what she'd been told to do. She'd followed orders. She wasn't supposed to have to make this choice.

"I—I have to follow orders. I can't choose you. There's too many people at stake," she said, her voice shaking.

"I know."

Her mouth opened and closed, but there was nothing else to say.

"All right," she finally managed, her voice far away. She felt as though she'd been knifed, reality cold as tempered steel driven into her heart.

"Do you—" Her voice broke. "Do you want it to be me? Or does it—not matter?"

She knew Ilva probably wanted the Stone back if it could be recovered, but she couldn't bring herself to care.

He scoffed. "You lost your chance."

Her throat worked several times before she could speak. "I'm sorry."

He didn't reply. There was not even a flicker of remorse in his eyes. He looked cruelly satisfied.

There was no air in the room. She kept trying to breathe, but there wasn't any oxygen. A dull ringing filled her ears. She looked blindly for her satchel, trying to remember where she'd left it. She knelt, wavering, willing her mind to function.

"So, what happens to you now?"

Helena blinked. "Me?"

"Yes." He leaned forward and caught her chin, tilting her face so that the light from the windows fell across it, a pale slice of winter. "What happens to you?"

"When you're—gone?"

He gave a short nod.

"I don't know," she said with a short hysterical laugh. She pulled away. "Like you said, I've always been expendable, so maybe they'll offer me to the next spy."

"Don't joke. I want a real answer." There was a sharp undercurrent to his voice.

She met his eyes then. "I promised I was yours. You made me swear it. I didn't make plans."

Anger darkened his face. "Surely there's something you're looking forward to now."

She reached out, her fingers brushing over his heart. "No. I'm—spent."

As she stood, she thought of Luc standing on the top of the Alchemy Tower, so close to the edge. She hadn't understood why he'd gone there. How she and everyone else who needed him weren't enough to hold him back, but now that edge called her, the abyss that would open once she'd split across the marble.

The air swam, her eyes struggling to focus because all she could hear was the drumbeat of her heart inside her skull.

Everyone who touches you dies.

"What do they want?" His voice was almost a whisper.

She looked back. "What?"

"Is it—actual crawling? Or was there something more constructive Ilva had in mind?"

Her throat closed. "I—I'd have to ask."

"Find out. I'll do it." He looked exhausted, but now there was an edge of something seething in him.

"Are you really offering?" she asked, certain it was a trick.

He gave no response.

"*Why* are you offering?" Her voice rose, a note of hysteria in it.

He looked up at her a moment. "I realised just now that I'd miscalculated something. It hadn't occurred to me that I'd made you marketable."

The words thudded against her chest. "Oh."

Apparently, Crowther was right after all. The Ferrons were possessive enough to eat themselves alive before they'd let go of anything they considered theirs.

"I'll bring an answer back," she said.

He gave a short nod and looked away from her, saying nothing else as she went and pulled on her cloak, using it to hide her ripped clothes. She slung her satchel over her shoulder.

His hand twitched as she reached the door, but when she glanced back one last time, he'd looked away, still leaning against the wall, staring across the room, so pale he could have been a ghost.

She walked out of the tenement into a downpour of rain. She stood beneath it, trying to gain her bearings, drawing rapid breaths. She was on a precipice; she could still feel that edge, the plunge if she misstepped.

She kept her hood pulled up at the checkpoint, but she was familiar enough that they waved her through without being thorough. A security failure, but she was grateful for it. She split from her usual route, heading to the drop point. She couldn't show up at Headquarters like this.

As she neared it, signs of the war began to appear, as they did in every part of the city below Headquarters. The walls were scorched and distorted from combat.

The drop-point safe house was little more than a sub-basement storage room.

Her hands were stiff and trembling as she shoved the door closed. She focused first on lighting a fire in the portable stove using the discarded pile of kindling and old newspapers.

She was struggling to coax the fire to life, wishing her knowledge of pyromancy extended beyond the theoretical, when the door opened. She turned quickly, hoping it wasn't Ivy, although a stranger might be worse.

It was Crowther who entered. He stopped short, irritation pinching his face.

Helena looked back to the fire.

"Are you injured?"

She shook her head. He nudged her out of the way.

With the snap of his fingers, there was fire, the wood igniting with a crackling roar. Helena held her hands out towards the flames, saying nothing. He went into the next room and returned with a towel. She took it wordlessly, scrubbing until water stopped trickling from her hair. She could feel him scrutinising her.

"Is it done, then?" he asked when she lowered it to her lap and reached towards the fire again.

Her throat caught. After a moment's hesitation, she nodded. "Yes, I did it."

He released a soft breath of relief, and his right hand briefly patted her shoulder. "You can give the talisman to Ilva."

She kept staring at the fire. "He was being honest when he said he wanted to avenge his mother."

Crowther sighed, but Helena kept speaking.

"Back when Atreus was arrested, Kaine was safe at the Institute, but his mother wasn't. You know vivimancy for torture doesn't always leave evidence behind. Kaine killed Principate Apollo because it was the only way to save her. But she never recovered from it. Certain kinds of stress for too long can damage the heart."

There was a tense pause, and she could feel Crowther's doubt permeating the air.

Helena didn't look away from the fire. The heat singed her hands, but she didn't draw them away. If her hands were scorched, maybe she wouldn't feel the rest of her body.

"Atreus used to make Kaine swear he'd take care of his mother, because he blamed him for Enid being sickly afterwards. She wouldn't leave Paladia, though, and eventually the torture caught up with her. She died at home, but there was nothing natural about it."

There was no sound but the crackle of fire.

Perhaps Crowther already knew all that. She had no idea how much he and Ilva had lied to her, choosing to present Kaine's motive as power because that was how they'd wanted Helena to perceive him.

She closed her eyes, wanting to sink into the floor. "He wants to know what you want. You and Ilva. What proof of loyalty you expect from him."

The air shifted and then Crowther's fingers grasped hold of Helena's shoulder, pulling her to her feet and turning her to face him. His eyes swept from the top of her head and slowly down, catching on various points along the way.

"What did you do?" he finally said.

She met his eyes, lifting her chin. "I completed my mission. I made him loyal."

She was used to Crowther being unfazed by nearly everything, but he looked as if he'd been struck by lightning. Then he pulled her over to the window where the light was strongest, pushing her cloak off with his right hand, so he could get a good look at her.

Her braids had been pulled loose, the sections hanging haphazardly. His fingers dropped down to her neck, brushing against a spot that made her flinch. Before she could stop him, he flipped the clasp on her cloak; heavy with rain, it slid off her shoulders and to the floor with a wet thud, revealing her torn clothes, and all the bruises from the training that she usually healed before she got back.

She recoiled, shrinking back towards the shadows. She wanted to say it wasn't what it looked like, but she didn't think he'd believe her.

"I'm fine," she said, but her voice shook. "I only came here to clean up. You said not to go back to Headquarters if I wasn't put together."

Crowther's mouth was pressed into a hard line, and he started to speak—but then his eyes swept over her again and he slowly let go.

Helena twisted free, shoulders hunching inward. There was a small bathroom through the next room. She locked the door and stared at the reflection in the mirror; she was so pale that she was nearly grey, but her lips were red and bruised. Her hair looked like a bird's nest, only made worse by the rain.

She turned away, rummaging for a cloth, anything to clean herself up with. Stripping off her underclothes and trying to scrub them clean. The cold, stinging wet between her legs had her feeling almost hysterical.

Her hands were shaking as she threw the rag into a bin under the sink, barely steady enough to remove the hairpins tangled in her hair.

Her lips were trembling, eyes burning as she braided her hair.

She bit down on her lip as she coiled the long braids carefully at the base of her neck.

Her fingers were trembling too hard to make her resonance stable, so she left the bruises.

Calm down. You only have one chance to convince Crowther.

But the more she thought it, the more unsteady her breathing became. She crouched on the floor, pressing her hands over her face until she was quiet.

She looked at her reflection again. She was thinner now than she'd been when she first saw Kaine last spring. Her cheeks had hollowed, there were craters of exhaustion under her eyes, and her collarbones jutted out. Stress had carved her away like water cutting through sand.

She rummaged through her satchel and found a salve for bruises, spreading it across her lips. Eventually her hands were steady enough that she could conceal the bruises with a tingle of resonance, watching the only colour in her skin slowly fade.

She pulled on a fresh shirt and walked out. The rooms were silent.

"Crowther," she called, her voice hollow.

There was no answer. She went to the front room; the fire had dimmed to embers, and he was gone.

She swallowed hard, trying not to cry. Of course he'd gone. He wasn't going to listen. No one would. He'd picked up whatever he'd come for and left again.

A pit of despair opened in her stomach.

Your failure was always the plan.

The room seemed to stretch as she reached the door. Her hands were shaking too much to manage the knob.

It swung open, Crowther reentering. He was dripping wet, his thin hair plastered against his scalp. He looked like a wet cat.

"What are you doing?" he said as he came back in. "Sit down."

He had a paper packet in his hand, already tearing from the rain. He ripped it open, and several bottles tumbled out.

"I wasn't sure what was needed," he said.

She looked at the vials. He must have gone back to Headquarters and taken them from the hospital. The drop point kept basic medical supplies but nothing too valuable or prone to supply shortages. She recognised her own handwriting on the labels.

She stared at them, and considered taking the laudanum, something to smooth down the razor-sharp edges of her emotions, but she needed to stay clearheaded.

She inspected the next option. A contraceptive.

Her throat worked as she set it down. "You know I don't need that."

The only useful thing he'd brought was a valerian tincture, which the hospital used to calm patients who were in shock.

"What happened?" Crowther asked as she unscrewed the lid and swallowed it.

"You know what happened," she said. "Exactly what you expected when you sent me there. I'm just a bit slow."

"Marino." His voice was sharp but then he seemed to catch himself and softened it. "*What* happened?"

She'd planned to go to Headquarters and make her report without any explanations about exactly why or how, to be calm and assured, but Crowther had caught her before she was ready. Her jaw began trembling uncontrollably.

She felt so used. She understood rationally that it had to be like that. The war was larger than any one person. Even Luc, whether his family legacy was real or not, was a figurehead, an idea greater than himself.

She knew that and she was willing to follow orders, knowing the consequences, understanding the sacrifice. She didn't need any promises of reward or acknowledgement or eternity; she would do what was necessary because it was necessary. They knew that, and they had still *lied* to her.

"I told Ilva that all I needed was more time," she said simply. "It was just—abrupt. We'd been training. The bruises were from that."

Crowther said nothing, but she could feel him watching her like a hawk. She could only wonder what he was noticing, dissecting her behaviour, organising all the details of his observations into a mental file.

Helena pressed her hand against her sternum, trying to make the warmth from her palm seep into her, to speak calmly so that Crowther would believe her, not write her off as hysterical.

"He was so upset afterwards that he told me everything. He started crying after he told me about his mother. He always knew you were going to betray him. It was part of his plan. That's why he's kept climbing rank; he figured the more important he was, the greater the blow—when it happened."

There was a long silence after that.

Crowther gave a low sigh that sent Helena's heart skyrocketing.

"If he's such a suicidal martyr, why would he cooperate now?"

Her throat closed. Her fingers twisted at the loose fabric of her shirt. "Well, now that he can't deny the obsession to himself, I don't think he knows how to let go. Like you said, the Ferrons are self-destructively possessive. The array made it worse. He regards me as—" She swallowed. "—as his. I think that's what changed things. He still doesn't care about survival, but he also doesn't know how to let go."

Crowther's lips pursed. He ran his thumb slowly against them, considering.

Helena watched him, twisting her fingers, squeezing until her knuckles ground together. "Will you—will you tell Ilva? I know you both think I'm compromised, but I did what I was told to. He said he'll do whatever you want. I did it—I did—"

Her voice failed, and she started shaking uncontrollably. She gripped her arm, using her resonance to force the valerian to take effect. *Calm down.*

"Yes," Crowther said, "I'll speak with Ilva. You—did do as instructed." He cleared his throat. "If he's prepared to prove himself, that changes things."

Helena nodded, glancing blindly around the room, unable to feel relief. "Thank you."

She started towards the door, although she wasn't sure where she was going to go. She didn't think she was calm enough to return to Headquarters, but she couldn't stay here.

"Marino."

She winced. Crowther was still watching her. There was an odd look in his eyes, like he was seeing more than she wanted him to.

He swallowed several times and pressed his fingertips together. "I was about the same age you were when the Holdfasts brought me to Paladia."

Helena drew back. She knew that Crowther had been one of the Holdfasts' sponsored students, but he'd been brought in as an orphan after the Holdfasts had saved him. Helena had never considered their experiences as similar.

"My family and village were murdered at the hands of a necromancer. They crawled up from the ground and left me in the snow to die. When the Eternal Flame came, there was no saving them, only lighting the fires to erase the atrocities they'd become. I chose to distinguish myself with my willingness to do what is necessary. Not for glory or for the Faith, but because someone must do whatever it takes to stop the rot. I've never regretted my choice."

He looked down at his right hand, slowly opening and closing it. It was thinner than his other hand—the muscles had wasted over the years.

He was silent for so long that Helena finally realised the speech was meant as a sort of apology. That in some way he regarded them as alike, and she had done something for him and now he regretted treating her so poorly.

She didn't want an apology, though.

"Are you—" He blinked and started again. "Is there—healing you require?"

Her spine went rigid. The last thing she wanted was Elain or Ivy anywhere near her.

"He wasn't violent," she said sharply. She folded her arms tightly around herself. Her voice was very tense, her throat refusing to relax. "It was just—abrupt. Besides"—she let her voice grow venomous—"wasn't healing myself part of your instructions from the very beginning?"

Crowther looked away. "If you need clearance for anything, I'll see that it's signed off."

"I just came here to fix my hair and get a new shirt. I wasn't injured," she said, growing angry at this sudden and belated attempt at concern.

They'd been so clear that she was alone in this, and now that the ruse was finally up, now that it had come out that they hadn't *really* sold her off, forever, without a second thought, they thought she'd *want* them to care?

A sick heat burned in the pit of her stomach.

"You should allow people to look out for you."

A harsh, sobbing laugh split her chest at the absurdity of his words.

His expression grew pinched. "There was no time to train you for the assignment. We thought it best to let the deal run its course and—collect the pieces afterwards. It made you more convincing."

A lump rose in her throat. "Well, he saw through you both. I was the only fool in the end. But you got what you wanted. Lucky you, I guess."

"You—" He said it heavily and then paused.

"What?" she asked sharply, anger evaporating as panic closed around her again.

Was it not enough? Was he trying to break it to her gently that Ilva would still choose to kill Kaine? That the month had been a lie, too. That there was nothing Kaine could do that was as valuable as betraying him?

Crowther's eyebrows furrowed as he studied her. "I've spent a year working on the logistics of replacing you . . . I must admit, you are the most exceptional asset the Eternal Flame possesses. And I am sorry for that."

Knowing now the Holdfasts' method of selecting their "prodigies," she did see the parallels between them: both brought to Paladia as talented children with nowhere else to go, their lives spent being lonely and useful because it was all they knew.

Perhaps, looking at her as his successor, he did find her tragic.

Crowther went with Helena to the Outpost the next week.

After his brief interlude of humanity, Crowther had retreated back into his shadows, and when he reemerged, he'd reverted to his normal self. Still, Helena could feel how her place in his strategy had shifted with the new developments.

She said nothing to him on the way there. They took a lorry as far as the gate and then walked to the Outpost. It was startling how quick the journey was when not taken on foot. There was a light, misting rain draped like a shroud over the city, frothing into a thick mist near the dam.

The necrothralls on the Outpost faded into the rain when they passed.

Kaine was waiting inside the tenement as though he'd never left. He looked gaunt. Tired. He didn't meet her eyes. He barely even looked at her. The cloths that had covered the floor had all been folded and lay in a pile against one wall.

If Crowther had any reaction to the tenement, he didn't show it, but Helena felt a visceral sense of discomfort as his eyes swept over the room. She was used to it, but now she saw all the dirt, chipped paint, and cracked tiles again. Remembered how degrading it had felt the first time she'd arrived.

As he stood surveying the space, the air in the room grew tense. Like a forest going abruptly silent.

Crowther had not seen combat in years, but Helena had healed enough of his interrogation victims to know he had a talent for precision pyromancy, and now he had two hands to wield it with. She wasn't sure about the extent of Kaine's abilities, but even the Undying struggled against flame alchemists.

The feeling of hatred between Crowther and Kaine was so tangible, the air sang with it.

Crowther was the one who spoke first, eyes glittering. "I understand you wish to make a new deal with the Eternal Flame, Ferron."

There was mocking insinuation in his tone.

Kaine had gone startlingly pale. "So it would seem."

Helena had thought she was supposed to act as an intermediary between them, but Kaine glanced towards her.

"You can go now, Marino. I'm sure Crowther can find his way back on his own."

Helena hesitated, looking between the two men.

Amusement lit Crowther's face as he glanced at Helena, too. "No need to walk back alone. Wait outside, Marino. I'm sure Ferron won't let anything happen to you on the landing."

The muscle in Kaine's jaw ticked, but he didn't speak.

Helena looked between them and then turned reluctantly and went out to the landing. She only heard Crowther utter one word before the door sealed shut:

"Beg."

She wandered the hallway, peeking through the tenements missing doors at the identical units. She followed the stairs to the top floor and wandered back down.

The rain was falling through the broken skylight, creating a constant drip and patter. As she reached the second floor, a glimpse of something hidden in the shadows caught her attention.

She went closer, rising on her toes and squinting, trying to see clearly what it was. It had been strategically concealed to make it almost invisible in the shadows.

A human eye encased in glass stared down at her. When Helena moved to the side, it rotated, following her.

A shiver ran down her spine. She hadn't even known that it was possible to animate only a part of a body, but it was undeniably animated. Perfectly preserved. Angled to see the entire landing from the shadows.

That was how Kaine always knew when she was there.

She sat on the steps for half an hour before Crowther emerged from the room. She knew he probably wouldn't tell her the terms, but she hoped that after having her wait, he'd tell her something.

He merely paused, studying her. "Good work, Marino."

CHAPTER 49

Februa 1787

THE MOOD IN HEADQUARTERS GREW SOMBRE AS the winter crawled on. The days felt endlessly dark, the air so cold and damp that even quick walks across the commons were bone-chilling.

After months of largely successful defence and fortification, the Resistance was hit hard and sudden. One of the walls along the East Island was blown up by a bomb blast so large, it took down several buildings. Then more blasts, and before they'd even begun to evacuate the survivors, the necrothralls and chimaeras poured in.

The Resistance lost a battalion and an entire swath of the East Island.

Luc's battalion was trapped inside a building, pursued down to the river level where they ended up cornered for more than a day until the Resistance assembled a large enough force to get them out. The casualties were terrible. Half of them were badly injured. One medic was killed in the retreat, and another died from injuries during the siege. Luc had held back the chimaeras and necrothralls by maintaining a wall of flame for hours on end. He and Lila had been coated in smoke and grime, too exhausted to even speak when they were brought back. Soren sustained a shattered right arm when the floor collapsed under him and several others. He'd been held back from defence during the siege, caring for the injured and watching them die one by one.

He refused to talk about it.

BEFORE HELENA COULD RETURN TO the Outpost, Crowther informed her that she would see Kaine only once a week now. No explanation about why; those were simply the new terms of the deal. When Martiday came, she didn't know what to expect, how different things might be, but when Kaine arrived, he wordlessly kicked the padding cloths across the floor and began training her as if nothing had changed, except he didn't look at her anymore. His eyes seemed to go through her.

"How do you know all this?" she asked when he paused in attacking her to show her several techniques for breaking arms in ways that would shatter the bone or pierce the skin, slowing regeneration.

"The same way I know any of it," he said, staring across the room. "When you can't die, people keep hurting you until you can hurt them more."

"I'm sorry."

He looked at her sharply, fury in his eyes. "I'm sure you are."

There was no more conversation. He attacked and she had to fend him off. She managed to get a jab in under his arm but experienced only a moment of triumph before his fingers were wrapped around her throat, dragging her close.

They both froze, eyes meeting, and it was as if time stopped.

He snatched his hand back with a scathing glare. "Unless you start thinking faster than you move, you're going to be killed."

She failed twice more.

"That's enough for today." He finally turned away from her, reaching into his cloak, and pulled out an envelope, setting it on the table.

Helena's chest clenched in dread as she went over to her satchel and pulled out an envelope of her own, fidgeting with it as she turned to face him.

"Crowther said to give you this."

A sort of deadness filled his eyes as he looked over. "Right . . . My orders for the week."

He pulled it from her fingers with a listless jerk.

"Kaine—"

"Run along, Marino. I have work to do."

IT WAS HELENA'S JOB TO examine Luc to ensure he was healthy before he was allowed to leave Headquarters. He was still so shattered he scarcely seemed to notice her, which was for the best, as they hadn't spoken since the solstice.

He and Lila watched each other with a fervent intensity, as though the other person were their only touchstone.

If it were possible, Helena would have recommended a break—a few weeks to recuperate at least. Luc was dangerously haggard, and his lungs worried her, but they could not afford the luxury. Both were dispatched back to the front in their newly polished armour to reassure the now nervous battalions.

Soren was only a few days behind them.

Each week Kaine would train her, hand over intelligence reports, take his orders, and leave without even a backwards glance.

They didn't talk anymore. If she asked questions and it wasn't about combat, he ignored them. It felt as if there were a canyon between them now.

It was fine, though. He was alive. Every week she got to see him and know he was alive.

However, that was not something he seemed to care about. There was a raw despair visible in his eyes. Even his rage was smothered, as though he were existing out of sheer obligation.

After three weeks, she caught him by the wrist as he was taking Crowther's envelope from her. "Please—look at me."

He snatched his hand back but then stared squarely at her, that cold rage briefly reappearing. "Is this not enough for you? Is there something else you want, too?"

"No—" She looked at him helplessly. "I'm sorry. I thought—"

He gave a dry laugh. "Perhaps someday, if I have time again, I can make you a list of all the things that apologies don't fix."

Her hands dropped. "Kaine, I—"

"Don't—use my name. I hate the way it sounds on your tongue." He ripped the envelope from her fingers and left.

There was another deluge of injuries. Helena could barely keep track of all the battles and skirmishes, the victories and losses. In the hospital it all blurred together into endless screaming. Time seemed to morph into a horrific monotony, punctuated only with Kaine's cold resentment.

She tried to stay busy. With Rhea's permission, she attempted a tentative treatment of Titus, but he reacted poorly, becoming severely sick with a fever, putting an immediate end to the attempt.

She was cut loose. Left to her own devices. Everyone else seemed to come and go—even the other healers got dispatched down-island to the new hospital every few weeks—but Helena was always at Headquarters.

Ilva and Crowther no longer made any demands of her except to pass on their orders.

She was a collar around Kaine's neck, and her job now was to bear it.

SHE WAS RETURNING FROM THE Outpost when her hospital charm grew hot. She sprinted the rest of the way back. There was blood smeared across the ground of the gatehouse.

The guards were waiting for her. "Where were you?"

"Who? What—" she gasped out as they cleared her.

"Lila," said one of the young guards. "And Soren."

Dread flooded through her like poison. "Where's Luc—"

There was a pause and she knew before the older guard spoke.

"Missing."

Helena's body moved but her mind had stalled as she raced to the hospital.

No. This couldn't happen.

The casualty ward was in a frenzy as Helena entered. Elain immediately turned to Helena, hands covered in blood, her face white with panic.

"My resonance doesn't work!" she said, her voice rising with panic. "I can't stop the bleeding."

Lila was laid out on a bed, covered in dust and dirt and blood. The remains of her armour were smashed and split, her clothes shredded, as if she'd been caught in an explosion. Nurses were cutting off the straps and transmuting her armour to get it off her. A wide gouge ran down her face, from temple to cheek, and below that, at the base of her neck, a large puncture was pouring blood.

"I don't know what's wrong!" Elain was saying as Helena washed her hands under scalding water and doused them in carbolic dilution. "I think there's something inside her, but my resonance doesn't work! When I try to feel her, it's like—my hands—"

"Soren too? Or just Lila?"

"I don't know, I haven't tried him. We just got them in. She's bleeding out, and I can't feel anything!"

"Check Soren," Helena said. "I need medics for Lila, and Pace. Tell her I need her now."

She moved next to Lila. The neck was one of the few openings in her armour if her helmet had been off. Her blood was soaking the bed. She'd been hooked up to an intravenous drip with plasma expanders, but it wouldn't do any good if they couldn't get her to stop bleeding.

Lila's head was lolled back. She was still conscious, muttering under her breath, over and over. ". . . told him—to run. I—told him—t-to run—"

Helena reached out with her resonance and felt the horribly familiar disruption of nullium.

She'd hoped to be wrong. That Elain was just hysterical. Or even burned out.

Anything but this.

The nullium was much stronger than the shrapnel Helena had retrieved from Kaine. Altered in some way to intensify the effect.

She tried to at least get a vague sense of the size of what had been driven into Lila's chest cavity. Trying to determine if there was a risk of puncturing her heart if they put pressure on the wound. It was like peering through fog. Her hands felt as though they were asleep, needle-points pricking across her nerves as she tried to search for the most intense sense of dissonance.

It was long and slender. It had likely pierced her lung, possibly grazed her heart, but it was hard to tell.

This was so much worse than she and Shiseo had been prepared for.

"What is it?" Pace appeared at her side.

Helena was pressing gauze over the wound, trying to keep it from bleeding more. Lila had gone silent.

"It's nullium. She's going to need manual surgery to get it out. Maier isn't trained, but you were in the hospitals, back when they still used it, right?"

Pace went very white. "It's been a long time. I only assisted."

Helena drew a harsh breath. She couldn't disclose her own surgical experience with nullium. "I—used to help my father, sometimes. If you'll lead, and I keep her stable, then maybe. Is Soren—?"

She was afraid to know if Soren had nullium injuries. If she and Pace had to choose which twin to save, protocol dictated that the person with better odds of survival should receive priority, but as paladin primary, Lila had priority.

"The others can heal him," Pace said. "He took a bad blow to the head, but it's nothing Elain can't manage."

Helena closed her eyes as she fought to stay calm, trying to will Lila to survive, because this time she could not make her do it.

"Move her into the operating theatre," Pace said. "I'm sure Maier will help as much as he can. We'll need medics and nurses for support. I'll brief them. You keep her stable."

It had been only a handful of times that Helena had assisted her father with surgery. Before the massacre.

Observant with a good head in a crisis, he'd said. But that was a long time ago.

Handing over surgical instruments was very different from performing surgery without resonance. No one was prepared. The nullium they'd been familiar with only interfered when they worked with it directly. This was much more diffuse.

When Lila was sedated, Matron Pace used a long pair of clamps to reach into the puncture just above Lila's collarbone and pull out a long, rusting spike. It was fragile, degrading already due to the unstable fusion. Shards kept breaking off, forcing Pace to reach in over and over, removing them piece by piece.

Helena could feel through her resonance that even with the bulk of the spike removed, there were shards dissolving into Lila's blood. The nullium was spreading through her body like a fog, thicker and more impenetrable with every passing moment.

The fragility of the nullium was both a gift and a curse. It had taken the path of least resistance. There was a small puncture in Lila's lung, but her heart was not damaged, nor her oesophagus. It had stayed within the cavity. But the pieces were everywhere, and the alloy was so unstable that it was rapidly dissolving.

Pace wiped her forehead with a cloth. "We're going to need to do a thoracotomy to get the pieces out. Is she stable enough?"

An alchemical surgeon like Maier could normally perform a thoracotomy without needing to open a patient. It only needed incisions large enough to get slender tools inside; with training and resonance, their instruments were an extension of their fingers and senses.

Helena held back her resonance, using ordinary touch to check Lila's vital signs, because it was easier than trying to parse all the interference. "She's holding on."

They made an incision between Lila's ribs, using makeshift retractors to pry the bones apart so they could reach all the remaining shards. The pieces varied in size and crumbled if they weren't picked out carefully enough. There were little cuts and grooves in Lila's lungs and heart where shards had nicked her—wounds that could be easily repaired if Helena could use her resonance but were laborious and dangerous now, each requiring manual sutures.

The procedure was all unfamiliar, and they were racing against time. The longer the nullium had to break down and distribute into Lila's blood, the greater the likelihood that she might die from the metal toxicity. The surgery was pushing her body to its utmost limits, and Lila had to survive on her own.

Helena manually siphoned the blood, keeping Lila's heart beating as Pace worked. A nurse had taken the larger shards to Shiseo to analyse and synthesise the sequestering agent, but that treatment was hours away.

It was possible that until they managed to purge the metal from Lila's bloodstream, they would be unable to use any kind of resonance on her.

"A thoracic lavage next," Pace said at last, setting down her tools. Her eyes were bloodshot from strain by the time they finished.

Maier took over the sutures. His stitches were beautifully neat, but he looked shaken as he worked.

Helena looked up and found it was growing dark outside. "I should check on Soren."

She felt so strange as she washed her hands. She'd barely used her resonance, but the pressure of the last several hours had her head throbbing. Stepping out of the operating theatre, she found most of the hospital crowded around one bed.

Soren was awake and propped up. All the privacy curtains had been pushed aside, and at the forefront of the people surrounding him was Ilva.

Soren's arm was in splints, and bandages covered half his face. He kept shaking his head. "I don't—remember. It happened so fast."

"Did you recognise anyone? Even imagine that you saw a face?" Ilva said, grasping Soren's wrist.

"I don't know," Soren said again, his voice straining. "There was—an explosion. Something hit me. Might have been out seconds or minutes. When I got up, I couldn't see. Luc was gone, and Lila was on the ground, bleeding out. She kept saying, *Told him to run.* I didn't know where to look—so I came back."

"There was no warning?" The questions seemed to be exploding from Ilva. She was visibly agitated. "No signs at all? Who was leading the unit?"

"I—" Soren's expression twisted, and he seemed to struggle to remember.

"I always said it was a mistake, allowing a female paladin," Matias said. "If I had been Falcon at the time, I would never have allowed such a violation of tradition to be entertained. I warned you, Ilva, Luc was partial to her, but no: Lila Bayard was too exceptional to separate from him. Now look what's happened."

"Shut your mouth!" Ilva snarled over her shoulder at Matias, her fingers still digging into Soren's wrist. Then she turned back and shook him. "Did she say Luc surrendered himself? Did he hand himself over because of Lila?"

"I don't know," Soren half whispered.

Elain was standing near Soren's bed, too awed by the number of Eternal Flame members currently flanking the bed to interfere.

"Pardon," Helena said in a curt voice, and she pushed herself through the crowd. "Soren Bayard has a head injury. It's inadvisable to stress him."

Everyone turned to look at her.

"Is Lila awake? Can she answer questions?" Ilva said, instantly rising to her feet.

Helena shook her head sharply. "She is not available for anything. We performed an extensive manual surgery to remove a spike of nullium that she'd been stabbed with, but the alloy deteriorated and distributed through her bloodstream, which will interfere with *anything* involving resonance until it's removed."

"How long will that take?" The panic on Ilva's face was clear.

Helena shook her head. "We have her under anaesthesia right now, but we're working blind. She may wake in the next few hours, or it could take days. Lila is very strong, but this will still be harder on her than past injuries. Nothing's certain yet."

Soren had slumped back and looked as if he was on the verge of a panic attack, but Ilva drew herself up like a viper.

"I thought you had prepared for this eventuality," Ilva said. "What have you all been doing?"

Helena's jaw tensed. Why was it always the hospital's fault when things went wrong? If Helena had come out and said that surgery was a success and Lila was already getting out of bed, they'd all be off to the perihelion to offer Sol flames of thanksgiving. But bad news was always the hospital's fault.

How nice it must be, to be a god.

"The alloy has been altered, and the interference is much more intense. Manual procedures are not simple, especially in a hospital where only *two* people have any experience performing them. If you want the hospital prepared to perform manual surgery, the Falcon will need to approve the cadavers for practice, as we requested *several* months ago."

Matias coughed as if he'd swallowed something the wrong way and suddenly stopped looking like he wanted to be present.

Ilva was gripping her cane but looked ready to topple. It was as if Luc's loss had ripped the ground out from beneath her.

"Examine him, then," Ilva said, moving unsteadily away from Soren's bed. "There will be a Council meeting in an hour. I want full reports on both the Bayards."

Everyone filed out. Helena glared and jerked her head, indicating that Elain put the privacy curtains back as she sat down next to Soren.

He was leaning back amid the pillows which had propped him up, covered in newly healed cuts. She could tell, as soon as her resonance touched him, that he'd lost his right eye. Whatever had hit him had fractured the socket and crushed it.

Her fingers trembled.

"She's never going to forgive me," he said, his voice a near whisper.

Helena didn't know if he was referring to Ilva or Lila.

She squeezed his hand. "If you'd gone after Luc in this state, all three of you might be dead. That wouldn't have been any help. I'm sure there's more people looking for him because you came back."

Elain had done well with her healing. He'd had several broken bones, including the same arm he'd shattered just a few weeks ago. It hadn't fully healed, and it was likely to have lingering issues now.

"Do you think he's still alive?" Soren asked.

Helena's heart caught. She couldn't think of any reason the Undying wouldn't immediately kill Luc.

"Until we know he's dead, he's still alive. And we're going to get him back," she said, forcing her voice to sound hopeful. "Stop worrying now. I need to check your head."

He had a concussion, but his eye and brow bone had absorbed most of the blow. All her visits to Titus had made her more familiar with brains; she felt as if she understood them better and could at least diagnose accurately, rather than shying away.

Elain hadn't known what to do with the destroyed eye and had left it, just wrapping gauze over it and repairing only the bone.

"Soren, your right eye's—"

"I know," he said brusquely, as if it didn't matter. "I can still fight, though, right?"

Her hands stilled. "You've broken your arm and lost half your range of vision. That's going to require adapting. You're going to be vulnerable. You won't see things from the right."

"I'll just turn my head," he said in a flat voice. "Handy thing, necks."

She sighed. "You're not going back out. Not for weeks at least."

He shook his head. "Lila's out. I have to bring Luc back before she wakes. She can't wake up and find out I didn't go after him." His chin trembled. In twelve years of knowing him, Helena had never seen Soren cry. He looked down. "I didn't tell them, but she told me to leave her. To go find him. But I didn't. I told her I'd go, as soon as I got her safe—"

He started trying to climb out of the bed. It only took one hand to push him back. He was barely strong enough to sit up.

"Soren, I need to deal with the ruptured tissue in your eye," she said, trying to sound firm.

He ignored her, trying to shove her off, but she was adept enough at combat now. She deflected his hand and slipped her fingers behind his head. It took only a frisson of resonance and his remaining eye rolled back as he collapsed, unconscious.

She closed his eye gently so it wouldn't dry out. "I'm so sorry," she whispered as she set to work.

If there was anything intact inside the socket, there would have been a small chance of saving some of his sight, but Soren's eye was wrecked.

She removed all the tissue that couldn't be repaired so that it wouldn't rot or cause infection, then carefully rebandaged him. In a few weeks, someone would make a beautiful glass eye for him, or perhaps shape a gem.

Assuming there still was a Resistance in a few weeks.

Rhea arrived just as Helena finished.

It had been a long time since both twins had been in the hospital.

Rhea's expression was stoic, but her eyes were searching as she moved towards Soren.

Helena stood up. "I just finished. I can wake him," she said, quickly covering all the eye tissue with a cloth.

"No, let him rest." Rhea sat down slowly on the edge of the bed, studying the parts of Soren's face that weren't obscured. "My little boy," she said softly, her voice a murmur, as if she feared Soren might wake.

Helena stepped back, not sure if Rhea would want privacy or answers.

"You know, he was such a little thing when he was born," Rhea said, one of her hands reaching and covering Soren's. "Titus could fit him into one hand. The doctors didn't think he'd make it. Lila came out bright red and screaming, but my little Soren was just a wisp of a baby. Quiet and pale. Even when he needed to nurse, he'd barely make a sound. He always followed Lila around, never caused trouble himself, but was always right there, getting into hers."

Rhea gave a sobbing laugh. "I thought I was doing such a great thing when they were born. Twins. Two babies for the Bayard family. Our little paladins." Rhea's body trembled as she held Soren's hand. "And now Titus doesn't even know what's been done to our beautiful children—all my family, I only have *pieces* of them left."

She folded over Soren. Her body was shuddering, but she cried silently.

There was a trick to sobbing like that; it was something a person had to learn to do.

Helena slipped away, to give her space to grieve.

THE MEETING WAS SOMBRE. ILVA sat at the Council table, looking almost drugged while the reports were being given. The attack had occurred on the lower part of the East Island. Luc and Lila had been leading the battalion towards Headquarters; they'd passed a condemned building, and just as Luc and Lila stepped beyond it, there had been an explosion. The building had collapsed.

Soren had been on the edge of the blast and thrown by it. Only two others had survived, because they'd fallen behind. They'd been caught in the rubble with only minor injuries.

There'd been signs of a fight, char marks and a pool of blood, presumed to be Lila's. Burned human remains, presumed to be necrothralls, a lich with his talisman ripped out. Luc's sword, rings, and other weapons were found discarded, as if he'd left first and then been stripped.

There'd been no word from the Undying. No proclamation that Luc was dead or even captured. The guards had all been told to prepare for the possibility that he might return reanimated or with his body possessed by a lich. If Luc reappeared, all due diligence must be performed. No one was to believe in any miraculous escapes.

As time passed, the questions grew. Why would the Undying keep him alive? Wouldn't they announce if he was dead, or were they keeping him hostage to negotiate a surrender?

If he was a hostage, why hadn't they reached out?

"Until we know that Lucien is dead, we will assume that he is alive," Ilva said in an icy voice, rousing herself when one of the lead metallurgists referred to planning for contingencies. "The Undying have no reason to conceal his capture. It's been twelve hours, and we haven't received word. It may be a sign that not everything is as it seems."

As the meeting closed, Matias stood, announcing his intention to entreat the heavens to return Luc to them safely. Many people followed him.

Ilva remained at the table, speaking to Crowther.

"Marino, a word before you go," Ilva said when Helena rose to return to the hospital.

Helena waited until the room was empty. Ilva flicked a hand, and the guards closed the doors.

"You'll head to the Outpost. We're going to use Ferron," Ilva said in a brusque voice. "Every piece of information he has or can obtain about the circumstances of Luc's capture—I want it all. As well as an explanation as to why we received no warning about this."

"Of course." She'd expected as much.

"Tell him this is a critical mission," Ilva added as Helena turned to go. "Those precise words, Marino. A top priority. If he has an opportunity to get Luc back for us, that would be preferable to the losses we'll suffer with a rescue."

They meant to sacrifice Kaine to recover Luc. It was the obvious choice. An easy trade-off. The kind that any strategist would make.

But—

"All right." Her voice was lifeless.

LUMITHIA HUNG LIKE A GIANT silver disc in the sky, so near full Ascendance that she blotted out the planets, leaving the night sky as an endless black abyss overhead. The bright silver light cast glaring shadows across the city.

When Helena reached the landing in the tenement, she paused and stepped intentionally into the silver shaft of light cascading from the broken skylight, looking up at the eye hidden in the corner. Then she waited.

It was a long wait.

The windows rattled in the wind, but she didn't hear anything until the door clicked and Kaine strode in. Everything about him seemed sharper. "What happened?"

The instant he asked the question, she realised he didn't know.

Ilva had been right: If the Undying had Luc, it was being kept secret.

"There was an attack today. A bombing," she said, and her voice trembled. "Killed most of a battalion, the Bayard twins barely survived, and Luc—is missing."

"Are you sure?"

She gave a stiff nod. "They used a weapon made from that resonance-interference alloy. We call it nullium. Lila was stabbed and nearly killed with it. You didn't know this was in the works?"

He shook his head slowly. "I didn't. There's suspicion of a spy due to—recent sabotage. And I haven't had the leisure to be as present as I used to be."

She looked down, drawing a deep breath before she spoke. "We have to get Luc back. I was told to tell you it's critical. Your top priority."

"Right . . ."

"Any information you can get on his capture, who did it, where he is, if he's alive . . . The Council wants you—" Her words caught. "—to do anything you can."

"Of course," was all he said, and he turned to go.

She watched his back, the shift of his shoulders, one dipping as he reached for the knob. She didn't know if she was ever going to see him again.

"Wait," she said.

He paused but didn't look back. "I'll call you when I have something."

"Kaine . . . when I kissed you, I—"

He turned suddenly. In one moment he was across the room and in the next, he was in front of her, his expression venomous, his teeth bared. "Really, you want to discuss this now?"

Her throat was so thick with guilt, she could barely speak. But she was desperate. "Will you look at me, at least?"

A cruel glint entered his eyes as they locked squarely on her face. It was like being punched to have his full attention again.

"You want me to look at you?" His voice was light, almost cajoling, but there was fury beneath the surface. He leaned towards her. "Fine. I'm looking. I must say, it's delightful, seeing all the guilt in your eyes."

He sneered, drawing back. "You know, I used to think the circumstances of my servitude to the High Necromancer as cruel an enslavement as anyone could conceive, but I must admit, it *pales* beside you."

He tilted his head. "At least before, I could console myself that it wasn't my fault; acceptance was the best I could do to keep my mother safe. It's different when I have no one to blame but myself."

His hand came up, his gloved fingers wrapping around her throat, pulling her forward. "After all, I did choose you."

She met his eyes, that deadened despair so visible when he looked at her.

"I envied your naïveté, how you credited me with goodness and failed to realise that it was a setup from the very beginning. When you begged for a chance to heal me, I gave in. When you touched me, I didn't push you away. I thought, Where's the harm? It all ends soon enough, and life has been cold for such a long time."

She didn't realise she'd started crying until his thumb brushed across her cheek.

"By the time I realised I'd miscalculated, you'd already forced your way in. You were so obvious, but that only made it worse; knowing you'd let me do anything to you in the hope it would save everyone else, even the people who'd sold you in the first place. At least when I sold my soul, my mother prostrated herself, begging to take my place. I suppose, in some regards, I am luckier than you."

She gave a low sob.

"After you nearly bled to death here, I thought, at least I can keep her alive. She deserves to have someone who cares enough to *try* to keep her alive. I thought eventually you'd give up. But you will do anything to save the people you feel responsible for. Of course you'd weaponise your guilt in order to use mine." He gave a low bitter laugh. "I'm sure there's something poetic in it all, but right now all I feel is a new set of manacles."

He let go and stepped away from her, heading for the door. "So forgive me if I dislike looking at you. I'm still adjusting to the ways these new ones chafe."

SOREN WAS SITTING NEXT TO Lila when Helena returned to the hospital, heart dead in her chest.

In her absence, nothing had happened except meetings and arguments in which no one agreed about what to do. Helena had known it was Luc who held everything together, but it was startling to see how fast it all crumbled.

Lila's hair was cropped short like a boy's, the area near the wound was shaven. Her face was so swollen and bruised, she was almost unrecognisable. Maier's careful sutures had tried to rejoin the torn skin, but that scar would stay with her for the rest of her life.

"She's younger than me, you know," Soren said. Helena nodded. "No one ever guesses that."

He leaned forward and whispered something in Lila's ear, his voice so low Helena couldn't make out the words. Then he straightened, walking out.

Helena followed him. The hollow under his remaining eye looked like a crater. His face was drawn, pain lines visible around his mouth and the corner of his eye. Someone had removed his cast already. Elain.

"Come on," she said, taking him into a curtained-off area and making him sit down.

She worked on his arm and hand first. The bone had been mended well, but it was a new injury, which made it more at risk of being broken again. She knew he wasn't going to be careful. He'd be out in the field as soon as there was word. The best she could do was heal as far as she could, imitating the way Kaine's body regenerated, not merely to "fixed" but all the way back to its prior state.

"I need your help," he said as she placed new gauze over his eye.

Her hands stilled. "For what?"

"I need a healer, and you're the best."

She drew back, tilting his head to study his face even though his expressions were always evasive. "Soren, what have you done?"

He raised his eyebrow. "Nothing . . . yet." A helpless smile just barely touched the edge of his lips. "You have to promise to help first before I can tell."

Helena hesitated. With Luc or Lila around, Soren had never needed to create his own trouble. He was, Lila once joked, like a cat, feigning indifference but somehow always in the same room with you.

Soren alone was a mystery. She didn't know what he might do when all the choices were his to make.

"All right. I promise. Tell me."

"Not here," he said, standing up.

They left Headquarters, wound through several alleys, and entered an abandoned shop.

"I got a healer," he said as they entered the back room, his hand on Helena's shoulder to push her through the door as if she might bolt otherwise. Which she might have, given how clearly planned her presence was.

Waiting there, fully armed, stood the two remaining members of Luc's unit, Alister and Penny, as well as Sebastian and Crowther's informant from the hospital, Purnell, who carefully avoided Helena's eyes.

"Marino?" said Alister. "I thought you were getting a medic."

"A medic's not good enough," Soren said as he walked up to the table in the centre of the room. Helena hung back. "We need a healer. Helena's the best."

"Maybe . . ." Alister said, dubiously, "but she's never been in combat. She'll be deadweight in a fight. Same as this one." He pointed at Purnell. "You're going to get us all killed if we don't get this perfect."

"We don't need her to fight. *We* can fight. The thing none of us can do is make sure we can get Luc out alive. Hel's the best bet for that. We don't know what kind of condition he's going to be in when we find him. She can fix anything."

Helena wasn't sure she appreciated the degree of confidence Soren was placing in her.

"Have you ever been to the front?" Alister was staring at her.

"No."

"This is insane," Alister said. "I'd follow you anywhere, Soren, but this is not a good plan. What if Luc's in a bad way, and all we have is her; is she going to carry him out?"

"I'll help!" Purnell spoke up abruptly. "After I show you the way, I can help with Luc. I'm good in the hospital."

"Soren." Helena's voice was tight. "Can I talk to you?" She dragged him back outside. "What are you doing?"

"We're getting Luc back," he said.

"Yes, I've gathered that," she said, shaking him, not caring that he was injured, because he was about to go commit suicide. "You're barely recovered. Why is Purnell here?"

"Sofia?"

Since when was Soren on a first-name basis with a hospital orderly?

"Yes, the orderly. Do you know who she is?"

"She's the one who knows where Luc might be."

Helena stared stunned as it dawned on her why Purnell was there. This had Crowther's fingerprints all over it. This wasn't Soren's rescue, this was Crowther, pulling the strings once again.

But then, what was he planning to do with Kaine? Was Kaine a distraction? Or was this because Crowther hoped to avoid losing Kaine prematurely?

Helena's molars ground together.

"And how would she know that?" she asked, trying to get Soren to see how insane this all was.

Soren gave a tight smile. "Crowther uses her to keep an eye on us, but she doesn't like it. She came clean with Luc a while back. She's seen maps for a secret prison that can be accessed from the West Island's waterways."

"Soren." Helena exhaled, closing her eyes. "Why would she have seen maps like that?"

Soren shrugged, not seeming concerned about it. "Crowther uses her for carrying messages. I guess she peeked."

If Crowther was the mastermind behind this, Helena wanted him directly involved, giving clear instructions about how he thought it was going to work, not some shadowy *an orderly saw a map* sleight of hand.

She was sick of how Ilva and Crowther both defaulted to manipulation to get their "miracles" to show up. As if people couldn't be counted on unless they were tricked.

"If that's the case, then that means Crowther knows about this prison, and he might have a lot more information than just a map. We should talk to him."

Soren immediately shook his head. "No. The Council is adamant that no one can take any action until they 'know' who has Luc. Ilva somehow thinks she's going to negotiate a trade to get Luc back. No mention, though, of what she possibly thinks we could offer."

Helena knew exactly what it was that Ilva probably had in mind.

"My duty is to Luc," Soren was saying, "not the Eternal Flame. As long as Lila's out, I'm primary. The Council doesn't command me, my duty is to my vows and my vows are to Luc."

She'd thought they wanted Kaine to rescue Luc—to risk his cover to spare their own troops. But if that failed, Ilva would sell him out without a second thought.

Which meant Crowther was being forced to go behind Ilva's back. That was why he was using Sofia Purnell to pass the relevant information to Soren, the one person with the ability to act on his own.

"All right," Helena said, nodding. "I'll come."

Soren looked startled, then sagged with relief. "Good. I don't think I can do this without you."

Helena scrutinised him. "What do you mean?"

His eyes were heavy-lidded. When he was pensive, they got soulful. Now there was just one, but she still recognised the expression.

"I need you to do anything, Hel, whatever it takes, to save him. No matter the price. Anyone in the Resistance would die for him; I need you there because it might take more than that."

Her eyes went wide. "Do you realise what you're asking?"

He held his head high. "My vow is to protect my Principate with my life and my death. You're the one who said that if someone's willing to die, why not give them a chance to keep fighting."

Her hands had gone numb. "You can't volunteer the others for a mission like that. Are you planning to tell them that's why I'm here? *That you chose me because you want necromancy as your backup plan?*" Her voice dropped to a furious whisper as she retreated, but he caught her by the arm.

"That's not the only reason," he said. "You *are* the best. I'm not volunteering them, just me. If something goes wrong, you do anything you have to to get them out. This is me giving you permission."

She shook her head. "I don't even know if I can. I've never—"

"We both know that if someone can do vivimancy, they can do necromancy. And if there's anyone who can figure it out on the fly, it's you. I'm not going to do anything stupid. I just—" He swallowed. "I need to know this is going to work. Hel, this has to work."

She wavered a moment longer, but what were the alternatives? Every choice had become unbearable. And this was the price she'd already offered to pay.

"Fine." She swallowed. "For Luc."

"For Luc. Come on."

Helena wanted very much to corner Purnell and interrogate her about exactly what Crowther knew, and how he expected the mission to unfold, but Purnell was constantly in motion, moving around the room, staying out of reach.

"How do you know all this?" Helena asked pointedly, after she was told about the location of the prison and how there was a floodwater cathedral that they would use to reach it.

"I know people who use them. The scouts—and others, when they need escape routes and safe places to go," Purnell said.

"Why aren't they more patrolled?"

Purnell shrugged. "It's a maze. The greys can't see in the dark, or they get lost, and the Undying don't like crawling in sewer water."

Helena's own throat convulsed at the thought. "I see."

"It won't be bad, though. It's flood season now," Purnell said. "The water will mostly be mountain water. It'll be cold, but nothing like it is in the summer."

Small mercies. Helena was well acquainted with how cold the river snowmelt was; the mere thought of crawling through it was enough to make her bones ache. "And these tunnels are connected to where Luc is?"

Purnell was avoiding Helena's eyes again. "A lot of old access points to the sewers were built over, but they're easy to reopen if you have the building schematics. Someone investigated it a few months ago. It's very high-level compared with the other prisons, but almost completely empty. Like it's being reserved for something."

"If Luc's there, then this means his capture is something they've been working towards for a long time," Sebastian said in a tight voice.

Fear sliced down Helena's spine. "Why are you so sure Luc's there?"

"If it's a secret they have him, they'd have to put him in a secret place," was all Purnell said.

Helena couldn't help but feel that the girl's involvement had already destroyed Crowther's chance at plausible deniability. Surely he could afford to be less opaque.

"If he's not there, no one will even know we went in," Soren said. "We have to go tonight. Ascendance is tomorrow; the floodwaters are already high, and none of us will be clearheaded enough to go. We'd have to wait two more days, and Luc can't afford that."

Helena hadn't considered that aspect. They captured Luc just before Ascendance. Why? Just to increase the complexity of the rescue efforts? Or was it a coincidence?

The plan was only the vaguest shape of a plan. *Get in, find Luc, get out.*

Helena's job was to keep Purnell close and out of the way. The others would deal with any fighting. When they found Luc, she'd examine him, make sure he was still alive, and, if necessary, heal him as rapidly as possible. Then she would get him out. Purnell would help her carry him if he couldn't walk on his own.

Helena's job was getting him back to the East Island by any means possible. If she had to leave everyone else behind, she was to do that. Once Luc was safe, the others would scatter and regroup.

"Let's go," Soren said, pulling on his armour as Alister and Penny snapped to attention.

"Wait!" Helena said, fighting to keep her voice steady, overwhelmed with the feeling that the plan was wrong. "I need to get my medical kit."

Soren's eye narrowed with suspicion. "Don't you just use your hands?"

She shook her head. "No. If Luc's really hurt, there's elixirs and salves, restoratives that will make him recover faster. Relying on vivimancy would—drain him or me. If I have my medicines, we'll have a better chance of him making it out if he's badly hurt."

Soren relaxed marginally. "All right. Go fast. If you don't come back in fifteen minutes, we'll leave without you."

She ran out the door, straight to Headquarters and the Alchemy Tower. The lift had never felt so slow as it cranked upwards.

"Please be there, Shiseo," she prayed as the doors opened and she hurried to her lab, beginning to doubt whether she was making the right decision.

Shiseo was there, synthesising chelators when she burst in.

"I need your help," she said as she rushed to her satchel. She went to the cabinet filled with all her medicine and snatched up vial after vial, enough doses for everyone twice. She found needles, bandages, manual medical tools, then packed everything she could into waxed, water-sealed bags and put all of it into her satchel until it was full to bursting.

Then she opened a small drawer that held her knives and started strapping them on.

"You got the titanium-nickel," Shiseo said, watching the knives mould against her skin. "May I see them?"

"Not now," she said, pulling the satchel over her head and buckling the extra strap to her waist so she could run with it. "I need you to do something for me. I can't tell you all the details, but I don't have anyone else to turn to."

She snatched up a piece of paper and started scribbling notes. Everything she knew, all the relevant details. Location. Strategy. Exit.

Written out plainly, it was obvious there was no way it would work, but she didn't know what else she could do but go along with it.

She looked up. "Do you know the way to the old factory Outpost?"

Shiseo nodded. "Yes. I visited when it was operational."

She nodded shakily. "I need you to go there, as quickly as you can. It's—enemy territory, but if you see a necrothrall, say 'Helena sent me' and they should leave you alone. Take this route." She sketched it roughly on a slip of paper. "You'll find a tenement building with the iron symbol on it. On the second floor there's a door. Shove this under the door and then come back. Or—if you don't want to do any of that, give this to Ilva. I can't—I don't know how to make this choice."

She held the paper out.

Shiseo looked from her to the paper, an odd gleam of interest in his dark eyes. "I always knew you were very interesting."

"I have to go," she said.

He took the paper, and she turned and ran, not waiting to see which choice he made. She kept running.

Soren and the others were emerging from the shop as she careened down the alley.

“Thought you’d split,” Alister said, giving her a sideways grin. He seemed to have accepted her presence now.

“No,” Helena said, breathing raggedly. “I’m all in.”

CHAPTER 50

Aprilis 1787

Accessing the West Island's flood cathedral was a mission of its own. There were Resistance patrols they had to hide from until they finally found a weak point in the wall that Alister could open. They crawled through, straight into ice-cold floodwater. The spring floods had started early, and with Lumithia at near Ascendance, the tributaries had climbed out of their banks and threatened to drag them all downriver. They had to cling to the wall as they made their way to a crossing point, one of the old pre-war bridges which was nearly destroyed. It swayed dangerously, threatening to collapse as Helena crawled across it, not daring to look down at the swirling, freezing death below.

Things only got worse once they were across. The flood cathedrals were immense towering underground rooms, designed to fill with several storeys of water and redirect it downriver, and they were filling. The grate to access one was half covered in floodwater and made of inert iron, which required time to break through to reveal a terrifyingly deep drop. Even with electric torches, they couldn't see the bottom. The roar of water rose from the dark.

The others were unfazed. They were used to traversing the city levels, rappelling up and down dozens of storeys during combat. Their armour had harnesses built in, with spools of wires and hooks to anchor themselves.

Penny, a reconnaissance scout, went first. She was terrifyingly quick. In seconds, she was anchored and dove headfirst into the dark without a backwards glance. For a minute, there was nothing but the taut wires; then they slackened and drew tight again, and began to vibrate at intervals.

Alister touched them with his fingers. "All clear," he said, flicking the wires so they'd vibrate back down.

The anchors came loose, slithering into the darkness after Penny like a pair of serpents. The rest of them followed. Helena and Purnell, without their own armour and harnesses, were deadweight in the literal sense. Alister took Helena with him, and Sebastian carried Purnell, and the water poured down on them like a waterfall. They were soaked to the bone, nearly numb by the time they reached the bottom. It was too loud to hear anything but water crashing down, echoing off the walls with a cacophonous roar.

Alister was shaking with cold, but he knelt down, putting his hands underwater for several minutes.

"It's shallow along the edges but about ten feet left, there's a drop, and the water's fast. I can't feel the bottom." He had to shout to be heard. "If we go straight, it should be fine, but let's anchor a line before we cross. I'll go first, I know the safest route."

Once they reached the far wall, there was a ladder leading to an upper walkway that ran above the dozens of huge tunnels feeding into the cathedral. Helena used her vivimancy to warm everyone, but there was nothing to be done about their soaking clothes except to keep moving.

Penny took the lead again. She'd memorised the route through all the tunnels that wound bewilderingly. She had a slight limp from an old injury, but she was still quick and light-footed. She moved forward, checking the route, making sure things were clear before using her torch to signal the rest of them forward.

They did not encounter a single necrothrall.

Helena's dread grew.

They climbed an endless ladder that connected to a tunnel, and after crawling so long that Helena began to wonder if she'd ever see light again, they emerged into a basement.

"Wait here," Soren said.

Penny leaned against a wall. She was breathing hard, stooped over, her hand pressing against her knee.

"Let me see," Helena said. There'd been a torn ligament—it had been healed, but she should have been on bedrest for a few days and then worked slowly back into active duty.

"I'm fine, I'll get fixed up again once we get back," Penny said, but Helena could tell she wouldn't.

There was a muffled shout, the quick snick of steel, and a thud. Soren's head popped back through the doorway to those waiting in the basement. "Clear," he said softly.

They ascended three floors. Helena had never seen Luc's unit in actual combat, only their practices. They were deadly. Dark blurs of steel and spilled blood. Their weapons morphed like water in their hands, the blades twisting and altering, reaching out and slaughtering anything that crossed their paths, using their harnesses to make gravity-defying attacks.

The prison was unquestionably occupied. There were too many guards and necrothralls for it to be abandoned, but not as many as would be expected for keeping Luc prisoner.

Helena kept telling herself it wasn't a trap, but it felt like one. They moved fast, trying to search every room before their victims were discovered and the alarms went off. There was no point in hiding the bodies; Soren left a trail of blood in his wake.

Alister was defence. He had spectacular resonance reach. He could throw up a wall, or shove back attackers by moving the ground under them. He'd hang back and queue them so that Sebastian and Soren could kill methodically without getting crowded or overrun in the narrow hallways.

Penny, no longer scouting, acted as Alister's cover, protecting him from any attacks.

They checked every room. Cell after cell. No Luc. No prisoners at all. The place seemed empty. Except there were guards.

They finally found a prisoner in the last cell in the block. A huddled figure under a blanket.

"Luc?" Soren's voice was ragged with desperation.

The figure lying on the cot stirred, and a grey-haired man lifted his head. When he saw them, his eyes went wide and he lunged towards the bar, jabbering in broken Northern dialect.

"Resistance?"

That was all Helena managed to make out among the many words she didn't know. He sounded western.

"Save?" The man pointed at himself.

"No," Soren said, shaking his head. "We're looking for someone else."

"Save." He pointed at himself again.

"We're only here for one person," Soren said, already turning.

The man's eyes narrowed. "Boy?" He touched his own hair. "Gold?"

They all turned back.

"Is he here?" Helena asked.

The man set his jaw. "Save." He pointed at himself again.

"We don't have time to drag around a prisoner," Soren said. "We'll find him ourselves."

"No!" The man sounded terrified now.

Helena studied him. "What's your name?"

"Vagner," he said slowly.

The name was familiar. Vagner.

Wagner? That was the name Crowther and Ivy had tortured out of Lancaster.

She turned to Soren. "We've been looking for him."

"Helena." Soren looked at her with exasperation. "We can't deal with a prisoner."

"This one is important. Crowther's had people trying to find him. If this is where they're hiding the prisoners they don't want anyone knowing about, that's all the more evidence this is a prisoner we need."

Soren hesitated. "If he slows us down or does anything that puts the mission at risk, I will kill him, and you won't stop me. Agreed?"

Helena nodded.

Luc wasn't anywhere on that floor. They ascended again. Hope dwindling. Maybe all these guards were just for Wagner, who followed them, cowering behind her and Purnell as though they were human shields.

They turned a corner and found an immense grey-skinned necrothrall standing in front of the door. He smiled.

Not a necrothrall, then, a lich.

"There you are," he said in a rasping voice, raising a huge spiked club, as his other hand rapped a warning on the door behind him. "I wondered if the remaining Bayards might show up. Two down and two to go." He paid no attention to Soren, his focus on Sebastian. "That pretty niece of yours made a sound like a rotten gourd when I ran her through. You should have seen how fast your Principate dropped his sword when she fell."

Sebastian stilled Soren. "Who are you?"

The lich smiled again, the corpse's bloated lips splitting into a rotten grin. "Don't you recognise me, Sebastian? I'd think you would, after all the effort you and Apollo put into executing me. Afraid it didn't stick. Not like the axe did when I split your brother's skull."

"Atreus," Sebastian said, his voice soft, but his grip on his weapon tightening.

Helena stared in horror. Kaine's father was still alive?

Before she could process the revelation, both paladins attacked, and Atreus swung at them. The wall exploded, tile and stone flying, dust filling the air. The hallway was narrow, a tiny combat space in which speed was a far greater advantage than size and muscle. If Atreus landed a blow, he would have killed Sebastian and Soren, but he had to hit them. They were faster, slicing at him a dozen times before he could raise the club and give it momentum.

The other wall cracked open as Atreus swung again.

The air was so thick with dust, it was almost impossible to see anything but the gleam of metal. There was a horrifying crunch and squelch and something came flying through the debris and hit the ground. The lich's head.

"Come on," Soren's voice barked from amid the choking dust. The rest of them moved forward. Soren was favouring his right arm and

Sebastian was bleeding at the temple, but they were mostly unscathed. The huge corpse that had been Atreus Ferron lay at their feet, gouged all over with deep wounds that would have killed anyone who wasn't already dead.

"Shouldn't we get the talisman?" Helena asked as they all stepped around it.

"There's no time to search a corpse that big," Soren said as he stumbled forward and shoved the door open.

There was Luc.

They all froze.

He was strapped down on a medical table, a mask fitted over his nose and mouth attached to several tubes. There was a cluster of people around him, swathed in surgical gowns.

His torso had been sliced open, peeled back to expose all the organs, but they were blackened, almost necrotic.

"Fuck!" said a woman's voice, and she glanced over towards them.

They were clearly trying to finish what they'd been doing when Atreus knocked to warn them.

Two people lunged across the floor and through a door on the far side without a backwards glance, leaving the rest.

The room exploded into violence.

Soren had been waiting for this moment. He shot across the room, his weapon sweeping into a long curving blade. He killed everyone violently. There was nothing quick or clean about it. Warm blood spattered across her face as Helena went for Luc.

Despite being strapped down, his hands had been pierced through with spikes of nullium that Helena instantly recognised by the telltale way they were dissolving into his blood.

Her fingers trembled as she reached out, looking for a pulse, not sure if her resonance would work. She pressed her fingers below his jaw and gave a small sob of relief. He was alive. Drugged and cut open, but alive.

She ripped the mask off his face as Purnell twisted a nozzle on the tank, cutting off whatever they'd been using on him.

What had they done?

Her hands shook as she searched for a talisman inside him, but she felt no signs of lumithium or any other metal. His organs were darkened, as if he'd been poisoned with something, but there was no time to try to heal it all.

She closed the incisions, working carefully, aligning everything. Purnell was prying the spikes from his hands, her breath coming out in rapid pants as she struggled to get them loose. There was a stark look of terror starting to creep across the girl's face.

The veins and arteries in Luc's arms had been constricted, the gas administered keeping his heartbeat impossibly sluggish. The combination had kept his resonance inactive while allowing the now dead scientists to use their own on him. He was also conscious, but just barely.

Soren and Alister were trying to force open the door that two attackers had attempted to escape through, without success.

Helena worked as fast as she could, speeding up Luc's metabolism and forcing his damaged kidneys back into action, making his heart beat more rapidly once Purnell had the spikes out. Helena shoved a decoction into her hands, ordering her to wash the wounds and get them wrapped in gauze.

Then her ring burned.

Pain like fire ran up her left hand. She gave a choked gasp as she kept working. The sensation barely faded before it burned again.

"Is he alive?" she dimly heard Soren asking, his voice shaking.

"Yes. Just give me a minute," she said, touching Luc's face desperately. "Come on, Luc. Do you hear me?"

Her ring burned again.

Alarms started. A deafening ringing that filled the air.

"We've got to go!" Soren yelled over the din. "Fuck. We'll just carry him."

"Luc, wake up." Helena shook him.

They didn't have the manpower for Luc to be deadweight. There was no way that Helena and Purnell could carry him all the way out if there was fighting.

She had a vial and a needle. Her hands were shaking as she filled a syringe. She'd never used this—epinephrine combined with painkillers and a few other things to jump-start his body into action. If it was too strong, it would kill him. It would all be for nothing.

"Come on," she muttered, and jabbed it through his chest into his heart.

Luc lurched, giving a sudden gasp as his body jolted into violent consciousness.

Helena saw a flash of sky blue as his eyes cracked open.

"Hel?" he croaked, his voice dry. He reached out, touching her face with his bandaged hand as if he couldn't believe she was real.

"Yes," she said, trying not to cry. "We've come to take you home."

His eyes rolled around, searching, skimming past everyone clustered around him. "Where's—where's Lila?"

"Headquarters," Soren said, his voice gruff, "waiting for you."

Luc stiffened. "Is she really—?"

"She's alive," Helena said quickly. "We took care of her. It's your turn now. Come on."

Luc gave a shuddering gasp of relief. "They said if I went—they wouldn't kill her. She was—bleeding—so much. Wouldn't even let me burn it closed. She's—she's all right?"

"She's alive, getting better," Helena said. "Come on. Take this. We've got to go."

She pulled him upright and he groaned, clutching at his chest.

"What did they do to me?"

"I don't know. I'll fix you better once we're safe," she said, breaking a tablet in half and pushing it past his lips. She just had to hope he was still strong enough that everything she was doing wouldn't kill him. "Hold still."

She pressed her hands on each side of his neck, and used the dissolving tablets to manipulate his physiology, getting his internal systems working the way they needed to.

He'd crash terribly once it all wore off, but she'd be there. She could make up all the difference once they were safe.

"Up now," she said. He was breathing too fast; she could feel his heart racing dangerously. She tried to slow it a little, but the more conscious he became, the more he comprehended their danger.

She pulled one of his arms over her shoulder and Purnell took the other, and they dragged him to his feet.

"You came . . ." Luc said, slumping heavily on her.

"You're my best friend," Helena said, staring ahead. "Of course I did. Come on. We need to get you out."

He kept tripping over his feet, his body bearing down so hard that her knees nearly buckled. She was grateful he was not in armour, or she didn't know how they'd manage. The floor was slick with blood and gore.

"You shouldn't be here. You're not—trained," he said when they were halfway down a flight of stairs.

"Helping you is exactly what I'm trained for," she said.

Her ring kept burning, again and again. She ignored it.

She had been afraid that after all the fighting to get there, Soren and the others would be too exhausted to keep going, but recovering Luc had reinvigorated them.

However secret the prison had been, it was not so secret that there weren't plenty of necrothralls now that the alarms had gone off. Not shoddy, damaged necrothralls that shambled and ravaged carelessly; these greys were expertly reanimated, so capable it was hard to believe they were dead except they kept coming no matter how Soren and Sebastian sliced them apart. The narrowness of the hallways and tight corners was both gift and curse.

"I need a weapon," Luc said, trying to pull away from Helena as Soren was slammed against the wall and crumpled. A necrothrall nearly took his head off, but Sebastian rammed into it, buying Soren enough time to scramble to his feet and decapitate it.

He was fighting left-handed, his right arm cradled against his body.

The drugs were taking effect. Luc was strong enough to resist Helena's attempts to hold him back and alert enough to realise how outnumbered they were. Still she tried to stop him.

"Luc, you're injured. I'm not even sure how much. You're just not feeling it."

"I'm not watching them die." He tried again to shove her and Purnell off.

She dug her fingers into his arms. "Luc, you don't have resonance."

"Then heal me again later," he said, finally ripping himself free and throwing himself into the fight. He kicked a necrothrall so hard his foot went through its chest. He snatched up its sword.

Soren called him several names, but there was no time to do more than curse as they kept fighting their way down.

Helena pulled out a knife when they reached the basement. Wagner was huddling behind Purnell as if he expected her to protect him. Purnell's eyes were wide, the whites glaring with visible panic as she clutched back. They shouldn't have brought her. The girl was beginning to fall apart. She didn't have the nerve for combat.

They got into the room and blocked the door, but it was barely secured before the whole wall shook. They fled into the tunnels, scrambling after one another into the sewers, trying to reach the flood cathedral. Alister brought up the rear, crushing and sealing the tunnel behind them, step after step, so that pursuit would be slow.

They reached one of the larger tunnels and paused, gasping for breath.

"You're not supposed to be fighting, you moron," Soren said, slumping against the wall. In torchlight, he'd turned very grey and his nose was broken, blood streaming down his mouth and chin.

Purnell was crouched on the ground, rocking and muttering, *Mummy? Mummy, please don't,* over and over.

"Don't tell me what to do," Luc said, breathing hard, shifting his grip on the sword. "This sword is shit. You could have brought a weapon for me. Do you have my rings at least?"

"You don't have resonance," Helena snapped.

Luc grimaced but gripped the sword harder.

"I don't know how Lila's never killed you," Soren said, pushing himself up but looking ready to topple over.

"Hold on." Helena went over and checked him. His arm was broken again. Three times in a year. It was unlikely to ever heal properly after this. She aligned the bones again and fused them.

"Do you have something for pain?" Penny asked in a small voice. "Or maybe you could block off some nerves."

When she was done with Penny, she made them all take her blood tonics, so that if they required healing, what she'd need would already be there. She'd brought two for everyone but hadn't expected an extra prisoner. Wagner drank hers while she was passing out the others.

"We need to keep moving," Soren said. They had to drag Purnell with them; she was completely gone, staring blankly as if she didn't know where she was anymore, still saying *Mummy,* her voice chillingly childlike.

They retraced their steps, following the maze of tunnels back to their entry point. At first it was a relief that they weren't being pursued, but the closer they got, the eerier it was.

Helena's ring burned again.

"Sol save us. It's Blackthorne!" Penny said, her voice strangled with terror as they rounded the corner.

The shallow sections of the flood cathedral were filled not only with a horde of necrothralls but also a number of what looked to be the mortal Aspirants, lined up and blocking their path.

"Go back!" Soren immediately said, but he'd barely spoken the words before there came a scream of metal behind them, followed by a savage roar.

Chimaeras.

They were penned in.

Blackthorne stood at the front, barely armoured. "Capture Holdfast, kill the rest, and you will receive the immortal reward!"

There was an eager roar among the Aspirants, while the necrothralls just stood still, waiting.

"Stay close," Luc ordered as he fell in, shoulder-to-shoulder, with Soren and Sebastian.

"Get across," Soren said.

The plan, as much as there had been a plan, fell apart. There was no escaping with Luc when he was in the thick of the fighting. Helena's fingers went for her daggers.

The first wave of necrothralls hit, and the group splintered like a wrecked ship.

Several necrothralls rushed towards Helena. There was no time to think. She moved on instinct, blocking, slicing, her dagger morphing to chase after crucial joints, while her other palm pressed flat and she jerked back, ripping their reanimation free.

The energy struck her, a blistering flare of power, and she sent it outwards, pulverising the necrothralls closing in. There was light somewhere, fire, torches, reflecting across the frigid water that was already up to their knees. The noise was deafening. The roar and chaos shattered the senses. She looked for the others, but it was impossible to see them in the throng. So many bodies, living and dead, moving through the dark. Kaine had trained her to defend herself and flee, not fight in a melee. She tried to key up her resonance, but there were so many bodies and movements and weapons swinging, it was dizzying. She ducked a swinging club and lashed out with her knife, the blade singing with resonance as it tore through the waxy decaying skin, up the torso and throat, slicing through bones like butter, into the brain.

She twisted her resonance and the blade curved, severing the head completely.

Something collided with her, bowling her over. A warm hand, wrenching her up. *Ally,* she thought, until she saw the steel-gauntleted fist, gripping a sword and swinging it towards her head. She drove her knife up, the handguard just barely large enough to deflect, and then she stabbed towards the weak point near the shoulder, narrowing the blade as thin as she could until her resonance with the metal told her she'd pierced flesh. She flared out the knife blade as it sank into the hilt. She jerked it back and felt the warm, heavy spurt of hot blood across her hand as the grip on her loosened. The sword fell, barely missing her head, and the Aspirant crashed into the water on top of her.

Cold water hit her head-on, painful as a kick to the ribs. She scrambled to her feet, fighting to get free of the body nearly drowning her.

She stabbed blindly, the water and noise and disorientation making it impossible to sense anything clearly.

She crawled out of the throng, found a wall, and got up, trying to catch her breath, trying to find the others in the flickering dark. There was screaming. It kept going on and on. It was Purnell. She'd snapped out of her daze and was now screaming at the top of her lungs, the sound bouncing off the walls, drawing attention. A group of necrothralls was closing in.

Wagner, who was nearest to Purnell, shoved her straight at them as he tried to escape. As she fell, Purnell seemed to become lucid again, comprehending terror sweeping across her face.

She was weaponless but quick. She leapt, somehow evading the clawing hands, and fled into the centre of the flood-filled room.

Half a dozen steps and then Purnell stepped too far, vanishing underwater.

Helena watched, praying that she'd resurface, that somehow she'd escaped the current. Something rammed into Helena, knocking her sideways. A boot came down on her wrist, and she inhaled water when she gasped with pain.

Fire tore along her ribs.

She crawled back towards the wall. Her clothes freezing on her skin. She turned, looking desperately for the others, coughing up water.

Wagner had somehow managed to reach the far wall and had a spear he was beating off necrothralls with.

Luc and Sebastian were fighting together in the centre of a horde, while Soren had broken away and was trying to reach Alister and Penny, who'd been backed into a corner far from everyone else.

The light flickered madly off the water, only giving glimpses. The chimaeras had caught up. Fangs and claws were flashing as Alister tried to raise a barrier. Penny gave a cry as her weapon caught in the shoulder of a chimaera and was ripped from her hands.

Soren raced through the water, his weapon morphing as he ran, trying to reach them before the chimaeras closed in.

An axe came swinging through the air, barely missing Soren's leg.

Soren caught himself, stumbling in the water, and turned hard, looking around wildly to find his attacker. His weapon flashed, barely blocking a blow that nearly threw him off his feet. Now he was facing his opponent. Blackthorne barred the way.

Blackthorne, realising the disadvantage of his opponent, kept moving to the right. Making all his attacks from Soren's blind spot. Tiring him.

"Soren!" Luc suddenly shouted.

Soren pivoted sharply as a chimaera leapt at him. He beheaded it in one clean sweep of his blade.

There was a horrible, wet cracking sound.

When Soren turned, Blackthorne had swung from the right.

The axe head was buried all the way through his ribs to his spine.

Blackthorne jerked the axe free and licked it as Soren dropped, vanishing into the water.

Everything went out of focus.

Luc was screaming, but Helena's body seemed to abruptly come alive. She stumbled forward, slashing at anything in her path, trying to reach Soren before the river took him.

Luc was faster. By the time Helena reached him, Luc was already on his knees, pulling Soren up into his arms, stained with the rush of blood that poured out of him. Sebastian was a moment behind him, immediately throwing himself into Blackthorne's path and holding him off as Luc knelt in the water, Soren clutched against his chest.

Luc looked up when Helena reached him.

"Y-You can heal him, right?"

"Luc—"

But he was already pushing Soren into her arms, the weight dropping her to her knees in the water.

She held on to Soren with trembling hands, ignoring the throb of her wrist.

"I'll cover you," Luc said, picking up his sword. And then he was gone.

The battle did not stop for Soren.

Helena tried to ignore the fighting that raged around her, trying to focus. A thread was all she needed. She could keep him alive.

Just like she'd kept Lila alive.

But the wound was so big. Wounds like this didn't survive a journey to the hospital. This blow had been lethal. Soren's remaining life was feeble, slipping away as her resonance tried to grasp it.

Fingers brushed against her hand.

Soren was staring at her. "Two souls is still a bargain."

The words had barely passed from his lips when a surge of cold deathly energy hit, slamming through Helena's resonance.

She was so raw with exhaustion, so focused on trying to keep him alive, her vision blotted out as a jolt of death ran through her. She doubled over, for a moment too dazed to comprehend what had happened. Her vision cleared and Soren's blank, sightless gaze met hers.

He was gone.

"No. No. No. Soren!"

He hung in her arms, his blood still flooding against her skin, the only warmth.

Helena looked around. Alister was calling to Penny to fall back as she fought the chimaeras using a knife, letting them get dangerously close before she could hit them. One mistake was all it would take.

Soren was dead. Purnell was dead.

Sebastian was doing everything he could to keep Luc protected, holding off Blackthorne. Luc was fighting, but his focus was split. He kept checking on Helena where she knelt with Soren clutched in her arms. She could see the desperation in his eyes. The certainty that she was going to save Soren. That she could.

She met his eyes for one guilt-stricken moment and turned back, pulling Soren's body against her.

"Anything," she said, pressing a hand against his neck. "Whatever the price."

She pushed the energy out of her body and brought him back.

It was more than just easy. It was instinctive.

She knew Soren, knew exactly what it felt like when he was alive.

Her resonance wound through him like a current, knitting the wound closed with absolute efficiency, stitching the severed sections of his organs back together, rejoining the bones, but she didn't stop there.

She felt his mind return, a shadow, the barest glimmer of him, and she poured her energy into that.

Come back. Come back. You can't go yet.

Soren blinked up at her, and she felt a connection materialise between them, a wisp. She strengthened it, because she couldn't let him go.

"You can't rest yet, you have to protect Luc," she said, and heard the words echo through him.

Soren knew her. She could feel it. The familiarity she represented. It was horrible, feeling this abomination of life in her arms. For all her efforts, this was a shadow. Soren was a puppet she'd slipped her hand inside.

After so many years of healing, necromancy was effortless. There was nothing to hurt. She simply told Soren's body that it could not die. He would fight as he'd always fought. He would protect them, because he knew how to do that.

He stood and helped her up, weapon already in hand.

Muscle memory lingered, like a sleepwalker's habits, even when the person was gone.

She could see herself through him. Her consciousness kept flickering back and forth along the connection forged between them. He turned then and saw Luc, and she felt the pull towards him. He looked for Lila next.

Luc saw Soren standing, and for an instant, relief flooded across his face. Then vanished.

Luc knew. In an instant, he somehow knew.

Still Soren started towards him. Helena stopped him.

"You need to protect Penny and Alister," she said, both in her mind and aloud, pointing, turning his focus away from Luc. "Get us out."

Soren turned and obeyed. Helena watched, her mind swimming from the disorienting secondary awareness in her mind. Her consciousness didn't know where to go.

A chimaera leapt towards her face.

She dodged. A scythe flashed before her eyes.

Soren.

She blinked, trying to make out her own surroundings.

Soren killed the chimaera without breaking his stride as he reached Penny and Alister, shoving Penny to safety before turning back.

A blur from the left. Helena lurched sideways, trying to dodge, not sure if she was seeing her assailants or Soren's. Her focus narrowed for an instant, bringing her surroundings back into the forefront of her own mind.

If she died, Soren would be gone, too. She had to stay alive until they got Luc out.

She tried to block out Soren, but he was rooted in her mind. She sensed something and turned an instant before it slammed into her. The air was knocked out of her lungs. She looked down, blinking through her fragmenting consciousness.

Soren. Helena. Soren.

There was a knife driven to the hilt into the right side of her chest.

Helena.

If she'd turned a split second later, it would have gone through her heart, but—as she squinted, struggling to focus—she didn't think it had hit anything immediately vital.

Pain was what it took to drag Helena's consciousness securely back into her own body.

She managed to slice off the hand of the necrothrall that had stabbed her before it could pull the knife out. Using her throbbing right hand, she held the knife in place, trying to keep it from being jostled as she stomped down on the inside of the necrothrall's knee.

She stumbled away, gasping, the edge of the blade slicing the wound wider as she moved.

A chimaera's fangs closed around Soren's leg, tearing it open. He cut off its head, unmindful of the injury.

He was being torn apart. She could feel the injuries, even though pain didn't register. She hadn't brought that part of his brain back.

He didn't stop fighting.

Get the knife out, close the wound. She went towards the far wall.

She huddled in the freezing water. Another chimaera had attacked Sebastian and Luc. The size of it, it had to be part bear. Luc's strength was flagging.

The chimaera was huge, mostly mammal but with longer, reptilian jaws and skin so thick, their weapons glanced off. It screamed like a human.

She tried to focus, biting down on her lip, bracing herself to pull out the knife.

Fingers dug into her braided hair, and Helena was abruptly dragged up until her toes barely touched the ground.

Basilius Blackthorne peered at her, teeth bared in a grin, bloodstains from mouth to chin.

He ate his wife and children with those teeth . . .

"The Eternal Flame has a necromancer, I see." His voice was raw and rasping.

She tried to stab the arm gripping her, but he batted her hand away with a blow so hard, her left hand nearly went numb. Her knife hit the water with a splash.

She grabbed for his wrist.

Her fingers grazed his skin, her resonance lashing out.

But Kaine had always warned her: Once the Undying knew what she was, they'd be wary.

Before her resonance could connect, he wrenched her hand off, fingers closing around the knuckles of her left hand, squeezing and twisting. His grip was like iron, and her bones broke like twigs.

Helena screamed. The knife in her chest shifted, painful pressure growing inside her lungs.

Blackthorne looked at her shattered hand expectantly and then laughed. "Forgot, you won't regenerate."

His gaze turned to her right hand, eyeing the awkward way she had the knife braced. "I think this one is already broken, but let's make sure."

With unexpected gentleness, he pulled it away from the knife hilt and snapped her wrist. Black spots of pain danced in her eyes as another strangled scream burst out of her.

"I should keep you alive," he said as he pulled the knife from her chest very slowly, savouring the glide of the blade.

Helena was in so much pain that her mind kept flickering over into Soren's, seeking an escape.

He was mobbed by necrothralls. The chimaeras were dead, but there were too many necrothralls, dozens of them, shoving him down into the water, tearing him apart. His leg twisted as teeth bit down, tearing out the tendon behind his knee.

He was still fighting. His weapon was gone, but he had a knife. Penny was screaming behind him, but Alister held her back. Soren kept stabbing, tearing, clawing his way through, following her instruction not to stop fighting even as he was ripped apart. Dead fingers scrabbled across his face, finding his remaining eye. His jaw was torn down, his throat left gaping.

Helena jerked reflexively each time a little more of him was ripped away, but the pain was all with Helena. She couldn't feel her fingers; there was just a beacon of agony radiating up her arms.

A warm gush of blood ran down the side of her body.

She thought Basilius would stab her again, but he dropped the knife into the water. He touched her side, fingers light across the wound. Her raw nerves screamed in protest.

His fingers traced along the slit between her ribs, and without warning he shoved two of them into it. Helena screamed as her skin tore wider. The bones bowed as he forced his fingers inside the wound, slick with her blood.

"Did you know, my favourite things are wounds," he said, the words breathless. "Wetter, hotter, and tighter than anything else."

Helena's legs thrashed, her broken hands scrabbling to push him away, the ruined bones grinding, but it was no use. She screamed and screamed but no one noticed, bashing her head against his chest until he gripped her by the throat with his free hand, his thumb shoving hard against her trachea until she stilled. Her lungs seized, spasming.

"Yes, just like that," he said with an approving groan. "Don't worry, I won't let you die. You'll still be alive when I hand you over. Bennet is going to love you."

Her consciousness had frayed to its outermost limit. Her vision blurred. She couldn't even breathe to scream anymore.

She was only half aware as Soren was ripped from her mind, his body washed downriver, the connection unravelling like blood in the water.

"One more scream. You do it beauti—"

Blackthorne stumbled, gasping as if the breath had been knocked out of him. His grip on her loosened, fingers sliding free an instant before he was wrenched backwards.

Helena dropped like a stone. The frigid cold drove her back into consciousness or she would have drowned. She cowered back, looking for Blackthorne in terror and spotted him being dragged by his throat through the water, a wire or rope wrapped around his neck.

The person dragging him wasn't one of the Resistance.

It was one of the Undying. Immediately identifiable by the helmet and black uniform.

By the time the two were in range of each other, Blackthorne had recovered himself and lunged at his attacker. He'd snatched up a sword from the water and swung, going straight for the head, but the other Undying sidestepped.

Blackthorne tried again, and again. His attacks were precise, the movements of a highly accomplished combat alchemist, but his opponent simply dodged. No weapon. No counterattack. Quick and light, evading as if it were a dance, until Blackthorne left himself open for an instant. An instant was all it took.

The Undying stepped past a blow and with his bare hand, punched through Basilius's armour and into his chest as easily as if reaching through water. A pale, long-fingered hand dripped red with blood as it pulled out a gleaming piece of metal from Blackthorne's chest cavity.

Blackthorne collapsed into the floodwater, vanishing.

The entire fight had not even lasted a full minute.

In the chaos, no one else had noticed. Helena tried to breathe in but choked from the pressure inside her lungs. She pressed her arm against the wound, trying to prevent more air from seeping into her chest cavity.

The necrothralls began to drop. A few Aspirants noticed the newcomer and seemed confused about what had happened. Before they could react, they were dead. A weapon gleamed so quick that she barely saw it, just watched the bodies fall.

It was Kaine.

She'd never seen him fight. He'd never really fought with her. But she knew. There was no mistaking that brutal efficiency.

He was as deadly as she'd imagined.

She could see the techniques he'd tried to drill into her, the fluidity that she'd lacked, how quick he was. No movement wasted. The momentum of one kill led to the next.

Bodies fell like stars.

He stalked through the water towards Helena. Not a step wavering, cutting down everything that crossed his path.

When a chimaera leapt at him, he lifted his hand, and the instant it touched the creature, the body unravelled, limbs sloughing apart as if he'd ripped out all the invisible stitches assembling it. One minute a monster, and the next dead in the water.

It wasn't combat, it was slaughter.

A numbers game. Minimum effort, high return.

It was impossible that he'd ever fought to his full potential before. If anyone had ever fought like that, everyone would have known about it.

He reached into a pocket, pulling out a fistful of something and flinging it outward.

They looked like shimmering bits of metal, and as they flew, she felt his resonance expand, carrying them.

The metal sang through the air, moving like an avian murmuration, and hit like a spray of bullets, tearing through the necrothralls' skulls.

Rather than fall, the metal stayed suspended in midair, sweeping back, dripping blood and gore. Kaine drew his hand up and they came darting back, cutting through more bodies. A flick of his fingers and they shot out again.

When he reached Helena, his eyes were burning with rage behind his mask, glowing bright as molten silver.

"You idiot," he said, and dragged her up out of the water, crushing her hard against his chest.

His resonance in the air grew heavier. A wave that swept outwards. She watched it hit the nearest necrothralls and Aspirants. They began jerking and seizing, dropping into the water. The necrothralls crumpled, while the chimaeras and those living were gasping as if their lungs were being compressed, clawing at their throats.

Helena could still breathe, although laboriously, but everyone around her was suffocating.

Sebastian was trying to reach Luc but collapsed into the water. Luc was tearing gouges down his throat as his face turned blue, eyes bulging.

"Stop it," she gasped, realising that Kaine was making no distinction between the Undying and the Eternal Flame. He was killing everyone. "Stop it! You can't kill them! Stop!"

She tried to wrench away as Luc's eyes rolled back and he slumped in the water.

The invisible wave reached the walls. Penny collapsed. Alister followed.

The struggle was coming to an end.

"Stop. Stop! Stop!" She fought to get free. "Stop!"

"Shut up," he snarled through his helmet, letting go of her. "Wait here."

He stormed over to Sebastian and Luc, Penny and Alister and even Wagner, although she hardly cared if he died. He placed a hand on their chests, and one at the back of their heads, and she watched them jerk and start breathing again without regaining consciousness.

She tried to stand up, but her legs wouldn't hold her. By the time Kaine was coming to her again, everything was swaying.

He dragged her to the far wall, where several tunnels disappeared into darkness.

"Can't leave them," she rasped, trying to pull free.

"Shut up." The water was only to their ankles, and there was a ladder leading up to a walkway that was shoulder height.

"You can't leave them," she said, struggling. "Bring them, or I won't go."

He turned without a word and went back, kicking most of the necrothralls into the current, but pausing beside a few dead Aspirants and reanimating them. They crawled to their feet and began helping to carry Luc and the others over and shoving them up onto the walkway while Kaine lifted her as gently as he could. She nearly bit through her lip at the pressure on her ribs. His palms were red with her blood, but he said nothing as he swung up the ladder and scooped her up again.

The necrothralls hauled the rest of the rescue team up over their shoulders and followed.

Helena faded in and out of consciousness in the dark, briefly coming to as she heard the sound of grinding metal and a loud roar of rushing, rising water coming from the flood cathedral before they continued on.

Kaine stopped walking and kicked the wall. A door almost invisible along the endless passages swung open. He carried her into a small room.

There was a table against one wall, and he laid her on it. He turned away, shoving the door closed, and reached up to rip off his helmet. His face was twisted with fury.

"Tell me you can last long enough for me to get a doctor." His voice was shaking.

She shook her head.

He was breathing fast, but he swallowed. "Then you'll have to tell me how. Can you still do that?"

"All right," she said unsteadily, even though she wanted to pass out more than anything. "The first is—my liver. It's where the blood is coming from. I think. There's air—in my chest, collapsing my lung. After—after you—fix my liver, you can—stimulate blood generation. I don't have the tonic, but you should be able to manage some."

He unbuckled the straps on her satchel and cut away her soaking clothes so he had clear access to the wound between her ribs that had been ripped wide.

She flinched, trying not to recoil as he staunched the bleeding. He listened carefully as she described what he needed to sense to identify and repair biliary ducts.

Without her hands working, without resonance, it was like instructing the blind.

"Shut up," he told her when she apologised for not being sure of what was wrong. He reached into his cloak, pulling something out. "This one's for blood, right? Does it work for you?"

He held up a familiar green-blue vial.

Her throat tightened and she nodded. "Yes. That works for me."

The process of siphoning the air collapsing her lung was difficult because she didn't have the supplies for it. She swallowed hard. "There's a tube in my satchel."

He found it, and she gingerly indicated where to numb and puncture, giving only a small whimpering gasp as it sank through the tissue and into her chest cavity.

She swallowed, staring up at the ceiling overhead, able to think more clearly as breathing grew easier. "You need to look for damage to the lung tissue next, then you wash the wound and close the diaphragmatic muscle and—"

His fingers brushed near the wound, and her mind stalled, careening violently.

"Don't—don't touch it!" The words came out a strangled scream. She almost fell off the table, trying to get away.

He snatched his hand back as she collapsed and lay there, drawing sharp laboured breaths as she tried to calm down, choking back panicked sobs.

Her heart was pounding so hard, she could feel it in her temples.

"He was going to—going to—" She tripped over her own tongue, trying to protectively cradle that side of her body. Keep it from being touched.

"He's gone." Kaine's expression was pulled taut, a forced flatness to his entire demeanour. "He won't ever come back. Should I just cover the wound and fix your hands instead?"

She shook her head. "No. I'll stay still. Just—" She swallowed. "Sorry."

The muscle in his jaw set. As he worked, he began telling her each time he was about to touch her, what he was about to do, his voice low, calm, and she realised he was imitating the way she used to narrate her treatment of the array.

It was the simplest part of the procedure, but she wanted to throw up because she was so sick with terror.

"There."

The immediate danger had passed. Kaine also seemed to finally breathe.

"Why were you there?" he finally asked.

She stared at him for a moment and then looked away. "The Council was going to do whatever it took to get Luc back."

"You aren't experienced in combat," he said. His hands trembled as he wiped blood off her face. "Why would they bring you without even giving you a partner."

"I had a partner," she said. "She died in the fight."

"Who?"

"Purnell. She was an—orderly."

He glared at her.

"It had to be a small team; we were supposed to get in and out without being noticed. Sofia and I weren't supposed to fight."

"You knew it was a suicide mission. That is what the Bayards do, they die for the Holdfasts. They know nothing else."

"Yes, but if Luc dies it's over, for *all* of us. It was worth it to go."

"And if you'd died?" He looked up, his eyes glittering with rage.

"There's plenty of people to replace me. I've always been expendable, remember?" She used her elbows to sit up. "I need you to fix my hands now."

The strain showed around his eyes. "I know."

She forced herself to inhale. "Start with my left. It won't matter as much if it doesn't all set right."

He blocked off most of the feeling from her elbow down but left enough that she could sense if he was setting it correctly, working as gently as he could. The broken pieces ground together, sending a sudden pain through her arm into her shoulder, even with most of the sensation gone.

"Good," she choked out, dropping her head onto his shoulder as she fought back tears.

He rejoined the bones in her wrists before he worked on her hands directly. He had to physically move several bones back into alignment, twisting the parts that Blackthorne had mangled.

The pain without the adrenaline surge of battle bore into her. She was sobbing into his shoulder by the time he finished aligning the bones and began fusing them.

Her hand was swollen, purple and red from bruising when he finished.

He cradled it in both of his and ran his thumbs across her palm and up to her wrist, his resonance like a balm, repairing the damaged tissue and the broken blood vessels with the sweep of his thumbs, then working along each finger. He was so gentle.

She recognised the technique. She hadn't realised he'd paid attention.

"You could be a healer," she finally said as he removed the block on her nerves. She flexed her hand, opening and closing. It was still sore, and fragile as though hairline-fractured. "You have a natural talent for it."

"That's one of the most ironic things anyone has ever said to me," he said quietly.

He turned his attention to her other hand.

"You can numb it all the way," she said. "I can use my resonance now."

Working together, it was surprising how quick the process was. When he finished, he massaged her hand again, in the same way he had with the first.

"Don't ever go on another mission," he said without looking up, her hand trapped in his.

She looked away, drawing a deep breath.

"That's not your call," she said, slipping her hand free and standing. The room swam. She was dangerously lightheaded. She didn't have a saline drip or the plasma expanders that would be on hand in the hospital. Tonic or not, she didn't physically have the resources needed to regenerate all the blood she'd lost.

She pulled her satchel gingerly over her head, trying to be gentle with her hands as she prepared to leave. They'd never said goodbye before, and she didn't see any point in starting now.

He blocked the door, his eyes gone cold. "Remind Crowther that if the Eternal Flame wants my continued assistance, they will keep you alive."

His eyes had that cold silver gleam in them as he stared at her. Her heart wavered for a moment and then turned to lead. He'd been quite clear about what she was, how he regarded her, and how much he hated her for having any hold on him.

This concern, this obsession with her preservation, wasn't about her at all. It was about his mother, Enid Ferron, and his failure to save her. To him, Helena was an opportunity to try to get it right. A consolation prize he didn't even want but couldn't bring himself to give up on.

No wonder Crowther had been so pleased. *Well done, Marino.*

She knew she was supposed to accept that, but she couldn't bear it anymore. "You're doing this for your mother, Kaine. Would you really give that up because of me?"

She knew that would anger him: to outright insinuate that what he felt towards her was in any way comparable to his feelings for his mother. He would make a point of proving her wrong.

He went very still.

She stepped around him, reaching for the door, but he caught her shoulders, turning her back, the expression on his face stark.

"She's dead," he said. "You are not. My loyalty was to those least responsible for her suffering, but if the Eternal Flame has decided that you are an affordable casualty, I will not be noble or understanding. I can exact dual revenge. I will make them pay if they get you killed."

She stared at him, startled. She hadn't accounted for this. She knew Kaine wasn't a spy because of any ideological reasoning; it was purely a sense of personal interest. He hated the Holdfasts and the Eternal Flame but he hated Morrough and the Undying more. That fact was immutable. The source of all his motivation.

But now, because of a careless comment from her, he was reevaluating whether the Eternal Flame served his interests.

She swallowed hard. She should be cold. She should remind him that she would always put the Eternal Flame's interests first. If he expected more than that, he would have to wait. And earn it.

She looked up at him, willing the words to form, but they stayed trapped in her throat. She was so tired. Life had been cold for such a long time.

The others are hurt. You don't even know what's been done to Luc, and you're wasting your time here.

She flexed her hands, feeling the new tissue, focusing on it as she attempted to pull away. "I *have* to go." Her voice shook.

He wouldn't let go. He gripped her tighter. "You are not expendable. You don't get to push everyone away so that they'll feel comfortable using you and letting you die."

She shook her head.

"This is war," she said, forcing her voice to stay steady. "It's not some sort of tragic self-condemnation to be expendable. It's a strategic liability not to be." She met his eyes. "That was why you picked me, remember?" Her voice broke. "Well, thanks to you, I'm worth less now. They added all these new healers after you asked for me. I had to train all my replacements." She gave a bitter laugh. "You made me as expendable as I am now. And you didn't even want me, either."

He flinched, his grip loosening enough that she pulled free, turning again. He caught the door as she opened it, shoving it closed.

"You are *not* replaceable," he said, his hands trembling against her shoulders. "You are not required to make your death convenient. You are allowed to be important to people. The reason I'm here—the reason I'm doing any of this—is to keep you alive. To keep you safe. That was the deal." He searched her face. "They didn't tell you."

She shook her head, giving a broken sob and—before she let herself think—she kissed him.

CHAPTER 51

Aprilis 1787

KAINE CRADLED HER FACE IN HIS HANDS as he returned her kiss, pulling her closer, his arms wrapping around her.

She was half crying as she kissed him, tracing her fingers along his face and under the curve of his jaw, trying to memorise every detail: his pulse under her fingertips, his lips pressed against hers. The taste of him.

Her eyes fluttered shut, trying to savour it all. This one moment. She could have this.

She'd earned it.

Then, all too soon, she forced herself to step back, pulling away. "I have to take care of the others."

He didn't try to stop her again, but the rest of the team wasn't outside the door as she'd expected; Kaine's necrothralls had moved them deeper.

Her fingers trembled as she checked for pulses. They were still alive, although Luc's skin almost burned to touch.

"How do we get out?" she asked as she started checking for injuries, trying to work out how hurt everyone was, how much work it would take to get them conscious and moving.

"Down this tunnel. Go right, then right again, and then straight. There's an upper floodgate in the far north."

"Where they released the chimaera?" She remembered the place.

"You'll have to break it down, but it'll get you out."

She nodded. "You have to go before I wake them."

"I know," he said, but he didn't leave, lingering until she looked up. His eyes shone in the dark, as if there were moonlight underground.

He touched her cheek, tilting her face up and kissing her. "Use the ring, call me, if you ever need anything."

She wanted to say she would, but she couldn't bring herself to.

He was a spy that they depended on. And she was—

Not his handler. No, that role belonged to Crowther.

She was—

A prison.

"Go," she said instead. He disappeared down one of the tunnels, his necrothralls following him, as silent as wraiths.

She woke Sebastian first, hoping that he'd be calm and easier to manage. He'd also know what to do. She searched what supplies they had. She'd lost both her daggers, and everything in her satchel was contaminated with floodwater. Only one of the electric torches still worked, providing dim light in the darkness.

When he woke, Sebastian just sat silently staring at Luc's still face while she gingerly fixed his dislocated shoulder and several shallow wounds that had already stopped bleeding on their own. Finally, he looked at her.

"What happened?"

She shook her head. "I don't know. Everything went black. When I woke, you were all unconscious. I was afraid more of the Undying would show up, so I brought everyone here."

His eyes swept pointedly over her. "Helena, I know you used necromancy. There's no chance you moved us all here on your own."

She started to shake her head in denial.

"You reanimated Soren. There was no surviving the blow he took."

She went still. She didn't know if it would be better or worse to tell Sebastian that Soren had asked her to.

"That was why he brought you, wasn't it? I did wonder."

Helena said nothing. Soren's death felt like a wound too deep to even wrap her mind around. She didn't think she could even say his name without choking.

"Is he still—nearby?" Sebastian's voice was wistful.

Helena's throat ached. "No. He—he's gone. I'm sorry."

There would be no holy fire to liberate Soren's soul from his body. Somewhere downriver, he would decay into the earth. Lila would never see her twin again. Not even in the afterlife.

Sebastian said nothing for a long moment. "We'll tell the others we brought them here together."

There was blood crusted around Alister's eyes, ears, and nose from the strain of all the transmutation he'd done. She woke him slowly, but he seized into consciousness, clawing at his neck, his eyes wild as they locked on Helena.

"What happened?" he gasped.

"We're not sure," Sebastian said, leaning over him. "Are you all right? We need to move before we freeze. Luc's sick."

"Where's Soren?"

"Killed in combat," Sebastian said shortly. "Marino, can you get Penny up?"

Penny's leg was wrecked, the tendons ripped out with teeth. There was no saving it. Helena blocked the nerves and fused the bone so she could limp on it. Penny didn't even cry when she woke, just scrubbed at her face and struggled to her feet.

Wagner was unscathed. Of course he was. Coward. At least she didn't have to waste any of her energy healing him.

Helena tried to wake Luc. His fever was searing. He'd somehow gotten hotter in the minutes after she'd left him. She tried to cool him, but his body kept fighting it, pushing the fever higher and higher. She'd drugged him too much.

When he regained consciousness, he screamed. The noise reverberated through the tunnels.

"Knock him out!" Sebastian said, lunging forward. "Keep him cold. We'll carry him back."

It was fortunate they could smell clean air ahead, because Helena couldn't have explained how she knew the route out.

Sebastian had an entangled medallion like Helena's ring. He used it to send a pulse code to Headquarters.

A few times, they heard sounds echoing through the tunnels. Screams. Roars. Splashing. They moved quietly. Helena worried first whether Kaine could have gotten clear and then began to wonder if the reason they did not run into anyone was because he was lurking in the shadows.

When they reached the locked floodgate, Alister broke through the stone wall to get past it. A torrent of icy water rushed by. They struggled through, fighting to find stable footing as they clambered out.

A dense fog hung in the air, and a slim smuggling boat shot into view, moving silently across the water towards them.

Sebastian sighed with relief. "Althorne."

General Althorne glared at them from the boat as it pulled to shore. His men silently slipped into the water, not even splashing as they came towards the straggling unit.

"Where's Soren?" Althorne asked, his expression hard as Luc was carefully lifted into the boat.

"Killed in combat," Sebastian said quietly.

One of the men was lifting Penny into the boat. Alister scrambled aboard himself, smearing away the fresh blood around his eyes with shaking hands, clearly on the verge of burnout.

Althorne looked at Luc, his expression a mixture of concern and relief. "We'll need to keep him restrained until he's cleared."

Helena gestured towards Wagner. "We found him in a cell. I think Crowther wants him. Don't trust him, he killed Sofia Purnell."

Althorne jerked his head, and two of his men came over and seized Wagner's arms.

He grumbled but didn't resist, clearly preferring Resistance captivity to the Undying.

"You are all currently in custody for your violation of orders," Althorne said, once the boat was pushed off. There was no bite to his words.

They'd rescued Luc; any censure for that would be a formality.

Helena slumped against the side of the boat. The journey passed in a blur—docking on a concealed wharf, being herded up a staircase and into the back of a lorry.

When they arrived at Headquarters, Penny, Alister, and Luc were taken away to the hospital ward. Wagner was placed in a cell. Helena and Sebastian were checked, cleared of serious injury, and escorted to their rooms to be locked inside with guards stationed at the doors.

Helena was glad not to be kept in the hospital, even though she could have used the saline and plasma expanders. She stripped out of her wet, ruined clothing, hands shaky and trembling, and took a shower, washing away the filth of the tunnels and spring melt.

As the traces vanished, she grew eerily removed from what had happened, as though at some point during the battle, she'd left her body and couldn't return to it. Back in her room where everything looked familiar, it felt as if it had been a dream.

Soren wasn't dead. He couldn't be.

She would go out and see him sitting next to Luc in the hospital.

The memory of him, dead in her arms, felt like a tear in the fabric of her mind, as if the way she'd tethered him back to life had been ripped out when the connection between them broke. The person she knew and the body she'd reanimated had been tied together, and now there was a wound left.

He couldn't be dead.

It was a horrible dream.

She stared down at her hands. Somehow she'd expected them to be stained or blackened by her necromancy.

What would Sebastian tell the Council? He'd have to tell the truth in a report. Once the truth came out, there'd be consequences.

It would have been a lesser crime to have murdered Soren. Murder was only a mortal crime; necromancy was a crime upon this life and the afterlife.

She packed away all her possessions in her trunk and sat waiting.

There was a loud banging on the door. She stood, ready.

"Helena! Helena! There's something wrong with Luc!" It was Elain outside. "We need you in the hospital!"

All thoughts of arrest vanished.

"What's wrong?" Helena opened the door, and the guards stepped back to let her out. She rushed towards the lifts with Elain.

"We've done all the examinations and doubled-checked for talismans, and he's clear. But his organs—they're all poisoned. I don't know what they could have done. We tried reversing the damage, but they won't regenerate. We were trying to get his fever down and Pace had me wake him, but he started screaming. Now he won't stop, and he doesn't let anyone near. He's hurting himself."

Luc was in a quarantine room at the far end of the hospital. She heard him before she saw him.

His eyes were deranged, his face gaunt with scarlet stains in the cheeks. There was a ripple of heat coming off him as if he were molten gold.

Ilva was standing helplessly in the doorway, along with Althorne, Maier, Pace, and several medics. Ilva kept trying to talk to him, but Luc didn't seem to hear anything. The screaming faded as his throat stripped itself raw. He'd seemingly forgotten how a body worked. He seized, his arms and legs and fingers and head all tilting into bizarre angles, and then he slammed himself into the wall.

"I brought Helena," Elain said breathlessly.

Luc's head swivelled. He stared at Helena. His eyes seemed to grow, bulging from their sockets, head weaving like a snake.

"Hel—" he croaked. He reached for her. His fingers looked broken, but he didn't seem to notice. "Hel—"

"Careful, he's been violent," she dimly heard Pace say. She paid no mind.

She reached out, laced their fingers together, and touched the side of his face with her knuckles. His skin was so hot, it almost burned. He somehow bent his fingers, not seeming to notice the pain, clutching her hand, pulling her close.

"I'm here. What's wrong?" She numbed his hand, setting his fingers quickly.

His eyes had gone out of focus, and he started shuddering. "Out—" he moaned, shaking his head. "Inside—"

She pressed her hand against his forehead, ignoring the way his skin scalded her hand, letting her resonance flow into him, trying to find the source of what was wrong. What was she missing?

"Hel—" Luc was saying again.

Pain exploded through her chest.

The world went careening, spinning. Vicious red burst across her vision, slamming into the back of her head. An endless ringing filled her ears.

She struggled to focus her eyes. She couldn't breathe.

She clutched at her chest. Noises were elongated. Faces loomed over her.

Something grabbed her. She gave a panicked scream, going for her knives, but they weren't there. She clawed wildly to free herself.

"Calm down, Marino," Matron Pace was saying. "You're all right, just a bad scare. Knocked your breath out."

The raw terror ebbed. The room came slowly back into view.

She was on the floor, breathing raggedly, pain consuming her chest as she tried to make sense of what had happened.

Luc was on the other side of the room. His expression had turned scorchingly lucid.

"You—" His eyes were suddenly clear and burning. "You used necromancy on Soren."

The accusation hung in the air like the lull between lightning and thunder.

Everyone froze.

Helena pushed herself upright.

"I'm sorry," she rasped, struggling to speak. Her lungs were seizing for air, sending jolts of pain through her ribs. She knelt and almost doubled over on the floor of the hospital. "I tried to heal him. I'm sorry."

"He was alive. Why didn't you just heal him?" Luc's voice was racked with grief.

She couldn't breathe enough to explain herself, to describe how quickly Soren was gone, that he'd known he'd die, and that he'd asked her to do it.

"I'm sorry, Luc."

"Get out . . ." He wasn't looking at her anymore. His gaze lost focus, and he swayed.

"Luc, you're sick—"

"Get out!" He closed his eyes, starting to shudder again, his breathing coming faster and faster as if being in the same room with her was about to drive him mad. "Get out! Get out! Get out!"

He started clawing at his chest, screaming, tearing grooves into his skin as if trying to tear his own heart out.

"Luc?" another voice broke in.

Lila stood in the doorway, a crutch under one arm. Rhea was beside her, helping her walk.

The scars on Lila's face and chest showed vividly where she was stitched together.

Luc's eyes shot open at the sound of her voice.

"Lila . . ." he said, his voice both grief-stricken and filled with relief, as if he hadn't believed she was still alive until that moment.

Several people tried to hold her back, murmurs of *Careful,* but Lila let go of her mother, reaching desperately towards Luc. She let her crutch fall and toppled into his arms, clinging to him.

"I told you to run," Lila was saying, clutching him close. His hands were shaking as he touched the laceration running down her face.

Lila brushed across the gouges he'd clawed in his chest. "What did they do to you?"

He just shook his head and pulled her closer, burying his head against her shoulder, arms wrapped around her.

It was painfully intimate. If there had been any doubts about whether or why Luc had handed himself over, they were all gone now.

There was a touch at Helena's elbow. She looked up and found Ilva, who nodded towards the door.

Helena pushed herself to her feet and slipped out before Luc noticed her again. When she passed Rhea, she looked away.

It was Lila who coaxed Luc into bed, who persuaded him to let Pace and Elain examine him again, to accept an intravenous drip in his arm, and take the medicine needed to bring his fever down.

Helena sat on a hospital bed in the main room, an intravenous drip in her arm, while Elain fixed a fracture in her sternum and spread a salve across the bruise that spanned most of her chest, then treated the back of her head, where she'd hit the far wall.

It wasn't the first time Helena had been injured by a patient, but it felt different.

Luc was never going to forgive her for what she'd done to Soren. She'd broken him.

The curtain around the hospital bed rustled, and Ilva stepped through. Elain lingered until Ilva glared, and then the healer fled. Helena closed her shirt and didn't look up.

"We're taking reports on what happened," Ilva said, her tone unreadable.

Helena sat numbly. Would they put her on trial now? Or would it wait until after the war?

"What have you heard?" she asked in a dull voice.

Ilva cleared her throat. "Luc is delirious, his version of events hardly reliable given that he was not only severely injured but also heavily drugged. Alister and Penny both gave statements that Soren Bayard died protecting them. Sebastian Bayard—" Ilva paused for a moment. "Sebastian corroborates this, and claims that the two of you managed to drag the others to safety after the rising floodwater washed away a large number of the attacking forces."

"And?" Helena asked.

"Lucien—hallucinated Soren Bayard's alleged reanimation. Perhaps Soren fell briefly. In the confusion of a battle, it is impossible to know. The point is, this was a heroic rescue. The Principate was saved though the price was great. Sol's will was done."

Helena knew she was supposed to be grateful, but she also knew the lie wasn't for her sake. It was all for the story. It didn't matter what had really happened, only what people believed.

"The obligations of Soren and Sebastian's vows supersede any orders by the Council," Ilva said. "Alister and Penny were obeying the orders of their direct superiors. You would have a reprimand on your military record for your participation, but as a healer you're not part of the military. Matias will be the one to decide what sort of reprimand you deserve. Until then, you'll be off duty. I believe it would be best if you stay out of sight until the official story has circulated."

Helena went back to her room and collapsed into her bed, exhaustion rolling over her like a wave. It was dark oblivion at first, but then the landscape of her mind morphed.

She was sinking, down, down. There were teeth sinking into her. Hands clawing, curling around her limbs, tearing her apart. She kept fighting. Cold fingers carving gouges through her flesh, stabbing into her bones. She tried to fight. The weight bore down on her.

Her bones cracked. Teeth sank into her flesh. The tendon behind her knee ripped out. Wet hands found her mouth, clawing in so deep she couldn't bite down. Her jaw gave way, ripping until her throat tore open. She was still fighting as water closed over her head.

Helena started violently awake, gasping to breathe, hands clutching at her open throat.

Just a dream, just a dream, she tried to tell her pounding heart.

Not really a dream, though. A memory. Soren's memories postmortem were lodged inside her consciousness as though they were her own. Bright and lurid in all their details.

She hadn't known necromancy was like that. That she would never be free of the person she brought back. No wonder necromancers went mad. Who could stay sane with the minds of the dead inside them?

The place where Soren had been was like a pit of festering guilt. Her body and mind had been cored, and now something dead and rotting was left there. Everyone always talked of what a curse necromancy was. Warned against it and its consequences, but Helena had been so convinced of its necessity, and so distracted by the eternal consequences, that she'd never paused to consider there being immediate ones.

She lay there, still feeling phantom fingers tearing her apart; her body was unutterably cold, reliving the cold, snowmelt water. She pulled more blankets onto herself, stealing Lila's bedding, and huddled, trying to sleep, to escape from the deadness Soren had left inside her. Every time she closed her eyes, Soren's final memories and sensations flashed through her mind.

She hadn't brought back his ability to feel pain or emotions, but her own mind dutifully tried to fill in those blanks, phantom sensation and terror rippling through her until her mind threatened to fissure, splitting between two realities.

It was only pain that drew her back into herself. She kept pinching at her skin, scratching at it. It wasn't intense enough. She needed something stronger.

She blinked and found herself holding one of Lila's knives, a second away from shoving it through her left forearm.

She dropped it and fled the room, wandering half blindly through the empty hallways of the Tower. It was night, quiet; almost everyone was asleep. It was so eerily still. She was consumed with a sort of mania.

She stumbled outside, hoping that the clear air would help centre her.

Lumithia hung overhead, bright as a white sun in the black abyss.

Helena's eyes throbbed just looking up at her. The Ascendance always put everything on edge, but Helena was already on edge. Ascendance had shoved her right over.

She closed her eyes and she was drowning again, nails dragging welts across her skin.

Kaine.

Kaine would know what was wrong. He'd understand. He used necromancy; he must know how to deal with this.

Without pausing to think, she headed for the Outpost. The destination was deliriously urgent. Curfew would be soon. She had to get through the checkpoints.

The streets of the city were like silver ribbons gleaming under full Ascendance, the shadows like teeth.

Just a little farther, she kept telling herself with every step. Until she was across the bridge, the river high and roaring beneath her, the tenement looming in front of her.

It was only when she reached the steps that she stopped to think.

She'd promised Kaine she would never come to the Outpost unless there was a Resistance emergency. He was a spy. It was dangerous for him. She'd given her word.

She'd risk his cover—endanger him.

She turned away.

Without a destination, her focus fractured.

Soren. Helena. Soren.

She felt her jaw give way, cold air and blood as her oesophagus tore open. Fingers gouging into her eye sockets. Water closing over her head. She was drowning but couldn't die, so she just kept drowning.

When her consciousness found her again, she was lying on the ground. The black sky, dark as ink, loomed overhead as Lumithia bore down, a scorching cold in Helena's resonance.

"Marino, what have you done to yourself?"

She was barely conscious of being lifted off the ground. Hot hands touching her face and forehead, driving away the drowning cold. She burrowed into the heat.

She was delirious. Truly delirious now, because Kaine was there with a giant winged dog standing behind him.

She'd never had a hallucination before, but all things considered, it was oddly pleasant. Kaine was like a furnace, and when she buried herself in his arms, face pressed against his chest, she could scarcely feel the cold dead fingers anymore.

"Soren Bayard died and I—I brought him back, but the other necrothralls tore him to pieces. I can't stop remembering how it felt. I think he took part of me with him. How do you do it again and again without going insane? Is it like this forever?"

One of his hands tilted her head back so she could see his eyes. In the moonlight, the grey glowed almost as bright as Lumithia, his hair gleaming that same colour.

"Had you ever used necromancy before?"

She shook her head.

"I don't suppose anyone told you how to do it, did they?" He exhaled, the back of his fingers pressing against her forehead. "You had the shit luck of knowing him, too. You're going into shock."

A hysterical laugh bubbled up from her. Of course no one had told her how to perform necromancy.

He shushed her, pulling her back against his chest, warding off the way her skin crawled with the memory of decaying fingers burrowing into it. "You tried to bring him back, didn't you? Idiot. You're freezing cold."

She didn't struggle as he half carried her towards his giant dog.

On closer inspection, it wasn't a dog, but a wolf with bright-yellow eyes, and it was the size of a warhorse, with wings the size of—

She didn't know of anything on earth with wings that large.

Kaine pushed her up and set her on a saddle cinched behind the wings, and then swung atop behind her. Helena's eyes fluttered shut as she sagged against him, tensing at the sensation of icy-cold fingers tearing open her skin. The creature hunched down, muscles rippling beneath thick fur. There was a lurch, then a sickening jerk that nearly threw Helena off.

Without warning, they were airborne.

Wind stung across her face, and her eyes rolled back. She was barely conscious of anything except Kaine behind her and the cold wind screaming in her ears.

Then she was sliding down, her legs giving out, and Kaine caught her before she hit the ground. They were standing somewhere so high up, the night so bright, that she could see beyond the mountains. She'd never been so high.

She looked around. She was on a balcony and alone with Kaine. For the first time in years, she felt a sense of distance from it all, looking down onto the East Island, cratered by years of war, cast in moonlight.

The air was thin, as if she were back in the mountains, the world dreamily still.

She held out a hand, letting the silver coat her skin.

"Do you think this is what my subconscious thinks I want?" she asked, peering towards the light of the Alchemy Tower's beacon gleaming like a small golden sun. "To run away from the war with you?"

Kaine's expression was unreadable as he pulled her back from the railing. There was a dark doorway, and he led her through it and into a hallway. After the silver brightness of the city, her eyes struggled to adjust.

"What do you want?" he asked.

His voice seemed to come from the darkness.

Her eyes burned and she reached, feeling the wall under her fingertips.

"I don't want to always be alone," she said. It was easier to be honest in the dark. "I want to love someone without feeling like if they know, it'll end up hurting them. People who love me always die. No matter what I do, it's never enough to save them. I have to love everyone from a distance, and I'm *so* lonely."

Her eyes blurred, and then the darkness fell away, revealing a large room with a roaring fire. The place was lavish. The Holdfasts' city residence had once been like this, filled with gilded furniture that glittered in the firelight.

It was elegant but impersonal. There wasn't anything to make the place feel lived-in.

She looked back; Kaine was standing behind her. His black clothes were limned by the glowing firelight, adding a flush of gold and ember red to his almost monochrome appearance. He still had that otherworldly glow about him.

"You don't have to be alone," he said.

She looked down, wanting to fall headlong into the fantasy of believing that; to feel good for a little while, and tell herself it would do no harm.

But she knew that was a lie. Her mind was never quiet enough to let her enjoy anything without thinking about its consequences.

"Why? Because of you?" she asked bitterly, going towards the fire instead, sinking onto her knees in front of it. She couldn't think she was drowning here. She shook her head. "I don't get to care about you."

Her chest clenched, fingers curling into fists. "If I care about you—I won't be able to use you. And you're the only hope I have of keeping everyone else alive."

She curled in on herself, staring at the dancing flames. Somewhere on the Outpost, she was lying on the ground, going into shock, possibly freezing to death.

"Then use me," Kaine said. He was right next to her. He pulled her close and tried to kiss her.

She jerked away. "No! No, I can't." She shook her head. *Wake up, Helena.* "I don't want to do that to you. You don't—deserve that. I can take care of myself."

He wouldn't let go.

"You don't have to push me away to protect me," he said in a hard, familiar voice. "I can take it. You can stop being lonely. I won't misunderstand. I know you just want someone to be with."

She looked for a door. An escape.

He didn't let go. "Helena . . ."

She stilled at her name.

"I'm alone, too," he said.

A lump rose in her throat, her heart pounding. "But I don't want to hurt you, you don't deserve—"

He kissed her, swallowing her objections. She didn't struggle when he pulled her into his arms. The heat of the fire faded until there was only the heat of him, his lips warm against hers, his hands cradling her face. Then there was the softness of a bed beneath her back, pillows and sheets, and she pulled him closer, fingers seeking the buttons on his coat and unfastening them, but he caught her hands in his, holding them captive against his chest, and drew back. He tilted her face into the light.

She stared dazedly at him as he pressed the back of his hand against her forehead and tucked her in as if she were sick and needed nursing.

When she tried to sit up, he sat down next to her and let her huddle close, face buried against his chest.

"Necromancy doesn't—bring someone back . . ." he said, "but that can be hard to remember in the moment. When it's someone you know, when you can feel the span of their loss, it's instinctive to think it costs that much to bring them back. What you did with Bayard was put a part of yourself into reanimating him. In other circumstances, you could have reversed it, untethered yourself, but he took all of it with him when he was destroyed."

There was a pause.

"You'll recover, but it'll leave a scar. You just have to stay grounded until your mind learns not to go there. Lucky for you, animancy should help with that."

"Did this ever happen to you?"

He was silent for a minute. "Something similar once, but it was a long time ago."

Helena curled closer to him, listening to his heartbeat.

He was alive. She had kept him alive. She found his hand, pulling it up near her chin, holding it in both of hers, tracing the ridges of his knuckles, lacing her fingers along them. Just holding on.

She lifted her head to look at him.

He didn't move, not even when she let go of his hand to reach up and touch his face. Or when she shifted near enough to brush her lips against his cheek. Her fingers traced across his cheekbones, and she kissed his temple and his forehead. Then, hesitantly, she pulled him closer and kissed him on the mouth.

He was fire to touch.

She kissed him slowly until his arms slid around her back and he returned it.

She didn't know if what she was doing was holding on or letting go.

The first thing his fingers found were the pins in her hair. Her braids tumbled down her back, his fingers combing through them until her hair was loose. His hand tangled through it as he kissed her again.

The kisses were slow. It wasn't seething or rushed or guilty, but it was still desperate, because he always made her desperate.

She kissed him the way she'd wanted to. The way she'd secretly wished she could.

She could have this.

Once.

She gave a low sob. He paused, but she held on, not letting him go.

"This—is the way I wanted it to be," she admitted. "With you. I wanted it to be like this with you."

He went very still.

"I'm sorry. I'm sorry it wasn't," he finally said, pulling her closer.

Had he ever actually been like this? She wondered sometimes how much of her drunken memory of kissing him was real. Or if she'd invented all the intimacy to replay when her life felt too void of any tenderness.

"It doesn't matter," she said, resting her head on his shoulder.

"Yes, it does. Let me give you this now." He drew her face to his and kissed her. Slow and intent.

Like a star, he was glittering and ice-cold from afar, but when the space was bridged, the heat of him was endless.

His lips didn't leave hers as his hands found the buttons on her shirt and underclothes, unfastening them slowly this time. The fabric whispered across her skin as his fingers traced along her spine. His mouth followed the curve of her collarbones, fingers drawing her head back so he could taste the dip of her throat.

She fumbled at his clothes. Her fingers were unsteady, but there was no rush this time. She managed the buttons one by one.

He was unfathomably gentle. His touch light, and yet it made her feel as though a flame were kindled inside her, a desire that made her ache.

It wasn't too fast, or too much before she was ready. He went as slowly as she wanted him to.

When he pushed inside her, his eyes were fastened on her face. "Is this all right? Is it good for you?"

She gave a gasp and nodded. Because it was good this time.

"It's good. Don't stop," she said, gripping him by the shoulders, pulling him nearer. She could feel the scars of the array spanned beneath her fingers. She didn't know how he could be so calm with all that power humming beneath the surface of his skin.

His forearms were around her head as though framing her, his fingers laced in her hair. When he started to move, he pressed his forehead against hers, their breath intermingling.

When he kissed her, it felt like the beginning of something that could be eternal.

It happened so gradually, she almost forgot that there was more to it. They could have stayed like that, lost in each other, and it would have been more than enough. She breathed in against his neck, tasting his skin with the tip of her tongue, memorising his scent, the feel of him in her arms.

The world beyond them had ceased to exist. He knew how to trail his fingers across her skin so that she was gasping, kiss her so that her legs wrapped tight around his hips, and move so slowly that, at first, she didn't notice the coiling tension inside her. That lurking hunger.

But of course there was more, and Kaine was looking for it. All his meticulous attention to when her breath caught, what angle made her hips rise in response, when she caught her lip between her teeth to hold back a low moan, body shuddering. He entwined their fingers and noticed when she gripped him, squeezing so tight her nails bit into his knuckles, breath growing short.

The pace and friction and contact increased, growing into something larger and deeper than comfort.

When he slid his hand between her legs, she instantly flinched away. The comfort vanished. She went cold all over, trying to twist, wanting to escape, turning her face away.

"No." She tried not to panic, but this was all a mistake. "No, don't."

He withdrew his hand and cradled her face, kissing her. "You get this part. This is yours."

She shook her head. "No. It's not." She drew in on herself, chin down, speaking rapidly. "When I became a healer, I had to promise I wouldn't ever—I took the vows—and—and then you said—about Luc, if he knew. I can't stop thinking about that. That—that I'm a whore—"

Her voice failed.

"I'm sorry." His hand still entwined with hers tightened. "I'm so sorry. I ruined so much of this for you. This is how it's supposed to be. Let me give this to you now."

She didn't move, her heart pounding against her ribs.

"Please, Helena."

She gave the barest nod.

"Close your eyes." His breath whispered against her cheek.

Her eyes fluttered closed as he kissed her.

Without being able to see, her focus was on the sensations, the feeling of his body pressed against hers. The movement of air across her skin. When his lips brushed against the pulse-point of her throat, she moaned. His palm cupped her breast, stroking as he started to move.

He kissed her as he slid his hand between their bodies again, deepening the kiss until her jaw loosened, mouth slack, and pleasure flooded through her, so intense her spine bowed. She gave a ragged gasp against his lips.

She was being wound up, fire igniting, growing, running outwards along her nerves, through her arms and legs until her fingers twisted, tangling in the sheets. Every time he moved or his lips found some new sensitive place, the tension ratcheted inside her, notch by notch, until she was on the verge of fracturing open.

Her breath caught inside her lungs as she struggled, trying to hold herself together, overcome by the terror that she would break apart. She couldn't.

If she broke, there would never be anyone to pick up the pieces.

"I can't—" she finally gasped out.

"Helena." Kaine's lips brushed across her cheek and temple, his breath ragged. "You get to have this. You're allowed to feel good things. Don't be alone. Have this with me."

He pulled her leg up with one arm, deepening and shifting the angle, drawing the tension higher, and crushed their bodies together, kissing her.

Her eyes shot open.

She stared up at him as her whole world shattered into shards of silver.

"Oh gods—" She sobbed the words out. Her fingernails sank into his arms. "Oh—oh—oh . . ."

She came apart under him, and he watched every moment of it.

As she lay panting, trying to catch her breath, his speed increased. Gripping her closer, tighter, his expression going tense. When he came, his mask slipped. He met her eyes for a moment before he buried his face against her shoulder, and she saw all the heartbreak in him.

Afterwards he held her close, not letting go.

She looked up. He was watching her, his expression distant, his emotions carefully hidden away.

She reached up and ran a finger along his cheek, looking for any trace of that boy who'd first greeted her at the Outpost, but there was so little of him remaining. Even his hair was all silver now.

"I think I've nearly memorised you," she said. "Especially your eyes. I think I learned to read them first."

The corner of his mouth twitched, and he caught her hand, capturing it against his chest.

"I memorised yours, too," he said after a moment, and then sighed, looking away. "I should have known—the moment I looked into your eyes, I should have known I would never win against you."

She gave a small smile, struggling to stay awake, afraid it might all fade away if she did. "I've always thought my eyes were my best feature."

"One of them," he said quietly.

CHAPTER 52

Aprilis 1787

When Helena woke, she found herself in a large bed, in a large room, and through the windows, the Novis Mountains were arrayed around them, gilded by a golden sunrise.

She was tangled in juniper-scented sheets and wrapped up in Kaine's arms, and she had no memory of how she'd gotten there.

She glanced around the room again. From the angle of the city, she could tell she was on the West Island. Probably one of the towers so immense they often disappeared into the clouds.

She'd always imagined Kaine on an estate or in one of the old houses in the city. Why would he be somewhere like this?

He lay, arms wrapped possessively around her as though he were keeping her from being stolen, features relaxed in sleep. She studied him.

What had she done?

Kaine Ferron was a dragon, like his family before him. Possessive to the point of self-annihilation. Isolated and deadly, and now he held her in his arms as if she were his. The temptation to give in, to let him have her, and to love him for it terrified her.

Her need to love people and her desperate longing for them to love her back—she had given that up, locked it away and buried it, giving its place to the coldness of logic, realism, and the necessary choices of war. This could only lead to ruin.

She had to be gone before he woke.

She tried to slip away as she had before, but this time his eyes snapped open. He pulled her back immediately but then caught sight of her terrified expression.

His eyes flickered, and he let go.

She went still.

The fear and anger that he'd inspired a year earlier had all but disappeared. The danger was still there, cast in sharper relief now that she had seen how lethal he was. Yet somehow knowing it made her less frightened. Now she knew how much he was holding back. Despite everything he'd achieved, this was Kaine Ferron using restraint.

"This was a mistake," she said. "I shouldn't have come here."

His throat dipped as he looked away.

"Don't worry," he said quietly. "This won't complicate anything for you. You wanted someone to be with, and I was available. I know it didn't mean anything."

Helena's breath caught, and she swallowed. He wasn't just someone. To her, he was—

That was the mistake of it, what she was so scared of.

Before she could even begin to invent a lie, something must have shown in her face. Her eyes always betrayed her.

Because his expression was withdrawn, and then, in an instant, triumph flashed across his face and he reached for her again. Hunger and heat splintered the air like lightning.

Before she could bolt, he pulled her back to him and his lips found hers, and all her fears and guilt and resolution became lost to her. All she could think of was how much she wanted to be there, being touched by him. He was fire, and she was already consumed.

"You're mine," he said against her lips, his fingers sliding along her throat, tangling in her hair, holding her fast as he dragged her nearer.

It was not like the previous night. It wasn't comfort. It was claiming.

His mouth was hot on her lips, his teeth nipping possessively along her jaw and her throat, over her shoulders. She tangled her fingers in his hair, arching into his touch. She tried not to cry from how desperately she wanted him, and how grateful she was that she didn't have to ask. He pulled her closer, arms entwined around her as he aligned himself and sank into her with a sharp thrust, his breath burning along her neck.

He was exacting. Determined to prove to her that this was where she belonged, to ensure that she could never deny what he made her feel.

She could feel his resonance along her nerves. He made no effort to hide the way he attuned himself to her, overwhelming her with sensation and pleasure all at once.

In the moment his control slipped and his expression was laid bare again, there was no more heartbreak; he was possessive and triumphant.

He pulled her close, crushing her to his chest. "You're mine. You swore yourself to me. Now and after the war. I'm going to take care of you. I'm not going to let anyone hurt you. You don't have to be lonely. Because you're mine."

Helena knew she should go, but she had lost herself there.

She was locked in the dangerous embrace of Kaine Ferron, and it felt like home.

She slept in his arms, nearly dead to the world, waking only briefly when his fingers trailed along her shoulder. She looked up, found him watching her, his eyes dark.

She arched into his touch and dropped a kiss over his heart. He picked up her hand, and she felt his resonance in her fingers as she fell asleep.

When she woke again, it was nearly evening, and the mountains had turned purple with dusk, gilded a burnished red as Sol began his descent.

Kaine was dressed, but he was just sitting beside her, watching her sleep, her fingers laced in his, as if there was nothing else to do.

"How are you here?" she asked, dazed with exhaustion. She somehow felt more tired than she ever had before, as if her body had finally remembered how to sleep and now intended to recover all the years of deprivation.

He raised an eyebrow. "I live here. Did you think my primary residence was the Outpost panic room?"

She shook her head, rolling onto her back. Her hands didn't hurt at all anymore. "No, but how are you able to spend a whole day in bed with me? Aren't you a general or something? Don't you have meetings, or crimes to commit?"

Rather than answer, he leaned over her until she was stretched out beneath him. His longer arms pinned her hands above her head, and he kissed her.

"I'm off duty," he finally said when she was breathless. "A concept I fear no one has ever acquainted you with."

She rolled her eyes. "But why do you live here? I thought old families had property."

He let go then and sat up, looking out at the view. "My mother was tortured at our country estate, and all the staff murdered. We moved to the city residence, and that's where she died. I wanted somewhere else to go, away from it all."

Helena sat up.

"I'm sorry, I shouldn't have asked, I just never imagined you high like this," she said, reaching up and resting a hand on his cheek. He dropped his head against her palm and closed his eyes for a moment, the strands of his hair falling across her fingertips.

Then he abruptly lifted his head. "Well, it's mostly practical. Amaris flies better from the roof. She's better at it now, but it used to be hard for her to get airborne."

"Amaris?" Helena repeated slowly.

"The chimaera. You saw her last night."

She blinked at him, a memory of an impossibly enormous, winged wolf resurfacing. "I thought . . . I'd hallucinated."

He gave her a look. "I told you I was getting a chimaera."

"Well, yes, but I assumed it was something—smaller, and you never mentioned it again. I assumed it had died."

He shrugged. "Well, she was small at first. About the size of a foal when she arrived."

"What is she?"

"Bennet isn't forthcoming about such things. A lot of Northern wolf and some kind of destrier. I don't know where he got the wings, though."

"And she's—tame?"

He shook his head. "No. Just fond of me, but you should meet her. I meant to introduce you, but the moment never seemed right. Come on."

Helena didn't move, not wanting to go anywhere yet. Everything was so different between them now. The tension and wariness finally absent.

She'd never known him outside of that context, even as children.

Secreted away from the rest of the world, she felt that she could finally see him for his own sake, rather than only through the lens of the Eternal Flame's interests.

Glancing around the impersonal rooms, she could see them for what they were, a place to exist. There was not a single item of personal significance. Temporary. Uncommitted.

"When did you realise that I didn't know you were supposed to die?" she asked rather than stand.

He released a long breath. "The first time you arrived on the Outpost. I could tell by the way you looked, you thought it really was forever."

Her throat tightened.

He looked away. "It was—funny at first. I kept waiting for you to catch on."

Heat spread across the back of her neck.

"I thought that when I pointed out that you should've known about my punishment, you'd realise it was a setup, but you didn't. Then I assumed that it would have been explained to you by that evening or the next day, but you just kept coming back. I figured there must be something else they wanted, but it was clear by then they weren't going to tell you. I almost did, a few times, but—" He sighed. "—I suppose I enjoyed the way you wanted to save me."

She nodded slowly, fingers running along the seam of the linen sheet. "Crowther talked so much about the long term and making sure you didn't lose interest, and how I had to keep it secret, that no one could know. I thought they trusted me." She was quiet for a moment. "Ilva told me just before the solstice. You probably realised."

She took his silence for confirmation.

There was a pause as she remembered something. "Kaine, I don't think your father's dead."

Kaine looked at her sharply. "What?"

"When we rescued Luc, there was a lich. He told Sebastian that he was Atreus. He was guarding the door to the room Luc was in."

"No," Kaine said, his voice shaking. "No. He died. If he were still alive, he would have come back. For my mother."

His pupils had shrunken into sharp points of black, the denial stark.

"He was a lich," she said as gently as she could. "Would he have wanted her to see him like that?"

He started to speak several times as if to protest but then stopped. "What happened?"

"Soren and Sebastian killed him. He was between us and Luc. We didn't have time to find the talisman, though. You didn't know he was Undying?"

He shook his head. "I thought he was arrested before all that began." He drew a scoffing breath, his expression growing bitter. "So in the end, he didn't even manage to die for her."

"Your mother?"

He nodded slowly. "It was all because of her. I know what people said about them, about why he married her, but he—adored her. She was life itself to him. When I was born and she was sick, he grew obsessed with keeping her well, not allowing visitors or any potential disease near her. Morrough claimed he could cure her, that she'd live forever."

"He must not know what happened after he was arrested," Helena said.

There was a strained look in Kaine's eyes. "Likely not."

"If he knew, do you think—?"

Kaine shook his head. "I'm sure he'd blame me. He always did."

There was a pause, and he looked over at her. "Speaking of dying, or rather, not dying . . . would you mind telling me why I haven't?"

Helena suddenly found the thread count of the sheets fascinating.

"It was a failed experiment. Bennet spent weeks trying to heal it, and everything he did made it worse. When it was finally deemed a failure, he tried to scrap my body, but the array was pulling so much energy from the talisman, he couldn't touch it. He assumed that eventually the energy would run out, or my body would incinerate around it, so they sent me home, because they didn't want the potential fallout to contaminate the new lab.

"Since my miraculous recovery, Bennet's tried to repeat the experiment. Every subject has died, slowly and terribly, and Bennet cannot find any explanation for why I alone survived. You are the only person who has never questioned my survival, and I would like to know why."

There was a long pause. Helena cleared her throat. "I had this amulet of the Holdfasts'. A holy relic, you could say. Ilva gave it to me when I became a healer, and it helped."

"Helped?" The scepticism in his voice was heavy.

"I could—work longer." She avoided his eyes. "I didn't get tired or—burn out when I had it. When you were injured, you'd deteriorated so much that the array was using more energy and resources than you had. I thought since it had helped me maybe it would work for you, too, give you enough strength to recover."

His eyebrows rose. "What kind of relic would have the power to do that?"

She coughed. She should probably lie, given that telling the truth was possibly treason.

But she couldn't think of a lie to tell. She'd already committed treason anyway.

"The Stone of the Heavens," she said. "I didn't know that's what it was, and it's not—really what the stories said. It was something made by the Necromancer, but Orion ended up with it, and people just assumed it was heaven-sent."

"And they gave it to you?" Kaine's eyes were narrowed.

"Apparently, it—chose me. It doesn't work for most people."

Kaine had his hands on his hips. "And that's how you healed me?"

She gave a tight nod. "That's how I healed you."

He was silent for a long time. She couldn't read his expression, couldn't tell if he believed her.

"Where is it now?"

"Gone," she said, averting her eyes. "It's gone now."

He sighed. "Well, I suppose it makes sense they wouldn't let you keep it, if I'm what you used it on."

She forced a self-deprecating smile. It was probably best he thought that. "Ilva wasn't pleased."

"I imagine not. Were there any other repercussions?"

"Well, I was supposed t—" She swallowed. "—to kill you, but I got out of that. So I guess it all worked out in the end."

She managed another smile, but he did not return it.

His expression had gone cold and empty. "This is your idea of things working out?"

Her face fell, and just as suddenly it was all back: the reality of all that existed between them. That he would have preferred it if she'd killed him; that that was what he'd wanted. Instead she was sitting on his bed, smiling over how it had worked out so nicely for everyone else now that she had him on a leash.

"No, no, of course not. Sorry."

She drew back, turning, trying to find her clothes.

"What are you doing?" Kaine leaned forward and caught her by the ankle before she was halfway across the bed.

"I think I should go now," she muttered, her throat tight, trying to slip free.

"Why?"

Her heart was in her throat. "I know you didn't want any of this; I didn't mean to act like it was all fine."

His expression hardened, and he dragged her back across the bed.

She tried desperately to get free. "Can I—at least put my clothes on before you get angry? Please."

He stared at her. "I wasn't talking about me. I was talking about you."

"Me?" She was confused enough that she stopped struggling.

"Yes. You. The Resistance has latched on to you like a parasite, and you think it's all worked out because they're kind enough to keep you alive while they eat you?"

"It's not like that," she said sharply.

"Six years in a war hospital. How many people have you saved for them? I doubt you know. But was that enough for them? No. The moment there was another advantage to gain, they sold you for the ports. I've seen workhorses treated better; they would have turned you into glue once you weren't good for anything else." He sneered. "But I suppose that's how it's always been. It's only the war stallions like the Bayards who are retired to the countryside."

"Shut up," she said, kicking sharply and freeing herself. Her face was hot with anger. "You think I don't know I'm expendable? When you see fit to remind me of it at every turn? Well, you don't have any right to be angry about that, when you're just as much a part of it as any of them. You knew what was happening, and that I didn't, and you still chose to be as cruel as you were. At least Ilva and Crowther manipulated me for a reason." She looked away from him. "When were you even *that* kind?"

He was silent. She looked away.

"I'm sorry," he said after a moment.

She gave a mirthless laugh. "Yes, you've apologised before, but you don't change, so it doesn't really mean anything."

"You're right."

He sat down on the edge of the bed and pressed his face into his hands. "I'm sorry for that, too. I never meant for any of it to go so far. I knew the mission you'd been sent with, and I was sure I'd be immune, but realising it was all real for you—when it would work, and I'd find myself falling for the trap I'd chosen—I'd do whatever it took to make you stop. It hadn't occurred to me that they wouldn't tell you."

She bit the inside of her lip. "They thought I'd be more convincing that way."

He nodded slowly. "I thought if I was just cruel enough, you'd give up. That you'd have a limit, that once I found it, you'd stop—finding ways to emotionally blindside me." He gave a low sigh. "I spent such a long time waiting to be betrayed, I didn't want to care when it happened. I *was* trying to hurt you, but I am so sorry that I did."

She stared out at the horizon, shaking her head slowly. "I don't know why I kept trying. You just had these moments when I could see how little of you was real. When you'd forget to pretend, you always seemed so lonely. And I was lonely, too." She looked down at the scar in her palm. "I used to think that we were the reverse of each other. Now—" She looked at him and extended her hand. "—I can't help feeling like we're mostly the same."

He entwined his fingers with hers and pulled her close, and this time she let him take her into his arms, his face buried in the curve of her neck.

Life was not cold.

Then he sat back enough to look at her. She watched the way his eyes moved, taking her in piece by piece as if he didn't want to miss a single detail.

His hands slid up around her throat, warm and possessive, thumb covering the scar below her jaw as he kissed between her eyes. "You're a far better person than I am. This world doesn't deserve you at all."

She shook her head. "I could survive without having to go as far as you did. That doesn't make me better."

"You keep people alive. You touch them and your instinct is to save them, no matter who they are or what they've done to you. That is not a trait we share. It's far more difficult than calculating all the ways to kill someone. And it costs you more."

Their foreheads touched, and she closed her eyes. It was as though their souls were touching, too.

She wanted to spend her life lost in that moment, but she'd been gone for a day, and no one knew where she was. She couldn't stay.

"I have to go back."

He didn't let go. "You should eat."

"I have to go," she said firmly, trying to rise.

"Take a bath," he said, catching her waist. "I'll order something to be brought up. Anything you want."

"Kaine." She pulled his hands off. "You can't keep me here. I have to go."

His expression flickered, just enough to reveal a shard of possessiveness, something ravenous and desperate. Then it vanished and he let her stand, resignation sweeping across his face.

She reached out, her fingers brushing back his hair. "Don't worry. I'm always going to come back to you."

CHAPTER 53

Aprilis 1787

KAINE'S CHIMAERA WAS SOMEHOW EVEN LARGER WHEN encountered lucid. When Helena was dressed and ready to leave, rather than be smuggled through the city, Kaine led her to the high open roof. The creature stood, stretching and yawning, baring fangs longer than Helena's fingers, wings spreading so wide they nearly blanketed the rooftop.

The chimaera cantered stiffly towards Kaine, eerie yellow eyes watching Helena, the whites showing, muzzle curled in warning.

"Be nice, Amaris," Kaine said chidingly, scratching the chimaera behind her ears.

Amaris drooped her head, her lip still curling to the gums, eyes fastened on Helena. It was for the best that Helena had been delirious the night before; she would never have climbed on that animal knowing it was real.

Kaine patted the wolfen monster and then knelt, running his hands up and down a foreleg. Helena could see the horse shape of the leg, but it ended in a paw with huge talon-like claws.

She backed away, giving more space. Despite Kaine's desire that they all be friends, it was obvious that Amaris did not like anyone but him.

"She's not growling at you," Kaine said before Helena could take another step back. "Bennet spliced the legs wrong when he made her. Whenever she grows, the nerves get stretched out, and I have to fix them."

"What do you mean?" Helena watched. She could tell he was using his resonance as his fingers brushed along the length of the foreleg.

"Bennet only cares about the aesthetics when it comes to the chimaeras. He forces things to fit together even when they shouldn't. The reason the chimaeras are so dangerous is that they're all rabid with pain. They usually die because the stress kills them. When Amaris arrived, she bit me about fifty times during the first week. You may recall that my back was still in tatters at the time. I nearly snapped her neck after the tenth time, but I thought, I'm in so much pain I'd love to bite someone. Why would it be different for her? She was all puppy then, but legs like a foal. Constantly tripping and breaking her wings." He glanced back at Helena. "I had a notion of the taming capacity of pain relief, and you'd mentioned how flawed the transmutations were, so I tried to fix what I could. Once she realised I wasn't there to hurt her, she stopped biting."

He straightened and patted Amaris just below a huge wing. The feathers were as long as Helena's arms.

He rubbed his knuckles between Amaris's eyes. "She warmed up to me after that. She's the only survivor of the whole batch. Bennet tried to take her back, wanted to see why she'd worked. She nearly took his head off. Didn't you?"

He rumpled the thick fur.

"Come meet her, she'll be nice now." He gestured Helena over. He took her hand and let Amaris sniff it. Her teeth remained bared, but her tail slowly began to swing and her wings relaxed. He guided Helena to bury her fingers in the thick fur and scratch behind an enormous, pricked ear.

Helena could feel his eyes on her as she tentatively let her resonance creep in. Amaris trembled but didn't move or snarl.

She could feel how haphazardly assembled Amaris was, bones and tissue not meant to be combined but forced together nonetheless. Unlike the chimaeras she'd examined in her lab, it was clear someone had tried to correct the excessive flaws, to properly join the muscles, smooth the bone fusions and misjoined ligaments, to block off nerves that caused nothing but pain.

She tried to imagine this monster as a puppy, a foal, a hatchling. Innocent and juvenile and then—

Pain and mutilation.

Of course the chimaeras were savage. How could anything endure so much hurt and not learn only to bite?

"You've done remarkable work on her," she said, her mouth dry. "Is this how you learned to heal?"

"I suppose it was some good practice."

He looked out over the city, spread below like a glittering crown. Lumithia had yet to rise, leaving whole swaths of the East Island in darkness, but the Alchemy Tower stood above it all, its beacon ever burning.

"We should go now. It's dark enough to fly without being sighted."

It was one thing to pet Amaris; it was quite another to mount her. Helena was certain the wolf could bite her in half if so inclined. Kaine stood at Amaris's head, scratching her ears, while Helena grasped the leather harness and clambered up.

It took an embarrassingly long time, like scaling a furry mountain. Helena was worried about kneeing or elbowing Amaris and struggled to get a good grip. Kaine swung up behind her in one easy movement.

He was barely seated before Amaris leapt off the roof.

They plummeted straight down and then the huge wings spread out, catching the air and carrying them skywards.

Kaine flew Amaris so high, the air grew thin. They kept their distance from the city and towers, flying near the mountains until they reached the dam. Amaris banked sharply, so fast the Outpost blurred and the wind from her wings rattled the windows as they sped past. One of the factories had a large open roof that they landed on.

Helena's legs scarcely held her as she slid off, desperately grateful for solid ground and convinced that humans were not meant to fly, and it was an abomination for them to do so. She tried to appear grateful and not look too green as she scuttled away from the chimaera.

Kaine followed her. Now that the introduction to Amaris and the journey were over, there was an undeniable look of resentment in his eyes again, as if letting her return to Headquarters was not yet something he was convinced of.

Helena pretended not to notice as she headed for the gate, but it only made his mood darken. Finally, she stopped. "What is it?"

"Don't go," he said softly.

"You know I have to."

He shook his head. "No, I don't. They don't care about you."

The words were like a raw nerve being plucked. The pain hummed inside her. Before, she would have denied it, because Luc was there and he would never turn on her, but that was no longer true.

Still, she was unmoved. She shook her head. "We can't let the Undying win. There is too much at stake. I have to go where I can do good."

A look of fury joined his resentment. "No, you don't. It doesn't matter how many times you break yourself, the gods don't care. There's no reward. This"—he threw his hand out, gesturing at the city, the mountains, and the black sky that Lumithia now radiated down from—"is the Abyss. We're already in it. None of it matters. Sacrifice and pain, the universe does not care."

"You're wrong," she said.

He opened his mouth to argue, to offer an endless list of examples of how cold and uncaring the world was, but she didn't need to be told.

"You're wrong because I'm part of the universe," she said. "A tiny piece, I admit, maybe never an important or mathematically significant one, but still a piece. You and I are not separate from it. No one is. It matters to me, everyone who's died and everyone who will, and everyone who suffers. As long as I exist, I will always care. And that means that part of the universe does." She smiled at him. "Doesn't that make it all a little brighter?"

He looked despairing.

She gave a helpless shrug. "I want to do good in the world. That was what my father wanted most for me." She looked down at her hands. "I know most people won't think I have. I've done things now that I don't think I'm supposed to be forgiven for. But I want to be remembered as someone who tried at least."

She stepped back, but he caught her.

"Helena—"

She pulled free. "Be careful, Kaine. Don't die."

"CROWTHER'S LOOKING FOR YOU," THE gatehouse guard said as he let her in.

Helena nodded and headed to the Tower.

Crowther was seated in his office, his right arm strapped to his body as if it were paralysed again, and he looked at Helena with a degree of disgust unlike anything she'd ever seen before. It reminded her of how the guild students used to look at her, but intensified by magnitudes.

The fingers of his right arm were squeezed into a fist. Which meant it still worked and he was intentionally depriving himself of it.

It took her a moment to understand. This was because she was a necromancer now.

"I was told you wanted me," she said, pretending not to notice his expression.

"Hours ago," he said through clenched teeth.

"I'm here now."

Crowther snapped the ignition rings on his left hand, and a deep red orb of flames filled his hand before his fingers squeezed into a fist, skin glowing for a moment before the light extinguished. "The prisoner you brought back refuses to cooperate without you, and Ilva . . ." His expression twisted with fury. "Ilva insists on a light touch until we know who he is. I have wasted an entire day waiting for you. Where were you?"

Helena avoided his eyes. "Ilva said it would be best to keep out of sight until the official story had circulated."

"That's not what I asked."

Helena set her jaw and met his eyes. "I was with Ferron, but I'm sure you already worked that out."

He gave a scathing laugh that made her scalp crawl. The venom in his expression was so shocking, it was as if she were not even human anymore.

"It's not as if I wanted to use necromancy," she said, deciding to drag the unspoken source of his fury into the open. "There was no other way. Soren wasn't near recovered enough for a mission like that. What was I supposed to do? Let Luc die?"

"What were you supposed to do?" he repeated slowly, standing. "You were supposed to stay in Headquarters. You have one job, Marino, and that is to stay alive and intact so that Ferron can have his weekly proof of life. But it seems I have expected too much of your skills of deduction, so let me be crystal-clear: Unless you are liaising, you will not set foot outside of Headquarters *ever* again. The only reason I am not having you thrown in prison to stand trial for necromancy is because you now exist to keep Ferron in line."

Helena's throat closed. "It was your plan. I was working with what I had."

Crowther's eyes bulged. "My plan?"

"It was your informant from the hospital who gave Soren all the information. Where else would Purnell—"

Before she could finish the question, the door burst open, and a boy flew into the room.

"Where's Sofia? I tried to find her, but no one will talk to me. Where is she?"

It was Ivy, her face dirty, hair tucked up in a cap.

Crowther's gaze slid to Helena. "Marino, perhaps you'd like to tell Ivy here where her older sister, Sofia Purnell, is?"

Ivy turned, and Helena noticed then the resemblance between the hospital orderly and Crowther's little protégée. A few years apart, different colouring, and Ivy's features were sharp and foxlike where Sofia was soft. But as she looked, Helena could see the likeness.

"Your sister?" Helena said, her voice straining. "Sofia was *your* sister?"

Beneath the dirt, all colour drained from Ivy's face.

"Sofia was part of the rescue team that saved Luc. She showed us the route through the tunnels to the prison, but during the escape, she was caught in the flood current. I thought—I thought"—Helena looked at Crowther—"you sent her. You didn't send her?"

Ivy stared at Helena for a moment and then screamed. Helena had never heard such a sound from anyone. It exploded out of the girl, so sharp it felt as though the lightbulbs might shatter. White rage swept across Ivy's face.

Helena braced herself, but Ivy whirled on Crowther. "You promised to protect her if I did everything you said! She wasn't supposed to work for you. She was just supposed to be safe!"

She lunged at him, going right over the desk, as if she intended to claw his eyes out, but before her fingers reached him, a burst of flames materialised and slammed her into the wall. Ivy hit the floor, and books toppled from the shelves onto her, catching fire as they rained down.

Crowther had moved, darting like a cat. His years of combat experience showing as he closed in on Ivy.

"I never told her about tunnels or waterways, or any prison," Crowther said as his hand clenched in a fist, the fire vanishing. "If she knew that information, it was from *your* indiscretion. I warned you to tell her nothing, but you had to talk about all the ways you could travel through the city unseen. Are you glad you impressed her now? I'm sure you made it sound so easy."

Helena expected Ivy to spring up, but the girl just stayed there on the floor.

"I wanted her to know the ways out. I showed her the map and told her about the prison so she wouldn't go that way," Ivy said, her voice a whimpering sob.

"If you had listened to me, she'd be alive," Crowther said, his voice callous. "I upheld my end of the deal; none of this is my fault." He kicked her. "Now get out of my sight. If Lucien Holdfast had been killed in that ridiculous rescue, I would have blamed *you*."

Ivy picked herself up off the floor without a word, but as she slipped through the door, she looked back for an instant, and there was murder in her eyes.

When she was gone, Crowther stepped over and pulled out a radio from inside his desk, holding the transceiver up as it crackled to life. Helena recognised the voice of the guard. One of the higher-ups.

The string of jargon that Crowther muttered was nearly incomprehensible, but Helena did pick up two phrases: "extremely dangerous" and "neutralised."

He set the transceiver down and looked around his charred office.

"Is that really necessary?" Helena asked.

Crowther looked up. "You've seen what she's capable of. Without her sister keeping her in check, Ivy is of no use. Bear in mind, that rule applies to Ferron as well."

His eyes raked over her in disgust, as if he could see every place Kaine had touched her. "I would strongly advise keeping yourself alive, Marino."

WHEN HELENA SAW WAGNER, HE smiled at her, but all she could think of was the terror in Sofia's face as he shoved her towards the necrothralls.

A translator had been found, a rheumy old man named Hotten who worked in the kitchens. His son had been a graduate of the Alchemy Institute and died early in the war.

"Now then," Crowther said as they entered the cell. All his anger had vanished, and he was almost convincingly convivial. "Why are you so important?"

Hotten translated. Hevgotian was a low West dialect that had a folky cadence and very round-sounding words. Wagner gave a few long-winded answers that Hotten summarised after trying and failing to keep up.

"He knew Morrough in Hevgoss. Morrough was given a prison unit, sector four criminals. Wagner was a guard," Hotten translated slowly.

The only thing Hevgoss liked more than expansionist war was their prison population. It was vast, multigenerational, and the source of their labour force and the bulk of their military. Sector four criminals were usually political prisoners, sentenced to four generations of imprisonment, lifetime after lifetime of indentured servitude that only their great-great-grandchildren would have a chance of escaping.

Labour sentences were passed down for almost any infraction, lasting anywhere from days to generations. Much of their low-ranked military was composed of sector one and two criminals, who were promised pardons in exchange for a successful military record. Whenever there were labour shortages, or rumours of political or economic instability within the country, Hevgoss had a habit of going to war, stretching their borders to encompass some new population to refill their prisons.

Officially Hevgotian prisons were all state-run, but that didn't prevent the "rental" of prisoners when it suited them to whoever could pay. Slavery was illegal on the Northern continent, so Hevgoss had reinvented it.

"Morrough had made a deal with the militocrats. He was trying to find a way of controlling the power of life. He said that mastering it, harvesting it, was the key to immortality. He promised the leaders that he'd teach it to them if they provided him with the materials to test it, but the prisoners"—Wagner shrugged—"were resistant. They didn't want to cooperate. They knew they would die."

Wagner smiled as he recounted this, as though the story evoked fond memories.

"My job was to deliver the prisoners each day and take them back at night, but there were never any to take back when he was done with them. Morrough was friendly to me. He would talk to me, tell me his frustrations. The energy, you see, could not be taken by force; it had to be given willingly. He had already found many tricks to get it, but when the prisoners were dead, the energy, he said, remembered. They would lash out. Resist, so that it was difficult even for him to control."

Helena and Crowther shared a quick glance. Clearly Crowther was also acquainted with the true story of Orion's victory against the Necromancer.

"It was my idea that solved it." Wagner thumped his chest. "My father, he was a warden, so was my grandfather. Prison uprisings are a dangerous thing. There are prisons the size of towns. To keep order, it is important that the guards are not the enemy. Instead, you make the prisoners think their trouble is other prisoners, a different unit or sector. Those prisoners are the reason this prisoner has less; the rules they hate are those prisoners' fault. By making privileges always at the expense of others, the prisoners forget who has made those rules. Morrough liked this idea. To take the souls, he must make the prisoners blame someone else. Even after the energy was taken, the blame must continue to be misdirected."

Wagner looked from Helena to Crowther, seeming to expect their awe.

"He succeeded in this, I presume," Crowther said.

Wagner nodded. "He stopped trying to contain or bind the energy to himself. Instead he used another prisoner inside the array." He spread his hands wide. "He had a strange alchemy. With his power, he pulled the energy out and bound them to the soul of a chosen prisoner. The other prisoner would suffer all the anger, and Morrough took the power."

"But how would he control it," Helena said, "if the souls—the energy is bound to someone else?"

"With his bones," Wagner said, raising his eyebrows. "I saw it. He used his alchemy to contain all the souls inside pieces of his own bones. It was strange, but if a piece stayed with the prisoner in the array, they could not die, even if they tried. Then Morrough could keep the power."

The phylacteries. It was exactly what Kaine had described.

"The souls of the others, they would feel that life, they would try to resist, but the prisoner could not be killed. Still . . . slowly their mind would—" Wagner touched the sides of his head, pulling invisible strings as though unravelling something.

"Are you saying that the Undying are just a power source for Morrough?" Helena said slowly.

"Yes! That is what he called them. Undying. Not living or dead."

Crowther placed paper and pen down in front of Wagner, indicating that he sketch as much of the procedure and array as possible.

It was clear that Wagner was no alchemist, or artist, but he'd seen the process done at least a few times. He sketched a massive array unlike anything Helena had ever seen. Neither celestial nor elemental, it had nine source points, and in the centre a platform was suspended by which Morrough could access the body of the prisoner designated to survive.

The sacrificial victims were placed on the nine points. Morrough would open the chest cavity of the chosen recipient prisoner and place a piece of one of his own bones inside as the final component of the array. After somehow tethering their life force to that bone, he would activate the array.

The array created a pull so terrible that the sacrifices shrivelled into husks, stripped of life until it was drawn into the recipient, trapping their soul beneath the layers and layers of the others, like an insect trapped in a spiderweb.

Morrough would cut off a shard of the bone, coat it in lumithium, and leave it inside the prisoner's body. Then he'd place the rest back inside his own.

The information fell in line with what they knew, but Helena's mind refused to believe that such a thing could be possible.

Ilva's story about the first Necromancer had been horrifying enough, manipulating and deceiving a multitude, but the scale made it impersonal. This process was so intimate and intentional. The repetition. The scope. Nine victims, over and over, tearing bone shard after bone shard each time. For power. For immortality.

This was how Kaine had been made.

"How did you survive so long, knowing all this?" Crowther asked Wagner.

Wagner smiled. "He was a selfish man. The lives of others were, to him, a resource. I am no fool. When it was a success, I ran. I knew he would try to find me someday. He would not share credit in his great discovery. I thought he had forgotten, until I woke up in Paladia. Now the world will know of me."

He smiled craftily at Crowther, clearly anticipating being used by the Resistance to counter Morrough's claims of power and scientific genius, but Helena couldn't imagine anyone caring whose idea it was; Morrough was the one with the power and ability.

"How are all the Undying able to use necromancy?" she asked.

Hotten translated the question.

"Accident," Wagner said with a barking laugh. "He never knew why."

ONCE THE INTERVIEW WITH WAGNER was over, Helena was left at a loose end. Headquarters security was thrown into chaos after the guards failed to apprehend Ivy.

Any information Ivy knew was now considered compromised. Crowther immediately moved the prisoners under the Alchemy Tower to a different location, somewhere south of Headquarters, and a team of alchemists went down into the warren of tunnels, trying to seal them off to keep Ivy from sneaking back in.

But when Ilva and Althorne went with Crowther for a follow-up interrogation, Wagner was found dead, hacked to bits by the reanimated corpses of the two guards stationed outside his cell. The remains had been assembled to read: CROWTHER NEXT.

Luc was still in the hospital, under constant watch. Information about his condition was kept carefully controlled. According to the daily reports, he was recovering and only needed a few more days before he'd be transferred to his rooms.

Elain was the only healer allowed to go in to see him. She was tight-lipped for the first time in her life. She would hurry in and out, retrieving medicine from the supply room, talking to Pace in a hushed voice, and then hurrying back.

Helena covered Elain's usual shifts. Among those patients was Penny, whose leg had been too damaged for healing and had been amputated at the knee. Alister was sitting at her bedside, keeping her company when Helena pushed back the curtains.

Helena was surprised at first that Penny had so few visitors, but then she remembered that, aside from Alister, Luc and Lila were the only ones left. All the rest were still being searched for beneath the rubble.

"I should go," Alister said, standing up. "The tribunal has follow-up questions."

Penny nodded wordlessly, her fingers clutching the blankets on her lap.

"What tribunal?" Helena asked, sitting down when Alister had gone. "You two aren't being punished for saving Luc, are you?"

Penny shook her head, picking at a lump in the thread of the linen sheets. "No. We just got a reprimand. I'm even supposed to get two medals. The tribunal's for Lila."

Helena looked up sharply. "What do you mean?"

"They're replacing Lila with Sebastian as paladin primary," Penny said without looking up. "Lila's probably going to be stripped of rank for compromising Luc's safety."

"You can't be serious," Helena said. "Lila has saved Luc's life more times than—"

"I know," Penny said sharply. "We all know, but they're not going to do anything to Luc—he's Principate. So Lila takes the fall. People have been complaining for a while—I mean, they always were, because she's a girl and paladins are supposed to be boys—but Lila always outweighed the risk before, but after that last time with the chimaera, and now . . . the higher-ups see her as a liability for him. They think that if it hadn't been for her, Luc wouldn't have been captured."

"But—"

"They've been doing interviews, and the thing is," Penny continued, looking a mixture of guilt-stricken and resigned, "we all knew. I mean he tried to be subtle about it, but you could tell just looking. Especially lately, everyone thought it was all going to be over soon. I think Luc thought it'd be fine because no one cared when it was his dad and Sebastian. But there's always more rules for us girls, and no one under oath can say that Luc's not compromised. Could you?"

Helena looked away.

Poor Lila. She'd straddled the impossibility of her role for years, rarely making a mistake, but now she was left paying for Luc's.

What would happen?

Helena swallowed hard, forcing herself to focus on the task at hand. There wasn't anything they could do about the tribunal. "How's the leg?"

Penny seemed to shrink. "Fine," she said too quickly.

Helena reached out slowly. "You know, sometimes the nerve endings don't realise the amputation has happened, and it can make you feel like the leg's still there and in pain. I can use my resonance to block it so it doesn't feel that way."

"Really?" Penny's voice had a hint of desperation.

Helena set to work, but even this made her think about Lila.

As far as lost limbs went, it was a good amputation. Maier had been able to salvage as much of the leg as possible and perform a clean cut, without the rush of an emergency. "You know, you might be able to get a prosthetic."

"I don't think my repertoire is good enough for much," Penny said with a bitter smile, but the strain in her expression was already clearing. "Maybe a basic one, though, so I can stay on, maybe man the radios. I don't want to get sent off."

"The forge-masters are very talented. Titanium bonds well for most people, and it's a lot lighter than the old models."

"I guess we'll see," Penny said.

There was silence while Helena worked, and then Penny spoke again. "Is it true, what Luc said? When Soren came to save Alister and me, was he dead?"

Helena flinched as if she'd been kicked through the skull, Soren's name striking like an anvil. She was drowning again.

Penny's leg wavered in Helena's vision.

"When I first heard the rumour, I thought it was ridiculous. I was sure I would have noticed if he was dead. But sitting here, I keep thinking about it, the way he didn't stop fighting no matter what they did to him. He never screamed—not even when they started tearing him apart." Penny's voice shook. "I think I'd rather believe he was dead."

Helena's skin crawled as if those cold fingers were dragging across it. She blinked, pushing the thoughts and memories of Soren back and away, again wilfully forcing her consciousness to swerve around the wound that his memory evoked.

She knew better than to outright confess. She bit her lip for a moment. "Soren said we had to do anything, no matter what it took, to save Luc."

Penny was quiet for a long time. "I don't know how to feel. I know I'd be dead if he hadn't come right then . . . but—" Her lips trembled. "—what if *that* was a test? All these years of fighting the good fight, but then in the final moment, instead of staying true, we chose the easy way."

Helena was glad that she was nearly done working on Penny's leg, because the conversation was making her hands shake. *Easy.* She hated that word.

She swallowed hard. "If one person's actions are enough to damn everyone, then the gods are terrible, and Sol is the worst of all."

"You don't mean that," Penny said sharply, catching her by the wrist, clutching at it until her fingers bit into her skin. "Look at me, Helena. You don't mean that. It works the other way, too. Orion passed the test, and think of all the blessings that came from that."

Penny seemed desperate to convince her.

"I remember when you first came here. We were in the same dorm. You said that Paladia was the most beautiful place in the whole world. The Shining City, you called it. You said that in Etras people didn't really believe in the gods, but here in the North, you understood why they did, because how else could a place be so beautiful. Don't you remember that?"

She found Helena's hand and squeezed it. "That's what you said. I think you still believe that, deep down. You were just—you were just scared and you—made a mistake, but you can repent. If you talk to the Falcon, he makes it all so clear. The journey, all the suffering, it's what we need. How else can we be purified? Even—even when it's hard, we have to be grateful for it, because that's what makes us pure."

Penny was smiling at Helena, fervently trying to convince her. "That's why it's better for all of us to die true to what we believe than to live on by betraying and corrupting ourselves. I know you meant well, saving us, but you should have trusted Sol."

Helena pulled her hand free. "Penny, if I thought we'd all die, I wouldn't be so afraid of losing. What they'll do to us if we lose will be far worse than death." She shook her head. "There will be nothing purifying about it."

EVEN AFTER DAYS OF CHELATING treatment, Lila's resonance failed to return. The Council was trying to keep the news quiet, not wanting to cause a panic. The chelators were supposed to sequester the metal in Lila's blood to flush it out, but it wasn't working as effectively as expected.

Shiseo had said nothing about the message Helena had sent him to the Outpost with, asked no questions, but he'd looked very relieved the first time she returned to the lab. It communicated more than words could.

They spent days analysing and re-analysing the shards and new samples of Lila's blood, trying to determine what they were missing. Every time Helena had to leave for a shift, she always returned to find Shiseo still working. He finally fell asleep, slumped over the workstation.

Helena sat quietly, watching a flame under the glass alembic before her, steam rising in the cucurbit, collecting in the ambix and running down the tube into a vial beside it.

Elain Boyle had been made the Resistance's lead healer earlier that day. It was a new position that Matias had created for her. Elain had arrived in the hospital wearing a large and ornate sunstone amulet around her neck, and now her general duties were managing and scheduling the other healers' shifts, while she worked exclusively as Luc's "personal" healer.

Helena told herself she didn't care.

Her chymiatria was becoming the default for the healers. Pace had quietly created a section in the storerooms for the tonics and medicines, letting Helena's chymiatria bear some of the load of healing.

Helena curled her fingers into a tight fist. She'd built up a large supply of ingredients since they'd recovered the ports, but she was worried about running out now that Crowther had banned her from foraging anymore. Some could be made using imported materials, but there were a few things that were hard to get her hands on if she couldn't gather them herself.

She sighed. She used to love the quietness of lab work—such a stark contrast with the hospital—but now it left her to her thoughts, and everything she pushed away in her mind crowded around, suffocating her.

She missed Kaine.

Whenever she thought of him, she felt as though a piece of her was missing.

The war had drilled itself into her bones, carving away at her until there was hardly anything left except what made her useful, an ideal component in an elaborate machine, but Kaine had reminded her that she was human; that not every trait and ability and quality she possessed only mattered insomuch as it was useful to someone else. That she was allowed to breathe sometimes.

Now, in his absence, she felt herself suffocating.

CHAPTER 54

Aprilis 1787

When Helena stood on the dam, staring across the bridge to the Outpost, she hesitated.

She'd missed Kaine the whole week, but now, returning, she felt dread. He could be so unpredictable. Every moment of softness between them tended to be followed by its direct inversion.

She drew several steadying breaths, set her jaw, and made herself cross. A necrothrall was waiting outside the tenement when she arrived. Her heart dropped, and she swallowed hard, opening her satchel and pulling out the envelope along with replacements for his medical kit.

Her face was burning, but she tried to control her expressions and not look directly at the necrothrall as she held it all out.

"Here." She shoved everything into the necrothrall's hands and turned away.

"Marino."

She nearly jumped out of her skin at the sound of her name. She whirled around.

The necrothrall was the only one standing there.

"Did you—talk?" She'd never heard a necrothrall speak. Motor function was one thing, but reanimation of the language parts of the brain was too much. Necrothralls didn't talk. They never talked.

"Come," it said.

She followed him warily, relaxing when she realised they were headed for the panic room. He couldn't have just told her to go there last week?

She was half indignant when she arrived, and then forgot, because before she was through the door, Kaine had her in his arms and was kissing her as if starved.

Her fingers caught his cloak and her eyes fluttered closed as she kissed him back. The whole world dropped away. She felt his teeth, hungry against her lips and tongue.

His hands found her hips, guiding her backwards. Then his lips were on her neck as she gasped, the dip of her throat, between her clothed breasts, and he was on his knees, pushing her back on the sofa, and she was under him and she had not even put down her satchel.

His hands were sliding under her clothes, lips burning a trail of desire across every inch of skin his mouth could find.

She had never felt so intoxicated.

His resonance hummed beneath her skin, following the pathway of her nerves and veins, mapping her. Not erotically, but in the same panicked way her own resonance sometimes flared when she was afraid someone was hurt and wanted to find the injury. It reached all the way to her toes and then vanished, but she scarcely noticed as his tongue ran up on her inner thigh, and then a haze of hot pleasure consumed her.

Her shirt was undone, skirts up around her waist, when he sank into her. She wrapped her arms tight around his neck, pulling him close, burying her face against his shoulder. The world had reduced itself to a single point, Kaine, his breath and body and touch.

As they lay entwined on that too-small sofa, limbs entangled, it was like that horrible hungover morning and yet completely new. This time, they'd gotten it right. Her eyes fluttered closed, tracing her fingers across his skin, but he sat up after only a few moments.

He was looking her over, his eyes searching.

She lifted her head, still catching her breath. "What's wrong?"

His thumb found the scars on her ribs. "I worried about you. Had a lot of time to wonder if I'd done everything right when I healed you."

She caught his hand. "You did everything perfectly."

He still looked worried. "And nothing's happened since?"

"No," she said. "I haven't left Headquarters at all since I got back. And I—I won't anymore—except to come straight to you. I'm not—" The words caught, tangling in her throat. "I'm not allowed to. Got very strict orders about that, so you won't have to worry anymore."

He gave an audible sigh of relief and sank down to her, brushing a kiss against her forehead.

Helena closed her eyes, trying to let him have this, but her stomach clenched and her jaw trembled as she tried to swallow her emotions.

"What's wrong?"

She looked up and found him watching her again.

"I—I liked foraging. I used to go with my father, during the summers."

There was a pause. "I didn't realise it was important to you."

She was silent for a moment. Thinking of the wetlands stretched out around her, nothing but the wilds and the mountains and the brilliant blue sky above, the only place where she could breathe without smelling blood.

"Sometimes it was the closest thing to freedom I still had."

She felt him freeze.

"It'll just be until the end of the war," he said, the words half plea and half vow.

A bitter laugh caught in her chest as she looked at him. "Just till then? When'll that be? And what end do you think will somehow go well for either of us?"

He couldn't meet her eyes.

She looked away, too. "There are things I've been a part of that I know the Eternal Flame would never officially approve of. I don't know what will happen if it all comes out."

Her chest tightened as she thought about those rooms underground where Crowther had taken her so many times now. The blood. The burns, the flayed body parts, tangled nerves, split open and twisted apart in horrible, terrifying ways. Helena's name was beside Crowther's in those prisoner logs. Her handwriting cataloguing in clinical terms the injuries she'd healed, the condition of the prisoners when they died or were placed into those horrible underground cells. She knew it was intentional on Crowther's part, having her listed as the medical personnel on-site. Leverage.

At one point, he might have let it remain a latent threat, but she expected no mercy now.

If the war was won, without Luc on her side, she had few friends.

Kaine took her hand. "You can run. Say the word, and I'll get you out."

A craven, exhausted part of her sparked to life at those words. Out. Free. Away from the war.

She hadn't known how much she'd wanted it until she heard it offered by someone who meant it. She'd been so quick to refuse her father when he'd wanted to return to Etras, but now she physically longed for it.

But the war would continue, no matter where she went, and Kaine would be there. He couldn't run. If she was gone, Crowther would not keep him alive.

"No," she said, meeting his eyes.

"The offer stands. Say the word, and I'll get you out."

She reached up, combing a strand of pale hair back from his eyes.

"What about you?" she asked.

He grimaced. "If I could run, I would have vanished while my mother was alive."

"Would you go now, if you could?"

His eyes seemed to ripple with heat. "With you, I would."

She forced a smile. "Then we'll go together. After the war." She gripped his hand and pressed it against her chest, letting him feel her heartbeat. "When the war is over. We'll run away somewhere no one knows us. We'll disappear—forever."

His eyes flickered, but he smiled back. "Of course."

He was lying.

They both were. It was daydream to think it possible.

She squeezed his hand tighter until the illusion faded.

She swallowed hard, dreading what she had to say. "The Eternal Flame has recently obtained new information about the process that the Undying undergo to gain their immutability. I was asked to question you about the details. To verify the information."

Kaine just stared at her for a moment. Then his gaze turned dissociative.

"Kaine." She touched him, and he started.

"It's a blur," he said quickly. "I don't remember."

"Anything helps. It really does."

He was silent, his chest rising and falling several times before he spoke again. "What do you want to know?"

"There was an array involved?"

He nodded slowly.

"Could you describe it? Or draw it?"

He shook his head. "I never got a good look at it. I remember there were nine points, and I was in the middle. I was cooperating, but they still drugged me and strapped me down so I couldn't move."

He was staring at the far wall.

"They started to bring the staff in. The ones they hadn't already killed. I hadn't known how it worked, that they were going to—when I asked what they were doing, I was told I was lucky we had so many servants, they didn't need to use my mother."

"They used your servants?"

He nodded slowly. "We never had much company in the countryside. My mother was sick so often, and with all the rumours, my father didn't trust anyone. He was busy managing the guild, so it was just the two of us there, and the servants. They were almost like family, some of them. My mother's lady's maid, Davies, had been with her since she was a girl, and came with her to Spirefell when she married. After the birth, when my mother was—Davies practically raised me the first few years."

"I'm so sorry, Kaine."

He was silent for a long time, not looking at her. "There was this platform over me, and then Morrough was leaning down. He had something in his hand. The bone shard, I think. I remember screaming. When I woke up, there was still screaming, but it wasn't me anymore. I couldn't hear it, I could just feel it. Like they were sutured inside me, all mangled but still alive."

She stared at him in horror. "Do you still—hear them?"

He blinked slowly. "They're quieter now."

She swallowed hard. "According to the information we have, the Undying are a by-product of Morrough's attempts to harness power without suffering from ill effects."

He was silent a moment. "So if we kill the Undying, that weakens him."

"In theory, yes. Would destroying the talismans affect the phylacteries? Does that kill the Undying?"

Kaine shook his head. "No. He can make another, but they're—only slightly more intelligent than necrothralls then."

"There must be some way, though. We'll figure it out."

He looked at her, his expression beginning to clear and sharpen again. "If the Undying are the source of Morrough's power, that means this won't be over until they're all dead."

She knew instantly what he was trying to prepare her for. "No. I'll find a way to reverse it. If it's possible to bind a soul, surely it can be unbound."

"Helena . . ."

She shook her head. "You already thought I couldn't save you once. You should give me more credit." She cleared her throat, refusing to have this conversation.

She stood, dressing quickly. "I have to take this information back to Headquarters."

She didn't really care about reporting to Crowther, though. She wanted to begin reviewing the array that Wagner had sketched. She needed to do research.

"Wait. I have something for you, although I *hope* you won't need them again." Wrapped in oilcloth were her daggers.

She'd been sure they'd been washed downriver.

"How'd you find them?"

"I had spares made. It took long enough to find a metallurgist with a resonance for your alloy. I figured a few extra sets might be wise."

"Thank you," she said, touching them fondly and then putting them carefully in her satchel before she began to fix her hair.

"I hate your hair like that," he said, startling her.

She looked up. "I could crop it instead."

He looked so offended that she laughed.

"I have to keep it out of the way when working, and I'm always on call for emergencies. It's practical."

He looked unconvinced. "I want to see you more."

Her fingers stilled. She could see the hunger in his eyes. Possessive. Ravenous. He would drag her from the war and hide her the instant she let him. The conflict was visible in his eyes.

Want. Want. Want. She felt it like her heartbeat.

If he couldn't hide her, he would hoard her to himself as much as he was able to. She'd fallen for a dragon.

"I've always been on call for you," she said. "If you call me, I'll come here as soon as I can."

He shook his head at that. "No. We can't use the Outpost much longer. There's plans for repairing it under way."

Her heart sank. "Oh. Then how would we—"

"The Resistance doesn't watch the skies," he said. "Now that Amaris is older, it's not difficult to fly to the East Island at night. I'm sure there's a rooftop somewhere. I'll find something before next week. If the ring activates only once, it's not Resistance-related. Signal back when you're there, and I'll come for you."

She lifted her left hand. She'd feared the refraction effect might eventually wear off, but it still held; she could barely see the ring unless she focused. It was so light, she almost forgot about it at times.

"I thought you said if I ever burned you—"

He captured her hand and pulled her close. His other hand slid possessively up her throat, fingers tilting her head back, and he kissed her, long and deep, before he drew away to meet her eyes.

"Call me, and I will come."

CHAPTER 55

Aprilis 1787

KAINE CALLED HER. OFTEN.

Sometimes his duties came to an end in the late evening, but most of the time it was past midnight. When she wasn't on shift, Helena would work in her lab until her ring burned.

There were many buildings that were abandoned. Kaine had found one with a large open roof and working lift. Helena didn't have to pass through any checkpoints to reach it.

Sometimes Amaris wouldn't even land.

Helena would stand in the open-most part of the rooftop, and silent as a wraith, Amaris would drop from the sky, Kaine leaning over and snatching Helena up, and they'd be airborne, riding the wind, climbing over the buildings without being seen.

They'd land, and he'd pull her off Amaris, checking her over.

"You're all right? Has anything happened to you?" he'd ask, even though she'd felt his resonance beneath her skin while they were flying, and he knew she wasn't injured.

She hadn't expected him to be so obsessively worried. She'd observed his quick arrival at the Outpost, the careful way his eyes would track her, but she hadn't considered how deep the fear cut into him until he didn't have to hide it.

They'd go inside, and she'd let him see her in the light, holding her arms out to prove she was in the same condition she'd been the last time.

"I'm fine. See? You don't need to worry."

The reassurance never seemed to have any effect. Whatever had happened to his mother had been hidden, and Enid Ferron had never told him fully—either because she couldn't, or to spare him.

Withholding it had probably been the worse choice. Kaine was like her. He obsessed over what he didn't know more than anything else.

She'd meet his eyes, hold his face in her hands. "I'm fine. Nothing has happened."

Once he was finally convinced that she had no hidden injuries, a tension inside him would break. He'd gather her in his arms, and she'd feel his heart pounding.

You did this to him, she reminded herself whenever she was tempted to grow impatient with the ritual. *You guessed where he was vulnerable and you exploited it.*

She'd run her own fingers over him, trying to detect any injuries on him before he kissed her again.

He'd hide them or ignore them as if they didn't exist unless she managed to discover them. Nullium injuries had begun appearing among the wounded after battles. Sometimes Kaine would end up with a shard in his body somewhere, and while its effects on him were limited, when it entered his bloodstream, it could slow his regeneration for hours unless she intervened.

She never had and never would heal anyone the way she healed Kaine: in his arms, pressed against his body. She'd bribe him into cooperation by pressing openmouthed kisses across his shoulders, hands, and face while her resonance found every place he was hurt, checking him over meticulously until he'd grow impatient and pin her hands down, pushing her back on the bed and taking her slowly. It was always deliriously slowly.

He'd stare into her eyes until she almost felt their minds touching.

"You're mine. You're mine." He'd repeat the words over and over. "Say it. Say you're mine."

He'd entwine their fingers, press their foreheads together, and sometimes his whole body would tremble. She'd wrap her arms around him, trying to reassure him.

"I promise, Kaine. I'm always going to be yours."

There was a possessive terror in him—in the ways he touched her—as though he always expected it to be the last time he ever saw her.

When he didn't summon her, time stretched, filling Helena with a bottomless dread until her ring burned again.

Then she was the one who would desperately demand to know if he was all right. On the nights she slept alone, she had nightmares of him being killed. Sometimes gone forever, other times as a lich, or discovered and caught. She didn't know which possibility to fear most.

"Be careful." It was always the last thing she said to him before he left her on some rooftop. She would hold his face in her hands, staring into his eyes. "Don't die."

He'd dip his head forward, kissing her inner wrist or the palm of her hand, his silver eyes locked on her face. "You're mine. I'll always come for you."

He always did.

Yet each day it felt as though the odds were being pushed higher. Steeper. The war teetered on the brink of calamity. She wasn't sure how far the array and his own determination could take him before everything came crashing down.

He was walking a razor's edge.

When he slept, she'd stare at his face and will his survival.

She'd make it happen. They'd go away, across the sea so no one would ever find them. She promised herself she'd find a way. She promised him: There would be an after.

"I'm going to take care of you. I swear, Helena, I'm always going to take care of you." She heard him muttering the words against her skin or into her hair in such a low voice, she could barely make them out. Some days the compulsion seemed worse than others.

She heard him repeating it over and over one night. He usually stopped after a little while, but this time he didn't.

She lifted her head and held his face between her hands so that she could meet his eyes. "Kaine, I'm all right. Nothing's going to happen to me."

He stared at her with the same bitterly resigned expression he'd worn while training her and whenever she turned to leave, like he was bracing himself, waiting for what he regarded as inevitable.

The war was a cage with no escape.

He subsided and rested his head on her chest, listening to her heartbeat, arms framing her. She tangled her fingers through his hair, and it was quiet, but she could feel him mouthing the words.

She hesitated before she spoke.

"Tell me about your mother, Kaine. Tell me everything you could never tell anyone."

He went silent. She slid her fingers over his shoulders, tracing the interconnected scars from the array. "You can tell me. I'll help you carry it."

He didn't speak for such a long time, she wondered if he'd fallen asleep. Then he turned his head, just enough that she could see his profile.

"I'd never seen anyone tortured before," he said at last. "She was—the first person I ever saw tortured. He—" His jaw trembled as he struggled for words. "—they experimented on her. Even though she wasn't even—she hadn't done anything."

As he spoke, his eyes grew wide. He stared across the room, his gaze far away.

Helena watched and she could see him, just sixteen and home for the summer holidays.

Home, walking unknowingly into a nightmare that he would never escape.

"I thought—" His voice was suddenly younger. Boyish. "For a while I thought that if I killed the Principate soon enough, she'd recover. That I could fix it all. But she was—a shadow of herself when I returned. I think—I think she tried to hold on over the summer, show a brave face while I was there, but—

"I wasn't even gone a month." The words were low, wavering.

Helena laced her fingers through his hair. He closed his eyes and drew his chin down, his body contracting inwards.

"After I killed the Principate, it took more than a day to get back, and they knew I'd done it. They'd heard, but they didn't let her out until I gave him that fucking heart—still beating. She kept having these fits; she'd crumple on the floor, or stop breathing, or sit rocking and muttering. I brought in doctors, but they said there was nothing wrong with her but a weak constitution and tendencies towards hysteria. They recommended institutionalising her, or administering all these tonics and injections that left her in a stupor."

Helena squeezed his hand, running her fingers across the array.

Calculating, Cunning, Devoted, Determined, Ruthless, Unfailing, Unhesitating, and Unyielding.

To avenge his mother. In penance for all the ways he believed he'd failed her.

"I'm so sorry, Kaine."

He was quiet. He closed his eyes and drew a sharp breath.

"Then—" His voice cut off.

"Then—" It failed again. "She'd been doing better, I thought she might even recover, but I—I—We'd taken a new district. There was a list of families we were supposed to make examples of. Father, mother, two children. After we killed the parents, they reanimated the mother, had her with the older girl. I was supposed to come up with something with—with the father and the younger one. Little thing, wearing two braids with bows on them. There was a birthday cake. I think it was hers. Durant dragged her over by her hair and handed her to me—I knew what they wanted but I ran."

He swallowed. "I booked a ship, passage for two. I thought my mother and I could just sail away together, and she wouldn't know I couldn't really go with her until it was too late. But when I went to get her, they'd gotten there first. They'd brought the corpse."

"Oh, Kaine . . ." Helena was too horrified to say more than that. He was gripping her hand so hard, she suspected there'd be bruises where his fingers were entwined.

"I tried to find a way to run with her." His voice shifted, starting to grow familiar as the story moved through his life. Traces of his hard, controlled tone beginning to emerge. "I had everything prepared, every detail and contingency, but she wouldn't leave without me. I thought about forcing her, drugging her, putting her on the boat and sending her away, but I was so afraid she'd come back for me, and I didn't want to have her locked away. I didn't want to be someone who caged her again."

His voice grew deadened. "If I hadn't gone home that night . . . she wouldn't have died. I don't know why I did."

He fell silent.

Helena shifted out from under him enough to sit up. She couldn't look at him without a tearing pain spreading through her chest.

She touched him lightly on the forehead. "Kaine—I'm not your mother."

He flinched, opening his mouth to deny, but she continued without letting him cut her off. "The Eternal Flame is not going to hurt me if you fail an assignment. They aren't going to torture or endanger me to punish you. I'm not a hostage. I'm in this war because I choose to be. I'm not fragile. I'm not going to break. Please." She brushed her thumb over the arch of his cheekbone. "Believe that about me."

He shook his head. "Let me get you out. I swear it won't affect my aid to the Resistance. Just let me get you out."

"I'm not going to run while everyone else is fighting. We can do this together. Let me help you. You don't have to do everything alone now."

Despair flooded across his eyes.

"You can't ask me to run away from the war."

His lip curled. "Why not? Haven't you done enough for them? They sold you. What if I'd—" His voice cut off, and he couldn't meet her eyes. "What if you'd had the same offer from someone who'd meant it. You would have still gone—and if I hadn't trained you, you would have died rescuing Holdfast."

"And I agreed to it. All of it. No one ever made me. We don't get to choose when we've done enough and leave others behind to bear the consequences. There are no civilians in a war like this. If they win"—she spread her hands—"everyone loses."

He clenched his jaw, and she knew what he wanted to say, that he didn't care. He didn't care whether anyone survived except her.

Helena gave a sad sigh and dropped her head, burying her face in his shoulder. He wrapped his arms around her.

She was almost asleep when she heard the faint whisper of his voice. "I'm going to take care of you. I swear, I'm always going to take care of you."

KAINE WAS HELENA'S ONLY SOURCE of solace as things within the Resistance deteriorated.

When Lila finally recovered her resonance, her long convalescence seemed to have sucked the life from her. She was unable to spring back the way she usually did, and the scarring from all the surgery on her chest and shoulder was so severe that it bound her movement, requiring extensive healing and therapy to regain mobility.

Helena planned out a potential treatment regimen, but then it was assigned to one of the other healers. Luc had requested that Helena be kept away from Lila as well as himself.

Helena sat staring at Pace's desk after she was informed of it.

"You'll still work casualty shifts," Pace said.

"Right," Helena said, in a dull voice. "I take it that means Luc's more lucid, then? If he's making requests now."

Since Luc was moved to his private quarters, Helena had not seen or heard a word about him or his condition, although the Council insisted that he was still steadily recovering.

The matron's lips twitched. "Well, 'lucid' is certainly a word you could use." She cleared her throat. "I'm sure that with time, he'll even out again. You don't need to worry about him; there's plenty of other people doing that."

Helena nodded slowly, but time was not something that the Eternal Flame had.

Luc was the keystone for the Resistance. Without him, everything grew quickly volatile. Crowther began leaning more heavily on Kaine, using him to seed misinformation and sabotage, as though the Undying army were a machine to be deconstructed. The envelopes with orders were thicker every time Helena delivered them.

Kaine made no mention of what he did, but she could tell he was on the verge of breaking under the pressure. He grew steadily more desperate each time he saw her.

It ate at Helena, watching him erode under everything he was expected to maintain and produce for both sides while Helena was trapped in Headquarters like a caged animal.

Without foraging, she filled her hours with new research, Shiseo taking the lead as they tried to perfect alchemy suppression upon the Council's request. The Undying were almost impossible to take and keep captive, but with suppression, it might be possible. She knew from Kaine that nullium interfered with the Undying's abilities and regeneration the same as any alchemist.

Shiseo designed a nullium cuff to create targeted resonance suppression, locking around the wrist to blur the resonance into a feeling like static.

Helena tested it, locking one around her own wrist, flexing her fingers, sliding it up her arm. When it was near her elbow, she could push through the interference. She shook her head. "These don't fully suppress the resonance."

She took it off, inspecting the interior Shiseo had lined with nullium.

"If we really wanted to completely erase it, I think it would have to be internal," she said. "If the nullium were encased in ceramic, that would prevent the corrosion and biointerference. If you put a thin tube of it right through the wrist here"—she pressed her fingers against the space between the radius and ulna—"the cuff could slot around a suppression spike and alchemically lock in place. I bet there wouldn't be any resonance then."

Shiseo looked so disturbed that Helena realised the reality of what she was proposing beyond its practical function.

It was one thing to think about cuffing the various Undying, all hidden behind their helmets and their dead, but when she thought about Kaine, a more likely prisoner, a pit opened inside her stomach.

She shook her head. "Never mind. That's too much. We don't need to suppress that much."

"It would probably work."

She shook her head. "It's not necessary. This design is good enough."

SOMETIMES HELENA'S RING WOULD BURN twice, and often when that happened, Amaris would arrive, and Kaine would practically collapse off her back. Other times, Amaris would appear alone. Helena would climb onto the chimaera's back, clinging to the harness as the air whipped around, and they'd fly into the underbelly of the city, to a basement, a wrecked building, or sometimes an alley, and she would find Kaine. Usually a piece of nullium shrapnel would be buried into him somewhere, deep enough that he couldn't get it out.

She learned to always have her satchel stocked with medical tools and bandages and all kinds of different medicines. As the nullium grew increasingly effective, the injuries often required surgery. She grew adept at manual surgery with only an electric torch for light.

He wouldn't let her knock him out, wanting to keep watch in case someone came, but he'd often be half delirious, his eyes nearly glowing silver, muttering under his breath, "I'm all right—I barely feel it. Don't worry. We'll go soon . . . Got it worked out. Just—a little longer . . ."

She'd sit with his head on her lap, singing softly to him while he stabilised, holding his hands in hers. Nullium slowed his recovery so much. He'd have lost so much blood, he'd float on the edge of consciousness or begin trembling and go into shock. She'd run her fingers and resonance across his palms, and murmur apologies.

You're killing him. You're killing him. This is because of you.

She'd only let herself cry over him when he wasn't conscious to see it. She gripped his hands in hers, trying to fix him.

"I'm sorry. I'm sorry. I'm so sorry," she said over and over.

She'd wipe her eyes and then clean up the blood before he regained consciousness. She'd feel the tension tear through his body the instant he came back to himself and feel him breathe when he looked up and saw her.

On the long nights, Amaris would curl up behind Helena, nuzzling at Kaine's limp hands. Helena would sit, tracing her fingers along Kaine's face, following his every heartbeat and promising, "I'm going to take care of you. I promise, I'm always going to take care of you."

CHAPTER 56

Maius 1787

THE UNDYING USED THE FIRST NULLIUM BOMB in the middle of spring.

The Resistance had known an attack like that was coming; the use of nullium had been growing ever since the Undying had used it against Lila, and although the injuries were severe, as a combat weapon nullium was limited in its utility because of how fragile it was. As a bomb, however, it was devastating.

A few tiny pieces of shrapnel were all it took to wipe out an alchemist's resonance. If it dissolved and was distributed through the blood, the hospital had to manually suture the wounds, administer chelating agents, and then wait for the patient's resonance to recover.

Expert alchemical medicine combined with healing had made recovery for Resistance fighters efficient; so long as a combatant didn't die from blood loss, injuries that in other parts of the world would take months to recover from could be healed here in days or weeks.

With nullium, however, convalescence slowed to a crawl.

The hospital had prepared as much as they could, medics and surgeons learning about manual surgery and the chymistry department producing a large supply of chelating agents, but logistics were not enough to improve morale. People were terrified. Alchemy and resonance were everything; the idea of being without was like returning to a pre-alchemical stone age.

Ilva, who took so much in stride, seemed knocked permanently off balance after Luc's capture, failing to comprehend and proactively address the fallout. Perhaps because she was a Lapse, she was incapable of understanding the emotional severity of the mere threat, its impact on morale.

The only bright spot was that Luc seemed to abruptly realise his responsibilities. Largely cloistered in his rooms, he suddenly reappeared at an assembly that Althorne had called to soothe Resistance unrest. Luc appeared dressed all in white and gold, burning with righteous indignation. Physically, he was shrunken. Though his armour concealed most of it, his features were visibly gaunt. Still, it was as though his body were merely a shell now, and his soul shone through. He seemed to radiate life.

"Morrough, like every necromancer before him, wants the Resistance to be afraid, and for the Eternal Flame's light to be extinguished," he said, his blue eyes burning. "We will not give them that satisfaction. Paladia is ours. We built this city as a beacon; that light has protected the world from necromancy's stain for generations. The gods are on our side. Sol is unconquerable. The laws of nature will not give victory to corruption. We will not fail; we know the rewards our ancestors received for their faithfulness and bravery, and we will taste the same!"

There was a grimness in his voice, and yet he was strangely breathtaking as he spoke, like the sun at its zenith. She could feel the mood in the air shift from uncertainty and fear to conviction. To faith.

Luc kept speaking, describing the city in the loving detail of one who knew it intimately, describing the dreams he and his father had had for Paladia's glorious future.

The next thing Helena knew, there was a counteroffensive being assembled. Squadrons readied. Luc's new battalion, who had not yet even seen combat together, went out with four others and seized a district of the West Island.

Helena watched from a skybridge as they all returned in a victory parade, followed by cheers. Luc was standing on the back of a lorry, Sebastian beside him, waving as they swept through the gates.

Lila had not gone. Officially it was because she was still in recovery, but the reality was that the tribunal had not yet begun, the leaders concerned over how Luc might react. If he used his power as Principate to directly oppose the Council and military leaders, there was no real means to overrule him that wouldn't result in a complete collapse of leadership, potentially fracturing the Resistance.

So long as Luc acknowledged Lila as his paladin primary, Lila could ignore what the rest of the Council said—her vows were to Luc. And so Lila remained in limbo. Not cleared for combat, but not really injured anymore, either. She stood at the door of the Tower, applauding with everyone else, but grief shone in her face.

The counterattack had been so sudden, so brazen, the Undying had hardly mounted a defence. Similarly, the Council was blindsided by Luc's abrupt embrace of full leadership, and left scrambling in the wake of his decisiveness. The success of the offensive made him difficult to argue with, especially when Resistance morale rose with his ascent to claim his place on the Council.

The battles began to blur together. Except now there was a medical ward for nullium injuries, and the casualty rates skyrocketed, infections and disease becoming an increasing threat. First came overcrowding, followed by shortages in clean linens and bandages, and then the blood infections began and sickness followed.

Helena was on shift for days sometimes, ignoring Kaine's signals unless they were messages for Crowther. Work at least kept her from wearing grooves of worry through her mind.

When she was alone, she lay in bed, staring at the ceiling as she twisted Kaine's ring around and around her finger, thinking about the array sketch Wagner had drawn. Nine points.

Northern alchemy almost always used either five or eight, the elemental or celestial numbers. Those were the only array formulas even taught at the Institute, the exception being the Holdfasts' pyromancy, which operated with a seven-point array, but Helena only knew of that because she'd helped Luc with his homework.

She'd never heard of a nine-point array. She had no idea how it was supposed to work, and her only sample was full of obvious errors and drawn by someone wholly unfamiliar with alchemical principles.

How could she reverse what had been done to Kaine if she didn't understand the method? She moved her fingers, trying to visualise the energy channels. Her mind kept going back to Soren.

She smothered the thoughts, burying them with animancy, trying to force her mind to go around her memories of him. It kept niggling at her, though—not his destruction but the moment in which he'd died. She always tried to break the resonance connection before a patient died, but she'd been fully focused on Soren in that moment.

The energy, the sensation of it, running through her like an electric current kept coming to mind whenever she tried to imagine channelling through a multiple of three.

It made her wonder. If Morrough could trap living souls inside bone, and the first Necromancer placed an entire town of living souls into a Stone, what would happen if someone captured the other form of energy? Had anyone ever done it?

The next time she felt a patient on the verge of death, rather than break away, she left the connection open and tried to hold the energy as it struck. It seared through her resonance, leaving her hand numb and twinging for hours.

Well, it made sense that she couldn't just hold it. It would need a container of some sort. The sunstone amulet had been . . . quicksilver? Or glass? Maybe crystal. She tried a variety of substances from the storerooms, smuggling odd metals and other compounds into the hospital inside her pockets, to see if the energy would channel into any of them.

Sunstones cracked, while metal set her pocket on fire. In a box shoved to the back of a storage room, she found several large chunks of obsidian. Volcanic glass did have a higher melting point than normal glass.

She stuck a piece in her pocket.

She gripped it when she felt a patient's vitality grow thin. He was one of the nullium patients, hit with shrapnel that had ripped apart his organs, and the infection hadn't responded to treatment. She could force his heart to keep beating, but it would only make his death take longer; he'd die the moment she left. His skin was burning with fever, and he was gripping her hand, speaking to someone unseen, the words coming slower and slower.

She swallowed hard and kept her resonance open as his eyes went still. The death surge ran through her like an electric shock straight into the obsidian.

Her arm went briefly numb. When sensation returned, he was dead, and the obsidian hummed warm against her fingers. She could feel it, that strange dark energy.

Her fingers trembled as she closed his eyes, pulling the sheet over his face. Had she just trapped a soul in volcano glass? She squeezed it. No. She knew what that energy felt like, the amulet and Kaine. This was different.

Still, she tried to pretend it wasn't there while she finished her shift.

She hurried to her lab. She opened the door, and stopped short at the sight of Lila, curled up on the floor, her face swollen, eyes red.

Helena froze. Gods, the tribunal. It must have begun.

She'd hardly seen and hadn't spoken to Lila since before Luc's rescue. She'd returned to her room one day to find all of Lila's things gone and heard about a private memorial service held for Soren only afterwards.

As much as she had wanted to try to explain herself, she couldn't, because officially Soren had simply died.

But Luc would have told Lila the truth.

Helena stood frozen, not sure what could have possibly driven Lila here.

"Lila." Helena set the obsidian down, moving tentatively. "Lila, what's wrong? What happened?"

Lila stared at Helena without responding for a long time.

"I made a mistake," Lila finally said, her voice barely a whisper, "I've made such a mistake."

Helena swallowed hard. "It's—all right. I'm sure it'll be all right. Whatever you've done—I'm sure it can't be that bad."

Soren's ghost seemed to hang between them.

"No." Lila shook her head. "I've been lying to everyone. My whole life, I've been lying. Now—now I don't know what to do . . ."

Her voice was so strained, it trailed off.

"Soren was the only person that knew," Lila whispered. Her eyes were swimming, but the tears didn't escape. "He always kept my secrets. Knew what to do about things. Said it was his job—looking out for me."

"What happened?" Helena reached out tentatively.

Lila looked up and drew a deep breath, her chin trembling before she finally spoke. "I—I'm pregnant."

Helena didn't move. Couldn't speak. She was too stunned to even believe the words Lila had just uttered.

To know she was pregnant meant she had to be at least two or three months along, and that was assuming her cycle was regular, which Helena knew it wasn't. She'd been in the hospital at that time.

"How?" was the only question Helena could even think to ask. Never mind everything else that this meant.

Lila swallowed, her head moving jerkily, wincing when it pulled at the scars on her neck. "I know. I didn't think I could. After—everything. I always assumed that it wasn't even possible."

"No," Helena said impatiently. "I mean, yes, that too, but you weren't pregnant when you were in the hospital. You've only been out for—How would you possibly know you're pregnant?"

Lila looked down, avoiding Helena's eyes. "That's—that's the secret. I *know* I'm pregnant."

It was then that something incredibly obvious, which Helena should have realised years earlier, finally dawned on her.

Lila Bayard, who so often came back from battles nearly unscathed, who always recovered miraculously from her injuries, who adapted to a prosthetic leg in months when everyone said it would be a year. Who had never struggled to recover from an injury until she lost her resonance.

"You're a vivimancer," Helena said.

Lila didn't meet her eyes as she gave a small nod. "I never used it on anyone except me. Soren a couple of times, but only when he asked. He said I couldn't let anyone know. Not even Mum and Dad, because if people knew I wouldn't be allowed to be Luc's paladin."

"All this time?" Helena said softly, startled by the sense of betrayal she felt.

"I'm sorry. I wanted to tell you but—you know what it's been like for you. I couldn't risk that, not with Luc at stake. I couldn't be like you—fighting's all I'm good at."

The revelation was more than Helena felt she could process right then.

"Who's the father?" Helena asked, as if it wasn't completely obvious.

"You know it's Luc."

Helena nodded. She wanted to be angry, but her own secrets were worse, and the fact that Lila had turned to her in Soren's absence spoke volumes.

"You've probably heard, they're planning a tribunal unless I step down as paladin voluntarily." Lila's voice was empty and despairing. "I used to tell myself it would all pay off in the end, but the war just kept going. I didn't ever—I mean, a few times he tried—but I told him off every time." Lila shook her head. "Doesn't matter, though, seems everyone thinks we've been fucking each other at the front lines. Doesn't mean anything that we didn't." She looked down. "When he came back from taking that district—I know it wasn't about me, but I felt so ruined. Being left behind and knowing I always will be now. He came and found me after and told me that he'd been thinking about me the whole time, and—" She shrugged. "Everyone thinks we are anyway, so—"

Helena rested a tentative hand on her shoulder. "It's all right. I can take care of it. If it's early I can get ingredients or just use vivimancy, whatever you'd prefer. No one will know."

"No."

Helena stared at Lila, certain she'd misheard.

Lila drew a deep breath, avoiding her eyes. "I mean, that's why I came. I knew you could do it, but—while I was waiting, I couldn't stop thinking, what are the odds?" She shook her head. "I can't remember the last time I had a cycle. It's been years. I didn't think I could. I always thought Soren would be the one who'd marry and have the next generation of Bayards, but now I'm all that's left."

Helena had no words.

Lila looked down, curling smaller, as if she could feel Helena's judgement. "It probably won't stick. So maybe I could just wait, and—have this for a little while."

"And if it does—stick?" Helena asked.

Lila didn't answer.

Helena's chest grew tight. She wanted to say Lila was being stupid. A baby, during the war. Lila wouldn't be the first, but still, those girls were different. Lila was an alchemist. A warrior. Neither of those things paired with motherhood. The rules were strict.

"It won't stick," Lila said.

"That's not an answer," Helena said sharply. "What if it does? You are going to have a baby during a war when you're already facing a tribunal. You won't be a paladin after that. They won't ever let you fight again."

Lila was picking at her nails, her cuticles bleeding. "Luc's going to leave combat to take over leadership now. Ilva's too old to continue as steward, and there's no one he trusts to replace her. They say that if I step down as paladin primary, they won't call a tribunal, Sebastian will replace me, and I'll be cleared for combat again." Lila drew a deep breath. "I'll be in command of my own unit. First woman."

Lila's voice showed no pride or excitement for what would be a historic accomplishment, because there was no chance that she could reenter combat, stripped of her former rank, without the scandal following her. Her reputation and legacy were irrevocably stained.

"If you said I was sick with something, no one would know I'm pregnant—and if it doesn't take, I'll go back into service like it never happened."

"Or you could retire from active combat and train recruits who could use someone with your experience," Helena said. "Those aren't your only two options."

"I'm not going to retire. That's not how it works for us Bayards," Lila said, her blue eyes snapping. She winced. "Sorry. People keep telling me that it's not all over, but—" She scoffed. "—I know how it works. What will be remembered. It won't be anything I ever did in combat."

Now Helena understood. A pregnancy altered the narrative. It didn't erase the scandal, but it did reframe it; instead of a violation of vows that nearly led to calamity, it became a love story.

The Principate had already been in desperate need of an heir, but it was hard to make it a stated priority when Luc's life was supposed to be shielded with divinity, and Luc had, for obvious reasons, always been resistant to the idea of a political marriage, which was what the Council wanted.

A Holdfast heir could reinvigorate the Resistance. How could it be a doomed war when there was such a tangible symbol of the future?

Of course Lila would prefer that version of her story, rather than the alternatives she was faced with.

Lila had always seemed unstoppable, but now Helena could see all the cracks she'd hidden. The desires she'd never let herself have.

Helena knew something about that.

"Will Luc know?"

Lila drew a breath, shaking her head. "No. I think it would distract him. He's under so much pressure, and the transition will be a lot. If he knew and then it came to nothing—it would crush him, to have hoped."

"Does Luc—want children?" Helena asked hesitantly. She didn't think she'd ever heard Luc speak of children. His hopes for the future were of the war being over, of travelling. Then again, the matter of Lila had always been carefully unspoken. Helena had known, but he'd never admitted it outright, not even to her.

Lila nodded. "He talked about them that night. How he's not like his father, he doesn't want to just do his duty. That he wants to have a family for himself, not because of the Principate, or because he needs an heir, but just because he loves someone so much that he makes one. That's what this would be."

Helena swallowed hard. She still hated this, but she couldn't refuse Lila. "I'll need to talk to Crowther and see what the options are."

Lila's face screwed up. "Why would you go to him? He's awful. Luc can't stand him."

Helena looked away. "He's the most pragmatic choice. I don't have the seniority to quarantine someone. I don't think you want Elain or Matias involved. The choices are Crowther or Ilva, and Ilva hasn't been very reliable lately."

"Fine," Lila sighed, wincing. "Crowther, then."

CHAPTER 57

Maius 1787

ACCORDING TO RECORDS, LILA BAYARD CONTRACTED A bad case of bog cough after helping deliver supplies to the water slums at the south end of the island.

Bog cough tended to crop up every year in the early summer after the floods, as the air grew warm and damp, and the dark, recessed levels of the city, far from sunlight, found their interiors blackened with mould.

The symptoms were a deep cough coming from low in the lungs, and an occasional rash. While mostly dangerous to children and the elderly, sometimes it would linger and transform into a virulent sickness that could sweep through the city like a plague. That was the ostensible reason why the upper levels of the city preferred to be restrictive with the lower sectors of the population.

Helena was familiar with the symptoms because her father used to treat it every summer. Most of the people who caught it couldn't afford to travel up-city to a licensed apothecary. Helena could replicate the symptoms almost perfectly using vivimancy, creating purplish rashes on Lila's inner wrists and the sides of her neck, and agitating her lungs enough to make her cough violently while Pace examined her and gave the diagnosis.

With so many people in tight quarters, plague was a constant fear.

Lila was promptly placed in isolation in the Alchemy Tower, and everyone else involved in the supply delivery was quarantined for three days until they were declared symptom-free.

Such a common sickness did not dampen morale, particularly since it was considered primarily an affliction of the poor and unsanitary. That Lila had caught it was taken as a sign that she was still too weak from her injuries. High in the sun-soaked rooms of the Alchemy Tower, she would recover.

Luc, however, was distraught. He demanded to see her, but he was flatly refused. His own lungs still showed signs of deterioration and damage; under no circumstances was he permitted to go anywhere near Lila.

Helena hardly knew where to begin with this new secret. Pregnancy was not something she'd ever studied. Her experience with newborns was mostly limited to emergency situations. She looked in the library for a few references but found the options lacking, until she remembered that Matron Pace kept most medical textbooks in the records office for easy access.

"I never thought I'd find you interested in pregnancy." Matron Pace's comment made Helena jump as she was caught hurriedly perusing one of the books.

Helena slammed it shut, cramming it into place. "I'm not. The title just caught my eye."

"You're welcome to borrow it."

"No." Helena shook her head. "Passing curiosity was all."

She made for the door.

"Marino." Pace's voice was commanding.

Helena turned. Pace was watching her like a hawk.

"Are you in a family way?"

"No."

"Accidents happen," Pace said mildly, leaning back against her desk. "Especially during wartime. You wouldn't be the first."

Helena released an exploding little scoff. "I'm *not* pregnant."

"I just hope your fellow is the responsible—"

"I can't be pregnant. I've been sterilised," Helena snapped, too mortified to keep listening.

Pace froze, shaking her head. "No. They wouldn't. They couldn't have possibly found that necessary at a time like this."

Helena's cheeks were burning, but her stomach had a gnawing pit inside it. "Well, they did. Maier did it. Ligature, same week I got back. It was—it was one of the Falcon's conditions. So, like I said, not pregnant."

She started again for the door.

"Helena, wait." Pace's voice was beseeching.

Helena winced, turning reluctantly back. Pace had one of her red, chapped hands pressed against her chest. "I shouldn't have teased you. I had no idea. Maier never said anything."

"It's fine," Helena said stiffly. "I wanted to be an alchemist more, and women don't get to do both." She lifted her chin. "Now I won't ever have to worry about choosing. Besides—" She looked squarely at Pace. "—I'll probably die young, so I'd be a terrible mother."

Pace studied her. "Was your mother terrible?"

Pace couldn't have hurt her more if she'd kicked her. The room swam.

Helena's throat closed. "How dare you."

"I'm sorry, I shouldn't have said it that way," Pace said, but she didn't really look sorry. "But Helena, I don't think you know how to be honest with yourself about what you want."

"It was the only way to become a healer—we needed a healer, Ilva said I was the only person who could do it." Helena's jaw trembled, and she had to set it hard. "It was the choice I had, and I made it. Would you really rather I hadn't?"

"You weren't even seventeen. You'd barely lived enough to know what you wanted."

"I feel pretty alive right now," Helena said through gritted teeth. "And I'm *fine.*"

"Being alive is not the same as living. I hope someday you'll have a chance to realise the difference."

Pace went over to the bookshelf and pulled the book that Helena had been reading off the shelf, holding it in both hands as she stared at the cover. "I was a midwife, you know. Long time ago now." She shook her head. "I should have realised. You've always poured your all into the present moment, as if that's all you expect to have."

She turned back to Helena. "Perhaps a glimpse at the next generation will make the future feel a little more real for you."

She held the book towards Helena. The title, *The Maternal Condition: An In-Depth Study on the Science and Physiology of Gestation,* glinted in the light from a window high overhead. "Lila Bayard will need the best care you can provide."

Helena stared at her in astonishment. "How—?"

Matron Pace pressed the book into her hands. "I've been a nurse for twice as long as you've been alive. Your vivimancy skills are remarkable, but Lila would have had to be sick for a good three weeks before developing a rash like that."

As Luc began taking over leadership, Ilva's health began a sudden and rapid decline as if all those years, she'd just been holding on until he was ready. Some days she was barely lucid. Crowther had become so concerned about Ilva's sudden deterioration that he'd had Helena examine her. There was nothing wrong; she was just old and tired.

The war seemed to pitch back and forth in favour between the two sides. The constant fighting seemed to grant little advantage beyond leaving the city more battered.

Luc led another aggressive attack on the West Island, and they captured a warehouse. It was found filled with large tublike tanks of fluid with bodies inside, tubes connected to veins, and breathing masks fastened over the noses and mouths. Resistance fighters. All dead, but their bodies still warm.

When the perimeter had been breached, a gas had been released into the masks, killing them all mere minutes before the Resistance reached them.

A procession of lorries returned to Headquarters, filled with the bodies to cremate. There were only a few captives, but one was the Warden, who proved difficult and refused to answer questions.

Because the Warden was Luc's captive, they couldn't be disappeared into one of Crowther's underground holes and tortured for information. Crowther remembered then that Kaine had taught Helena a unique method of extracting information; she had mentioned it once as an alternative when trying to dissuade him from torture.

Helena was as horrified as everyone else at all the healthy, intact, familiar faces being prepped for cremation, so close to rescue. She'd immediately agreed.

Some strings were pulled and Crowther managed to get a few hours alone with the Warden, bringing Helena with him.

The Warden was a woman, with a thin face and short cropped hair and a wide mouth. Her pale-blue eyes instantly narrowed when she saw Helena. Each sized the other up.

Crowther settled into the shadows, leaving Helena to make her attempt.

"Who are you?" Helena asked, not sure how to begin.

"What's it to you?" the Warden asked.

"Can't say I've met any women among the Undying or their Aspirants."

"Men generally like our bodies a lot more than they like us." The Warden looked over into the corner where Crowther was watching. "Guess I'm one of the special ones."

"How are you special?" Helena asked, even though she had a pretty good idea.

"Probably for the same reason you are." The Warden had looked back and was studying Helena now. "The difference is that I'm not a traitor to my kind."

"I'm not the one who just murdered more than a hundred people," Helena said, struggling to keep her voice even. She didn't know why it bothered her so much that this Warden was a woman, but it made her angrier.

"They would've killed me, given half a chance. I killed them first."

The Warden lifted her chin, jutting it towards Helena. "What are you?" Her eyes flicked over Helena. "Healer? I bet. I was a healer once."

Helena was doubtful about that, but the woman was talking without coercion, so she let her.

"Didn't want to be a healer, but there's not a lot of choices out there for us. He tried to make me a nun. Wanted me to raise other brats born like me. Teach them how to keep their abilities in and punish them if they didn't. Didn't you?"

Helena turned to stare at Crowther, who watched, his expression unreadable.

"You know her?" Helena asked.

"Oh yes. Kestrel Jan often came to see us whenever someone misbehaved at the orphanage. Always brought a pet along, someone with a long leash whom we could aspire to become like as long as we'd do *anything* he asked. I'm surprised, though. They're usually younger." Her eyes flicked over Helena.

"That's enough, Mandl," Crowther said sharply.

Mandl grinned towards him. "See, I knew you'd remember me."

"Pull the information and let's be done," Crowther said to Helena.

Helena took a deep breath.

Mandl looked unfazed. "You're not going to make me talk," she said. "I used to break my bones and gouge myself open just for fun. Just to feel something inside that hole they raised us in. You're too weak to hurt me, Traitor."

"You'd be surprised," Helena said, heart pounding.

Mandl just laughed.

The bodies from the warehouse were such a fresh tragedy. All those people, moments from rescue, and now they were gone because Mandl wanted to hurt the Eternal Flame and the Resistance even more than she cared about freedom.

Helena didn't delude herself that the Eternal Flame had the degree of moral superiority that they tried to claim, but how could anyone find the Undying better?

"Why were you keeping the prisoners in tanks like that?" she asked, maintaining a calm, steady voice.

Mandl smiled, her wide mouth stretching across her face. Her fingers twirled even though her wrists were shackled with inert iron. "Come on, try touching me. Let's see who breaks first."

Helena's anger sat like a boulder in the pit of her stomach as she moved towards Mandl. "I'll admit, you're probably better than me at hurting people. I can't beat you at your own game, but we're playing mine."

Mandl's eyes flicked over to the door and then at Crowther, the first glimmer of nervousness. She forced a laugh. "What can you do?"

Helena was behind Mandl now. "I don't think you know this trick."

Mandl tried to crane her neck, attempting to twist and see what Helena was doing. She jerked away as Helena slid her bare hand up from the nape of her neck, fingers lacing through the short hair. Mandl's hands twisted, trying to break loose from the shackles.

"It's all right." Helena's voice was as practised and clinical as her resonance as she blocked the right nerves along the spine, making sure not to stop Mandl's heart or suspend anything vital. "I guess there's something to being Institute-trained after all."

Helena slowed her heartbeat, stifling the rising terror. Like a gas valve, tinkering with the cocktail of hormones racing through Mandl, telling her to be calm, that Helena was not a threat.

"You want to tell me everything I ask," Helena said softly.

Mandl seized violently, trying to resist, her body lurching. Her resonance flared, trying to push back against Helena, but she was too late.

"Bitch—traitorous bitch—" she slurred as Helena winnowed through her raging emotions.

Mandl's eyes lost focus. Her mind and body were in direct conflict, and it was impossible for her to struggle as Helena slipped into her memories.

Kaine had made the process seem simple. It was much more difficult than Helena had expected. The noise of another mind. There was so much sound and energy, and Mandl's panic and attempts at resisting made it so much harder. Kaine had always let Helena's thoughts wander, catching them as they passed. Helena couldn't help but think there were easier ways to do it.

"What's your name?"

Elsbeth.

The name rang from a dozen directions all over inside Mandl's mind, coalescing at the forefront.

Mandl's face was slack, a trickle of drool running down one side of her mouth, but her eyes followed Helena with growing fury. Her mind trying and failing to recoil at the way Helena was manipulating her.

"Why were you keeping prisoners in tanks like that?"

Mandl tried to resist, but a memory flitted across her consciousness. A man in uniform was speaking: "—keep the best specimens . . ." Mandl's attention in the memory wandered to a buzzing fly and everything went out of focus.

Helena tried again. "If you had a new prisoner, what would you do with them?"

Memory fragments were like tatters of moving pictures, sounds and sensation all whipping by as if carried by wind. She heard voices, but they were too distant to make out.

She saw the walls of a warehouse, greenish light from the tinted windows. A boy whose face she half recognised, writhing.

Everything blurred, but a tingle of anticipation ran along her spine.

The gleam of a hypodermic needle in the low light. A finger flicking it to knock loose an air bubble. A glimpse of the boy again.

Blur.

Rows of the bodies laid out on gurneys next to the tanks. A bloated corpse with yellowish eyes, grey discoloured skin. Squeezing the arm of a young man and saying, *I'll take this one next.*

A printed form requesting ten female subjects. Signed Artemon Bennet. Mandl's hands pushing a cart with the boy lying on it, the mask and tubes still attached as she wheeled him into an empty room.

Shutting the door softly. Another shiver along her spine.

Helena ripped her mind free, snatching her hands away, wanting to scrub them until the skin came off.

"What is it for?" she asked. Her skin was crawling. She didn't want to go back into Mandl's mind.

Mandl was breathing unsteadily, her pupils dilated so wide that the blue irises barely showed.

"I'll pull it out if you don't answer," Helena said, gripping Mandl by the hair. "Do you prefer that?"

Mandl's expression twisted, and she spat. "It keeps them fresh."

"Fresh for what?"

"Anything. New bodies for the Undying. Test subjects. Thralls. The thralls last longer when they're new." Mandl was panting openmouthed, her lips growing chapped.

"How long are they kept there?"

Mandl smiled cruelly. "There's high demand, so usually not more than a few months. Electric shock keeps the muscle toned. We slow the vitals."

It felt an eternity before Crowther was satisfied with the amount of information Helena pulled out. By that time, Mandl's eyes were so disoriented that they looked in different directions. She'd grown feverish and was slumped forward, trembling.

"Well," Crowther said, sneering down at Mandl, "it seems you'll make a passable replacement for Ivy."

Helena said nothing. She never wanted to do it ever again. She regretted agreeing to it.

She turned wordlessly to leave.

"Traitor . . ." Mandl called after her.

CHAPTER 58

Junius 1787

Successful as Luc's recent offensives were, the new territory was stretching the Resistance thin. Despite the widespread admiration for Luc's decisive and successful leadership, the higher-ups were less enthused. There were rumours of Luc having an explosive argument with Althorne and several other members of military command, for not consulting them.

Some of the districts were surrounded on three sides by the Undying, requiring constant patrols and defence while providing very little strategic use. The districts in question also had not received their "liberation" with enthusiasm. Many of the Paladians on the West Island were quite happy under Undying occupation and fearful of being labelled Resistance sympathisers if the district was eventually taken back. As a result, the Resistance was forced to fend off not only attacks from the Undying's forces but also civilian rebellions.

The summer Abeyance was approaching, and the troops were concentrated down-island to defend the ports and the anticipated trade influx.

The hospital remained ceaselessly full. No longer were the sharp deluges of battles followed by a lull to recuperate. Now it was constant, an unrelenting strain that ran everyone ragged.

"I don't know what to do," Helena said one night, sitting up because she couldn't sleep, not even in Kaine's arms. "I don't know how we can win. I can't see any way."

"You can't save everyone," he said quietly.

Her jaw started trembling, and she clenched her fists. "I'm not even trying to save everyone, though. I don't know how to save anyone. I can't figure anything out. Everything I try is a dead end. We're running out of time."

He said nothing.

"I'm just—" She scrubbed her eyes. "I'm so tired. Everything I do feels like I'm delaying the inevitable, saving someone one day so they'll die in a worse way tomorrow. I wish I'd never become a healer."

She'd never admitted it to anyone before. That she hated it.

She told him everything now. The truth about the Stone, and where it was, the true story of the Holdfasts, the array from Wagner, and how no matter how she tried, she couldn't work out how the channelling was supposed to work. She even told him about the obsidian, and how useless it had proven to be.

She was so tired of finding possibilities that went nowhere.

"Bring me a piece," he told her. "Maybe you haven't been able to test it the right way."

She shook her head. "There's already too much you need to focus on. You don't need to worry about my pointless experiments." She cleared her throat. "Did I tell you, I'm working with my lab partner to reverse the nullium alloy, so we can use the compound from it to make inert metal? I was thinking, I could use transmutation to make a really light mesh armour with a high tensile strength, and then use the compound to remove the resonance. You would wear it under your clothes. It wouldn't interfere with your resonance, and no one could use theirs to break through it." She traced a finger over a silvery scar on his arm. "I think I've almost got it all worked out. Then you won't get hurt so much."

He kissed the top of her head. "I'm still healing just fine. Bring me a piece of the obsidian. It'll be more interesting to experiment with than dealing with all of Crowther's self-defeating sabotage orders. Everyone in the Undying is paranoid about spies now, and Morrough's been taking more precautions than ever."

HELENA WAS SORTING THROUGH THE various pieces of charged obsidian she'd accumulated when the windows exploded. A roar shuddered through the air and Tower. Lab equipment shattered across the floor.

The sirens started. All of them.

Another bomb.

Helena headed for the stairs before her bracelet burned, running over the broken glass that covered the floors.

They got scattered reports of what had happened. Several buildings had fallen, and the interconnected skybridges conjoining the cityscape had wrought massive destruction across the centre of the island. The hospital prepared for the inundation they knew would come, but as they waited, only a few lorries arrived, all carrying people from the outermost edges of the collapse.

Helena was healing a heavy gash across a woman's head when she heard the clamour that meant gurneys were being brought down the hall, but before they reached the hospital, there were voices bellowing from the hallway.

"Don't bring them in! Get them outside. Cover those windows. Get every entrance sealed."

There was muffled arguing and protests until a voice roared, "The nullium's in the air. They're covered in it. Take them back out!"

Helena turned to stare in horror at Elain, who looked bewildered, her suncrest trembling below her throat.

"Why does it matter if it's in the air?" Elain asked.

"Because if we inhale it, we could all lose our resonance," Helena said, nearly frozen as all the ramifications of that began dawning on her. Nullium shrapnel had been devastation enough, but they weren't prepared for inhalation.

She looked around at the hospital with all the high windows open, trying to catch the mountain breeze as the basin sweltered in the early-summer heat. The air was hazy with dust.

They were already breathing it.

THEY WORE CLOTH MASKS AND the casualty ward was relocated into the commons, trying to keep the new patients away from those already in the hospital, but it was impossible to tell on sight if the dust covering someone had nullium in it or not.

All the protocols were forgotten as more and more stretchers arrived, the injuries growing progressively worse as the rescue and recovery efforts neared the blast zone.

They washed off as much dust as possible, trying to reduce potential contamination while sorting out life-and-death injuries and identifying those already showing signs of nullium exposure.

How long would it take for nullium in the air to penetrate the lungs and reach the blood? Once it did, how long would they have before their resonance began fading? No one knew.

Helena worked with a degree of ruthless abandon that she had never before dared. Every second counted. She healed and healed, working with mindless desperation. The day was hot, and the dust in the air grew thick as a rare southerly wind brought it up-island towards them.

The mask on her face sealed the dampness against her skin. Her hands grew caked with dust that she kept washing off after every patient. The mask stopped working; it was so clogged with dust, it nearly suffocated her. She replaced it with a wet cloth, which was what everyone without masks had already begun using.

"Marino! Where's Marino?"

Helena looked up from washing her hands. "What is it?"

She squinted through the haze at the man in front of her.

"What are you doing here? You're supposed to be down-island. I've been looking for you." He was in a lorry uniform, and he took her by the arm.

She stared at him in confusion as he pulled her towards one of the lorries. "What?"

"There's too much of a risk of the nullium contamination spreading if we keep bringing the wounded up-island. Takes too long anyway. There's a hospital down-island but they're overrun, not enough experience with the nullium. You're in charge of the nullium ward here, so you're lead. Orders are right here." He shoved her up into the passenger side of the lorry and handed her a piece of paper.

"I'm not in charge . . ." She squinted at the paper, her eyes gritty with dust. "I'm not allowed to leave Headquarters."

She stared stupidly at the words that indicated that Helena Marino, as head of the nullium ward, was to be dispatched to the field hospital to lead the medics in treating the nullium-poisoned combatants. It was signed by Falcon Matias.

She couldn't even remember the last time she'd been given written orders from him.

"This can't be right. Was there a meeting?"

The engine rumbled beneath her.

"I just follow orders, Marino. They don't bring me in for Council meetings. You were supposed to be there right off. Kept waiting, finally went looking for you." The driver twisted at the ignition, shifting a gear, and the lorry lurched forward. Before she had more time to argue, they were speeding out of Headquarters and down-island.

She could already see the ruined skyline.

"I need you to go back and tell Crowther where I've been dispatched. I don't think this was Council-authorised," she said as they drove.

"There's a radio at the field office. You can check in when you arrive."

She always forgot how fast it was to travel by vehicle on military roads. In no time at all, the lorry stopped at a hastily assembled checkpoint.

Everyone sent down the island into the blast zone was fitted with layers of protective clothing, masks as well as veils to try to keep out the dust. They stopped to dress and then continued deeper. The dust hung in the air, and the road deteriorated, covered in rubble. It was midday, but the dust blotted out the sun so that everything glowed an eerie orange.

Two bright lanterns showed through the smog, and they pulled up at the hospital. There were already medics there, no healers, although it was hard to tell who anyone was.

Medical workers all wore red ribbons tied around their arms. Here Helena saw the devastation she'd kept expecting to arrive at Headquarters.

This was the worst of it.

There were so many crushed bodies. The armour of soldiers had splintered and sliced them apart. Medics with the right resonance were transmuting the armour off, but when it came loose, blood would immediately begin pouring out.

Dust and smoke and metal and blood stained the air. Helena could taste it despite all the layers.

There was no running water.

She could barely see. No one had any idea where the radio was, or if they still had one. They were drowning in injuries.

Half of the medics had already lost their resonance, and there was no time to do anything but switch to manual protocols. Without running water, it was impossible to keep anything clean.

Helena could feel her resonance starting to fail when General Althorne came through the door, pulling a cart with several bodies on it.

"I think they're alive," he said, breathing heavily. He was coated in dust, no mask and only light armour on. "There's at least forty trapped under a wall. We can hear them, but we don't know how to reach them without potentially collapsing it on them."

Helena let the others check the bodies and try to find space for them. The hospital was already overflowing. Althorne's fingers were bloody from digging through rubble. He sat down heavily, coughing violently, struggling to breathe.

"You should be wearing a mask," she said.

"Can't breathe in those damn things," he said, gulping water. "No point. Already lost my resonance." Then he blinked and peered at her. "Marino?"

"Yes?" She didn't know Althorne had any idea who she was.

He leaned towards her, his voice dropping. "What are you doing here? Get back to Headquarters before Ferron finds out about this."

She was speechless, but of course Althorne had to have known. She looked at him helplessly. "Matias signed the order and dispatched me here, and I can't find the radio to get permission to return."

"Go back to Headquarters. First lorry. Tell them I ordered it. The last thing we need is Ferron going off the rails." Althorne dragged himself up on his feet.

"Wait." She caught him by the arm, and to her surprise, he collapsed back onto the chair. She reached out with her failing resonance, but all she felt was a blur.

"Althorne, you need a mask. It'll give you lung damage to keep breathing this dust. You're too valuable to risk," she said, searching him, trying to find the injury she could tell he was hiding. It was a testament to how weak he was that he sat there, letting her.

He said nothing.

"When are reinforcements coming?" she asked. "There's not enough people here to handle this much. We're running out of everything."

"They're not," Althorne said quietly, as if to keep anyone else from overhearing. "We're all there is."

Helena's heart stalled.

He watched as several soldiers dragged in bodies on makeshift litters.

"We can't risk our remaining combatants down here, losing their resonance. The fallout has to be contained," Althorne said, his voice tight with resignation.

He stood and swayed.

"Where are you hurt?" Helena asked, blocking his path.

He shrugged her off, straightening, his breath laboured. "It's shallow. Falling rubble. Everyone's bleeding. I'll be fine."

"Althorne." She stepped into his path. "You're hurt. Badly. If I had my resonance, I'd sedate you by force, because you're not in any condition to lead recovery efforts. You are too valuable. You know that. The Resistance can't lose you."

He patted her on the shoulder as if she were a child. "My men are in that rubble. Buried and suffocating because I sent them there."

A warning shriek rose from the rubble. Long and piercing, followed by another and another. Whistles. Helena didn't know what it meant.

Althorne's face hardened. He pushed her aside with a sweep of his arm. "Block the doors. They've sent in necrothralls; they'll be coming for the bodies."

He strode past her, and Helena stood, torn between trying to stop him and the urgency of securing the hospital. Before she could decide, he vanished into the dust. She turned to face the hospital.

"We need to move all the bodies as far back into the building as possible," she said, her voice shaking. "If there's not enough room—stack the dead. We have to secure the doors."

The thought of being locked in a field hospital again made her vision blur. She forced herself to stay focused, curling her fingers until she felt the scars on her palm.

"Can't we let Headquarters know we're under attack?" a medic asked, voice muffled through protective gear. "They have to send people."

Helena shook her head. "They're not coming. The nullium has to be contained."

Everyone around her froze, staring. She probably wasn't supposed to tell them that.

Helena had never been a leader, and she had no idea how to suddenly begin being one. She was not the kind of person that anyone believed in, and standing, covered in dust, soaked in blood and gore—it was not the time for it. She focused on practicalities.

"Our job is to keep everyone here safe. We'll move them back and put up obstacles. The Undying won't come here themselves; nullium affects them, too."

"But there's no room to move anyone unless we can break through the walls, and no one here has the resonance for that. We're already out of space," a medic said. "And how are we going to block the doors?"

Helena looked around. He was right. If they protected the survivors, they'd have to leave the dead to be taken. Which would cost them dearly later on.

There was no room, and no means.

She was in command. She had a stupid slip of paper declaring it.

"We'll evacuate," she said, not caring whether the nullium was supposed to be contained down-island. It would be worse if the Undying got hold of all their casualties. "We won't go into Headquarters, but if we get close enough, they might not pursue. If the Council minds, they can blame me."

A flurry of activity followed as bodies were prepared for transfer. Helena went and commandeered all the lorries, using the crumpled slip of paper that named her as head of the nullium ward as proof of legitimacy.

They crammed as many bodies as possible into the lorries. Dead at the bottom, injured on top. A medic or nurse departed with each lorry.

The wait for their return felt interminable as they readied group after group.

They could hear the fighting. Fire glowed through the smog. Whistles kept sounding on all sides, like a signal of wolves closing in, except it wasn't night; the world was red.

Helena's muscles were burning from lifting, over and over. The bodies never seemed to stop. She and one other medic were left, even though there were still wounded and more bodies that they had to get out.

"I'll stay," he said. "Take this one."

Helena shook her head. "I'm lead. I go last."

He stepped back, thumping the lorry.

"I'll wait with you, then," he said.

She could only see his eyes, and they were crusted all around until they were black with dust.

He reminded her of Luc.

"No," she said quickly, looking away. "Go, that's an order."

She watched him swing up into the cab next to the driver as the lorry pulled away, driving carefully through the debris. She could just barely make out the Alchemy Tower in the distance. The flame at the top like a small sun.

The lorry stopped.

Helena squinted through the dust, trying to make out why. There was another lorry approaching, swerving back and forth so that the departing lorry couldn't pass it.

Suddenly the approaching lorry sped up, and Helena could see through the dust enough to make out the bloated grey face of the driver.

The Resistance lorry's wheels screamed as it went into a rapid reverse, but rubble scattered across the road prevented evasion. The approaching lorry crashed into it head-on.

There was a bright flash.

CHAPTER 59

Junius 1787

HELENA LAY SQUINTING, STRUGGLING TO SEE, BUT everything was dim, blurring. When she tried to breathe, pain radiated through her, so sudden it jolted her back into consciousness. She clutched her chest, trying to draw breath, but she couldn't.

What had happened? She couldn't remember. She fought to breathe, and a low whistling sound came from somewhere. Then it all rushed back. The lorries, they crashed and—

There must have been another bomb.

She struggled, trying to pull herself up.

She tried to spot the explosion, but the landscape was wrong. Where was the road? There was just fire and a crater.

Agony bloomed through her. Her vision turned red.

A whistling sound like a boiling kettle kept coming from somewhere. She tried to find it and realised it was coming from her throat.

She moved cautiously. If she'd damaged her spine—

Calm down. Focus. Assess your condition and act from there.

She forced herself to look down and gave a strangled whimper.

There was a piece of metal buried in the centre of her chest, splitting her sternum.

She kept staring at it, too shocked to move at first. She was going to die. She was going to die in a field hospital, just like her father. All that vivimancy just to run into the same fate.

She closed her eyes, struggling to stay calm as feeling crept back over her. She could sense her fingers. Toes. Her spine was intact at least.

She kept trying to breathe, but she wanted to scream with every hitch of her lungs. It was worse than a knife wound; the agony seemed to radiate outwards, seething like cracks through every rib. It consumed the whole of her consciousness.

Get up. You have to get up.

She could barely make herself move. She looked towards the road again. There was just a hole. The road was gone, but there were still people in the hospital.

She managed to get her hand up and peel the mask off. She didn't think that lung damage from dust mattered anymore.

The air was so much cooler. She managed a half breath.

She couldn't die.

She fought to her feet, managing shallow, panting breaths, and nearly fainted when she got upright. Every movement was agony. The need to breathe warred with the excruciating misery of forcing her ribs and lungs to shift. She bit down on her lip as she tried to shuffle towards the doors. One step at a time.

Her lungs kept agitating her with the urge to cough, but she fought it back. Pain exploded through her each time, bright white, so searing she'd waver, unable to see.

If she coughed, she would faint, and she'd be dead before she regained consciousness.

She would not die. She would wait. Someone would come back and find her. Maier could operate. Shiseo would work night and day to find the right chelator, and she would make herself recover quickly.

She'd promised Kaine that she was safe, that nothing would happen to her. She could not die.

She made it through the doors. There was a tray with a few discarded instruments and bottles on it. She fumbled through them until she found a vial of laudanum.

She managed to unscrew the lid and forced down a sip of the tongue-biting contents.

Not too much. She had to stay lucid. She searched the rest of the supplies, looking for something, a stimulant to keep herself going.

She'd kill for a cough suppressant.

She forced herself to look down at her chest. She was wearing so many layers, she couldn't see exactly where the shrapnel went in to tell if it was nullium dissolving into her blood or just a stray piece of the lorry.

She wanted to pull it out but knew better. If it had punctured her heart or aorta, she'd bleed to death in seconds. It might be keeping her alive.

Someone would come. She could wait until a lorry came back.

She made herself keep moving, because it was easier than sitting, feeling the injury.

She checked the remaining patients. The nearest was a boy who'd been cut out of his armour. He was missing an arm. There was an intravenous drip in his remaining arm, but there was so much blood pooled beneath him. Reaching feebly for a pulse and finding none, she drew his eyes closed and moved on.

Most were dead, several unresponsive; only a few were still conscious. She checked all of them, noting where they were.

The laudanum had managed to numb her enough that she could move a little easier.

"Mum . . . ?" one of the soldiers moaned, catching her wrist as she passed.

Pain ripped through her chest and up her spine, shattering the relief. Her legs nearly gave out, and she bit down on her tongue so hard her mouth flooded with blood.

His helmet was crushed around his skull. Through the openings, one side of his face was mangled. There was thick blood oozing from his head onto the pallet underneath him.

"Mum . . ." he said.

"She'll be here soon."

He wouldn't let go of her wrist. He tugged again. Her vision flashed white.

"Mum . . . sorry. Forgot to say goodbye. Sorry."

"It's all right, d-don't worry," she said.

His fingers relaxed enough for her to slip her hand free. She looked down.

He was dead.

She took another sip of laudanum. It was growing harder and harder to keep from coughing. She couldn't tell if the blood in her mouth was from her lungs or her tongue.

She tried to listen for any sound of the lorries. The sounds of fighting were fading. She headed for the doors.

She was growing increasingly certain that her injury was beyond the Resistance's means. The bone and potential heart damage would require extensive manual surgery beyond what Maier could manage without alchemy. One of her lungs was likely punctured. She'd need at least two surgeons, possibly three.

If triage protocols were in place, which they would be given the mass injuries, no one except Luc or Sebastian would qualify for three surgeons.

She leaned her head against the wall.

Even with a successful surgery, her likelihood of survival would be low. She'd be at high risk of complications and infection, a drain on their limited supplies. The hospital would save far more people if they passed her over. Any half-rate medical assessment would realise that.

Whether the lorries arrived or not, she was going to die. She looked down at her hand, wishing she had the resonance to send a pulse code to Kaine. Some way to tell him she was sorry. That she had tried.

The edge of her vision was beginning to fade, unravelling like fabric, slowly shrinking smaller and smaller.

When she blinked, there was someone standing in front of her. Her mind stumbled through the fog of pain before realising it was a necrothrall. It stood studying her as if confused about whether she was dead or alive.

Her lungs seized, trying to force a cough, to clear the fluid inside her chest. A rasping whimper escaped her as she tried to hold it back.

Movement caught her eye. There were more necrothralls. The sounds of fighting had ceased. Althorne and his men had died or fallen back. The necrothralls were coming for the hospital. For the dead and the survivors.

She couldn't let them take the survivors.

She stepped back, trying to find a scalpel, something sharp, something that would be quick and painless. She wouldn't let them be taken to West Port. All she could find were filthy bandages and empty bottles of medicine. She needed one scalpel.

Something under her clothes bumped against her leg. It took her a moment to remember what was there. The obsidian. She had been holding it when the bomb went off; she'd shoved it in her pocket without thinking.

She fumbled for it and slit her finger open. The piece must have shattered in the explosion, but it was sharp at least.

She was too slow. The necrothralls were already inside. There were bodies by the door, and several necrothralls had stopped there, dragging them away, while the rest moved deeper.

They weren't moving fast, but they were faster than Helena. They reached the survivors before she did.

"No!" Helena rasped out, her raised voice splitting her chest.

One of the necrothralls moved towards her. She tried to fend it off. All she had was the obsidian. She slashed at the necrothrall with it. The soft, deteriorating skin split easily on contact, and then the tip hit bone.

She'd used barely any force, but that pressure alone caused enough pain that her legs failed her.

When her head cleared, she was on the ground—and so was the necrothrall.

Blood dripped from her fingers where she was gripping the obsidian, the edges of the black glass buried in her skin. There were still so many necrothralls.

They moved towards her, bodies blotting out the reddish light filtering through the door. Wind fluttered across her face.

Her eyes slid shut.

When she tried to open her eyes again, they were heavy, as if her lashes had tangled. When she tried to move—her body wouldn't.

She tore her eyes open. There was glaring light, and everything was blurred until she found a vague dark shape near her. She recoiled, then squinted.

Kaine was standing beside her, pale and wide-eyed, his face impossibly haggard.

"You . . ."

The word emerged cracked and croaking. Her tongue was thick and dry, as if she hadn't touched water in days. She couldn't feel anything below her neck.

She tried to look down but couldn't move.

She was paralysed.

Her eyes crossed as she tried to look down her body. All she could make out was an intravenous drip in her arm. When she squinted, she could see saline and other things in upended glass vials all running down into the tube.

"What?" she asked. The words crackled in her throat and slurred across her tongue. "What'd you do . . . ?"

"What did I do?" Kaine repeated slowly. "I saved your life."

He was breathing unsteadily. "Crowther, with his endless demands, has the High Necromancer taking a myriad of precautionary measures. Only three people knew about that bombing before it happened. And I wasn't one of them. When I got word, I thought I was being paranoid sending my thralls in. Surely, they'd understand that I can't stop every fucking thing. This was for my peace of mind, I told myself. To see the fallout, so I'd know how bad things were. You wouldn't be there, of course. I told myself you wouldn't be there, you'd be safe in Headquarters, because that is the damned deal. Isn't that what you promised? That they wouldn't punish you? I *knew*—I *told you* this would happen—"

His voice broke.

"Wasn't . . . Crowth—" Speaking moistened her tongue at least, but she was dying for water. Her mind was still foggy. She couldn't understand how she was there.

"Don't defend them!" Kaine looked feral with rage. "Do you have any idea how close you came to dying? It took an entire medical team to keep you alive. Why would they leave you alone in that fucking hospital if they weren't trying to kill you?"

"Were . . . evacuating," she said slowly, pacing her words, her tongue gradually complying.

"Alone?"

"I was—in charge." She felt eerily lucid. "Soldiers—didn't deserve to die alone."

She tried to get up. She felt as if she'd be able to think more clearly if she could just sit up for a minute and figure out what had happened to her.

"Well, I didn't see anyone there while you were dying."

She wasn't sure why she was trying to reason with him, but she wanted him to calm down so that she could reorient herself.

"It's a war, Kaine. People die. Given your personal death toll, you should know that better than anyone else. You know that I'm not going to prioritise my survival over everyone else's."

He stared at her for a long terrible moment, the rage stark on his face. "Well, you should." He was suddenly ice-cold, and his eyes gleamed so silver that they were almost white. "Because I have warned you, if something happens to you, I will personally raze the entire Order of the Eternal Flame. That isn't a threat, it's a promise. Consider your survival as much a necessity to the Resistance as Holdfast's. If you die, I will kill every single one of them. Given that the risk to their lives is the only way to make you value your own."

Helena stared at him, dumb with shock that slowly twisted into rage.

"How dare you? How—dare you!" Her voice rose so high, it cracked.

If she could have moved, she would have thrown herself at him and tried to beat him to death with her bare hands. She wanted to scream at him.

But beyond her fury was an even greater sense of horror at what this meant. He'd become the very threat that Crowther had feared. Once he would have been loyal to them for the sake of avenging his mother, but Helena had usurped that, given him a new and uncontrollable source of obsessiveness and rage.

She closed her eyes, unable to look at him, and the ouroboros flashed through her mind, that image of endless self-annihilation. A dragon forever consuming itself.

She gave a rasping sob that rattled her lungs violently, and as she fought to breathe, the room went still.

The surface beneath her shifted. Fingers tucked a stray curl behind her ear before brushing across her cheek.

"I know your face too well." He sighed. "You're thinking you'll have to kill me now, aren't you? That I'm too much of a liability."

She said nothing, refusing to open her eyes.

"Would you really do it?"

She looked at him. "You know—you know I will not choose you at the price of everyone. It wouldn't even save you if I did."

He looked away then. "You'd never forgive yourself."

Her jaw trembled. "No. I wouldn't—" Her throat grew thick. She struggled to swallow, unable to lift her head. "But it wouldn't be the first unforgivable thing I've done. What's one more line for the history books?"

He was silent for a long time.

"What will you do when I'm gone?" he asked, as if that was all that mattered.

"I'm sure you can imagine."

The ceiling blurred at the thought of a world where Kaine was gone and she was alone, with no one to blame but herself.

She hated this war. She had thought she could do anything. That she was strong enough for it. That there would be no limit to what she was willing to do or endure. Apparently, Kaine had become her limit.

She couldn't imagine herself without him. She didn't think she'd even exist anymore.

She gave a choking gasp, struggling for air, lungs rattling.

Suddenly Kaine was over her, holding her face in his hands, tilting her head so she could breathe. That was all the embrace possible.

"Just live, Helena." His voice was shaking. "That's all I'm asking you to do for me."

Helena gave a low sob, lungs whistling as she fought to breathe. "I can't promise that. You know I can't promise that. But I can't risk what you'll do if I die."

He kissed her. She could taste the plea on his lips.

"I'm sorry," she kept saying again and again, "I'm sorry I did this to you."

A harsh buzz broke the air. Kaine went rigid and jerked back with a curse. Another buzz. Two long and two short. Each time the noise came, the lights in the room dimmed, flickering ominously.

He looked around, his teeth gritted. "Fuck. I'm being called back to the city." He stepped away but kept staring down at her. She could see the calculation in his eyes as he seemed to hesitate over something. Finally an expression of despair flashed across his face.

"Davies," he said. His voice barely carried, and his eyes went out of focus for a moment. "Come here."

The door behind him opened, and a woman entered. Helena didn't know enough about servants' uniforms to place what she was, but she recognised the name.

Enid Ferron's lady's maid stood beside Kaine, looking down at Helena with rheumy blue eyes. A faint whiff of something dry but organic drifted into the room with her. She was dead but so expertly reanimated, she looked almost lifelike.

Helena looked around the room and towards the window, realising that she couldn't see any buildings, just sky and trees.

"Where are we?" she asked abruptly. She didn't even know how long she'd been unconscious.

"Spirefell. My family's country estate," Kaine said, pulling on his uniform, the black coat and cloak. "I'll explain more later. I have to go. Don't be afraid of Davies. She won't hurt you."

Helena kept staring at the necrothrall. One of the servants who'd died when Kaine became Undying, whose life was responsible for his immortality and immutability. He'd reanimated her?

"I'm sorry," he was saying, "I thought I had more time to explain. You'll be safe here. No one will find you. I'll be back as soon as I can.

"Davies, take care of her." He leaned over Helena one last time, stroking her hair. "You're safe. I promise."

Then he was gone. She could hear something in the walls and floor moving but couldn't see what it was as she was left paralysed, in the care of a necrothrall.

She looked at it—her—again. Davies stood watching Helena, her gaze vague but constant.

"Can I have water?" Helena finally asked.

Davies poured a cup of water from a pitcher on a table nearby and then brought it over to Helena and helped her sip enough to wet her mouth. It was bitter; Helena recognised the taste of laudanum.

She had no idea it was possible to reanimate necrothralls to this degree. The woman seemed alive.

"You were Enid Ferron's lady's maid, weren't you?" Helena asked, fighting the wave of exhaustion the drug brought upon her.

Davies nodded slowly as if she understood the question. Helena struggled to focus.

"You've been here, all this time?"

Another nod. Davies mouthed a word silently. *Kaine.*

If that were true, it meant she'd been reanimated for nearly seven years without showing any signs of decay. Helena hadn't known that was even possible.

"Why? Why would he do that to you?"

If the necrothrall answered, Helena wasn't conscious enough to see it.

She slipped in and out of lucidity, in more pain each time she came awake. Davies was sitting in a chair beside her, knitting what appeared to be socks. The numbness was wearing off. Pain was shifting from a distant impression to a weight steadily bearing down harder and harder.

Her throat was bruised and raw inside; she must have been on a breathing apparatus at some point.

When the pain grew oppressive enough to wake her again, she found that Kaine had returned. He was standing beside her, replacing several of the vials connected to the intravenous drip.

"What happened to the medical team?" Helena asked, her tongue thick and dry again. "The people you had save me. What did you do to them?"

He stared down at her. The room was dark; his black uniform made him blend into the shadows, but his pale hair and eyes almost glowed.

"Don't ask questions you don't want answers to."

"Did you kill them?" Her voice sharpened.

He flicked a switch, filling the room with dim orange light.

"No, I didn't kill them. An entire medical team turning up dead would have raised questions. They think they saved a woman who died under interrogation yesterday. And they do not care at all that they spent hours saving you for the ostensible purpose of my torturing you to death afterwards. They were proud to be of service. You are, after all, a terrorist, they said."

She knew he was trying to distract her. "So you would have killed them but didn't because it would have raised inconvenient questions."

His eyes flashed. "Yes, I did all of this for convenience, which you know I have so abundantly in my life with my two mutually exclusive masters."

Guilt caught in Helena's throat like a stone. "I don't want you to kill people because of me."

He gave a barking laugh. "What exactly is it that you think I do with all my time? I kill people. I order other people to kill people. I train people to kill people. I sabotage and undermine people so that they will be killed, and I do it all because of you. Every word. Every life. Because of you."

She gave a ragged gasp as the room tilted, swimming as the blood drained from her head.

The viciousness in his expression vanished. "Wait. Helena, I didn't—"

"No," she said harshly. "Don't even try to take it back."

"I—" His voice was soft. Pleading.

"No," she said again. "It's true. What you said is entirely true. Everything you do is on my head, too. Every life . . ."

"Don't." He sat on the edge of the bed, picked up her right hand. "Don't carry it. It's not yours. Stop trying to carry a whole damned war on your shoulders."

"This is all my fault, though," she said. "I did this to you. I made you like this. Someone should regret that, and you can't. But if I do—maybe that will be enough to make you stop someday."

He looked away and said nothing. She watched his fingers move across hers, wishing she could feel it.

"What's happening in the city?" she asked.

He was silent for a few seconds. "Althorne's dead. There were several units trapped in one of the buildings; they got them out, but he died during the retreat. From our estimates, the Resistance has lost at least half their active forces. We retook the ports two days ago."

There was nowhere for the despair of that information to go but to lance into her mind. No twisting horror in her gut; no sense of emptiness. She could not feel her body. She could only think.

"There has been considerable backlash to the bombing, though. They didn't expect the dust to contaminate both islands. There's been panic and outrage over the widespread loss of resonance, the hospitals are overwhelmed with patients needing chelators, and the death toll for the Resistance, while significant, has provided us almost no new necrothralls because Durant forgot that the nullification compound would interfere with reanimation. They have to pump fresh blood into the corpses to reanimate them. So I doubt it will happen again. At least not on that scale."

A paltry source of comfort, but it was something.

"I don't know what to do," she finally said. "I can't ignore a threat to the Eternal Flame."

He sighed, head dipping. "I was just angry."

"You're always angry, but you can't make threats like that or reduce a war like this into a simplistic blame game. And you *can't* hold the Resistance hostage to control me."

His shoulders slumped. "If you die, Helena, I'm done. I won't continue this. I'm tired."

He looked at her, and she could see the whole war in his eyes, the toll that came from struggling with no end in sight, driven by a terror of what might happen if he ever stopped.

"I mean it. I won't kill them—but I will be done. You are my terms of service. The contract is void if you die."

She managed to turn her head a little. "There is a life for you on the other side of this war. You have the Stone. If Morrough dies, you might be fine, and you'd be free. You could do—all sorts of things. Don't reduce your world to me."

His lip curled, a flash of teeth. "Oh, and do *you* have a list of post-war plans that you've forgotten to mention?"

She averted her eyes. "Do as I say, not as I do."

He laced their fingers together as they lapsed into a silence as empty as the future.

"You could—become a healer," she finally said, straining to feel the sensation of his hand against hers.

A smile ghosted at the corner of his mouth. "I hadn't considered that."

"You should. You have a talent for it—although your bedside manner is terrible."

"It would be something to balance out that death toll of mine," he said, not looking at her.

"I shouldn't have said that. It's not your fault."

He shook his head, staring at the wall. "Maybe that was true once, but I believe I own it all now."

She swallowed, willing her fingers to move so she could squeeze his hand. "You are so much more than what the war has done to you."

Her voice shook with conviction, but he still wouldn't look at her.

"You are," she said desperately. "Just—just like I am. There's more to both of us—it's just waiting to get out. Someday, we'll leave all this behind. Go far away, and you'll see. The two of us—I think we could."

He made no answer, but she dimly felt his fingers grip hers tighter.

"I promise—you'll see . . ." Her eyelids began to droop.

"Go to sleep. You have a long recovery ahead of you."

She resisted, trying to stay awake. "How long have I been here?"

"Don't worry about that."

"How long?"

". . . It's been four days since the bombing."

Four days? Blood was suddenly pounding in her ears, and her lungs rattled when she tried to breathe.

"Kaine—you have to get word to Crowther that I'm alive."

"Don't worry about them." His voice was hard.

"No, listen. You have to tell him."

He stroked her cheek. "Just rest."

She fought to move, needing him to understand. "No. Promise me. Promise you'll send word. Make sure he knows that I'll come back."

If Crowther thought she was dead, he might decide that Kaine was too much of a risk to keep alive.

"Promise me—promise you'll get word—"

"All right. I'll send word, I promise. Rest."

The throbbing pulse of blood in her head slowed, and she relaxed. He tucked a curl behind her ear.

"You'll be here at least three weeks unless the nullium clears from your blood before then."

"There's a chelator the Eternal Flame developed—"

He tapped the tip of her nose. "The Undying have chymists and are also familiar with metal-sequestering agents."

She rolled her eyes.

"You'll get your resonance back . . . but it will be a long time for you. You had several shrapnel injuries, and you inhaled a significant amount as well. It's hard to say how long it'll take. You'll have to recover the old-fashioned way. Go to sleep. Loath as I am to admit it, the war will still be here when you wake."

CHAPTER 60

Junius 1787

Being injured was horrible. Helena was accustomed to the efficiency of healing to circumvent the slowest and more unbearable aspects of recovery; having to suddenly endure the natural speed of healing was utter misery.

She spent much of the first week in a drugged stupor, feverish with an infection. When she finally grew lucid again, she found Kaine still beside her. He had a large stack of books and folios that he was flipping through.

"What are you doing?" she asked after watching for a little while.

His eyes flicked up. "Studying human anatomy for my future career as a healer," he said in a dry voice.

She knew that the real answer was that he would have to be her healer once the nullium was cleared from her system, but she played along. "We can open a practice together, like my parents did. Up on a cliff. We'll be able to look out the windows and see the tides."

He raised an eyebrow. "Do I get any say about this future life of ours, or are you making all the decisions?"

"Do you *have* ideas?"

There was a pause. "Can't say I do."

She drew a slow breath. She could move her fingers now. As her fingers flexed, she realised her right hand was bandaged, the fingers splinted, and she remembered the last moments in the field hospital.

"I almost forgot," she said. "I think I discovered something in the hospital."

He looked up.

"The obsidian I told you about. I had some in my pocket when the necrothralls came. I think—I think I severed a reanimation with it."

"Are you sure?"

She squinted, trying to remember more details, but all she recalled was the red-orange light, and the pain. "Not entirely, but I think we should test it again."

"Well, don't worry about that right now." He snapped his book shut and came over to change the bandages.

She'd regained enough mobility that as he peeled off the gauze, she lifted her head, determined to see. Running like a ragged seam down the centre of her chest was a huge incision, sewn closed with black thread and bone wire. The skin was swollen, yellow, and white and pink.

Helena had seen more wounds than she could count, watched innumerable people grieve over the loss of who they'd been before and what their bodies had become. She knew all the things to say, the encouragement and reassurances, that it would be all right, that it would get better.

Staring at the wound, she forgot all of it.

"My gods," she said, head dropping, her throat convulsing, too horrified to keep looking.

"It'll heal. Give it time," he said quietly as he checked for signs of infection.

She knew from treating Lila that she would scar. Even if she tried to heal herself afterwards, organised all the matrices, there was a limited time frame for preventing scars, and something about nullium seemed to have a mild keloid effect on the tissue.

She drew several sharp breaths.

She was lucky to be alive. A few scars were nothing compared with the injuries others in the Resistance would carry for life. She still had all her limbs, both eyes and ears. Even all her teeth.

She was very lucky by any metric. What did a scar matter? It would be fine.

She could feel Kaine watching her and forced herself to speak. "I think your scars are prettier than mine," she finally said.

"I have a better healer."

IT TOOK THREE WEEKS JUST for the nullium in Helena's blood to reduce enough that Kaine could use resonance to monitor her healing, although actual transmutation was still far off.

Her own resonance was barely a hum in her veins.

Whenever Kaine was absent, Davies stayed with her. Helena's head was finally clear enough to notice more of her surroundings.

The room was sterile. Almost bare. There was a bed, a towering wardrobe, a desk, and a chair. Falcon Matias had more indulgent quarters, and he was supposed to be an ascetic.

When she teased Kaine about it, he grimaced. "This is my room."

Helena fell silent, looking around again, abashed. "Oh. I thought that a country house would have bigger rooms."

He nodded. "There are larger ones. I moved in here because it was closer to my mother's room, then never left."

"I'm sorry I brought you back," she said.

He shook his head. "You didn't. I come back to check on the servants."

She hesitated but then asked, "Are they all dead?"

He nodded.

"Why did you—?"

He looked away, his throat dipping as he rubbed his hands together. "It was just after. I don't remember everything. I could feel them screaming inside me. I found their bodies piled up in a corner like discarded rags. They were still warm. I'd never—I didn't even realise what I was doing. I was trying to put them back."

"So they're—them?"

He shook his head. "I don't know what they are. I like to think I was able to put a part of them back, that it's why it got easier after that, but it's more likely that they act like themselves because I want them to. I just—can't seem to let go."

When Helena was finally able to have a pillow, Davies would prop up books for her to read during the hours when Kaine was absent. She was curious about the kind of library that existed at Spirefell, but Davies unfortunately did not seem to be literate, at least not anymore. The books Helena received were largely at random. One day, she received an encyclopaedia of butterfly species, the next a florilegium of Cetus's earliest writings.

Because "Cetus" had written thousands of alchemical texts and letters, dated across centuries, excerpts were often assembled into various collections by scholars based on which parts of his work and history they happened to consider legitimate. Depending on the florilegium's edition, Cetus was born in ten different countries. Sometimes he was a king, other times a priest; some letters even claimed he'd worked with Orion himself.

In the florilegum Helena received, Cetus was very taken by an ancient Khemish cult, which claimed that human resonance was the alchemisation of mankind. That alchemists were an ascendant form.

"Sounds like something alchemists would believe about themselves," Kaine said in the late evening while she was telling him about it. He was much more interested in Helena's lungs than in ancient cults.

Helena tried not to wince as the bandages came off. "Do the Undying have a religion?"

"The High Necromancer is our deity," Kaine said, tracing his resonance carefully along her ribs where several had cracked. "Our lives are in servitude to his infinite power."

"If he's that powerful, why doesn't he come out and win the war?"

He glanced up for a moment. "He's a god. You'll notice that making humans die for them is the gods' primary mode of operation. You'd think Sol could personally smite a few necromancers if he hates them so passionately, but somehow, it's always the Holdfasts coordinating those efforts. Makes one wonder if he really cares."

Ever since she'd told him about Orion and why the Holdfasts had become Principates, he seemed to think that if he just criticised the Eternal Flame enough, she'd give up on the Resistance.

Her sigh made her lungs rattle, and Kaine seemed to completely forget the conversation for several minutes.

"Since Holdfast started showing up in combat, Morrough has stayed far away from the front lines," he said at last.

"But if he's so afraid of Luc, why didn't he kill him when he was captured?"

Kaine shook his head. "I don't think he wants him dead. The orders have always been to take him alive. I used to think it was because Morrough feared usurpation from whoever made the killing blow, but now, after that capture, I think it's something else. Holdfast has been at the front lines for six years. Do you really think that if Morrough wanted him dead, he couldn't have found a way to kill him by now?"

It was four weeks after the bombing before Helena could get up without feeling like she'd shatter. Her resonance had feebly returned, and the bandages were off, but the wiring remained because her sternum was still worryingly delicate. Before lacing on a chest brace, she sat with a mirror, looking at the scar that ran down between her breasts.

It was far from pretty.

She'd always admired the way Lila wore her scars, her jokes about naming them; it was only now that she began to realise how difficult it was to be proud of them.

The visual evidence of the injury would never go away. In a moment of intimacy it would be all there was to see. Staring at it in the cold light of day, she couldn't help but think that someday Kaine might not want someone who had the war so overtly carved into them. Surely he'd want to be able to forget sometimes.

Now, with her, it would be impossible.

He was sorting the vials of medicine on the table, but she could feel him observing her from the corner of his eye.

"It'll fade," she said quickly.

Her face was burning. She dropped the mirror, putting her hand over the scar to hide it. It took the span of her entire hand.

"Once I'm better, I'll treat it every day so—it'll fade more," she said. She could feel a divot in the bone where it had refused to regenerate. She could attach titanium plating there to reinforce the bone, but given her repertoire, it might interfere with her work. Part of the reason titanium was so medically useful for alchemists was because the resonance for it was rare.

Her jaw trembled. "It won't look like this forever."

He set a vial down. His silver eyes were intent, his attention like a beam of light through a magnifying glass, suddenly focused solely on her. He stepped over and gently but firmly pulled her hand away.

She knew he'd seen the scar more than she had, and in far worse stages than this, but she hated having him look at it.

"Do you see my scars that way?" he finally said. "When you look at me, are they all you see?"

She flinched. "No."

"Well." He met her eyes. "I don't see you that way, either. You're mine." He let go of her wrist and lifted his hand, the fingertips tracing the scarring until it was covered by his palm, warm against her bare skin, then sliding up to curve around her neck. "You are. It doesn't matter what happens to you, you will *still* be mine."

HELENA SAW ONLY BITS OF the house. Spirefell. They took walks through the dim hallways as she tried to adapt to the way her chest ached when she moved. Breathing deeply made it feel like her sternum would snap. The house was an old, heavy style long abandoned in the city. Everywhere was detailed in dark wrought iron, even the floors run through with it. There was a melancholy beauty to it.

In the foyer, an intricate mosaic of the ouroboros dragon was inlaid in the marble floor. Meticulously rendered in both grandeur and savagery. She studied it from the landing above.

The Ferrons must have been so proud when the house was built. They must have thought they'd defeated god.

That night, she pulled Kaine into the bed. He'd slept in the chair beside it every night, her hand in his, ignoring her arguments that surely there were other beds in his house.

Now he finally gave in to her.

She curled against him, having missed the warmth and comfort of his body.

A few more days and she would go back. She'd convalesced there longer than she'd meant to, but the return trip would be hard, and she'd be no use at Headquarters if she wasn't recovered.

Everything would be different. The bombing had decimated the Resistance, wiped out their supplies. Everything they'd gained in the last year, gone, and now Morrough knew there was a spy. The Undying were looking for Kaine, trying to lure him out, but that would not stop Ilva or Crowther from coercing him into doing whatever they deemed necessary.

She had to go back.

She held him, her heart beating so hard it made her whole chest throb.

She pulled him closer, tilting her head back, and kissed him. His hand rose up to caress her cheek, but he began to draw away. She knew he was going to say she was still recovering. She was so sick of her convalescence. Of having so little time and never getting to spend it in the ways she wanted.

"It'll be fine if we're careful," she said, not letting go. "Please. I want you before I go."

He was careful. Slow and gentle. He touched her as though she were glass.

He pushed into her and she caught his face in her hands, pulling him close so that their noses and foreheads brushed, her fingers trembling.

I love you.

It was right at the tip of her tongue, but she hesitated, biting the words back.

There was a part of her that felt she might doom them if she said it. If there were important things left unspoken, tomorrow would come.

She kissed him instead.

I love you. She told him in the way she held him close; in the way her mouth met his; in how her hands trailed across his skin, mapping him, memorising every detail of what it was to be with him, his scars under her fingers.

I love you.

I love you.

She told him in the way she let go of herself and held on to him instead. With every beat of her heart. *I love you. I will always love you. I will always take care of you.*

It was dusk when she left. She stepped outside for the first time. Spirefell was a sprawling house which curved in, connecting with the other buildings to form a large courtyard with an overgrown garden in the centre.

Amaris was there, waiting restlessly. Her wings fanned out and fluttering.

Kaine lifted Helena carefully, the chest brace absorbing the pressure of her weight. As he swung up behind her, she looked towards the house. In the summer gloaming, it looked almost like an immense slumbering dragon itself, curling inwards, the spires like spines. It was covered in vining roses which crept all the way up the front, nearly covering it.

Davies and an old male servant, possibly a butler, stood at the top of the wide flight of stone steps, watching.

When Amaris launched herself into the air, it was like being punched in the ribs. Helena doubled over, gasping from pain, and she felt Kaine tense and nearly turn Amaris back.

She gripped his leg. "I'm all right."

They were airborne for longer than Helena had ever been before.

Amaris flew towards the mountains, trying to beat the moonrise. It was close enough to the Abeyance that Lumithia was a crescent, not too bright as she rose. They landed on the top of a building dangerously close to Headquarters. When Helena looked south, she saw why.

A wall had been erected, marking off Resistance territory. It was more than halfway up the island. Beyond, she could see the gash bisecting the city where the bomb had gone off, the buildings fallen. The centre of the island was cratered.

"We lost that much?"

"No, but you don't have the forces to hold more," Kaine said grimly, swinging down and helping her carefully off Amaris's back.

She was nauseated with pain, fighting hard to breathe as she squeezed Kaine's hand, but she couldn't bring herself to say goodbye. She had a growing fear of anything final. She could feel it all coming to an end.

"Be careful," was all she said.

"Helena, please—" His voice broke, stopping her in her tracks.

She turned back, and he gripped her shoulders.

She knew what he wanted to ask her, could see it in his eyes. *Run away and don't come back.*

But he knew she wouldn't. He swallowed, not meeting her eyes. "Don't get hurt again," he said instead. "Don't—"

She rose up on her toes and cut him off with a kiss.

"Be careful," she whispered. "Don't die."

When Helena appeared at the gates in boys' clothes, struggling to breathe, her reception was one of far more suspicion than joy. She was placed in a holding cell for an hour before Crowther appeared to have her let out.

"You sure?" the guard said to him. "She's been listed among the dead for almost a month."

"Yes, she was found by one of the splinter factions," Crowther said. "I knew they'd send her back eventually. Let her out."

Helena didn't know if the splinter factions of Resistance fighters existed at all, or if they were an invention to cover up all of Crowther's illicit activities. A great deal of Kaine's intelligence and activities were attributed to these alleged groups.

Crowther looked as if he had not slept in weeks. His face was haggard, his eyes bloodshot, and he appeared mostly angry about having to go out of his way to get Helena released.

Helena wanted to know what had happened while she'd been gone, but before the door of the holding cell was unlocked, he was already walking away.

"Go to the hospital. The matron's on shift. I'll deal with you tomorrow," he said over his shoulder.

Matron Pace wept at the sight of her. "You're alive! I should have gone. When I heard they sent you—I—"

"I'm glad you didn't," Helena said. She was exhausted from the flight and journey back. There was a grinding pain in her chest. She pressed her hand gingerly against her sternum, trying to relieve the pressure.

Pace ushered her into a space enclosed by curtains. "How did you survive?"

Helena stuck with the vagaries of Crowther's excuse. "I don't really remember. We were in the hospital and there was another explosion. When I woke, I'm not sure where I was. I'd had an operation, and I was mostly left to recover."

"Let me see."

If she were Pace, she'd be the same, so she allowed her clothes to be removed and the chest brace carefully unfastened to reveal the scarring down her chest.

"Oh." Pace's hand trembled, but then she inspected it more carefully. "This is . . . good work."

She'd clearly expected some kind of back-alley surgery utilising twine and kitchen knives. "Whoever their surgeon is, we should try to bring them in."

"I never saw who it was," Helena said. "I'm getting better, but my resonance is still unstable."

Pace attempted a smile, but it was more grimace. "Fortunately, chelator is one of the few things we still have in sufficient supply."

“How bad are things?” Helena asked.

Pace did not stop moving as she continued to examine Helena and began prepping her arm for an intravenous drip. “I only hear things secondhand.”

“How bad are people saying it is?”

Pace shook her head. “Of our remaining combatants, more than a third are still showing signs of the nullium poisoning. The wind’s shifted, so we’re spared most of the dust now, but even the parts of the island that are still intact are dangerous. At least until there’s rain.”

“I heard that Althorne died.”

“And Ilva.”

“What?” Helena stared at Pace in shock.

“A little more than a week ago. Her heart failed from the stress. Luc is inconsolable. You should go see Lila tomorrow. She was devastated when she learned you were listed among the dead.”

No mention of Luc’s reaction to Helena’s presumed death. Her throat tightened.

“How is she?”

“Progressing. Everything is quite healthy.”

THE BOMBING HAD DAMAGED THE island’s structural foundation and flood infrastructure, and it was impossible to repair due to the risk of nullium exposure. The Resistance had also lost almost all their prisoners because the building had collapsed, including Crowther’s, whom he’d moved to keep from Ivy’s grasp. They were all presumed dead, but it was impossible to verify much of anything within the blast zone.

Even the smuggled aid received from Novis was now difficult to obtain, and the scale of injuries too great to let patients evacuate to Novis. Their monarchical neighbour was beginning to signal a dwindling enthusiasm for both providing resources and absorbing Paladia’s injured.

The war had gone from teetering in the balance to a Resistance free fall. Without Althorne or Ilva, the Council was reduced to three: Matias and Crowther, who had almost entirely opposing views, and Luc, who distrusted both of them.

Crowther had always operated from the shadows, allowing Ilva to take the lead with his tacit support. Now he was alone, seeming to shrink and writhe under the glaring scrutiny of Luc, like a spider without its web, fumbling about on overlong legs.

There was a part of Helena that wanted to leave him to his fate, but she knew that the more powerless Crowther felt, the greater his danger to Kaine.

She sat, watching him move around his office, pausing at various maps and diagrams now riddled with black slashes of ink.

"How much communication have you been in—with Ferron?" she asked, exhausted from the journey from hospital to Tower.

"None, except that you were alive and would be returned once you were out of danger. Why?"

Helena drew a labouring breath. "I think I've discovered something. Ever since Wagner—I was studying the array, thinking about the different kinds of resonance energy to understand the process Morrough uses."

A wary look entered Crowther's eyes.

"You know, normally arrays are elemental or celestial, five or eight axis points. But Luc's pyromancy uses seven, and Wagner drew nine for the ritual. Kaine confirmed it was nine, so I was trying to think differently about the energy. When I'd try to envision how it would work, I kept thinking about a feeling I have in the hospital sometimes—"

"Marino, get to the point."

"When a patient dies, there's an inverted form of the energy that Morrough utilises to make the Undying. The vitality changes, and there's this moment as it dissipates when I feel it."

"And . . ."

"Before the bombing, I figured out a way to channel it and trap it inside obsidian. It didn't seem to do anything, but when I was at the field hospital, I cut one of the necrothralls with it, and it collapsed—as if the reanimation had been severed."

Crowther looked over sharply. "Are you sure?"

She shifted and grimaced as pain fractalled like lightning through her chest. "Well, I was injured, but I'm pretty sure. I've replayed it again and again. We should test it." She swallowed hard. "I have a few more pieces, and once my resonance is stable again, I can make more."

"Bring them, I'll see who I can pass the idea off to." He waved her away in dismissal.

Helena didn't move. It wasn't that she'd expected to be credited; she just had no intention of letting Crowther casually exploit her anymore.

"You must be very busy now," she said.

"Indeed. I am."

"I'll help you, but I want something in return."

Crowther's eyebrows rose. "And what is that, pray tell?"

"I want to know and approve every order you're giving Kaine."

Crowther's bloodshot eyes flashed dangerously.

Helena didn't blink. "I'm offering you a deal. What you do is illicit, and you have no allies on the Council to cover it up anymore. You need someone. I'm offering to be your shadow. I'll provide you with what you need, same way you did for Ilva. But Kaine is my condition."

His expression grew scathing. "You're overestimating your value, Marino."

Helena's mouth twisted in a bitter smile. "I'm not, though, am I? You said it yourself: I am an exceptional asset. Why else would you and Ilva spend so much time manipulating me? Always been so quick to take advantage of what I can do while treating it like it's of no use to anyone. By all means, replace me if you can."

Crowther's fingers curled into a fist, eyes narrowing, but he said nothing.

Her heart rammed against the damaged bone. "You have overutilised Kaine. If I were a lower-calibre healer, you would have killed him a dozen times over in the last several months. I have told you this, but you ignored it because you know I'll do whatever it takes to save him."

Her face contorted with anger. "But the fact that he will do anything you ask doesn't mean you can keep demanding it. I have done the unconscionable for the Eternal Flame, and I have let him suffer for it because what other choice do we have? But now everything we achieved, that he paid for, is gone. We have nothing to show for it. I won't let you keep forcing him to pay the price while you stall for time."

Crowther was silent for a moment. "A trade, then? Is that what you're proposing? Yourself—your cooperation—in exchange for Ferron's safety?"

Helena gave a tight nod. If Kaine had any idea what she'd come back to do, he probably would have ripped out his own talisman before letting her return. Clearly she was learning; she was not so easy to read anymore.

There was a pause, then Crowther laughed.

"What an odd turn of events." He stood, still chuckling. "Very well. Follow my orders, and he will stay alive. I'm not Ilva; I have no interest in seeing Ferron prematurely dead for the sake of vengeance. Why begrudge a weapon its uses? Even if that weapon is an abomination."

He walked around his desk, a ghastly smile on his face. "You know, I had a nearly identical version of this conversation with Ferron earlier this year."

Helena refused to react, meeting his eyes.

"So long as you make yourself useful to me, I'll let you approve Ferron's assignations. But if you ever disobey me, or cross me, I will—"

"Yes, I know what you'll do," Helena said.

IT TOOK A WEEK BEFORE Helena's resonance was stable again. During that time, she functioned as a test subject for Shiseo as they developed a tablet form for the chelators, to reduce the overcrowding and demand on saline.

In that same week, a weapons specialist gave an obsidian spear to an ambitious young man hoping to join Luc's unit. Even before he returned, the rumours reached Headquarters about a miraculously effective weapon.

The weapons specialist was evasive about his methods, although he was obliged to admit that Crowther was the one who'd given him the obsidian.

Everyone leapt to the conclusion that the properties of the obsidian came from pyromancy; that the obsidian must be infused with holy, cleansing fire.

The new weapon secured Crowther's place and influence not only on the Council but over the Eternal Flame. Once Helena was finally recovered enough to resume work, she was told that because of her injuries she would no longer work in the casualty ward but be assigned the less rigorous task of palliative care and last rites.

She wore a heavy black habit with myriad hidden pockets filled with obsidian glass and tended to the patients that couldn't be saved. She'd thought she'd seen the worst of the hospital, but she realised now that she was used to seeing those with some chance of survival.

Now she sat with men whose bodies seemed turned inside out, hearts exposed, faces lopped off, sometimes so little of them left that it seemed impossible that they were alive. They'd hold on to her, often mistaking her for someone else as she tended them like a carrion bird.

As unprecedented a breakthrough as the obsidian was, it was impossible to keep up with the demand, especially in the hands of soldiers trained with steel. Though its edges were sharper than razors, the glass shattered easily, making the weapons unreliable.

The obsidian was effective not only on necrothralls but liches as well. When one soldier managed a blow through the chest, the lich died, all his necrothralls collapsing with him.

The talisman was brought back, and Helena examined it. There was no sense of energy. She compared it with others. When it was cut in half, powder as fine as dust poured out.

Kaine summoned her that night. Her ring burned twice, and she practically ran out of Headquarters. She stood on the rooftop, hand pressed against her chest, numbing the grinding pain as she waited.

"What happened today?" he asked as Amaris landed heavily on the roof. He didn't dismount, which meant the conversation would be short. She could feel every second they'd been separated, the weight of it.

"What do you mean?"

"We've all been recalled from combat. Effective immediately. The thralls and Aspirants will continue to fight, but the Undying have all been withdrawn from the front lines."

"Someone killed a lich with the obsidian," Helena said. "Do you think maybe he—the lich—died? That Morrough can't bring him back anymore?"

Kaine was silent for a few moments.

"Seems you've found a weapon to kill us," he finally said.

She couldn't read the emotion in his voice. All the exhilaration drained from her.

She'd spent so much time afraid of Kaine's immortality, knowing that his discovery or apprehension would be without means of escape; he could be tortured forever, without even the hope of death. Now it was very likely that he *could* die.

She had made this possible. She had not saved him; she had created a new way to lose him instead.

"Be careful," she said.

He was studying her. "Did they let you recover before they set you back to work?"

She managed a smile. "Yes. Moved me out of the casualty ward. My duties are less rigorous now."

He nodded. "Well, that's something."

There was a pause. She had so much she wanted to say, to tell him, but she knew he was already lingering too long.

"If the obsidian does what we think, the Eternal Flame will be a real threat to Morrough now. He's sure to respond accordingly," he finally said. "You should prepare for that."

She nodded wordlessly, and he relaxed on the reins, Amaris immediately moving to spring, the wind rushing around her wings.

"Don't die."

She must have said it too quietly, because he didn't answer.

CHAPTER 61

Julius 1787

When Helena had no rites to perform, Crowther still kept her busy.

Since she'd proven her usefulness with Mandl, he saw no reason not to continue utilising her to increase his influence and control in the Council. She refused to use her vivimancy for torture, experimenting with her animancy instead, trying to perfect the methods for extracting information. She could not afford to fail.

The Helena of two years ago would not recognise the person she was becoming.

Every line she'd once believed herself incapable of crossing, she passed over without hesitation now.

Sometimes, she pushed too far, until it felt as though she were crawling beneath a prisoner's skin, their consciousness and her own briefly occupying the same mind-space. They'd grow sick with fevers afterwards, as if suffering from some kind of poisoning, but it was effective, so she overlooked the side effects, believing them manageable until Crowther told her that two of her "subjects" had died.

She had never caused a death before. Not like that. She became very careful, even though Crowther considered it a waste of time and mercy. She found that brief, repeated sessions were safer than long ones, the fevers milder, as if tolerance could be developed. And once that happened, it was even easier for her to extract what she wanted.

"I think I might be able to heal Titus Bayard," she said late one night to Shiseo.

The Eternal Flame had selected a new general for the Council. They'd lost so many in the bombing, the line of succession had been convoluted. Hutchens had a good record, but he was too awed by Luc.

Shiseo paused, looking up from an obsidian knife he was making.

Helena drew a deep breath. "When General Bayard was injured, I didn't understand what needed to be done—I didn't realise that an injury like his wasn't the same as other wounds. I had an idea earlier this year, but when I tried to test it, Titus reacted badly. Still." She looked down. "With my work lately, I realised the trick is working in increments and building a tolerance. Once I do that, I think it could work."

Shiseo tilted his head. "How?"

She wet her lips. "There are paths the mind follows, thoughts and memories. When I healed Titus, I didn't know, and I trapped him. It might be too late, but if I could get in, maybe I could make a way back out for him." She swallowed awkwardly. "I do something like that to myself sometimes. Use my resonance to alter how I think, where my mind goes."

Shiseo considered for a minute. "It sounds complicated."

She looked down. "I think I'm going to try at least."

Crowther showed callous interest. "If you wish. If you kill Bayard, it will spare us a mouth to feed."

She swallowed hard. "I'm trying to be helpful."

His lip curled. "When I want something, Marino, I'll tell you."

They'd just received word that Kaine had been dispatched to Hevgoss on a diplomatic mission without warning. He hadn't even had time to tell her, he'd just sent an encoded message on one of the radio channels, and then he was gone. No goodbye.

The only thing going well was Lila's pregnancy. Lila was bored but healthy, healthier than Helena had seen her in years. The pregnancy showed no risk of miscarriage.

"Are you all right?" Lila asked. Helena had her hand on Lila's stomach, her eyes closed, trying to separate Lila's louder heartbeat from the baby's in an attempt to tell if it felt healthy.

Foetal heartbeats were much faster, but it was confusing to sense two people simultaneously.

Helena opened her eyes, dry and burning from exhaustion.

"I'm fine," she said, though she felt as if she were bleeding to death inside. She'd seen so little of Kaine, and now he was gone and she didn't know when he'd return. Her days were spent waiting for people to die, no longer even trying to save them.

Lila looked sceptical. "You don't look fine. You don't look like you sleep at all. Pace said you were badly injured. Are you recovered? You know better than anyone how important full recovery is."

Helena shook her head. "It's not that. My shifts are longer now but they're not hard. I need to go, I have—more work."

Lila spoke as she started to stand. "You don't say it, but you think I'm selfish, don't you?"

Helena sighed, staring down at her hands. "You've been through a lot; I don't blame you for wanting something. I just don't understand why you want this right now. You should at least go to Novis where you'll be safe." She shrugged. "Maybe having the Principate's heir would be enough to convince them to send some medical supplies."

Lila had thus far refused to "come out of quarantine," and was still pretending to be contagious with bog cough.

"I want to wait a little longer," Lila said. "Just to be sure."

Rhea and Titus were waiting in one of the private rooms. Helena had written to Rhea, telling her that there was a possible treatment opportunity that she wanted to discuss.

"What would it entail exactly?" Rhea asked, gripping Titus by the arm to keep him from wandering.

"It would be a series of procedures," Helena said, rubbing her hands against her black habit, trying to get her palms dry. "It's similar to what I tried earlier this year, but I know how to control the reaction now. If we worked slowly, with short procedures, followed by recovery periods, I think Titus will adapt to the process. And then I can attempt to heal him without causing the reaction he had last time."

Rhea squeezed Titus's hand, leaning towards Helena, her eyes bright. "So you've done this before?" Her voice trembled with eagerness.

Helena cleared her throat, wanting to temper expectations. "Not this exactly. But a related procedure. It's not without risk, though. Are you familiar with mithridatism?"

Rhea shook her head.

Helena drew a deep breath. "It's a method of developing immunity to poison through low dosage. The process of going deep enough to heal Titus will have—similarities; he'll have a sort of immune response to my resonance, in the form of brain fevers. We'll have to monitor them, keep them under control. If they're too high, we'll have to take longer breaks. The goal will be building up his tolerance for my resonance in the delicate parts of the brain."

That was all mostly true, with only a few details omitted.

Rhea nodded. "Yes—yes—whatever you—"

The door opened before she could finish speaking and Luc entered, followed by Sebastian.

"Rhea, what are you doing?" Luc asked, his voice breathless.

Rhea looked startled by the intrusion. "Helena's found a way to heal Titus."

Luc looked at Helena, his eyes hard, bright, and feverish. "You can't be serious."

Helena started to answer, but it wasn't a question and it wasn't directed at her. He'd turned back to Rhea.

"You're going to trust her after what she did to Soren?"

Helena flinched, her mind nearly pitching itself into that clawing wound inside her. She swallowed hard. "Luc, Soren died. I'm sorry I couldn't save him, but this procedure for Titus could work. Think of how valuable it would be to get him back."

Luc looked back at her again, a look of disgust in his eyes. "That's what this is about to you? Value?" He looked at Titus, who'd grown restless from the tension in the room. "You look at what you did to him, and see a wasted military asset?"

"What? No. That's not what I meant."

He stared at her again, his eyes blistering as sunburn. "You lay as much as a finger on him, and I'll—"

"She won't," Rhea said, breaking in. "Thank you, Helena—Healer Marino, I appreciate the offer, but I think we'll pass."

Luc gave a sharp nod and then turned on his heel, walking out without a backwards glance. Sebastian wavered, looking at Rhea and Titus, his expression conflicted before he turned, following Luc. When they were gone, Rhea's face crumpled, and she gave an audible gasp before pressing her face in her hands.

Helena could find no words. She sat numb with shock as Rhea stood, not looking at Helena as she led Titus out.

Once she was alone, Helena pulled her gloves on and headed for the Alchemy Tower. When the lift opened, she was surprised when Sebastian stepped out alone, a weary expression on his face. He paused, resting a hand on her shoulder. "It was good of you to try."

Helena couldn't quite bring herself to look at him. She stared at his chest, at the suncrest on his armour.

"Why is he doing this?" she asked. "Everyone understands. Even if they think it was wrong, they understand. He won't even try."

Sebastian sighed. "You know why."

She wasn't sure that she did, but she nodded and stepped into the lift. There were three guards stationed outside Luc's door, and they shook their heads when she approached.

She went to her own room and climbed out the window, walking carefully up and around the low slope. Luc's hair gleamed golden in the setting sun. He was sitting hunched on his heels, twirling something in his fingers. He brought it up to his mouth, flames sparking in his fingertips as he inhaled.

His whole body seemed to come loose, and he sagged in on himself.

Watching, she was reminded of how soft his face used to be, the brightness of it. Now the war had chewed him down to the bone. He sat there, out of armour, so shrivelled he reminded her of an insect exoskeleton, like the shed dragonfly nymphs that clung to the water reeds. He was hollowed out.

Smoke curled from his lips as he slowly exhaled.

He was smoking opium.

She stared in horror at how casually he did so. As though it were an old habit.

He pulled the pipe from his mouth, catching sight of her. His expression hardened, growing more alert. "Go away."

"No," she said, and came closer.

He spun the pipe in his fingers again, his jaw rippling with anger. If he hit her again, she'd probably fall from the Tower and die.

She stood only a few steps away. "I couldn't save him. Even if I'd killed myself trying, it wouldn't have been enough. What is it you wish I'd done instead?"

Rather than answer, he shook like an autumn leaf on the verge of falling loose. He seemed to be trying to speak, but at the same time his hand was bringing the pipe back to his lips, fingers sparking a feeble flame. He inhaled so long that when he stopped, the pipe nearly tumbled from his fingers.

She feared he'd fall, and knelt to catch him, but he looked up, meeting her eyes, and he—he didn't look angry anymore, he just looked exhausted.

"What happened to us, Hel?"

She stared at him, and her pathetic, starved heart leapt for a moment before she realised the obvious. This wasn't Luc; this was the opium talking.

"A war." She looked away from him to the ruined city before them. A view which had once been so beautiful.

"You used to believe in me," he said, his voice faraway. "What did I do that made you stop?"

"I still believe in you, Luc," she said. "But we have to win this war. We can't make choices because we want a certain story to tell later. There's too much at stake."

"No," he said. "This is how we win. This is how we've always won. My father, and grandfather, all the Principates going all the way back to Orion. They won by trusting that good would triumph over evil, and I will do the same."

She looked at him in despair.

His index finger flicked against his thumb, ignition rings sparking, and again fire filled his palm, running along his fingers.

He cradled the flames like a kitten before his fingers closed around it, leaving only a tongue as he tucked the opium pipe between his lips and brought the flame close to the bowl again.

Her hand clenched into a fist, fighting a wince as she listened to him inhaling.

"What if it's not that simple, though?" she said. "Everyone who wins says they were good, but they're the ones who tell the story. They get to choose how we all remember it. *What if it's never that simple?*"

He shook his head. "Orion became sun-blessed because he refused to break his faith."

Helena exhaled, burying her face in her hands.

She heard his rings spark, and the pipe hissed as the opium vaporised.

"Luc—please, let me help you." She tried to reach towards him.

He flinched away, rage suddenly flashing across his face. "Don't—touch me."

He was teetering dangerously close to that immense fall, as if the Abyss still called to him. She didn't know how to draw him back anymore, what to say that he'd still hear.

"Do you remember what I promised you, Luc, that night you came out here?" she asked, her voice pleading.

He gave no response. His gaze had settled back into a dim stupor, the sunset limning his gaunt features as though gilding him.

"I promised I'd do anything for you." She curled her fingers into a fist. "Maybe you didn't realise how far I was willing to go."

"Don't say that," he said, suddenly alert again. "Don't make it all my fault. I thought you could heal him."

She closed her eyes. "Sometimes people die. You can't save everyone. Neither of us can. Please let me try to heal Titus."

"I can't." He stood, stumbled down onto the balcony of his room, and disappeared.

IT HAD BEEN OVER TWO weeks with no word when Helena's ring finally burned again.

She ran out of Headquarters without a backwards glance.

When she reached the rooftop and saw Kaine already there, standing beside Amaris, her knees nearly gave out. He was in uniform, clean and polished, wearing a row of medals as if he'd just come from a ceremony.

"You're back." It was all she could manage to say, already reaching out for him when he was still steps away.

He pulled her into his arms. "Have you been all right?"

She managed a nod but then her head dropped against his chest, and she was so tired, her eyes closed, listening to his heart, legs threatening to give out. He'd come back. She couldn't ask for more than that, but it had felt so long. As if every minute of his absence had cut into her.

"What's wrong?" he finally asked.

Everything.

"Nothing," she said. "I think I forgot to breathe after you left."

He wrapped his arms around her shoulders again, but he was tense, his attention elsewhere. Dread seeped through her like blood in water.

She lifted her head. "What is it?"

He wasn't looking at her; he was staring towards the blazing light of the Alchemy Tower. "I'm sure you realised: My trip was a diplomatic mission. We went to establish a formal alliance with Hevgoss, proprietary alchemical research in exchange for their mercenary forces."

"We guessed it was that."

"The new Hevgotian ambassador is—partial to my company. Keeping him entertained is my primary responsibility for the moment. Does Crowther have any outstanding orders?"

She shook her head. "No. We've been waiting to see what happened. He'll want a report, but that's all for now."

His eyes narrowed. "There's nothing?" There was a tension in his voice.

"Not yet. You just got back."

Rather than look relieved, his eyes got that strained look that appeared when he was sure she was injured and he just didn't know; he drew back, looking her over. "What happened?"

She furrowed her eyebrows, shaking her head. "Nothing."

He didn't believe her, she could tell. Panic was creeping across his features. She wished she'd come up with some errand for him; he was clearly certain that something must have happened to her for him to be given any reprieve. She sighed and caught his hand.

"After Althorne and Ilva died, I told Crowther that you were being overutilised, and I made him agree not to put so much on you."

He scoffed. "And he just agreed to that?"

"No. I made a deal with him. Because of the obsidian and the Council being less stable, he's vulnerable, he needs someone, and I told him that could be me, but only if I got to approve your orders from now on."

Instead of looking relieved, he snatched his hand away from her.

"You did what?" He spat the question. "You thought *that* would help me? That is the last thing I want."

A stab of exhausted, furious hurt cut through her. "Why? Is protection exclusively your right? Am I supposed to sit around while you win the war for me? Is that how you see this?" She gestured furiously between them.

"That was the deal," he snapped.

"Well, I didn't agree to that. Besides, I'm not doing anything dangerous. I'm not even allowed to go outside anymore."

He stared at her, enraged.

"Kaine—don't be like this."

He didn't budge. The space between them was ice-cold, as though all their ghosts surrounded them. They were both drenched in the dead.

The war was an abyss that took everything and was never satisfied. There was always more required. Another life. An additional measure of blood. Be better. Smarter. More ruthless. Quicker. More cunning. Accept a second portion of pain.

It was never enough.

Helena had nothing left to sacrifice. Everything remaining would cost too much to lose. Yet she was expected to be docile and cooperative, a comforting possession, and she was not.

She swallowed bitterly. "What did you expect me to do?"

"I don't want you in this fucking war." The rage in his voice was raw. "All I do is worry about what will happen to you if I fail to meet all requirements. If you get captured, you have no idea what they'll—"

"I do know," she snapped, cutting him off. "What do you think I do with all *my* time? I heal the people the Undying don't manage to kill. Everyone—everyone from the lab near the East Port, I treated them—watched them die. They all died. I am so aware of the risks, I think sometimes that I will go mad from knowing them. Why do you think I fight so hard?"

Her voice splintered. She turned away, despair clawing through her. She'd told herself that it would all be better once he was back. That she'd breathe again.

But all she felt was renewed terror, the feeling that everything was crumbling, and she couldn't stop it until she was left living every second bracing herself, unable to enjoy even the moments they had.

"I'll tell Crowther you're back." Her voice was empty. "And let you know what he wants."

She wanted to vanish. She was so tired of everything, of begging him not to get caught, not to die, to come back to her. Of trying to convince herself that a promise meant anything in a war like this.

"Be careful," she said.

He caught her by the arm. "Wait. Don't go."

She shook her head. "Kaine—I'm so tired—I don't want to fight."

"We won't." He was looking at her more closely now. "Come with me. You're worked to death. They can spare you for a night. We won't fight."

She managed to nod. The flight was a dull haze; she barely felt the wind. She was half asleep when Amaris landed. Kaine carried her inside and laid her on the bed. She felt him pulling off her shoes, and then he sat on the edge of the mattress, his hand resting between her shoulders.

He was safe. He had come back.

She roused the instant his hand withdrew.

He paused. "I need to eat and wash."

She caught his hand, gripping it so tight her nails bit into his skin. "I was afraid you'd die. You said you couldn't leave without special arrangements, and you were gone so suddenly, I thought—you might not come back." Her voice was thick. "You're always in danger, and I can never ask you to stop."

He ran his thumb across her knuckles. "You know I would if I could. I'd run with you and never look back."

"I know—" Her voice broke. "Don't die, Kaine. You can't leave me behind."

He sank back down beside her, and didn't leave until she stopped crying and fell asleep.

When the bed dipped, she woke to find him on the far side of the mattress. His hair was damp and hung over his eyes. She shifted across the bed and into his arms, burying herself there, letting her eyes close as she traced her fingers across his skin. She would know him blind.

He caught her hand and rolled her under him.

He studied her, that ever-present grief visible in his eyes, until she lifted her head and kissed him.

His hand slid up to wrap around her throat, and his thumb nestled under her jaw. A gradual, deepening kiss. She laced her fingers through his silver-white hair.

She never thought she could know a person with such slow intimacy. She knew exactly how he would press his lips against the pulse-point of her throat, the way his body shifted when she was beneath him. The grip of his hands on her hips, his teeth grazing her inner thighs, and the heat of his tongue.

"Mine. You're mine," he said as he kissed her.

"Always."

CHAPTER 62

Augustus 1787

News of the Undying's alliance with Hevgoss was of no surprise.

Letters were dispatched to the surrounding countries, urging them to object, to pressure Hevgoss into withdrawing, but there was little response. Even Novis was slow to reply and tepid in their condemnation.

"Let's focus on the bright side: This alliance with Hevgoss is a clear sign that our obsidian offensive is having an effect," General Hutchens said with casual assurance to the assembled members of the Eternal Flame.

On paper, Hutchens had an excellent record—he'd been in command of the ports and only given them up after the bombing because the Resistance couldn't maintain control of them without leaving Headquarters vulnerable. Not only had Hutchens managed to extensively sabotage the ports prior to retreating, but he'd done it with almost no casualties. He was a good choice, but he was also a true believer in Luc and Sol and the Eternal Flame, and his confidence in their eventual victory was implicit.

Details like supplies and the humdrum labour of war tended to fall beneath his consideration. Sol would provide.

Crowther could not and did not trust him, and it was creating an ever-widening gap between the true circumstances of the war and how Hutchens and the rest of the Council understood them.

"What we need to do is increase our obsidian supply and hit them hard before the Hevgotian mercenaries arrive."

Helena wanted to throw up at the mere thought of producing more obsidian. Even if she could, only so many people died in circumstances in which she could be present.

"We lost more than half of our forces and territory the last time we were about to perform a similar offensive." With all the upheaval in the Council, Crowther was forced to speak for himself, and even when his comments were pertinent, he lacked the charisma to make anyone agree with him. "While I am optimistic about the effect of our obsidian, there is a risk that Hevgotian mercenaries means more nullium usage. Hevgoss has few alchemists; the battalions arriving will be from the prisons."

Hutchens shook his head. "I doubt we'll see more nullium. I don't think they can afford to blow up any more territory. The dust affected the West Island, too."

"We'll plan better this time," Luc said. He had a certain tone that he used in meetings now. It was deeper, more authoritative. In the past he'd speak tentatively unless riled. "Regardless of what happened in the past, we can't afford to lose more. The Undying have never wanted living soldiers before. This change in tactics is an undeniable sign that we're doing something right. Ask anyone who's been in combat lately—they've pulled all the Undying out, living and lich alike, it's all necrothralls and Aspirants. The obsidian's changed everything. Negotiating for an alliance is an admission they can't win on their own. I'm with Hutchens, I say we hit them hard. The Undying are trying to go to ground; we'll dig them out."

"Even if it were possible to win so decisively, there's still the risk of Hevgoss trying to sweep in and collect the spoils of war regardless of which side emerges victor," Crowther said. "This may be the time to negotiate with Novis. Reticent as they've been in recent months, I doubt the queen is pleased by the threat of Hevgoss obtaining Paladia's resources. With the right incentives, she may renew her support. Perhaps a high-profile diplomatic visit as a show of respect—"

"I'm not leaving Paladia," Luc said, cutting Crowther off with a look of overt disdain. "You think it would inspire confidence in our troops if they see me leave on a diplomatic mission amid rumours about reinforcements coming from Hevgoss?"

Crowther's eyebrows pinched together. "You would be the most effective negotiator. Your appearance in the Novis court would be a greater compliment than any other resources or representatives we could afford to send. Any proxy would—"

"It's out of the question. If you want to send someone to Novis, by all means. But I'm not leaving Paladia." There was furious vehemence in Luc's voice.

Helena had known that Crowther intended to make such a proposal. He'd even weighed the possibility of revealing Lila's pregnancy, trying to coerce Luc into taking the trip under the pretence of escorting her and his "heir" to safety. However, Lila was still adamant about concealing the pregnancy. To reveal it in the context of her fleeing to Novis would be a dangerous gamble.

In the end, it was Matias who went, along with a box of gold that Luc transmuted. It wasn't what anyone wanted, but as Helena watched Matias ceremonially depart, an old knot in her chest unravelled at seeing him gone.

He was barely across the border before the Resistance was readying for battle.

It was suicide. They didn't have the combatants or nearly enough resources for it. Scavenging groups went into the ruins, trying to recover what weapons and armour they could. They were strictly banned from bringing back any of the dead. Those who'd died in the fallout zone had to be left until a means of safe ceremonial disposal was possible.

Anyone who wanted to fight could fight, alchemist or not, adult or not, man or not. There was no time to train anyone. They didn't even have weapons for them. There were boys and girls practising with sticks, trying to make themselves slingshots. No armour because there was none in their sizes.

The sight made Helena sick.

They were battle fodder. They'd be slaughtered in minutes.

But they would do that rather than allow necromancy. This doomed assault was relying on a miracle, on the conviction that by risking everything, they would be rewarded. Glory and blessings and eternity to those who believed.

Just as Sol had blessed Orion.

But there was no Ilva now to create a miracle.

"I want to build a bomb," she said, entering Crowther's office in the middle of the night and finding him sitting there, wide awake. He was always awake. His already narrow face had grown skeletal. He looked eighty, but she knew he was not even fifty.

"I didn't know that explosives were anywhere within your field of expertise," he said with dry contempt.

She sat without invitation. Crowther sighed.

Helena had once thought that Kaine had tested the outermost limits of her capacity for internal conflict, but Crowther was a new realm entirely. She had never hated and needed someone so intensely.

He was the only means by which she could do anything meaningful, the only member of the Eternal Flame who listened to her at all. Yet he held her obedience at Kaine's throat like a knife.

The hunt for spies within the Undying had intensified. All their other informants had disappeared without a trace. The risk of using Kaine or even the information he sent was too great.

"I used to help Luc with his pyromancy fundamentals. I'm familiar with the technical processes of incendiary function. The rules apply with or without resonance," she said.

One of Crowther's eyebrows rose, and the fingers on his left hand fluttered, ignition rings brushing against each other.

"I've been thinking about it for a while . . ." Her throat was aching from nervousness. "We'll use the obsidian in the same way the Undying used the nullium bomb. We could use nullium, too."

"Wouldn't an explosion melt the obsidian?"

"No. Shiseo has some experience with pyrotechnics; they're used in Eastern celebrations. Between the two of us, there's a decent amount of technical knowledge. If we build it right, we can harness the explosive force but limit the heat. It won't be anything near the scale of their bombing, but we don't need it to be."

"You are remarkably confident for someone with nothing but a basic alchemy certification."

Helena's jaw tensed, but she pressed on. "We have a lot of scrap obsidian. Knapping an edge with obsidian leaves a lot of discarded shards and pieces that are either too thin or too small for use. Those are all I'll need, so it won't interfere with production."

She pulled out a folded stack of papers. "We'll need these components forged in the Athanor Furnace."

He glanced at the designs. "I can't make any promises. But . . ." He sighed. "I suppose it might be of use."

HELENA WAS BOTH DESPERATE AND terrified of what was to come. If the attack was a success, if the bomb could do enough to weaken Morrough, could Luc kill him?

If he did, what would happen to Kaine?

When she slept, she had endless nightmares of digging through Morrough's corpse in the darkness with her bare hands, arms coated in his blood, ripping out his bones, trying desperately to find the piece that held Kaine's life. In her dreams, Luc always approached, like a rising sun.

She would plead for time, try to explain herself, but Luc never heard. Every time she burned, too.

In the cold light of day, she knew it wouldn't be like that. She would be in Headquarters, in the hospital. She wouldn't know anything until it was too late.

Every day she wondered if she was working towards her own doom and Kaine's destruction.

After how poorly he'd reacted to Helena's mere involvement in the war effort, she didn't tell him about the bomb. It wasn't difficult to hide it; he was so busy with the ambassador, they scarcely had any time to do more than exchange urgent information.

It was only when she and Shiseo completed all the components that she went to the roof and called for him. She had to wait a long time. When Kaine arrived, he was dressed in formal attire, sharp and polished.

"I can't stay," he said. "What is it?"

"We have a new weapon," she said quickly. "Is there a time or place where a lot of the Undying will be in proximity? Somewhere you won't be. It could be planted up to two days in advance."

His expression hardened. "A bomb?"

She gave a tense nod.

"Obsidian?"

"And nullium, so you need to be well clear."

He nodded and looked at her pointedly. "I hope they're not building it at Headquarters."

She shook her head. "No. It's off-site."

He exhaled. "Well, the Resistance is taking this final assault seriously at least. The Hevgotian force will cross the western border within the week, but several militocrats and officials will arrive in a day. There's to be a welcome banquet for them the following evening. Most of the Undying will be in attendance; even Morrough may be there briefly."

She nodded. That would work. "Can you place it without suspicion? And then get away?"

His eyes softened. "No one pays attention to necrothralls the way they should. They assume anyone using them must be on their side. If I rip out the reanimation, I can take over someone else's and use them to make a delivery. It won't be easily traced back to me."

"And you won't be there? When it goes off." She was afraid that he was evading the question.

Standing there, the two of them looked worlds apart. He was clean and pristine, in a tailored uniform, wearing a row of intricate medals, while she stood ragged, in male-sized standard-issue clothes washed to threads.

"How far away do I need to be?"

"Far enough not to breathe it in. There will be micro-shards in the air. We don't know what effect they'll have. You should be far away."

"I'll run an errand around that time. The ambassador enjoys making himself inconvenient. I'm sure I can convince him to want something unreasonable and distant."

She nodded. "Make it a long errand. I'll bring it tomorrow evening."

"No." His voice cracked like a whip, and all the softness vanished. "Crowther's not using you to transport a bomb."

She shook her head. "It won't be activated until the components are joined, and there's a countdown. I'm not going to get blown up carrying it," she said. "You can't put it together on your own if you don't know how to join the pieces."

"I don't care. Tell Crowther to figure out another way." He'd turned bloodlessly pale, that inhuman gleaming rising beneath his skin.

"But if I don't come," she said, ready to resort to anything if he'd just cooperate, "that means I won't see you again until—until after."

He didn't waver. "Then I'll see you after. Send someone else."

Her breath caught in her lungs. "Kaine . . ."

He glared at her. "I found you after a bombing. I had to watch them cut you open, trying to get the shrapnel out. You nearly died so many times on the operating table, I lost count. If you'd been an inch closer to the blast, that shrapnel would have gone through your heart. You want me to set a bomb, I will do it, but you will not touch it. Do you understand?"

She swallowed bitterly, grateful that she hadn't told him any details that might have revealed her involvement. "Fine. If that's what you want."

She turned to go. There was so much she needed to do. Take inventory, finish the bomb, help prep the hospital. She'd been assigned to the casualty ward again.

Kaine pulled her to him. "Come back here in a few hours."

She shook her head. "Now's hardly the time."

He didn't seem to remember that he was the one who couldn't linger.

He wouldn't let go. She wished that all of this had begun sooner; there was so much time they'd missed.

"All right," she said finally, giving in. "But you have to leave now."

He let go slowly. "I'll call for you."

After reporting to Crowther, she headed to the off-site lab where she and Shiseo used their resonance in tandem to assemble the final components. They'd built the bomb to be as compact as possible, but it was still nearly the size of a child. It would need to be placed in the centre of a room.

Bombs themselves were not a new alchemical development, but they'd been banned for almost a hundred years after it was decided they were uncivilised. Although banning them had done nothing to stop their development; Hevgoss was famously partial to such technology, viewing it as an equaliser against alchemists.

With the right manipulation of the air and flames, Luc held firebombs in his fingertips. A great deal of his homework had involved arrays and technical studies, drilling all the various ways in which fire could be manipulated and weaponised. Helena had utilised much of it.

The trick had been designing something that would cause a powerful explosion without melting their obsidian.

Shiseo had taught her a technique for a combination alloy fusion utilising dual array transmutation. It was complicated and dangerous. Even with all the arrays stabilising their resonance, Helena burned several fingertips nearly to the bone.

"Are you all right?" Shiseo asked as she sat trying to quickly regenerate the tissue.

Her fingertips hurt so much, it was hard to even feel her resonance, but years of practice made it natural to soothe the damaged nerve endings and regenerate them. Later she'd fix the dermal layer so that it wouldn't be obvious to the eye.

"It's nothing," she finally managed to say, blinking hard and staring at her hands, at the lines that ran across her fingers and palm. Out of habit, she pressed her fingers against her sternum, feeling the faint dip in the bone. The scar had faded some, but the ache where the bone had split lingered. "Is it done?"

He set the two pieces on the worktable, and she eyed them wearily.

He looked at her. "We'll finish this tomorrow. Your hands need to recover, and you need rest."

She gave him a faint smile. "I will tonight."

SHE STAYED PREOCCUPIED UNTIL LATE into the night, rechecking the medical inventory. Her epinephrine injections were nearly out, but there was no record of who'd taken them. Helena left a brusque note. If Elain was going to run everything, she could at least enforce the rules.

She was rolling a mountain of sterilised bandages into spools when her ring burned.

Amaris barely landed; Kaine swept her off the roof and they were airborne. The instant they were inside, he had her pinned against the wall, his lips ravenous on hers.

She gripped him tightly. Her fingertips were still numb, but she hardly noticed.

His hands slid up until her face was cradled in them. His forehead pressed to hers, breath mingling a moment before he kissed her again, drawing her farther inside. Their every step hurried. They were always running out of time.

Someday, she promised herself, *someday I am going to love him in a moment that isn't stolen.*

"Are you all right?" he asked once they were inside, where it was lit enough that he could look at her.

He reached out, and she knew that if he touched her, he'd use his resonance and realise her hands had been recently injured, so she caught his hand in hers, curling his fingers closed and clasping it against her chest.

"Yes." She nodded. "Now I'm all right."

He stared at her, and she knew she looked tired, thin, and so sallow from being always indoors with little natural light. The bombing had broken most of the windows, and even the few that survived were boarded up and sealed in case the wind brought the nullium towards Headquarters again.

"I should have called you sooner." His thumb traced along her cheekbone.

She shook her head. "It wouldn't have been worth the risk. It's dangerous for you to fly so near like that. Someone could shoot you with obsidian." A tremor ran through her just saying it aloud. "We shouldn't be doing this. It's stupid to take this risk."

She was suddenly struggling to breathe. He pulled his hand free and then held her head in both his hands, as if trying to quiet her mind for her.

"We're safe here," he said.

For now. For this moment.

But not really. Not ever.

Still she nodded, trying to believe it, not wanting to poison what little time they had left. She rose up on her toes, kissing him, pulling his arms around her.

Don't let this be the last time.

She didn't close her eyes. She kept them open and watching him, trying to notice every detail. She wanted to commit everything to memory, the way he felt under her hands and against her skin, as if sufficient detail could make this secret thing real enough to endure; as if she could write it into the universe so deeply that even a war could not erase it.

Afterwards, he gathered her against his chest, chin resting on the top of her head as his fingers drew patterns across her skin.

I'm going to take care of you. I'm always going to take care of you.

He didn't say it audibly, but she could hear it in the shifting of the air, the way his jaw moved when he mouthed the words.

She'd hoped to sleep, to experience one last hour of peace, but she was too afraid. When she sat up, Kaine's quicksilver eyes were instantly guarded. She didn't say anything for a moment, holding his hand in hers, studying his face, this aspect of him that was hers alone.

She entwined their fingers, trying to find the right words.

"Kaine," she finally said, "there's a chance—we're hoping that this attack will be the end of the war. We don't—we aren't sure how much longer we're going to last if it isn't."

His hand twitched.

"If it isn't—" Her chest jerked, and she gave a tight, half-sobbed laugh. "—well, we'll just keep fighting, then. But if it is . . . I—I don't know what will happen to you. I'm sorry. I tried to find a way"—she looked down—"I couldn't figure out—"

"It's fine," he said.

She shook her head. "Maybe if Morrough's killed, your soul just goes back to you. We don't know that it won't. There's a chance. Or maybe the Stone would be enough to—"

She was grasping, and they both knew it.

"It could," she said insistently, squeezing his hand. "So, if that happens, if you're all right when it's over, you have to run. All right? Get away as fast as you can. Don't let yourself be captured."

His eyes narrowed. "Where will you be?"

Helena looked down, playing with the ring on his hand. It had been so long since she'd seen hers.

"You know me, I'll be in the hospital. There will be a lot of injuries, so I wouldn't be ready right away—so you just go, and I'll catch up."

He scoffed. "If I survive, I'm not going anywhere without you."

She pressed her fingers to his lips, hushing him. "No. You can't risk getting caught."

He pushed her fingers away from his mouth, but she wouldn't let him interrupt. She had thought about this in circles, and there was little chance that Crowther would let her slip away without paying for her necromancy. If she was lucky, she'd just be expelled from the Eternal Flame. It would be the quickest and quietest resolution, but even that might take weeks or months.

"Go south, towards the sea. When I can, I'll come, I'll look for you, and it'll be just like we said—we'll disappear."

His eyes narrowed into slits. "And how long do you expect I'd be waiting?"

Helena's eyes dropped. "I don't know. It might be—a little while."

"Why?"

"Because—there will be a lot of things that will happen once it's over. But I'm sure once it is, they'll rather I just disappear, so then I'll come look for you, all right? I think it would be good that way. For you. You might realise you want other things once you have real choices—"

His fingers curled around the back of her neck, pulling her close until their faces were nearly touching.

"You're mine," he said almost against her lips. "Mine. You swore it. Your Resistance sold you to me. I'm not going anywhere without you. And if anyone touches you, immortal or not, I will kill them."

He didn't wait for a reply; he kissed her as though his lips were a brand on hers.

SHISEO WAS THE ONLY OTHER choice for delivering the bomb. He and Helena coated the very exterior of it with a fine layer of mo'lian'shi which Shiseo had extracted from nullium dust. After that, it was coated in Helena's mirroring elixir. Shiseo had tinkered with the composition and made it workable on larger surfaces.

Once it was all assembled, it would be difficult to notice, and the exterior inertia would make it invisible to anyone searching by resonance.

As they finished, Helena slipped her ring off, studying it. The mirroring was rubbing off. If she was arrested, she'd be searched, and any metal removed. That would include Kaine's ring.

"Would mo'lian'shi interfere with an entanglement?" she asked.

Shiseo studied the half-visible ring. "If you left a small part exposed, you could probably still use it." He eyed her knowingly. "That would keep it hidden if someone searched you using resonance unless they were very thorough."

That was all she needed to know. Muttering an apology to Kaine for the burn he was about to get, she coated all but one section. Once it cooled, she dipped her ring into the mirroring elixir, refreshing the concealment, watching it vanish.

WHILE SHISEO WAS DELIVERING THE bomb, Helena went to check on Lila. If the hospital ended up inundated, it would be a while before she'd come again.

The bump between Lila's hips had grown undeniable, but Lila was almost manic with regret, questioning her decision for the first time. Her nails were all bitten to the quick. "I can't believe that the final battle is happening now," she said, watching the combatants as they milled below. "I should be out there."

"It's not as if you knew," Helena said, tiredly. It was too late for Lila to change her mind now.

"Do you think this'll be it?" Lila asked. "Are our chances good?"

"As good as they can be," Helena said.

Win or lose, all she felt was dread, but it had to end now. It could not go on.

"He's awake," Lila said, holding out her hand for Helena's. "Come feel. Right here."

Lila caught Helena's hand and pressed it on her stomach, just above her hip bone. There was a pause, then, without using resonance, Helena felt a strange flutter against her palm.

"Feel that?" Lila asked.

Helena nodded, letting her resonance sweep through Lila to the baby, finding the heartbeat quick as the flutter of a bird's wings.

There were no more kicks.

"He probably went to sleep," Lila said. Helena still didn't know where Lila got the conviction that the baby was a boy, but she'd named him Apollo and referred to him as Pol. "You should feel him at night—I think he does somersaults. Gets his feet all the way up to my ribs."

"I can't imagine where he gets his athletic troublemaking genes from," Helena said in a dry voice, pulling her hand away.

"He'll have all the fun we missed," Lila said, letting her shirt fall over her stomach. "You know, I think I'll be happy for him to be a peacetime baby. I bet there will be a lot of babies in the next few years. They'll all go to the Institute together like we did. D'you think you'll ever have children?"

Helena shook her head without a word.

"You might change your mind someday," Lila said coaxingly. "Just have to find the right sort for you. You'd be a good mum."

"I'm a healer; we don't do things like that," Helena said.

"But you only became a healer because of the war. No one's going to expect you to keep doing it once it's over."

For all of Lila's exceptionalism and understanding of the perilous role *she* occupied, somehow she didn't seem to realise that most people never had the chances she did, whether by birth or by ability. Lila was a once-in-a-lifetime talent, with the beauty to match, and a name with centuries of legacy behind it. The rules did not bend like that for anyone else. Especially not Helena.

She changed the subject.

"I really think you should tell Luc. He should know before this battle starts. That way if things go wrong, the Eternal Flame will know the importance of getting you to safety."

Lila was silent for a surprisingly long moment.

"He already knows," she finally said quietly, averting her eyes from Helena's.

"What?"

"He broke in, through the window, when I was first placed in quarantine. He was so worried that I told him the truth. He said if people knew, they'd make me leave. Send me to Novis. He needed me, so I kept saying I wanted it to be a secret. He made me promise not to tell anyone."

Helena was struck dumb for several moments. "He's known this whole time? That you're pregnant, and I'm the one caring for you?"

If Luc knew and allowed this, why was he so opposed to her healing Titus? It made no sense.

Lila flushed. "Sorry. I wanted to tell you, but I didn't want him upset. He's still not doing very well."

"I need to go," Helena said, standing up unsteadily.

Lila tried to stop her, blocking the door. "No. You're angry, I can tell. Please, let me explain."

Helena stared at her. Lila looked so much like her father, cast in a feminine mould—the height, the pale hair and blue eyes, even a scar on one side of the head.

"I don't need an explanation from you," Helena said. "I need to talk to him."

She searched everywhere for Luc. Everyone she asked gave a different location: He was in a meeting, he was asleep, he was in the commons, the mess. Everywhere she went, he was always a few minutes ahead of her.

Finally, she tracked him down in the hospital, but he was in a private room, under guard, no admittance.

Helena stood waiting, and finally Elain emerged carrying a tray with several syringes and empty vials on it, and a tense furrow between her eyes.

"I need to see Luc," Helena said.

Elain started at the sight of her. "He's resting."

Helena looked down at the tray, and Elain tried to turn it from her view.

"Why are you giving him all that?" Helena asked, eyes flicking from vial to vial. "These shouldn't be combined, and he's too young to need half of them. And these—" She snatched up a syringe with her writing on it. "—these are for dire emergencies only. If you overuse them, you're going to give him heart failure. Who approved this?"

Elain's eyes flashed indignantly. "I'm his healer."

CHAPTER 63

Augustus 1787

Time slowed to a crawl the next day as Headquarters was emptied, the combatants dispatched. There was no time or opportunity to speak to Luc before he was gone.

Helena and all the other healers and medical staff waited in a prepped hospital ward, waiting for news, for injuries. The hands on the clock indicated that the bomb should have gone off, but there was no sound or shudder of an explosion.

No sign that anything had begun.

Of course, it was a smaller bomb, intended to be detonated inside an enclosed area. She wasn't likely to feel it, and the fighting would mostly be on the West Island.

Knowing that didn't make it easier to wait. After so many years, she could feel it all coming to an end and dreaded almost every possible outcome.

Perhaps it would end, and they would win and everything would be all right, but Kaine would vanish in the aftermath, and she wouldn't know if he was dead or alive, trapped under rubble, or had fled somewhere far away.

She would just have to look for him until she knew.

Every tick of the clock made her flinch. The orderlies, medics, and healers were talking among themselves, but Helena stood frozen, her ribs clamping around her lungs.

You made a mistake. You built the bomb wrong. Kaine was caught while planting it and he's being tortured, and you don't even know. Everyone is going to die and it's all your fault.

Her fingertips and arms were beginning to prick, going numb.

The doors burst open. The room was so blurred, Helena couldn't make out who it was, but she heard shouting: There'd been an explosion on the West Island. The Resistance had attacked.

Helena stood swaying, trying to feel something, but she still felt empty.

Heat flared around her finger. Just once.

She looked down at her hand, at the ring that was barely there, and her knees gave out.

She dropped straight to the floor and burst into tears, pain splintering across her chest.

There were voices around her, but she couldn't follow them. All she could do was try to breathe, but her lungs refused to open.

A warm hand wrapped around her elbow, pulling her to her feet.

"Let's sit a minute," Pace said as she wrapped an arm around Helena's shoulders and escorted her to her little office in the storeroom. "Elain can call when someone's brought in."

She pushed Helena down into a chair.

Helena let herself be herded along, sitting, eyes closed. She pressed her fingers against her chest, feeling the scarring through her clothes, easing her heart rate back down.

When she finally opened her eyes again, she found Pace watching her.

"What's happening?" Pace asked.

Helena shook her head. "Nothing. I'm just tired."

Pace's features were all pinched together. "You know, they say there's a point when the Toll becomes exponential."

Helena shrugged. "They say a lot of things about healers. I don't know that even half of them are true."

"Perhaps, but I doubt anyone has ever healed to the extent and magnitude that you have. You have not been well for a long time. You think I couldn't guess why you started supplementing your treatments with all those tonics and injections? Your trainees barely know how to heal without them, but you worked solo for years. For all you know, you could be risking years of your life every time—"

"I don't think it's that . . ." She reached up absently for the chain, but it was long gone.

Pace shook her head, worry etched into her broad face. "Is it the nullium? We're seeing so many side effects from the bombing, and you had some of the worst exposure of any of the survivors. That's not even considering your injury at the time."

Before Helena could shake her head, Pace continued. "We're going in blind on all this, without any idea of the potential long-term effects. I suspect Luc's brain fevers are a symptom of residual nullium in the brain."

Helena looked at her in confusion. "Luc has brain fevers?"

Pace sighed. "You saw what he was like just after the rescue."

Helena nodded. "I thought they'd stopped."

"He tries to keep them hidden, doesn't want to cause worry, but sometimes they're so severe that he still grows delirious, claws at his skin, won't let any men in the room, even Sebastian, screaming things like, 'Get him out.' Elain has to sedate him until they pass or he'll injure himself."

Helena felt as if she had been staring at a puzzle from the wrong angle for months; now she could suddenly see it clearly.

"He says, 'Get him out'?" Her voice seemed to come from far away.

"Usually."

Helena's head throbbed. "Can you—describe these fevers for me?"

Pace's eyebrows furrowed. "Well, I've only examined him a few times. Elain manages him now; he's more cooperative with her. She believes it's caused by recurring brain inflammation. The symptoms are delirium, with a rapid heartbeat. We thought it was related to his organ damage, but they appear to be separate conditions."

"What's the opium for?" Helena asked.

Pace sighed and looked away. "His fevers seem prompted by a condition of the nerves. Calming him keeps them from growing so severe.

We've tried everything, but inhaling the vapours is the only thing that prevents them. If he becomes fully delirious, it can take days before he recovers, and he requires extensive treatment to get back on his feet."

"That's just—masking the symptoms. That's not fixing anything. You should have told me this was going on."

This couldn't be.

"Helena," Matron Pace said firmly, "he's been examined over and over by myself and Maier and Elain. There's no cause. It's all in his mind. Managing the symptoms is all we can do. He was specific that he didn't want you involved. Every time your name was even brought up, he worsened."

"And you never questioned that?"

Pace looked at her pityingly. "It's not as if you have any particular experience with brain fevers."

Helena shook her head. Pace was wrong. She had a great deal of recent experience with brain fevers. She knew exactly what caused them. Animancy.

But that wasn't the only time she'd encountered brain fevers. She'd seen them before that. The exact symptoms Pace had described. The impossibly hot fevers, as if the mind were trying to burn something out from inside it. The self-mutilation, screaming, "Get him out."

She'd seen all of it just before her father had been murdered.

At the field hospital.

But Luc had no talisman like those liches had. He had been checked and rechecked. It would have been found.

. . . unless the talisman had not been coated in lumithium, which would make it undetectable.

Morrough had captured Luc but hadn't killed him, and they'd thought it was only because they'd arrived in time.

But maybe they'd been too late after all.

She jolted out of her seat. Pace reached out, trying to stay her, but Helena bolted from the room, running through the hospital and straight to the war room. There was no one there except a cadet, who looked up nervously and told her that she didn't have the clearance to be there.

She glared at him. "Do you know where Crowther is? It's urgent I speak to him."

He shook his head, clearly sullen about guarding an empty room. "No. They were looking for him earlier. Disappeared last night, it seems."

That made no sense.

It was as if she were standing in a trap laid with dominoes. She could feel them falling around her. Closing in.

"Do you know where Luc's battalion is?"

The boy rolled his eyes and drew himself up. "You don't have clearance to—"

Helena eyed the map on the table. There was a golden flag amid the sea of blue.

She turned and left before the cadet was done talking.

She ran to her lab, snatching up everything she could get her hands on. First, her new set of knives. Then a couple of obsidian knives Shiseo had been experimenting with. She ransacked her remaining healing supplies.

Shiseo entered with a box from the off-site lab as she was cramming a final vial into her overfilled satchel. He was probably the only person who would take a warning from her without asking for proof or an explanation.

"Get out of Headquarters," she said. "Take everything you can and go back to the off-site lab. I'll send word if it's safe to come back. I can't explain now, but something's about to go wrong."

She went to Crowther's office, but it was empty. Where was he? There was no time to search. She headed out.

She traversed the island on foot. She knew from flyovers which parts were still intact, and that she was headed in the right direction when the air began to smell of smoke and burning flesh.

Whenever she spotted Resistance units, she asked for updates. Reports were contradictory, but there were consistent stories of many necrothralls dropping, leaving whole districts with only a few bewildered Aspirants to defend them. They were making piles of the necrothralls and burning them to ensure they couldn't be recovered and reanimated.

With all the good news, Helena began to doubt herself. Was she paranoid? It was going so well. She refused to turn back, though; she had to find Luc.

A broad-shouldered commander that she vaguely recognised as part of Luc's battalion stepped out of a building.

"Marino?" He said her name doubtfully.

"I need to see Luc," she said, gripping an obsidian knife in her pocket so hard the handle bit into her skin.

"Well, he's not here, he's fighting," the man said.

She must seem insane. "I know, but it's urgent. I can work with the medics on-site until he comes back."

The commander looked confused but didn't object.

Healing at the front had none of the organisation used in the hospital. Most of her work was stopping blood loss by staunching and closing wounds, healing only the simple injuries. The priority was completing the most urgent interventions and then sending the patients on to Headquarters for full treatment.

The bombing was believed to be either an accident or an act of sabotage. No one even considered that the Resistance might have planted a bomb.

The miracles had begun, people were saying. The gods were on their side.

Victory Day, they were already calling it. They'd retake the whole city.

The injured combatants arriving slowed to a trickle because the battalion had pushed so far into the West Island, no one was being brought back.

The field commander was on the radio, wanting to know if they were supposed to relocate closer to the action. They'd had no instructions about whether to follow.

The current base of operations was in an old building on a mid-level of the city. It had solid walls and small windows. It was a good place to fall back, reasonably defensible. The air inside grew suffocating, warm from bodies and motion. The medical transport lorry had departed for the hospital and not yet returned.

Helena was closing a deep cut along an inner thigh when someone outside yelled, "They've taken Headquarters!"

Everyone looked up, staring at one another in confusion.

The lorry driver stumbled in, gasping for air, his head bleeding. "The Undying have taken Headquarters!"

No one spoke for a moment as shock rippled through the room. In all these years, Headquarters had never been touched. There were so many protective measures in place. It was the most secure place in the entire city.

Everyone seemed to snap back to life. There was a clamour of furious voices, everyone descending on the driver, demanding information. Helena pushed through, checking his head. He had a graze, and his hands were torn up.

"I went through all the checkpoints," he said, allowing Helena to tilt his head to the side and close the wound. "Showed my papers, got waved through. Everything was—normal. Pulled in, the patients were being unloaded." He mopped his forehead, smearing blood across his face. "Quiet, though. really quiet. I get fuckin' awkward when it's too quiet. Always rather talk, you know? Asked a guard a question. No answer. I thought all the blood on them was from carrying the wounded. Asked another question. They started moving towards me. That's when I realised. They were all greys. Fresh killed, still warm. I drove out—ran over a few, didn't look back. First checkpoint, tried to report it. They weren't talking, either. Barricade was up. So I ran. Didn't know where to go except come back."

The building was palpably silent as everyone tried to absorb this. It was beyond belief.

The Undying would have needed extensive information about their security protocols to infiltrate, a spy with a high-level security clearance to get in, and intimate knowledge to create necrothralls with the right instructions. How could it have happened? With no word? No distress signals?

The commander tried to contact Headquarters by radio, but there was only static.

"Signal to anyone you can, without setting off any alarms. You, you, and you," said the field commander, pointing at several men. "Go check the nearest checkpoint."

Only two men came back.

"They were all dead," said one, holding a hand against his stomach where blood seeped through his fingers. "They were waiting for us."

The field commander sent out anyone capable of carrying word to intercept and recall any units or lorries they encountered, and then he sat down at the radio and began uttering a string of jargon into channel after channel, arguing furiously with everyone who answered, because no one wanted to believe the report.

The door burst open, and Luc strode in, Sebastian only a few steps behind him, concealing a limp, the rest of the battalion milling in back of him.

Luc's face was pale and streaked with blood and smoke. Although he looked skeletally thin, his eyes were blistering, a brilliant feverish blue, but rather than acknowledge the field commander, his attention went directly to Helena.

"What are you doing here?" he said.

She stood up. "I need to talk to you, Luc. Urgently."

He blinked and finally turned to his field commander. "Who let her in here?"

Before anyone could respond, Helena spoke again.

"It's about Lila," she said.

The words worked like magic. Luc's attention snapped onto her, and his throat dipped as his eyes darted around the room.

"Fine," he said after a beat. "Let's talk. Sebastian, get everyone ready to move. We're retaking Headquarters."

"No, bring him, I'll heal him while we talk," Helena said. "It'll save time."

Luc eyed her warily but nodded. He seemed so familiar, and yet—there was something off about him.

You should have known. You should have noticed.

He turned to the field commander, who looked lost. "Take everyone who can fight and start moving back towards Headquarters. Sebastian and I will follow."

There were rooms deeper in the warehouse that connected to the next building, and as they walked there, Helena slipped one of the obsidian knives into the waistband at the back of her skirt, hidden under her jacket.

Sebastian had cracked ribs and a gash to the leg where a knife had gotten through a weak point in his armour.

Helena gave him one of her last vials of medicine to help sustain the amount of tissue and blood she was about to regenerate. Before she could stop him, he unfastened and began removing his chest plate.

"What's wrong with Lila?" Luc asked the instant the door was shut and the three of them were alone.

"Nothing," Helena said. "She's fine."

Anger lit Luc's face.

"I just didn't realise you knew about the baby," Helena said, meeting his eyes.

Sebastian started. "What baby?"

Luc tensed enough that his armour clicked, but his expression was controlled. He didn't even look at Sebastian.

"What baby?" Sebastian asked again.

"That's why you came here?" Luc asked, his blue eyes glinting cold. "Because of that?"

Helena's heart was beating so fast, it was a thrum in her chest. "No, I came because I don't understand why you wouldn't let me heal Titus but you've been letting me take care of your heir."

"Luc, what did you do?" Sebastian said.

Luc ignored his paladin; all his focus was on Helena. "Lila can protect herself. You've already done enough to Titus."

Helena's throat closed, but in that moment, she knew: This was not Luc.

She should have realised sooner, but she'd spent so much time fearing his rejection, dreading the inevitable schism, that she had not questioned its happening.

She looked away. "You know, I was in one of the field hospitals during the massacre. When the liches infiltrated using living bodies. Apparently, a living body won't accept another soul; it's like an infection, the body tries to burn it out. That's why they came in sick with brain fevers, screaming and clawing at themselves, saying, 'Get him out,' until they died."

She drew a slow breath as she finished healing Sebastian's leg. "Do you know anyone who suffers from fevers like that, Luc?"

Sebastian had gone very still.

Luc shook his head. "Can't say I do."

He said it calmly, but there was a growing pressure in the air.

Helena found the cracks in Sebastian's rib. "You surrendered yourself to save Lila. You knew it would cost everything, but you did it anyway. You told me that you chose her as your paladin because you wanted her by your side, so you'd have a chance of protecting her, even though you knew you weren't supposed to. I know how it killed you every time she got hurt. You didn't even want me to clear her for combat again after she lost her leg." She kept looking for any glimmer of the person she knew. "Now she's the mother of your child, and instead of getting her to safety, you've kept her in isolation for months. And right this minute, you have every reason to think she's been captured, that she'd be one of the first people they'd kill, but instead of running to her, you're here with me. Luc would never do that."

"Luc, what have you done?" Sebastian was staring at him in horror.

Helena asked, "Who are you?"

It was like watching a curtain being pulled back.

One moment, the expression and characteristics were still there, and then Luc sighed and seemed to vanish beneath his own skin.

"Well." He grinned at them both, a smile like a slit throat. "I thought you'd realise months ago, but you're all such fools when it comes to the Holdfasts."

Sebastian trembled beneath Helena's fingers as they both stared at this thing standing in front of them.

Helena's hand slipped to her back. "Who are you?" she asked again.

"I've gone by so many names, I don't even remember them all," said the person in Luc's body. "Once, long ago, my brother called me Cetus."

Helena's eyes widened.

"Cetus?" she said.

He inclined his head, but she shook hers.

That would make him older than Paladia, older than the Holdfasts, older than the first Necromancy War. No one could live that long. Cetus was an invention, centuries of alchemists pseudonymously writing under one name. Not a person.

It had to be a lie, an attempt to distract her.

"I checked Luc," Helena said, trying to keep her voice steady. "There was no talisman. How is this possible?"

"Cetus" tilted his head to one side so that Luc's neck popped, as if Luc's body were a suit of armour that didn't fit properly.

"My brother and I were born entwined. We entered the world as one when we slid from our mother's womb. We'd sucked her dry from within, and the fires of her pyre licked across our skin, branding us from birth. Cursed children, they called us, when they called us anything at all. Our shared blood has endured for centuries and now we're one again, as we always should have been." He gestured down at himself.

"You're—related to Luc?" Helena said in disbelief.

The smile split Luc's face again.

"You should have seen Orion. He had such a way about him. People worshipped the ground he walked on. He could charm with a look. He found us sponsors, lodging, funds so I could do the Great Work and he could find audiences to adore him. He would do anything for adoration, and I taught him the tricks to do it. Gold and fire, and he thought that should be enough for us; we could buy ourselves a kingdom." Cetus looked scornful. "But I had greater aspirations. Kings and kingdoms rise and fall. We were made for eternity, my brother and I, we were gods.

"I lacked my brother's natural charm, but I'm a fair actor. Orion drew so much attention, most overlooked me, so I pretended to be Orion, coaxed just a few of his followers into cooperation. I needed trust, the kind that he earned so easily. It was necessary for my work, and he had always benefitted most, but when Orion learned what I'd done, the source of this new power, he called me a monster and left me. I knew he'd come back, once I discovered the true secrets of immortality. When he realised that humans were mere puppets and saw what I could offer, he would beg for me to take him back."

"You were the Necromancer," Helena said, realising. "The one who built the cult in Rivertide. After you made that Stone, you called Orion here, but when he saw what you'd done, he tried to kill you."

Rage flashed across Cetus's face. "His mind was poisoned by those paladins of his. If he'd come alone, he would have seen reason—"

"Why did you come back now?" Helena asked. "You disappeared for half a millennium. The Holdfasts don't want anything from you. Why are you helping Morrough?"

She studied Luc, or what was left of him. Gaunt, sweated down to nearly bone. He was dying; it was just a slower death than what she'd witnessed in the field hospital.

Luc laughed. It was the timbre and note she'd heard a thousand times over the years, but the malice and mockery in it were all new. "I am Morrough."

Sebastian shot to his feet, but before he had even drawn a weapon, Luc had his sword out and stopped him, tsking.

"A piece of him, I should say. When young Luc so boldly surrendered himself, I was curious how alike we were. I have lived for so long now, and he was so—fresh. I bound a piece of my soul to my bone and placed it inside him. I'd hoped he would accept me—hoped that we could be one as my brother and I should have been—but he's as self-righteous as Orion. It's fortunate that healer Boyle is so eager to please, she keeps him sedated for me."

"Luc's still alive, then?" Helena's voice shook.

"Of course. This is his body after all." Morrough, or Cetus, or whoever he was, gestured downwards. "I'm just a shadow in the back of his mind, or I would have been, if he hadn't gone so mad trying to tear me out that they drugged him to a stupor. Gave me free rein."

"You're puppeting him like a necrothrall? Is that how you infiltrated Headquarters?"

Luc's features twisted in offence. "I'm not a puppet. I know what's in the interest of my primary self, and I have found the means of pursuing it. You can kill me, and it'll do nothing—only Luc will die. As for your Headquarters—" He shook his head. "It seems that young Luc isn't your only traitor."

"But what is all this for?" Helena asked. Apollo, Luc, Lila . . . she couldn't understand. "Why come back to Paladia after all these centuries?"

"Because I want to erase my brother's legacy the same way he destroyed mine." Fury swept across Luc's face. "He tried to blot my name from history, to discredit any of my work that he couldn't steal and claim as his own. Attributed my discoveries to charlatans, taking my research and making himself a god with it. It's only fair to return the favour."

Helena shook her head. She didn't believe that. Morrough had too many opportunities to wipe out the Holdfasts; even Kaine had remarked on it, that Luc was being intentionally spared.

She thought of Luc, cut open on that table, all those decaying organs inside him.

"You're dying," she said. "Your original body, wherever it is. You came to Paladia because all the power in the world isn't enough to keep regenerating forever. There's a limit and you've reached it and you can't push beyond that no matter how much vitality and how many souls you harvest. When you had Apollo killed, you took his heart, and when you had Luc, we couldn't heal his organ damage because those organs were yours. You're harvesting Orion's descendants for parts. And—" It dawned on her slowly. "—that's—that's why Lila's pregnant. You're making yourself another descendant. That's why you wouldn't let her go to Novis: because you'll need that baby next."

Cetus stared at her, a bizarre look of calculation in Luc's eyes. "You're clever," he said. "The Holdfasts had no idea what they'd found when they imported you. An indentured animancer. Perhaps Apollo was more cunning than I realised. I knew what you were the moment you reached in with your resonance—if I hadn't thrown you across the room, you would have found me. Pity really. I had no choice but to have you sent off to the front. Matias was so happy to oblige. But somehow you came crawling back like a cockroach."

Cetus smiled, a cruel glint in his eyes that Luc had never possessed. "Never mind, though. I'm glad I get to do this personally. Sebastian"—he looked at Luc's last remaining paladin—"you're finally going to die protecting a Holdfast from a necromancer."

Luc moved so fast. There was a shriek of metal as Sebastian drew his weapon and blocked the attack. The room was small. Helena flung herself out of the way as Sebastian shoved Cetus back, drawing another weapon, slamming the hilt down on Luc's hand before he could unleash a wave of fire.

Luc's body was weak, tired from battle, and dying, and Sebastian was a fury unlike anything Helena had ever seen before. In an instant he'd hammered Luc into a corner, smashing through his defences, raising his arm to make a killing blow.

The instant before Sebastian brought his weapon down, Cetus's expression morphed, mockery vanishing as it became Luc's face, blue eyes wide in shock.

"I'm sorry," he said.

Sebastian hesitated for less than an instant, and Luc's knife sank into the base of Sebastian's throat. There was no armour to stop it. Cetus dragged the blade down, sundering Sebastian's ribs and gutting him.

Sebastian fell without a sound.

Cetus didn't even watch Sebastian die; he'd already turned to Helena. "Your turn."

He was blocking the door, and if she screamed, no one who came would take her word over Luc's.

As Cetus came towards her, she focused on everything that Kaine had ever drilled into her. She needed direct contact.

An instant would be enough.

He swung his sword at her head, but he was tired, his hand injured by Sebastian. The blow was slow and weak. She whipped out one of her titanium knives and managed to transmute it quickly enough to block the blow.

Cetus's knife flashed, Sebastian's blood spattering, aimed at her throat. With her other hand, she slammed the hilt of her obsidian knife into his wrist. The sight of black glass captured Cetus's focus. Helena dropped her titanium knife, her empty hand shooting out, her palm against his forehead, fingers tangling in his hair.

Her resonance slammed into his head with the force of an arrow, using the same trick of paralysis that Kaine had used on her so long ago.

The knife and sword in Luc's hands clattered to the floor, and his knees gave out. She let him slide to the ground, her palm still firmly pressed against his skull, shoving her resonance deep into his mind.

Helena had never been inside Luc's consciousness, but she knew from her interrogation work that a mind was like a home. It had the feeling of the person. Luc's mind was like walking into a house and finding the walls covered in blood and torn apart. A parasite had grown through his consciousness and fed on every glimmer of the person who should be there.

Cetus had cannibalised Luc, wearing him like a skin.

She ripped her consciousness back out and nearly doubled over with nauseous horror.

Cetus's eyes danced even though his face was strained by his inability to breathe.

"Luc, come back," Helena asked, her voice tremulous. "I know there's still a part of you in there. It's Hel. Come back. I'll help you."

She moved the paralysis enough to let Luc breathe.

Cetus studied her with interest. He was not afraid at all. "You're talented. If you joined me, your abilities would be valued."

She stared coldly at him. "Let me talk to Luc."

There was a strange hunger in his eyes. "You're the one making that obsidian, aren't you? I should have realised. Crowther was so tight-lipped. Tell me how you do it."

Her eyes narrowed. "Let me talk to Luc, and I'll tell you."

Anger flashed across Cetus's face. "Why bother with him? He's weak and useless, just like Orion, so satisfied with mere tricks that he suppressed his true power, denying his animancy."

"Luc is an animancer?" she said in shock.

Cetus's expression was jeering. "You never noticed? Never felt the way he could alter a room, entrance an audience?"

Yes, but she'd always assumed that was related to his pyromancy. The feeling of pressure that could come over her when he was upset. She shook her head.

"That's not animancy."

"It's a form of it, one Orion was especially talented in. He wanted people to love him and he made sure they did, while he repressed and rejected all the rest of it. And then hunted everyone else with similar abilities out of existence."

She shook her head again, but Luc had always had an uncanny magnetism. She had never questioned it. Had he even known?

"Let me talk to Luc," she said again, "and I'll tell you how to make the obsidian."

Cetus's expression morphed. "Hel?" The voice was wavering.

Helena's fingers clenched into a fist, closing his throat, choking him. She shook him. "That's not Luc. You think I can't tell? Give me Luc."

Cetus glared at her, and his eyes rolled back. This time Helena felt a shift through his mind as though something were being ripped out from beneath layers of membrane.

Cetus gave a ragged groan, and his eyes rolled dazedly back into focus.

Luc's face drained of all colour.

"Run," Luc rasped. "Hel, run. He's going to kill you."

"No, I'm not going anywhere," Helena said, wanting to cry. "I've got you. I'm here now. I'm sorry I'm so late."

She sensed the landscape of Luc's mind shifting again. That he was being dragged back under, but she'd paid attention, found the shape of Cetus, how he was entwined through Luc. After years as a healer, months of interrogations, and the difficult task of learning to sense Lila's baby—one spark of life hidden inside another—her resonance was surgical. It wrapped around Cetus, crushing him into submission.

Luc's eyes went out of focus, and he gave a pained gasp, wavering as if he were about to faint.

"Luc?" Helena said sharply. "Luc, focus. Listen to me. I am going to figure out a way to save you. I'll get rid of him."

Her voice was shaking, as her focus was split between talking to Luc and trying to keep Cetus at bay without injuring Luc further. "I just need you to hold on a little longer."

"Hel . . ." Luc's voice was barely more than a whisper. "I tried to—fight. He killed Ilva."

"I'm so sorry." Tears welled up in her eyes and fell onto his face. "I'm going to fix this. I promise."

Luc shook his head. "No. Kill me, it's the only way to stop him."

"No!" she said sharply. "Look at me. I'm going to save you. That's why I became a healer, remember? So that someday, when you needed me, I could save you."

He didn't seem to hear her. He was talking, the words all coming out in a rush.

"Lila—she thought he was me—"

"I'm sorry." She didn't know what else she could say.

His jaw trembled. "Don't tell her."

"You're not going to die, Luc."

Her mind felt as if it were about to rip in two from the effort of keeping Cetus subdued.

She could barely see straight.

"You have a chance. Kill him. No one else can—"

"No—"

There was a knife in Luc's hand. She saw it too late.

She was so focused on keeping Cetus back, she'd let the paralysis slip.

She didn't think.

She blocked it on instinct and completed the parry exactly the way Kaine had taught her to: a quick sweep of her knife, so fast it knocked the blade from his fingers. In the same motion, the obsidian knife sank to the hilt into the left side of Luc's chest, in the place under the arm where the armour was weak.

He gave a guttural gasp, body seizing uncontrollably. Helena gave a panicked scream as he collapsed in her arms.

"Sorry. I'm so sorry," he said.

She ripped the knife out, wrenching his armour out of the way with her resonance, trying to reach the wound.

"No! No, no. Don't do this to me. Luc, don't." She closed the wound as quickly as she could. It only took seconds to stop the bleeding and repair the place where her knife had sliced the aorta.

Fingers clamped around her throat, digging into her trachea, and she looked into Cetus's expression of pure hatred.

"You stupid—bitch," he said as she felt a quick pulse of that dead energy.

Luc's face cleared as he gave a gasp of relief.

"Got him," Luc said, letting go of her, forcing a smile.

Before Helena could speak, there was a hard knock on the door. "Principate, are you all right?"

Helena expected the door to burst open, for the room to fill with soldiers who'd find her kneeling over Luc with a bloody knife while Sebastian lay slaughtered beside them.

"I'm fine," Luc immediately called, his voice straining. "Be out soon."

The footsteps retreated, but Luc wasn't fine.

Helena had closed the wound, there was nothing physically wrong with him, but she knelt there and felt that he was dying. It was happening slowly. Not a sudden cold pulse, but as if he were bleeding to death, his vitality slipping out rather than blood.

There was no cause for it, nothing to fix, but she felt it through her resonance. As though he were unravelling.

"What's happening?" Her fingers scrabbled, trying to find a way to fix it, but she had never encountered a death like this.

His hand closed over hers, squeezing tight enough to stop her resonance. "It's all right."

"No, it's not," she said, trying to pull her hands free. "I can figure this out. But if you'd given me time—I would've—"

"I died months ago, Hel—" he said, his breathing forced.

"No—you're still alive—I'll fix this if you just—" She tried to pull her hand free.

"Stop," he said more forcefully, pulling her close and making her look at him, at his gaunt, nearly skeletal face. "Listen to me. You have to get out of here before anyone realises. I'll help you. I think I can last that long. Get Lila, take her far away, where Cetus—Morrough—whatever he is, can't find her. She won't leave if I'm still alive."

"She won't leave if you're dead, either. You'll come with us. We'll all go. I'll heal you, and then—"

Luc swallowed hard. "She has another—another Holdfast to protect. Not me—anymore."

Helena shook her head. "Luc, don't do this to me."

"I'm sorry. It shouldn't be you, but it has to be."

She tried to touch him again, to push his life back where it was seeping out through his skin.

"We have to go now." His voice rose, hard and commanding. He shook her as if trying to startle her into compliance. "Get Sebastian up. People will notice if he's not with me."

She stared at him, before looking to Sebastian lying in a pool of blood.

"Y-You want me to use necromancy?"

"We have to leave together," Luc said, the remaining traces of colour draining from his face as he pushed himself up, strapping on his armour. "Get him on his feet."

Her heart was in her throat as she closed the wounds on Sebastian, regenerating only as much as was necessary, and brought him to his feet. She had learned her lesson reanimating Soren. She was careful and brought back only a shadow.

He stood up, blank-eyed. Empty. She put his armour back on to hide the blood.

She braced herself as she looked towards Luc.

Luc sat looking at his last paladin with open grief, but when his eyes rested on her, there was only that same sadness. "You've always done the worst things because of me."

The words cut her to the quick. She should have known. She should have known Luc better, enough to know he wouldn't turn on her like that. He was too faithful.

She drew a harsh breath. "I promised I'd do anything for you."

She helped him stand, and he pulled her closer, into a hard hug. His chin resting on the top of her head.

Helena's eyes were burning. His armour dug in through her uniform hard enough to leave bruises behind. His hand clutched at her shoulder as he caught his breath and opened the door.

He straightened as they walked out. The warehouse was mostly abandoned; only a few of the uninjured lingered, waiting for Luc. Everyone was blood-spattered; they barely noticed the fresh blood on Luc or Sebastian. They all stood at attention.

Luc walked with his head high, shoulders squared, his shrunken frame naturally falling into the posture he'd been raised to assume.

"Sebastian and I are heading out," he said. "You all stay here; this is a solid base, and we need it to remain defended. If we can't recover Headquarters, we'll depend on places like this for our forces to fall back to."

"But—" one of the soldiers started.

"Those are my orders," Luc said. Beads of sweat formed along his temples, and Helena could feel him wavering, fading away, that cold energy seeping into the air around him. "Sebastian, with me. Marino, you too."

They made it up one street and around a corner into a narrow alley between two towers before Luc's legs failed. He was too heavy for Helena alone; Sebastian had to catch him, dragging him out of sight.

Luc sank against the wall, his breath shallow as he blinked up at the little bits of sky visible overhead between the towering buildings.

"Is it dawn?" he asked, his voice almost wondering.

Helena nodded. "First light."

He exhaled. "We were—going to see the world together, remember?"

His fingers scrabbled to find hers, his eyes still on the sky.

She took his hand, squeezing tightly, as if she could keep him longer if she held on.

"Never did see Etras . . ." he said, his voice faint. "Sorry. Promised I'd—take you back."

"It's all right," she said.

"Will you—take care of Lila? And the baby?"

She nodded.

"Don't tell Lila—"

"I won't."

His hand trembled in hers. "Promise . . . ?"

She swallowed hard. "I promise."

He said nothing else. When she looked up, his eyes were unseeing, the dawn reflecting in the empty blue.

CHAPTER 64

Augustus 1787

Helena left Sebastian with Luc, pulling free the reanimation and leaving the two of them hidden in the alley.

Her only thoughts were of Lila.

The air was thick with smoke and blood. She could hear fighting as she moved through the city, trying to stay out of sight. She couldn't save everyone. Anyone.

She had to reach Lila.

She neared the last wall that was intended to mark Resistance territory. There were necrothralls guarding it. Familiar faces. The field commander from Luc's unit with a gash in his skull that showed brain tissue underneath.

Kaine had said no one paid close attention to whose necrothralls were whose. A necrothrall was presumed to belong to one of the Undying. If she pulled the reanimation from a few, she could use them to escort her into Headquarters as a prisoner, but these were too well armed.

She needed easier targets. She turned and fled, hiding in buildings, climbing and descending old stairs and evacuation ladders, trying to find a way back to Headquarters. The combatants all had harnesses that they used to swing and rappel through the streets, navigating the levels of the city easily, but she had to find a route on foot.

The necrothralls kept tailing her. She could tell she was being herded, hunted with persistent predation. She could not out-endure the dead.

She hid, crouching behind a pillar half covered in rubble, trying to catch her breath.

Footsteps came nearer. Her heartbeat was a drum. She drew a gasping breath and jumped up, fleeing her hiding spot. She ran straight into one of the Undying, all in black.

Before she could react, a large hand gripped her head, and everything went dark.

HELENA WOKE WITH A PANICKED gasp. Kaine was leaning over her, his fingers at the base of her head. She jerked away, eyes roaming, not recognising where she was. Her head was swimming.

"It's all right. You're safe," he said.

She stared up at him in confusion, trying to remember how she'd gotten there.

Everything came rushing back. Luc. Luc was dead.

She'd killed him.

The memory was like being punched in the throat.

"What—what happened?" Her mouth was dry. She looked dazedly around, trying to pinpoint their location.

Kaine's fingers slipped away from the back of her head. His expression was calm, but his eyes were furious.

"The war is over," he said. "The Undying have taken the city, including your Headquarters. The remaining Resistance factions are cornered; if they don't surrender, they'll be buried in rubble by the day's end."

She pushed herself up, too dazed to think clearly. She'd been trying to reach Lila . . . and then? She couldn't remember anymore.

Kaine began pacing around the room.

"How did this even happen? What kind of plan was stretching yourselves across the entire city and leaving your Headquarters unguarded? And where the fuck is Holdfast?"

Helena flinched. "He's dead."

Kaine froze and turned sharply. "What do you mean?"

Helena stared down at her hands. She was in the same clothes. Luc's blood was among the stains, but she couldn't pick out which ones belonged to him. She couldn't bring herself to speak.

"How?" Kaine asked.

She swallowed. "It was—an accident."

She told him everything. What she'd realised, and who it had been, and everything over the months. That Luc had tricked her, and she'd reacted, and then it was too late.

"I tried to heal him . . ." she said, her voice shaking. "But it was like there wasn't enough of him left to hold on. He was unravelling and I couldn't—" Her chest seized, threatening to crack. "*I was supposed to save him—*" The words came out a whisper.

Her throat contracted and her whole body shook and she couldn't make herself speak. Kaine was silent until she managed to compose herself again.

"Morrough must be so old," she said. "Paladia's more than five hundred years old."

"This whole war was just two brothers fighting over who gets to play god?" Kaine gave a disbelieving, bitter laugh. "You think you're picking a side, and you're just on the opposite end of the same fucking coin."

Helena didn't speak, gripping the blankets draped over her until her knuckles turned white. She had to get up, but she felt like glass a breath away from shattering. "I have to get Lila."

"The war is over, Helena."

She flinched at the way he said her name. That he'd used it to say that.

"I know," she said, going hot and cold all over. "You don't need to tell me. I know we've lost!"

She pressed her lips together, grinding the heels of her hands against her eyes as she tried to control herself.

"I'm not saying it's not over." Her voice still shook. "But we have the obsidian now, we can both make it, and if we're more covert—we could still bleed him dry by killing off the Undying."

"There is no 'we' anymore," Kaine said. "You're leaving Paladia."

She looked up sharply. He stood over her, arms crossed.

"I'll kill them, but you're done. Holdfast is dead. The Eternal Flame is gone. It's time for you to go."

She shook her head. "I can't leave you here."

His expression was hard as stone. "I don't *want* you here. It'll be easier for me to work if Morrough assumes a complete victory."

Helena's jaw tensed. "Fine," she finally said in a tight voice. "I'll collaborate long-distance initially, if you think that'll make things easier."

"Good." He stepped back, turning away. "I'll have everything arranged."

She watched him warily, not sure she believed him. Reasonable as it was, she knew he'd already wanted her out of Paladia. There were no other choices, though. She had to get Lila to safety. Until Lila was secure, Helena had no room to negotiate.

"I'm only going if Lila's with me," she said.

Kaine rocked back. "No chance. If she goes missing, they'll hunt her across the continent. She's not worth it."

Helena stood. "I'm not asking. I have to take her. If she's not with me, I won't leave. I promised Luc I'd take care of her. She's been under quarantine at the top of the Alchemy Tower. They might not have found her yet. The sooner we go, the better our chances are of getting her without being noticed. We could—we can find a body and I'll use vivimancy, disguise it, so it looks like her. No one will know she's gone."

Something about Kaine suddenly shifted, a tension around his mouth.

"You can take me as a prisoner, use that as an excuse to go inside. It's only been a few hours—"

"Helena . . ."

He said her name slowly, a note of warning but also a plea in the way he said it. His eyes flicked around the room, pausing briefly on the curtains. Her voice died. Half in a daze, she stood up and walked forward, pushing the curtain back. It was dark outside.

It was night.

But how could it be night? It had been dawn; the sun was just rising when Luc died.

"How . . . how long did you keep me unconscious?" Her voice shook. "How—how long has it been?"

He gave no reply.

She turned and lunged for the door, but he caught her, dragging her back. "I can explain—"

She struggled, trying to rip herself free. "What did you do?" Her voice rose. "How long have I been unconscious?"

"Listen." He shook her, and there was a wildness to his eyes. "After the bomb went off, when the Resistance began to attack, Morrough had everyone remaining fall back. They knew your numbers, how many combatants you had left. It was obvious that Headquarters would be vulnerable. They expected an attack before Hevgoss arrived—they were waiting for it. They had someone on the inside. Once your forces had been lured onto the West Island, they sent us to infiltrate. When I got there, you were missing. No one knew where you'd gone. I abandoned my post to find you. Once I had you safe, I had to go back."

"So you—left me here for how long? A day?" Her voice was raw with betrayal.

"I came back as soon as I could."

She started to tremble, her body going into shock. "I was going to get Lila. That's where I was headed, but I kept getting cut off—and—" She flinched. "That was you, wasn't it? You knocked me out. You didn't even—"

All those necrothralls tailing her. He'd killed those soldiers, set them up, all watching and waiting for her. There was so much blood on his hands.

He cradled her face with them. "What did you expect me to do? Let you walk back into that massacre? The orders were to kill anyone who tried to resist."

"Are they all—?" She couldn't even finish the question. It didn't matter. "I won't leave without Lila. You can help me or I'll go alone, but I'm going back for her."

Kaine was unmoved. "If you want Morrough defeated, there's no rescuing anyone."

"We won't defeat him if we don't rescue Lila. She's pregnant. Morrough needs another Holdfast, and Lila's the one carrying it. I promised Luc I'd get her out—it was the last thing I told him before he died. It was all that mattered to him."

"Why should I care about what Holdfast wanted?" he said, his voice implacable.

He was not going to do this. Not even for her.

Her chest tightened. She could feel her ribs curved around her heart like a cage.

You always lose.

Everyone you love dies.

"Because if you do, I'll stop—everything," she said. "I'll leave, and I won't come back. Just like you want, if you'll help me get Lila Bayard. Whatever you want. Anything you ask. I'll do it, I swear."

Her fingers shook as she reached out for him.

"Please."

He'd gone very still. "Will you?"

She nodded. "Yes . . ." Her voice struggled and failed. "Yes, I promise."

He studied her, eyes narrowed and calculating. "Those are your terms? The Bayard girl, and then you'll do anything I ask?"

Her throat closed. "Yes. Anything you ask. I swear."

He nodded slowly. "All right. If those are your terms, I'll get her for you."

Helena gave a shuddering gasp of relief. "Thank you."

He just nodded, but he seemed distracted. She waited to hear how they'd do it, but he was silent, just studying her.

"What do you need me to do?" she finally asked.

Irritation instantly flashed across his face. "Stay here."

Her eyebrows furrowed. "But I could help. I can—"

"I don't *need* help."

When she opened her mouth to argue, he looked her up and down. "You're too memorable. It'll be easier for me to look for her alone. If you want me to get her out, stay here and let me work in peace without succumbing to your desperate need to insert yourself into everything I do."

She tried to protest, and he raised a finger, pointing it at her face.

"If you leave this suite while I'm gone, if I have even the slightest inkling that you're trying to help me in any way, I will come back and the deal will be off. Do you understand? Stay here."

Her jaw tensed, throat tightening, but she nodded.

"There's food in the cupboard. Keep the curtains closed. It shouldn't take too long."

"Where is this?" she asked, looking around.

He sighed. "This was the suite of the Hevgotian ambassador, who tragically died in a recent explosion."

"The one you were—?"

He nodded and left without another word.

Helena waited. Kaine had recovered her satchel when he'd apprehended her, and she took inventory of her remaining supplies. She was out of most things beyond what she kept for Kaine. She went through it carefully, hoping he wouldn't need any of it when he got back with Lila.

There was a good chance Lila would be injured. She wouldn't let herself be taken without a fight. How would Kaine convince her to cooperate?

Helena stood and went to the door but refrained from touching it. Surely he had a plan.

She went back to inventorying. Kaine had put her knives back into the outer pocket.

She tried to keep herself busy, because if she stopped to think, her grief and guilt would crush her to death. Luc. It was all her fault. She could have saved him if she'd only noticed. Now she was leaving everyone behind, knowing what was likely to happen to them.

All her worst fears coming true and there was nothing she could do.

You can't save everyone. You never could.

This was the only way.

Once Lila was safely away, if Kaine could slowly kill off the Undying, eventually the nightmare would end.

Time seemed to crawl past. Helena showered, washing away the blood and grime from the city. Luc's blood. Sebastian's blood.

She found clothes in the wardrobe. Hevgotian traditional clothing, which involved an unexpected number of tassels. In the cupboard was bread and very strong, hard cheese, which she forced herself to eat even though everything tasted like chalk in her mouth.

She was about to ignore Kaine's orders and go looking for him anyway when the door abruptly swung open and Kaine walked in, Lila hanging limp in his arms. Her prosthetic was gone, and there were metal bands locked around both her wrists.

Helena flung herself across the room as he laid Lila on the bed.

Helena searched for any signs of injury, but Lila was not injured at all beyond a few bruises. As Helena searched her, her resonance failed at Lila's wrists, and she realised they were alchemy-suppressing cuffs.

They were crudely made; she would only need a few tools to get them off.

"Was she still in the Tower?" she asked as she pushed an eyelid open, trying to pinpoint whether Lila had been physically knocked out or sedated.

"No," Kaine said. "They'd already transported her when I got there."

The alchemy suppression was external, and since the effects were at Lila's hands, Helena could still use her resonance everywhere else.

"Where was she?" she asked, checking for the baby's heartbeat.

"They'd taken her to Bennet's lab, but I was able to retrieve her. We need to move quickly now. You both need to be out of the city before dawn."

Helena was so panicked over Lila that she didn't immediately notice that there was something unnerving about Kaine's voice. She looked up. He was staring at her with a look that was almost starved; she'd never seen him look that way before.

Reaching out, she took his hand, feeling for any sign of injury. He wasn't hurt, though. His pale hair was smoke-stained, but he looked unscathed. And yet there was something off about his expression.

"What's wrong?" she asked, standing up, forgetting Lila.

The corner of his mouth curved into a wistful smile, and he inhaled.

"Kaine?" She searched his face. "What happened?"

He stared at the floor a moment before finally meeting her eyes. "I blew my cover getting the Bayard girl for you."

The world stopped spinning. Time stalling as the air froze, and it was just them, and nothing else existed.

"What?" She tried again, shaking her head. "You—you what?"

She was certain she was misunderstanding him, but it was there in his eyes. He was saying goodbye to her.

She shook her head again. "No."

He said nothing. Her protest vanished into the silence replaced by a horrible, waiting stillness, like the space between slowing heartbeats, when a heart finally stops. The sound of ending.

"*No,*" she said, her voice straining, breaking the quiet again, refusing to believe him.

"There wasn't any other way," he said gently, catching her by the arm as she swayed.

Her heart had started to beat again, and now it was beating faster and faster. She kept shaking her head, backing away from him, her eyes going for the door, looking for an escape, a way out. This was not happening.

He caught her, held her by the shoulders. "You know they've been looking for the spy. There were counter-espionage measures in place at the lab, and there wasn't time to find a way past them. To get to Bayard, there are entry records indicating that I was there, that I entered a laboratory with highly controlled access. I couldn't burn down the building and fight my way out carrying an unconscious, pregnant woman. When the next security shift begins tomorrow, the lab will be found and the records will show that I was the only one who left alive."

She shook her head again, twisting free. "No. No, we can go back." She turned to get her satchel. "There must be a way to destroy the records—I can—"

He jerked her back, his expression set. "You're leaving, remember? That was the deal you made, Marino. I met the terms."

Helena gave a low, pained sound as she shrank away from him.

His eyes were aglow, as if he was willing her to understand. His gaze flickered across her face as if trying to take it in, memorising her, because this was the end. The last time he'd ever see her.

She might have forgiven him for that, but the adoration in his eyes was tempered by a sharp-edged triumph. The satisfaction of getting his way.

"Anything I wanted if I went and got Bayard for you; those were *your* terms."

He would have hurt her less if he'd reached in and ripped her heart out.

"You gave your word," he said, when she refused to reply, his voice hardening.

"No—" Her voice broke.

His expression softened as she stopped struggling. "We had a good run, but we were never going to last." His fingers slipped a loose curl behind her ear before his hand drifted down to rest briefly at the base of her throat. "You knew that."

"Kaine, please, let me—" she started, her voice shaking.

His expression turned cold again. "Anything I wanted. It was your deal."

Her lungs were beginning to burn. She tried again to pull away, but she couldn't breathe. The crisp edges of him were blurring. He was speaking, but the words were growing rounded.

Kaine pulled her closer, and the cold determination on his face was shifting into worry.

"Helena—breathe."

Her vision tunnelled, all darkness except him.

He shook her. "Helena—don't—come on—breathe—Helena, please . . ."

Her fingers grasped at him as she fought to speak.

"No—" Her voice was broken. "—don't do this to me."

The devastation swallowed her like a tidal wave, and he vanished.

WHEN SHE REGAINED CONSCIOUSNESS, KAINE was leaning over her once again. She stared at him. Her left arm hurt as if there was a deep bruise just below the shoulder. Her body felt wrong. Numb. Her mind sluggish.

She blinked, and even that took effort and concentration. Then everything came back with almost violent anguish.

She struggled to focus. The pain in her arm was likely some kind of injected sedative. Kaine had drugged her, but there was also a mineral salt aftertaste on her tongue that she recognised as her tablets. He'd used them to erase the panicked surge of adrenaline, to set her heart at a slow, steady rhythm. He'd made her calm and malleable.

She glared up at him, trying to find words.

"I'm never going to forgive you for this," she finally managed. The words came out slurred, giving them an irregular lilt.

Kaine's lips tightened into a flat line, but then he nodded. "I know you won't, but you'll be alive and away from the war. Those were always my terms."

Helena went silent, trying to think despite being transmuted to the verge of incoherence.

There was a well of rage seething through her that she couldn't quite reach, as if it were just beyond her fingertips.

She had to think slowly, laboriously, struggling to keep her focus razor-sharp because when she let it falter, her thoughts turned nebulous. She was surreptitious as she curled her fingers against her palm, just enough to send her resonance through her own body, trying to reverse Kaine's tampering, but it had settled.

"If you die, who's going to stop Morrough?" Her voice was dull.

His expression turned cold. "He can have Paladia for all I care. If the Eternal Flame wanted to win, they should have made better choices. They all knew the risks, but that was never enough incentive for them. They refused to pay the price that victory demands, and I am sick of watching you try to pay it for them."

He tried to take her hand, but she recoiled from him. Hurt flashed in his eyes, but he swallowed, his jaw set.

"It's time to go," he said.

"No."

His eyes narrowed and grew flintlike. "You gave your word."

Helena inhaled through clenched teeth. "I know. And I will go, per your demands, but I need to speak with—Shiseo. If I can teach him how to use the obsidian I have left, he can pass on the information to the survivors, and then at least they'll have a chance—"

"You gave your word."

Helena met his eyes. "You know I will always choose the Eternal Flame first."

He stared at her, eyes widening as if she'd struck him. His mouth pressed into a hard line, and his gaze dropped. She watched his throat dip, and she kept talking.

"If you force me to leave without speaking to Shiseo, the last thing you will ever do is betray me and everyone I love. A traitor is all you'll be to me, but if you let me do this, maybe—someday I'll be able to forgive you."

Hurt shone from his eyes, an empty look of despair, but she glared back. Too drugged to show more emotion.

"Fine." His voice was raw with bitterness, and he didn't look at her again.

She sat up laboriously and drew a map that showed which part of the city the off-site lab was in, hoping that it had escaped notice. She added a vaguely termed list of things she wanted Shiseo to bring. "He should be there if no one's found him. I'll need him to bring all this so I can explain how it works."

Kaine stared at the map and list, his eyes narrowing. "Who is he exactly?"

"An Easterner. He helps here and there."

"And you trust *him*?"

"More than I can trust you," she said.

Kaine turned white, but he crumpled the list into his pocket. "Don't leave," he said.

She turned away from him. Lila lay beside her, still unconscious.

The instant he was gone, Helena pushed herself and began ransacking the suite, finding and prying free every piece of metal she could. She was indiscriminate in her destruction; anything that was not immediately visible, she ripped out, and then identified its components and transmuted it down into compact bars of various alloys and metals, pausing every few minutes to clear her head of the drug.

She was certain that Kaine would take her and Lila into Novis first. It was in range. He'd use Amaris to get across the river without dealing with checkpoints or the paperwork of commandeering a boat. However, large as Amaris was, Helena doubted the chimaera could carry three. The river was wide in the basin. Two riders would be enough to wind Amaris and require her to rest before returning.

Helena didn't trust Novis with Lila, not now with Luc dead. In the hands of Novis, with Falcon Matias circling him, Luc's son would be little more than a pawn, a Principate raised with the same lies and manipulation that had haunted Luc.

Lila would have to be hidden.

Kaine had somewhere already in mind, but travel arrangements would not be quick. Even if he had money on hand, obtaining safe and discreet passage would be complicated.

She went to the window, peeking out, trying to gauge how high she was, and found a street only a few storeys below. The suite was in one of the higher parts of the city, far removed from the violence, but there was a large skybridge connected to all the nearby buildings, with a plaza and gardens overlooking the lower parts of the city.

There was also a fire escape just outside the window. Not a functional one, but a decorative sort of balcony made of wrought iron.

She heard footsteps sooner than she'd expected and rushed back to the bed, trying to look dazed when the door opened and Kaine entered, Shiseo behind him.

She pushed herself up, rubbing her eyes. "You found him."

"Give him your information so he can go."

Helena slurred her reply. "He's just an assistant. I'm going to have to go over everything."

Shiseo blinked at Helena, and she was grateful then for how unreadable he was.

Kaine gave a hiss between his teeth, hands clenching into fists. "Fine."

She was interfering with his timeline. She could feel his desperate impatience.

"You'll use Amaris, right? To take us across the river?" she asked.

Kaine's eyes flicked to Shiseo, but he gave a faint nod.

"Can she carry all of us that far?"

His jaw went tense. "It'll have to be two trips."

She nodded vaguely and went to him, noticing the way he leaned towards her without seeming to be aware of it.

She stopped short and lowered her voice. "You should take Lila, before she wakes."

He drew up. "You want me to go?"

Her expression twisted bitterly. "Well, there's no point in teaching you any of this, is there?" She lifted a shoulder. "I just thought—if you took her first, maybe we'll have some time to say goodbye when it's my turn. But maybe that doesn't matter."

She turned away, grateful that she was so drugged, she could finally lie without effort. She could feel Kaine's eyes on her as she found a stack of thick, high-quality paper in the desk drawer and searched for a pen.

Helena's heart was pounding, a slow drumbeat of dread as she sat and began to write, slowly and methodically, not looking at him again.

"When I get back, you'll go, whether or not you're ready."

Helena's heart was in her throat. It took a moment to speak.

"Fine." She didn't dare look up.

She watched from the corner of her eye as he went over and hauled Lila up.

He stopped at the doorway and looked back at her. "I'll be back in a few hours. Don't leave this room."

Helena's throat tightened. She looked over, and her lips parted, to say—

To say—

She looked back down to the paper in front of her. "I'll be waiting for you."

The door shut and she didn't move, expecting it to burst open again. There was a long silence before she finally looked up.

"How did he bring you here?" she asked Shiseo, pressing her hand against the side of her neck and trying to alleviate all the tampering in her body enough to think coherently.

"There was a motorcar. He took it underground. He had a special card that let us through, and we came up in a long lift."

She turned and went over the box of supplies Shiseo had brought, sorting them as quickly as she could, laying them all out in the small kitchen. She had to work in rushed spurts to stay ahead of the sedative. Taking an etching sheet, she hastily began sketching an array to stabilise her component construction.

"He said you needed me," Shiseo said after several minutes.

"I'm sorry, I don't," Helena said, her fingers quickly shaping the various metal bars into a multitude of spheres. "I just needed an excuse so he'd leave and bring me these supplies. I imagine he told you, we lost. Luc's dead. You should get to Novis, you'll be safe there."

Shiseo seemed unconcerned. "What are you doing?"

She paused. "I'm building a bomb. I need to blow up a laboratory."

There was a long silence. "We used the Athanor components already."

Helena twitched one shoulder as she began divvying up materials, calculating how much she had. Not enough. She scrounged through the kitchen cupboards and found a bag of flour.

"This is going to be a different kind of bomb," she said. "It'll still use some obsidian, but I'm using a different pyromancy principle for this. Luc's books always warned about using pyromancy in enclosed spaces, because if the flames consume all the oxygen, it creates a vacuum. Obviously, I'm not a pyromancer, but when I was little, there was a mill fire. The flour in the air caught fire, and it burned down the entire building."

She paused, using her resonance to stall the effects of the sedative again before measuring carbon disulfide into sealed spheres, careful to keep from inhaling any.

Her hands had to be steady, her focus razor-sharp.

"You will burn down a lab?"

She nodded. "The West Port Lab. Do you remember Vanya Gettlich? The woman with nullium in her blood? That was West Port's doing. If I burn it down, they won't realise that Kaine rescued Lila. If they think she died in a fire, they won't look for her. And it'll be—" She swallowed hard. "It'll be a quicker death for everyone inside than what will happen to them otherwise." She pressed her hand against her head again, clearing it, and then nodded him away. "You should go. You won't want to be here when Kaine gets back, and if I get any of this wrong, I might blow up this building instead."

"You will not come back?"

Helena used the mortar and pestle to grind obsidian into micro-shards. "Of course I'm going to come back. I told Kaine I'd be waiting for him. It's just—"

She paused and blinked back tears. "I made a deal to leave, and I have to keep it." She swallowed hard. "He'll be—he'll be alone here. I have to make sure he's safe before I go."

She couldn't breathe. Her lungs made that awful whistling sound, and she doubled over, clutching at her chest, trying to get her fingers under the chest brace.

Shiseo took the mortar and pestle from her.

"Your wrist motion still needs practice," he said as he ground up the obsidian for her. "Like this, see?"

She watched, the sedative taking effect. Her chest slowly stopped convulsing. She let him finish before straightening with a wince.

When he was done with the obsidian, he helped her transmute metal bars into the various shapes she needed. He was better at delicate transmutation work than she was; he made beautifully delicate pins that would be removed to allow the carbon disulfide to evaporate and ignite the white phosphorus.

Helena made as many bombs as she could. The Hevgotian ambassador had a very large, sturdy rucksack that Helena filled with them, hoping that all the spheres were even and wouldn't break during the journey. She took her knives from her satchel, shoving them into the pockets of a tasselled jacket, along with the few remaining supplies from her emergency kit, and pulled a cap down low to hide her face and dark hair.

After hesitating, she lay one of the obsidian knives on top of the note she'd written. Kaine should have one, if he didn't already.

She slung the rucksack onto her back, careful not to jostle it, and then went over and unlatched the window, leaning out. There was a red haze rising from the north end of the city, but the beacon of the Eternal Flame, which had burned for centuries, visible for miles, was gone. Extinguished.

She was about to climb out the window when Shiseo spoke up.

"Wait."

She looked at him.

"You will come back?"

She pressed her lips together and nodded, slipping one leg over the sill.

"Wait," Shiseo said again. He drew a deep breath. "I am not in the habit of holding on to—things. People." He shook his head. "I was very young when my father regretted his marriage. I was a disappointment. My mother's family did not rise as expected, so he put us aside and began again. When my half brother became Emperor, I was seen as a threat, but he sent me to oversee the imperial mines, and I thought perhaps he did not want to kill me. But when I was accused of stealing imperial metals, I realised I must always wander."

Helena knew he was trying to communicate something important, but she was too stuck on one point. "Your *brother* is the Emperor?"

Shiseo waved the question off and seemed very focused on the story he was telling her.

"I always thought it better to let life flow by quietly. For many years, I did."

Helena was not sure if she was touched or exasperated by his sudden need to tell her this.

"When they said you had died, I—I regretted that I did not know you well. I do not like to presume. To ask questions. But I—enjoyed our lab." He smiled at her.

Helena exhaled, smiling back. "Me too. I wish we could have worked on other things." She slid through the window onto the metal balcony.

"Wait."

She tensed with frustration.

He reached after her. "I should go. If I am caught, I will tell them about my brother. They will not kill me. You see?"

He held out his hand for the rucksack, the urgency visible in his face.

Helena looked at him for a moment and then pushed his hand away. "I'm going to use necromancy to plant the bombs. It has to be me."

His hand dropped.

"Take care, Shiseo," she said. She started to turn, then paused. "If I don't come back—if you ever see Kaine, tell him—tell him that I—"

Her head dropped down, and she quickly brushed her fingertips across her cheeks. She cleared her voice and shook her head. "Never mind. I imagine he knows."

CHAPTER 65

Augustus 1787

HELENA HAD RARELY VISITED THE WEST ISLAND even before the war, but she knew she needed to head south, and down to the lower levels of the island, to reach its small port.

It was dark and quiet; in the plaza, one might not even realise there was a war. The lifts would require fare and identification, assuming that they were even operational, but there were always stairways, some large and others designed for maintenance and service workers. They would be the most efficient. When she came across gates, the locks were usually simple enough for basic transmutational lock picking.

She was almost to the lowest levels before she saw anyone. She reached a gate, and just as she got it unlocked, two people came around the turn of the stairs, heading up. Helena tried to tuck herself against the wall and let them pass without drawing attention to herself, but when she risked a glance up, she gave a gasp of surprise.

It was Crowther. He met her eyes dully, no expression on his face, but he stopped in his tracks as the person beside him turned and looked at Helena.

Ivy gave a small smile. "You got out, too. I hoped you would."

Helena stared at her in horror, looking again at Crowther, blank-faced and empty-eyed. He was dead.

"What did you do?" Helena's voice shook.

The smile on Ivy's face vanished. "The Necromancer has Sofia. He said he'd give her back to me if I gave him the Headquarters and Crowther. They wanted him alive, but they said it was all right if I had to kill him. So I did."

Because Crowther was believed to be the one making the obsidian. Helena's head swam.

"You're the one who gave them all the information?" she said. "Who let them into Headquarters?"

It wasn't Cetus. Here stood the real traitor.

"I had to," Ivy said. "It's the only way to get Sofia back."

"Ivy, your sister's dead."

"No!" Ivy shook her head. "She's alive. I've seen her, she knows me when I visit her. He'll give her back to me when I bring him Crowther."

"How could you?" was all Helena could say. "All those people—"

"They would have all died anyway," Ivy said with a callous toss of her head. "This way, it was quick. I made sure the plan had them all die quick." She shook her head. "I'm not a traitor. They were going to die no matter what."

Ivy turned and continued, Crowther's corpse behind her.

THE WEST PORT LAB WAS a huge, windowless building, originally built as an industrial shipping warehouse. Kaine had given the Eternal Flame an interior blueprint for the lab earlier that year, but there had never been any context to use the information.

There were only small pipes for airflow throughout the building, intended to ward off external pyromancy attacks. The ventilation was poor. Which was exactly what Helena needed.

There were a few smaller buildings scattered around it, and she eyed them warily as she passed.

As she stood studying the warehouse, a necrothrall approached her;

her casual presence was enough to merit investigation, but a solitary, unarmed figure wasn't cause for alarm. As it neared, Helena pressed her hand against her neck, clearing her head again, and then reached out and pulled the energy out of the necrothrall, as easily as plucking a piece of lint off a jacket.

The corpse sagged against her, the smell of rot closing in. She shoved her own resonance through the dead body, reanimating it again.

It wasn't a very good corpse. It was in the early stages of bloat, the tissue and ligaments all damaged.

She was careful to use only a little energy.

Her new necrothrall turned and held the next necrothrall in place while she repeated the process until there were more than twenty greys gathered around her.

Her focus blurred as the edge of her consciousness fragmented into all the different shadowed minds, but it was only the edges this time; her mind remained her own.

"Find the openings," she told them as she began activating and distributing her bombs.

The effect of the sedative was worse now with the necromancy. The focus required was exhausting. It was fortunate they were all intended to perform nearly identical tasks. She gritted her teeth as she began transmuting each bomb, performing the final step before sending the necrothralls away as quickly as possible.

It was a delicate balance between staying far enough away that she wouldn't get caught in the blast zone, but near enough that the phosphorus wouldn't ignite prematurely after the initial activation.

She watched them reach the warehouse and start climbing up the walls.

She started to back away, and her eyes went out of focus as she followed the greys, up, up. No pain centres to feel their fingers shredding.

She squeezed her eyes shut, trying to focus on their progress.

They reached the pipes and slits in the warehouse. A few were on the roof, pulling off the vent covers. Her heart pounded as one of the necrothralls with clearer vision held a sphere up to the pipe and confirmed that it would fit through.

In unison, the necrothralls pulled out the delicate pins that Shiseo had transmuted for her, then dropped the spheres down the pipes. Sending them into the reinforced, sealed-off warehouse.

As the last of them dropped, Helena turned and started running.

There was an almost perfectly simultaneous muffled bang behind her as the initial blast went off. She looked back and saw tiny clouds of dust, some glittering, some white.

The world exploded.

The air was shattered with the violence of the blast, a wave that twisted the air as Helena ran, a searing heat that seemed to chase her down.

The fire was trying to swallow everything, cannibalising itself as it burned, raging and starved, dragging in the air to fuel itself until it created a tornado of wind. Every pyromancy sin Helena had ever warned Luc over, she'd committed.

Warehouses were designed for storage, not structural integrity. The blueprints had shown exactly where the few structural supports were located. The building collapsed in on itself and then blew apart with another sudden explosion. Whatever weapons Bennet had been developing, whatever dangerous, flammable, incendiary resources they had from their own bombs, the fire had found them.

The ground moved like liquid under her feet. The paving stones cracking open.

She was flung against one of the buildings.

Fire was still roaring when she blinked again. The sedative had absorbed the pain of the blow. She lay on the ground, trying to catch her breath, a pulsing throb that should be agony pressing against her skull.

Everything was on fire. She could feel the heat, could dimly make out more explosions. There was a sharp, painful ringing in her ears that muted all other sounds. She looked where the lab had been, but there was only rubble and flames.

Her legs wobbled, giving out when she tried to stand. She collapsed, gasping unsteadily. Her lungs were burning, but breathing made her head swim.

There might be nullium.

She pulled off her jacket and pressed it over her mouth and nose, trying to breathe slowly.

Get up. Run.

But she was so tired. Nothing felt real. It had to be a nightmare. All that time. All those years, everything she'd done, telling herself it would all be worth it in the end. All lies. She'd killed Luc. The first person she'd ever been meant to save, she'd stabbed through the heart.

She lay falling into her loss. Pinned by the weight of her grief. How could she get up now? How could she bear it?

Kaine.

Her eyes snapped open, and she clawed at her throat, trying to push back the sedation, fumes filling her lungs. She'd told him she'd be waiting for him.

If she didn't go back, he'd return to find a mess of hastily assembled explosives and her scrawled note.

I love you. I love you. I love you.

She forced herself up. She wasn't going to die. She wouldn't leave him behind. She had to go back.

She managed a few steps before her legs gave out again. There were figures approaching through the smoke, but she couldn't make her legs hold her.

She scrabbled in her pocket, finding the vial and syringe she'd put there. Last resort.

She pulled it out, hand shaking as she stabbed the needle into the vial and pulled up the plunger, filling it. She drew a deep breath and braced herself as she jabbed it straight into her heart and injected it.

The cocktail of stimulants had been formulated for Kaine. It hit like a shock wave, energy roaring through her body, ripping away any last remnants of the sedative and Kaine's transmutation. Energy seemed to hum inside her veins. She could feel her mind sharpening, everything growing brighter, clearer.

She leapt to her feet and ran faster than she'd ever moved in her life. She could barely feel her body. She knew she needed to run.

Something tackled her to the ground. She twisted, going for her knives, but she felt fur. She grabbed hold of her attacker and shoved her resonance through, finding all those places where transmutation had stitched the creature together. She unravelled them.

The chimaera died instantly.

She scrambled up, whipping out an obsidian knife as necrothralls reached her. She tore through them, barely feeling their attempts to grab her. Her eyes were locked on the high towers of the island. She was going that way. She'd get back. She'd be there, waiting for Kaine.

She was not going to die.

There was no time to reanimate the necrothralls to fight for her. She destroyed everything in her path with savage efficiency. There was so much power exploding through her body, her heart threatened to tear in two if she didn't keep moving. She fought free and bolted again. The blood was roaring in her ears. More figures emerged from the smoke. Helena stopped short in horror.

Among them stood Althorne.

She had no idea how they'd managed to reanimate him with the nullium contamination. They must have made a special effort for the general. Beside Althorne stood someone else, a young man with wheat-coloured hair and a square face.

Lancaster.

Crowther had said his prisoners had all died in the bombing. Clearly he'd been mistaken. She looked around, dreading who else might emerge from the smoke.

"Look at that, you were right," Lancaster said to Althorne. "There is someone out here."

"Take her," rasped the lich. Althorne's eyes squinted through the smoke towards her. "She may know who attacked the laboratory."

"If I get her, can I have her?" Lancaster said, eyes lighting up, glancing at Helena again. It was clear he recognised her in some way.

"When the interrogators are done with her," the lich said. "Hurry up."

Helena watched as Lancaster advanced, switching out the obsidian blade for her long titanium dagger. If he was being sent while the lich hung back, that was probably a sign he was still an Aspirant.

But it also meant the lich was the one controlling all the necrothralls.

She had to get rid of him or she'd end up being chased through the city. Lancaster first, though.

Her primary advantage in this was being wanted alive.

"Let me pass," Helena said as Lancaster came closer and the lich began to disappear back into the smoke. She tried to keep an eye on him, track where he was going.

Lancaster shook his head. "Come on, don't make this harder for yourself. You're outnumbered. Drop the knife."

The necrothralls had fanned out around her. They had long-range weapons. Helena's eyes swept left and right, looking for an escape, trying to plot out what to do. Her blood was roaring in her ears, telling her to move, to attack, to run. She had to be smart.

She gripped the dagger a moment longer, feeling the texture, all the finely wrought details, swallowing hard as she let it slip from her fingers and clatter to the ground. She lowered her head and moved submissively forward as her fingers slipped down to grip the other.

She walked hesitantly towards Lancaster.

"Take her."

The necrothralls stepped forward, lowering their weapons as one started to seize her arm.

Helena struck.

Her knife flashed, transmuting mid-motion until it was double its length. She cut off the hand, gutted the necrothrall, and buried a shortened blade into the skull of another.

She dodged a sword that sang as it sliced over her head and lodged in a necrothrall behind her. He screamed.

They weren't all necrothralls, then. Well, that made them easier to kill. She wasn't trying to win, this wasn't a battle; she only wanted to escape. She kept herself aimed in the direction that the lich had disappeared.

You cannot die here.

Her left wrist was caught in a brutal grip. She twisted, wrenching to get free, hot white pain enveloping her shoulder as her arm rolled out of the socket. She whirled back, getting a hand on the attacker. She didn't stop to think, she just ripped apart everything her resonance touched. There was an animalistic scream of agony as her wrist came free.

She dragged herself away, trying to pull her shoulder back into its socket. She could barely move her fingers, but she refused to stop.

Fast and clever, Kaine had said. That was what she needed to be to survive.

Lancaster swung into her path, a grin of triumph on his face, thinking her beaten. She slammed her dagger into his chest. He dropped like a stone.

She found her feet and ran straight into the smoke. She could see the city beyond, glittering with all its false promises.

The necrothralls were still in pursuit; she could hear them through the smoke. She was winded to the point that her vision was blurring. The combination of stimulants and sedatives was doing a remarkable job of keeping her from feeling how injured she currently was.

She saw a large figure in the smoke and went towards it. Althorne. She reached for her obsidian dagger, wishing her left arm worked. She keyed up her resonance until it sang around her in a torus as she rushed forward.

Through the smoke, something huge and heavy swung towards her. She barely dodged in time. It slammed into the ground.

The lich was fighting with a glaive, the way Lila did, but with far less speed and elegance. Helena had never fought a lich, but this one didn't seem accustomed to the body. If she could hit it with the obsidian once, it would sever the reanimation in the body. If she stabbed close enough to the talisman, it would kill whoever he was.

"You're quite the alchemist," came Althorne's voice. The glaive rushed past, so close its wind nearly sliced her cheek open. "What are you?"

Helena was too winded to reply. Her focus was on his weapon and getting past it. She could see Althorne clearly now. His face was grey, and he had a festering head wound. He was in armour, which made it harder to stab him.

When she finally got too close for his glaive, he backhanded her. She went flying but the obsidian caught his wrist, slicing the grey skin wide open. She hit the ground so hard, she couldn't breathe. She forced her head up, gasping as she watched the reanimation unspool from Althorne's corpse, like an infection moving up his arm.

She struggled to her feet. The necrothralls were still coming but slower. The lich didn't fend her off as she closed in again.

Helena only had one fully functional hand, and she hardly managed to grip the obsidian in her left hand while her right ripped the armour out of the way. The lich noticed then, tried to grab at her, but she caught him by the throat and wrenched. Althorne's oesophagus came out. He dropped. She swayed, shoving his armour out of the way, trying to feel for the talisman, to identify where to stab. Purple dead blood oozed from his throat, covering everything, the clothes and armour and the silver chain that hung around his neck. A pendant, coated in blood, had nearly tumbled into the gaping wound.

It was a dragon, with wings arched above it and its tail caught in its teeth.

She paused, staring. This was Atreus Ferron.

She tried to grip the dagger, but her left arm was numb. Was it better to kill him, or to give the talisman to Kaine and let him choose what to do?

No. She had to do this. Kaine shouldn't have to kill his own father.

She reached out with her resonance again, trying to feel for the talisman.

Thwack!

Red exploded in her vision as something slammed across her skull. She toppled across Althorne's corpse, and when she tried to get up, everything spun. She got halfway up and collapsed again.

Lancaster stumbled towards her, half his chest coated in blood. He was gripping the glaive. He'd used the pole section to crack Helena across the back of her head.

"I'm going to kill you," she said, trying again to push herself up.

He gave a wheezing laugh. "Try." He gestured at her. "Get her up."

Two Aspirants pulled Helena off the ground, kicking the obsidian knife out of her hand. Her legs would barely hold her. Everything swayed, but the drug still screamed through her veins, and her resonance was razor-sharp. She didn't fight, instead slumping against the more heavily armed of the two.

They were stupid to fall for the same trick twice.

She found a knife loose enough to slip from its sheath as they dragged her over to Lancaster. Standard-issue combat knife. She was very familiar with the model.

Lancaster was pale with blood loss, but he smiled and kept his distance, clearly preferring to risk his compatriots. "I'm going to have so much fun with you. Once I'm Undying, I'm going to have them keep you alive as they turn you inside out."

She used the last of her strength to lunge at him.

She would have stabbed him straight through the heart, but he managed to dodge. It was a pity for him that she had such broad resonance. She rammed the knife through his armour as if it were paper. She transmuted it, twisting, mangling his lungs before her hand went for his throat.

Fingers clawed into her hair, wrenching her off before she blew his brains apart with her resonance. She clawed at everyone gripping her, her fingers sinking through flesh, tearing at anything she could grasp.

"Break her hand. Break her fucking hand!" Lancaster was screaming as he clutched at the knife buried in his chest, unable to pull it out without ripping out his own lungs.

A hand closed around her forearm, and there was a horrifying crunch as a boot came down on her right wrist.

She watched the heel grinding her wrist into the stones.

They let go and she lay there in the street. Lancaster had already collapsed.

She tried to push herself up with her dislocated arm.

Run, Helena. You have to run.

One of the Aspirants had only one hand left, but he pulled out his sword and brought the hilt down on her head.

HELENA WOKE TO SCREAMING.

She was lying on something cold and hard, and when she tried to open her eyes, they were crusted shut. She lifted a hand to rub them, and white searing pain set her entire brain on fire. Her eyes tried to wrench open, but they still refused to part.

"It's all right. Gentle. There's blood in your lashes." It was a familiar voice. She felt fingers rubbing along her eyes. "There."

Helena peered out, vision swimming, and found Matron Pace staring down at her. Helena was lying with her head in Pace's lap. It was still dark, the only illumination torchlight.

Her senses trickled back. She was in so much pain, but she could tell that she wasn't even feeling all of it yet. She could smell blood. Dried blood and fresh.

There was screaming that kept going on and on.

And laughter, too.

She tried to sit, but Pace held her down.

"None of that. You're badly injured," she was saying. "I got your shoulder back in place, but they took your chest brace and your wrist is badly broken."

"Where are we?" Helena managed to ask. Her eyes wouldn't focus, but she recognised one of the healers as well as medics and orderlies. They were clustered around her.

Pace gave a strained smile. "At Headquarters. In the commons."

Helena looked past Pace; there was something overhead. They were in a cage. A large kind used for animals. There were dozens of cages scattered around them.

"Let me up." Helena struggled to sit up, her body beginning to scream in protest as the stimulants and sedative wore off. Without her chest brace, the strain bore down on her sternum as she peered past the bars. Looking for the source of the screaming.

Hanging by her wrists, Rhea was screaming. Titus stood beside her. He was covered in blood, and there were knives and sticks and spears sticking out of him. He pulled a knife from his leg and began slicing Rhea's skin off with it.

Then he put it in his mouth and ate it.

He was dead. He had to be dead, but the sight of it still left Helena horror-stricken.

And Rhea was not dead.

Beside her there were pieces of meat dangling from chains. Helena squinted in the low light.

Severed arms.

A torso.

Alister's head.

Her throat contracted, and she rolled to her side and vomited so violently, there was tearing pain through her back as her body convulsed.

She looked up again as Pace used a scrap of fabric to wipe her mouth for her.

Helena turned away. "How long have they been—"

"It started at dusk," Pace said, her voice wavering, "once they were sure that Headquarters was secured. They don't have Luc, though, or Sebastian. There's still hope."

Helena's throat tightened so much, she thought she'd choke. She couldn't bring herself to tell Pace that Luc wasn't coming, that he couldn't.

She looked down at herself. She'd been stripped completely and put into a grey smock. Everything was gone: hairpins, ties, hospital call bracelet. The only thing that remained was Kaine's ring, hovering in the corner of her vision even when she looked directly at it. It had worked; even resonance hadn't found it in a strip search.

Now her left wrist bore a suppression shackle, like what had been locked around Lila's wrists. Her right wrist was bare, apparently too swollen for the matching shackle to fit around.

Rhea's screams were growing fainter.

There was a roar of excitement, and Helena looked up, terrified of what would come next.

A long, low motorcar was pulling in through the gates. Helena's heart dropped as it stopped at the steps leading to the Tower. The door opened, and Luc stepped out, his expression hesitant, almost bashful, as if arriving late to a party.

A hush fell across the courtyard. Everyone stared in shock as he surveyed the scene around him.

"No . . ." Helena said at the same time as Pace.

Luc turned and gave a low, obsequious bow as someone else emerged from the back of the motorcar. The person was tall, dressed in intricately decorative robes and a cloak of blue and gold, with a crescent-shaped crown rising from his head. Morrough.

He walked in front of Luc, ascending the marble stairs, which ran red with blood. All the remains of the Eternal Flame's military leaders were in pieces on the ground or dangling against the walls.

Morrough turned as Luc ascended behind him, revealing a masked face; the crescent, like an eclipsed sun, concealed the upper half. The little bit of skin that showed was a pale, lipless mouth.

Helena had never seen Morrough. There had been stories of his appearance at a few early battles, but he'd let the Undying fight his war.

So this was Cetus. The first Northern alchemist.

The silence remained as Luc followed him up the steps obediently, while Morrough surveyed his audience.

"Paladia has followed this family of false deities for too long," Morrough said in a rasping voice that barely seemed like it could carry. "They showed you fire and gold, and you thought these paltry tricks divine." The mouth twisted in derision. "I have conquered death. Immortality is my gift, and I do not hoard this secret knowledge but grant it to all who are worthy."

There were loud cheers at this. But that was not the worst of it. As Morrough spoke, Luc sank to his knees as if he were one of those begging for immortality.

Helena watched Luc's every movement, trying to make sense of what she saw.

Luc was dead, she knew he was dead. Morrough must have found and reanimated him, made him seem so lifelike in order to have the satisfaction of being his executioner.

As everyone watched, Luc leaned forward, pressing his head to the stones which were slick with blood; it stained his clothes, his skin, his hair. The blood of those who'd followed him and his family so faithfully.

"Do you beg for immortality?" Morrough asked.

Luc paused as though hesitating, as if ashamed, then he lifted his head, looking up at Morrough like a supplicant, blue eyes wide, and nodded.

“You are unworthy,” Morrough said, but he held out a long bony hand as if extending it to Luc. Then his wrist turned, palm faced down, above Luc’s head.

Even from the distance, Helena felt the resonance in the air, and Luc’s head slammed down into the marble, skull splitting, breaking apart like a cracked egg. His face caved in, and his body toppled over, brains smeared across the blood-soaked marble.

The air filled with screams of horror.

Morrough turned away from the body. “Store him. He will never burn.”

Then he entered the Alchemy Tower, the monument his brother had built to memorialise necromancy’s defeat.

TIME PASSED IN A HAZE. Those who hadn’t gone into the Tower with Morrough began sorting the remaining prisoners, dividing them up, marking the numbers on the shackles into files.

Now that the “festivities” had come to an end, additional cars were arriving. The more decorated members of the Undying, in their black uniforms. Others who appeared to be government officials. The Guild Assembly. Governor Greenfinch.

Most were entering the Alchemy Tower, which had been rinsed of all the blood.

The door of the cage Helena was in screamed open, and guards began pulling the prisoners out, shoving them towards various areas.

“Careful!” Pace snapped as Helena was seized by the arm and dragged to her feet. “Her wrist is broken. She needs medical care. These are smart, capable women. You should—”

The guard sneered at Pace. “We’ve got plenty of prisoners of all sorts.” He looked Helena over. “She’ll go in the cull group, same as you, crone.”

He ignored Pace’s attempts to reason with him, not for herself but for Helena, trying to convince him of her exceptional abilities, as he copied the number on Helena’s shackle onto a list along with Pace’s.

They were pushed towards another cage and grabbed by another guard, who shoved them carelessly inside.

Pace tried to resist, still protesting, and she tripped, falling too fast for Helena to react. Her head struck one of the iron bars with a sharp crack, and she didn't move.

Helena's left hand was shaking as she braced herself against the bars, using her body to cover Pace as more prisoners were shoved into the cull cage, searching desperately for a pulse. Everyone shoved inside was either badly injured or extremely old. The cadet guarding the war room was slumped beside her, deathly pale, his bowels oozing through his fingers as he tried to hold them in.

She couldn't help him.

She slumped down next to Pace, lifting her head onto her lap, hoping she was dead, that she wouldn't witness whatever happened next.

A shadow fell over her.

She looked up, heart in her throat, and then froze at the sight of Mandl.

"My, my," Mandl said, her wide mouth splitting into a smile, "I thought I recognised that hair of yours."

Helena was too exhausted to feel anything at the sight of her.

Mandl gestured with a quick flick of her wrist. "Take her out."

The guards who'd shoved Pace glanced over. "This is the cull cage."

Mandl turned on him. "I don't care what 'cage' it is, get her out."

Helena was dragged out, her hand bumping roughly against other bodies. She bit back a moan of pain, and her shoulder was nearly wrenched from its socket again.

"It really is you." Mandl appraised her as Helena was dropped at her feet. "You certainly put up a fight. Were you afraid I'd find you?"

Helena had scarcely thought of Mandl since she'd finished interrogating her.

"I hoped I would." Mandl's breath rushed across Helena's. She smelled sharp and acrid, like formaldehyde. "I'm going to make sure Bennet gets you for one of his special projects."

The guard cleared his throat.

"What now?" She turned on him sharply.

"They're saying Bennet's gone."

"What?"

The guard lowered his voice. "Rumour is that Hevgoss was responsible. Bombings are—their sort of thing. No one's saying much, though. Stroud took a batch earlier and had to bring them all back. Says the whole lab's gone. Bennet and all the rest. But word's not supposed to get out among the—" He gestured around the commons.

A glimmer of triumph sparked in Helena's chest. Bennet was gone; he would never hurt Kaine or anyone else ever again.

Mandl stood, stunned. "But then what about the stasis warehouse. Will it be decommissioned?"

Before the guard could reply, she answered herself. "Of course not. The Undying will still need pristine bodies in reserve. Even without Bennet."

She looked down at Helena again, who tried not to look as if she was listening.

"Well, if he's gone, that means that I'm responsible for the selection process." She leaned forward and grabbed Helena by the back of the arm. "I think I'll have you as my first pick."

Mandl's resonance stabbed through Helena's hand. Her nerves were suddenly on fire, being torn apart. Agony shot up her shoulder, through her body, and into her brain as if a splintering spike were being driven into her.

Her muscles began spasming as she screamed.

"Oh dear," Mandl said with false concern, still holding Helena fast. "That wasn't what I meant to do. I was trying to do this." She grabbed Helena by the back of the neck.

Renewed pain burst through her, shooting down her spine and along every nerve ending. Building and building until Helena's heart threatened to explode. She'd break all her own bones if it would let her escape. She'd chew her limbs off.

She could feel her mind scrabbling to break free from the agony. *Just break. Just break.*

"I'm not fragile. I am not going to break. Please believe that about me."

She'd promised. Her body was seizing, but eventually it stopped. She was dropped heavily to the ground. Her muscles kept twitching. Mandl knelt, reaching towards her again, and Helena cowered away.

Mandl's wide mouth stretched across her face. "See how quickly you can learn to be afraid?"

She took Helena's right hand, resetting and healing the broken bones. She would indeed have been an exceptional healer if she hadn't been a psychopath.

Then something cold pressed against Helena's newly healed wrist, clicking as it was locked in place.

She stared at it dazedly, struggling to breathe. It was another cuff. The number was different. She couldn't quite make it out.

Mandl stood, brushing herself off. "Put her in the transport lorry."

As Helena was being dragged up off the ground, a young man stepped forward, stammering.

"Wait. That—that one, we got her. She's supposed to be interrogated. I think. Pretty sure someone said something about that."

Mandl gave a slow reptilian blink. "She was in the cull cage."

He flushed and scratched his head. "We had orders."

"Whose orders?"

"Um, it was one of the dead ones. I don't remember. He told Lancaster something about it."

"And Lancaster is?"

"Well, he's in surgery."

Mandl's lips pursed, and she looked as if she were about to eat the Aspirant. "So you want me to do what? Put her back into the cull cage? Do you have jurisdiction to take her?"

He stammered and backed away. "I just—it's what I heard. Maybe someone else would know."

Helena wasn't sure if she'd just been saved or damned. Interrogation was what Atreus had wanted. To find the bomber. She struggled to think. Her body kept spasming. All the drugs in it had her mind spinning as they faded away.

Several liches came over and dragged Helena and several other prisoners towards a lorry, shoving them into the back.

Interrogation would be dangerous. If anyone realised she was the bomber, they'd want to know how. Why.

She knew all too well now the dangers of interrogation. There were points where the mind broke, where pain became all there was. The Undying would hurt her in whatever ways were necessary to get the answers out.

Kaine said animancy was special. Rare. If Bennet was dead, Kaine and Morrough might be the only ones left with the ability, which meant they might bring him in and torture her in front of him or make him torture her.

If Morrough interrogated her personally, he'd find Kaine in her thoughts and memories. No amount of evasion could hide him; he was the fabric of her thoughts. Her every action tied to him.

Even if her death was quick, Kaine's punishment for his betrayal would be eternal. Or else they'd use her, just as they had his mother.

It would be everything he'd feared.

If they found him in her memory.

If.

She had to push him away, like she had pushed away the memory of—

Soren.

She would redirect her thoughts, transmute her memories until her mind stopped running to him. She couldn't confess to something she didn't remember.

She pressed her hands against her temples, wincing as she moved her right hand. The bones were repaired, but the tissue damage and bruising remained. The nullium in the manacles hummed, blurring her resonance, but suppression like that was imperfect.

She still had her resonance, though it wasn't as powerful. But she didn't need power; she needed precision and patience. She closed her eyes, using that feeble strain of resonance on her own consciousness. After spending so much time navigating the minds of others, it was easy to manipulate her own mind—no reaction, no resistance.

The last two years of her life, she pushed down beneath the surface as if to drown them. There was no other way. Kaine was almost everything now.

Without him, there was just emptiness. Her routines. Hours and days in the hospital that bled together, years of an unending nightmare.

Alone. Everyone dead. Because they always died. She tried to save them, but in the end, they always died. Her life was a graveyard.

Where there was space she couldn't reconcile, she filled it with Luc. Not his death, not Luc from the war; the Luc she'd promised to save.

The version of him he'd tried to be. The Luc who'd always believed in her.

It was the way he deserved to be remembered.

She was lost in her own mind when the lorry pulled into a warehouse. An old slaughterhouse with meat hooks overhead and metal tables everywhere, and a cement floor that could be easily sprayed down to wash away the blood. The other prisoners began to panic, jostling her from her thoughts.

"They're not going to kill us yet," Helena said, her voice raw. "They're putting us in stasis. To keep us fresh."

They were pulled out, one by one, and injected with something.

The process was horrifyingly well synchronised. Rote. As the prisoners went limp, they were hoisted onto long tables, side by side. A guard went down the line stripping their clothes off.

A few tried to fight. One boy got kicked in the gut for his efforts before the needle went into his neck. He called out for his mother, for Sol, for Luc.

The woman—Mandl, her mind belatedly supplied—stood observing, and when Helena was pulled out, she waved her towards the far end of the warehouse. "Put her over there. I'll deal with her personally."

A needle sank into the side of Helena's neck. It was thick, the dose of paralytic unnecessarily large.

Her muscles went numb, but not her sensory nerves. She could feel things, just not move.

Mandl's face appeared above her, a satisfied smile on her lips, eyes skimming from head to toe. "You think you know what's about to happen to you, don't you?"

Helena lay there as Mandl pulled her hair out of the way and placed something adhesive at the base of her neck, over her spine.

"This is to keep your muscles in order."

An electric pulse caused Helena's body to seize, muscles contracting and releasing several times.

Mandl's fingers trailed across Helena's cold skin, seeming to tremble with excitement. Needles with tubes sank into her arms.

"Pity about Bennet," Mandl said. "I always found his ideas inspirational. If he got you, he'd keep you alive for ages if I asked. Interrogations are so quick, and you'll be completely spoiled after that."

She placed a mask over Helena's face that stretched from above her eyebrows all the way down over her chin. There was some kind of adhesive that sealed it against her skin. It was transparent enough that Helena could just barely see through it and watch as Mandl picked up a large syringe with a pale-blue liquid inside. "This would put you in a nice little coma. Bennet said it's like making meat tender by keeping the pigs calm before slaughter."

She squeezed the plunger. Helena heard it spatter onto the floor.

Then there was the sound of paper tearing as Mandl ripped a form off a clipboard, crumpling it. For a moment she could make out the number at the top, 19819.

Without that form, there would be no record that Helena was there. She'd vanish. A clerical error.

Mandl combed her fingers through Helena's hair. "While you're waiting, I want you to think about all the things I'm going to do to you when I come back."

Mandl turned away. "All done here. Put her under with the rest."

Helena was lifted onto a cart that went rattling across the floor into a second room. It was bitterly cold. Helena could see the rows of sectioned tanks from the corner of her eyes. The photographs from the raid flashed in her memory, all the bodies floating inside them. All dead.

The guards, wearing large rubber gloves to their shoulders, lifted one prisoner after another and slid them into the tanks, hooking the tubes and wires into a row of machines that ran along the far end.

Helena's heart was pounding harder and harder as she was picked up and the cold fluid closed around her.

She couldn't move. She was trapped inside her own body, like a cage sealing her within her mind. The cold seeped into her, slowing her heart, dropping her metabolism. It felt like forever and like no time at all before the light vanished, too.

Helena was left in darkness and silence.

Her heart was pounding in unadulterated terror. The lid was inches from her face, but she couldn't see it. Freedom so close but utterly beyond reach.

She tried to breathe slowly but couldn't. She started panting, heat and steam filling the mask over her face.

She tried to scream, but all that came out was a weak uneven whimper. Her body grew colder and colder, and her lungs spasmed as her panic used up the limited oxygen coming through the mask. Her chest began aching and burning for air. She kept trying to breathe, but there was nothing to breathe.

She was relieved when she passed out. It was better than being awake.

Something burning hot jolted her back to consciousness.

She'd forgotten where she was and panicked as it all rushed back. The tiny, enclosed space beneath the surface, in the dark. Not enough air, and she couldn't move.

The burning came again, cutting her panic short as she tried to place where the sensation was coming from. She knew that feeling.

Her hand. Her left hand was burning. The ring. Her heart stalled.

Kaine. He'd come back and found her gone. She'd told him she'd be waiting, and she wasn't there. The ring burned again and again and again.

He was looking for her. He'd come for her.

He always did.

But she could not think about it.

She had to forget. If she remembered and was interrogated, Kaine could not be found.

She couldn't think about him. Trapped, frozen, without use of her hands, she could only draw her resonance inwards. She was used to pushing it out for combat. Now it was like a net she closed around her own mind.

She could feel the faint texture in her mind of her manipulations, altering her thoughts, bending them around all the things she must not think about. She followed the new paths, over and over, wearing new grooves into place, teaching her mind to settle there and look no further. She counted. She made routines. She tried not to remember.

If Kaine found her, he'd understand.

She could wait.

Hold on. You promised you wouldn't break.

PART THREE

CHAPTER 66

Maius 1789

CONSCIOUSNESS SPLIT HELENA'S MIND OPEN.

She lurched up, head throbbing, mad with pain. All she could think was *Get away, run.* The need to escape consumed her. Everywhere she looked, it was all darkness.

She tried to move, but her body failed her. Her motions jerked, and pain bloomed from her wrists, across her hands, and into her arms when she tried to get up. She struggled to breathe as her ribs had clamped tight around her lungs.

It wasn't the tank, but it was still so dark, and she could barely move.

A hand brushed against her shoulder.

She gave a strangled scream, her head snapping up. It was Kaine. He was leaning over her, his pale hair and silver-bright eyes visible in the dark. His fingers trembled as he stared at her.

She studied him in shock.

He was different. Older. He wasn't old, but his eyes had a look as if it had been decades since she'd last seen him.

She gave a sob and reached for him.

"You're alive," she said.

He flinched back as despair swept across his face. She didn't understand why. Then Grace's fearful voice rose from some distant corner of her mind.

"Lila Bayard was the first one he brought back."

It all came rushing back: The manacles. Transference. Imprisonment in Spirefell. Everyone was dead because the High Reeve had killed them.

He was the High Reeve.

Her blood ran ice-cold and she snatched her hand back, shoving herself away from him, ignoring the screaming pain in her wrists. Something was tangled around her elbow, and she ripped it out as she scrambled away. Her arms and legs shook under her own weight, and she nearly toppled off the far side of the bed. She slid onto the floor and knelt, peering across the mattress at him in that dark room in that dark house where she was a captive.

Kaine was *still* alive.

But if he was alive, that meant he had not come for her, and she had waited.

The mental dissonance made her want to scream. The past and present shattering against each other as she knelt in their ruins.

It couldn't be him. Ferron had hurt her. He'd *raped* her. And he killed everyone.

Kaine wouldn't.

He'd promised he'd always—

Pain lanced through her brain. Her vision disappeared. An anguished moan escaped her. She buried her face in her hands as it grew, boring through her mind, so excruciating she could hardly keep conscious.

Her head was on fire, skull cut open, pressure emulsifying her brain. She screamed, trying to let it out. She kept screaming until she was gasping for air. When she looked up again, she was alone.

Perhaps she always had been, and Kaine's face had been an apparition she'd conjured.

Perhaps this was all a dream. He was dead, and she was still in the tank, rotting and forgotten in the dark where no one would ever find her.

She slumped, and a hand grasped her shoulder before she hit the floor. She started, and he was there again. As their eyes met, his expression crumpled.

"You're remembering, aren't you?"

She managed a nod, reaching up and gripping his wrist, feeling his skin and bones beneath her fingers. He was real.

He was still alive. She'd been so sure that everyone was dead, but he wasn't, and yet that felt worse.

She turned her face away, pressing it into the duvet, wanting to scream again. All the contradictions and horror clamoured as she tried to untangle her mind. Nothing felt real. Everything was lies.

Clarity struck, and she gripped him tighter, nails biting his skin.

"The obsidian—Mandl and the rest—was that—was that you . . . ?"

"It was."

Her jaw trembled, her eyes burning. "Was it—always you?"

"Yes."

All the Resistance fighters, secret members of the Eternal Flame that she'd convinced herself were out there, all melted away until only Kaine remained. Her captor and nightmare.

She nodded, looking away, unable to reconcile her simultaneous relief and horror.

He was alive. She'd kept him alive. That was what she'd wanted but—

Not like this.

"Why'd you kill Lila?" Her voice cracked.

"I didn't. She's alive."

She stared at him. The pain in her head seemed to make him glow. "Grace saw her body. Everyone at the Outpost saw it. Mandl kept her at the gate."

"She was pregnant, and she was the only surviving Bayard. They weren't going to stop looking for her until they found a body. I produced one. It was your idea."

Helena had no memory of that. She didn't know how to believe anything he said, so much deceit lay between them.

"She has a son now. An exceptionally noisy child, named for his grandfather. And every time I've seen her, she's tried to murder me at least twice."

That did sound like Lila. Helena lifted her head, her throat aching with the desire to believe him. "Where is she?"

He shook his head. "Not in Paladia, but you'll see her soon. You promised Holdfast you'd take care of them, remember? They've been waiting for you."

Her heart rose, but then she remembered all the other things he'd told her, said to her. She shrank away.

"I don't believe you." Her jaw trembled uncontrollably.

"I know."

She shook her head. "I don't understand. I can't remember—I only remember you."

She wanted to reassure herself that he was real, but he couldn't be real. The person in her memory couldn't exist because Kaine Ferron had killed everyone. Eradicated the Eternal Flame, hunted down anyone in the Resistance who'd dared to run. He was drenched in blood.

His throat dipped. "What—do you remember of me?"

He was familiar and yet so utterly changed, as if he'd been carved out of the likeness of the person she'd known.

"You—you spied for the Eternal Flame," she said, her voice barely more than a whisper. "You used to call me, and I'd come and heal you—and—annnn—"

Her tongue stuck on the word as bright scarlet pain burst through her head and everything tilted.

She blinked rapidly, struggling to think. She'd been saying something—something . . . Her tongue was fuzzy. When she tried to open her mouth, her jaw jerked, snapping repeatedly.

Her limbs and fingers all curled rigidly inwards, as if she were a dead spider. She toppled, and Kaine caught her just before she slammed face-first into the floor.

She couldn't speak.

Her jaw kept snapping, lungs rattling as she gasped. Her head began jerking, slamming against his chest until he pressed his hand flat, holding her still. Her heart raced with panic.

"It's all right," he said. "Give it a minute. It'll pass."

She felt him inhale as she kept jerking in his arms.

"Did quite a number to that brain of yours." His voice was calm. "All your transmuted barriers are coming apart now. It'll pass."

Her throat contracted, and every tendon and muscle inside her body seemed to be drawn inwards, threatening to snap. He'd said it would pass but it wasn't passing.

"Just a little longer," he said.

Her head finally stopped jerking, and her body went limp in his arms, mind hazy and disjointed. He picked her up. Her bones jutted out, the joints pressing against him as he placed her back onto the bed, tucking her under the duvet. She wanted to protest, but her jaw was rigid, mouth refusing to move properly.

There was a reason he shouldn't hold her. She didn't want him to, but she couldn't remember why anymore. Yet she was terrified that if he let go, he'd disappear into the dark and leave her there alone.

He moved quietly around the bed and lit a candle, sorting through a tray of vials beside the bed. The dim light flickered between them.

"You've been unconscious for a week," he said without looking up, as if he could feel her watching him. "You—" He stopped, lips pressed together as he inhaled. "You had a seizure and wouldn't wake afterwards. A-Apparently you've been subconsciously maintaining all those barriers inside your brain. All this time. When you got pregnant—the Toll from it all was too much. Burned yourself out."

Pregnant? She'd forgotten that she was pregnant. A panicked rasping gasp shook her as it came back to her. The baby that Morrough wanted. She'd just lain there and let it happen and—

"Why—" One word was all she could manage.

Kaine wavered, eyes darting from the items in front of him to her. He set them down and leaned over.

"Look at me. I know you want to remember everything, but your mind has to stabilise; everything is fragile right now." His eyes were imploring. "It will make sense eventually."

He didn't use resonance as he spoke. It would have made things worse if he had. Just being close to him, her body intuitively calmed even though she remembered so vividly all the ways he'd hurt her inside this cold prison of a house.

A tremor ran through her.

"It's just a little longer," he said, "and this will all be over."

She had so many questions, though. *What happened? Why didn't you come? Why did you hurt me? Why did you rape me?*

Why did you become High Reeve?

"Why—" Her voice broke. "—why did you kill everyone?"

He seemed startled by the question, as if he'd expected one of the others. "I was trying to find you."

Her heart stalled, body and mind torn between horror and relief.

"You looked for me?" Her voice cracked.

A look of anguish flashed across his eyes. "Of course I looked for you. I looked everywhere for you. Did you think I left you there?"

She tried to remember what she'd thought. "I was supposed to be interrogated. There was so much of you in my head. I thought, if I didn't remember, they wouldn't be able to find you. No one ever came. I thought everyone must be dead."

He looked as though she'd gutted him and stepped back, turning away from her.

"I looked for you everywhere. In the wreckage first, then Central and the Outpost, but you'd disappeared. There was a transfer slip about a person of interest captured near West Port, and you'd been listed as too injured for rehabilitation and culled. I went through all the dead trying to find you, but you weren't there. I went through every prison, every file, but you'd disappeared, so I volunteered to track down anyone missing. I thought eventually something would lead to you." His jaw clenched. "I had to bring them all back. If I'd failed, the job would have been reassigned."

He didn't meet her eyes as he said this, staring across the room. "I went to Hevgoss quite a few times. Thought maybe you'd somehow ended up there. I was even in that warehouse once, checking all the files there for anyone who might match your description. But I didn't open the tanks so—"

His jaw trembled visibly, and he didn't say anything else—just turned back to sorting through the tray.

"Why didn't you assume I was dead?" she asked.

His hands stilled. "I had to know."

He drew a deep breath. "This room is safe, but Morrough has eyes in the house. He watches from the hallway sometimes. Now that you're pregnant, he's unlikely to have you brought in again, but as long as it was a risk, there was always the chance he'd see anything that happened here."

Understanding slowly dawned on her. All these months, Kaine had been performing for Morrough through Helena's eyes, knowing that any moment that passed between them might be seen.

What had been real, then? Any of it? None?

A wave of exhaustion struck. She felt as if all her memories had been shaken and lay jumbled and upended, out of order. It was hard to even think clearly.

She wanted to sleep, to sink back into the abyss, but she was afraid that her memories might slip away again. That Kaine would vanish, and when she woke it would be Ferron again, ice-cold and cruel.

Try as she might, the two were categorically separate in her mind.

Kaine, she knew.

But Ferron was a monster. Her fear and hatred of him were rooted in her bones. That horrific chair of bodies, his pile of victims. She couldn't forget that.

Her head throbbed, her skull threatening to crush her eyes out of her head. She squeezed them shut. The bed dipped, and Kaine took her arm. She felt her veins swell, and there was a prick of a needle as he put in a new intravenous drip.

"Don't pull this one out," he said as he worked. "All your years in a hospital, and you're still a terrible patient."

He laid her arm down and began going through the vials again, finding one and adding it to all the tubes that joined with the saline running into her arm.

"You should sleep now," he said. "We'll talk tomorrow."

"What if I forget again?" Her voice was small, nearly trembling with fear.

He didn't answer.

"Will you—will you go back to being the way you were, if I forget?"

"It's almost over now," he said, not answering the question.

She could feel the drugs in her veins, a heavy shroud bearing down on her. She fought to keep her eyes open, to stay awake, to remember.

"Then what?"

The room seemed darker.

"You'll take care of Lila, the way you promised you would."

THERE WAS A CRACK OF faint light cast between the curtains when her eyes opened again. She could see the room, her prison. Kaine was gone.

She was only awake a few minutes before the door opened, and one of the necrothralls entered. Helena stared.

"I saw you before . . ." Helena said as the necrothrall set down a tray with a bowl of soup on it. "I was here, before."

Why would she have been here?

"Shhhhh . . ." The necrothrall released a soft, hissing breath through her teeth, shaking her head as if in warning.

She reached into a pocket and withdrew a folded piece of paper, holding it out to Helena.

There was only one word, written in clear strokes.

REST.

The paper slipped from her fingers and the necrothrall took it immediately, returning it to her pocket before offering soup.

Helena forced a few spoonfuls down, but her body recoiled, trying to hurl them back up. She tried not to think, to stop trying to remember, but it was like trying to ignore Lumithia in Ascendance.

All that time, Kaine had known her. From the moment she'd arrived.

The transference process . . . it was *her* idea. The procedure she'd wanted to use on Titus Bayard.

And Shiseo . . .

She looked down at her wrists in renewed horror.

Transference, the manacles—those weren't things that Kaine had known of. It was Shiseo who'd known. Transference was the reason Morrough had wanted the repopulation program started.

Her throat convulsed, and she vomited all the soup onto the floor beside the bed.

She tried to stop thinking about it. To remember herself from before, to reconcile who she was with the person she'd forgotten. In the process of forgetting, she'd flattened herself, forgotten all her anger. Her capacity to be monstrous.

That was the person Kaine wanted. Who he'd done all this for.

But that Helena didn't exist anymore. All that was left now was a shadow.

It was dark when Kaine returned.

Her heart rose with relief, but dread rushed through her at the sight of him. She stared at him in the dark as he stayed by the door, clearly not intending to linger, coldly appraising her from across the room.

She didn't know what she wanted him to do. She didn't want him there, but not seeing him was worse because when he was gone, he might be dead; she'd never see him again.

"Are you angry with me about something?" she asked when he didn't speak.

His lips vanished into a line, and he entered, shutting the door. "No."

He went to a window, pushing back the curtains enough to let in a soft gleam of silver light. He was in uniform.

Helena watched him, trying to pinpoint what it was about him that was so different now.

"You are," she said. "I feel like I know you are, but I don't remember why."

He didn't look at her. "It doesn't matter. It's all in the past."

"Why look for me, then, if the past doesn't matter?"

His jaw clenched. "Do you remember how you were captured?"

She nodded. "I blew up the West Port Lab."

He gave a short nod, still staring out the window. "Do you remember why?"

She furrowed her eyebrows. The answer felt obvious, but she couldn't remember exactly.

"Don't push if you can't recall," he said, glancing towards her sharply when she was silent.

"It was because of you, wasn't it?" she asked, somehow sure it had to have been, although she didn't remember anything except the fire, her ears throbbing, trying to run.

He looked away again but nodded.

Helena wasn't sure why he'd be angry about that. She closed her eyes. She felt so tired now that he was there, as if she'd waited for him in order to rest.

"When you were asleep, I used to promise I'd take care of you," she said.

"No." He said it harshly. "That was me. I was the one who used to say that."

She opened her eyes. "I used to say it back. I guess you didn't know."

His expression grew stricken and then he looked away, flicking the curtains closed so that it was too dim to make out his face anymore.

"What's the plan?" she asked into the darkness. "You said it was almost over? What does that mean?"

His eyes seemed to glow. "We're just waiting for the summer Abeyance. Get you as far away as possible. You'll blend in if you go south."

"Is that where Lila is? South?"

"Yes, she's still on the mainland, near the coast. She stayed at a midway point while we tried to find you."

"We?" Hope rose in her chest. There were survivors.

"Shiseo."

Helena recoiled at the name.

Kaine was closer now, she could tell by his voice, but the room was so dark that she couldn't see him. "He turned himself in, providing papers and a seal identifying him as a member of the imperial family, and offering research. He designed those manacles in the hope that if you ever showed up, he'd be the one called in to put them on."

"Well, he certainly managed that," Helena said hoarsely. "This is all his fault. If he hadn't told them about transference—"

"Morrough would have vivisected your brain the day they found you if Shiseo hadn't intervened," Kaine said. "He had no way of knowing what Morrough would do with the method."

She fell silent.

"It was the only thing he could come up with that would give me access to you and buy enough time. He'll be the one to take you to Lila."

"But what's the plan for Paladia?"

Kaine was silent for several moments. "Morrough's weakening. He tried to use Holdfast for spare parts, but it wasn't enough, even though he mutilated himself adding his bones. Enough of the Undying are gone now that he can't move or breathe without that monstrosity of his. That's why he's so desperate for an animancer—he thinks it'll let him start over."

Luc's bones. He'd used Luc's bones.

"It's all about striking at the right moment," Kaine was saying. "Morrough's activities and the extent of the slaughter here have begun to impact the continent. The surrounding countries will intervene soon. There are rumours of an alliance that even Hevgoss is cooperating with. Paladia's a critical source of lumithium, and it's an industrial power that isn't easily replaced when so many alchemists are dead. The other countries may not have cared when it was a civil conflict, but now they'll act to secure their interests. Once they're confident Morrough's weak, they'll move quickly."

There was an assurance in the way he said it, as if it was all arranged, every detail already in place. Helena brightened with interest, trying to remember what she'd read in the papers.

"How will you—?"

"You don't need to worry about the specifics," he said, cutting her off. "You'll be gone before then. If you want to help, eat and get strong enough to travel."

He left without another word.

He didn't come back again for several days.

It made her anxious as evening after evening passed and he failed to even briefly appear. She couldn't stop herself from trying to remember, to piece together answers of why he was angry and why he didn't come back. Memories would burst open, staining her vision red, upending her thoughts, leaving her drowning in disjointed spurts of emotion and snatches of conversation.

She had fits all through the day. Davies added vials of various drugs to the saline drip until Helena lay in a stupor, unable to think.

It was dark when the mattress dipped and a cool hand brushed back the curls clinging to her face, tucking them behind her ear. Her hand was picked up, long fingers entwining with hers. Kaine's thumb stroked across her knuckles, finally stopping at her ring finger, spiralling something there slowly.

The ring.

She'd forgotten all about it.

Once the fits stopped, Kaine withdrew again, but he didn't disappear entirely. At first she thought she was imagining it, but it was undeniable that he was distancing himself.

He'd stand, hands clasped behind his back, not even looking at her, giving only short answers to her questions. She rarely knew what to say; everything felt either trivial or too devastating to put into words. She didn't know where to begin.

Hold on, she'd told herself over and over inside the tank. *Don't break.* She'd thought she'd succeeded, but now she knew, there were only pieces of her left.

She sat in bed, watching him stare out the window. It was night and there was nothing to see; he simply didn't want to look at her. She knew he'd leave in a moment, if she didn't say something.

"How—have you been?" she finally asked in desperation, then winced because it was a stupid question.

"Fine," he said.

She blinked down at her lap. "You're married."

He went rigid at that, and she watched him inhale. "Yes, to Aurelia Ingram."

She nodded. She didn't know why it mattered, given everything else. She'd never at any point imagined Kaine marrying her. Yet her mind couldn't move away from the detail. He had a wife now. Which made her—

She wasn't sure what she was. What she'd ever been.

"Morrough ordered it," he said, even though she hadn't said anything else. "The Guild Assembly wanted a high-profile event, proof that things were back to normal. I didn't have any choice."

She nodded again wordlessly.

"I—" He looked towards her and started to speak again but then stopped.

The space between them was like a chasm filled with every sin they'd ever committed against each other, but even from that distance, she could feel his anger.

No matter what he said, she knew he was angry at her.

"You're able to travel now?" she asked. "You said you went to Hevgoss lots of times."

"Yes."

She twisted the linen hem of the sheet between her fingers. "Then . . . after things here are done, will you—will you come south, too?"

"Lila has a rather abiding hatred for me."

Helena kept waiting for an answer. *We're supposed to run away together. You promised.*

He glanced back out into the courtyard. "With luck, I won't be in Paladia for long afterwards."

"So you'll come—eventually?" Her voice was hopeful.

It felt impossible for things to ever be repaired within the suffocating confines of Spirefell, but if they went somewhere far away, maybe it could be done. They'd found each other once, after all. With time, they could do it again.

His eyes glittered for a moment, and she saw the briefest curve of his lips as he quietly said, "If that's what you want."

It felt like a lie.

CHAPTER 67

Maius 1789

TIME DID NOT HEAL ALL WOUNDS, BUT it did make a difference for Helena's mind. With each day, her memories seemed to settle, falling into a semblance of order.

She gradually remembered tricking Kaine and finally understood why he'd been so deeply paranoid from the moment of her arrival. Why he had checked her mind, wanting to know even her most inconsequential occupations.

He'd underestimated her once; now he would never trust her again. He was still lying to her.

She'd suspected, but it was difficult to rely on her judgement or interpretation of anything. Lacunae were scattered across her consciousness. Her thoughts still compulsively turned away from their conclusions, and her mind was habitual in its tendency to overlook what was missing. But as time passed, she grew certain of his deceit.

He was managing her, "maintaining her environment," and trying to trick her even now. What the deceit was, she wasn't sure. She mulled over it, trying to sense the holes in the carefully crafted narrative he'd begun feeding her from the moment she'd regained consciousness. She needed more perspective, a stronger sense of what was real and what was not.

She went out into the hallway, staring down the passages. It used to terrify her, the hallways, the house, the ghastly sense of death and mourning that permeated it.

She stood there, watching the space around her disappear into shadows. It was haunted after all.

She had been the ghost.

She wandered slowly down the hallway, her feet bare. The cold iron in the floor kept her present, sure of what was real.

Kaine appeared on the landing below her as she reached the stairs. He was all in black except the pristine white at his throat, and the barest edges of his cuffs visible at the wrists. His colouring was so stark now, he looked almost like an ink drawing, the sharp lines and contrast of black and white.

"I thought you'd be out," she said when he didn't speak.

"I noticed you were up. Do you think you could manage a trip to the main wing?"

No, but she nodded, curious where he'd take her.

He maintained a conscientious distance as they made the journey, warning her quietly of the places where Morrough could be watching.

She kept looking at him, noticing the edge to him, the over-precision. He was exacting to a degree that left him nearly inhuman. It was the array, she realised with slow horror. He was more than distilled. It had transmuted him until there was nothing left but the qualities it permitted.

In his search for her, he'd let it consume him.

They stopped outside a large pair of doors that had always been locked during Helena's exploration of the house. Opened, they revealed a library.

"I would have brought you here earlier, but I worried Aurelia might be suspicious if you were in this wing too often," he said, stepping to the side so she had space to enter. "I'll be gone until evening, but I thought an incentive to exercise and a way to pass the time might suit you."

Helena didn't move, peering into the cavernous space. On the far side, she could see a few north-facing windows. Even in late spring, the light in the wing was feeble, the aisles shadowy, and the ceiling so high she could scarcely make it out. The darkness threatened to drop down and swallow her.

She'd just disappear.

"Aurelia might notice now," she said, not stepping through the doorway.

"She's gone."

She looked at him sharply.

"Staying in the city at present. I doubt she'll come back, but you'll be warned if she does."

Helena swallowed. "Maybe—maybe we could come back later."

Kaine had clearly expected this to tempt her. After all, she had been desperately bored in captivity, and now he was offering a world of pre-occupations. His eyes ran over her in a rapid catalogue.

Helena rested her fingers on the wall, feeling the texture of the wall-paper as she wet her lips.

"It's just a bit dark—in there," she said. "The ceiling. It wouldn't be very good if I had a fit . . . and there's the—the baby." She tripped over the word. It was the first time she'd managed to acknowledge it since she'd regained consciousness. Her mind swerved hard around that reality, unable to face its implications.

Kaine flinched, too.

"I'd rather not go in. If that's all right," she said.

"Hel—" He started to move towards her, but she tensed, and he stopped short.

He stood, staring at her, one hand barely outstretched. Her cheeks burned, and she looked away.

What must it be like to be stuck with this version of her when she used to be so much more? She couldn't even fully remember and still found it intolerable. Her jaw trembled.

"I know it's illogical—being scared of the dark. I know," she said, and her voice shook. "I'm trying—I know . . ."

He stepped back, pulling the doors shut, and her heart dropped as the distance between them grew larger. Even though she didn't want him to touch her, she felt desperate for him to hold her again. Her mind and body were at perpetual odds.

He could not occupy the impossible in-between where she wanted him because there was no distance large enough to erase what had happened that still left him within her reach.

"It's fine," he said without looking at her. "I thought you might want to, but of course, you're not familiar with the space. If there's anything you want, I'll bring it to you."

She gave a stilted nod.

"I'll walk you back," he said.

"No, you should go," she said, pressing her hand against the wall until the manacle twinged inside her wrist. "I'll slow you too much. I know the way."

His eyes flickered. "If that's what you want."

He turned away, and she reached out on instinct. "Kaine . . ."

He stopped, and she instantly withdrew her hand.

She forced a tight smile. "Be careful. Don't die."

He stood unmoving for a moment, staring at her, and then turned away. "Right."

IT WAS PAST NIGHTFALL WHEN he returned. Helena was sitting on the sofa in her room, staring at the pattern on the rug as she waited. She had spent the whole day trying to be sure of the lie, piecing everything together again and again.

He paused in the doorway, not entering, as if to make clear that it was to be a brief, impersonal visit. She watched him carefully. He'd always been prone to being still. She remembered that about him.

"Do you know what books you'd like?" he asked at length.

She shook her head. "I've been thinking today."

He raised an eyebrow.

"Your plan doesn't make any sense to me," she said.

"Well, not all of us have your exceptional intellect," he said lightly, but he didn't move from the doorway.

Helena studied the space between them. If Morrough were watching, what would he see? Nothing. There was nothing to see, there was only emptiness between them.

"Today, you didn't say you'd always come for me," she said. "You used to say that when I had to go. When I—" She blinked, one hand spasming. "I think. Didn't you?"

Kaine's face twisted into a grimace, and he stepped into the room, shutting the door, and leaning against it. "I thought it a rather empty promise at this point."

She shook her head. "It wasn't your fault. You looked everywhere. Mandl—"

He gave a harsh laugh. Helena started, her heart slamming into her throat.

"Right. Thank you. Of course," he said, the sarcasm bright in his tone. "Everywhere. Yes, I looked everywhere, didn't I?"

She stared at him as his voice turned musing but his eyes remained hard and glittering.

"Through wreckage, and piles of corpses, through prisons and mines and laboratories, and across a damned continent. I looked everywhere—except the *one* place that mattered." His voice cracked, but he grinned. "Thank you, truly, for crediting my *exceptional* efforts."

There was something familiar about the way he was speaking. Her stomach curdled, and her vision flickered. His face suddenly loomed and she wasn't sure where she was. Past? Present? Both?

He gave another laugh, startling her back into the moment.

His expression had warped. "Not my fault?" he was saying; his teeth showed, bared at her. "Is that what you expect me to tell myself?" He laid a pale hand over his heart. "Do you think embracing eternal victimhood will make me feel better?"

He was seething with so much rage, she could feel it in the air. She looked down, trying to breathe slowly.

There were so many things she was trying not to think about, struggling to keep her face above the surface before she drowned in the morass of her mind.

But she knew that he was lying to her. There was something he didn't want her to know, that he was determined to keep her from realising, and if she could remember more clearly, she'd know what it was.

"That's not my point," she said. "I'm not trying to talk about that. What I don't understand is why you're waiting until I'm gone. Morrough will know you've either betrayed or failed him if I escape."

He drew a breath, composing himself, sharp and cruel as a steel trap. "As I said, there is very specific timing to it all, but none of it concerns you."

He was trying to wound her into silence, but she refused to let him.

"If I'm gone, Morrough will know you're the traitor," she said stubbornly. "Even if he doesn't, he'll blame you for letting me escape. He's desperate, and this—this baby is his best chance. If you could hurt him enough to topple the regime, you would have already done it unless there's something holding you back."

Now Kaine said nothing.

She drew a deep breath. "You said things are unstable, and that's true, but there's one thing that's keeping everything together, one thing preventing a collapse. The High Reeve. That's who everyone is afraid of. They all assume that if anything happens to Morrough, the High Reeve will take over. And now the world knows that's you.

"Considering it in that light, then there's only one thing I can think of that would make Morrough seem weak enough for the other countries to finally attack."

He gave a smooth shrug. "I'd hardly consider you well-apprised about the current political climate. Just because you can only think of one thing doesn't mean that nothing else exists."

She met his eyes. "Why don't you tell me what you're planning, then? And we can see if I'm missing something."

He cocked his head, a freezing, mocking intensity suddenly surfacing. "Which part of 'it doesn't concern you' do you not understand? Has the meaning of one of those words slipped your mind? Should I bring a dictionary, perhaps?"

Her throat tightened, her fingers spasming. He was always cruellest when he was vulnerable.

She met his eyes. "If you had a way to weaken or kill Morrough, you would have done it already. You wouldn't have—" Her throat closed. "I wouldn't be—pregnant. Which means there's something preventing you from doing it. And it's me, isn't it? You're waiting until I'm gone, because it won't matter then if Morrough knows you're a traitor, because you'll be dead. Because that's the only way left to weaken Morrough, losing the High Reeve."

He stood unmoving a moment longer, and then the façade fell. He gave a long sigh.

"I had really hoped the library would keep you busy for at least a week," he said, looking exhausted.

Helena waited for him to explain himself, but he didn't.

"That's your plan?" Her voice rose, trembling with disbelief. "All this time and you've gone with the same plan of hiding me somewhere and getting yourself killed as a traitor, and you think I'll be all right with it?"

He gave a laugh so low, it hummed in her bones.

"Do you have a better solution for us this time, too?" he asked quietly. "After all, not every single horror that I've ever imagined has happened to you yet. Losing you and spending fourteen months trying and failing to find you. Finally getting you back, tortured and broken. Keeping you prisoner—the transference—raping you—" His voice was growing raw with grief and rage.

He had gone white, that scalding gleaming white. "Is this not enough? There are, undoubtedly, still unexplored depths to the potential misery between us. Shall we endeavour to achieve all of it?"

She was silent. There was so much she wanted to say, but finding a way to begin, to reconcile it, felt impossible. Her mind was too small now, too simple to contain it. If she tried, it would shatter.

He released a sharp breath, and his expression closed, the gleam vanishing. His jaw trembled. "This is the best I can do, Helena. I'm sorry, I know it's never been enough for you."

"Kaine—" His name came out jagged.

He sighed, resting a hand against the doorframe as though it were propping him up. "I know you want to save everyone; you always do. Unfortunately, that's not a talent I possess. At least this way you'll see the war ended. I can give you that."

"No!" she said forcefully.

He looked up at her, his face hardening. "You always said you wouldn't choose me over everyone else. I am chained to a sinking ship. I will not take you with me."

"I was lying!" The words came out a scream. "I didn't—I couldn't—I wasn't g-g—"

She gasped for air, clutching at her chest. Her heart was pounding so unevenly, it wouldn't let her breathe. She pressed one hand hard against her sternum, ignoring the pain that shot through her arm. The room swam.

Kaine's fury vanished, and he came towards her hesitantly, kneeling as if she were a skittish animal. He gently took her by the shoulders, holding her upright.

"Helena . . . breathe. Please. You have to breathe." His eyes were pleading.

She remembered him. This. That they were like this once. She grasped at him, fingers clutching at his shoulder, her forehead meeting his.

"Please breathe," he kept saying, the weight of his hands on her shoulders grounding her until her chest stopped spasming.

"There has to be another way," she said, when she could speak again. "We said we'd run away together. Remember? Why can't we run away? You said you travelled; we could run and I'll find a way to reverse what happened to you. The other countries will deal with Morrough if you're gone. Why can't we do that?"

"I would have already taken you away if I could've. Morrough allowed me to have my phylactery while I was hunting fugitives, but he—grew suspicious last year. That's why it has to be Shiseo who takes you."

She shook her head. "No . . ."

He took her hand in his. "You promised me whatever I wanted if I saved Bayard for you, remember? Well, here is what I want. I want you to leave this accursed country behind and go live a whole life somewhere far away. You swore to Holdfast that you'd protect Lila and his heir. I expect that promise will keep you busy for a long time."

"I promised to take care of you first," she said, snatching her hand back. "Always. I promised you always. If you'd gotten your way, you would have sent me off, and I wouldn't have even remembered you. Wouldn't have had any idea until it was too late—"

"Well." His voice was strained. "The last time I was honest with you, you disappeared and never came back."

She flinched, and her breathing stalled again. "But I tried. I was—I was coming back. I tried to—"

"I know you did. You were quite the force of destruction, if the reports were anything to go by. If my father hadn't been there, and you hadn't realised, you might have escaped. I know you tried." He drew back. "But it wasn't enough in the end, and that wasn't your fault, it's just the way it is."

She gripped him, not letting him pull away, keeping his face close to hers. "But what if we'd been there together? If we'd saved Lila together, it could have all been different. Why can't we work together now?"

Something flashed across his face, and he just looked at her, eyebrows drawn together. She realised the absurdity of her question. Because she was not even that person anymore; she was little more than a ghost.

He just looked down. "We have a long goodbye in front of us. I don't want to fight you, but I will not do anything that puts you at further risk."

"Let me try to find another way," she said. "If I could research, there might be something we haven't considered yet."

He was silent. She watched him weighing the costs and the risks, and finally he sighed. "I will let you try under two conditions. If your health deteriorates from the stress, you will stop, and when Shiseo arrives, regardless of how close you think you are to a breakthrough or an answer, you will go without making me force you. You won't trick or manipulate me again; you will say goodbye, and you will go." He met her eyes. "Do you agree?"

Helena swallowed hard. "One condition."

His jaw ticced. "What?"

"Don't lie to me anymore. I don't want to wonder, every time, whether you're telling the truth."

CHAPTER 68

Maius 1789

As soon as he'd agreed, Kaine stood, letting go.

"It's late. You should rest," he said. "Tomorrow I'll see what I can find. I think Shiseo collected some things for you."

"Wait," she said quickly, grasping at him, the equilibrium threatening to vanish as the physical space between them reopened. "Don't—don't go."

He looked at her sharply before that feigned look of detachment slid back into place. "Why?"

Her fingers curled into a fist. "Whenever you leave, I never feel sure of what—what version of you will come back. My memories—they're all out of order, and it gets confusing. You're always so—so cold when you're out of reach."

His hand spasmed as it vanished behind his back. "What would you like me to do, then?" he asked, the words seeming forced.

"I want you to stay," she said, her voice a whisper.

She stood up and went towards her bed. It was as she passed him that she slid firmly back into the present, but not *this* present.

She was going to the bed, and he was taking off his coat to drape over the sofa. She would lie down and look at the canopy and try to stay still . . .

She froze midstep, lungs closing until she was suffocating and her head throbbed, threatening to split it apart.

How would they ever fix this?

"Helena . . ."

His voice snapped her out of her reverie. She looked back at him.

He shook his head. "Let's not do this," he said. "I'll come back tomorrow, and I'll—try to—"

"No." She shook her head. "I need to get used to you again. I need to remember it."

He exhaled and sat on the edge of her bed, as he so often had before, her hand laced in his, staring across the room.

His fingers kept spasming. He was trying to keep them still, but tensing only made it worse. She couldn't understand why he'd have tremors.

"Why don't you heal anymore?" she asked.

He didn't look at her. "With so few of the Undying left, Morrough pulls more heavily on those remaining. Regeneration takes longer now. But—I don't know why my hands won't stop. Price of hubris, I suppose."

All these months, she'd watched him crumbling. He'd been slowly eradicating the Undying, despite knowing that with every kill, the punishment he'd be subjected to would grow as his ability to recover from it diminished.

"I'm so sorry, Kaine," she said softly.

He flinched and nearly ripped his hand away from her.

"Don't apologise to me," he snapped, glaring down at her.

"But you're angry with me, aren't you?"

He looked back across the room, throat working. "That doesn't mean you have any reason to apologise."

"Why not?"

"Because—" His voice failed him, and he looked down. "I have to apologise first and I—I . . . don't know how to begin. I'd hoped you'd never remember any of this. If I'd just lied to you about how I got Bayard out. If I'd just let you go, none of this would have happened."

Helena sat up. "It would have killed me. If you'd sent me away and

I'd found out later you were discovered because I made you go back for Lila, it would have killed me. I'd do it all again, every second, to save you."

He turned to look at her, shock and rage sweeping across his face.

"You didn't save me," he said when he was finally capable of speech. "You just put us in hell for two years."

If he'd struck her, it would have hurt less. The blood drained from her face, her body going ice-cold.

"I tried to come back—" she said, her voice shaking. "I *really* did."

His expression had turned regretful. "I know. I didn't mean—"

She drew away from him, feeling like she might throw up if she looked at him then.

"You shouldn't have assumed I'd be willing to lose you," she said. "Did you think I cared less because I had other obligations? That I don't feel things as much as you? I did *everything* I could to keep you safe. You don't know all the things I did."

"I just meant—"

"Every time you asked, I promised I was yours. Always. There aren't any exemptions or expiration dates on always."

HELENA WOKE TO A CRUSHING pain in her head. She lay in the dark, trying to find her bearings. She could feel Kaine's fingers, still entwined with hers. She searched for him and found him on the floor, sitting beside the bed, his head slumped to the side.

She shifted closer, studying him in the dim light.

It was the in-between spaces she struggled with, when her memories spun like a flipped coin, warring between past and present. But this close, despite the alterations of time, he was hers. Still. Just as he had been.

He'd loved her, even though he never expected them to be anything but doomed. He'd loved her all the same.

"I'm going to take care of you," she mouthed silently.

She felt the moment he woke. Tension shot through his body, eyes snapping open, fingers spasming. He went rigid and then relaxed for a moment when he saw her. His eyes narrowed and he stood, leaning over her. "Are you all right?"

"Just a headache," she said.

He touched her forehead, his resonance numbing the pressure behind her eyes.

"Can you get me the research today?" she asked.

His eyebrows knit together. "I think you should rest."

"No. I'll be anxious if I don't have something to think about."

He sighed but didn't argue, but she could tell he was debating something as he studied her. Finally he drew a breath, picking up her hand. "I'm trusting you—begging you—not to make me regret this."

She wasn't sure what he meant until he wrapped his fingers around her wrist and the ribbon of metal suddenly unspooled.

She watched, wide-eyed, as he unwound it and the tube of encased nullium slid out of her wrist. The puncture was torn along the edges, scarred from all the occasions when she'd fallen or used too much force on her wrists.

She was startled how small the tube and puncture were. It had felt larger—as though it had filled all the space between the bones in her wrist. Her fingers unfurled, feeling her resonance inside them for the first time in so long.

"You'll still have to wear the cuffs," he said, voice strained. "But I'm trusting you to be careful and not murder the servants or run away."

Helena managed a shaky nod, too overwhelmed to do anything else.

"I'll have to put the nullium back in when Stroud visits, or she'll notice. I hope you understand why I couldn't do this sooner."

She nodded again.

He drew a deep breath and took her other wrist, removing the manacle from that one, too. He let her have a minute, twisting her wrists and feeling her resonance reach her fingertips.

"I didn't realise how much a part of me it was till it was gone," she said, pressing her palms against her head and calming the frenzied inflammation of her brain. Her mind was a bizarre landscape, as if two versions of herself were overlaid with each other, her consciousness veering between them.

She looked up. "I think I can eat."

She kept unfurling her fingers, relishing the sensation of her resonance. Kaine watched, clearly torn between his desire to keep her in a state and place that he could fully control and not wanting to be her captor any longer.

He'd had to choose, and he'd set her free.

She didn't want him to regret that.

She spent several minutes trying to repair the muscle and tendon damage done by the tubes, but most of it was too old and compounded upon to restore. Time and injury had left her fingers clumsy, their previous dexterity all but gone. Eventually she gave up and held out her wrists towards him, so that he could wrap the copper ribbon around them.

Kaine pocketed the nullium tubes. "I'll send what I can find of the research."

He started to stand, but Helena caught his hand. She could grasp at things now without forced feebleness, and so she held on until he looked back at her.

"Be careful," she said. "Don't—" The word caught in her throat. She squeezed his hand. "Come back to me, all right?"

"I will."

IT WAS MIDDAY WHEN DAVIES brought in a folio and Helena sat deciphering a variety of accumulated notes. Most of it was written in an unfamiliar hand, using an alchemical shorthand and notation that she wasn't familiar with, but there were some notes that she recognised as Shiseo's flowing script, and even Kaine's handwriting.

There were numerous partial arrays and formulas. Some felt oddly familiar. She kept staring at them, racking her mind until symbols blurred, smearing across the pages.

She curled on her side, arms wrapped around her head, and passed out.

When she woke, Kaine was sitting next to her. He had her pregnancy guide open, eyes skimming across the pages.

She winced at the sight of it.

She didn't want to think about the pregnancy. She knew it was there, but it was too much. Other things were of greater urgency.

He closed the book immediately.

Her head still hurt, so she closed her eyes. "Where are those notes from?"

"Some are Bennet's, I believe. Shiseo collected any non-metallurgical array work he encountered. Said it was something he saw you working on."

A new gap in her memory seemed to rise to the surface. She'd worked on something like that?

"I don't remember." How much was still missing?

"I'm sure it'll come to you," he said.

But there was so little time. She opened her eyes, mind grinding like jammed gears. "I never used arrays for vivimancy, or animancy, I don't think." Her eyebrows furrowed. "Maybe they wouldn't work with celestial or elemental formulas. Have you ever used any other numbers for an array?"

Kaine shook his head.

The conversation was painfully stilted. She was walking blind through her own memory, trying to solve a puzzle without remembering which pieces she held. As she talked about her ideas, Kaine nodded, expression appropriately attentive, but his eyes kept glancing at the clock, and he showed no emotion when she tried to engage him in the subject.

She slowly began to realise that he was indulging her. The notes, removing her manacles: It was all an attempt to appease her. It was the library. He was keeping her occupied and motivated to recover her strength, but he had no expectation that it would make any difference. He was managing her.

She stopped talking.

He nodded again, as if agreeing with something she'd said, and stood. "I'll make sure you have what you need."

He started for the door, then halted suddenly and turned back. He stood staring at her and the room for a long time before he finally spoke.

"I know we—" He stopped, and his hand curled into a fist, vanishing behind his back. He blinked, staring just past her.

"From what I understand," he finally said, his voice eerie and removed, "simple methods of abortion are unlikely to be feasible by the time you'll escape. There are other methods that can be done by vivimancy or surgery. When you go, I'll try to ensure you have the materials necessary to resolve it, but if there's anything in particular you'll need, just tell me. I'll make sure that you have it."

Before she could respond, he turned and left.

Helena leaned back, pushing the folio away and forcing herself to look at her body.

Hesitantly, reluctantly, she reached down and pressed her fingers against her stomach, just below her navel, finding the slight swell of her uterus. Her hand trembled almost violently as she let her resonance reach in.

She'd seen the resonance screen, but it was different reaching out herself.

It was startling how small it was.

She snatched her hand away, her heart pounding unsteadily.

Helena had never thought about children. Not until they were something that she couldn't have and so it didn't matter what she wanted. A month ago and she would have killed herself in an instant to prevent a baby, any baby, from falling into Morrough's hands. The pregnancy had not existed for her beyond that context.

But if she escaped, if the choice was hers, what would she do?

When Davies arrived that evening with dinner, she brought etching plates and a stylus. Helena held the stylus in silent disbelief at first. If she'd ever found one searching the house, she would have tried to stab herself through the heart with it.

Kaine really had known her too well.

"Is Kaine here?" she asked.

Davies shook her head.

"When he comes back, can you tell him that I want him?"

It was dusk, the light soft when the door opened and Kaine stood there as if he wasn't even sure he should step over the threshold.

Helena looked up from the folio, hating the space.

"Had I told you I was sterilised?"

He entered then, shutting the door. "No, but I assumed. It was standard practice for the Faith. It was one of my father's greatest concerns if I were ever found using vivimancy—that they'd cut me and end the family line."

"Oh."

She was glad they'd never had that conversation, then.

His jaw clenched. "It hadn't occurred to me that Stroud could reverse it. I thought you were safe from the program."

Her hands crept towards her stomach. "I want to talk about what you said earlier, before you left."

His expression closed.

Helena's chest tightened. There were too many moments, both past and present, when he'd looked at her like that. She closed her eyes, trying to block them out.

"Can you come closer?" Her mouth had gone dry. "It's hard to talk when you're so far away."

It was clear that he didn't want to be anywhere near her for this conversation, but she *needed* him near.

She stared at her hands. "I didn't realise you expected me to terminate the pregnancy when I escaped. I mean, I understand why you would, but I'm not going to."

She looked up, trying to gauge his reaction, but he wasn't looking at her.

"You may change your mind once you're free," he said, his voice void of emotion, as if it had nothing to do with him.

She shook her head. "I won't."

His jaw ticced, tension growing visible around his eyes. "There's no reason to make any commitment like this to me." His voice shook. "Do whatever you want."

"I am," she said. "And I want you to know. If I didn't, I'd wonder about everything. If our baby would get your eyes or mine. What kind of resonance they'd have. If they'd have any, or if they'd just get to be ordinary." She was speaking quickly, because her throat was growing thick. "I'd wonder if they'd have hair like mine or if it would be straight like yours. If I have to go without you—if you—if you die—I'd want to tell them all about you." She swallowed hard. "I've never gotten to tell anyone about you. I'd want someone to know what you were like."

He looked at her then.

"What I'm like?" he finally said. "What exactly do you think I'm like?" he scoffed, shaking his head. "You have a chance at a new life. Don't drag my memory with you."

Helena shook her head, and his expression hardened, everything about him sharpening.

"Do you really want to spend the rest of your life with one of the Undying's bastards chained to you?" he asked. "The whole world knows you're here, who you were sent to. Do you think they won't guess who the father was and *how* it came to be? No matter what colour eyes it has, or how old it gets, it will be the child of a murderer, conceived because I *raped* you while you were my prisoner, and everyone will know that. Everyone."

His face was furious, his fingers curling as if he wanted to shake her, but he turned away, his expression contorting.

"Just leave it behind." He drew a ragged breath. "You want children? Have them with someone else."

She stared at him, incredulous. "Is that what you think I'm going to do? Run away and pretend you were a monster I was lucky to escape?"

He glanced at her, empty resignation in his face before he looked away again. "It's the truth."

Her chest constricted, crushing her heart.

"Kaine . . ." She reached towards him. "You're not a monster. You didn't have any choice. Neither of us—we were both raped."

He jerked away, evading her fingers. "Don't."

She stepped forward and caught his face in her hands, holding on to him.

"You're mine," she said, heart pounding unsteadily against her ribs. "Did you really think I would still hate you once I remembered?" She shook her head. "Even before I did, you were the only thing that ever felt safe. I thought I was going mad, but a part of me always knew you. I left a note. Didn't you get my note? I love you."

He flinched as if struck and started to shake his head, but she stilled him, forcing him to meet her eyes.

"I do," she said more firmly, her voice shaking with intensity. "I love you. And I always will. Always."

She rose up on her toes, pulling him closer, and kissed him.

He stayed frozen when her lips touched his.

"I love you," she said the words against his mouth, as if breathing them into him.

He was still a moment longer and then shook, his palms cradling her face, fingers tangled in her hair, pulling her closer, his mouth burning as he kissed her.

He kissed her like he was starving. As though he were trying to pour himself into her or consume her.

He's mine. He is all mine, was all she could think. She wrapped her arms around his neck, meeting every caress of his lips on hers.

He drew back just enough to speak, his palm curved around the nape of her neck, his forehead resting on hers.

"I'm sorry—I'm sorry—I'm so sorry for everything I did to you," he said, his voice hoarse and broken. "I love you. You left, and I'd never told you."

HELENA SPENT HER DAYS SCRIBBLING notes, going through every book and scrap of information she could find, trying to make sense of the piecemeal array concepts that Shiseo had collected. She remembered now about Wagner and her repeated attempts at making sense of his amateur array sketch.

The task of reconstructing it felt impossible, but it was the only thing she could think to do, the only solution she could envision. Upon request, Kaine provided her with the complete works of Cetus, all the various letters and florilegia, all those centuries of writings dubiously attributed to him. She hoped that if she could work out which were legitimate, she might have a better understanding of his alchemy methods.

As she worked, she ignored the nagging fear that it was all pointless, that she was delusional; if she hadn't been able to find a solution before, what chance did she have of solving it now? She kept working; there simply could not be a future in which she left Kaine behind to die.

She dragged her mind forcefully from where she had constricted and suffocated it in order to accept the empty tedium she'd limited her memories to, but the effort gave her such headaches she could only work for short periods.

She woke one morning to the servants gathering up all her books and research and ferrying them into a room which adjoined hers. The doorway between the two had always been locked in the past. Kaine was standing by the bed.

"Stroud is coming today," he said. "I have to insert the nullium."

Helena's mouth went dry. "Of course," she said, forcing herself to hold out her hands, and not to flinch as the tubes slid into her wrists, her resonance vanishing. She knew it wasn't his fault, but a sick sense of betrayal swept through her as she stared down at her hobbled hands.

She curled back into bed, her heart pounding with dread, trying to rub the nauseating dead sensation from her wrists as Kaine left to escort Stroud in.

"Look who's conscious again," Stroud said as she entered. "The High Reeve was very concerned about you. I think he expected you to die. Seems you did listen to your father in the end."

Kaine's jaw clenched, and he made no attempt to hide his disdain for Stroud. "Perhaps focus on the reason for your visit."

Stroud sucked her teeth, setting her satchel on the table beside the bed and leaning over Helena, prodding with finger and resonance.

"Well, it seems the sickness has passed. She's beginning to regain some weight." She pressed several fingers against Helena's forehead but used only the smallest frisson of energy, tsking. "Her brain is still severely inflamed, though. I wouldn't depend too much on those memories surviving the rest of the pregnancy. The most severe Toll generally happens at the end, assuming this child is what we hope."

Stroud was focused on Helena, or she would have seen Kaine go grey.

"Now that she's eating, you need to make sure she's getting outdoors and exercising. The weaker she is, the less likely we'll achieve viability."

Stroud let go of Helena and reached into her satchel, pulling out a resonance screen. "Now let's see how things look."

She pulled the blankets down and Helena's clothes up. Kaine turned away.

"Very healthy," Stroud said with a smug smile, nodding at the vaguely pulsing shape visible in the gas. "It doesn't appear the coma or fits had any impact on the foetal development. That would be quite unfortunate. I think we're far enough along that I can . . ."

Stroud squinted, and the screen morphed, the shape stretching and ballooning. Stroud's face suddenly fell.

"It's female."

CHAPTER 69

Junius 1789

A GIRL.

Helena had not even considered seeking out the gender. She remembered Lila trying to figure it out, but there were so many other things to worry over, it hadn't occurred to her.

The pregnancy was suddenly so real, it was jarring. Before, the baby was a concept, little more than an ephemeral possibility. Now it was a girl.

Stroud pushed more firmly against Helena's lower pelvis, the lines in her face darkening.

"Well, this is disappointing. We wanted a male," she said, glaring down at Helena as if she'd purposely conceived the wrong gender. Helena kept her face blank, staring dully up at the canopy, as if she were too weak to have an opinion.

Stroud turned to Kaine. "The High Necromancer will not be pleased. A female is—out of the question. Practically unthinkable."

"It was always a fifty percent chance," Kaine said, appearing unconcerned. "I was under the impression that *any* animancer child would do at this point."

"Yes, but a *female*." Stroud sounded as if she were referring to some kind of rodent. "He will not be pleased."

She pressed a hand against her forehead, exhaling loudly. "Too late now, though. There's no time to start over. And with the state of her, she might not survive a second attempt. We'll have to proceed. Once we have the process perfected, I'm sure we can manage a boy. This will be temporary. You are keeping a close eye on her? Keeping her calm?"

"Yes," Kaine said through gritted teeth, gesturing towards the door. "So let's talk elsewhere, why don't we?"

"Yes, yes," Stroud said impatiently, packing her bag and heading out, followed closely by Kaine. Helena sat up as the door closed.

She looked down at her stomach, pressing her hand against the bump between her hips. Without resonance she could only feel stillness; it was too early for movement.

A girl.

Kaine still barely acknowledged the pregnancy beyond how it related to Helena's health. It was *her* pregnancy. Her baby. He refused to treat it as having anything to do with him.

Still, she couldn't help but wonder: Would he mind that it was a girl? It was sons who carried the name and inherited within the guilds. A girl child with talent for alchemy was often considered a waste, only good for a marriage alliance. Not that it mattered either way with an illegitimate child.

Her stomach twisted into a tight knot.

When Kaine returned, his expression was wary. He came over, his hand resting on her shoulder. She could feel his resonance through her nerves and knew that he was looking for something.

"I'm fine," she said. "The baby's not doing anything to me, if that's what you're worrying about."

He studied her face carefully. "It could get worse later. And you—"

He touched the side of her head with his fingertips. She could see him estimating her years in the hospital, the number of patients, how it added up, how much time she might have left.

She shook her head, catching his hand in hers. "You said vitality doesn't get taken like that. With your mother, the vivimancer said it was because she didn't realise she was doing it. Lila's a vivimancer and Rhea never had any trouble."

Kaine still looked as if he were watching her slip away before his eyes.

"Besides, you did something to me, didn't you?" She studied him. "I thought it was a dream, but you used the Stone somehow."

"I don't know how much it did, though," he said, "you were so far gone, and then you slipped into that coma. I won't be there at the end if—"

"I'll be careful," she said. "I'll be able to feel it. The Toll has signs. It's not like it happens suddenly."

He nodded slowly, but she knew any risk was too much to him.

"It's a girl," she finally said, trying to draw his focus elsewhere.

He just nodded absently.

Her heart sank. She'd spent so much time worrying about this baby when it hardly existed, because it was all she'd had to care about. Kaine had been right when he'd called her desperate to love someone. It seemed to be her fatal flaw.

Now there was so much to care about, she'd stopped worrying about the pregnancy at all, thinking it could wait. But it couldn't. It had been there all this time, and now it was a girl that no one wanted, except her.

Faced with indifference, Helena felt herself grow reactively possessive. She slipped her hand away from Kaine and went to the wardrobe, getting dressed slowly.

"What are you doing?" Kaine said as she buttoned her dress.

"I'm going to go for a walk," she said without looking at him. "It's good for the baby."

"I'll go with you."

She wasn't sure she wanted him to if he was just going to brood and scrutinise her, but she nodded.

He removed the nullium from her manacles, and then instead of going into the courtyard, he took her to the rear of the house, with the hedge maze and the overgrown gardens. There was a pathway canopied with climbing roses.

Helena hesitated. "Won't Morrough notice?"

"He only watches the courtyard."

They walked in silence until they reached a gnarled apple tree, blossoms all faded, covered in fresh green leaves. Kaine stopped short and stood staring at it.

"I used to climb this tree when I was a boy," he said. "It's bigger in my memory."

He'd never spoken of his past without prodding before. All she knew of his childhood was the loneliness of it. An absent father, a sick mother, and the servants whose ghostly memories still lingered around him.

"I got stuck right here once," he said, reaching out and touching a large branch that barely reached Helena's waist. "I was sure I'd fall and break my head if I moved. I stayed there half the day, shouting for my mother. She wasn't supposed to get out of bed, but I wouldn't listen, I wanted her to come for me. Wanted her to see how high I'd climbed. Eventually she did." His hand dropped. "When I was older, I felt so guilty about it. All those stupid things you do when you're young and don't understand."

Helena could scarcely imagine Kaine that young.

He pointed to a break in the hedges. "If we go that way, there's a pond. Used to be all kinds of frogs and newts there. I used to think I could tame them, teach them to do tricks."

He said all of this without any emotion, a flat recitation. He looked around.

"I should take you up to the spires," he said at last. "I'd remember more from up there, I think. It's strange . . . I don't know why I have so much trouble remembering moments."

He started to walk back, his eyes wandering as if he was searching for something there in the gardens. He paused, his lips moving several times before he finally spoke.

"My mother's name was Enid."

Helena nodded. She remembered that.

He looked towards the garden, fingers curling into a fist. "I always liked that name."

Slowly Helena realised what he was doing.

This was his attempt at giving her what she wanted. For him, acknowledging that he would have a child, a daughter, meant acknowledging that he wouldn't live to meet her. He was telling the stories so Helena could tell their daughter about him, about what he'd been like, before the Institute and the war.

He stared towards the city where it rose above the trees. "I'm not sure what will happen to the estate and inheritance. I've transferred as much as I can to a foreign account, but if you did ever come back, I'm not sure if she'd be able to claim it. I can look into it, if you want."

Helena's throat closed and her shoulders started to shake, and she couldn't make herself breathe.

Kaine looked over. "I've brought you too far."

She shook her head but couldn't move. There were so many things she wanted to say, but she didn't know how to without having them break her open.

He stepped closer. "Can you walk back?"

She managed to shake her head.

Moving slowly, he slipped his arm around her waist and lifted her into his arms.

She wrapped her arms around his neck and buried her face in his shoulder.

"Enid is a good name," she finally managed to say, her voice hoarse. "I like it, too."

KAINE LAY ON THE BED beside her, her head resting on his chest as she watched the hands on the clock. She was running out of time. Always. She never had enough. The Abeyance was less than a month away.

Kaine was awake, too, fingers tracing patterns along her arm.

She sat up, leaning forward, and kissed him slowly, memorising the sensation of their lips meeting, the tip of his nose tracing against her cheek.

She slid her fingers through his hair, deepening the kiss, wanting to lose herself in the familiarity of it. She had felt this before.

Kaine's hand rose up to curve around her neck, sending a shudder of heat through her, her blood alight in her veins. She'd buried the memories of this in the deepest recesses of her mind.

She leaned closer, her hand sliding down his chest.

His hand closed instantly around her wrist, stilling it. "What are you doing?"

She sat up, drawing a deep breath. "I want to have sex with you."

The tips of her ears burned at saying it so baldly, but she watched him as she spoke. Searching for his reaction.

There was a hard, flintlike look to his eyes, visible even in the dimming moonlight.

"No."

She tugged at her wrist again, and he let go. She pulled her knees up against her chest, wrapping her arms around them. Her heart was pounding a hard, unsteady tempo.

"I don't want the last time to be when you were—" She swallowed. "—when we were being forced."

"No," was all he said.

Her fingers spasmed, but she nodded, and sat, staring at the deepening shadows across the room.

"Why?" he finally asked.

"I just told you."

"There's never only one reason with you," he said.

She didn't answer for a long time. "I can't remember what it was like. Before. I know it happened, but when—when I try to remember any details, I'm always here. If it never comes back—that'll be all I'll remember."

She paused then, thinking of all the ways it could go wrong. There was no going back. What they'd had was gone. It wasn't something they could just re-create. Attempting it might destroy the fragile safe haven they still had in each other.

"Never mind." She shook her head. "You're right, it's a bad idea."

He said nothing, but the next day, when he kissed her, it was different.

Hungrier.

After he was gone for several days, he came back and his touch was like fire, his teeth grazing her neck, his face buried against her skin, breathing her in. Heat rushed through her, and she gave a shivering moan, body turning liquid against him.

"Tell me to stop," he said, his mouth over her throat. "Tell me to stop."

She pulled him closer. "Don't stop. I don't want you to stop."

His teeth dragged across her skin, and she drew his hands to the buttons on her dress, helping to unfasten them. His fingers slid over her bare skin as she shuddered into his touch, aching for him.

It used to be like this. Feeling it again, she could remember it, the way he used to touch her, hold her, consume her.

He kissed her neck until her head dropped back and she was gasping. Her hands trailed along the curve of his jaw, down over his shoulders, as the physical memory of him awakened beneath her skin.

She brought his face back to hers. "I love you," she said, kissing him. "I wish I'd told you a thousand times."

She found the buttons on his shirt and began unfastening, pushing his clothes away, running her hands across his skin, fingers craving the warmth of his body.

"Tell me to stop, and I'll stop," he said, his voice ragged.

"Don't stop," she said, fingers trembling as they grazed the familiar patterns carved into his back. Her clothes were slipping off, and want pulled at her from within.

She was pushed back on the bed, her body under his as he kissed across her breasts, but then everything inverted; she was lying there, trying to hold still and stay quiet, frozen with fear of what might happen if she didn't, the bed canopy above her, and the body over her, every sensation a wretched betrayal.

Her hands froze and her eyes went wide as her ribs clamped down around her lungs, suffocating her.

"Stop." The word was ripped out of her, so painful that it took her lungs with it.

Kaine froze, jerking back, but she caught him, pulling him to her, not letting him go, burying her face against his shoulders, and breathing in and remembering that it was him. And he was hers, she could not let him go.

Her body shook, as she choked back a sob.

Kaine was not even breathing.

"It was just for a moment," she said, her chest hitching. "It was just too much for a moment. It'll be better now that I know I can say stop. It was good." She wouldn't let go. "It was good. It was just for a moment that I—It was good."

But he pulled away until she finally let go. He sat up slowly, his face drawn, pupils contracted so that his eyes resembled cracked ice. He looked so fragile.

He was covered in scars. Her hand shook as she reached out and touched one that ran nearly the length of his torso. "What has he done to you?"

He looked away. "Anything he wants."

She rested her head on his shoulder, entwining her arm with his as they sat there in the lengthening dark, amid the ruins of all they'd once been. They just needed more time.

HELENA HAD READ THROUGH ALL the works ever attributed to Cetus, organising them in order of likely legitimacy. She felt that she was beginning to grasp what Cetus's fundamental ideas were regarding alchemy, but she was in desperate need of a more recent glimpse at his methods, and she knew exactly where she might find one.

When Kaine was gone, she left her room, moving slowly, avoiding the shadows, using the walls as a touchstone.

She knew which rooms Morrough might be watching from, and she was careful to avoid as many as possible.

Davies materialised as Helena reached the foyer, but Helena passed through the main wing, moving onwards.

She finally stopped, looking over. "Can Morrough see me here?"

Davies shook her head slowly.

Helena went over to the far door. The frame was warped to lock it in place. Without iron resonance, a person would never get through. Helena's resonance hummed in her fingers as she placed her hands on the frame and pushed the iron back as if it were a curtain. She gripped the knob; it was a simple lock mechanism.

She glanced back at Davies, who had a look of terror on her face, the only emotion she seemed to still express.

"I'm sorry," Helena said. "I need to see it."

"No . . ." Davies said; her voice came out warped, hollow and gasping. She didn't know if it was Kaine or the remaining shadow of the woman protesting.

Helena shook her head. "I have to know how it was done."

Davies did not follow but hovered near the door, stricken, uttering her ghastly pleading *No*s as Helena turned on the light and went towards the array.

The lights flickered unsteadily overhead. Looking at that too-small cage, knowing who had lived inside it for months, Helena felt sick. Her heart was beginning to pound. She forced her eyes past, focusing.

She stood at the edge of the array, surveying all the careful work to obscure what had been there, trying to superimpose the sketch that Wagner had provided and the drafts in Bennet's folio. Somewhere amid those three was the complete array.

Her fingers moved slowly, trying to feel out potential patterns, but it had been so long since she'd done more than simple vivimancy.

She got on her knees and began to trace her fingers across every shape and pattern. It was incomprehensible the first several times she crawled across the floor following the lines, trying to visualise the patterns of the energy. It was the third time that it finally began to make sense.

It was an animancy array. She recognised the feeling of the energy, the patterns it would follow.

Her resonance trailed through her fingers as she swept them along one line of the array. Yes, she knew that feeling. Another line. False. The energy would never twist that way.

She crawled across the floor again, more slowly, tracing every line again and again, ignoring the splinters catching in her fingertips.

Her heart began to pound with relief. She could solve this. She could figure it out. An ache spread through her chest at the unsteady tempo of her heartbeat, but she ignored it, trying to finish. It began to race faster and faster, until her lungs began to hurt. Just a little more. She needed to have the whole array complete in her mind so she could etch it.

The floor blurred. She blinked hard, trying to focus.

Her fingers were bleeding as she reached up to press them against her heart, her body going cold. Her heart was racing uncontrollably. She tried to slow it, but it was like trying to catch a running horse.

The room swayed. The iron cage and the door gracefully swung to the side, upended as her shoulder hit the ground.

The room dimmed, the lights' flickering click fading away.

SHE WOKE, DAZED, LYING IN bed in her room, her chest aching as if there were a lead weight crushing it. Kaine was sitting beside her, her hand in his.

She couldn't remember how she'd gotten there. Her wrists throbbed, and she could feel the dead sensation of nullium inside them.

"The doctor just left," he said without looking at her. "It seems you developed an irregular heartbeat from the strain and distress of your imprisonment and pregnancy. They detected it during your coma, but I was told that if I could keep you calm, it might resolve itself. Seems unlikely now, though."

Helena didn't know what to say.

His jaw worked several times. "Do you have any idea what it was like, finding you collapsed in the middle of that damned array inside that torture chamber?"

"I'm sorry," she said. "I didn't want to make you go back in."

He exhaled, his head dropping. He'd seemed furious except he was clutching her hand in his.

"It wasn't a panic attack," she said. "I think I know how Morrough used the array—how the design works. I've figured out how he did it. I was just relieved. My heart lost control."

He looked at her, his eyes burning. "Do you think that makes it better? Your heart could fail, and if I'm not here, you'll be gone. Just like—" He went silent. "Don't do this to me."

Her mouth went dry. "But I have to save you."

"No." The word was sharp. "You don't. And you can't. You are the only person who has never understood that."

She opened her mouth, but he cut her off.

"We made a deal to tell the truth to each other, and that is the truth. You cannot save me. I cannot be saved."

She struggled to sit up, her chest aching as if her sternum had split again. "You don't know that. Let me try."

He wrenched away from her and stood. She thought he'd storm out. She slipped from the bed, reaching after him.

"Kaine."

He stilled at the foot of the bed. "You don't get to have everything, Helena," he said at last. "There's a point when you have to realise that you aren't going to get everything you want. You have to choose and let it be enough for you. You have other people. You promised Holdfast you'd take care of Lila and her son. You have a baby who needs you, and you know that."

She shook her head. "I don't want to choose. I always have to choose, and I *never* get to choose you. I'm so tired of not getting to choose you."

He looked back at her. "You're not choosing. You promised me anything I wanted. I want you to stop breaking yourself trying to save me. Go. Live. Tell our daughter I saved you both. That—is what I want."

"But I'm so close. I can figure this out."

He came back towards her then. "You promised me that if the research was having an impact on your health, you'd stop."

"I know, but—"

He gave a gasping laugh, almost more of a sob. "Did you know, you are the worst promise keeper I have ever met?"

Her throat tightened. "I keep the ones that matter."

"No." He shook his head. "What you do is make so many conflicting promises that you can pick and choose depending on what you want. I've devoted some thought to your methodology." He looked down.

"That's why you never seem to keep any of the promises that I care about."

He reached towards her, his fingers brushing her hip. "You care about this baby. You worried about her so constantly, you wrecked your heart with fear over what would happen to her. Now you're so preoccupied trying to save me that you're letting yourself forget that *she* is dependent on you. I can't protect her from you. Endangering yourself trying to save me risks her."

Helena's throat closed. She tried to back away, but he caught hold of her, gripping her by the shoulders, forcing her to look at him. "You have to let me go now."

"I can't." She shook her head. "You think I'll be calm if I stop? If I have nothing to do but to sit in this room and wait to lose you? You wouldn't. You never would."

They compromised in the end.

Kaine took her back to the room and let her spend hours crawling around the floor, copying down every detail of the array onto etching plates. When he had time, he went with her to the library, and let her use her animancy on him, studying the talisman inside his chest, but she did not set foot outside her room without him anymore.

One evening he came back after more than a day's absence, his expression stony. "You'll have to stay in tomorrow. There's to be a dinner party. Aurelia is returning for it, and the remaining Undying."

"What's it for?"

He gave a thin smile. "I'm supposed to convince them that there's nothing wrong."

CHAPTER 70

Julius 1789

HELENA WATCHED THROUGH THE CURTAINS AS ADDITIONAL servants, both living and dead, were brought in from the city. Kaine had bolted the door shut to ensure that she would receive no unsolicited visitors, leaving one of the maids inside the room with her.

She had never noticed just how heavy and reinforced the door was.

The motorcars arrived in the evening. It was almost funny watching the Undying filing into the house of the very murderer they feared.

She tried not to worry. Kaine had not seemed concerned about the evening, but he was a convincing liar.

As the evening dragged by, she tried to focus on her attempts at reversing Morrough's array structure when the maid, who'd been standing still as a statue, abruptly sprang into action, rapidly gathering up Helena's books and notes and shoving them all under the bed.

Someone was coming.

They'd just hidden the last of the papers, ensuring everything was covered by the bed skirt, when the room was filled with the sound of shifting iron. Helena flung herself onto the bed, curling onto her side.

A moment later, the door swung open, revealing Stroud, followed closely by Kaine.

"I don't see how this could possibly help," he said as Helena blinked at them in feigned confusion. "You know the delicacy of her condition."

"There are a great many delicate positions right now," Stroud said, walking over and shaking Helena. "The High Necromancer was very clear that we are to project an image of strength. All these assassinations have threatened their sense of invulnerability, and if their fears are allowed to undermine the regime, we'll all suffer. We must show them that a solution is under way."

"And you think parading a pregnant prisoner famously sent here for interrogation will reassure them?"

"I think explaining why she's pregnant will do it. They're too paranoid to take our word for it, but they'll believe it once they see her. She was the Principate's last sponsored student." Stroud looked down at Helena. "Get up and put on something thin enough that your stomach will show."

The pregnancy hardly showed at all unless she was naked; Helena doubted there was anything she could wear that would make it visible. A detail which was immediately obvious when she stood up.

"Oh, for heaven's sake." Stroud went over to the wardrobe and pulled out a chemise, then stuffed it up the front of Helena's dress so that her stomach looked visibly distended.

"There. Come along now." Stroud took Helena by the arm and began pulling her towards the door.

Helena glanced at Kaine, but there was nothing to be done.

The journey to the main wing was simultaneously longer and shorter than Helena remembered. As they reached the large foyer, Helena's chest tightened. She fought to keep breathing slowly as she was pulled into the large room where she'd first seen Kaine at Spirefell.

Stroud's fingers dug into her arm. "Don't say a word."

Everyone turned as Stroud entered with Helena, and she felt lurid and obvious, her hair loose, made visibly pregnant, a condition which no respectable Northern woman would be seen in.

Her appearance was met with silence. Helena's eyes darted around the room. She recognised few faces; Aurelia was present, standing sulkily beside Crowther.

Atreus, Helena reminded herself. His skin was grey with faint mottling along his temples, and he wore ignition rings now.

"This is the secret project?" said one man in angry disbelief. Helena recognised his voice. He had long sideburns and a receding hairline. "The project the entire country read about in the papers?"

"Of course not," Stroud said, a note of defensiveness in her voice. "Do you think the High Necromancer publishes his true plans in the newspapers? She was brought here for another purpose, and you are the privileged few who will know of it. As I'm sure you all recall, this is the foreign student that the Holdfasts went to such great expense to bring here."

Several faces darkened at this reminder.

"The High Necromancer has discovered that she possesses a rare form of resonance which he has a great interest in cultivating. Once the process is complete, the High Necromancer will achieve heights of power never seen before."

"So you admit there is something wrong with him?" This was from a lich on the far side of the room. Helena's heart stilled at the sight of Sebastian Bayard, his pale hair and eyes, but grey-skinned now.

Stroud's lips pursed. "What I admit is that the High Necromancer has defeated mortality in ways never dreamed of by any other soul on this earth, and when he succeeds in this, as I know he shall, it will be to the benefit of us all. Some of you may recall that during the war, Bennet pursued a method of placing talismans into new living bodies. It was a goal of much importance."

Several of the liches nodded.

"Those initial attempts were unsuccessful, and due to the constraints of the war, it was necessary to focus our efforts elsewhere. However, since then, a new method has been discovered, which the High Reeve and I have closely collaborated in perfecting. The High Necromancer's physical form is in—decay, but no one dares deny his power. He will transfer his soul into a new body and thereby ascend to heights of power unimaginable. And when he has done so, he will allow you to do likewise."

"What new body?" It was the first man who spoke.

Stroud smiled, pushing Helena forward so that she was more visible. "The one our prisoner is producing for us."

Everyone stared at Helena. Her heart was pounding, and she couldn't hear what was being said because she was focused on trying to remain calm. She could feel Kaine's rage simmering beneath his skin.

There was jeering laughter.

The room blurred.

"Don't think of it as a baby," Stroud said sharply, loud enough that Helena could hear over her pounding heart. "It is simply human materials with the right resonance." Stroud's face was flushed red. She had clearly expected admiration instead of the mockery she was receiving. She dragged Helena roughly back.

"I worked with Bennet on the chimaera project; I'm well versed in the methods of growth acceleration. A few more months and the foetus will be viable, and I will have the materials with the necessary resonance to craft a new body for our leader. Once he has ascended to his new form, he will allow those who served him *faithfully* to follow and receive new bodies as well."

Several of the liches straightened, their longing visible.

"So this is what your program was for?"

Helena shivered at the sound of Crowther's voice, emerging from the back of the room, where Atreus was still standing beside Aurelia. He seemed to like the new Mrs. Ferron much more than his son did.

"The economic benefit of the process is legitimate," Stroud said with a prim look. "But I admit to ulterior motives."

"Wait." Aurelia's voice cracked through the room like shattering glass. "Who is the father?"

"The High Necromancer obv—" one of the Undying said but then paused, staring at Helena and seeming to reconsider.

Another one, a man with an oil-bright face and a thick moustache, gave a barking laugh. "I knew you were having your fun with her, Ferron."

Aurelia's cheeks flushed scarlet.

"The parentage was determined on the basis of resonance. The High Necromancer deemed your husband the most suitable," Stroud said in a conciliatory voice. "I assure you, Mrs. Ferron, your husband's cooperation was in no way a reflection upon you—"

Several people laughed.

Aurelia grew dangerously pale. "Get out! All of you, get out!" She picked up the nearest thing, a vase, and flung it straight at Helena.

Helena was wrenched forcefully from Stroud's grip. The porcelain passed her head, shattering on the wall behind her.

Kaine was standing beside her, his eyes glowing so that they were almost white. "I agree." His voice hummed like resonance in the air. "If anyone has further doubts about the power or stability of the regime, you are welcome to see me for personal reassurance."

There was a pause and then several of the Undying muttered excuses, edging towards the door.

As the room emptied, Stroud rounded on Kaine. "The High Necromancer was specific that this was to be a diplomatic meeting, and you were not to threaten them into compliance."

Kaine's eyes were still gleaming. "The only thing they understand is power and fear. There's no reasoning with someone whose sense of entitlement is threatened. Now I have an unpleasant domestic situation to resolve, thanks to you. You may see yourself out and assure our great leader that the Undying will continue to keep their heads down, because they know it's their only means of keeping the ones they have."

Stroud's face puckered, but she drew herself up and left.

Helena glanced around as the last stragglers departed and blinked when she recognised two more faces. They were the only other women in the room beside Stroud and Aurelia. They'd been near the windows. Both were pretty, although one had a slightly grey cast to her skin; her features were soft, and she had a detached look in her eyes. The other had an almost foxlike quality about her. She was staring at Helena, her lower lip caught between her teeth.

It was Ivy and Sofia Purnell.

Ivy glanced towards Kaine, a look of confusion on her face. She turned back to Helena, seeming as if she wanted to speak, but then averted her eyes, taking Sofia's hand as she left.

Finally, Helena and Kaine stood alone with Atreus and Aurelia.

Kaine stepped past Helena, towards his family. "Take her back to her room," he said over his shoulder.

Two servants came forward, but Aurelia spoke up.

"No! She should stay. You were always hiding her away, ensuring you're the only one allowed near her. It's just as I thought after all."

Kaine's expression tensed. "As Stroud said, it was at the High Necromancer's personal command. I assure you, nothing about the process was pleasurable for anyone involved."

"Well, that's a pity," Atreus said in Crowther's low voice. Crowther's clouded eyes drifted slowly across Helena as he came forward, an awful scent of astringent chemicals and lavender rising from him. "I'd hoped to hear this had at least invigorated you to do your duty to your family. I have it on good authority that you were once a regular at certain city establishments during the war. So clearly you do not lack experience or capacity, leaving me to assume you lack motivation."

"I have better uses for my time than worrying over your legacy," Kaine said, his eyes glittering with malice.

Atreus glared at him for a moment and then moved suddenly towards Helena. She shrank towards Kaine on instinct.

Atreus looked sharply at his son. "For a captive, she doesn't seem very afraid of you."

Kaine reached over and snatched Helena away from his father. "Well, that's all thanks to Aurelia here. After she assaulted my prisoner in a fit of rage, I ended up in the heroic role of saviour." Kaine smiled down at Helena, his eyes ice-cold and mocking. "Isn't that right?"

Helena did not have to pretend to tremble. Her heart was pounding so hard, the room was swimming.

"It's time I put her away for the night. You can both see yourselves out." Kaine turned to leave, seemingly dragging Helena behind him.

Atreus spoke up again. "The High Necromancer may have given you a long leash in the past, but you have overestimated both your skills and importance by letting him use you as a dog. Now he treats you as one. It seems killing is the only thing you've *ever* done well."

Kaine's expression betrayed nothing, but Helena felt him flinch.

"You may threaten the others in compliance, but I am not afraid of you," Atreus said. "You have flown too high, and all that is left for you is an immense fall."

Kaine's fingers spasmed against Helena's arm.

"This is my house," Atreus said, "and now that your failed tasks are mine to complete, you do not command me. Perhaps, when I have finished, I will ask our great leader to order you to produce an heir, since slavish obedience is the only quality you seem to possess."

Kaine didn't look back. "Do as you wish. I don't care."

He walked quickly and did not stop until they reached the west wing of the house, leaving Atreus and Aurelia far behind. He stopped then, turning and holding her face, studying her eyes, and she felt his resonance in her nerves, slowing the unsteady pounding of her heart.

He pressed his forehead against hers. "I am sorry. It didn't occur to me that Stroud would do something so asinine."

"It doesn't matter. It's over now," she said. "What did your father mean about your failed tasks being his now?"

"It's nothing. Come, let's get you back to your room."

She wouldn't budge. "What's happened?"

He exhaled. "The task of hunting down the killer has been reassigned to my father."

"What does that mean?"

"Nothing. He won't find anything. Shiseo's envoy will be back in a little over a week."

The news was like a punch in the gut. She knew time was running out, she could see it every time she looked into the night sky, but news of Shiseo's return made it so much more final. She was silent until they reached her room.

"That girl who was here, with her sister. Do you know her?"

Kaine's eyes narrowed. "She was the one who let everyone into the Institute."

"She was one of Crowther's. She killed him because her sister died when we rescued Luc," Helena said, nodding. "She's convinced that the necrothrall with her is alive."

"The reanimation is one of Morrough's. He rarely bothers with such elaborate work, but that explains why. I would have killed her already, but she makes it difficult because she never goes anywhere without the necrothrall and doesn't keep any others."

SPIREFELL FELT HAUNTED ONCE MORE with the presence of Atreus and Aurelia.

With a room facing the courtyard, Helena would hear when anyone arrived. She watched Kaine and his father standing on the steps as a lorry drove in and prisoners were dragged into one of the storehouse buildings.

Kaine started to walk away, but Atreus called harshly after him. Kaine turned slowly, following his father inside.

The screams that followed pierced the windows, floating through the twisting halls of the house. They would not end.

Helena closed the curtains and huddled in the far corner of her room, trying to block out the sounds. She had too many memories of screams like that.

She flinched at a touch and looked up to find Kaine in front of her. She studied him. She could tell he'd washed recently; his hair was damp.

They stared at each other, feeling the weight of it all.

"Did—did any of them say anything that could incriminate you?" she asked, her voice hoarse.

His eyes flickered. "No. None of them knew anything."

She swallowed hard.

Every word. Every life. Because of you.

She couldn't speak.

"It's late. Will you eat?" Kaine finally asked.

She looked over, catching sight of a tray set on the table across the room. The shadows in the room were long. She had hidden in the corner for an entire day.

Her jaw trembled, throat thickening.

"Why is he doing this here?" she asked, as if it somehow made a difference where it happened.

"He believes there are spies, and that's why the killer has been so effective. He's convinced Spirefell is the only place that remains secure." He looked down. "You should try to eat. I'm expected to have dinner with him and Aurelia tonight."

He started to stand, but she reached out. "Will you come back, after?"

She could see his silver eyes in the darkness.

"If you want me to."

In the quiet, she went and pulled out her arrays, all her notes, studying them, altering certain components of the design she'd developed, squinting as she ran her fingers along the patterns, trying to feel the energy and remember if it felt right.

There were no books, no sources to reference for alchemical arrays designed for animancy. She had to rely on fragments of information and her own experience.

Arrays could take years, sometimes decades, to perfect.

At best, she'd have only one chance to get it right.

"SHISEO WILL REACH EASTERN NOVIS in a few days," Kaine told her. They were walking in the hedge maze, because they couldn't be seen there from the house and it was far away enough that she couldn't hear the sudden screams. "He'll be here within the week."

Helena's stomach dropped. "Oh."

She knew he was telling her to brace her for what was so soon to come, but it didn't feel like being braced—it felt like being struck.

Her throat worked several times. "Do you think there's any chance I could go to the library with you? I just want to see if I've overlooked anything."

"If that's what you want."

In the library, she could feel the weight of his gaze as she made her way slowly through the aisles, looking for old histories and commentaries on the qualities of alchemy. When he watched her, there was such visible grief in his eyes, she didn't know how she hadn't recognised it sooner.

She knew that to him, what she was doing was stealing time from them. If she found nothing, it was all wasted. Moments they could have had together, she had spent searching for a solution that did not exist.

Still, she pulled another book down from a shelf, fingers trembling, and added it to a stack.

"These too."

"I THINK—I'VE FIGURED OUT THE array and all the materials I'd need to restore your soul," she said when Kaine came the next day. She was sitting on the edge of the bed, empty-handed, her meal untouched.

He paused, shutting the door. "Oh?"

Her left hand kept spasming uncontrollably, and her heart was beating like a fist inside her chest.

"If we alter the base of the array, I could use the inner components of it to hold the energy while I use my animancy to separate your soul from the others."

"But?"

She swallowed. "When Luc died, it happened slowly. Cetus—Morrough had damaged him so much, his soul couldn't hold on once Cetus was dead. I didn't know how to—Your soul was ripped out of your body. If I can get it back in, with time maybe it might reintegrate, but we'd need to secure it at least initially, like—like the servants' souls are doing now, to the phylactery."

"You'd need a sacrificial soul."

She nodded. "They'd have to be willing. It wouldn't hold together, it wouldn't work if they weren't."

"Ah," was all he said.

She swallowed hard, jaw trembling. "Maybe if I start over, I can find something else. I might have come at it from the wrong angle."

He was silent.

Her chest convulsed. "Or—I was thinking, what if we prioritise just getting the phylactery first, and go. Then I'll have another month to study it, right? I could build a bomb—we could—you have an old forge here. It wouldn't be high heat or a large detonation. If we used nullium, once Morrough was injured—you could get the phylactery and then we'd run, and—and I can figure something out then."

Kaine's expression was closed, his gaze infuriatingly patient as he walked over to her. "Can you safely handle explosives while pregnant?"

Her throat closed. "We could work together—I could tell you how to—"

Kaine picked up her hand and laid it against his. His fingers twitched several times, and Helena's entire hand spasmed.

"Which of us has hands steady enough to build a bomb?"

Helena snatched hers away, curling her fingers into a fist so tight she could feel metacarpal bones under her fingertips. The room swam, threatening to topple her from the bed. She braced her other hand firmly against the mattress to steady herself. "Well, maybe if I—"

"Helena, I'm tired."

She looked up and saw it in his eyes. The war had eaten him; it had carved him to the bone and not stopped even then. He was scarcely more than a ghost.

She had known, from the moment she'd seen the array on his back, that if he survived it, it would drive him to distil his world to a single point and he would never stray from it. He had made that point her.

He could not stop so long as she was in danger, and it had worn him almost to nothing. He just wanted an endpoint to look towards.

Her shoulders shook. "But . . . I want to save you back."

"I know." He said it gently. "And if anyone could, it would be you. But I would like to say goodbye to you before you're gone, and you are losing yourself in this."

He pulled her into his arms, his chin resting on the top of her head.

But her mind would not stop racing. When he left, she went back to her research. Starting from scratch. When she heard him coming, she put everything away and didn't mention it. He knew anyway, but they pretended.

She kissed him. Pushed him back against the bed and slid her legs up until she was on his lap, fingers threaded through his pale hair as she moulded her body to his, wanting all of him.

As he kissed down her neck, she found the buttons and fastenings on his clothes until she could touch his skin, shoving his shirt down off his shoulders, guiding his hands to her waist.

His hands gripped her, thumbs pressed against her lower ribs, arching her closer.

Her hands shook as she began unbuttoning her dress, fingers trembling so badly that they fumbled with the buttons. Kaine tried to close his hands over hers, but she jerked them free.

"I want this," she said, voice shaking. "I want this on our terms before I go—please . . ."

Her voice cracked.

"This was ours . . ." She swallowed, blinking hard. "They took it from us, but it was ours."

She managed the rest of the buttons and let her dress slip off, pooling at her waist. She wrapped her arms around his neck, pulling him close, kissing him.

She stayed astride him, her thighs bracketing his hips as their bodies joined. His fingers curled against her waist, but he didn't push her down, didn't make her move beyond the pace that she felt ready for. He gave a low groan as she rolled her hips forward.

She tried not to remember, not to compare it to any other time, just trying to dwell on the now, grounding herself in the moment, but it was familiar . . .

She remembered it being like this before, slow and intimate. The burning reverence of his touch when he'd made love to her.

That's what it had been. Making love. It was what they'd had.

CHAPTER 71

Julius 1789

HELENA WAS CORRODING LIKE METAL; DISSOLVING, DECAYING, flecking away into pieces. There was a constant pain in her chest as she felt herself come apart.

There were so many things she wanted to say to Kaine, but she could scarcely think them without her throat beginning to ache and her heart pounding and she would start crying. She'd never been particularly prone to crying before, but the pregnancy seemed to rip it out of her. The countdown to her departure was slowly tearing her apart.

One day, instead of crying, she snapped and raged at him.

His plans were stupid and selfish. It wasn't fair that he got to die and she was left to live with everything. If he'd let her help rescue Lila, none of this might have happened. If he'd just trusted her and not been so controlling, if he'd let them work together—everything might have been different. It was all his fault.

He let her say it all, until she was gasping for breath, hand clawing at her chest, trying to force her heart to beat evenly, and when he had to do it for her, she tried to tear his hands off.

When his father called him away, she was left to seethe and realised he was doing this intentionally.

He knew the destructive ways her mind tilted. Since the moment she'd arrived at Spirefell, he'd gone out of his way to needle and antagonise, trying to provoke her. He'd given her a target. When she'd hated him, she'd been less self-destructive.

If she was angry now, it would make leaving easier.

He was managing her. She swallowed her anger, but all her emotions sat like poison inside her.

A LORRY BROUGHT A FRESH batch of prisoners to Spirefell, and Kaine was gone again.

Helena couldn't help but wonder at the relationship between Kaine and his father. They were both unveiled in their contempt for each other. Atreus seemed to find so much in his son to despise, and yet seemed to constantly find reasons to need him. Kaine blamed his father for the tragedy of his mother, and yet Atreus was among the Undying he'd spared, despite seeming an easy target.

Helena was sitting numb with despair when the door opened.

She looked up, blood running cold as one of the uniformed lorry guards stepped into the room.

He tilted back the cap on his head, and it was Ivy.

Helena stared with deadened surprise as Ivy gave a tentative smile.

"You were hard to get to."

Helena didn't move. "What are you doing here?"

"I'm here to rescue you."

Ivy had no sooner spoken than there was a scream of metal as the iron around the door warped inwards, barring the door. Ivy whirled and tried the door, finding it completely immobile. She turned and started to move towards Helena.

"Don't," Helena said sharply, standing up. "The last time someone came and got too close, he broke almost every bone in their body before he arrived."

Ivy froze, the look of a caged animal filling her eyes. However difficult Helena had been to reach, this was clearly not a well-plotted rescue.

"Why are you here?" Helena said, staring at the girl. She was a girl. She was so young. "You've known I was a prisoner here since last year. Why are you here now?"

Ivy drew back and then moved around Helena in a wide arc, making for the window, rattling it forcefully, and trying to break the panes of glass. The girl had lost her touch, or perhaps been too impulsive, too misguided in what she thought the difficulty of the infiltration would be.

"I thought you were here for interrogation," Ivy said. "I didn't know the High Reeve would do—" Her eyes flicked to Helena's stomach. "—that to you."

Helena scoffed. "They're doing the same to plenty of girls in Central. Why do you care about me?"

Ivy stilled. "Sofia liked you. Wanted me to be your friend. She was always telling me that I should be more like you. That I should help people. I never listened."

"I don't want to be your friend," Helena said coldly. "Your sister is dead. You betrayed us all for a corpse."

"I know!" Ivy's voice rang with grief as she whirled to face Helena, face pale, eyes bright. "I know, but I couldn't—I couldn't let her be dead. I thought—" Her face crumpled. "—I told myself she was just hurt, but she would come back. But she doesn't. She—can't. Even if she did, she would never forgive me for all this. Would she?"

Helena felt no sympathy. "You cost us everything. Even if we were always going to lose, there were people who could have run, they could have fled if they'd had time. But *you* made sure they didn't."

As she spoke, the doors warped, metal screaming, and Kaine walked in. The wrought iron peeled itself from the floor, elongating into countless points, all aimed at Ivy. A flick of his hand and Ivy would be run through from every side.

She could try to flee, but she would not make it two steps.

Ivy turned to face him, her face strangely resigned.

"What an unexpected traitor," Kaine said with complete insincerity.

"I have to admit I thought you were too smart to fall into a trap this obvious."

Ivy gave a bitter smile and shook her head almost sadly. "You don't remember me, do you? I thought eventually you might."

Kaine studied her. "I can't say I do."

"I was different when we first met. Smaller. Screaming."

Kaine shook his head, as if that could have been countless people.

"I used to wear two braids. With bows." Ivy gestured along her shoulders with both hands. "After the Undying killed my parents, they used them to drag me across the floor and put them in your hands. You were younger then, too."

Recognition slowly dawned in Kaine's eyes.

Ivy pressed her lips together, inhaling. "When you ran away, the other Undying went after you. Forgot all about my sister and me. I tried to cut my mother's head off with the cake knife to make her stop what she was doing to Sofia. That was when I realised what I could do with my hands." She looked down at her fingers. "After we got away, Sofia was still alive but she—it was like she was in a dream. She didn't move unless I moved her or eat unless I fed her. We hid in the slums. When she finally woke up, the last thing she remembered was that it had been my birthday. She didn't remember any of it. We would have died, if not for you."

Kaine's expression grew contemptuous. "Another reason to regret my actions that day."

Ivy turned confused until Kaine reached into his coat and drew an obsidian dagger. Then her sharp eyes widened, not with fear but surprise, almost joy. "You're the killer."

He smiled. "Yes, and you, in particular, I've been looking forward to."

Ivy turned towards Helena. "And you knew?" She looked between them. "Is this all pretend?"

"In a way," Helena said. She hadn't thought she'd mind seeing Ivy killed, but it seemed she was doomed to feel some pity for anyone she understood. Crowther had mentioned that Ivy had come from the slums and worked for him in exchange for her sister's protection. If Sofia had been in a fugue state, it was no wonder Ivy had been able to cling to the fantasy that Sofia was still alive.

"Don't kill her," Helena said.

Kaine glanced at her. "You can't expect me to spare her."

Helena shook her head. "I don't think she expects to be spared," she said, suspecting she was about to make a terrible mistake, but there was so little reason left not to risk everything. She looked towards Ivy. "The Undying are all doomed. You know that, don't you?"

Ivy nodded. Helena doubted that she had become Undying out of any interest in immortality; more likely it had been a condition of Morrough's, like Kaine, a leash around a lethal vivimancer's throat.

"Will you help us?" Helena asked.

Ivy's sharp eyes jumped between Helena and Kaine, her expression wary and calculating, but she inclined her head.

"No," Kaine said sharply. "She can't be trusted." He turned on Helena, and his resonance hummed ominously, the iron in the room giving a bone-shuddering groan. "She'll say anything to get out of this room alive, and then she'll betray you, just like she betrayed everyone else."

Helena looked at Ivy and back to Kaine. "I think we can. She owes you. She owes you years of her sister's life. She'll do this for Sofia."

"What do you need?" Ivy asked. Her eyes were sharp and curious, that bright look that Helena remembered well.

Helena looked at her. "Kaine's phylactery. It's part of the outer bone of Morrough's right arm."

Ivy trembled almost imperceptibly. It was clearly more than she'd bargained for. "Why?"

Helena looked at her and then at Kaine. "I need it to save him."

Ivy nodded slowly. "I'll try. If there's a way, I'll find it."

"You won't survive, if you do this," Helena said, watching Ivy, beginning to doubt herself but unable to stop. Any chance was better than none.

Ivy lifted her chin. "I'm doing this for Sofia. She can't be hurt anymore. It doesn't matter what happens to me." She looked at Kaine. "You were the reason I could save her once. So this will be my thanks for that."

"I don't want your thanks," Kaine said, his lip curling, but Helena clasped his wrist, urging him to lower his arm. He glared at her. "This is not worth it. She's not even competent."

Helena rose up and spoke softly so her voice wouldn't carry. "Tell me, truthfully, would you have been any different if you thought it could save your mother? Say no, and I'll let you kill her."

His jaw clenched, and he lowered the knife.

"Get out before I change my mind," he said.

Ivy hesitated a moment, and Helena nodded, urging her to go. Quick as a flash, she darted across the room, weaving around the iron and out the door. The room slowly reassembled itself, and Kaine stared at Helena, accusation in his eyes.

"After everything, you'll risk it all on this?" he asked.

"If it saves you, it's worth it."

"And if it doesn't?"

She looked around. She didn't even feel any sense of hope or trust that this could work; she simply couldn't sit in idle despair any longer. "Then I'll die knowing I tried everything, which is more happily than I'll live if I leave you here. She has nothing to gain from betraying us. She's already lost everything."

He shoved the obsidian knife back into its sheath. "Well, I imagine we'll find out in short order."

He left and returned with two knives, one the obsidian and the other a part of her old set he'd recovered from the bombing, and a suicide pill. If Ivy betrayed them, and he couldn't reach her in time, she'd have a chance of a quick escape for herself and the baby.

The day passed with a relentless intensity. Night came, and nothing happened except word that Shiseo's envoy was crossing into Novis. A few days were all that was left, and time would run out, regardless of what Ivy did.

When the house was dark and silent, Kaine came to her. They took every moment together slowly. There was no time left; they couldn't waste it by rushing.

She lay in his arms, listening to his heart. When she tried to picture home, this feeling was all she could imagine. She rolled onto her back and found his hand, pressing it against the swell between her hips.

"That's her," she said. "I'll—" Her throat grew tight. "I'll probably be able to feel her move within the next month. The book says it feels like fluttering at first."

She had to swallow hard to keep speaking.

"It's called quickening—when you first feel a baby move." She drew a deep breath. "If you use your resonance, you'll be able to feel her now. If you want."

His hand twitched and he hesitated.

"We can do it together," she said. "You should meet her."

THE NEXT DAY, RATHER THAN walk the hedge maze, Kaine took her back to the courtyard.

She froze, heart in her throat at the smell of old blood and decomposition trapped there in the still summer air. Her stomach threatening to upend.

At least thirty prisoners had been brought to Spirefell since Atreus had returned. Helena didn't know if it was better or worse if any of them were still alive.

"Do we have to walk here?" she asked.

Kaine looked at her. There was a risk they were being watched, and so his expression was chilly and indifferent, but his voice was soft. "Just this once. It won't take long."

She forced a nod.

The courtyard was much more beautiful in summer. The vines that had covered the house like blackened veins in winter had bloomed into climbing roses.

There were still two necrothralls stationed at the front of the house, barely more than bones now, and Helena eyed them warily as Kaine led the way across the courtyard garden.

"You don't need to worry about them," he said under his breath. "Morrough is too preoccupied with himself to waste effort on his necrothralls. Their senses are nearly gone, and he hasn't noticed. Come. There's a reunion that's rather overdue."

It dawned on her then where they were going.

"Amaris . . ."

Kaine unlocked the stable door. "She had a hard time when you first arrived."

The door swung open, and in the dim light of the stable, an enormous black shadow unfurled itself from the corner and stood, wings arching and stretching. The chimaera came forward, the heavy chain dragging behind her.

"I was afraid she'd give us away if I let her near you. She has quite the reputation nowadays," he said. "You were the only other person she's ever taken to."

Helena considered that a rather generous description of her relationship with Amaris.

Her mouth went dry. Amaris had grown. She was several hands taller, and her immense yellow eyes glowed in the low light. Helena remembered the chimaera being so careful and gentle around Kaine when he was injured, the way she used to curl against Helena's back, blocking out the cold, but she had a far starker memory of entering the stable and being nearly bitten in half.

She took a nervous step back. "I'm not sure that she remembers me."

Kaine held up a hand, and Amaris stopped. "Oh, that. That wasn't you. That was the necrothralls. She can't stand them." Amaris was bobbing her head impatiently. He stepped closer and rumpled her fur. "She tolerates the staff, but any of Morrough's reanimations that get close—well."

He glanced at Helena. "She very much remembers you. Howled for half the day when you arrived."

Helena stepped hesitantly closer and let Amaris sniff and nuzzle at her fingers. When she didn't lose her hand, she took a step closer.

"You and Shiseo will take her with you when you go," Kaine said when she hazarded to rest a hand on Amaris's head. "Fly at night. It'll take a few days to reach Lila, but you'll be hard to track down that way." He rubbed Amaris's shoulder just beneath an immense wing. "You'll leave her, when you take the ship."

Helena's hand stilled. "Leave her?"

"She'll be fine," he said, but his voice was gruff. "She can hunt for herself, and she doesn't like most humans, so she'll avoid populated areas. With luck, she'll head back to Paladia looking for me. End up in the mountains."

"But doesn't she need someone to—the transmutations on her have to be maintained if she's still growing."

His jaw ticced. "There's only one surviving chimaera from the war, and everyone knows who it belongs to. If she's sighted, that will be enough to give an ambitious Aspirant a direction to hunt you down. You have to leave her."

He rested his head against Amaris, and her wings fluttered. She turned her neck to nip at him.

"We'll go out together, won't we, old girl? Bennet's last two monsters."

The air in the stable was burning her eyes. Helena turned and walked out.

The air near the house was fresher, and she drew several forceful gasps, her hand pressed over her heart until she heard quick steps and looked up to see Aurelia storming down the stairs towards her.

Aurelia was pale, her eyes flashing with rage. She was wearing a pale-pink dress splashed with scarlet detailing. As she got closer, Helena noticed that the hem and her shoes were also scarlet.

"Where is Kaine?"

"Aurelia." Kaine's voice emerged from the dark interior of the stable. "What did I tell you about speaking to my prisoner?"

Aurelia whirled towards the stable. "I need to talk to you! How am I supposed to stay away from her and ever talk to you when you're always with her?"

Kaine stepped out of the stable, eyes glittering. "What do you want?"

Aurelia's throat worked several times. "I need you to talk to your father. He's ruining the house."

Kaine raised an eyebrow, looking unconcerned. "I thought you were pleased that he'd come to stay."

Aurelia's eyes bulged in her head. "That was before he turned the house into a torture chamber. It was one thing when it stayed in the storehouse, but he's bringing them inside! There are *piles* of body parts all over, and I walked into a pool of blood because he flayed someone in the middle of the foyer."

Helena realised then that Aurelia's dress was not scarlet-detailed at all.

"I advised that you stay in the city," Kaine said, appearing indifferent to all this. "But you refused because my father said something about domination livening the blood, and you thought, what?" He leaned towards her, lip curling. "That I might set my sights on you?"

Aurelia had gone white as a sheet with two scarlet blotches staining her cheeks. "I am your wife."

Kaine cocked his head to one side. "I didn't ask for you."

"What's this?" Atreus had emerged from the storehouse. There was blood up to his elbows, and a long knife used for gutting fish in his hand.

Aurelia started, clutching at her throat with her iron-ringed hands, shrinking towards Kaine, but Kaine drifted away from her, just happening to insert himself between Helena and his father as they faced each other.

"I'm afraid Aurelia doesn't care much for what we've done to the house, Father," Kaine said. "I believe she finds us rather—uncivilised."

Atreus stared at Kaine for a moment, Crowther's narrow nostrils flaring in a way that Helena recognised as suppressed anger. "Does she? I suppose it is rather excessive. I was waiting for *you* to object. I thought at some point surely you'd feel a sense of ownership. You did grow up here . . ." His voice trailed off as he turned to stare at the immense house which towered around them. "This was your mother's house. She planted those roses the summer we wed."

Atreus's grip on his knife tightened, and for a moment Helena felt Kaine's resonance in her teeth.

"I'm afraid the estate has never had much sentimental charm for me," Kaine said. "Perhaps if you'd come back sooner, you might have made the effort of maintaining it."

"Yes, you seem intent on destroying everything this family has ever built," Atreus said, his face contorting so much, it seemed the dead grey skin might tear as he glared at his son. "What sin did your mother ever commit to deserve such a son?"

Kaine leaned forward, a razor-thin smile spreading across his face, pure contempt in his eyes. "I believe it was when she married you."

Fury seemed to ignite inside Atreus, but Aurelia broke in.

"See? See? I told you. It is all his doing! I have been a perfect wife. You should have seen this hideous mouldering place when he brought me. I've done everything to be a proper wife that I have had means to, trying to restore this house, to get rid of all the ugly, fussy old-fashioned things everywhere, and to make it the heart of society. Everything decent in this house is because of me. I'm just like your wife, I—"

Atreus turned sharply. There was a wet snick and a gasping burble as Aurelia stopped speaking.

She reached up towards her neck as a line of blood gushed from a slit across her throat. She blinked once, mouth opening, but no sound came out, only a blood-filled gasp, and then her head toppled backwards, slit throat opening, body following, and she collapsed onto the white gravel. Her pink dress turned redder and redder.

Helena had to cram her hand against her mouth to smother the sound that nearly escaped her.

The side of her neck burned as her heart began pounding, but she couldn't move as Atreus glared down at his former daughter-in-law, the fish knife dangling once more from his fingertips, a drop of blood on the curved tip.

"Do not *ever* compare yourself to *my wife,*" he said, staring down at Aurelia.

Kaine made no move except to step forward and block the sight of Aurelia's slit throat from Helena's view.

"I hope you intend to deal with the Ingram family," he said. "Given that you contracted me into marrying her."

"What can they do?" Atreus said with a sneer that Helena knew well. It was eerie seeing Kaine's traits in Crowther's dead face. "You clearly had no intention of ever putting an heir inside her."

Atreus leaned down, pulling Aurelia's body up off the ground by an arm. "I'll deal with this, but once this matter is resolved, you will give me the name of a woman you will cooperate in marrying and producing a guild heir with. Otherwise, once I've found the last member of the

Eternal Flame and gifted them to the High Necromancer, I will request that he *order* your cooperation in producing an heir, and I will choose the bride."

Atreus turned and disappeared into the house, dragging Aurelia with him. The scent of the roses mixed with the coppery tang of fresh blood.

Helena turned and walked away, heading towards the far wing of the house. Once they were inside, in a hallway where they couldn't be watched, she stopped. Kaine was only steps behind her. She knew he was about to ask if she was all right, but she spoke first.

"You planned that."

He froze for an instant. "What makes you say that?" His voice was light.

"Because she's a loose end. If you'll let Amaris die, you won't let Aurelia live."

His expression hardened. "What did you expect? She tried to gouge out your eyes."

Helena flinched at the memory of Aurelia's talons hooking behind her eyeball. Her terror of being blinded, left in the dark forever. "I haven't forgotten."

"I would have killed her then, but it diverted suspicion to have a pretty wife in the house. Living here alone with you could have attracted attention. That was the only reason I let her live."

Helena nodded listlessly. None of that surprised her, but it didn't change anything, either. "I hate it when you kill people because of me," she said.

She reached up, pressing her left hand against the scar on her neck, remembering her father's face and the horrible gash below his jaw. That mockery of his smile as her last memory of him.

There was so much easy, indifferent death. It had bled together. The quantity had grown beyond a tragedy, into a figure so large it was almost abstract. Even for her, after so many years of fighting for every life, pouring herself into preserving them, eventually she had ceased to bleed. There was so much now, it was scarcely comprehensible.

She and Kaine stood in the centre of it.

"There's so much more to you," she said, "but sometimes I feel like all I do is bring out the worst. You would never go so far if it weren't for me. You wouldn't be like this. I did this to you."

"You're right. I don't imagine I would."

"I used to have so many dreams for us," she said, voice thickening. "When I'd worry about you, when I'd do things I didn't want to, when the war felt so heavy that I was sure I'd break under it, I'd tell myself: Someday you're going to run away with him. Somewhere quiet. You won't ask for very much, just you and him, and that will be enough." A lump welled up in her throat, and she shook her head. "That was all I wanted. It was my whole dream, to see what we could be away from the war. I thought it would all be worth it for that."

She exhaled, right hand clenching, feeling the scars from the amulet across her palm. "But look at everything we've done, and it's still not enough. I guess in the end, I am like Luc. I thought that we could suffer enough to earn each other."

He said nothing, and she was so tired of his resignation.

"Why are you always so ready to die?" she said, whirling on him even though she'd sworn to herself that she wouldn't be angry anymore. "Even at the beginning when you made your offer to Crowther, you were already planning to die, like it didn't matter to anyone. But why are you still like that now, when it does?"

Kaine sighed, jaw jutting forward. His thumb pressing against the ring on his hand. "I didn't have anyone, Helena," he said quietly. "After my mother died, I was alone. My life was blown apart when I went home at sixteen, and everything I did from that point on was to keep from losing the only thing I had left. When she died—it didn't matter. Revenge was all I could do to make up for it, and dying for that didn't matter to anyone—not until you came along."

His voice grew bitter.

"I didn't make plans past the war because there were never any plans to make. Holdfast, the Eternal Flame, they were never going to win, and I always knew that. Falling for you didn't change that—it just . . . it just made knowing worse."

The lights flickered, and a distant buzzing came from the main wing.

Kaine tensed, his head snapping right. "Something's wrong. He never uses that to call for me anymore. Go to your room and bar the door."

He left quickly. She watched from the window as he emerged in uniform, including the helmet that concealed his hair. He led out Amaris, swinging onto her back, and then they were gone, flying towards the city.

Helena waited. In less than an hour, a motorcar came. She watched it pull up, knife in hand. Had Ivy been captured or betrayed them? Was the summons meant to lure Kaine away from the estate?

Instead Atreus emerged in uniform, sliding into the rear. The motorcar pulled away.

What had Ivy done?

It was the middle of the night when she heard the door disbarred from the outside.

Kaine entered, still in uniform, his helmet in his hand.

His expression was unreadable.

"We received word that while the Eastern envoy was passing through Novis, the train was attacked. Everyone on board was killed—including Shiseo."

CHAPTER 72

Julius 1789

SHISEO WAS DEAD.

His return had hung over Helena like a raised sword, so long a foregone conclusion. He would return and she would go. That fact had felt immutable.

Kaine was shaking his head slowly, as if he could scarcely believe it himself.

"Is it confirmed?"

"They sent his head. Novis is claiming they had no direct part in it, that it's a surviving faction of the Eternal Flame, but—there isn't one. Not with those kinds of abilities. This was an experimental salvo. The queen is calculating, and she wants to see if the allying countries will distance themselves if pressured to choose a side, and whether New Paladia has any recourse." He lowered his head, and the air warped with his resonance, but then he laughed. "The irony is, this is what we orchestrated, this was our plan, except they weren't supposed to do it until I was gone."

He threw his helmet against the wall. "Now they've given Morrough warning and time to assemble forces and recall the necrothralls from the mines, and I am still here and I can't refuse orders. Fuck!"

So they were all going to die, then. Kaine was going to die, she would die, their daughter would die. Spirefell was a cage and a tomb.

She reached out to him, her fingers almost numb. "It's all right, Kaine. You did everything you could."

I'd rather die in your arms.

His eyebrows knit together for a moment. "You're still leaving."

Helena stared at him, not understanding. The escape plan had hinged on Shiseo.

He pulled off his gloves. "There are other ways, they're just . . . not as clean. There's more risk of being tracked down if they move quickly to pursue, which is likely to happen. Morrough will do anything to recover you. If you can reach the coast in time, you'll disappear into the islands long before they can catch up. But—you'll have to get to Lila alone. Unless you think you're strong enough to take Amaris by yourself."

"How—alone?"

Even before, during the war when she'd been stronger, not prone to fits of panaphobia, flying on Amaris was something she'd endured only out of necessity. The height and speed had always terrified her, and Amaris had known where to go, requiring no guidance from Helena.

Flying at night as Lumithia's crescent shrank out of sight was almost unimaginable. It would be black as pitch, the world an abyss beneath her. Her head felt light just thinking about it.

"I'll take you as far as I can, and there will be a ship downriver that will sail to the coast. I'll show you maps and the route you'll take inland to find Lila. I can arrange transportation, but it would be safest if you travelled at least part of the way on foot, if you think you'd be able to manage the distance. Just before the Abeyance, you'll go to the ports; there is passage booked and false identification papers waiting. You'll take a ship to Etras. I've arranged a place there."

Her heart stuttered, tripping over itself as she tried to think.

"You don't have to decide now," Kaine said, his hand on her shoulder. "I'll arrange for both, and you can choose. I know it'll be hard, but it will be worth it. Lila's been waiting for you a long time."

She nodded shakily.

Everything had to move fast. The Abeyance wouldn't wait, and if there was a war about to break out between Paladia and the surrounding countries, Kaine did not want her there for it.

After all the years spent hoping that Novis or any of their neighbours might intervene on their behalf, they now acted at the worst possible moment.

"I have to go," he said after a bit. "I'll come see you when I can. Try to eat and rest as much as you can. Keep the doors barred. Fortunately, with Aurelia gone, the door is more secure. Crowther had no iron resonance to speak of, despite my father's efforts to plumb some from the decrepit depths of his corpse. As long as the door's locked, he can't open it."

He was rambling, because he was nervous; things were slipping out of his control. All his carefully laid plans destroyed by the very intervention the Resistance had been waiting for when annihilated.

SHE BARELY SAW KAINE AFTER that. For days, he was gone; she didn't think he slept at all. She tried to do her part, to eat and perform callisthenic exercises inside her room to build up stamina and get a little stronger so that preparations were not so limited by her.

Atreus returned to Spirefell, apparently no worse off for having murdered Aurelia, assuming it had become known. He seemed to have run out of prisoners; instead he prowled around the house. She heard his footsteps in the hallway outside her door and spotted him entering and leaving the chantry several times.

When the windows rattled from the wind of Amaris's wings, she knew Kaine had returned at least briefly. He was busy with more than merely preparations for her escape. He was the High Reeve; he'd be expected to coordinate the response to the attack.

She was surprised when only a few minutes later, the door opened and he walked in.

His eyes were so bright, they seemed to actually glow. He was the furthest from human he had ever appeared. He walked towards her as if he sensed but did not actually see her.

"Kaine?" she said, her heart in her throat.

He didn't respond. The wrongness of whatever had happened to him was visceral. Cold swept through her. The instinct to run frayed her every nerve, but she went towards him.

She touched his face. "What happened?"

He blinked, and a little humanness seemed to seep into him. She held his face, tilting it down towards hers.

"Kaine?"

"I've never killed so many at once before . . ." he said softly.

"How many?"

His eyes flickered, darting as if trying to calculate the number. Then he shook his head.

"What happened?"

He was looking through her, as if he still wasn't quite there.

"I was ordered to make a show of strength. A warning." He swallowed. "There were rows and rows of prisoners. I don't know where they got so many."

As he spoke, his expression slowly thawed, growing younger and younger until he looked painfully boyish, his eyes huge. He was going into shock. He didn't seem to be talking to Helena so much as trying to explain it to himself.

"I didn't know there'd be so many," he said. "This wasn't supposed to happen until I was gone."

She pulled him closer, wrapping her arms around his shoulders. He felt cold, even though it was nearly the peak of summer, and his skin was clammy.

It seemed impossible that he could continue much longer. As if he were trying to outrun fate, but every time he managed to outpace it, Morrough demanded something else.

And she couldn't do anything. The impotence burned inside her. "Have you seen Ivy? Has she said anything to you? Is she still trying? Maybe if you both—"

He blinked and seemed to come back to himself. He shook his head, straightening. "Don't. I'm fine . . . just tired. I'll be fine. Almost over now."

He meant it as reassurance, but the words left her empty as he vanished back through the door.

SHE WAS SO ON EDGE after Kaine left again that when she felt a sensation in her lower abdomen, her first reaction was pure panic.

She went utterly still, heart faltering, and it came again. Fluttering.

She stared down, pushed her dress flat so she could run her hands over the swell between her hips.

She still forgot sometimes that she was pregnant.

As unbelievable as Lila getting pregnant during the war had been, she had always liked children; they were drawn to her, and Lila knew exactly how to make them laugh.

Helena had never had that kind of allure. She didn't know if she could be a good mother, or if wanting to keep this baby wasn't just her selfishness rearing its head. Her inability to let go.

To love someone. To be needed.

Her hand trembled violently as she pressed it against her stomach, letting her resonance reach hesitantly inwards, sensing the tiny bones softer than cartilage, veins like threads.

Soon this would be all that was left of Kaine in the whole world.

"I'm going to take care of you," she whispered. "It's—our way."

She'd barely spoken the words when the door opened and Kaine strode in. It had been nearly a day but his colour was still unsettling, his eyes too bright.

"Stroud's coming," he said, his voice tense. "I came as fast as I could, but I have to—"

As soon as he reached her, he was removing the manacles and sliding the nullium tubes into place. Helena winced as her resonance vanished like an extinguished light.

Kaine was barely done fastening them when his eyes lost focus. "She's here. Make sure everything's hidden."

When Stroud arrived, it was clear that the current tensions disagreed with her. There were hollows beneath her eyes. Her cheeks were red from split capillaries.

"Central is specifically designed to accommodate gestation," she was saying in a strident voice. "Marino is our most crucial subject. She should be there, where I can keep a close eye on the foetal development and we can move quickly once viability is achieved."

"And you think that the 'gestational environment' you've set up is conducive for someone with a heart condition agitated by stress? You might as well *ask* her to attempt a spontaneous abortion," Kaine said, sneering at Stroud. "Marino is my prisoner. The High Necromancer entrusted her to me, and he has not changed his mind on that point. I will not have you tampering with my assignment just because you'll no longer have Shiseo's work to legitimise yourself with."

Stroud turned a furious shade of red, as if a fresh wave of capillaries were splitting beneath the surface of her skin. "I will be appealing this."

"You're welcome to try, but I did tell him of your interference and its contribution to her current state. She might not have a heart condition at all if you hadn't rushed her interrogation by injecting her with a nearly lethal dose of stimulants and threatened to cut her tongue out if she didn't get pregnant. Now get on with whatever pretence brought you here."

Stroud's entire face was nearly beet red as she performed a perfunctory check of Helena's heart condition and pregnancy. She'd seemingly hoped to sneak into Spirefell and commandeer Helena while Kaine was busy.

In a few minutes, she was done and furiously repacking her satchel so that Kaine could escort her back out.

Helena watched from the window as Stroud climbed into a motorcar and pulled away. The car was barely through the gates when the lights in her room flickered, and she heard the distant buzzing from the main wing. Kaine was already being summoned again.

She watched through the window as Kaine emerged from the house, swinging up onto Amaris's back. The chimaera ran half the length of the courtyard and was airborne.

Helena pressed her hand on the window, the nullium tube pressing against the tendons of her wrist.

The day's paper arrived with lunch. The photograph on the cover was enough to turn her stomach.

It was taken from the main gates of the Institute, which opened directly across from the steps of the Alchemy Tower. There on the steps stood Kaine, no helmet, nothing concealing his identity; his face was visible for all to see, his eyes so bright they distorted the photograph. Between him and the gate, covering the commons, were rows of bodies.

She kept waiting for Kaine to come back, but hours passed and he didn't. It wasn't like him to leave her in the house with Atreus unless she could secure the door.

Night fell and Lumithia was little more than a sliver of light, as if the night sky were a black curtain concealing the daylight, and someone had pierced it with a knife.

A low howl floated through the house. Helena went to the window.

Amaris was standing in the courtyard, a huge shadow, only her edges catching the moonlight. Her head kept dipping down to nuzzle something on the ground, and then she'd tilt her head back and give a soft breathy howl with those horse lungs of hers, like a moaning gust of wind.

As Helena watched, Amaris circled and pawed the ground, wings fluttering nervously. For an instant the feeble moonlight reached the ground, illuminating pale hair.

Helena ran to the door, finding one of the servants in the hall.

"Get Davies and the butler, I don't know his name," Helena said. "Kaine's in the courtyard."

It moved, but very slowly.

Helena barely had time to think about the dark or the shadows, clutching at the wall as she descended the stairs, willing her heart to stay steady. She faltered at the doorway. The house was all dark; there were no signs of Atreus. She tried to tell herself that it was good it was dark, Morrough wouldn't be able to see well if he was watching.

She drew a deep breath and rushed across the gravel to where Amaris was giving another helpless howl.

The chimaera snarled, whirling when Helena got close. Helena stopped, showing her empty hands.

"It's me," she said. "Remember? I'll help him."

Amaris stopped snarling, but her muzzle remained curled back. She let Helena kneel and crawl the remaining distance to Kaine.

He was lying face down and when she rolled him over, her hands came away wet with blood. He smelled of rot, of that awful hall underground. His skin was cold, and he was barely breathing.

"Kaine? Kaine? What did he do to you?" She shook him gently. She'd seen him injured by nullium before, but she'd never seen anything like this. She had no resonance to reach out and find what was wrong. It was so dark outside, she could scarcely see more than his outline. She felt his pulse, but it was irregular in a way that would kill a human. Stopping intermittently and then restarting, pulsing and stopping again.

She tried to lift him, but with the nullium in her wrists, she couldn't hold him. She hooked her elbows under his arms but didn't have the weight or strength to move him across the ground. She sank back into the gravel, and his head lolled against her shoulder.

"Kaine—"

He didn't respond.

She looked around for the servants and spotted Davies and the butler and several other servants coming out, carrying electric torches. They moved as if only half there.

Amaris snarled, and Helena quieted her, petting her ears and urging her back enough for the servants to reach Kaine.

"Take him to my room," she said softly. "Be gentle, I don't know where he's hurt."

The butler pulled Kaine carefully over his shoulder.

Amaris was trembling, a low groaning whine as her nose followed Kaine up the steps, head bobbing like she wanted to go with him into the house.

"He'll be all right. I'll take care of him. You did everything you could." Helena stayed a moment longer, pressed against the immense, reassuring warmth of the chimaera, and then she forced herself to turn and cross the open gravel back to the far door.

Calm. Stay calm, she told herself over and over, willing her heart to stay even, not to let her mind slip into the shadows. *You have to get upstairs to Kaine.*

She reached her room before the servants did, in enough time to turn down the bed and clear the table of everything except what medicine she thought might be useful. She started wetting towels while she waited.

The butler was smeared with blood where Kaine's body had pressed against him.

"Hold him so I can get these clothes off," Helena said, pulling off his clothes and discarding them onto the floor, trying to find the source of the injury now that she had light. There were no wounds anywhere. Not anymore. What had they done to him? Where had the blood come from?

The more she couldn't find a cause, the more her chest clenched in dread. Had they done something inside him?

"Bring me all the medical supplies you have in this house," she said to the other two servants who hovered uselessly, their eyes even more unfocused than usual. "And hurry if you can."

The butler laid him on the bed, and she wiped the residual blood away.

She wrapped all the bedding around him, trying to keep him warm, and then hurried back to the pile of blood-soaked, stinking clothes lying on the floor, rummaging through his coat until her fingers grazed a familiar shape. She gave a small gasp of relief and pulled out the medical kit.

It was still intact right down to the waxed sheet of written instructions, carefully folded and stored. Several of the vials were long empty, but in the slot she wanted was a new, full vial and the necessary syringe. Clearly it was something he used regularly.

She pressed her forehead against the kit, sighing with relief, and hurried back.

She checked his pulse. It was still intermittent, starting and stalling and failing and then beginning again.

She wiped his chest clean of any remaining blood.

"Sorry," she said as she filled the syringe, tapping it to knock out any bubbles, and then she sank it into his chest, right over his heart, pressing down on the plunger, injecting the full dose.

Kaine slammed upright almost faster than Helena could pull the syringe away, clutching at his chest. Then he dropped back down on the bed, going limp. He was conscious now, his eyes roving blindly around the room.

"Kaine?"

"—H-lena . . . ?" Her name slurred from his lips.

He sounded bewildered. She set the syringe down and came closer, but his eyes weren't following her. They kept roving as if trying to find something to land on. She leaned over him, stroking his hair back.

"I'm here. What did he do to you?"

He furrowed his eyebrows. "Whe're we?"

Her throat tightened, and she glanced around. The lights were on, the room familiar. Her face was just above his, but he was staring through her.

"We're in my room. You collapsed outside, and I had the servants bring you here. Can you see me?"

"Can't—g . . ." His mouth worked, and she'd never seen him look so scared before. "Can't—sseee . . ."

Suddenly his expression changed, and he grasped blindly for her, hand bumping against her arm. "You all right?—your heart? Is your—heart—"

She caught his hand and pressed it to her chest and then her face. His fingers spasmed against her cheek. "I'm fine. My heart is fine. I'm a healer, remember? Patched you up a lot of times. Calm down."

She cleared her throat, sitting on the edge of the bed so he could feel her nearness, checking his heartbeat and pulse again. Now it was racing, too fast, but at least it wasn't failing. "I had to inject you with the stimulant to keep your heart going. It kept giving out, but I don't have my resonance. Can you try to get my manacles off so I can check you?"

She led his hands to her wrists, placing them on the manacles, but his movements were disjointed, and his fingers kept twitching oddly. Whatever had been done must have been neurological; he'd never had symptoms like this before. He tried several times. She finally grasped hold of his fingers, stilling them.

"Never mind," she said as she fought to keep her voice steady. "Never mind that. I'll work manually." She swallowed. "Can you tell me what happened? Why did he do this to you? You've been doing everything he wants."

He was quiet for a while; when he finally spoke his words were smoother, no longer so disjointed. "Hevgoss announced their alliance with the Liberation Front this afternoon."

That should have been good news.

"In their—declaration, they cited my 'barbaric slaughter' as the reason. Seems I should have foreseen this and refused orders. I was made an example of—the cost of failure and incompetence."

His chest convulsed as if he were attempting to laugh.

"What did he do?" Helena said, afraid of the way he'd avoided the question.

He exhaled. "He ripped out my heart first. Said it was—f-fitting . . ."

Helena was speechless. It had never even occurred to her that something like that could be survivable.

He managed a grimacing smile. "I think I owe the Principate an apology—terrible way to go. Although growing back was the worst part . . ."

His voice trailed off again.

She was glad he couldn't see as she forced herself to breathe slowly several times. She pressed her hand over his heart, feeling the heartbeat.

"And then?" she prompted.

His face twisted. "I'm not—I was still—" He gestured at his chest. "It was something—to my spine, I think. I couldn't see. Couldn't move. I don't remember when my eyes stopped—"

Helena's throat closed, but she kept her voice steady. "Well, your heart is stable now. I don't know how long the neurological symptoms might last. The best thing is to rest and give your body time to recover."

The servants finally returned, carrying several wooden cartons of medical supplies.

Helena sat beside him, going through their contents. Many more vials of the stimulant, which she hoped not to need. Kaine fell asleep after a little while but kept jerking, his fingers twitching spasmodically. He'd start awake, still blind, searching for her, his fingers grasping, trying to feel her heartbeat.

Helena would reassure him that she was fine, and he'd pass out again.

She worried the most about his spasticity. He kept tensing, twitching, his muscles curling inwards, hands and fingers curving into claws.

Helena knew the stimulant caused withdrawal symptoms like that, but she was worried about those symptoms being combined with some kind of brain or spinal injury. Should she have let him be? Was it possible for him to end up with permanent nerve damage? He regenerated so poorly now.

She took his right hand in hers, working at it slowly, knuckle by knuckle, until the muscles were no longer curved and rigid. Every time she moved her thumbs, the tendons twinged against the nullium, but she didn't care. She kept going, working up his arm to his shoulders, and then she started on the other hand. A gnawing pain radiated up her left arm, but she couldn't stop.

This was all she could do, and she would do it.

She checked his heart. It was finally steady. His expression relaxed when she spoke. So she talked to him softly, about anything she could think of. All the things she'd always meant to tell him.

After half a day without waking, she hooked him up to a saline drip. He still didn't stir. A few times, she heard footsteps in the hallway, but if Atreus was lurking about the house again, he didn't come too near.

Finally, Kaine's eyes fluttered and opened, falling on her.

She went very still. "Can you see me?"

He squinted. "Shapes at least." He squeezed his eyes shut, wincing and reopening them. "I think it's getting better."

"Good." She nodded shakily. "I was thinking perhaps the heart injury could have caused blood clotting, or maybe there was nerve strain. Either could cause temporary blindness."

He gave an absent nod because it hardly mattered either way. His fingers trailed over, finding her. "Are you all right?"

"Of course," she said, grateful he couldn't see clearly, because she was too exhausted to lie convincingly.

He started to close his eyes, but then they snapped open again. "My father is at my door." He sat up stiffly with a groan. "I need to go deal with him. There's still arrangements I haven't—"

Helena caught him by the shoulder. "You can't get up yet. You're not recovered."

He placed his hand over hers, trying to squeeze, but instead his fingers spasmed. "My father cannot find me here. I don't need to recover anymore. You have to leave tonight. I can't make it a perfect trip, but there's enough in place. You'll be able to manage."

"T-Tonight?"

He said nothing else. He stood up, pulling the needle from his arm, and dressing quickly. He struggled with the buttons on his shirt; Helena had to help him.

"My eyes are getting better already," he said, his voice hoarse. "I can see how disapproving you look."

He took her hands in his and after some difficulty managed to get his fingers steady enough to remove the manacles. She locked the copper back around her wrists herself.

"Keep the door locked," he said. "I'll be back by nightfall."

CHAPTER 73

Julius 1789

Helena studied the room around her. It was still cold there, even in the heat of summer. All the iron did not allow for much warmth. The sheets of her bed were stained with blood. The scent of decay lingered on the air, a creeping necrotic rot that had infected everything in her life.

It was strange to stand inside a prison, and dread leaving it.

She heard shouting and went to the window in time to see Kaine emerging from the front doors. He was moving more easily now. Atreus stood in the doorway, screaming at him with such rage that Helena couldn't make out his words.

Kaine just went into the stable and brought out Amaris, pulling himself onto her back with almost convincing ease.

Atreus was still shouting as Amaris flew away.

She watched him shake his fists at the sky. Seeing Crowther's living corpse never failed to unnerve her.

Atreus finally stopped screaming at the sky and stood a moment longer, before looking directly at the window where Helena stood.

She stepped back instantly, but it was too late; he'd seen her watching. An inexplicable sense of dread pierced her to the marrow.

She went and checked that the door was securely locked, feeling all the iron inside the door and walls. It was barricaded and reinforced. There was no way for him to get in.

Reassured, she sat studying the array she'd designed, tracing her fingers along the lines. The design would work, it would create the power and stability she'd need, but it didn't matter because it required five components, and she only had three of them.

She'd wasted so much time.

She buried her face in her hands for a moment, but her head jerked up at the smell of smoke and charred meat.

There was black smoke wafting into her room, and then the door began to char, the iron barring smouldering, as a dim red glow grew slowly brighter.

"Come out, come out, little prisoner." Crowther's voice came from the other side. "I want to talk to you."

Helena watched in horror as the wood charred away, and Atreus became visible through the iron bars. He looked almost alive, the red glow giving colour to the dead grey skin.

The bars keeping him out grew hotter and brighter, changing from a red to orange, and the room began to burst into flame, the wallpaper spontaneously igniting. There was a sharp crack as the glass casing in the corner broke, the eye plummeting into the fire that was crawling up the wall.

Crowther would never in his life have bothered to utilise his pyromancy to manipulate something as inferior as iron, but Atreus Ferron, the iron guildmaster, was trying to bend iron to his will once more.

If he couldn't, he'd probably burn her alive in this room instead.

"What do you want?" she said.

"I have questions for you," Atreus said. "Come here."

She hesitated.

"You don't want to smother to death inside that room, do you?" The rug began to smoke. "Come. Here."

Helena went forward, carefully, trying to stay back from the most intense heat. She could only hope that Atreus still lacked Luc and Crowther's talent for distance pyromancy.

A terrible smile spread across his face. "I've had many bodies over the years, but it's strange—this one has a violent reaction to the sight of you. You knew him, didn't you? Well, I believe."

Helena's steps faltered. She'd never heard of liches retaining the memories of the corpses they occupied, but there was no reason why some remnants might not linger.

"I didn't remember you at first. I thought it was only the corpse reacting, but when you attacked my son, it reminded me of that night. I barely recalled that body, it was too long dead before they brought it back, but I remembered you. The High Necromancer was pleased to finally get some answers about that bombing. As a reward, he shared some of the technique this resonance requires." Crowther's spider-like fingers twisted, and the heat intensified.

Helena said nothing. The iron between them glowed brighter, and the wall smouldered as it charred away. Atreus was keeping the fire contained, but he could burn the room down around her if he chose.

The heat of the glowing iron was distorting the air and threatening to scorch her skin.

"Strange attack, that bombing. That Lancaster mongrel was beside himself at the sight of you. I was told you did it all alone, but I've seen your records. You were nobody. No training, no combat experience. I'm expected to believe an unranked healer was single-handedly responsible for one of the most devastating attacks we sustained?"

Stroud had also commented on the lack of records surrounding Helena. She hadn't questioned it at the time—much of her healing had been treated as religious intercession rather than medical work—but Crowther had made her put her name down in the prisoner files, chaining her to him. And there had been all her work with Shiseo, the medicine, the chelators. The bomb. There would have been records of that.

Unless . . .

Kaine wouldn't have wanted her to be a person of interest to the Undying. And Shiseo, if he had been planted, waiting in Central in case Helena ever reappeared—he couldn't have any records tying him to her.

"You were a decoy, weren't you?" Atreus said, interrupting her thoughts. "Everyone knows how the Eternal Flame saw your kind; who better to use as a sacrificial pawn to protect the true last member of the Eternal Flame."

He grinned maniacally as he said it, his face aglow with triumph.

Helena had assumed that Atreus had come because he was suspicious about Kaine's injury, but no, this was about his mission. All his interrogations and victims had yielded no results, and so he'd turned his sights to Helena.

"You were sent here because you know something of vital importance. The High Necromancer entrusted my son to find it, but now he's grown so concerned with the thing growing inside you, he's forgotten that you know who the killer is. The one who bombed the banquet and the West Port Lab. Once I've caught them, the High Necromancer will have nothing to fear."

The iron glowed yellow, and the bars were beginning to droop as they turned molten.

"I don't remember," Helena said, her blood becoming a roaring pressure in her ears as the growing heat rippled across her skin. It was getting hard to breathe. "I can't remember anything about that. The High Reeve tried to find out, but if I ever knew it, it's lost."

"I don't believe you." Atreus stepped back and kicked the door. The drooping iron bars folded in on themselves, collapsing. As he stepped through, Helena caught sight of a charred mass crumpled on the floor.

One of the servants had tried to stop him.

Atreus forced her to fall back. With each snap of his fingers, fiery red flames materialised around him.

Atreus tilted his head. "My son is always worrying over you. Your delicate heart. One would think you were quite the exotic flower. He thinks that success comes by acting as an obedient enough slave." Atreus shook his head. "He's always been too terrified of failure to understand that success requires risks . . ."

Atreus's voice trailed off.

Helena's eyes darted towards the window, hoping desperately to catch sight of Amaris.

"Are you hoping he'll come for you?" Atreus was suddenly terrifyingly close. He grabbed her by the arm and dragged her to the window, pinning her chest against it. "My son. Do you think he'll save you?"

Helena's throat closed as Crowther's thin, spider-like fingers dug into her arm, the iron window lattice biting against her skin. The sky was empty.

She was on her own.

She'd never fought a pyromancer. If she tried to fight back using her resonance, she'd give Kaine away. Atreus would immediately know who'd removed the suppression on her manacles. She'd have to go for the kill. No hesitating this time. The obsidian knife was hidden under the mattress of her bed, but the bed was on fire. The room was on fire.

Atreus pressed his face close to hers, looking up at the empty sky with her. The powdery lavender scent on his skin almost overpowered the stench of blood on his clothes.

"You're fond of him, aren't you? You can admit it to me. After all, he takes you for walks and keeps you so comfortable in this room, with protective servants at your beck and call. I do believe he enjoys keeping an eager creature like you around. The Holdfasts must have trained you well."

Helena only managed to draw one ragged breath.

Crowther's lips brushed against her ear. "My son will enjoy you far less if I'm required to burn the information out of you."

One chance. She had one chance to catch him off guard and rip out the talisman.

"I don't remember," she said again, trying to gauge how fast she'd need to move, which direction to twist free.

"Maybe you just haven't wanted to *enough*," Atreus said, and before she could move, his fingers snapped.

Pain exploded across her back as her dress caught fire. Pain like a brand across her shoulders. Her knees gave out as she screamed.

There was a hiss and the fire across her shoulders vanished, but the pain didn't stop, the heat didn't disappear. Her mouth worked soundlessly, her vision turned white.

All she could smell was smoke and burned hair.

"That was your only warning. Don't lie to me," Atreus said, dragging her back onto her feet and pinning her against the window, his weight bearing down on the burns, forcing a rasping scream from her. "I don't ordinarily move so quickly during interrogations, but I don't have time to build your dread." His mouth moved against her ear. "Tell me who it is, or I will hurt you exquisitely."

"I don't know—" she said. The words came out a half sob. "I promise I don't."

Atreus sighed. "Kaine will be so disappointed when he finds you."

His fingers snapped again. Fire ran down her back like the lash of a whip.

She seized so violently that her head slammed against the window, nearly knocking her out.

Her ears were ringing from the blow, and everything seemed to slow, her panic giving way to a slow lucidity.

Kaine wasn't going to come in time.

They'd used up all their luck surviving this long. Half a day short, and it had run out.

Atreus dragged her upright again. "I'm no fool. Everyone knew there was a spy among the Undying in the year leading up to the Eternal Flame's defeat. The Resistance knew too much. The High Necromancer suspected that one of his most trusted had betrayed him, but they were never identified. They are the piece that remains unaccounted for. The evidence is undeniable. The massacres and acts of sabotage that were so uncharacteristic of the Eternal Flame. That person was responsible for the bombings, including the one that destroyed the West Port Lab. They disappeared after the final battle only to reemerge shortly after you did. You know exactly who it is."

Helena tried to twist free, fingers clawing, trying to reach his face. Contact was all she needed, but Atreus crushed his weight against her burning shoulders, forcing a strangled scream from her. There were black spots in her vision.

"Tell me who it is." He shook her.

"Kaine will be killed—if you hurt me," she choked out. Her body was going numb, sinking her into a dissociative shock, as though she were a prey animal already hanging by her throat.

"The High Necromancer will forgive my means if I find the killer," Atreus said. She could see his face reflected in the glass. His eyes had a burning look of utter desperation. It was strange how reminiscent of Kaine his expressions could be even in Crowther's face.

"Kaine will survive. He can have more children," he said.

Helena's head grew light. She could hardly breathe in the smoke. The room was engulfed in flames behind them.

Knowing she'd never see Kaine again, she couldn't help but look for any traces of him in Atreus. There was a similar evasiveness of their eyes in the way they spoke. The same look of furious desperation that Kaine wore all too often when he was cornered, when he thought he had nothing left to lose.

Despite their contempt for each other, Kaine had inherited his fatal flaws from his father.

Enid had been everything to Atreus, and now she was gone, and he was left grasping after shadows.

What would Kaine be like with someone who glimmered with constant reminders of what he'd lost? Perhaps something like Atreus, who could neither stand his son nor stay away.

She finally understood.

"He's going to kill Kaine . . . if you don't find the killer, isn't he? That punishment—it wasn't just because of Hevgoss, it was a warning for you, wasn't it?"

Atreus's expression turned black. He shook her so violently she nearly fainted. "Who is the last member of the Eternal Flame?"

"He looks like your wife, doesn't he? It's the eyes and mouth; they're so much like hers. He's all you have left of her now. But every time he sees you, he hates you with your wife's eyes."

Atreus raised his hand, ignition rings glittering.

"I'm the one who blew up the West Port Lab," she said quickly, before the rings could spark. "I used to help Luc study pyromancy theory. I wasn't supposed to, but he did better with companionship, so I studied it, too, even though I didn't have the resonance. I used those principles and theory to design the bombs, and then I used necrothralls to plant them. Because *I* am the last member of the Eternal Flame."

She drew a deep breath. "But you're right—there was a spy. I was his handler."

There was a flash of triumph in Atreus's eyes. He saw victory in his grasp.

"But you won't save Kaine by finding him. The killer you're searching for is your son."

Atreus stared at her dumbfounded before his expression contorted into fury. He forgot his pyromancy. His fingers wrapped around her throat. "My son would *never* ally himself with the Eternal Flame."

"Yes, he would. He hates Morrough," she rasped out. "He always hated him. Did you never wonder what happened to your family after you were arrested?"

Atreus sneered at her. "Nothing. When Kaine killed the Principate, my failure was forgiven."

Helena shook her head. "Then why is there an inert iron cage in this house, and a transmutational array carved into the floor? Why are all your servants dead? Do you really think someone like Morrough was understanding during all those months before Kaine went back to the Institute?"

Doubt flashed across Atreus's face.

"He kept your wife in that cage; he tortured her. He made her watch as he ripped out your son's soul. Kaine killed Apollo trying to save her. And it was all your fault."

"You're lying!"

She knew she should go for the kill, but she wanted to *hurt* him.

She grabbed hold of his head, even though her shoulders screamed in protest, and shoved her resonance through his skull. He was too startled to stop her.

She'd never used any type of animancy on a lich before. It was easy, like shoving her hand into a rotted gourd. There was a simpleness about the mind; it lacked the noise of the truly living. Atreus's thoughts were linear, flattened. They all ran towards Kaine and Kaine alone, because that was all he had left of Enid.

She knew that when Kaine had checked her memories, she could feel his consciousness, his emotions. There was no reason why she couldn't push her own memories through that connection instead of looking for Atreus's.

She wanted him to know. To understand the consequence of what he'd done.

Her mind was a cacophony of rage, and she shoved it all through Atreus's skull.

Kaine was kneeling in front of her as she was reaching towards him.

"Did—did any of them say anything that could incriminate you?"

No. That wasn't what she wanted to show him. She tried to focus.

Kaine kissing her, hands cradling her face, pushing her back onto the bed, his body over hers, pressed close.

Her memories were so disjointed and overlaid, she wasn't even sure if that memory was old or new.

"Your soul has been ripped out of your body. With time I think it will re-integrate, but initially it would need to be secured, like—like the servants' souls are doing to the phylactery."

"A sacrificial soul."

She nodded, unable to look up. "The person would have to be willing."

Not this. Enid. Something about Enid.

"My life was blown apart when I went home at sixteen, and everything I did from that point on was trying not to lose the only thing I had left. When she died—it didn't matter . . ."

She could feel Atreus's shock, his outraged disbelief. He tried to tear free, and she nearly lost her grip. The connection between their minds turned red.

Kaine's face, clearly younger, his hair still dark, appeared in front of her, fury radiating from him. "Who do you imagine was alone with the High Necromancer when word came that my father had been caught and confessed?"

Atreus stopped struggling. Helena's lungs were fighting for air, but she was lost in her memories, trying to crystallise them.

"I'd hear her screaming for hours sometimes."

Searing heat was swallowing her, but Helena wouldn't stop.

"She kept saying it was all her fault, and her heart stopped—"

Helena was jerked up. Her head lolled back, and everywhere she looked fire was crawling across the walls, consuming everything.

A pale face loomed in front of her. She struggled to focus.

"Hold on."

The voice was distorted, but she knew it. She reached out dazedly as Kaine's face flickered in her vision.

"You came—" She reached for him. "I guess you always do."

"Hold on, I'll get you out," he said, pressing her hand down and pulling her close.

Something painfully heavy was wrapped tight around her, and he lifted her into his arms. She arched in agony as his arm pressed against her raw shoulders, but he gripped her tight, carrying her through the flames. The hallway was thick with smoke, fire creeping out from her room, but he didn't stop until they were outside.

She gasped the clean, fresh air greedily as he laid her down.

"What happened? What did he do to you?" Kaine's hands were shaking so hard, he couldn't form a stable resonance channel.

Something huge and black suddenly closed in on her, blotting out the sky until Kaine snapped an order and Amaris backed away.

Helena couldn't manage words. Her lungs kept spasming for air, and everything was swimming. Breathing made her want to scream from pain. Kaine kept asking questions, but her mind struggled to focus.

Atreus came staggering out into the courtyard. His face was streaked with smoke, and his expression alight with rage.

At the sight of him, Helena clutched at Kaine's arm. "He knows about your mother. I'm sorry. I told him."

"Doesn't matter," he said as he stood.

Black smoke was filling the courtyard as if the house were a smouldering corpse.

"Why didn't you tell me what happened to your mother?" Atreus asked, his voice a low snarl.

Kaine faced him, his shoulders stiff. "What difference would it have made?"

Atreus lunged at Kaine. "You should have told me. She was mine!"

Kaine sidestepped, but not as easily as he ordinarily would have. The movement was stiff, his fingers spasming unnaturally. Helena caught sight of his face. His eyes were aglow.

"Yes, and what a terrible curse for her that was. You told Morrough, after all. You never cared what rumours they spun in the city, but you told *him* about her, that she was everything to you, that you'd do anything for her. She was your proof of how loyal you'd be to the cause." Kaine's voice was filled with fury. "Do you think he cared how long it took for torture to break you? No. All that mattered was that you broke, and she was right there. Your most treasured possession. You loved her right into her grave."

Atreus's long, thin, spider-like fingers curled, ignition rings gleaming on his hands.

Kaine laughed bitterly. "They must have found you terribly amusing when they brought you back and you stayed loyal. And you called me the dog."

Atreus's grey skin purpled with rage. "You should have *told* me."

"Why? What would it have done if I had? What grand vengeance would you have exacted that I should have risked my work to tell you?"

"What work is that? Crawling, snivelling between the legs of Holdfast's pet whore?" Atreus sneered at his son. His rings flashed against each other.

Kaine's resonance split the air. The spark of fire hung in place as Atreus flew in one direction, and his ignition rings were ripped into another. Atreus hit the gravel, skidding several feet. The flames vanished. When he lifted his head, purple blood seeped from gouges down one side of his face.

"Oh dear," Kaine said, standing over him, pure malice in every word. "Seems you've lost your fire again, Father."

CHAPTER 74

Julius 1789

THE WROUGHT IRON THAT FILIGREED THE HOUSE unfurled like serpents and wound around Atreus, pinning him like an insect. He'd snap all the bones in his body long before he'd escape.

Kaine went back to Helena. His hand trembled as he touched her face. "How badly did he—"

"Just—just my back, and it's not—too deep. The nerves are still intact." Which was a good thing, but it was also why the pain was excruciating. She sat, leaning on her knees as she felt his resonance sweep along her back, numbing the searing pain.

"I just need to catch my breath," she said, but she was shaking uncontrollably.

"It's almost over now. Once you're healed, you're going to go on Amaris. Do you think you can?"

She wasn't sure if she could even stay conscious much longer, but she couldn't say no to him.

"Is that what this was for?" Atreus's furious voice broke in from where he lay contorted on the ground. "All this because you're trying to save *her*?"

Helena thought Kaine would ignore his father, but he looked at him. "It seems I am cursed to love as you do."

"After he has killed you, Morrough will have her hunted to the ends of the earth. There is nowhere she can hide. You're wasting yourself for nothing."

Kaine ignored him, his eyes going briefly out of focus. "The fire is out. Let's get you inside."

Before she could try to stand, a loud blaring split the air. For a moment, Helena thought it was the buzzer, that Kaine was being summoned again, but it came from the wrong direction.

They turned in time to see a lorry come roaring up the road, approaching so quickly it threatened to crash through the gates.

"They're coming! Let me free!" Atreus shouted. "Let me free!"

The lorry stopped short, and a figure tumbled out of the driver's side, clutching something against their chest, as if fleeing with a child in their arms.

"I got it! I got it. Take it quick."

It was Ivy. She was pressed against the gate, her eyes wild, and she kept looking over her shoulder as if expecting pursuit.

Helena stumbled across the courtyard to the gate, grasping towards her.

"How did you—?" Helena's voice shook with disbelief as Ivy shoved the bundle through the gate at her. It was wet and smelled like gangrene and formaldehyde. The fabric fell aside, revealing a rotted arm, ripped off at the elbow, missing dozens of bones as the skin sloughed off, three fingers remaining. They twitched as if still alive.

"Sofia did it," Ivy said, her voice breathless and shaking. Her eyes were red, her face streaked with tears and smeared with rot. "I tried all kinds of ways to get close enough." She shook her head. "Couldn't. She did it."

"How?"

"Morrough doesn't watch his own necrothralls," Ivy said, her face twisting at the admission. "But she does what I tell her. Always does. She walked over and he didn't even notice her there. She ripped it off and threw it to me. He attacked her first—so I was able to run." Her face crumpled. "Do you think she'd forgive me now, if she knew?"

Helena didn't know what to say. "She loved you."

Ivy stood trembling.

Kaine had reached them now, his expression unreadable, but he reached into his uniform and pulled out an obsidian knife.

"What are you—" Helena started, but he flipped the hilt away from himself and offered it to Ivy. She took it without hesitating.

"Through the chest, near the heart," he said. "It's quickest that way."

Ivy nodded and turned, scrambling back into the lorry. In a minute she was gone, the rumbling engine fading until the only trace she'd ever been there was the dust above the road and the bundle clutched in Helena's hands.

"Kaine," she said, her voice hoarse from smoke. "You can come with me now. We can escape together."

He shook his head. "Come inside."

She stared at him in disbelief, not moving when he tried to guide her back towards the house. His jaw set, and he picked her up.

"What do you mean?" she said, still clutching the bundle in her arms, trying to get down even though she knew she was tearing open the burns on her back. "This was what we needed. This buys us a month, I'll be able to find a way . . ."

"I can't go with you," he said, walking towards the house. "My father is right. When you escape, war or not, you'll be hunted. If I went with you, we'd have a month, and I could protect you, but then I'd be gone, and Morrough would know what direction the hunters didn't come back from. Eventually they'll find you. If I stay, now that we have this, and he can't control me anymore, I can make sure that no one he sends makes it out of the city until you've safely disappeared."

She clutched at his shoulder, trying to make him listen. "But what if I reverse it—"

He shook his head as they neared the door. "You need a willing soul for that, and you're not going to find one, because the only person who'd die for me is you."

She stared at him as if he'd struck her in the throat.

"What? You're not even going to ask me?" Atreus's voice rose tauntingly from the ground.

Helena gasped, wrenching at Kaine's shoulder in order to look past him at his father. Atreus still lay on the ground, bound in iron, barely able to move even his fingers.

"Would you?" Helena said.

"I'd rather die," Kaine said before his father could reply.

"You need someone willing," Atreus said, looking at Helena. "Isn't that right, a willing soul? You have my phylactery there. It's the middle bone of the index finger."

She looked down at the rotting arm. It was oozing a thick, black slime in place of blood, but the middle bone of the index finger was among those remaining. Her heart thudded in disbelief.

"Why would you be willing?" Kaine asked, sneering down at him, his eyes scorching. "You've hated me since before I was born."

Atreus looked away. "Your mother would want me to save you."

"Well, you're too late," Kaine said.

He carried Helena inside, refusing to stop, even when she begged him to.

"I'm not having this conversation," he said. "The only thing left is getting you out as quickly as possible. It's lucky those necrothralls' eyes have practically rotted inside their heads, or we'd already be caught."

He passed the charred remnants of her room, stepping over a corpse. It was one of the maids. The remaining servants were inside the room, casting water to ensure there were no residual flames, gathering the bits and pieces of things that had survived. The windows were open, the air clearing, but it still stank of burned carpet, the sour scent of doused wood, and the tang of melted iron.

He set her down and unlocked a room a few doors down. There were medical supplies inside it, as well as packed bags. He pulled out a box.

"How do I—? For burns, I've never—"

"If your father . . ."

"We are not talking about this until I've healed you," he said, his voice hard. "Now give that to me."

He pulled the arm away from her, dropping it into a closet and closing the door to block the smell.

She doubted that he had any intention of discussing it after she was healed, but it had to be done either way.

"Cut off my dress; we'll have to use saline to try to loosen the fabric where it's sticking."

He brought the crisped remnants of her hair forward and pulled out a pair of shears, carefully cutting away the back of her dress.

"I hated these dresses," she said as he was washing her back, trying to soak free the remaining fabric. She touched her shoulder, using her resonance to feel the damage. The burn was deeper than she'd realised. The nerves were intact, but given the burn's size and depth, it would take more time than they had to heal it completely. Kaine's hands were spasming too badly for that kind of repetitive tissue regeneration, and Helena wouldn't be able to contort her shoulders to reach it. He managed the shallowest sections, but eventually his fingers grew so uncooperative that his resonance kept failing. He stepped away, breathing hard.

"It's fine," she said.

"It's not."

"Even if your hands were steady, it'll take too long to heal all of it now," she said. "If it's clean and numb, it'll keep until later."

He nodded slowly and rummaged through a carton, pulling out a familiar jar of salve. "Would this do?"

She gave a faint laugh. "Yes, that'll do."

He applied it carefully and wrapped her back in silk bandages, because they were gentler than linen.

"Your poor back didn't get nearly such luxurious treatment," she said as he worked.

She felt his resonance across her skin in all the places that were sore from the scalding air, and a small cut across her forehead that she hadn't even realised was there. Little things he could manage.

"Kaine," she said as he finished. "I need to talk to your father."

"He won't help; he's just trying to make you hope in order to hurt you. And even if he wasn't, I am enough like him already, I don't want a piece of his soul inside me."

She turned his face to hers. "You are all he has left of your mother.

When he looks at you now, he sees her. He knew the risk he was taking, coming after me. He did it because he thought it would save you."

She inhaled. "I know you don't want to believe it's possible, because hoping terrifies you. But I would rather die trying to save you than live knowing there was a chance and I didn't take it."

She could feel him wavering.

"You promised we'd run away together," she said. "Remember?"

He dipped his head. "Why is it that I have to keep all my promises, but you never seem to keep a single one of yours?"

She shook her head, tilting up her face so their foreheads touched.

"The first promise I made to you was that I'd be yours for as long as I live. I'm keeping that one."

HELENA'S ROOM WAS IN RUINS, her clothing nothing but ash. Fortunately, Kaine had travel clothes ready for her. Sturdy, neutral-coloured riding clothes. She dressed carefully, trying not to worsen the burns on her back.

The hallway was soaked with water, reduced to charred ruin, but the iron remained like the bones of a beast.

Atreus still lay on the ground where Kaine had left him, his eyes closed. They opened at the sound of approaching footsteps, his head lifting. He looked between Kaine and Helena and laughed.

Helena gripped Kaine's arm before he could react.

"I want to talk to him alone," she said.

"No."

"He can't do anything to me. Just wait here."

She felt Kaine's eyes on her as she walked towards Atreus. Atreus watched her approach with equally piercing interest.

"I didn't make my offer to you," Atreus said when she got close.

She knelt beside him. "You know he won't ask."

He looked away from her. "Then consider it withdrawn."

Her chest clenched in dread. She was tempted to beg, but she knew that Atreus wouldn't care about her humanity or humiliation.

"I'm going to escape regardless of what you do. Refusing will only kill him."

Atreus looked past her, towards Kaine, who stood watching them.

Longing like hunger shone in Atreus's eyes as he stared at his son. She wanted to speak, but waited. Finally Atreus broke the silence.

"I only realised how much he resembled her when I returned. I'd never noticed it when he was a boy." His eyes were straining, struggling to make out Kaine from the distance. "I never understood why she wanted a child so much. I would have adopted an heir from another family in the iron guild if need be. I should have been enough for her."

Helena watched him pityingly. He was pathetically jealous.

"He's all that's left of her now."

He finally looked at her. "Can you really save him?"

"Yes, if you truly want him to live."

He didn't answer immediately. Her heart dropped like a stone. If he wasn't completely willing, the bond would fade away, and Kaine would slip away just like Luc had.

"Enid was my life," he finally said. "If she were here, she'd tell me to save him. I never could say no to her about anything."

Helena reached out and bent the iron away. He rose slowly. He did not look at her or Kaine, but turned and walked into the house.

WHEN THEY ENTERED THE DRAWING room, Atreus could not tear his eyes away from the cage. Had he not seen it? Or simply never stopped to wonder at its purpose?

"How long was she—?" His fingers trembled as he touched the bars. He sank to his knees, as if intending to crawl inside to occupy the same space.

"Four months," Kaine said, his voice dull. His eyes were darting around, the way they always did inside that room.

Helena wanted to comfort him, but they were running out of time. There was so much to do.

She began working across the array on the floor. The array she'd etched had been melted and destroyed by the fire, but she had every detail memorised. She only needed the central part of the original array, but the defacement had to be repaired and altered. She needed it to hold Kaine's soul in place until she could secure it.

The new array was laid in iron. It was perfect for their purposes and readily available.

She and Kaine knelt on opposite sides. He closed his eyes and when they opened, they were glowing. Unsteady as his hands were, his resonance was stronger than hers. The air shivered as the house groaned, and iron began to flow towards them like water. When it reached the array, Helena used her own resonance to direct it, sending it morphing down certain pathways carved into the floor, moving towards the containment circle in the middle.

Industrial guild arrays could be as big as buildings, but Helena had never worked with an array larger than she could hold. The array on the floor was too large to see at once, and she had to crawl across it, verifying that every line and symbol was correct. It had to be perfect.

Her heart was in her throat, its jerky unsteady rhythm taunting her.

One chance.

"It's ready," she said at last, standing up in the centre of the array. "We can begin."

Kaine nodded but then went towards the door. The remaining servants were gathered in the hallway beyond, Davies standing in the front.

"Is Amaris ready?" he said.

One of them nodded.

Kaine stood there, not moving. "I never—I never told you—I'm sorry I couldn't save any of you."

Davies took a hesitant step forward, mouthing his name as she often did. She smoothed his hair back the way a mother might and then placed both hands on his chest and pushed him back. Away from them.

Helena went over to where Kaine had left Morrough's arm. The stench of it was like a kick in the stomach each time, and she worked quickly, disassembling it. The thing was repulsive. Holding it, she could feel all the power it contained, the lives of so many running through each bone. In the section of the ulna nearest to the hand, there was a horrible sense of familiarity. The piece used to bind Kaine. She removed what she needed and discarded the rest.

Kaine was standing in the centre of the room, stripped to the waist, covered in violent scars, the array on his back the starkest of all. Atreus was staring; it was obvious he'd never seen it before.

Kaine's focus was entirely on her.

There was no platform over this array. She would be in it beside him.

"Lie on your back," she said.

She knelt, guiding his hands to places she needed them on the array and then met his eyes. Her heart was struggling, threatening to grow uneven.

"This will work," she said. "I promise. I'm going to *save* you."

She pressed her hands on the cold iron and let her resonance flow into it.

She had never poured her animancy into an array except for small experiments on the etching plates. It took so much more power than she'd expected. As the array activated, a glow crept slowly along the iron until the entire array was humming. Kaine seemed to grow so translucent that she could see through him, his bones and organs and the talisman tangled beside his heart.

She pulled out the phylactery. The bone was so old it threatened to dissolve into dust, and she had to focus to feel the energy in it. It was like a package bound with thread, so tangled up it was hard to tell the strands apart. But she had to work carefully or risk causing damage. She unwound and unwound with her resonance, and the threads seemed to go on forever, until there was a sudden thump, and she looked up as one of the servants in the hallway collapsed to the ground.

She looked away.

She kept going, flinching as another hit the floor. And another. And another. And of course the last one, which meant she'd been the first to die, was Davies. She met Helena's eyes the instant before she fell.

There was a rush of energy as the bone shard crumbled, the convulsion before the energy altered into that cold death surge, but instead of transforming it was dragged down into the array.

The air illuminated, and Helena's hair lifted from her shoulders.

Kaine began to scream.

His eyes went stark, wide, and unseeing. His back arched up, his hands clawing at the floor until his fingertips and nails were torn bloody. Helena leaned over him.

"No. Don't do this. Hold on," she said, struggling to pin him down. He had to stay in the centre.

She forced his heart to calm, paralysing his limbs until he couldn't struggle, but he didn't stop screaming.

Her fingers fumbled for Atreus's reliquary. She was frantic as she freed it, tearing the tangled threads of energy off. The bone crumbled, and the energy in the array tried to drag in Atreus's soul, too.

She gripped it in her left hand and wouldn't let go. It couldn't mix with Kaine's. She strained her resonance so hard, her hand cramped, pain shooting up her forearm. Using her right hand, she pressed down on Kaine's chest, pulling at the sea of energy swirling through the array, trying to drag it into him, but his agony pushed his resonance outwards, against her, and no matter how she strained, she couldn't push through.

She leaned towards Kaine until her forehead touched his. He'd stopped screaming because his voice had failed. His eyes were unfocused.

"I need you," she said. "We're almost to the end now. But you have to come back to me. We're running away, remember? You, me, and our baby. We're going to be free. I'm going to save you, but I need you to fight with me."

There was a sudden shock of pain in her left hand, and two of her fingers lost sensation, falling limp, and she barely managed to hold her resonance to keep her grip.

She lurched forward, kissing Kaine's face. "Come back to me. Stay with me."

His eyes seemed to find her.

She pressed against his chest again, and it was like breathing in a roomful of oxygen, trying to force all the energy inside him. The outer edges of the array ceased to glow, slowly seeping inwards until the light vanished beneath Kaine and the strain on her left hand finally stopped.

He was barely breathing, a rasping, rattling sound emerging from him every time he drew a breath.

Helena worked fast. She wouldn't allow what happened to Luc to happen again. She could fix it this time.

She mangled Atreus's soul, her animancy resonance stretching it fine as a thread and binding it in the same way the souls had been bound around the reliquaries, wrapping the energy again and again, like a tangled spiderweb, through Kaine's ribs and around the talisman.

Not enough to make a new parasite like Cetus, but enough to buy time until Kaine's body remembered what it was to have a soul.

When she was done, Kaine lay still. She pressed her hand against his chest, feeling him. Alive and mortal.

No signs of seeping cold.

Helena slumped down, so tired she could have passed out beside him, but it wasn't over yet. This was only the beginning.

She pushed herself unsteadily to her feet.

Crowther's corpse lay dead once more beside the cage.

Her left hand was still cramped into a contorted fist, still holding the tattered remains of Atreus's soul.

She touched the corpse, and it took only a little of the nothing she had left to reanimate him. She pressed her left hand against his chest and pushed what was left of Atreus back into it.

His eyes slowly came back into focus. Kneeling beside him, she could feel the same sensation she'd felt as Luc gradually died. That slow bleed of life ebbing away, but for now he was not dead.

He looked towards Kaine, lying still on the floor. "Is he alive?"

She nodded. "Will you help me carry him? I can't lift him on my own."

Atreus stood and went to Kaine, while Helena paused, trying to repair her left hand. She followed Atreus where he was pulling Kaine up, dressing him quickly. It took them both to lift Kaine off the floor. His head lolled back and his feet dragged. She paused again, reanimating the servants, one last time, needing their help.

It was past nightfall; Lumithia was barely visible, Luna a waxing crescent, the night sky lit with stars.

Amaris stood just outside the doors, stomping nervously. She was already saddled with travel bags cinched on. Her wings fluttered as the servants carried Kaine out.

"It's all right. He's all right," Helena said, going hesitantly towards Amaris and shushing her, trying to calm and coax her to the ground because it would be impossible to lift Kaine onto the chimaera if she remained standing. She pulled down at the halter on Amaris's head. Very reluctantly, the chimaera crouched, her yellow eyes following Kaine.

Kaine seemed to have just barely begun to regain consciousness, his eyes sluggish as he was draped across the saddle. There were straps and a harness, which had likely been intended for Helena. She secured him to the saddle.

Amaris kept trying to turn her head, a low whine in her throat.

"It's all right," Helena kept saying as she scrambled up behind Kaine on the saddle. She reached into her pockets, finding Atreus's ignition rings and holding them out.

"The array has to be destroyed," she said as he took them. "No one can know he's still alive."

Amaris rose to her feet, wings already extending in readiness for flight, and Helena was about to release the reins and let her run when Atreus spoke.

"Kaine . . ." he said.

Kaine lifted his head just enough to look at what remained of his father. Kaine's face was exhausted, and pained, but the malice and hatred was gone as he stared at Atreus.

"Father . . ."

Atreus's whole face seemed to soften. He started to reach out, but Amaris snarled in warning, and his long fingers curled away.

"Your mother was always so proud of you. She said you were the best thing we ever made." Then Atreus looked at Helena. "Save him."

Helena didn't answer, she simply loosed the reins. Amaris raced across the courtyard, flight muscles tense and rippling beneath the saddle, and she leapt, launching herself. Her onyx wings beat against the black sky, and they were airborne, climbing higher and higher. The air whistled around them, and Helena clutched at the harness securing Kaine.

The city was bright, but the mainland was like a void, a black abyss they were attempting to flee, straining towards the stars.

As Amaris levelled out, something flickered below. It grew, becoming an immense, glowing ring of light as Spirefell was consumed by roaring flames.

CHAPTER 75

Julius 1789

THE NOVIS MOUNTAINS LOOMED STARK AGAINST THE starlit sky. Helena put their backs to them, flying south.

Amaris had been younger and smaller when Helena had last ridden her. Her wings were stronger and steadier. Once Helena pointed her south, she seemed to know to follow the river.

The darkness below was nearly endless, punctuated with the clustered lights of towns and villages.

Everywhere Helena looked there was endless dark. She buried her face against Kaine's back, trying to breathe.

"Don't die, Kaine," she kept saying, pressing her face between his shoulders, feeling the feeble thud of his heartbeat against her forehead to reassure herself that he was still alive.

She didn't know how long they flew; the night seemed endless.

Amaris began to descend without warning, and Helena nearly slipped sideways. For a terrifying moment, she thought she'd fall.

Kaine jerked from barely conscious to awake. His hand shot back and he grabbed her, holding her tight as she managed to get centred again. She tried to squeeze with her legs, but they were so tired she could scarcely hold on anymore.

Amaris hit the ground at a run and Helena nearly bit through her tongue. She looked around desperately, trying to make out where they were as Amaris cantered through the dark. There was an electric torch in one of the saddlebags, but she couldn't remember which anymore. Amaris halted, standing and waiting as Helena shifted to dismount, sliding down.

Amaris was several hands taller than she remembered. The ground did not meet her feet when expected. She fell the rest of the way, caught by thick, lush summer grass. She lay, staring up at the stars, a glittering path across the sky.

Before the Disaster, it was said people could travel by following the stars, but no one knew where they went anymore. She struggled back to her feet.

"Kaine," she said, fumbling through the dark until she found Amaris and then Kaine's leg, his boot hooked in the stirrup. "I don't know where we are. What do we do now?"

He lifted his head slowly. She could only see his silhouette in the dark. He tried to get off and then realised he was fastened to the saddle.

Helena felt her way to Amaris's head and urged her down to the ground before finding the straps and clips and unfastening them as best she could. Kaine leaned on her as he dismounted.

"Hunting cottage just . . ." His voice sounded raw.

They walked forward slowly, and then there were steps and a wooden door, and they stumbled inside. There was a shelf by the door that held a torch, and she flicked it on. It was barely more than a shack. Simple and rough-hewn, just a place to sleep.

There were two narrow beds, but Helena and Kaine collapsed into one, not bothering to remove their boots or cloaks.

"We did it, Kaine," she said. "Just like we always said we would."

SHE WOKE BECAUSE HER BACK was on fire, her left wrist throbbing with a nearly numbing pain. She struggled to open her eyes, staring around in bewilderment before remembering where they were.

Kaine was sitting beside her, awake but haggard. He was leaning forward, a hand pressed against his chest as though all his ribs were cracked.

"Are you—all right?" She struggled to sit up.

He nodded jerkily. "Fine. I'm sure it'll pass."

His throat was still hoarse and raw. He'd torn it apart screaming, and now things like that would take time to heal on their own.

"What will pass?" She tried to reach out but only managed to brush her fingers against his coat. Her body felt boneless. "What's happening?"

"It's nothing. I'm just not used to feeling—human anymore," he said.

She managed to get close enough to reach out. He was right, there was nothing wrong, but he felt delicate as a spiderweb inside. If a single thread snapped, it might all be for nothing.

She rested her head on his shoulder, breathing slowly. "You have to be so careful. It could take months, maybe even years before your soul fully integrates again. No vivimancy or animancy, nothing that could strain your vitality at all. One mistake could be enough to kill you. And you can't lean into the array anymore. You won't regenerate, and it could burn your back open."

He tucked a curl behind her ear. "You already told me all this yesterday. You know, I do make a habit of listening when you talk."

She nodded but couldn't help herself. "You have to be careful."

"I will be. Now, are you all right?"

"Just tired," she said, slumping, but the pain across her shoulders felt like she was being rebranded.

"How's your back?"

She winced. She hadn't wanted to bring it up, because she knew it would bother him that he couldn't heal it.

"I think the salve wore off," she said. "It's starting to hurt a little."

He started to reach.

"Don't," she said. "Give me a minute and then we'll use the salve so we can go."

"We'll rest till dark," he said. "Amaris is too recognisable for travel during the day. It's a few days' journey to the coast."

When her eyes opened again, it was dark outside. Kaine was packing the saddlebags. He looked up the instant she stirred. "Are you strong enough for more travel?"

They would have stayed if she said no, but she knew the more distance they put between themselves and Paladia, the less likely they were to be tracked down. They were racing against time. The Abeyance wouldn't wait.

"Yes," she lied.

They flew almost the whole night. The sky was silvering with signs of dawn when Amaris landed again. There was no cabin. Kaine removed Amaris's saddle, and they slept leaning against her furry sides, her black wings blotting out the daylight as the sun rose.

When Helena opened her eyes, Kaine was still asleep beside her, his face turned towards her as if he'd fallen asleep staring at her.

She traced her eyes across his face. His now mortal face, softly illuminated.

They were free.

Her heart swelled inside her chest.

It felt like a dream. One wrong move and it would all dissolve. Even staring at him, she could not shake the feeling that it wasn't real. And even if it somehow was, then it would not last.

The beautiful things in her life never did.

He was so still that she reached out, fingers trembling. At her touch, his eyebrows furrowed, and his eyes opened. She watched the light fill them as he looked at her.

"Hi," she said, because she was too overwhelmed to say anything else. She cleared her throat, sitting up. "I need to check you."

Amaris stood up, stretching, and abandoned them, wandering off into the woods, while Helena had Kaine open his shirt. She pressed her hand against his chest, trying to sense his condition now that she was no longer dazed with exhaustion.

He was still nothing natural, that was undeniable, but there wasn't anything they could do except give him time and hope that his body could find its way back to a semblance of normalcy. There was a fragile tenuousness to his vitality, as if a careless touch could shred it apart.

She was equally worried about his physical condition. It would have been better if they could have waited. He'd still been recovering from what Morrough had done to him, and now it was possible that he never fully would. Both his heart and his tremors worried her, and the thought of the array charring his back open if he ever leaned into it again made her throat close. Her hands shook.

"There are things you're used to treating as ordinary that you can't survive anymore," she said.

"I know," he said. His voice was still rasping. She shifted closer, pressing her hand against his throat to repair all the damaged tissue.

"I know you know rationally," she said, "but I mean instinctively. You have years of bad habits that you don't realise."

The thought terrified her. What if they were attacked? Kaine was highly competent in combat, but immortality was a crutch that he did not know how to fight without.

She should have planned more carefully. He'd told her to get her strength back, but she had focused on research, and that had saved him, but what if they were attacked, and she couldn't fight, and he was killed? What if it was all for nothing?

Fear ran like a fissure through her chest.

She looked around, trying to spot the saddlebag. There were knives in it. She needed to get them. She should be carrying them.

Everything was so bright, blurring—

"Helena—Helena, breathe. Look at me. I'm going to be careful. I'm not going to let anything take me from you."

She tried to nod, but her throat caught.

"But what if something goes wrong?" she asked, her voice straining. "It's going to fall apart. It always—falls apart."

She tried to pull away, eyes casting around. They were in the open, endless forest around them. Danger could come from any direction. It wouldn't even need to be the Undying. It could be anyone.

He turned her so she'd face him. "Look at me. We have not left any trace to follow. I've hunted fugitives, I know how you get caught. And we are not going to get caught. You've seen me fight carelessly because I could afford to in the past, but I have learned to be more careful.

Slower regeneration has taught me caution. Look at me: I trusted you, and you got us here. It's your turn to trust me."

She nodded jerkily.

"Now then," he said, reaching towards her lap, "are you going to tell me what's wrong with your hand?"

She looked down. The last two fingers of her left hand were curving inwards and didn't move with the others. She curled her hand into a fist to hide it.

"The array had quite a pull to it. It took a bit of straining to manage everything. The ulnar nerve just—came apart. I tried to fix it, but—there was too much long-term damage, it wasn't really salvageable."

Kaine took her left hand gently in his and straightened all her fingers. When his thumb stroked the last two, Helena couldn't feel it. Not in her fingers or along the outer part of her palm. His fingers trembled.

"It's fine," she said. "It's not even my dominant hand, so I can still do most alchemy. I bet I'll barely notice."

"Don't," he said through gritted teeth. "Don't act like it's fine."

She pulled her hand free. "It is fine if I get you instead."

There was food in the saddlebags, and Helena used retrieving them as a pretext for digging out her daggers and concealing them in her clothes.

The day wore on. The longer they were free, the more anxious she grew.

Kaine was restless, too, although he hid it better. The more he recovered, the more he wanted to patrol and verify that they were as safe as he claimed they were, but he stayed beside her so she could bury her face against his chest, fingers tangled in his shirt, sleeping restlessly.

After flying that night, they reached another hunting cabin. The travel exhausted them both. They barely spoke, just slept tangled in each other's arms until it was nearly evening. When she woke, Kaine was sitting beside her. His eyes had the faintest gleam to them again.

He looked almost like a painting.

She could see the possessiveness in his eyes, enough to realise how absent it had been in his attempts to let her go. He leaned over her and kissed her.

She wrapped her arms around his neck, wanting him nearer, under her skin, beneath her ribs, inside her heart. To hoard him so close nothing separated them and the terror of losing him would finally end.

Time always ran out for them. They'd spent years surviving on stolen moments, and now she finally felt how starved it had left her.

It was only after, as she lay beside him, her fingers tracing absently along the scars of the array, that she realised her back didn't hurt. That it should have by then, but it didn't.

She craned her arm around, touching her shoulders. Kaine sat up.

"What did you do? Did you heal me?" She whirled on him. "I told you, I warned you not to use any vivimancy."

He looked completely unapologetic. "I'm fine. I was careful, and you know that plenty of healing doesn't use any vitality. You're already too injured for this amount of travel without my father's torture still seared across your back."

She reached for him, fingers shaking as she pressed her hand against his chest, terrified of what she'd find, that he was already slipping away from her.

What if she'd woken up and found him dead beside her, and been left alone there to realise why? She checked over and over.

Her throat worked several times before she could speak.

"You shouldn't have done that," she said, her voice shaking. "It wasn't worth it. Plenty of people heal from burns without any vivimancy. I was *fine*. I was."

He held her face in his hands. "Helena, look at you. You have broken yourself into pieces, over and over, because of me, and you don't seem to understand that it kills me. Living is not worth it to me if you're the one who keeps paying the price for it. Let me fix what I can."

She closed her eyes, her face buried against his chest, listening to his heartbeat, willing herself to believe that he was all right.

"We have to stop hurting ourselves for each other," she finally said. "Both of us. We're not going to last if this is the only way we know how to love."

When it was nightfall, they flew onwards. From the darkness, something vast and faintly silver rose before them. Helena's breath caught.

It was the sea.

They veered off, travelling away from the river, the sea gleaming to their right.

Kaine seemed to know where he was going, despite the darkness. They passed over several small bodies of water, the lights of a village, and onwards through the dark until they saw a small flickering light visible through shutters.

Amaris descended straight towards it. The shutters rattled violently as Amaris's wings fluttered. Helena slid off, legs aching.

A door flew open, and warm light poured out. Helena squinted.

Haloed in the doorway stood Lila.

CHAPTER 76

Julius 1789

LILA GAVE A HEAVING, GASPING SOB AND stumbled down the steps. She had a rough prosthetic and a crutch, but it did not stop her from dragging Helena into her arms and hugging her ferociously.

"Hel, Hel. You're really alive."

Lila's hands were running over Helena, touching her face and shoulders as though she couldn't believe that Helena was real.

Helena stared at Lila in equal disbelief. Even though she'd known Lila was alive, she was so accustomed to the thought of everyone dead that she couldn't fully take it in even while staring at her.

Lila looked so different. Her blond hair was dyed brown, and there was a haggard weariness about her. The jagged scar still ran down her face, and she was crying as she hugged Helena.

"Lila . . ." Helena's heart felt as though it might explode. She'd been unprepared for how viscerally the reunion would remind her of everyone who was gone.

"I thought I'd never see anyone again. Look at you. You're so thin."

Her eyes ran down Helena's body, stopping at her stomach, and she froze.

Helena's chest clenched. "You know, right? Kaine said he was in contact with you."

Lila nodded slowly.

Behind them, Kaine dismounted.

Lila's head snapped up, as if she hadn't noticed him until that moment. "What are you doing here?"

Without warning Lila lunged towards him.

Helena had to throw herself between them, pushing her back. "We escaped together. Lila, don't hurt him, he's not Undying anymore."

A savage light came into Lila's blue eyes. "Really?"

"You're not going to have any more luck killing me now than you have at any point in the past, Bayard," Kaine said. "Lose any more limbs, and you won't be much protection for that little Principate of yours."

Lila gave a snarl like a wildcat, looking ready to tear out Kaine's eyes.

"Stop, both of you," said Helena, furious that they'd managed to ruin the reunion in less than a minute.

Lila stopped trying to assault Kaine and simply glared at him. "I guess I shouldn't be surprised you weren't really going to die saving her in the end."

"Shut up, Lila," Helena said sharply. "I brought him here. If you want to be angry that he's still alive, then you'll have to be angry at me."

Lila looked at Helena, disbelief and then despairing resignation sweeping across her face as she stepped back. "Fine. I'll keep my mouth shut. Put that monster of yours away, Ferron. I don't want it near Pol."

"Go on in," Kaine said to Helena. "Don't worry. I knew already that Bayard and I weren't going to be having a joyous reunion."

He turned to Amaris and led her towards the stable.

Helena watched them disappear inside and then looked back at Lila, feeling suddenly drained. She somehow thought there'd be enough joy to last an evening at least, but it already felt spent.

It wasn't that she'd expected things to be simple; a sea of loss surrounded them. She couldn't begin to imagine how Lila felt towards Kaine after all this time. Still, she hadn't expected to need to legitimise something as intensely personal as her relationship with Kaine so quickly.

"Lila, if you hurt him, I will never forgive you," she said.

Lila just shook her head. "You could do so much better."

"No. He's what I need, and he's what it took to save you."

She could see a multitude of objections rising to Lila's lips.

"Come inside," Lila said instead, looking away.

It was only when they were in good light that Helena realised that Lila was still wearing manacles. Not the full suppression that Helena had worn, but enough to keep her resonance weakened.

"He never took those off?" Helena said.

Lila looked down with a grimace. "He did for a while, until I nearly ripped out his talisman. When I woke up." She shook her wrist. "It's been a long time now."

Helena looked around. The house was small and visibly lived in. There was a kitchen, a table, and a bed in the far corner, mostly hidden behind a curtain. It seemed so ordinary for Lila. A world away from the Institute and Solis Splendour, the shining paladin armour.

Helena found herself at a loss.

"Have you been here this whole time?" she finally asked.

Lila shook her head. "No. Back when Ferron thought he'd find you soon, we were just across the river in Novis. It was later that he brought me and Pol here." She gave a wan smile. "He's sleeping, do you want to see him?"

Helena followed her tentatively, and they both peeked around the curtain, to be met with the sight of a golden-headed little boy, with soft round cheeks, thick dark lashes, and chubby limbs sprawled like a starfish across the bed.

Lila stared at her son, a heavy adoration in her eyes. "He's going to be so excited to have company," she said softly. "We don't go to the village much. It's just the two of us most of the time."

"You never ran?"

Lila swallowed. "I couldn't at the first place. First I was pregnant, and then with an infant. And no leg. By the time we got here . . . I'd realised I didn't have anywhere to go. Ferron said that even if I could get somewhere like the Novis court and they believed who I was, I'd be a disgraced paladin with an illegitimate child. If they decided to treat Pol as Principate, they wouldn't let someone like me take care of him or protect him. It would have been dangerous to look for my mother's family. Every time I'd think about leaving, I'd worry that the minute I did, you'd show up and we'd have missed each other."

Lila pushed the curtain to block the light from falling on Pol, turning away. "Ferron paid off someone in the village to make sure we don't starve since I'm not much good at farming. We have chickens and these awful ducks. I knit now, just like my mum did, although Pol grows out of everything about as fast as I can make them."

"You know we're not staying here," Helena said. "We're going to take a ship."

Lila's expression tightened, but she nodded. "Yes. Ferron's mentioned the plan. Although he's said a lot of things. I learned not to expect much." She exhaled. "Is he really—is he really coming with us? You're planning to—play house with him?"

Helena's shoulders tensed. "Yes. Running away together was always *our* plan. I added you to it because Luc asked me to make sure you and Pol were safe."

Lila's eyes went wide. "You saw Luc before he—?"

Helena's stomach shrivelled as she realised the lie she was about to begin telling. Could she really do this? Lie to Lila forever?

She started to speak, but Lila looked so desperate for any last pieces of Luc, his final moments. She swallowed.

"I was worried about him that day, so I left Headquarters. We—we reconciled just before his unit headed back to Headquarters. I think somehow he knew things were going wrong—he asked me to promise that I'd take care of you. It was the last thing he said to me."

Lila gave a strained gasping sound in her throat. "Do you know how he was captured—how they got him?"

Helena's lips pressed tight as she shook her head.

To the world, to history, Lucien Holdfast had died on the steps of the Alchemy Tower. Lila would have to believe that, too.

The door opened, and Kaine entered. Lila's visible emotions vanished, the temperature of the room dropping. Kaine paid no attention to her, his eyes for Helena only. He frowned.

"Have you fed her?" He looked at Lila.

"No . . ." Lila looked at Helena. "Are you hungry?"

"She's pregnant, and all we had was travel rations, so she's barely eaten in days," Kaine said, glaring at Lila.

"You could have mentioned." Lila went over to a cabinet and rummaged about, bringing over a pitcher of milk and some bread, cheese, and grapes, setting them on the table.

Helena picked at the food because Kaine was watching, but her stomach was still unsettled and she didn't know if it was from the exhaustion of travel or a general anxiousness worsened by the reunion and realisation that there was no point when things would be easy.

"Before we leave," she said, "we need to take Lila's manacles off. And is there some way to get materials so I can make her a prosthetic?"

Lila brightened at this, but Kaine's jaw set, then he sighed.

"There's no need," he said. He reached into his pocket and pulled out a small wire key, tossing it to Lila. With no further explanation, he went back outside. When he returned, he was carrying a metal chest that was covered in dirt as if it had been dug up. There was a lock that came easily open, and inside lay Lila's prosthetic, wrapped in canvas but looking little worse for wear.

"Has that been here the entire time?" Lila asked after a minute of stunned silence.

"I brought it here before you arrived," Kaine said. "But I didn't really trust you not to draw attention to yourself. I was going to tell Helena where to find it. It was in the wreckage from the bombing.

"The Abeyance is in three days," Kaine said while Helena was tinkering with the prosthetic, making sure the components still worked as she got it fitted for Lila again. "The trade routes have been open for a fortnight, but the sea is calmest now and the ships will be the most crowded, which will serve us well."

"Where exactly are we going?" Lila asked as Helena was adjusting the balance.

"There's hundreds of islands running from Etras towards the mainland," Kaine said. "We're headed for one of the smaller islands near one of the trade cities."

HELENA MET APOLLO HOLDFAST THE next day.

Pol was shy, burrowing his face in against Lila's neck and peering at Helena with dancing eyes as his mother introduced them.

He was a sturdy chap, with more of the Bayard build about him. He would grow up to be very tall, Helena could tell just from looking at him.

"Pol," Lila said, nuzzling her face in his messy blond hair, "this is your godmother, Helena. Do you remember that I told you about her? She was one of your father's best friends. She always looked out for him and me, and now—" Lila swallowed. "Now she's going to help look out for you. Isn't that nice? She came here with Ferron. You might not remember him, but you met him when you were smaller."

Pol peered through Lila's hair at Helena, with Luc's dancing eyes, and it was like meeting Luc again—the young version of him that she'd watched vanish.

Her throat closed, and she struggled to speak. "Hello, Pol, I'm glad to finally meet you."

Pol snorted and covered his face with his hand.

"He'll warm up to you soon," Lila said. "Never met a living creature he hasn't wanted to be best friends with."

"He looks so much like Luc," was all Helena could think to say. Her heart was beginning to pound, and she couldn't hear what Lila was saying, something about teething. Kaine's voice abruptly broke in.

"I think Helena needs to rest."

Lila's expression froze, but then she looked more closely at Helena and nodded. "Right. Pol and I need to feed the chickens. Come on, chappy."

Helena watched them head out the door, Lila moving easily again. She looked at Kaine and almost jumped.

His hair was brown, nearly as dark as it used to be. It made him look starker, given the contrast with his pale skin and eyes. He was dressed in common clothes, brown trousers and a rough-spun shirt. He looked entirely out of place. No one would ever look at him and believe he was a farmer.

"You don't like it," he said, touching his hair.

She couldn't stop staring. "It's not what I'm used to," she said, almost wanting to laugh as she reached out, touching it, remembering when it had first started to lose its colour. "I'm going to miss the silver."

"It'll wash out. You'll still see it sometimes."

He said that, but she didn't see Kaine much at all. Helena stayed inside the house; when she stepped out, the open and stillness unsettled her. After spending so much time in danger and on the move, the ordinariness of the cottage felt surreal.

Kaine and Lila seemed to alternate who was inside with her. When Lila was with Helena, he went out and would only reappear when Lila took Pol outside.

Helena assumed he was busy making final arrangements until Lila mentioned that he was in the stable. That he was always in the stable.

Hearing it, Helena immediately hurried outside, pausing only a moment before entering the shadowy interior.

Just as Lila had said, he was sitting on the floor in the stable, and Amaris was lying down, her enormous head resting on his lap.

He didn't look up when she entered; he was rubbing his hand through Amaris's fur behind her ears.

"I should put her down," he said softly. "It would be kindest. She won't understand if I leave her behind."

Helena's chest clenched as she came closer.

"You said she can hunt for herself," she said.

He nodded. "But the transmutations on her will wear off over time. It'll kill her eventually, like it did all the rest, assuming someone else doesn't first. And if she's seen in this area, it could point to us, where we went."

"Has there been any word?"

"None that's reached this far south."

Helena looked down at Amaris. "She's done growing, isn't she?

Maybe she won't need help as much anymore. She might be fine on her own."

He was silent for a long time. "It's not worth the risk."

Helena's throat tightened. "I don't think it's fair not to give her a chance. We wouldn't be here without her."

"She's just an animal."

Helena said nothing, because he wasn't saying it to her. She could tell this was an argument he'd been spending days making with himself. Amaris lifted her head and gave a low whine and licked across Kaine's entire face. He grimaced and pushed her nose away.

He sighed, tilting his head back. "I've killed so many people," he finally said. "I never thought I'd get stuck on an animal of all things."

The morning they left, Kaine got up silently and went out to the stable while Lila was packing up the last few things she wanted to bring. Helena sat tense as he disappeared inside, her stomach twisting into a sick knot.

A minute later he came back out. He stood there, staring up at the sky for so long that her heart began to pound in her chest. When finally he came back inside, he stopped behind her.

"Someday," he said softly, resting a hand on her shoulder, "your mercy is going to have consequences."

She held his hand in place. "There's blood enough on both our hands without adding hers."

He squeezed her shoulder.

"Bayard," he said after a minute. "It's time to go."

THE SEA WAS WILD AND roiling even at its lowest and calmest ebb. The port was crowded with people arriving and departing. There were false identity papers waiting for the group at the postal service in the port town.

Helena had forgotten how different the world could be. There was such consistency in fashion and feature in the North, she'd grown accustomed to it, but a port city during the Abeyance was a melting pot with sailors and travellers from every country across the sea, taking advantage of the annual opportunity to travel between the continents in a week rather than months.

There were enough Northerners that Kaine and Lila blended in, while Helena disappeared among the many Etrasians. She hadn't seen so much dark, curly hair and olive skin since she'd left Etras. It was shocking to hear Etrasian casually spoken, and to realise that it had been so long, she struggled now to follow it.

They descended the cliffs to the boarding wharf, and Helena clung to Kaine's hand in a near death grip as their papers were approved and tickets stamped.

The deck of the ship was crowded. Lila was so terrified that Pol would be knocked into the sea that they went inside to look out from the windows rather than standing on the bow.

Helena's heart hammered inside her chest, bracing for someone to recognise one of them. To hear a raised voice calling their names.

Kaine sat tense and wary. She could feel his resonance tracking her heartbeat as his thumb moved in slow circles across her palm, keeping her grounded. Amid the clamour, a loud Northern voice rose from the table beside them.

"Trying to get as much oil across as I can before the new war starts. The liberators will pay out of the nose for it once they hit Paladia."

Lila whirled. "What war?"

Kaine's fingers twitched, tightening around Helena's wrist. Amid the preparations and attempts at keeping the peace, Helena had avoided mentioning what she and Kaine had left behind when fleeing.

A Northerner with a large moustache and sideburns looked at Lila. "You don't read the papers? That High Reeve of Paladia is finally gone. Novis and the other countries are expected to be moving in any day. It's been in all the news lately."

Lila's face seemed to drain of colour. "Do you have a paper?"

The man reached into the pocket of his frock coat and pulled a pamphlet out. "See? There'll be a lot of machinery going in, dealing with all those corpses and whatever else those necromancers have cooked up. They'll need oil. If I get to Khem and back before the Abeyance, I'll make a fortune, but even if I take the land route, if I get the first order in, it'll still pay out. You should've seen how much opium was going for a few years back." His moustache rose. "There's nothing to rival war for money."

They were all too distracted clustering around the newspaper to reply. It wasn't a proper paper with full articles but instead a bulletin, the kind popular among businessmen.

At the very top the first bulletin read in bold, HIGH REEVE DEAD, and then in smaller text, *The world breathes a sigh of relief at reports that the steel magnate and iron guild heir Kaine Ferron, better known to the world as the High Reeve, was killed in the most recent Resistance attack, crippling the Undying regime.*

Helena clutched at Kaine's hand.

In the next bulletin were the words ETERNAL FLAME BANNERS RISE AGAIN: AS THE COUNTRIES UNITE AGAINST PALADIA, SOME DO SO IN REMEMBRANCE.

Lila finally spoke. "Did you know this was happening?"

Kaine said nothing.

Helena answered quietly, reaching across to squeeze Lila's now bare wrist. "We knew that there was an alliance developing, but we didn't know how fast it would move, or if they'd believe news of the death."

Lila sat back, clutching Pol in her arms, but she was looking out the window, back towards the mainland as the ship horns sounded, signalling cast-off.

Lila kept shaking her head. "I had no idea."

HELENA WAS SEASICK FOR MOST of the journey, the pregnancy making what would have been mild symptoms much worse. She still felt green when they arrived on one of the major trade islands. Kaine offered to get a room at an inn and complete the journey the next day, but Helena knew he wanted to leave as little trace of their journey behind as possible. The fewer places they stopped, the fewer people they spoke to, the harder they'd be to track down. They took a bus across the island. It was so different from the North. The city sprawling rather than climbing vertically as Paladia did. Stonework was a world apart from architecture utilising alchemy. They rode in a cart across a sea road leading to their destination.

The sea road was an immense causeway built up and paved smooth to allow crossing to the island during most of the monthly low tides. With the Abeyance dragging the tides away completely, the seabed lay bare, far below the causeway. There were people wandering across it, gathering whatever treasures the tide had left.

Helena and her father used to go down for the tides, searching for shells and treasures, studying the fish trapped in the tide pools. Treasure hunting was popular during Abeyance. There had been countless cities washed away in the Disaster, and even millennia later, their remnants lingered beneath the waves.

She looked over to see Lila's and Kaine's reactions to it all. Kaine was impassive, his eyes scanning the horizon. However, Lila looked more frightened than Helena had ever seen her. It took a moment to remember that the sea was regarded as terrifying in the North. Even the coasts were considered fraught with risk, as if it were a suicidal act of bravery for humanity to persevere in such a place. To those inland, the idea of living with the sea was simply too foreign.

"Don't worry," she said to Lila. "I'll teach Pol to be careful of the sea. But he'll like it. You both will."

Lila gave a nervous nod.

The residence they arrived at was high up on a cliff. It was a large stone two-storey house with a stable and a few other buildings. The island, Kaine mentioned off-handedly, was privately owned, and the house had belonged to the previous owner, which was why it was so much larger than those in the village they'd passed through.

It came mostly furnished. A woman in the village had been paid to maintain it and unpack the items that had arrived. There were warm stone floors, and raw beams, and sunlight streaming through all the open windows, carrying the strong scent of the sea.

Kaine entered the house first, walking through quickly. Helena could feel the wariness about him, his resonance tingeing the air. She bit her tongue, wanting to remind him to be careful, but his paranoia was ingrained—object and he'd just revert to deception.

"I need to make sure everything's in order here," he said, leaving Helena and Lila in the house.

"Well, this is definitely bigger," Lila said, cradling a sleeping Pol in her arms and looking around. "Shall we find the bedrooms? My arm's about to fall off."

They went upstairs, peeking into the various rooms in search of beds.

The first bedroom they managed to find was very large, but it also looked more like a library with a bed in it. Lila took one look at it and scrunched her nose. "I think this one's supposed to be yours. You should rest—you still look green. Pol and I will find somewhere else. What do you think the odds are that Ferron will let me have a sword if I promise not to use it on him?"

Lila departed, and Helena stepped into the room.

It was not too large; the ceilings were whitewashed with exposed beams overhead that made the space less overwhelming than the dark rooms in Spirefell. There were windows on the far side of the room, where the bed was, looking out over the sea.

She moved carefully along the wall, tracing her fingers over the shelves, noticing the various titles and collections. Alchemy books but also literature and histories, and travel diaries.

There was a desk and chairs, and a sofa, with a soft rug underfoot. She paused at the desk and found papers and pens, and etching plates and styluses, all arranged in the drawers as if waiting for her.

There was enough in this room to keep her busy for a lifetime.

That was what the room was, a life Kaine had tried to set her up with.

She wanted to appreciate the effort it must have required, but it felt all wrong. Too perfect. As if it were all a trap set specifically to lure her in and lull her with a false sense of safety.

Kaine was so vulnerable now.

Lila wasn't anywhere near fighting form, and even if she were, her priority would always be Pol's safety. If Helena let herself believe they were safe, let down her guard for an instant, something would go wrong. She was sure it would.

Her life was a perpetual countdown to disasters that she always failed to see coming. She huddled in the corner, between the bed and wall, her right hand gripping her chest, trying to keep her heart steady.

Calm down. She squeezed her eyes shut. *Breathe.*

Where was Kaine? Outside of Spirefell, he wouldn't know that she needed him . . .

Her eyes popped open, and she grasped at her left hand, finding the ring on her numb ring finger. Gripping it tight, she used her resonance to send a quick flare of heat through the silver.

A moment later, warmth pulsed back in response.

She stayed where she was, eyes closed, hand pressed against her heart, until she heard the door open.

"Helena?"

"Here." Her voice came out thin, wavering.

In an instant, Kaine was there in front of her. "What's wrong?"

She swallowed several times before she could speak. "I thought I would be glad to get here, but—what if they catch us? What if someone finds us because we've stopped running?"

His eyebrows furrowed as he ran his thumb across her cheek. "Do you want to keep running?"

Her stomach threatened to upend at the thought of more ships and new places and never stopping, always looking over her shoulder. "No, but why does everything feel wrong? Like it's not even real. This is what we wanted."

He pulled her into his arms, tucking her head beneath his chin. "I don't think that an ordinary life will ever feel real for either of us."

Exhausted despair tore at her as she realised that he was right. "I think I always saw running away as the destination. I never actually thought about what would be left of me by the time I got here."

She stayed there, numb at the realisation.

"Do you like the house?" he finally asked.

She looked around the room, trying to rally herself. "I do. How did you manage this?"

"It was mostly by correspondence. You talked about the sea, so I started looking before the war was over. I thought it would be easier for you, if you were going somewhere you liked."

"Just me. In this big house?" She said it lightly, but she was horrified at the idea.

"Lila was part of the arrangement by then. I came here briefly last summer. It was one of my last trips," he said quietly. "Before that, I'd just sent things along as I thought of something I thought you'd like."

She looked around again. All this, while he hadn't even known if she was alive.

"Come on now. You'll like it better once you've rested."

He closed the shutters, and Helena collapsed in bed. The linens were soft and airy from the sea breeze, and it was like coming home. Kaine sat beside her, their fingers enlaced, his thumb running along the ridges of her knuckles. There was an odd pause each time he reached the last two, and she couldn't feel the sweep of his fingers.

She was starting to drift off when he set her hand down.

She watched through her lashes as he walked slowly around the room, kneeling and running his fingers along the floor, then going over to the walls, peering appraisingly up into the corners of the room. He started towards the door, footsteps so light that they made no sound.

"Kaine."

He froze and turned back.

"Are we safe?"

His fingers spasmed, and he clenched them into a fist. "Yes . . . There's a few things I'd like to adjust . . . but we were careful. I doubt anyone looking could have moved fast enough to beat the tides. You don't need to worry."

"Do you need to worry?"

He looked baffled by the question. She held out her hand.

"We're supposed to get to rest now," she said. "You and me both. I didn't bring you here so you'd have to keep soldiering on."

His eyes flicked around the room, and he suddenly looked boyish and uncertain.

She studied him sadly, realising their difference: He didn't have any dreams about what he'd do or be after the war. He had never even allowed for the possibility. He had no idea how to do anything but be a soldier.

He opened his mouth to speak, but no sound came out.

"Stay with me," she said. "You're supposed to rest now, too."

He nodded as if he understood the idea conceptually, but he stayed standing by the door. She went to him, taking him by the hand. She found a surprising number of unusual weapons hidden in his plain-looking clothes, and he was wearing body armour beneath them, which she hadn't even realised he'd brought.

"Did you bring anything else?" she asked teasingly when she made him sit down on the edge of the bed and found an obsidian gimlet knife hidden in his shoe.

He avoided the question.

They lay facing each other, but his eyes kept flickering over to the weapons she'd taken. She touched his chin with her index finger, drawing his attention back.

"What did you want to do, before the war?" she asked.

"I was the iron guild heir—that was all I was allowed to be," he said. "The only thing I did that I wanted was staying at the Institute after I was certified. My father didn't think it was necessary, but my mother had wanted to study longer when she'd been there. Her family couldn't afford it. I had the ranking to qualify, so she convinced my father to let me. But when I returned, Crowther showed up, wanting to know why someone of my class wanted more than a trade education. My father was furious. I doubt I would have returned the next year if he hadn't been arrested."

"We'll have to figure something out now, then," she said, and pressed her head against his shoulder. He tangled his hand in her hair, holding her close. "Are we really safe?"

"We are."

She drew a deep breath and closed her eyes. "Good. I'm so tired."

When she woke, Kaine was asleep. He did not stir, even when she moved. It was as if years of exhaustion had risen up and swallowed him.

He slept for days. He didn't even twitch when Helena pressed a hand against his chest, her resonance reaching in. His soul finally seemed to begin integrating itself back into him.

Helena slept beside him for the first week. She hadn't thought she was tired enough to sleep for consecutive days, but it was as if a relentless tension had finally released and this was the first time she'd ever truly rested.

They woke to eat, and Kaine would go out, and she'd watch him walk along the edge of the cliff and survey the island and wander the house, and then he'd come back and pass out again.

But he only slept if Helena stayed near him. When she got up and went to peruse the various shelves to see what kinds of books there were, he immediately sat up.

"I can get up now," he said.

"No. I'm still tired," she lied. "I just want to read a little."

She brought a few books over and laced her fingers with his as she read, and he was asleep again in minutes. When she touched him with her resonance, he'd ceased to feel like something on the verge of unravelling.

He'd been sleeping almost two weeks when the door opened and Lila peeked across the room at them. "Pol's napping. Can I come in?"

Helena closed her book, nodding. They'd seen each other only in passing since their arrival.

Lila came over and stared at Kaine for a moment before she turned and sat on the edge of the bed, facing away from him. "I wanted to talk to you, but there's never been time. The people in the village say the tide will be rising past the sea road soon."

Helena nodded.

Lila inhaled. "You know, when he told me about you two, I didn't believe him. He said that Luc and everyone else was dead. He brought newspapers to prove it, and he said the only reason I was still alive was because of you. I believed him about most of it, but not what he said about you." Lila was staring hard at the floor as she spoke. "I couldn't believe it could have happened—that you wouldn't ever—but then I thought about how withdrawn you got, right when things started getting better. We used to talk about it, Luc and Soren and I, and none of us could understand why. When Ferron told me when everything started, I realised it was right around that same time. But I was sure you'd tricked Ferron into thinking you cared about him. Thought he was so pathetic for believing it."

Helena's fingers, entwined with Kaine's, spasmed.

"At first, he used to come check on me almost every week. It was like watching someone starve to death, him looking for you. I think he went mad for a while. He started threatening me, saying it was all my fault. If it weren't for me, you'd be safe, and he started telling me that when he found you, it'd be my job to take care of you for a change. Eventually he stopped saying anything about what would happen once he found you."

Lila pressed her lips together tightly. "Then I got word that you'd been found, but he said you'd forgotten everything, about him and me and Pol, that they'd try to smuggle you out before the Abeyance, but it had to be just before, because you'd be hunted when you escaped. Then I started hearing rumours about the repopulation program. I didn't think you'd be part of that—"

"He didn't have any choice," Helena said. "If it hadn't been him, it would have been someone else. It was that or kill me."

Lila drew an unsteady breath. "Well, I am glad that you're alive," she finally said. "But I still hate him, and I hate that you're trapped with him. Because you were right, and no one listened to you; you stayed with us despite knowing the whole time. You didn't deserve any of this. You shouldn't have to spend the rest of your life trapped by all the promises that people forced you to make."

Helena stiffened, and Lila noticed, her mouth tensing. "I don't just mean Ferron. I mean with me and Pol, too. Luc made you promise, and I know you'd stay with us for the rest of your life without ever complaining, but you don't have to. You've already done more than anyone should have ever asked from you. You deserve to make some choices for yourself. Don't spend any more of your life chained to old promises. Not for anyone. Not Luc, or me—or Ferron."

Lila closed her eyes and exhaled. "I just—I had to say that once, before we're all trapped on this island."

She stood up and left the room as quietly as she'd come in.

Helena sat in silence for a moment and finally looked down. "You can stop pretending to be asleep."

Kaine's silver eyes slid open, and he stared up at her, his expression carefully closed.

Helena raised her eyebrows. "Do you really think I went to all the trouble of saving you just because of an old promise?"

He said nothing, but she knew he did.

She shook her head, throat aching. "That's not fair. You said that I'm the worst promise keeper you've ever met. You can't have it both ways, you know."

"Helena . . ." He said her name gently.

She wouldn't let him finish.

"We said always, didn't we?" she asked, her voice strained. "Always. Well, if you don't want that promise in full any longer, I'll give it to you in increments." She clutched his hand tighter. "Every day. I'll choose you. That way you'll know it's still what I want."

She looked out towards the rising sea. "I'm sure there will be good days and bad days for us. Too much has happened to ever really put it behind us, but if you choose me, and I choose you, I think we're strong enough to make it."

A BUNDLE OF OLD NEWSPAPERS from the North had arrived just before the tides cut off the island from the rest of Etras.

A full article had been written about the High Reeve's death. Spirefell had been burned to the ground. A skeleton of warped iron was all that remained. Countless charred bodies had been recovered from the wreckage. Kaine Ferron, his wife, Aurelia, and Atreus Ferron were listed as dead. The killer had been identified as Ivy Purnell; she'd committed suicide nearby using one of the obsidian weapons developed by the Eternal Flame. Purnell was one of the Undying, but her family had ties with the Eternal Flame prior to the war. She was believed to be responsible for all the assassinations during the last year.

There were also articles about the Liberation Front, a confederation of armies organising against Paladia. It seemed only a matter of time before they attacked, but as Etras was once more cut off from the continents, the declaration of war had still not been made.

On the island, time warped. There was so much of it. Other than the tidal shifts, everything grew nebulous and unhurried.

Alchemy. Paladia. The war. It all barely existed in Etras.

Helena began to forage again, and soon the kitchen was strung with herbs, and she had decoctions and oil infusions, extracts and distillations. It was more medicines than four people would ever need, and so Lila—who was more sociable than Kaine or Helena—would take them to the village.

Kaine disliked the idea. He did not want Helena becoming responsible for a village of strangers, but he relented because having things to do kept Helena's anxiety from gnawing through her.

Instances of upper-class Northerners fleeing south to escape scandal were apparently relatively common. The previous owners of the house had been a minor Novisian noble family, and the arrival of new Northern strangers was predictably a source of curiosity on the island.

Kaine, Helena, and Lila frequently discussed the risks and the proper balance of keeping to themselves without seeming like they were trying to hide. A few careless rumours escaping the island might be enough to discover them. However, once Helena, an Etrasian herself, proved to be useful, the village grew protective and tight-lipped about their strange neighbours.

Kaine struggled the most to adapt. He was always paranoid, planning for the worst. When he wasn't with Helena, he was constantly walking the property and going to the village to bring back any news that came from the main islands, watching for signs of newcomers.

Late one evening, Helena sat working on a brace design for her left hand. The purpose was to make her two paralysed fingers bend and open with a transmutational device connected to her other fingers.

A low wind howled, and the shutters rattled. She thought nothing of it at first, until she noticed that Kaine had gone unnaturally still. She looked up as another gusting howl wafted through the house.

Her eyes went wide, and they both bolted to the front door. Running back and forth outside the house, wings outstretched, nose to the ground, was Amaris.

She looked up as Kaine came out the door and immediately dropped to her belly and crawled across the ground to him, wings and tail flapping, whining and whimpering all the way. He pulled her enormous head into his arms.

"You mad thing—how did you get here?" He could barely get the question out, because Amaris was licking his face over and over, her wings sending up a dust storm.

"I guess she couldn't let you go," Helena said.

Amaris was set up in the stable, which she was only allowed out of at night. It was the best solution they could come up with given her size and unusual qualities. She didn't seem to mind. In the evening, she would burst out and run in circles for a little while, and Kaine would take her flying out across the sea.

Helena was glad that he finally had something to do with himself. Until Amaris's reappearance, he had floated. He would read and keep Helena company, but he didn't seem to know how to want anything. He'd spent his whole life with a collar around his throat.

As weeks turned into months, the full breadth of his possessiveness began to reassert itself. During the day, he would watch Helena work with an intensity that she could feel in her marrow. When they were alone, she would stop what she was doing and let him consume her. His lips whispering *perfect, beautiful, mine* with every nip and caress.

"Yours, always," she'd promise.

It grew steadily apparent that Helena sat at the centre of Kaine's universe, and now that she was safe, his unrestrained attention had nothing else to obsess over. Everything except Helena was superfluous. She thought at first that it was a phase, but as autumn arrived, and Ascendance came and went, she began to suspect that he had no intention of taking interest in anything else. Lila, Pol, alchemy projects: It was all to indulge her.

Even the baby. Helena's pregnancy became increasingly an undeniable piece in their relationship, but his concern remained limited to Helena. The condition of her heart. The risk of the Toll manifesting again.

When he wasn't reminding her that "their daughter" needed Helena to breathe, and that she had to keep herself safe for "their daughter," his interest faded.

One night, when they were lying in bed and she was trying to show him how to feel the constant kicking that she was subjected to, she realised his attention had wandered to her wrists, the punctures from the manacles that still ran through each of them.

She knew he worried that her ulnar nerve snapping was only the beginning, and that there might be more damage. He was constantly watching how she worked and rarely allowed her to carry or lift anything that might strain her wrists.

"Kaine," she said quietly.

His attention snapped back.

"Kaine, you have to care about her."

He stared at her blankly.

Her mouth went dry. "You can't be like your father."

His expression closed, but she sat up and gripped his hand.

"You have to care. You have to *choose* to care. The way you are, if you don't, you won't—and she'll know. Just like you did. You cannot do that to her. She has to be someone that you decide to care about."

She swallowed hard, looking down. "We don't know how long I'll . . . after everything. I need you to promise that if I'm not here, you'll love her for me"—her voice cracked—"the way *I* would love her. She has to be *that* important to you. Do you promise?"

Kaine had grown pale, but he nodded. "All right."

"Promise me."

"I promise."

Helena was put on bedrest during the last month of pregnancy when her heart began to struggle with even simple things like the stairs.

She nearly fainted, and before the dizziness had passed, Kaine had her in bed and would not let her leave it.

Riding Amaris, he had gone to the larger islands and found several medical texts on pregnancy, which he had read from cover to cover, designating himself as obstetrician. He would not hear of Helena doing anything, and when she tried to protest, he cited passages from the books.

Several women in the village came to the house and helped Lila manage cooking and cleaning. With nothing else to do, Helena began writing, filling a journal with everything she could think of. She wanted it all written down: her version of events. Who she was, and what she'd chosen, and why. Answers to all the questions she'd ever wished she'd asked her own mother.

The winter solstice passed, and so did Helena's due date, and she thought she would always be pregnant and never leave her bed when her labour finally started. It moved at a relentless creep for more than a day with little progress as Kaine grew more and more worried. Lila was somehow the most levelheaded among them.

"We're all vivimancers. No reason to think we can't get one baby out," Lila said, kneeling by Helena's legs while Helena leaned against Kaine, his hand pressed over her heart, making sure the rhythm stayed even when the contractions crested and ebbed.

"I hate this," Helena finally said, beginning to feel like it was never going to end, her forehead slick, curls clinging to her face.

"I know." Kaine smoothed her hair.

"It hurts."

"Yes."

"I'm tired. I've been pushing for hours."

"I know."

"Stop agreeing with me."

Kaine stopped talking after that and didn't utter a word of protest when she nearly broke his hand squeezing it through a contraction, her whole body curling forcefully.

"Almost there," Lila said. "Head's out. Just one more and you'll get the shoulders through." She looked at Kaine. "Do you want to catch her?"

He shook his head.

Helena could feel her heart rate trying to rocket. So close, so close. Just one more and it would be over.

“That’s it! Yes! Shoulders are out, just breathe, she’ll come . . .”

There was a garbled wail as Lila lifted a wet, squirming bundle and thrust her into Helena’s arms. Helena gave a startled gasp as her daughter’s tiny, scrunched-up face nuzzled against her. The baby’s head was matted with dark wet curls.

All her exhaustion was forgotten. Helena’s hands shook as she cradled the baby close. The tiny head lifted, looking towards Helena, and a little mouth opened to utter an angry, protesting cry.

Lila was saying something, but Helena could only stare as the baby furrowed her featherlight eyebrows, eyes widening briefly.

They were as bright silver as a lightning storm.

Helena gave a sob and held her tighter. “Kaine—she has your eyes.”

CHAPTER 77

Janua 1790

Helena sat in bed, counting her daughter's fingers and toes, studying the tiny fingernails and the squashed profile. Lila had rubbed the vernix in thoroughly and swaddled the baby with expert speed before giving her back to Helena.

The matted brown hair was beginning to dry and stand in little tufts around her soft head.

"Looks like she got my hair," Helena said as she looked up, smiling.

Kaine was standing almost as far from her as he could without going for the door.

She stared at him in confusion. He had barely left her side for weeks, but now he looked cornered.

"Kaine . . . come and see her."

He swallowed. "Helena—"

"She's your daughter."

The muscle in his jaw jumped. "Yes. I know. I remember how it happened."

The smile on Helena's face vanished.

She looked down, the silence in the room so heavy that she felt as though she were being crushed by it. Some wounds would never heal, and sometimes she felt that she and Kaine had a nearly lethal number of that variety.

"I think I should go."

"Come here," Helena said, not giving him a moment to interpret her silence as agreement. Her voice was hard and flat.

He exhaled, his eyes despairing, as though his heart were being carved out of his chest, but he didn't move.

"Kaine . . . come here," she said forcefully.

He swallowed and stepped closer.

"We didn't have any choice. You didn't. But that's over now. We said we'd start over when we ran away. That's what we're doing now. She's never going to know that world."

Kaine was looking anywhere but at the baby.

"She's not going to hurt you, and you're not going to hurt her."

"Helena." His voice was strained. "I'm not supposed to have this life. Paladia is drowning in the blood I've spilled. You think that doesn't include children? Killing is the only thing I've ever done well. Do you really want someone like that near your daughter?"

Helena froze, staring at him, and finally looked down. "You didn't have any choice," she said. "And it's not all you've done. You saved me. You saved Lila and Pol. We—we did what we had to, to survive. But we get to be better than that now. We'll do it for her."

He finally dragged his eyes from the far wall.

Their daughter's silver eyes peered up at them. Her hair had dried into a halo of brown curls. Her face was squashed from birth, and both her hands had escaped swaddling and were up near her face. She was aggressively sucking on the knuckles of her right hand.

She was the loveliest thing Helena had ever seen.

"Look at her. She's ours. She's all ours. You're not going to hurt her."

Kaine was frozen as he stared at her. He'd stopped breathing, and his fingers spasmed, trembling as he finally reached out. He barely brushed the baby's palm, as if he thought his touch might poison or break her. The tiny hand instantly closed around his finger, gripping it.

Helena watched him and recognised the expression that slowly filled his eyes as he stared at the tiny person tenaciously clinging to him: possessive adoration.

ENID ROSE FERRON WAS, ACCORDING to Lila, the easiest baby ever born. The older she grew, the more she looked like Helena, except for her eyes, which were, in colour and angle, just like Kaine's and the grandmother that she was named for.

She slept beautifully and rarely cried. She would sleep for hours in her overly indulgent father's arms, snoozing on his chest as he watched Helena work in the kitchen or in the little laboratory set up in one of the outbuildings.

Enid possessed the solemn curiosity of an owl, head swivelling as she observed everyone around her. Helena would carry her in a sling, tucked against her chest, where she could wrap her arms tightly and protectively around Enid's tiny body when the shadows grew too long.

Once Enid could safely sit up, she would spend half the day sitting on Kaine's shoulders, riding about with him while he walked the perimeter of the property over and over, checking all the buildings and visiting Amaris, who would vibrate with excitement but hold utterly still when Enid tugged her ears and patted her.

Kaine talked to Enid more than he talked to anyone, even Helena. He would monologue to her about everything: the trees, the sea, the tide and moons, alchemy techniques and array theories, what the weather might be, and Enid listened to him intently, fretting if he got distracted or fell silent for too long.

When the next summer Abeyance arrived, it brought news from the North, detailing the siege currently in progress, how the city was being starved into compliance as demands of surrender were ignored.

They were all relieved when the Abeyance ended and there was no more unspoken question hanging in the air of whether they could or should do something more.

Enid might have been a perfect child, if not for the terrible influence of Apollo Holdfast.

The instant Enid could walk, the idyllic quiet of the island was forever shattered. The two children tore through the house, shrieking and shouting, oblivious to the ways their parents flinched and started at sudden noise.

From Pol, Enid learned to climb hills and trees, tearing her clothes to bits scrambling down the cliffs. She made mud pies and soups and "healing" potions in jars stolen from the kitchen. She learned to wrestle, and to fight with the play swords that Lila had made to teach Pol combat basics.

Pol planned to be a warrior someday, and Enid wanted to be one, too. Both children held Lila in high esteem because she was a warrior with a metal leg, which they found significantly more interesting than their own legs.

Pol showed an early and exceptional proficiency for pyromancy. Then Enid, apparently not to be outdone, healed Pol's lip after he split it open running into a door. Helena was horrified by the early manifestation, but Lila reassured her that she had been similarly young when her abilities began making intermittent appearances.

Enid was reading by the time news came that Paladia had finally surrendered. The allies had poured into the city, securing and dispatching necrothralls so stick-thin and malnourished that they scarcely put up a fight. There were stories about the conditions found there, of citizens so starved that they were mistaken for necrothralls as they swarmed the liberating soldiers, begging for food.

By all accounts, it was an exceptionally successful campaign, with few casualties for the allied armies. The Liberation Front was ceaselessly praised for bringing the tyranny of the Undying to an end.

But Helena felt sick reading of it, overcome by a sense of betrayal. How different it could have been if the international community had decided to put even a negligible amount of effort into caring sooner. If Hevgoss and Novis had been less concerned over which of them would control Paladia afterwards. They'd all bided their time, waiting until the situation grew intolerable for them, and only striking after their victory was assured, and still somehow they were heroic.

In the papers, all the horror stories about the conditions inside the city, described in lurid detail, were only shared to highlight what the Paladians had been saved from, rather than as an admonishment of what they'd been left to endure.

Morrough was not among the casualties or captives. Somehow he remained alive in the caves beneath the Institute, and after a few failed attempts to breach the underground, the Liberation Front left him there, hoping he would die on his own.

With the "liberation" out of the way, the focus of the allies turned to the urgent matter of getting Paladia economically productive once more, with debates raging about what Paladia should look like in the future, whether it should exist at all or perhaps become a shared territory that Hevgoss and Novis would collaboratively control.

Trials were expected to begin soon. The international community denied any knowledge of the forced labour on the Outpost, or that all the industrially vital lumithium had been extracted by necrothralls for the last several years. However, they couldn't deny knowledge of the repopulation program, so instead they insisted that as far as they knew, participation had been voluntary.

At some point in the siege or seizure of the city, Stroud had disappeared.

When the women began to be released from the Tower, stories about the program began to emerge—the abuse and torture that Stroud had permitted, and the children born and subjected to experimentation to study early-childhood resonance and how it developed—but they were regarded as too horrifying for print. Most of the focus was on the forced labour on the Outpost and the mines and the malnutrition among the surviving civilian population.

There was pressure for the matter of the repopulation program to be quietly resolved. The women urged to move on rather than be retraumatised in court; hysterical unmarried mothers could hardly be expected to provide admissible testimonies. It was a stain upon the Northern identity that such atrocities had occurred, and so it was treated as some evil and twisted idea that had sprung from the Undying's regime, as if selective breeding had not been long rooted in guild culture.

No, there would be convents for the mothers and, for the children, an orphanage where they could grow up to become productive members of society. And so it could all be forgotten.

Kaine was the only one who didn't seem surprised at how things unfolded. Helena was so upset that she was sick for days, and Lila started to disappear, leaving Pol with Helena and Enid for long periods.

After the children were in bed one night, Lila came into the kitchen where Helena was working on a chymiatria project that she hoped might help to manage her heart.

"I need to talk to you," Lila said. She was very pale; she'd been quiet and withdrawn ever since the Abeyance passed. She sat down and stared at the fire for a long time. "I have to go back."

Helena had known this day was coming, but her stomach twisted at the announcement. Lila was not made for a quiet life. She was never going to be happy on an island. She'd stayed because of Pol and Helena. But from the moment they'd read the bulletin on the ship, Helena had known that if Lila hadn't been a mother to a toddler, she probably would have jumped off and joined the Liberation Force.

"I've been thinking about it for a while. I can't let them do this. They're erasing everything. Everyone. They'll bury everything that happened. They don't care; they just want the manufacturing back. It's like watching vultures close in after they spent all these years watching us die."

Helena sighed. "What does going back do, Lila?"

"I'm going to kill Morrough," Lila said. "I'm going to go in, and I'm going to kill him. And then I'm going to make sure that no one ever forgets about the Resistance." Lila's throat worked repeatedly, the scar twisting her face. "So I need you to take care of Pol for me. And I need to learn how to fight using vivimancy, and get whatever obsidian's left. And, Helena, I need you to teach me how to build a bomb."

"Morrough might be dead in a year."

"I know. I won't wait that long. I'm going to go during the winter Abeyance."

"That's an incredibly dangerous voyage," Helena said sharply.

"I have to go!" Lila's voice rose. "They killed my family, they killed Luc, they killed—everyone. I can't tell Pol about how brave and wonderful his dad was and know that the person who killed him is still out there. No one cares about the way Luc fought and suffered trying to save us"—she gestured furiously—"because he didn't win. They'll forget all about him if I don't go back."

"You could die. Don't leave Pol an orphan."

Lila was staring at the fire, the expression on her face so intense, so yearning, she looked as if she might slip her hands into it if it would let her touch Luc again.

"I made an oath that I would die before I let Luc come to harm, but he died and I'm still here. I've tried to bear it, for Pol, but I can't. Not anymore."

HELENA RELUCTANTLY COMPILED HER RESEARCH on bomb-making. The technique used to bomb the West Port Lab had the most potential, especially if they could find the sources of oxygen feeding into the underground.

She'd thought about the design over the years. She'd been in a rush and improvised, using the materials available. With time, and resources, it could be far more effective.

In the meanwhile, Kaine trained Lila in combat vivimancy. To the surprise of no one, Lila had been training in secret. Objectively she was a better fighter, except that Kaine did not follow any rules. He switched from vivimancy to combat alchemy to sheer underhandedness constantly, so that the instant Lila had an advantage, the fight became something different. He was brutal with her, exacting and impatient to a degree that he'd dramatically softened with Helena. He gave Lila no such consideration. He beat her weaknesses out of her.

Helena hadn't realised how much time and consideration Kaine had devoted to thinking about killing Morrough. The strategy it would require. As if he'd spent the years on the island waiting for Lila to ask. Perhaps he had. Or perhaps he would have gone and tried to do it himself if he'd been physically able to, but he wasn't. He'd never fully recovered from the torture Morrough had last inflicted on him. Under stress, his tremors were worse than Helena's.

"You should put your name on this," Lila said when Helena finally gave her a design for the bomb. "Even if people think you're dead, you should get credit for your work. Luc always used to say you'd be the one to outshine us all."

Helena shook her head. "I don't want anyone to wonder about me or to look too hard. It's not worth the risk. Just say you took the design when you escaped, and you don't know who developed it."

Pol came to slowly understand that his mother was leaving. He was five by then, and he and Enid had birthdays close together. As an early gift, Lila and Pol went to one of the larger islands and returned with a leggy white shepherd puppy named Cobalt, named for his father's horse.

"He'll keep you company and keep you safe until I come back," Lila said. She'd let the dye in her hair fade, letting it grow blond again. It was braided and pinned around her head, because this was how she wanted Pol to remember her. "I won't be able to send letters, but I'll send messages sometimes, all right? And whenever you see Lumithia, that means I'm thinking about you, and when you see the sun shining, that's your dad, watching you for me."

Lila's eyes shone with tears. "And you'll look out for Enid? She's your best friend. You have to stick together, because that's what best friends do."

THE HIGH NECROMANCER, MORROUGH, ONCE known as the first Northern alchemist, Cetus, died on a spring day.

According to the newspapers, the underground stronghold was breached by an elite team of Novis and Hevgotian military, accompanied by Paladin Lila Bayard, the last surviving member of the Order of the Eternal Flame. A mysterious pyromancy bomb was used in the initial attack.

The blast caused the famed Alchemy Tower to collapse, and the wreckage was painstakingly excavated and infiltrated as the team was mobbed by necrothralls.

Many were killed in the attack. Lila Bayard was nearly killed. The general leading the attack ordered that everyone fall back, but Lila had refused. She went on alone.

Newspapers across the continent featured a photo of Lila Bayard emerging from the rubble of the Alchemy Tower, helmet gone, face filthy, her armour streaked with blood. The brutal scar across her face was starkly visible, sharpening the look of cold triumph as she dragged the remains of Morrough's mutated and rotting corpse behind her.

There was no denying Lila Bayard's heroism. She had done what a dozen countries had failed to do.

Having a living, breathing member of the Eternal Flame who had done the impossible made it harder for the allied nations to treat Paladia as an utterly failed nation that needed external control. Lila was offered all sorts of ceremonial roles, but she refused them.

She had not come back to rule. She wanted those lost remembered, and she wanted the tragedy of the war confronted, not buried, so that it could not happen again.

In Lila's absence, Pol and Enid grew intensely attached to each other, to the point that Helena and Kaine began to watch them with worry.

"She's not going to handle it," Helena said as they watched Enid and Pol run from tide pool to tide pool. "She's so much like us. I don't know if it'll be better or worse to begin preparing her for it."

Kaine nodded as the children teased a large crab which then chased after them, scuttling sideways. Enid and Pol both tripped, shrieking with laughter as they tried to drag each other away from the pursuing claws, and Cobalt barked wildly.

Word had come that Lila was leading reconstruction efforts to have the Alchemy Institute reopened. There would be a new Tower, a new school, but not all Northern alchemy would be funnelled through the narrow admissions rate of the Institute. Generations of knowledge and alchemy had been destroyed; the continent was in desperate need of more alchemists, as many as could be trained. Alchemy certification would no longer be exclusive to Institute students but overseen by external bodies and given to anyone who could pass the necessary resonance tests and exams.

The Institute would return to its original purpose of new heights and advancements in alchemy.

After fierce debate, vivimancy was added as a field of alchemical study at the Institute. Lila had insisted on it. Healers had been vital to the Eternal Flame during the war. The potential of the resonance was being villainised and wasted by superstitious paranoia; it should not be an ability exclusive to those willing to abuse it. Paladia's discriminatory treatment of vivimancers had played a role in how easily the Undying had recruited them. Paladia had to evolve.

It took a year and a half, but finally Lila returned, but she had not come to stay. She was taking Pol home.

Helena tried to change her mind, but Lila would not be moved. Luc's son had to go to Paladia and see what his family had built.

The only consolation to Helena was that Pol would never be the Principate, for there would be no more Principate.

The world had seen Lucien Holdfast grovel at Morrough's feet and beg for immortality before his execution. Even with claims that perhaps he'd been coerced, promised leniency for the rest of the Eternal Flame, the mythos surrounding the Holdfasts and the idea of a lineage of divinity had been irrevocably shattered.

Pol would go to Paladia as a Holdfast, and he and his mother would rebuild what had been dearest to his family's heart. The Alchemy Institute.

"Come back with me, Helena," Lila said as Kaine took the children on a walk along the cliffs. "You can run the vivimancy department; think of what a difference you could make. You'd be establishing a whole new formalised field of alchemy. You'd be perfect for it."

"How would that work?" Helena asked. She could tell that reality was setting in for Lila, the realisation of all the politics and pressure that were the price of her choices.

"Do I leave Enid here? Or take her with me while I try to clear Kaine's name?"

Lila looked away, staring out at the sea. "You can't clear his name. It'll never happen. I know you think he's a tragic hero with no choice, but he's done the most terrible things. People talk about Morrough, make jokes about him, but do you know who no one ever jokes about? The High Reeve. People look sick at the mere mention of him. His signatures and seal are everywhere. He was involved in everything. There was nothing that happened in that regime that Kaine didn't know about."

Helena's throat tightened. "Well, that's the thing about being a spy and destabilising a regime. You have to know about things. How else did you expect him to do it?"

Lila's shoulders drooped. Helena understood why Lila did not want to be a sole survivor, the lonely hero. In Paladia, she was still surrounded by vultures, watching her, waiting for any mistake, some means to tear her apart, just as they had when she was a paladin.

Now Pol would be in their clutches, but even knowing that, Lila couldn't leave her family, country, or legacy. It was not in her nature to give up a fight.

"I'm not going to leave him," Helena said after a pause. "There's no version of me that survived the war without Kaine. I was loyal to Luc, and I know you want Paladia to remember him, but that country killed him, as much as Morrough did. I can't go back to it."

Lila nodded, starting to turn, but then stopped.

"I know I said I wouldn't say anything else, but I have to say this before I go and leave you here." Lila's throat dipped, her scar growing stark on her face the way it did when she was upset. "You're all I have left besides Pol. I know you love Kaine, and he loves you, I don't deny that. But I don't think you realise how inhumanly cold he is to anyone who isn't you or E. The rest of the world could burn and he wouldn't care. I don't think he'd even notice. Is this really what you want?"

"I know what he's like," Helena said sharply. "It's the reason you and I are alive."

Frustration lit Lila's face, and she started to open her mouth.

"When you killed Morrough, what did you think about?" Helena asked.

Lila's mouth snapped shut, and she looked away, her face growing anguished. "Luc. I was thinking of everything he did to Luc."

Helena stared down at her left hand. The concealment on the ring had faded with time, but now the brace on her hand nearly covered it.

"Love isn't as pretty or pure as people like to think. There's a darkness in it sometimes. Kaine and I go hand in hand. I made him who he is. I knew what that array meant when I saved him. If he's a monster, then I'm his creator."

WHEN ENID REALISED THAT LILA was taking Pol away, she was initially uncomprehending and then hysterical.

"No! No, you can't! He's mine. He's my best friend. You can't take him away!"

She refused to be comforted by Kaine or Helena. She clung to Pol, not letting go. Pol was clearly conflicted, but he didn't let go of Lila's hand for even a second.

"She can come with us," he said, looking seriously at Helena. "I'll take care of her."

Helena's throat closed. "No. No, Enid has to stay here until she's older," she said, trying to untangle Enid.

"I want to go." Enid sobbed as Helena pried her fingers off Pol's trousers. "I want to live in Paladia, too. Why can't we all go?"

"I'm sorry, we can't," Helena said, holding her tight as Enid attempted to collapse onto the floor and crawl to Pol. "It's not safe for us. That's why we live on the island, remember? Because Mum's heart goes too fast when we do too many trips. Mum can't go places that make her heart go fast."

"But Pol is my best friend. I'll be all alone without him."

Kaine turned and walked into the next room for a moment, hands spasming.

Pol let go of Lila's hand and went over to Enid.

"E," he said tentatively, "you have to stay with your mum and dad. You can't come to Paladia yet."

"Why not? You get to."

"Yeah," Pol said slowly, his blue eyes huge and thoughtful, and then his expression grew pained. "But you have to take care of Cobalt. City's no place for a dog, you know. He doesn't come when we tell him, so he might get hit by a lorry."

Enid's head popped up. "Really?" she said in a trembling voice.

"Yes," Pol said. "And the boats are dangerous, too, you know. So you have to take care of him for me. He needs walks every day."

Enid nodded in fervent understanding of the serious responsibility being placed upon her, and Pol gave her the leash.

As Lila and Pol rode away, Enid sat on the cliff, holding Cobalt and crying.

CHAPTER 78

Four Years Later

"Mum."

Helena looked up from the tincture she was making. There were certain things always in demand in the village. Enid was sitting in the kitchen, watching her work.

Since Pol's departure, Enid had lost much of her playfulness. Kaine and Helena had tried to bring back the spark, to find children in the village for Enid to befriend, but she always held herself back.

There were too many obstacles: no alchemy, no mention of Kaine's or Helena's real names, or of where Pol and Lila had gone. The rules and barriers stressed Enid, and as a result she had retreated into the house, only going out with her parents or dutifully to walk Cobalt every day.

On the dark nights, Kaine would take her riding on Amaris. Sometimes they would fly to other islands together, but no matter where she went, Enid never wanted friends.

The bright spot of her life was the two weeks each summer when the family travelled to the Northern mainland, to visit Lila and Pol in the port city.

"Why do you have holes in your wrists?" Enid asked. "No one else has holes like that."

Helena's chest tightened as she looked down. She was usually careful to cover them, but she'd been distracted and pushed her sleeves up to work. Eight years was a long time to hide anything from a nosy child.

"No, there's not many people who have them," she said quietly. "During the war, people thought they could win if the other side didn't have their resonance, so they tried to find ways to make it go away. And—these holes were one of the ideas they had."

"Did it make your resonance go away?" Enid leaned closer, peering at them.

Helena pressed her lips together and nodded. "It did."

"But it's back now?"

Helena nodded. "Your dad got it back for me. It was a long time ago, but some scars don't ever go away. They look funny, don't they?"

Enid reached out and touched one inquisitively. "Did you get captured in the war?"

Helena's throat closed. She stepped away, going to the cupboard and tucking a tablet into her mouth and quickly drinking a glass of water. She'd known these conversations would come up eventually. Enid was getting too old to keep avoiding them, especially given how desperate she was to go to Paladia and study alchemy like Pol, who'd just begun his first year at the Institute.

"Yes," she finally said. "I was captured for a while, and it wasn't very nice, so that's why I decided to run away and have you instead. It's been much more fun."

Kaine entered the room, and Helena stiffened.

"E," she said, "do you mind running to the village and getting some cheese for dinner? We're all out."

Enid hopped up, curly hair flying, and disappeared out the door.

"What's wrong?" Kaine asked as soon as Enid was gone.

"Enid noticed the scars from the manacles just now," Helena said without meeting his eyes.

"What did you tell her?"

Helena inhaled. "As much as I thought she was ready to know. I didn't lie."

Kaine just arched an eyebrow. Helena set her jaw and went over to a shelf and pulled down a newspaper.

"A crate of them arrived today," she said. "I was looking through and this was there."

She lifted the paper. WAR CRIMINAL FOUND DROWNED IN HEVGOSS.

Kaine's eyes gleamed.

Helena looked down, studying the words. "It was Stroud. She was found in a lake. She appeared to have had a heart attack while swimming. Hevgoss is facing questions—apparently they took her in and gave her immunity in exchange for her research. Which is ironic given all those trials they presided over, where every guard was found guilty. But apparently the worst of them was quietly pardoned."

There was a brief silence.

"Pity someone didn't kill her," Kaine finally said.

"Someone did," Helena said in a voice that was almost a hiss.

Kaine stared at her blankly.

"Don't," she said. "Don't you dare lie to me."

Kaine gave a low sigh, and when he looked up, the sharpness of him reemerged like a raw blade.

The version of himself that he wore perfectly on the island whenever Enid could see him—softness, crooked smiles, quiet monologues. It all vanished, and now he was real again. As cold and gleaming as razor-edged steel.

"Why would you do this?" Helena said, feeling as if there were a chasm inside her. "Haven't we done enough? Why would you take a chance like this? Did you even think about what would happen if you'd been caught—"

"I was careful," he said, not defending himself at all. "Did you really think I was going to let her live?"

Helena tried to swallow. She'd spent the day working to keep her heart under control, but she was too upset to manage her distress. "You lied to me. It was when we were at the ports, wasn't it? When you said you had to go take care of some financial matter, but this is what you were doing. Now every time you go—anywhere—I'm going to wonder where you really are. And worry that you're never going to come back to me—"

Her voice broke.

Kaine reached for her, but she stepped away from him. Pressing her hand against her chest, trying to keep her heart steady so she could keep talking, keep being angry. She was so angry.

"Is this not enough for you? Is having this life so dissatisfying that revenge is worth the risk?" Her eyes were burning. "In a few years, we're going to have to tell Enid who you were. She's going to go to school soon, and even here in Etras, she'll hear about the war and hear your name. We both know exactly where she's going to end up, and there will be no hiding the things you did. It's going to shatter her world—even if she hears it from you first."

Kaine's jaw clenched. "I—"

"We don't get to have all the things we want in this life. Remember? You were the one who told me that. You said there was a point when I had to realise I wasn't going to get everything I wanted, and I had to choose and let it be enough. I thought we chose this. Have I been lying to myself this whole time?"

Her lungs started spasming so violently, an awful whistling rasped up her throat.

"She deserved to die after what she did to you." His voice was unrelenting, unapologetic. "I couldn't leave her once I knew where she was hiding."

She shook her head. "You shouldn't have looked. You should have left it alone."

She glared at him for a moment longer and then burst into tears. "I'm so glad she's dead."

Kaine took two rapid steps and caught her before she could back away, her fingers curled, gripping his shirt.

"I hope she suffered, but I didn't want it to be you—why is it always you?" She buried her face in his chest. "I hated her. I hated her so much. I'm so glad she's dead."

"I know," he said, his arms wrapping around her. "She's gone now. There won't be anyone else."

Ten Years Later

THEY STOOD, FINGERS ENTWINED, AS the last cloud of smoke from the steamship vanished.

"It's just the two of us now," Helena said wistfully.

Kaine was silent, silver eyes trained on the sea, as if he could still make out the ship over the curve of the horizon.

She squeezed his hand. "You realise why she's going, don't you?"

Kaine winced. "Yes . . ."

Helena rested her head on his shoulder. "I suppose it was inevitable. Letting things go isn't really a trait of ours."

He snorted. "I've had my moments at least. You, on the other hand . . ."

She laughed, looking up at him. His hair was still dyed brown, and she was surprised by how often she missed the silver-white. A few more years and he could probably stop dyeing it. However, his eyes were still the same. No matter how long she studied them, there always seemed to be nuances in the way the colour shifted, the glimmers of emotion that showed through.

When he looked down at her, the world around them faded away.

Her stomach flipped. "So, what do we do now?"

The corner of his mouth curved into a smile that had only ever been for her. "Anything. Whatever you want."

EPILOGUE

Julius 1808

THE RIVER FERRY CHURNED UP THE WINDING river, reaching the final bend and revealing Paladia to those aboard. The audible gasps gave away those who had never seen the famous city before.

It gleamed like a giant crown laid in the river, framed by towering mountains.

At the front of the ship, a young woman with large silver-grey eyes watched the city draw near, barely able to tear her eyes away as the ferry made port and passengers began to disembark.

She paused at the top of the gangplank, searching the crowd for a familiar face.

"Enid!" called a voice.

Several people turned to see former paladin Lila Bayard running towards the ship, her son Apollo behind her, and a few guards all trying to keep up.

Lila reached Enid first and crushed her into a hug before stepping back.

"Look at you. It's been too long." Lila dropped her voice down. "I was afraid I wouldn't recognise you, but you look so much like your mum."

Enid smiled. "Yes," she said in a faint Etrasian accent. "Father always says that."

Lila shook her head. "I can't believe they finally let you come. I thought they'd want you to keep studying in Khem, but I'm so excited that we're going to have you in the program."

Enid gave a sly smile. "Well, they knew I always wanted to study at the Institute. The apprenticeships in Khem are done differently—it's primarily metallurgical there."

Lila reached back and dragged Pol, who'd been awkwardly hanging behind, into the conversation. Enid's and Pol's eyes met for only an instant before darting away.

"Well, I wish they'd let you come sooner." Lila sighed. "Your academic qualities would have been extremely helpful here. Pol has unfortunately inherited the poor study habits of his father and me, and that's why he had to take a pyromancy certification exam *twice.*"

Pol turned bright red. "That was only on the written portion and that was years ago," he muttered. "I passed it."

"You're supposed to run the Alchemy Institute someday. How is anyone going to take you seriously with transcripts like yours?" Lila said. "We're lucky to have Enid here now. She'll give us some proper academic legitimacy."

Lila looked over to one of the guards. "Send her bags to Solis Splendour. We're going to take the scenic route back to the Institute."

A motorcar wound through the city, spiralling slowly up from the ports into the upper levels, headed north. It stopped at a plaza with a large open area. There were several tall columns encircling a statue.

Lila hesitated a moment and then began to open the door. "You should see this," she said, stepping out. "It's new, only finished a few weeks ago."

There was a small crowd present, and most people drew back for the approaching party as Lila led the way to the centre.

The statue was of a Resistance soldier in combat armour and rappelling harness. At his feet were the words GONE BUT NOT FORGOTTEN.

The columns were smooth marble, filled with names. APOLLO HOLDFAST, LUCIEN HOLDFAST, SOREN BAYARD, SEBASTIAN BAYARD, EDDARD ALTHORNE, JAN CROWTHER, TITUS BAYARD . . . they went on and on.

Lila stood looking around them. "This was where the nullium bomb went off. One of the last places rebuilt, because it was so difficult to protect from the contamination. I wanted a memorial for everyone who died during the war, and this is where they put it. I think I like it, but . . . maybe nothing ever feels like it's enough. What do you think?"

Enid shrugged, but her sharp eyes were rapidly scanning the columns. "I've never seen a war memorial before. I don't know exactly how they're supposed to make you feel."

Lila inhaled. "I don't know, either, I just hoped it would be more—"

Before Lila could finish her thought, a woman grasped hold of Enid's arm, pulling her towards her. "Helena?"

Enid turned to stare at the stranger, a woman with long scars sliced across her face.

The woman cut herself off, snatching her hand back. There was a small puncture straight through her wrist. "No. No, of course not. I'm sorry. I thought you were someone I knew."

Lila turned, and her lips trembled briefly before she spoke. "Penny, this is Enid Romano; she's come here to join the undergraduate vivimancy program. Pol and I were giving her a tour."

Penny stared at Enid for a moment longer, her eyebrows knitting together. "Oh." Her voice was strained. "I'm sorry, I probably scared you, grabbing you like that. From behind you looked just like someone I knew. Lila, doesn't she look like Helena?"

Enid's expression was blank, and she glanced questioningly at Lila.

Lila squinted as if trying to see what Penny was referring to. "It's the hair, I think." Lila looked at Enid. "Helena Marino, she was part of the Resistance, but she died before the Liberation."

Enid looked back at Penny. "I'm sorry for your loss."

Penny stood staring at Enid as if she were a ghost for another moment before she turned away.

They were scarcely alone for a moment before another voice interrupted.

"Lila, there you are, I haven't seen you here since the memorial opened."

A grimace flashed across Lila's face before she forced a smile and turned. "Mrs. Forrester, what an unexpected pleasure."

The woman was middle-aged and breathing heavily. "What's this I hear about the Holdfasts being back at their old antics of importing foreign students?"

The smile on Lila's face vanished. She straightened, taking full advantage of her height. "Enid was a celebrated student in Khem, and she's submitted a promising proposal on the use of vivimancy arrays for treating lung damage. The Institute invited her here to support her research because several of the illnesses associated with the nullium bombing still lack effective treatment."

Mrs. Forrester's face turned red, and she coughed several times, pressing a handkerchief over her mouth. "Oh, lung treatment, you say? That is interesting."

Enid stepped away, leaving Lila to accept the weak apology. She went over to the columns, scanning the names, but there were so many, crammed together, name after name.

Within minutes, Lila and Pol both had crowds gathering around them. The Principate might be no more, but the allure of the Holdfasts endured.

Across the plaza, one of the buildings had a row of shops. Enid walked towards them, casting a look back and meeting Pol's woebegone eyes before disappearing into a bookstore.

Just inside there was a large display of thick books.

A Comprehensive History of the Paladian Necromancy War by William Dover

Enid paused, staring at the books for a moment before picking up a copy.

"Just released this week," said a clerk, standing nearby and eyeing the book in her hands.

"I didn't recognise the title, so I figured it must have been," Enid said, flipping the book open to peruse the chapter index, finger pausing briefly along the way.

"Well, if you're wanting to understand Paladia and the war, this is definitively the best one there is. I mean, your dialect seems pretty good, but if you really want to know all the details and explanations for everything that went on—this is it."

Enid arched an eyebrow. The clerk seemed to take it as a sign of encouragement and stepped closer. "Dover spent more than ten years on it. Got special permission from the Assembly and the Liberation Front to access all the records, even trial transcripts that weren't public yet. It's shocking stuff. Some chapters—I don't recommend reading if your stomach isn't strong. But if you want to know what happened, this is the book that'll tell you. It's all there. Everything people should know."

"Do you?" Enid asked.

The clerk looked uncertain.

"Know everything that people should know about the war?" Enid clarified.

The clerk cleared his throat. "Well—for me it's hard not to. I was one of the ones born in the Tower. If you know what that means. There were trials. We kept getting moved around while they were arguing about what to do with us."

"I'm so sorry."

He cleared his throat. "Anyway. Reading that—helped put it all in perspective for me."

Enid looked down at the cover again. "I'll have to check it out, then. I'm from Etras, but even there, people still talk about the Paladian War."

Still holding the book, Enid stepped past the clerk, wandering farther into the shop. Once she found an empty aisle, she quickly flipped the book open to its index and ran her finger through until she found the chapter title she wanted.

She flicked to the page.

> Kaine Ferron, known to the world as the High Reeve, is the most infamous mass murderer in history. By all estimates, he was the youngest to join Morrough's Undying, only sixteen

when he assassinated Principate Apollo Holdfast, plunging the city-state of Paladia into one of the most devastating wars in history. Ferron devoted himself to climbing rank among the Undying. Not only was he the youngest to "ascend," but he went on to become the youngest individual to achieve the rank of general during the war.

Ferron's proficiency as an alchemist and a vivimancer was widely regarded as unnatural and the result of the horrific human experimentation that came to define the Undying's regime, but unlike most of Artemon Bennet's subjects, Ferron's participation was voluntary.

Many of the Undying retired from service post-war. However, Ferron's ascent was only beginning. He led the efforts to capture and interrogate all remaining Resistance members, killing them for use in the lumithium mines. His predilection for slaughter was key in achieving his status as High Reeve and his eventual acknowledgement as Morrough's successor.

It is the belief of many that if the Ferron family had not been murdered by Ivy Purnell, the Undying regime could have lasted decades longer. Morrough's condition was so deteriorated that many believe he would have handed control of Paladia to Ferron before the year's end.

Necromancy scholar Eustace Sederis wrote in his book *Ferron: A Biography of the High Reeve:* "Kaine Ferron was a monster long before Morrough ever reached Paladia. Joining the Undying simply enabled a born psychopath to indulge in his cruelty, and when even immortality and immutability could not sate his sadistic impulses, he submitted himself to brutal experimentation to achieve his ends."

EARLY LIFE

Kaine Ferron was born the only child of . . .

There was a sound behind Enid, and she snapped the book closed and turned. Pol was standing at the end of the aisle, a crookedly triumphant grin on his face.

Apollo Holdfast was an even mix of his parents. While many of his features were traditional Holdfast—sky-blue eyes, golden hair, and a smile warm as sunshine—he had Bayard bones, which made him taller than even his mother.

"Hello," he said.

A smirk played at the corner of Enid's mouth, and she arched an eyebrow, silver eyes studying him coolly. "Hello."

Pol rested his hand on the shelf above Enid's head so that he loomed over her. Enid simply raised her chin.

"Hiding from us already?" he asked.

The smirk on Enid's lips faded, and she looked down at the book in her hands. "No. There was a new book about the war, and I thought I'd look up the section on the High Reeve."

The grin on Pol's face vanished. "Don't. They're never going to tell it how it was."

Enid shrugged, nodding. "I know. I just—I feel like I have to know what they say. It's always the same thing, though. And I know it will be, but I can't help it. This one even had that Sederis quote included."

She gave another shrug that was almost convincingly indifferent. "What do you think the odds are that Mum's even in the index?"

Pol rested a hand on her wrist. "Don't."

But Enid didn't listen. She turned, resting the book on the edge of the shelf, and opened to the rear index, running her finger along until it stopped.

She released a slow breath. "Look . . ."

She flipped rapidly through the book, finally stopping at a glossy photo page in the chapter on Lucien Holdfast.

Enid and Pol both stared at the photograph.

Soren Bayard, Helena Marino, and Luc Holdfast sat together on a sofa, Luc's arm slung around Helena's shoulders, as they all stared at the camera.

Helena was in the centre, painfully thin in a medical uniform too big for her and a knitted pullover. Her hair was drawn back into two taut braids, pinned into a thick knot at the base of her head. Her face set with large, devastated eyes that betrayed the attempted smile on her face.

Enid stared at the photo for several minutes before reaching out and gently touching it. "I've never seen a picture of her from the war. Your mum sent her student photos from the Institute, but there weren't any others."

Pol didn't say anything, but when Enid wouldn't stop staring at the photo, he rested a hesitant hand on her shoulder. She looked up and met his eyes before giving a sad smile, reminiscent of the girl in the photograph.

She looked down again, and her fingers ran along the words captioning the photograph as if she wanted to rub them away.

"Someday . . . someone should set the record straight," she said quietly.

Pol cleared his throat. "You know Mum offered to. She wanted to tell what really happened to them, just up to the fire. Your mum and dad didn't want her to."

Enid nodded slowly, eyes still glued to the photo. "I know. I know they don't. I get it. If I lived through everything they did—I'd just want to leave it all behind. There's no point in trying to explain something like that; no one's ever going to even want to understand.

"But—" Enid's jaw trembled. "—she doesn't deserve to be forgotten like this. She shouldn't be a footnote. This shouldn't be the only entry she even has. She deserves her own chapter. She deserves a whole damned book of her own." Her voice quavered. "And the things they say about Dad—like he wanted it all, that he asked to have it done to him—" She scrubbed her eyes with the back of her hand and drew a deep breath. "Sorry. I always think I can handle this, and then I get so mad I feel like I'm going to be sick."

She blinked rapidly. "I'm glad I came here, though. I needed to see it.

The city, where it all happened. It's so hard not to have anyone to talk to about this. Mum says I can always talk to her or Dad, but she always has to take pills if I do and then she'll start pressing her fingers near her heart when she thinks I won't notice. I don't want to put her through that just because I want to talk. And Dad, every time any of it comes up, I can tell he thinks I'm never going to speak to him again."

Her knuckles were turning white as she gripped the book. She finally set it down and exhaled. "I don't know what I'd do without you and Aunt Lila. I think you're the only person who knows me."

Pol smiled at her, his eyes bright and earnest. "You'll always have me."

Enid nodded, lips pressed together, but then she slowly smiled back.

There was a pause as they stood together, both seeming suddenly aware that they were alone in an empty aisle.

Enid's cheeks flushed. Pol's eyes darkened and he shifted forward, closing the space between them.

The bell at the door rang out sharply. Pol straightened, drawing his hand back and running it through his hair several times as he cleared his throat.

"Mum'll probably show up any second. Or the guards. But once we get to the house . . . we should talk—more"—his head bobbed—"about—" He cleared his throat again. "Well, only if you want to—talk about—anything."

Enid blinked and then nodded jerkily. "Yes! We should. At the house, though. It's better to—talk there."

She nodded again and shuffled quickly past him and out of the aisle.

They hurried together towards the front of the bookstore, leaving the history book behind, still open to the page with the photograph. The photo caption read:

> HIBERNAL SOLSTICE, SOLAR YEAR 1786 PD. Principate Lucien Holdfast with Paladin Soren Bayard (See: Bayard, Soren; chapter 12, "A Life of Legacy") and foreign-born alchemist Helena Marino. Marino left the city at the start of the Paladian Civil War to study healing. She survived the war but

died during imprisonment prior to Liberation. She was a non-active member of the Order of the Eternal Flame and did not fight.

HIBERNAL SOLSTICE, SOLAR YEAR 1786 PD. Principate Lucien Holdfast with Paladin Soren Bayard (See: Bayard, Soren; chapter 12, "A Life of Legacy") and foreign-born alchemist Helena Marino. Marino left the city at the start of the Paladian Civil War to study healing. She survived the war but died during imprisonment prior to Liberation. She was a non-active member of the Order of the Eternal Flame and did not fight.

Content Notes from the Author

Alchemised is a work of dark fantasy containing wartime violence, religious abuse, depictions of complex trauma, suicidal ideation, self-harm, human experimentation, medical torture, eugenics, cannibalism, sexual assault, rape, and allusions to necrophilia. Please remember that depiction is not authorial endorsement. Because *Alchemised* is told in third-person limited point of view, it necessarily involves some distortions of vision as well as missed or misconstrued events. Reader discretion is advised.

Acknowledgements

The list of people I'd like to thank for supporting me in this journey is too long for this already incredibly long book, but allow me to express my heartfelt gratitude to each and every person who discovered my writing and has so enthusiastically supported me in every step of this unexpected journey. Your joy and excitement on my behalf have meant more than I can ever express.

To Caitlin Mahony and Rikki Bergman, my agents, thank you for your incredible patience, care, and protectiveness in this whirlwind experience, and for always taking the time to explain in text message the convoluted questions I should have sent you as emails. Suzy Ball, for wrangling the UK side of things. And Frankie Yackel for all your incredible work behind the scenes.

Emily Archbold, my dear editor, thank you for all your rambly emails that gave me an excuse to stop writing, for how thoughtfully you'd consider all my belated and harebrained ideas, and for your patient feedback and steadfast faith in my work. Jordan Pace, for dealing so expertly with all my preemptive panicking every time I was expected to promote my book in spoken rather than written words. To the incredible Del Rey team: Scott Shannon, Keith Clayton, Tricia Narwani, Julie Leung, Alex Larned, Marcelle Iten Busto, David Moench, Ashleigh Heaton, Tori Henson, Kay Popple, Maya Fenter, and Madi Margolis, thank you all so much for your vision, support, and enthusiasm at every step of the way.

I am forever grateful to the utterly delightful Rebecca Hilsdon, and the Michael Joseph team: Stella Newing, Riana Dixon, Sriya Varadharajan, Clare Parker, Jessie Beswick, Jack Hallam, Vicky Photiou, Bronwen

Davies, Kelly Mason, Akua Akowuah, Richard Rowlands, Jessica Meredeen, Helen Eka, Dan Prescott, Jill Cole, and Hayley Shepherd.

My deepest thanks to everyone involved in the foreign editions. It is such an incredible honour to have my story translated.

To Jame, for sticking with me for these years through the thickest and thinnest despite my chronic abuse of commas; I wouldn't be here without you. Rei, thank you for all your etymological research while navigating the convoluted lore I threw at you with zero context.

Avendell, your ability to take the thoughts in my head and somehow turn them into the most stunning art I have ever seen will never cease to amaze me.

To my extended family, thank you for all your excitement, support, and understanding when I've had to miss events in order to meet deadlines. Wren, for having a spare room for me to crash in when I needed somewhere to pull all-nighters, and for always ensuring that I was eating even if I wasn't sleeping. Kimi, who waited so patiently for years for me to finally tell anyone else in the entire family about my writing endeavours.

Andrew, thanks for stepping so gamely into the role of primary parent with all of zero warning. And to T and E most especially, thank you for being so proud of me and keeping me company by coming in quietly and reading fantasy books in my bed while I was writing fantasy books at my desk. I love you more than words can say.

About the Author

SenLinYu grew up in the Pacific Northwest and studied classical liberal arts and culture. They started writing in the Notes app of their phone during their baby's nap time. Their collected online works have garnered more than twenty million individual downloads and have been translated into twenty-three languages. They live in Portland, Oregon, with their family. *Alchemised* is their first novel.

senlinyuwrites.com
Instagram: @senlinyuwrites
TikTok: @senlinyuwrites